Edwin Abbott Abbott

Francis Bacon
An account of his life and works

D1670775

SEVERUS

Abbott, Edwin Abbott: Francis Bacon. An account of his life and works.
Hamburg, SEVERUS Verlag 2013
Nachdruck der Originalausgabe von 1885

ISBN: 978-3-86347-322-8
Druck: SEVERUS Verlag, Hamburg, 2013

Der SEVERUS Verlag ist ein Imprint der Diplomica Verlag GmbH.

Bibliografische Information der Deutschen Nationalbibliothek:
Die Deutsche Nationalbibliothek verzeichnet diese Publikation in der Deutschen Nationalbibliografie; detaillierte bibliografische Daten sind im Internet über http://dnb.d-nb.de abrufbar.

PREFACE

THE present work was undertaken six or seven years ago, at the request of the late Mr. J. R. Green, for the series of "Literature Primers." But although the rough draft was prepared as early as 1880, unavoidable delays deferred completion, till Mr. Green's lamented death destroyed the hope that the volume might receive his supervision. In these circumstances it was thought best that, instead of curtailing the work—which, from the first, considerably exceeded the limits of the primer series—it should be amplified and published independently. This ended in its being rewritten on a much larger scale.

By inserting the dates for all Bacon's letters and "Occasional Works," [1] and by adding references for all the philosophical and larger literary works, I have endeavoured to make the book of use not only to those readers of limited leisure who may be prepared to accept it on its own merits as a fairly complete account of the life and works of Bacon (so far as one volume on such a subject can be called complete), but also to such more leisurely readers as may desire to refer to that treasure-house of Baconian facts for which many

---

[1] The letters and "Occasional Works" are arranged in Mr. Spedding's edition in chronological order, so that, for these, the date is a sufficient reference.

generations of English-speaking readers will remain deeply indebted to Mr. Spedding.[1]

In the Second Part of the book, which deals with Bacon's works, rather more than usual prominence has been given to the less-known writings, some of which contain the germs of the *Novum Organum*, while others give the outline of the whole, or attempt to construct parts, of the *Magna Instauratio*. Several of these short treatises—for example, the *Redargutio Philosophiarum*, for which see pp. 367-70—are full of rhetorical beauty ; others throw great light on Bacon's system by exhibiting its main principles in brief ; and all are useful as showing the versatility with which he proposed to commend his philosophy to the world, and the changed mind with which at different times he regarded different parts of his system.

For the purpose of a summary, the *Advancement of Learning* has been preferred to the amplified Latin Translation called the *De Augmentis*, mainly because the former admits of quotations from Bacon's own inimitable English. Besides, the *Advancement* will be always more popular than the Translation ; and the *De Augmentis*, although much enlarged in detail, adds little in outline. But in the summary of the *Advancement*, attention has been called to most of the important differences of statement or argument between the English and the Latin Translations.

It is through Bacon's *Essays*, however, that he is most widely known, and of these Bacon himself tells us (in the cancelled dedication of the second edition to Prince Henry) that they are "of a nature whereof a

---

[1] "Spedding," in all following foot-notes, indicates Mr. Spedding's *Letters and Life of Lord Bacon;* references to the *Works* will be indicated by "Spedding, *Works.*"

man shall find much in experience, little in books."
Accordingly, it has been one of the Author's main
objects throughout these pages, and more especially in
the biographical portion, to call attention to such
passages of the *Essays* as are capable of being illustrated by Bacon's life, letters, and speeches, so as to
make this volume in some sense a commentary upon
Bacon's most popular, and perhaps most enduring
work.[1]

In the Alphabetical Index at the end of the book,
the italicised portion contains references to Bacon's own
words; under which head I have occasionally inserted
passages from the *Essays* and the *Advancement*, but
much more often from the less-read letters, speeches,
and minor works—the object being, not only to facilitate
reference to the incidents of Bacon's life and to the
accounts of his several treatises, but also, as far as
possible, to place at the reader's disposal a collection
of some of the brightest, and quaintest, but almost
unknown, sayings of one of the most varied and
suggestive writers of English prose.

---

[1] The references to the *Essays* include the *line*, as well as the number
of the essay. They refer to my edition (Longmans, 1876).

CONTENTS

PART II

BACON'S WORKS

APPENDIX I

APPENDIX II

INTRODUCTION

ONE advantage of the delay of the present work has been that its revision and rewriting have been facilitated by biographies of Bacon written during the last few years by Professor Fowler (1881), by Dean Church (1884), and by Professor S. R. Gardiner in the *Dictionary of National Biography* (1885), to the last of which I am more especially indebted.[1]

Professor Fowler (as also Mr. Aldis Wright in the biography prefixed to his edition of the *Advancement of Learning*, 1875) closely follows Mr. Spedding in his views of Bacon's character. Dean Church has been led to conclusions very similar to those which I endeavoured—very roughly and imperfectly—to express in my edition of the essays (1878), and to which I still, in the main, adhere. Professor Gardiner has viewed Bacon in a new light. He has called attention to the political aspect of Bacon's career. He has laid stress upon the grandeur of the work that Bacon *might have achieved* as a Statesman, if only he could have had his own way ; and has herein found some extenuation, not only for his desertion from

---

[1] By the kindness of the Editor of the *Dictionary*, and with the permission of Professor Gardiner, I was enabled to see the article on Francis Bacon, seven or eight months before it was published.

science to statesmanship, but also for his continuance in political pursuits even when it became evident that he could achieve nothing because he was forced to go the way of others. Accepting Bacon's claim as a prophet of scientific knowledge, he recognises "his equally great claim as a prophet of political knowledge;"[1] "the desire to rise in the world, consciously or unconsciously, went for much with Bacon: but the knowledge that his country could be saved, and that he was the man to save it, worked in the same direction;"[2] he alleges the keenness of Bacon's foresight, and the height of his political aims, "not in arrest of judgment," but as a plea for some modification of the sentence which we should otherwise pass upon his importunity for office and obsequiousness in office; and he implies that, had James I. been guided by Bacon, the latter would have accomplished a task not inferior to the highest of his scientific objects, "if it be admitted that to turn aside a coming revolution, with all its moral and material horrors, is as great a service to mankind as to enlarge a scientific scheme."[3]

I have endeavoured to give to this able advocacy the careful and respectful consideration which it deserves, keeping constantly in view throughout every discussion of Bacon's political letters and treatises these three questions: How far did Bacon anticipate the coming revolution? What were the means by which he hoped to avert it? What steps did he actually take to give effect to his hopes?

Professor Gardiner justly remarks that "the immensity of Bacon's genius is a sore trouble to his biographers." The complexities and inconsistencies in a nature so

---

[1] *Dictionary of National Biography*, vol. ii. p. 349.
[2] *Academy*, 3 May, 1884.　　　　[3] *Ib.*

many-sided will probably not be adequately explained by any single analysis—not by Pope's epigrams in verse, nor Macaulay's in prose ; not even by Dean Church's theory—subtle and truthful as it appears to me—that Bacon's life was a double one, the life of high thinking and the put-on worldly life, and that these two lives go on side by side, " the worldly one often interfering with the life of thought and discovery and partly obscuring it, but yet always leaving it paramount in his own mind ;" not by Professor Gardiner's suggestion that the greater part of Bacon's life was spent in shaping political history, and that "power to do good in politics was, according to the possibilities of his day, inseparably connected with high places and the good things of this world, to the advantages of which Bacon was by no means insensible ;" and most assuredly not by Professor Fowler's brief solution, that " carelessness about money matters was the root from which all Bacon's errors and misfortunes sprang."

Bearing in mind, therefore, the controversial nature which discussions of Bacon's character have frequently assumed, and the consequent neglect of important facts in his life while excessive stress has been laid upon isolated and sometimes petty incidents that seemed to tell in favour of some theory, I have endeavoured to avoid—at all events in the main body of the work— any lengthy psychological or moral disquisitions, and to set forth in a continuous story such extracts from Bacon's letters, speeches, and occasional works as might enable this much-accused and more-defended man to tell his own story in his own way, with as little as possible hindrance or interruption. In other words, I have tried to make this biography approach, as far as possible, the nature of an autobiography.

One difficulty in making Bacon intelligible to the world is this : the world will persist in believing that, because he was in some sense a man of science, he must needs have also been a man of at least ordinary accuracy and sobriety of statement; and people are confirmed in this prejudice by the fact that he does not appear to have been in any danger of being misled by passion ; that he was cold and calculating in his friendships ; not fervent in marriage ; and that he himself asked—as though there could be but one answer to the question—" Are not the pleasures of the intellect greater than the pleasures of the affections ? "[1] How, then, people naturally argue, could a scientific man of this cool, cautious, and almost cold-blooded temperament make mis-statements without deliberate purpose to deceive ?

The truth is, that in almost every great man there is pretty sure to be something of disproportion ; and, for success in active life, some excess of the self-persuasive faculty is almost necessary. The greatest living statesman in England was not long ago (1884) accused of being " able to persuade himself of anything." The accusation savoured of hyperbole ; but it by no means deserved to be treated as if it amounted to a charge of lunacy. No man can do great things if he is not persuaded that he can do somewhat more than he actually succeeds in doing ; no man can lead a party or work for a people if he does not believe in the party or people to an extent a little beyond what is warranted by facts. It is by this imaginative and illogical surplusage of belief (commonly called faith) that a man uplifts both himself and others : within ordinary limits it achieves ordinary successes ; beyond

[1] See below, p. 41.

those limits it achieves stupendous marvels or disastrous failures.

Bacon did not escape this disproportion. In him the immensity of his self-confidence and of his self-persuasive power more than corresponded to the vastness of his genius. Like Cæsar, he trusted not only himself but his fortune ; every one and everything that surrounded him *and could be useful to him,* Essex, Cecil, James, Villiers, his own life past and future, his scientific successes, his judicial prospects, his political future, even the largeness of his income and the smallness of his debts—there was nothing that came within the circle of things conducive to his prosperity, which he did not idealise or exaggerate. He could neither despair nor rest quiet under failure. His restlessness rose almost to the level of his self-confidence. If the good was unattainable, then he would make the best of the bad, and aim at that, and call that good. And as he made the best of his friends (as long as they were his friends), so he made the best of himself and of his own actions. Come what might, he could never bring himself to think ill of himself in the past, or to distrust himself for the future. For the purpose of appreciating Bacon's philosophical works as well as his political career, it is essential that the reader should understand that he has to do with a man who will never, and can never, confess, even to himself, that he has gone absolutely wrong.

If throughout his life, if even in his private prayers, he habitually used the language of conscious and superior virtue, he was not thereby imposing upon others more than he imposed upon himself ; however he might occasionally dissemble and justify dissembling, he never deserved to be called a hypocrite, for he was thoroughly persuaded of his own general rectitude, and even in his deepest disgrace and dejection he still retained his self-esteem. Yet to many readers, after perusing the following pages, Bacon's retention of self-esteem will appear nothing less than portentous. To describe it as bordering on insanity would be unpardonable, for Bacon's nature was eminently sane; but it would be nearer the mark to say that from his restless, perfervid mother, who is said on reasonable grounds to have been " frantic " for some years before her death, Bacon inherited some abnormal characteristics, one of which took the shape of an excessive and even monstrous self-confidence. But for this, Bacon's *Apology* would have been more humble and more accurate; but for this, the *Novum Organum* would never have existed; it was the secret alike of his great strength and his great weakness; it nerved him to superhuman enterprises, and blinded him to his own most obvious faults.

Having ventured to call special attention to one point in a theory, I will now venture to give equal prominence to a fact—not theory at all, but solid, substantial fact—brought to light for the first time in the course of Mr. Spedding's researches, but omitted by almost all Bacon's subsequent biographers, although it has a most important bearing directly on his judicial career, and indirectly on our estimate of his whole character.

All the biographies above mentioned with one exception [1]—while not denying that Bacon's own confession of "corruption" must be admitted to be in some sense true—nevertheless exonerate him from any perversion of justice. This opinion is based upon the absence of any attempt to reverse

---

[1] Professor Gardiner's Biography in the *Dictionary of National Biography*.

the Chancellor's decisions after his fall. "To be guilty of corruption, and to be guilty of perversion of justice," says Professor Fowler, "are widely different things;" and, without further argument, he accepts, as expressing the whole truth with regard to these transactions, an apophthegm of Bacon's in which, while declaring his censure to be "the justest censure in Parliament that was these two hundred years" he goes on to assert, "I was the justest judge that was in England these fifty years." Mr. Aldis Wright says, "that Bacon took bribes for the perversion of justice no one has ventured to assert. Not one of the thousands of decrees which he made as Chancellor was ever set aside" —implying that justice was in no case perverted. To the same effect writes Dean Church: "If he had taken money to pervert judgment, some instance of the iniquity would certainly have been brought forward and proved. *There is no such instance to be found;* though of course there were plenty of dissatisfied suitors; of course the men who had paid their money and lost their cause were furious. *But in vain do we look for any case of proved injustice.*" Even Professor Gardiner, in one passage of his biography, inconsistently argues in the same strain: "*As far as we know, his justice was as exemplary as his energy;* not only were no complaints heard at the time, which may be easily accounted for, but in later years when every man's mouth was opened against him, no successful attempt was made to reverse his decisions."

It is an obvious answer to all these inferences from mere silence, that if Bacon perverted justice, not for money—of which no one accuses him—but *out of servility to some great person,* the decisions could not be likely to be set aside, even after the Chancellor's fall,

as long as that great person remained in power. How
quickly complaints might have accumulated if Bacon
had forfeited Buckingham's favour, may be gathered
from the fact that when he *was*, for a few weeks, out
of favour, petitions against him were immediately
threatened : "There is laid up for you, to make your
burden the more grievous, *many petitions to his Majesty
against you;*" so writes Yelverton to Bacon, 3 Sept,
1617.[1] All the above arguments, therefore, are nugatory against a charge that Bacon perverted justice in
compliance with a request from Buckingham, who
remained in power for seven years after Bacon's fall.

Now who would have supposed that the biographers
from whom I have quoted above were aware : 1st, that
there *was a case* in which there was evidence tending
to show that Bacon *perverted justice* to please Buckingham ; 2nd, that Mr. Spedding entrusted to his
coadjutor Mr. Heath, who edited the legal portion of
Bacon's works, the task of thoroughly investigating the
case ; 3rd, that the results of the investigation are
found in an Appendix to the seventh volume of Mr.
Spedding's edition of Bacon's *Life and Letters;* and
4th, that the investigation results in *an unhesitating condemnation of Bacon's conduct, and a verdict amounting
to "perversion of justice for the purpose of conciliating
Buckingham"?*[2]

---

[1] See also page 286 for an implied complaint from a suitor that, although
the Lord Chancellor would not sell his justice for gold, yet he might not
always "hold the scales upright," when "Court or favour" interfered.

[2] Professor Gardiner (*Dictionary of National Biography*, ii. 345) after
briefly sketching Mr. D. D. Heath's "searching investigation" and the
inference from it, adds, "If this is a correct representation of the matter—
and it seems probable, though far from certain, that it was so—Bacon's
conduct was *distinctly blameworthy*, though the appointment of arbitrators
may have veiled from him the real nature of the offence, which consisted
in transferring to others the responsibility which should have been borne

Of course, it is open to any biographer of Bacon to surmise that the Editor of Bacon's legal works may have been led to erroneous conclusions by ignorance of the practice of Chancery in the seventeenth century. But at least some justification of such a surmise would appear necessary. At present, as far as I know, there has been no serious attempt to invalidate Mr. Heath's conclusions. Presumably he was requested by Mr. Spedding to undertake the investigation as being the fittest man to ascertain the truth. Moreover, his conclusions are consonant with probability; for it must be considered probable that the self-willed and unscrupulous Favourite would not have written letter after letter to the Chancellor in favour of parties who had cases pending before him, for the mere purpose of putting off his friends and dependants with a mere epistolary intercession that could result in nothing more than " a full and speedy hearing," or " such justice as the case may allow."

It is seldom that Professor Gardiner makes a mistake ; but there appears to be at least an error of omission in the following sentence : "Even in his court he was made to feel the weight of the Favourite's patronage, and was exposed to a constant flow of letters from Buckingham, asking him to show favour to this person or that, *of course under the reservation that he would do so only so far as was consonant with justice.*" *Sometimes*, it is true, Buckingham adds the qualification, " so far as may stand with justice and equity ;" but very often even this saving clause is omitted. Often, if

by himself alone." The reader will have the opportunity of judging for himself whether this sentence is not too lenient for justice ; but, in any case, this admission that probably Bacon was "distinctly blameworthy" is inconsistent with the statement just quoted that "as far as we know, his justice was as exemplary as his energy."

implied at all, it is passed over very lightly in the words,
" what favour you may ; " *e.g.*, " I desire your Lordship's
further favour therefore unto him [Sir George Tipping]
that you will find out some course how he may be
exempted from that fear of the sale of his land. . . His
offer, *which seemeth very reasonable and for his Majesty's
advantage, I desire your Lordship to take into consideration, and to shew him what favour you may for my
sake.*" [1] These words, says Mr. Heath, practically
amount to a request " for the reconsideration and modification of a decree pronounced ; " [2] yet the Favourite not
only presses his demand with scarcely the shadow of a
reservation in favour of justice, but plainly intimates that
he has formed an opinion on the case, and that his own
opinion and " his Majesty's advantage " admit of but one
result. Even where he inserts a qualification, Buckingham sometimes bases his request upon "information" or
" credible report," in such a way as to imply that his
mind is made up, and that the Chancellor must follow
his opinion. Thus, in the case of a young Mr. Hansbye,
who disputed legacies alleged to have been left by his
father, Buckingham first reminds the Chancellor that
the case had been previously recommended to him by
the King and himself, and then continues : " Whereas
. . . . I am credibly informed that it will appear upon
their report " [*i.e.*, the report of the Masters of the
Chancery] " and by the depositions of witnesses without
all exception *that the said leases are no way liable to
those legacies;* these shall *be to earnestly intreat your
Lordship* that, upon consideration of the report of the
Masters and depositions of the witnesses, you will for
my sake shew as much favour and expedition to young
Mr. Hansbye in this case as the justness thereof will

---

[1] *Life and Letters*, vi. 293.   [2] *Ib.*, vii. 579.

permit. And I shall receive it at your Lordship's *hands as a particular favour.*" [1] Not unnaturally does Mr. Heath refer to this case, in spite of the inserted reservation, as one in which "Buckingham seemed to be putting pressure upon Bacon."

In the following letter there is not a hint of reservation ; and its peremptory force is all the greater because it follows a previous recommendation :—

"To the Lord Chancellor,

"My Honourable Lord,

"Understanding that the cause depending in the Chancery between the Lady Vernon and the officers of his Majesty's household is now ready for a decree, though *I doubt not but,* as his Majesty hath been satisfied of the equity of the cause on his officers' behalf, who have undergone the business by his Majesty's command, *your Lordship will also find their cause worthy of your favour ;* yet I have thought fit once again to recommend it to your Lordship, desiring you to give them a speedy end of it, that *both his Majesty may be freed from further importunity, and they from the charge and trouble of following it ; which I will be ever ready to acknowledge as a favour done unto myself, and always rest*

"Your Lordship's faithful friend and servant,

"G. Buckingham.

"Greenwich, the 15 day of June, 1618."

On another occasion Buckingham writes, in behalf of some friends and relations, to request Bacon to enforce the performance of certain conditions by some contractors who had purchased a Patent "for the transportation of butter out of Wales" from some "who have near relation to me." Without inquiring whether the contractors could plead anything on their side—*e g.,* that they had already performed the conditions, so far as they were practicable and equitable—he desires

---

[1] *Life and Letters,* vi. 312.

the Chancellor, "out of his consideration of the matter according to equity, to take such course therein either that this said agreement be performed, or that they which refuse it may receive no benefit of the Patent, which upon reason thereof was passed in their names. And *herein I desire your Lordship to make what expedition you can*, because now is the season to make provision of the butter that for this year is to be transported, whereof they take advantage to stand out." (14 May, 1619).

But all these instances of pressure are trifling in comparison with the following, which refer to the special case above mentioned—the case specially investigated by Mr. Heath at the request of Mr. Spedding and left unmentioned by all but one of Bacon's subsequent biographers :—

"To the Lord Chancellor,

" My Honourable Lord,

"I having understood by Dr. Steward that your Lordship hath made a decree against him in Chancery, *which he thinketh very hard for him to perform ;* although I know it is unusual to your Lordship to make any alterations when things are so far past, *yet in regard I owe him a good turn which I know not how to perform but this way*, I desire your Lordship, if there be any place left for mitigation, your Lordship would shew him what favour you may for my sake in his desires ; which I shall be ever ready to acknowledge as a great courtesy done unto myself ; and will ever rest

" Your Lordship's faithful friend and servant,

" G. Buckingham.

" Newmarket, the 2d of Decemb. 1618."

There is little enough of " reservation " here in the words, " if there be any place left for mitigation," and " what favour you may." There is none at all in the blunt and intimidatory letter in which, on the following

day, Buckingham repeats and emphasises his request
or command :—

"To the Lord Chancellor,

" My Honourable Lord,

". . . . I have written a letter unto your Lordship, which
will be delivered unto you in behalf of Dr. Steward ; and besides have
thought fit to use all freedom with you in that as in other things.
And therefore have thought fit to tell you that, *he being a man of
very good reputation, and a stout man that will not yield to anything
wherein he conceiveth any hard course against him, I should be sorry
he should make any complaint against you.* And therefore *if you
can advise of any course how you may be eased of that burden and
freed from his complaint, without shew of any fear of him or anything
he can say, I will be ready to join with you for the accomplishment
thereof.* . . . . . .

" Your Lordship's faithful friend and servant,

" G. Buckingham.

" From Newmarket, the 3 of December, 1618."

On 11 December, disguising a shameful assent in a
hasty postscript added to a hastily-written letter, the
Chancellor's answer comes back as follows :—

"I forget not your doctor's matter. I shall speak with him
to-day, having received your Lordship's letter ; and what is
possible shall be done. I pray pardon my scribbling in haste."

What "the doctor's matter" was, and what Bacon
found it "possible" to do, I have been prevented from
describing in the body of this work by a regard for the
continuity of the narrative, which would have been
broken by a digression of this kind. But the matter is so
important, and has been so generally neglected, that I
shall make no apology for giving it a prominent place
here ; especially as Mr. Spedding, after retracting his
own favourable but erroneous conclusions concerning the
case, has printed Mr. Heath's ample investigation in
an Appendix where it is little noticed, and has himself

expressed no opinion about it. The following is a summary of the facts as set forth in Mr. Heath's Report.[1]

A bill was filed, May 1617, by a youth not yet twenty-one, against his two uncles, one, Dr. Steward by name, being a friend of Buckingham. To the plaintiff (when a child eight years old at the time of his father's death) had been left a legacy of £800,[2] besides a share in his father's property. The rents and profits were to be taken by the executors till the sons should respectively attain the age of twenty. The executors had legacies of £200 apiece. The executors *mixed the money coming to them as executors and trustees with their own*, and, when the plaintiff attained the age of twenty in March 1617, they disputed his claim to interest on the legacy, stating that they did not know whether they had "made any commodity out of the estate or not."

The Bill having been filed in May, the matter was brought before the Court on 17 July. Bacon heard the argument, on the defendant's demurrer to jurisdiction, in person, and overruled the demurrer by ordering the defendants to " answer over to the point of the legacy according to the charge in the Bill." The defendants did not " answer over " for three or four months. On 28 October, after the plaintiff had complained that the defendants, repeatedly refusing to attend, even when they did attend, would not account—the defendants, instead of being punished, were allowed to have a Master who was a "civilian" joined, at their request, with Master Norton, and were given a week to proceed with their accounts.

---

[1] Extracted from an article of mine in the *Contemporary*, vol. **xxviii**. pp. 157-9.

[2] Worth between £3000 and £4000 of our money.

On 3 November the defendants put in their answer, and—with the full knowledge of the opinion twice implied by orders in the cause—admitting that they have refused to make any allowance for profits from the estate and legacy, they add, by way of reason, " being a thing by law not due to the plaintiff, nor yet in equity, as these defendants verily believe *any man will think that shall be truly informed of this case.*" Upon this Master Norton and the civilian concur in a report against them.

On 28 November the Solicitor-General, appearing for the defendants, was heard by the Court against the report, which, however, the Court confirmed and decreed accordingly. It was still, says Mr. Heath, open to the defendants to ask for a re-hearing before the decree was signed, or, failing in this, they might have moved for leave to file a Bill of Review. Instead of doing this, they disobeyed the decree and kept out of the way of process. Not till six months after the time for paying the plaintiff, did Dr. Steward, when he was at last arrested, desire his objections to be considered.

One year after the decree had been pronounced, Dr. Steward, alarmed at the increasing severity of the orders made by the Court to enforce obedience, appealed to Buckingham, who accordingly, December 1618, wrote to the Lord Chancellor the letters quoted above.

In consequence of these letters Bacon first saw Dr. Steward *privately*, to concert measures, and then, having called the parties together, he *made* the plaintiff assent to all proceedings under this decree ceasing, on the mere payment into court of the undisputed sum *without interest.* " I say *made*," says Mr. Heath, " because it is certain he would have preferred keeping his decree and enforcing it." By way of preserving an appearance of impartiality and of seeming to leave the question of interest still open, the order (22 February 1619) ends with the award of a sham commission appointed by both parties to further investigate the disputed points. It is needless to add that not the slightest trace has been found of anything done by this sham commission.

"I do not suppose," says Mr. Heath, "that anything was ever seriously meant by it, *except to 'ease' the Lord Chancellor 'of his burden.'* The plaintiff must have known that to press this commission would be only to throw away more money and incur more vexation, besides making dangerous enemies."

" But," he concludes,

"suppose it was meant in earnest. And then read it in connection with Bacon's solemnly expressed opinions and promises (vi. pp. 187, 191) which he seems to me to have been hitherto observing. The Masters in Chancery were 'reverend men,' trained to their business. Yet he will not leave them without guidance in references, but will, 'as one that hath a feeling of his duty and of the case (? ease) of others, endeavour to cast his orders into such a mould as may soonest bring the subject to the end of his journey.' See also what he says about making, upon the matter, too many chancellors. Here, *after reverend Masters, as well as himself the supreme Judge, had considered the matter* and pronounced upon the law and equity of the case, he proposes to refer it again *to persons not likely to be so learned;* without casting the questions into any mould whatever—not pointing out, that is, any guiding principles whatever, or putting any bounds to their inquiries—and, after all, when these persons shall have certified what, in their judgment, 'law and equity' required in this case, the 'subject' may be no nearer to the 'end of his journey,' for the court is then 'to make such further order as shall be meet'—*i.e.,* may hear all the arguments over again, as before." [1]

---

[1] I understood from the late Mr. Cecil Monro that he arrived, quite independently, at conclusions still more unfavourable to Bacon than Mr. Heath's. Mr. Monro called attention to the fact that in the order of 22 February the money is paid not to the plaintiff, now of age, but into

I cannot but think that this Chancery trial, remarkable as it is in many ways—for the strong *prima facie* evidence that Buckingham was putting pressure upon Bacon; for the importance attached to it by Mr. Spedding; for the pains which he took to attempt to explain it; for the candour with which he admitted that his explanation had been erroneous; and for the clear, cogent argument in which Mr. Heath supplied Mr. Spedding's omissions, and interpreted the whole procedure—ought not to have been without some weight with the recent biographers who have endeavoured to form an estimate of Bacon's judicial career. If a biographer feels himself justified in rejecting Mr. Heath's conclusions, I submit that he is not justified in concealing his grounds for this rejection. If it be urged that in the biographies above mentioned, being but slight sketches, space could not be found for even a brief allusion to this important case, I reply that in every one of them (except Professor Gardiner's) room is made for the hackneyed account of Sir Francis Bacon's wedding costume as recorded by Carleton; and surely, any one who can admit contemporary gossip of this kind into a serious biography of a Lord Chancellor of England, ought not for shame to plead want of space as a reason for omitting all mention of the one case in which the Chancellor is apparently shown, after competent investigation, to have been guilty of a deliberate perversion of justice.

court, by reason of some *infirmity* in the plaintiff which made it doubtful whether the plaintiff "were in case to discharge the defendants of the said £900, if it were paid to him." Could the plaintiff be weak in intellect? or could it be that he refused to give the necessary discharge with such passion and absence of self-restraint as enabled his adversaries conveniently to impute "infirmity" to him? Had he recovered in the following June when the order was made to pay over the money to *him*.

EVENTS IN BACON'S LIFE AND TIMES [1]

A.D.

Born (youngest of eight children, six of whom were by a former
    marriage). Son of Sir Nicholas Bacon (11) [2] .   22 Jan. 1560—1

The Council of Trent breaks up 1563

Revolt of the Netherlands ; Execution of Counts Egmont and
    Horn . . . . 1566—7

Elizabeth is excommunicated 1570

The Turks are defeated off Lepanto 1571

Massacre of St. Bartholomew 1572

Bacon goes to Trinity College, Cambridge (13) 1573

Union of Utrecht between the seven northern provinces of the
    Netherlands 1575

He is admitted " de societate magistrorum " at Gray's Inn (14). 1576

The Earl of Essex, now ten years old, goes to Trinity College,
    Cambridge 1577

In France with Sir Amias Paulet (14—15) . . . . 1577 – 8

His father dies, and he returns to England ; his elder brother
    Anthony sets out on his travels (15) 1579

Admitted " Utter Barrister " (15) 1582

Conspiracies against Elizabeth ; the Parliament sanctions the
    Voluntary Association formed in defence of the Queen ;
    Severe laws passed against Priests and Jesuits (16) . . 1583—4

Represents Melcombe Regis in Elizabeth's fifth Parliament (15)
                                          23 Nov. 1584

William of Orange assassinated 1584

Writes *Letter of Advice to Queen Elizabeth* (16—23) . . 1584

About this time was written the *Greatest Birth of Time* [3] . 1585

Becomes a Bencher of Gray's Inn (23) 1586

Represents Taunton in Elizabeth's sixth Parliament . 29 Oct. 1586

---

[1] Numbers in brackets indicate the pages where the several incidents are
mentioned.

[2] This is our 1561. But in Bacon's time the " civil " year began with March 25,
the historical year with January 1. The dates that follow will be given according
to the modern reckoning.

[3] In 1625 (see p. 348) Bacon says : " It being now forty years, as I remember,
since I composed a juvenile work on this subject, which, with great confidence
and a magnificent title, I named *The Greatest Birth of Time*."

---

[1] The letter containing this request to Leicester was not known to Mr. Spedding till after the publication of his earlier volumes.

A.D.

[1] He had also been returned for St. Alban's and Ipswich.

The following letter exhibits the view Bacon took of his collective writings in 1625, the year before his death.

"MOST REVEREND FATHER FULGENTIO,

. . . . I wish to make known to your Reverence my intentions with regard to the writings which I meditate, and have in hand ; not hoping to perfect them, but desiring to try ; and because I work for posterity ; these things requiring ages for their accomplishment. I have thought it best, then, to have all of them translated into Latin and divided into volumes. The first volume consists of the books concerning the *Advancement of Learning ;* and this, as you know, is already finished and published, and includes the *Partitions of the Sciences ;* which is the first part of my *Instauration.* The *Novum Organum* should have followed ; but I interposed my moral and political writings as being nearer ready. These are : first, the *History of the reign of Henry the Seventh, King of England,* after which will follow the little book which in your language you have called *Saggi Morali.* But I gave it a weightier name, entitling it *Faithful Discourses,* or the *Inwards of Things.* But these discourses will be both increased in number and much enlarged in the treatment. The same volume will contain also my little book on the *Wisdom of the Ancients.* And this volume is (as I said) interposed, not being a part of the *Instauration.* After this will follow the *Novum Organum,* to which there is still a second part to be added : but I have already compared and planned it out in my mind. And in this manner the second part of the *Instauration* will be completed. As for the third part, namely, the *Natural History,* that is plainly a work for a King or a Pope, or some college or order, and it cannot be done as it should be by a private man's industry. And those portions which I have published, concerning Winds and concerning Life and Death, are not history pure, because of the axioms and greater observations that are interposed : but they are a kind of writing mixed of natural history, and a rude and imperfect form of that intellectual machinery which properly belongs to the fourth part of the *Instauration.* Next therefore will come the fourth part itself ; wherein will be shewn many examples of the machine, more exact and more applied to the rules of Induction. In the fifth place will follow the book which I have entitled the *Precursors of the Second Philosophy,* which will contain my discoveries concerning new axioms, suggested by the experiments themselves, that they may be raised, as it were, and set up like fallen pillars : and this I have set down as the fifth part of my *Instauration.* Last comes the *Second Philosophy* itself, the sixth part of the *Instauration,* of which I have given up all hope ; but it may be that the ages and posterity will make it flourish. Nevertheless, in the *Precursors*—I speak only of those which almost touch on the universalities of nature—no slight foundations will be laid for the *Second Philosophy.*" [1]

[1] Spedding, vii. pp. 531-2.

PART I

THE LIFE OF FRANCIS BACON

§ 1 THE COURT OF ELIZABETH [1]

SOMEWHERE in the correspondence of Anthony Bacon, Francis
Bacon's brother, there occurs the following description of the
Four Arts, without which no one could hope to succeed at Court
in the later days of Queen Elizabeth :

> "Cog, lie, flatter and face,
> Four ways in Court to win men grace.
> If thou be thrall to none of these,
> Away, good Piers ! Home, John Cheese ! " [2]

Criticism in verse is generally too epigrammatic to be accurate,
but certainly the doggerel just quoted will not seem very over-
strained to any one who turns over Birch's *Memoirs of the Reign
of Queen Elizabeth* or the MS. of Anthony Bacon's correspondence.
In the nation at large there was no lack of moral health ; but
the Court breathed an atmosphere of falsehood and intrigue.
Intellect had free play, literature throve, the English language
was in such perfection that it seemed impossible for the men
and women of those days to write weakly or nervelessly ; but
truthfulness seemed extinct about the Queen. The old religion
was dead, and the new religion had taken no hold of the royal
circle. Greece and Rome were recognised as the model states,
and Machiavelli as the great authority on politics.

---

[1] The greater part of this chapter is extracted from my *Bacon and Essex*.
Seeley and Co., 1877, pp. 1-12.
[2] These verses must have been quoted by the writer, whoever he was, from
Roger Ascham. (*Scholemaster*, Arber's edition, p. 54.)

As for applying the principles of Christianity to politics, we, in these days, cannot be surprised that the Elizabethan politicians did not dream of doing it; but they went far beyond us in their consistent disregard for truthfulness. Essex himself, though naturally one of the bluntest of men, confesses that, in order to serve the Queen, he is forced, "like the waterman, to look one way and row another." Walsingham is recorded to have outdone the Jesuits in their own arts, and overreached them in equivocation and mental reservation. The history, now generally accepted, of the famous Casket letters, convicts the leading statesmen of England of an attempt to bring Mary Stuart to the block by forgeries. Sir Robert Cecil urges his intimate friend Carew to entrap the young Earl of Desmond into a conspiracy for the purpose of getting rid of him. To be a politician meant in those days to be an adept in suspecting and lying. "Envious and malignant dispositions," says Bacon, "are the very errors of human nature, and yet they are the fittest natures to make great politiques of." To the same effect is Hamlet's pithy description of the politician— "One that would circumvent God."

Foreign policy was the principal, but by no means the only, sphere for the evil arts of the "politique." Untruthfulness, on a pettier scale, was the basis of Court life. The rival politicians of the Essex faction and the Cecil faction entirely distrusted one another. Anthony Bacon accuses Sir Robert Cecil of intercepting his letters. Bacon advises Essex to take care to flatter the Queen in face as well as in word, and to imitate the craft of the former favourite Leicester, in taking up measures (which he never intended to carry out) for the mere purpose of appearing to bend to the royal will, by dropping them in compliance with the Queen's command.

These Court shifts and tricks were reduced to a system, some of the secrets of which are to be found in Bacon's *Essays*. There was the art of procuring oneself to be surprised; there was the art of writing a letter in which the main point should be casually added or introduced; there was the art of being found reading a letter of which one desired to make known the contents, but not in a direct way; there was the art of laying a bait for a question; there was a whole budget of similar arts—all taken from life, all (as Bacon says in the dedication prefixed to the *Essays*) " of a nature whereof a man shall find much in experience, little in books." It is true that Bacon calls these arts " cunning," as distinct from " wisdom ; " and he does not like them. But there was no choice for a man who elected to live at Court. What the art of oratory was in democratic Athens, that the art of lying and flattering was for a courtier in the latter part of the Elizabethan monarchy. No courtier was safe of his position without it. Truth, Bacon declares, is noble, and falsehood is base ; yet " mixture of falsehood is like alloy in coin of gold and silver, which may make the metal work the better." [1] Theory on such subjects is generally purer than practice, and Bacon's theory is summed up in these words : " The best composition and temperament is to have openness in fame and opinions, secrecy in habit, dissimulation in seasonable use, and a power to feign, if there be no remedy." [2] If a courtier objected to " feigning "—" Home, John Cheese ! "

For the corruption of the Court it is usual to lay the blame upon the Queen's parsimony, which drove her servants to reimburse themselves out of bribes for the losses which they could not make good out of their salaries. But it was perhaps not so much the Queen's parsimony as the increasing expense of state services, which had once been performed by voluntary efforts, but were now becoming too burdensome for the old system. Be that as it may, the effect (whether of the Queen's parsimony, or of the collapse of the old system of voluntary service) was bad in every way, both for the country and the Court. The evil fell most heavily on the military officers and ambassadors, who were forced to supplement the public supplies out of their own purses. Burghley and Cecil, who for the most part stop at home, feel little of it ; but the ambassadors, Sir Henry Unton, Sir Thomas Bodley, Sir Robert Sydney, all write in the same strain, constantly complaining of their expenses, and imploring to be recalled. Essex hereafter will appear—in spite of the many estates and valuable offices which he enjoyed —overwhelmed with debt towards the end of his career.

But if the pecuniary evil fell most heavily upon those who went abroad, the moral evil fell on those who stayed at home.

---

[1] *Essays*, i. 66.   [2] *Essays*, vi. 110.

"My Lord," writes the Recorder of London to Burghley, "there is a saying, When the Court is furthest from London, then there is the best justice done in England. . . . It is grown for a trade now in the Court to make means for reprieves. Twenty pounds for a reprieve is nothing, though it be but for ten days." In 1598, Sir Anthony Ashley thus writes to Sir Robert Cecil: "I am advertised that Wm. Whorewood is very deeply to be touched in the treasonable matter of one Tydie, late a scrivener here in Holborn, not long since executed at Tyburn for having counterfeited her Majesty's great seal. . . . If you, either by yourself or in some other name, will deal in this suit, it will easily pay your extraordinary expenses in the French embassy; for his yearly revenue in land and leases is 2,000 marks, besides much money. . . . If you neglect it, the party will promote it to *the great one.*" The "great one" is probably Cecil's rival, Essex. There is no reason to suppose that Essex would have been much more scrupulous than Cecil in "dealing" in such a suit. Egerton was one of the most upright men of the time; yet we find Essex writing to Egerton, first on behalf of one party to a suit, and then (finding that he had been unwittingly supporting an enemy of Anthony Bacon) in behalf of the opposite party. To the same Egerton we shall find Francis Bacon offering something closely approximating to a bribe, and showing how the transaction can be arranged without any one's noticing it.[1] Lady Edmondes, a lady about the Queen's person, declines 100*l.* as too little to save the ears and liberty of a certain Mr. Booth, who has been condemned, or is likely to be condemned, to the pillory and imprisonment. Concerning this Booth, Mr. Standen (a correspondent of Anthony Bacon's) writes that he *heard* Lord Keeper Puckering say to Lady Edmondes, "Do your endeavour, and you shall not find me wanting;" and Standen unquestionably lays the blame in the right place when he adds, "This ruffianry of causes groweth by the Queen's straitness to give to these women, whereby they presume thus to grange and huck causes." Anthony Bacon, taking up poor Booth's case, offers 100*l.*, but will not come up to the lady's price, which is 200*l.* Even for this sum she will only save his ears, but not his fine—which has been already assigned to some

[1] See p. 86.

servant in the royal stables.   We must not be too hard on this
Lady Edmondes.   She was but one of a class, "these general
contrivers of suits," whom Bacon justly stigmatises as "a kind
of poison and infection to public proceedings." [1]

Apart from the corruption and mendacity for which the
Queen appears, in part at least, to be personally responsible, the
system of government was radically bad, demoralising both the
governor and the governed.   The sort of reverence that we pay
to "the British Constitution" is now, in our minds, quite
distinct from the feeling of loyalty to the person of the sovereign.
But to the courtiers of Queen Elizabeth the Queen was not
Queen merely, but Constitution too.   No minister could dare to
assume responsibility for the royal actions; and yet the Queen
could do no wrong, and was responsible to no one.

The increasing years and infirmities of the sovereign increased
the friction of the imperfect system and the debasement of
those who were subjected to it.   Gloriana in her brighter years
standing up against Duessa as the champion of the truth
against superstition, Britomartis in arms at the head of an
armed people defying the enemies of pure religion—this was a
fitting and worthy object for the homage of a court; but
Gloriana senile, yet destitute of the graces of old age, Gloriana
flirting and lying, Britomartis abusing her chief minister as "a
peevish old fool," or amusing herself with making Francis
Bacon "frame," or boxing Essex on the ears, or swearing at
her godson Harrington, or in her final stage of melancholy with
a rusty sword before her on the table hacking at the arras—who
could worship such an idol as this without becoming a hypocrite
or a veritable slave ?   To the outside world the Queen's imperfections were less visible, and they could still undebased
revere in her the fearless champion of their religion and their
national independence; but for the inner circle of the Court the
old reverence had become unnatural, hypocritical, and incompatible with the spirit of freedom and honour.

If the Queen's aims had been invariably directed towards
objects useful for the country, the mischief might have been
much diminished.   But it was not so.   She thought of England,
it is true; but she thought of the interests of England as being

[1] *Essays*, xlix. 62.

included in the interests of the Crown. She did not desire to see her courtiers too friendly together. " Divide and command " was her motto. Elizabeth, no doubt, was in Bacon's mind when he wrote that " many have an opinion not wise, that for a prince to govern his estate according to the respect of factions is a principal part of policy."[1] To the same effect writes Clarendon, though more approvingly, "That trick of countenancing and protecting factions . . . . was not the least ground of much of her quiet and success. Insomuch that during her whole reign she never endeavoured to reconcile any personal differences at Court." Well may Clarendon say that this is a policy seldom entertained by princes that have issue to survive them ! Elizabeth had no issue, and the maintenance of her own power seems to have been her first care. Grant that her policy of keeping the succession uncertain turned out ultimately well for the nation ; yet there is nothing to disprove, and everything to prove, that she pursued that policy and all her other policy, not because it was best for the nation, but because it was best for herself.

In any case her policy of dividing her servants against one another was injurious, not only to her immediate ministers, but to the nation at large. "There were in Court," says Wotton, " two names of power and almost of faction, the Essexian and the Cecilian, with their adherents." But he might have added that the bickerings of these rival factions at Court penetrated to the most distant parts of England, and weakened the action of the nation even in Ireland and France. If, for example, Sir Francis Allen seeks a post at Court and is supported by Essex, the Cecils are sure to have another candidate in the field Sir Thomas Bodley loses the post of Secretary of State simply becauses Essex takes up his cause out of spite against Cecil, and because Cecil consequently feels himself bound in honour to oppose him. Standen, applying to Burghley for a reward for the valuable correspondence with which he has supplied the Queen, is frankly told by the Lord Treasurer that, since he has chosen to send his information through Essex, and not through him, he must look to Essex for support. Anthony Bacon supports a certain Mr. Trott in his suit for the clerkship to the

---

[1] *Essays*, xli. 1.

Council of York, and procures for him the support of Essex. Immediately the opposite party at York send word to Burghley that Essex had put forward a candidate, and pray Burghley's support for a rival.

So keen is the rivalry between the two parties, and so absolute the necessity of always being in the Queen's eye, that the heads of the contending factions are ready to shirk the service of their country rather than to absent themselves from Court. Cecil refuses to go on an important embassage to France, unless Essex will promise to take no advantage of his absence, and will conclude an ἀμνηστία. Essex in the same way shrinks for a long time from taking the command of the Irish Expedition, although the unanimous opinion of the country designated him as the fittest leader in a dangerous crisis. Even when he has at last consented to go, he will not stir till he has it under the broad seal that he may return at pleasure. He is even guilty of the crime of designating for that responsible post Carew, a most intimate friend of Cecil's, simply with the view of bringing discredit on the Cecilian faction by Carew's probable defeat and failure.

For the same reason the cautious Francis Bacon most earnestly begs Essex to avoid foreign expeditions, and to stop at home in the precincts of the Court. That the Earl of Essex was, in the general estimation at that time, the fittest man to serve England abroad, does not seem to have been thought an argument worthy of serious consideration. Bacon warns Essex not to be like Martha, "cumbered about much serving," but rather to imitate the pious Mary: "One thing is needful," and that one thing is—the Queen: "win the Queen."

Cecil is equally emphatic on this point: "I desire you to know this, that men are never more in a state to desire to be freed from any tongue that conceives unkindness than when they are in foreign employments." This he writes to his friend Carew when the latter is serving the state in Ireland, and he proceeds to advise him to throw up his duty as soon as possible, and to return on the pretext of sickness: "Things done for absent men come not so easily . . . for my part I would wish that after the end of the harvest you wrote that you are sick, and desire but to return two or three months."

All this party bickering was encouraged by the Queen for her own ends. It was pleasant to her to play off one party against another, and to know that at any moment her finger could shift the scales. She was not content with being supreme—" one mistress at Court and no master "—as she told Leicester; she desired to have her courtiers absolutely dependent upon her beck and nod, and rather encouraged them to look upon one another as enemies. "Look to thyself, good Essex," she says, while giving him a gift of money; and in the act of assuring him that her hand shall not be backward to do him good, she begs him to *give no occasion to his enemies.*

If the Queen herself used such language, it is no wonder that the courtiers adopted it. Lady Ann Bacon most solemnly warns her son Anthony against the machinations of his cousin Cecil when the latter rises to power. Essex is continually influenced, especially towards the end of his career, by the belief that he is surrounded by "enemies," who are ready to assail, not only his honour, but his life. Francis Bacon shares and encourages the same belief, warning the Earl to beware of "such instruments as are never failing about princes, which spy into their humours and conceits, and second them; and not only second them, but in seconding increase them; yea and many times, without their knowledge pursue them farther than themselves would." We shall hereafter see how powerfully this suspicion of the "instruments" about the Queen impelled Essex towards his mad and fatal treason.

Torn by these contending factions—while the supreme arbiter held aloof, and, when she interfered, interfered out of mere caprice—the Court often presented the appearance of a transformation scene in a pantomime. No one knew what scene was to come next. Nothing in Ovid's Metamorphoses—writes Anthony Bacon to Essex during a moment of Essexian triumph—was so sudden as the change brought about by the Earl at the Court. At one time it is Essex who has the upper hand, and has (to quote Anthony Bacon's bitter expression) made "the old fox [Burghley] to crouch and whine," so that even Carew goes humbly to court the favour of the powerful Earl. At another time it is Cecil who is the great man, with all the business passing through his hands, the object of general homage or fear, picturesquely enough described with a bundle of papers under his arm, walking straight through the ante-room of the Court, and seeing no one as he goes ; while discom-fited Essex is sulking at Wanstead.

No wonder that under such conditions, the Court seemed to the poets of the day the very type of mutability and inconstancy. There was no law or order in it, no just recognition of merit, no certain condemnation of oppression, chicanery, or factious strife.   The sole regulation of the seasons of the Court-world lay in the fancies and caprices of a despot who would be flattered like a woman and obeyed like a god. Yet even sweeter than flattery to her was servile obedience.

Leicester estimated her character aright when he continually appeared to oppose her, that he might gratify her by the appear-ance of continually receding from opposition into subservience. Her courtiers countenanced her in her belief that her will should be their law.   " Yield," writes Egerton to Essex, when the latter had retired from Court after having been thrust out of the room by the Queen's orders, "let policy, duty, and religion enforce you to yield ; submit to your sovereign, *between whom and you there can be no proportion of duty.*"   Essex could at times shake himself free from such a debasing adulation.   To Egerton's letter, just quoted, he replies, " In such a case I must appeal from all earthly judges . . .   I keep my heart from baseness, although I cannot keep my fortune from declining." But, with few exceptions, the courtiers made no such appeal from earth.   The Queen's will determined for them what was honourable or dishonourable, what was right or wrong.   To be excluded from her presence is described by them as being equivalent to a living death.   Francis Bacon records, as a note-worthy event, a salutation from the Queen on her way to chapel ; to a disgraced courtier the little act of graciousness was a fore-taste of restoration to favour, and the royal favour was essential for a courtier's life.

When Essex was freed from imprisonment, and allowed to go where he pleased, it was with this significant qualification, that he must consider himself still under the royal "indignation." Modern readers may find it difficult to understand the force of this qualification.   But Cecil understood it, when he wrote to

Carew, that " this distinction of the Earl's being still under the
royal displeasure prevented any from resorting to him, except
those that were of his own blood." In other and more substantial ways the Queen's favour was essential to a courtier.
Estates, wards—for to make money out of the guardianship of a
rich ward whom you had " begged " from the Sovereign, was in
those days a recognised and respectable method of increasing
your fortune—offices, monopolies, flowed from the Queen; and
to many of the nobles, almost beggared by the expenses of
public services, these were necessary parts of income. Essex
we shall find hereafter depending upon one of these monopolies
as his principal revenue; the fear of beggary consequent on
his being deprived of it by the Queen, will be recognised as
one of the motives that will drive him into treason.

Such a Court as this may well be described by Wotton as
being a fatal " circle." Once drawn into the meshes of it, the
highest ambition and the most unselfish purity might become
entangled and defiled. The rivalry of faction, and the passion
for success, the traditions of courtier-like suppleness, the ever-
present power of flattery and finesse, the prospects of fortune if
one could but struggle onwards to the centre of the cobweb, and
the certainty of poverty and disgrace if one attempted to go
back, all together encompassing and clogging resistance, succeeded in breaking or bending the purest and proudest spirit.
Montesquieu has succinctly suggested these dangers for us in
the saying, "que la vertu n'est point le principe du Gouverne-
ment monarchique." Or if the abrupt force of this dictum is
too startling for us, we may accept the same truth more eu-
phemistically expressed in the courtlier period of Clarendon :
" There is a certain comparity, conformity and complacency in
the manners, and a discreet subtilty in the composition, without
which . . . no man in any age or Court shall be eminent in
the aulical function."

Such was the stage upon which Bacon received his first
training and preparation for the part of a Statesman.

§ 2 Bacon's Youth

As you walk westward from the City on the Thames Embankment, just before you come to Charing Cross, you may see on your right, about a hundred yards or so from the river's edge, a low, massive, three-arched stone structure with two weather-beaten lions at the top and some apparently purposeless steps at the bottom. This was once a water-gate, designed by Inigo Jones for the Duke of Buckingham, as the entrance to an intended palace, after the latter had at last succeeded in gaining possession of the adjacent house and gardens, dislodging from them their former owner, Viscount St. Alban, more commonly known as Francis Bacon, Lord Chancellor. Of the palace that Buckingham proposed to build, no more than this was completed; but all the streets around have turned traitors, and sided with the usurper—"Buckingham Street," "Duke Street," "Villiers Street;" not a "Bacon Street" among them! So this old crumbling gate (if we except the name of "York Buildings," given to a neighbouring block of houses) is all that now remains to mark the site of the old York House, formerly the residence of Sir Nicholas Bacon, Lord-Keeper of the Great Seal, where Francis, his youngest son, was born on 22 January, 1561. Sixty years afterwards, the disgraced and poverty-stricken Lord Chancellor passionately declared that to sell his father's house to Buckingham would be "a second sentence;" and from that we may judge how he loved the "ancient pile," as Ben Jonson calls it, and the gardens pleasantly sloping down to the Thames on the south, and looking to the Strand on the north, where the little Francis spent so much of his childhood as was not passed at his father's country residence in Gorhambury, Hertfordshire.

By his first wife Sir Nicholas had six children, and by his second wife (Ann, daughter of Edward the Sixth's tutor, Sir Anthony Cooke) he had two sons, Anthony and Francis, of whom Francis was the younger by two years; so that the future possessor of York House and Gorhambury was the youngest of a family of eight. Lady Ann's sister Mildred had married Lord Burghley (then Sir William Cecil); and their son, the hump-backed Robert Cecil—afterwards to become the real or supposed patron of Francis—was eleven years old when his baby cousin was born.

Lady Ann was a woman of strong character and solid accomplishments. In her twenty-second year (1550) she published the sermons of Bernardine Ochine, translated from the Italian; and to her Theodore Beza dedicated his *Meditations*.[1] When Francis was two or three years old, she was occupied with the translation of Bishop Jewell's *Apology for the Church of England*, published in 1564. The daughter of Edward the Sixth's tutor was naturally not left in ignorance of the classical languages; and in her most familiar letters she quotes Latin as freely and naturally as a lady of our times would quote French; occasionally, also, for secresy, she writes English in Greek characters when she wishes to speak her mind freely about great people or dangerous subjects. Vehement in all things, in her aversion to extravagance and trifling, in her love of Calvinism, and in her affection and anxiety for her two sons, she manifests throughout her correspondence a restless discursive spirit, of which some hereditary traces may perhaps be found in her great son's intellectual speculations.

She died in 1610, over eighty years of age; but after 1600 (when we hear that her health is "worn") no mention of her occurs in any of Bacon's letters; not even in the inventory of his estate made in 1608, although, had she been then living in the enjoyment of her dower, the inventory would have been incomplete without some reference to her. Bishop Goodman in his *Court of King James the First*, says that "she was but little better than frantic in her old age;" and it is at all events probable that, some years before her death, she so far lost the use of her faculties that the management of her affairs was taken out of her hands. But her influence on her son's religious views in his youth may perhaps in part (though only in part) account for the marked difference between Francis Bacon's earlier and later utterances on ecclesiastical affairs; and, in his old age, among three reasons which he gives for desiring to

---

[1] Strype's *Annals*, III. i. 110; ii. 197, quoted in the *Dictionary of National Biography*, "Anthony Bacon." But the dedication to Lady Ann is said to have been made out of respect for her son, Anthony Bacon.

be buried "in St. Michael's Church, near St. Alban's," one is that "there was my mother buried."

Sir Nicholas was a man of easier temperament and a humourist.[1] One of his favourite sayings was "Stay a little that we may make haste the sooner." His son says of him that, "All the world noted Sir Nicholas Bacon to be a man plain, direct, and constant, without all fineness and doubleness; and one that was of the mind that a man, in his private proceedings and in the proceedings of state, should rest upon the soundness and strength of his own courses, and not upon practice to circumvent others."[2] Possibly Sir Nicholas erred on the side of dilatoriness. At all events he "stayed" so long about making provision for his youngest son that the provision was never made, being anticipated by his sudden death; and when his death came, caused by the folly of a servant, he had no reproof but a good-humoured jest. If Francis owed his energy to his mother, he was probably indebted to his father for his placid self-control and his rich humour; and those who see in this most versatile of men the dualism of genius may perhaps trace something of that dualism to hereditary causes.

In his twelfth year (1573) Francis was sent, with his brother Anthony, to Trinity College, Cambridge, of which Whitgift, afterwards Archbishop of Canterbury, was then Master. As befitted the grandson of Sir Anthony Cooke, he applied himself to Greek; but although Aristotle was included in the books which he studied, the young student had already rebelled against the despot of science. The new star in Cassiopeia, appearing (1572) and disappearing (1574) in the region which had been pronounced by Aristotle incapable of change, was a mighty protest to the observant freshman against the infallibility of the Pope of philosophy; and accordingly Rawley, his biographer, tells us from the lips of Bacon himself, that "while still a

---

[1] "He had" (Naunton, p. 38, quoted in the *Dictionary of National Biography*, vol. ii. p. 370, "a very quaint saying, and he used it often to good purpose, that he loved the jest well, but not the loss of his friend." Ben Jonson rather implies that Francis inherited, a little in excess, his father's love of a jest : "His (Francis Bacon's) language, when he could spare, or pass by, a jest, was nobly censorious :" And the friendly Yelverton (see p. 263) warns Bacon, in the face of an impending storm at Court, that "it is too common in every man's mouth in Court that . . . . . *as your tongue hath been a razor to some*, so shall theirs be to you." [2] Spedding, i. 202.

commorant of the University he had already noted the un-
fruitfulness of a philosophy only strong for disputations and
contentions, but barren of the production of works for the
benefit of the life of man." Between August 1574 and the
following March, the plague kept them from the University, but
the two brothers remained at Cambridge till Christmas 1575.

Something of the valetudinarian may be traced in Francis
Bacon's habits and tendencies throughout his life, and this
turn of mind was probably encouraged, not only by a natural
delicacy of constitution, but by his early and close companionship with an ailing brother. Just before he went to Cambridge,
Anthony's sight was despaired of; he was afflicted with
permanent lameness; and Whitgift's accounts of the money
spent " for Anthonie being syck " between 1573 and 1575 show
that his studies were repeatedly interrupted by serious illness.[1]
When he was sixteen years old (1576) Francis and his brother
Anthony were admitted (as being sons of a Judge) "ancients"
of Gray's Inn ; and in the following year he was sent to Paris
as one of the suite of Sir Amias Paulet, the English ambassador.
In 1579 the sudden death of his father recalled him to England
at the age of nineteen, to find himself destitute of the patrimony
which Sir Nicholas had intended to provide for him. Inheriting
only a fifth share of his father's personal property, he was consequently under an immediate necessity to work for his own
living or else to run into debt.

Of all this period we have no record save a few anecdotes
which reveal an early predisposition to extend his studies beyond
the ordinary limits of literature, and to read the smallest print
of the book of Nature. A practical joke in a man's rooms at
Trinity illustrates for him the vibration produced by sound; so
does another story about a conduit in St. James's Fields, which
responded to shouts with " a fearful roaring ; " there is a
reminiscence of a conjuring trick which he attempted to explain
in his boyhood, a description of a remarkable multiplication of
echoes at a place near Paris, and an account of his deliverance

---

[1] See *Dictionary of National Biography*, "Anthony Bacon," by S. L. Lee, ii.
326. Burghley, writing (29 August, 1593) to Lady Ann describes both brothers
as being " so qualified in learning and virtue, as, if they had a supply of *more
health*, they wanted nothing."

from warts by a strange device of Lady Paulet.[1] We read also
in the *De Augmentis* that, during his stay in France, he invented
a system of writing in cypher.

Observer and student though he was, he does not seem at
this time to have clouded his bright parts by any bookish
bashfulness, by a retiring disposition, or by a too great predominance of the thinking over the speaking faculty. His
youthful reply to the Queen, asking his age, that he was " but
two years younger than her Majesty's happy reign," shows one
who, if he was by first nature a philosopher, was at least by
training and second nature a courtier. The Latin inscription
round Hilliard's portrait of Francis at eighteen years old, " Oh
that I had a canvas to paint his mind ! " [2] is but one among several
testimonies indicating that every one who approached him
acknowledged his remarkable powers. When he returned to
England in 1579, he brought with him a despatch from Paulet,
in which he is mentioned to the Queen as of great hope.
endued with many good and singular parts, and one who,
if God gave him life, would prove a very able and sufficient
subject to do her Highness good and acceptable service.

On his return home, he appears to have entertained the
hope that by Burghley's aid he might obtain some advancement
which might enable him to dispense with the ordinary routine
of legal studies. At all events we find him (16 September,
1580) writing thus to his uncle :—

" Although it must be confessed that the request is rare and unaccustomed,
yet if it be observed how few there be which fall in with the study of the
common laws, either being well left or friended, or at their own free
election, or forsaking likely success in other studies of no less delight and
more preferment, or setting hand thereunto early without waste of years ;
upon such survey made, it may be my case may not seem ordinary, no
more than my suit, and so more beseeming unto it."

But the request was not granted ; and after applying himself
to the study of the law Bacon was admitted in his twenty-
second year (1582) as an Utter Barrister of Gray's Inn.
Two years afterwards he took his seat in Parliament (23
November, 1584) for Melcombe Regis. But with law and

---

[1] Almost all these stories will be found in the same treatise, the *Sylva Sylvarum*, Spedding, *Works*, ii. 427-8, 670.
[2] " Si tabula daretur digna, animum mallem."

politics he was combining philosophy ; for about this time he composed a work on this subject, which—as he confesses to a correspondent forty years afterwards—" he named with great confidence and a magnificent title *The Greatest Birth of Time.*"

§ 3 THE "ADVICE TO QUEEN ELIZABETH"[1]

On an equally high level of confidence with the *Greatest Birth of Time* stands another treatise entitled *Advice to Queen Elizabeth* (written at the end of 1584 or the beginning of 1585), in which Francis Bacon advises the Queen upon all points of her policy, and in particular upon the treatment of those who objected to the religious supremacy of the Sovereign, and who were therefore called Recusants.[2]

During the twelve months preceding the meeting of Parliament in November 1584, three plots against the Queen's life had been detected ; and in the October of that year a voluntary association had been formed to prosecute to the death any person by whom or for whom violence should be offered to the life of the Sovereign, and to hold such person (Mary Stuart) for ever incapable of the crown. In the Queen's life, at that crisis, were bound up the interests of England, of liberty, and of the Protestant faith ; and to be a Roman Catholic at such a season seemed well-nigh equivalent to being a rebel.

But while the Queen and the House of Commons were at one in their determination to keep down, and if possible to suppress, Roman Catholicism, they were divided in their opinions as to the form of religion expedient for the Established Church.

The Commons would willingly have seen modifications introduced in the direction of Calvinistic Puritanism, and would have freed the Clergy from subscribing those of the Thirtynine Articles which related to discipline and Church government. The Queen, so far from making these or any concessions,

---

[1] Spedding, i. 47-56.

[2] It is interesting to know that, even before this date, in 1583, the Queen was in the habit of receiving from Anthony Bacon, the elder brother of Francis, confidential letters containing foreign information, which she highly valued. Through the Earl of Leicester she expressed to Anthony her satisfaction in having " so good a man as you to have and receive letters by " (7 October, 1583).— *Dictionary of National Biography,* " Anthony Bacon," ii. 324.

determined to inforce a stricter uniformity. For this purpose she appointed (1583) as Archbishop of Canterbury, John Whitgift, formerly Master of Trinity College, Cambridge, a man of honesty and good intentions, but of so narrow a mind as to be incapable of comprehending the scruples of those who differed from him, and devoted to the sole object of creating at least an outward uniformity among the Ministers of the Church of England. To second Whitgift's efforts she recalled into action the Court of High Commission which had been sanctioned by Parliament twenty-four years before, when religious differences threatened the nation with civil war. This court claimed a power, used by no other English court, of compelling men to accuse both themselves and others. By tendering to an accused person what was called the *ex officio* oath that he would answer truly twenty-four inquisitorial interrogatories, which he had drawn up—the new Archbishop could obtain information about the private and public lives of all suspected Ministers. Refusal to take the oath was punished by deprivation of benefice and imprisonment. The Commission had not indeed the power of torture or death; but these deficiencies they supplied, when occasion demanded, by recourse to the ordinary tribunals, "and men were actually sent to execution for writing libels against the Bishops, on the plea that any attack upon the Bishops was an instigation to sedition against the Queen."[1]

Not a single Statesman approved of the proceedings by the bigoted Archbishop; and even the placid Burghley was roused to remonstrance. He too, he said, desired to see order established.in the Church; but these proceedings resembled that of the Romish Inquisition, and were "rather a device to seek for offenders than to reform any."[2] Bacon's nature pre-disposed him to tolerance of almost all religious differences that did not affect the order of the State, and his mother's influence and home training would incline him to side with Burghley in favouring the persecuted Ministers. But in the paper written about this time (1584-5) he touches this subject lightly, and with a prudent—perhaps almost too prudent—discretion. His main business is with the present dangers of the

---

[1] Gardiner's *History*, i. 33-6.   [2] *Ib.*, 36.

State, and the principal danger is, in his opinion, the Queen's "strong factious subjects, the Papists."

It cannot be surprising if, in the general fear of Mary Stuart and the supporters of her faith, the "Advice" advocates strong measures against the Roman Catholics. Yet the pressure is to be one of continuous discouragement, enfeeblement, and coercion, rather than aggressive persecution. To suffer them to be strong, in the hope that they will be contented with reasonable concessions, carries with it but "a fair enamelling of a terrible danger." To leave them half content, half discontent, carries with it an equally deceitful shadow of reason; "for no man loves one the better for giving him a bastinado with a little cudgel." Nevertheless, the Papists, he thinks, have a grievance from which it will be safe to relieve them. The present oath of allegiance compels a Recusant to swear that he thinks "that which, without the special grace of God, he cannot think," so making him perjured; or else, if he refuses the oath, the refusal constitutes him a traitor, "which, before some act done, seems somewhat hard." The best course is, first, to frame the oath in this sense, "that whosoever would not bear arms against all foreign princes, and, namely, the Pope, that should any way invade your Majesty's dominions, he should be a traitor." Most Papists, Bacon thinks, would take this oath; or, if they refused it, no tongue, for shame, could say that the refuser suffered for religion; and the accepting of this oath would dissolve the present mutual confidence between the English Papists and the Pope.

Secondly, "their number will easily be lessened by means of careful and diligent Preachers in each parish to that end appointed, and especially by good Schoolmasters and bringers-up of their youth; the former by converting them after their fall, the latter by preventing the same." The mention of Preachers introduces the delicate question of tolerance for the Puritans. The subject of the paper is the Queen's "strong factious subjects and foreign enemies." Bacon says plainly at the outset, "Your strong factious subjects be the Papists." He does not dream of imputing "faction" to the Puritans, who are therefore altogether out of his legitimate scope. Yet he cannot help mentioning and protesting against the grievances to which they

were being subjected, at the same time that he apologises for
the digression and declares that he is not personally addicted
to their opinions :—

"For Preachers, because thereon grows a great question, I am provoked
to lay at your Highness's feet my opinion touching the preciser sort ; first
protesting to God Almighty and your sacred Majesty that I am not given
over, nor so much as addicted, to their preciseness ; therefore, *till I think
that you think otherwise,* I am bold to think that the Bishops, in this
dangerous time, take a very evil and unadvised course in driving them
from their cures."

Such persecution, he says, spreads abroad an impression of
disunion in England ; and besides, the Preachers are effectually
helping the State, and ought not to be discouraged : " their
careful catechising and diligent preaching bring forth that
fruit " which is desired, " the lessening and diminution of the
Papistical number."

"And therefore in this time your gracious Majesty hath especial cause
to use and employ them, if it were but as Frederick II., that excellent
Emperor, did use and employ Saracen soldiers against the Pope, because he
was well assured and certainly knew that they only would not spare his
sanctity.
"And for those objections what they would do when they got once a
full and entire authority in the Church, methinks they are *inter remota
et incerta mala,* and therefore *vicina et certa* to be first considered."

One advantage of the appointment of Schoolmasters will be
that, by making the parents of each shire send their children to
such fit and convenient places as may be at her devotion, the
Queen may, " under colour of education, have them as hostages
of all the parents' fidelity that have any power in England."
As for the punishment of death, it is useless as a means for
lessening their numbers; their vice of obstinacy seems to the
people a divine constancy ; and, as with Hydra, when one head
is cut off, seven grow up.

A third means for keeping down the Papists will be to disqualify all who will not " pray and communicate according to
the doctrine received generally in this realm " from all office,
" from the highest counsellor to the lowest constable." Fourthly,
Popish landlords are not to be allowed to evict or unreasonably
molest any tenants who " pay as others do : "

" And although thereby may grow some wrong that the tenants, upon that confidence, may offer unto their landlords ; yet those wrongs are very easily, even with one wink of yours, redressed, and are nothing comparable to the danger of having so many thousands depend upon the adverse party."

In order to enfeeble the Papists for military enterprises, no one is to be " trained up in the musters except his parishioners would answer for him that he orderly and duly received the Communion ; " and no one is " to have in his house so much as a halbert without the same condition."

Above all, let her Majesty, in her dealings with the Papists avoid " that evil shamefacedness which the Greeks call δυσωπία, which is, not to seem to doubt them who give just occasion for doubt." By modifying the Oath of Allegiance, and by enfeebling the Papists, the Queen will never need to execute any but those whom all will acknowledge to be traitors ; and while she will be dispensed from the necessity of seeming to trust them, they will be obliged, for their own sakes, to be faithful to her.

In foreign policy Bacon here avows himself, as throughout his life, the enemy of Spain. France ought to be made a friend ; Scotland to be distracted by supporting those noblemen whom the young King suspected, and by giving him " daily cause to look to his own succession ; " but against Spain help might be sought from Florence, Ferrara, and especially Venice. The alliance of the Dutch and northern princes, " being in effect of your Majesty's religion," ought not to be contemned ; Spain should be weakened by attacks both upon his Indies and Low Countries ; or, if war is not to be provoked, such help is to be offered the Low Countries as can be given without provoking actual war with Spain.

The whole paper is remarkable, not only for the lofty tone adopted by a young barrister of three-and-twenty in addressing the Sovereign, but also for the cool directness with which the writer advances straight towards his political object, keeping his eye much more upon the end than upon the means.

Here, as throughout the whole of Bacon's political writings, the influence of Machiavelli is manifest. Perhaps there is even some affectation of Machiavellianism in his eulogy of Frederick II., (" that excellent Emperor who did use and employ

Saracen soldiers against the Pope ; ") and in his recommendation to the Queen to use the Puritans in the same way as her mere instruments. Bearing in mind that about this very time (soon after Christmas, 1584) Bacon's mother was expostulating with Burghley upon the unfair treatment of the Puritans by the Bishops, and that the Queen was, at this crisis, placing herself in opposition to the feeling of the Commons by the persecuting policy for which she had just appointed Whitgift to the primacy, we can easily understand the reasons for Bacon's protestation that he was " not addicted to the preciser sort," and appreciate the extreme delicacy of touch with which he handled the question of the dispossession of the Preachers. This transparent veil does not however conceal his real sympathy with the " careful and diligent" Puritans, and his feeling that the Queen was making a mistake in attempting to crush them—an expression not obscurely expressed in his condemnation of the " very evil and unadvised course taken by the Bishops."

Herein Bacon shows the insight of a Statesman, no less than in his proposed modification of the Oath of Allegiance. But the reader must not omit to note the qualifying words with which the young barrister "lays at Her Highness's feet" his unacceptable condemnation of her policy. " I am bold to think it," he says, " *till I think that you think otherwise.*" From a very young man the phrase is excusable and natural, perhaps almost commendable. But it betokened more than a young man's excess of modesty. There was in Bacon an invariable pliancy in the presence of great persons which disqualified him for the task of giving wise and effectual counsel. In part, this obsequiousness arose from his mental and moral constitution ; in part, it was a habit deliberately adopted as one among many means by which a man may make his way in the world. In a little treatise entitled *The Architect of Fortune,* published in the *De Augmentis* (1623), he lays it down as a precept for the man who wishes to succeed, that he must " avoid repulse : "

" A second precept is, to beware being carried by an excess of magnanimity and confidence to things beyond our strength, and not to row against the stream. . . . We ought to look round and observe where things lie open to us and where they are closed and obstructed, where they are difficult and where easy, that we may not waste our time on things to which convenient access is forbidden. For in that way we shall *avoid repulse, not occupy ourselves too much about one matter, earn a character for moderation, offend fewer persons, and get the credit of continual success,* whilst things which would perhaps have happened of themselves will be attributed to our industry."[1]

Here then we have one secret of Bacon's failure as a counsellor. He had no political backbone, no power of adhering to his convictions and pressing them on unwilling ears. Young or old, from twenty to sixty, he was always the same in this excessive obsequiousness; if he strove against authority, if he forced himself to utter a possibly unacceptable " Yes " or " No," it was always " like Ovid's mistress, as one that was willing to be overcome." [2] This pliability he avowed so frankly that every one took him at his word ; and from the beginning to the end of his career his wiser counsels were neglected, and he was little better than an instrument in the hands of the unwise.

At the same time we must remember the circumstances in which a counsellor of those days offered counsel. Personal government was a necessity. There is no reason to think that Bacon considered it an undesirable necessity ; the great persons whom he sought to persuade seemed to him more fit to govern, and perhaps more open to his persuasion, than a House of Commons; the Queen and her Council had more means of information, more traditions of continuous policy, more responsibility, and far more power, than could be wielded by a mere representative and changeable assembly without organised parties. Desirable, or undesirable, it was a necessity. What counsels Bacon addressed to the House of Commons could not be heard outside the House, and might be ineffective within it ; the modern press and public meetings were non-existent. If, therefore, anything was to be done it must be done through the Queen ; and if his counsel was distasteful to her, it was impracticable and useless. How necessary, therefore, to show all possible

---

[1] *De Aug.* viii. 2, Spedding, *Works,* v. 73.

[2] See Bacon's opinion about the objectionable Patents in December 1602 (Spedding, vii. 151), "The King, by my Lord Treasurer's signification, did wisely put it upon a consult, whether the Patents which we mentioned in our joint letter were at this time to be removed by Act of Parliament. I opined (*but yet somewhat like Ovid's mistress, that strove, but yet as one that would be overcomen*) that Yes."

tact in avoiding unpleasant advice, and to be ready to exchange the counsel that was best, but unpleasing, for that which was less good but more welcome to her ears !

§ 4 "The Controversies of the Church of England"[1]

In the next Parliament (29 October, 1586) Bacon sat for Taunton, and, with other members of both houses, presented a petition for the execution of Mary Stuart. In this year he became a Bencher of Gray's Inn. The quarrel between the Puritans and High Churchmen, suspended during the general terror of Spain, broke out again after the destruction of the Armada in 1588, and the Marprelate controversy was at its height in the summer of 1589. Between the two contending parties, Bacon, in his *Controversies of the Church of England* (1589), arbitrates with stately impartiality, censuring both for their bigotry, but inclining towards the Puritans.[2]

One party, he says, is seeking truth in the conventicles of heretics, the other in the external representation of the Church,[3] and both are in error. The remedy is charity; the controversy being, as all confess, about things not of the highest nature, men must not forget the league of Christians penned by our Saviour, " He that is not against us is with us." St. Paul says, " One faith, one baptism," not " one ceremony, one policy : " and in such light matters, men should say with St. Paul, " I and not the Lord."[4] The causes of controversy are four, 1st, imperfections in the "conversation " and government of the Bishops and Governors of the Church ; 2nd, the ambition of certain persons which love the salutation of " Rabbi, master "— the true successors of Diotrephes, the lover of preeminence, of which disease the Universities [here he aims at Cartwright, the Lady Margaret Professor of Divinity at Cambridge] are the seat and continent ; 3rd, an excessive detestation of some former corruptions, which leads men to think that opposition to the Church of Rome is the best touchstone to try what is good,[5] and that the Church

---

[1] Spedding, i. 74-95.
[2] This treatise should be studied in connection with the Essay *Of Unity in Religion.*
[3] *Essays*, iii. 28.   [4] *Ib.* 65-80.   [5] *Ib.* 50.

must be purged every day anew; 4th, the imitation of foreign forms of Church government, whereas the Church in every country should do that which is convenient for itself.

Both parties have degenerated from their former moderation. The Churchmen, who once admitted the existence of defects, now maintain that things are perfect as they are; they condemn the Reformers; they censure the Churches abroad, and *even impugn the validity of holy orders conferred in the Reformed Churches abroad.* Why do the Bishops stand so precisely on altering nothing? A good husbandman is ever proyning and stirring in his vineyard; he ever findeth somewhat to do. But we have heard of no offers of the Bishops of bills in Parliament. Their own constitution and orders have reformed little. Is nothing amiss? Let them remember that the contentious retention of custom is a turbulent thing.[1] The wrongs inflicted by them upon the weaker party in the Church can hardly be dissembled or excused. They have been captious and uncharitable in inquisitions, in receiving accusations, in swearing men to blanks and generalities, in urging subscriptions; and in silencing preachers, they have punished less the preachers than the people. Let them not forget that " the wrath of man worketh not the righteousness of God."

On the other hand the Puritans, who began with projects of reform have advanced to projects of destruction; they are narrow and bigoted in their dislike of tact, study, learning, and critical acumen; they ramble and never penetrate; " the word (the bread of life) they toss up and down, they break it not; " they teach people their restraints and not their liberty, they vulgarise controversies, unduly magnify preaching, neglect liturgies, depreciate the authority of the fathers, and " resort to naked examples, conceited inferences, and forced allusions, such as do mine into all certainty of religion." Characteristically enough, he adds the accusation that in their excess of zeal, " they have pronounced, generally and without difference, all untruths as unlawful," forgetting the midwives in Egypt, and the example of Rahab, and even how " our Saviour, the more to touch the hearts of the two disciples with a holy dalliance, made as if he would have passed Emmaus."

[1] *Essays*, xxiv. 22.

Finally he warns the Puritans to "take heed that it be not true, which one of their adversaries said, that they have but two small wants, want of knowledge and want of love" and then—after deprecating personalities and public controversies on subjects on which "the people is no fit arbitrator," and which should be reserved for "the quiet, moderate, and private assemblies and conferences of the learned"—he concludes with the hope that he shall "find a correspondence in their minds which are not embarked in partiality, and which *love the whole better than a part.*"

Obviously either side of the controversialists might have replied that the real question was whether the "part" for which they were contending was essential to the "whole;" and indeed practical disputes are seldom settled by general propositions. Bacon writes like a sensible Erastian, with Puritan inclinations, who has a profound belief in the value of the Christian religion, and an equally profound indifference to small details of Church government or ceremonies. No Anglican, and no decided Puritan, could have written this paper. A Puritan could hardly have laid his finger so exactly upon the faults of his brethren, or have maintained so unhesitatingly that every Church should do that which is convenient for the Estate of itself ("*consentiamus in eo quod convenit*"): still less could a thorough-going Anglican like Hooker have made the implied admission that the Reformed Churches were superior to the Church of England in the absence of some "abuses" ("neither yet do I admit that their form is better than ours *if some abuses were taken away*") or have written the following sentence :

"Hence (exasperate through contentions) they are fallen to a direct condemnation of the contrary part, as of a sect. Yea, and some indiscreet persons have been bold in open preaching to use dishonourable and derogative speech and censure of the Churches abroad ; and that so far as *some of our men* (*as I have heard*) *ordained in foreign parts have been pronounced to be no lawful ministers.*"

As between the controversialists, it would be hard to detect partiality ; for Bacon's indignation at the oppressions of the Bishops is equalled by his scorn for the bigoted narrowness of some of the Puritans. But in his frank recognition of the existence of imperfections in the Church, and of the need of some reform, he appears to incline to the latter. It is creditable alike to his statesmanship and to his independence of character that, at a time when all deviations from the forms of the prayer-book were known to be distasteful to the Queen, Bacon should have pleaded for elasticity, and that he should have applied to Church policy his favourite maxim that " the contentious retention of custom is a turbulent thing."

§ 5 BACON'S CHOICE OF A LIFE

From political and ecclesiastical treatises, we turn to Francis Bacon's private life and attempts at domestic economy. It was a misfortune, and one of the greatest of his misfortunes that, during the first forty-five years of his life, he was almost always in debt and always in want of money. His elder brother Anthony, who was never tired of assisting him, was himself spending money freely, travelling on the continent from 1579 to 1592; and consequently in 1584 we find Francis arranging for the sale or mortgage of some of his brother's estates. From 1580 to 1588 he applies to Lord and Lady Burghley, to Walsingham and to Leicester, to further some suit of which we do not know the precise nature; but nothing was done for him till Essex came into the favour of the Queen in 1589; and in that year he received, through Burghley, his first token of favour, the reversion of the Clerkship of the Council in the Star Chamber, worth about £1,600. But it was of no present value, and was not enjoyed by Bacon till four-and-twenty years afterwards.

Meanwhile the want of money had an important bearing on the question to what was he to devote himself, to philosophy or to civil life. Like Garrick between the two muses of Tragedy and Comedy, so Bacon—courtier and politician by circumstances and breeding, but student by nature—stood distracted between Politics and Science, equally apt for either. But, without money, not even the author of the *Greatest Birth of Time* could find leisure for research or means for conducting his experiments. And for the nephew of the Queen's chief adviser, the son of the late Lord Keeper, who had himself been styled "her young Lord Keeper" by the Queen, how natural to expect some position worthy of his abilities and bringing with it leisure and wealth sufficient for his philosophic purposes! That this was one of his objects in suing for place, appears from a short autobiographical passage (subsequently cancelled) in the Preface, or Proem, to the *Interpretation of Nature,* written about the year 1603. In this the author describes his character and the motives that induced him to deviate from philosophy to politics.

"Whereas I believed myself born for the service of mankind, and reckoned the care of the common weal to be among those duties that are of public right, open to all alike, even as the waters and the air, I therefore asked myself what could most advantage mankind, and for the performance of what tasks I seemed to be shaped by nature. But, when I searched, I found no work so meritorious as the discovery and development of the arts and inventions that tend to civilise the life of man. . . . Above all, if any man could succeed—not in merely bringing to light some one particular invention, however useful—but in kindling in nature a luminary which would, at its first rising, shed some light on the present limits and borders of human discoveries, and which afterwards, as it rose still higher, would reveal and bring into clear view every nook and cranny of darkness, it seemed to me that such a discoverer would deserve to be called the true Extender of the Kingdom of Man over the universe, the Champion of human liberty, and the Exterminator of the necessities that now keep man in bondage. Moreover, I found in my own nature a special adaptation for the contemplation of truth. For I had a mind at once versatile enough for that most important object—I mean the recognition of similitudes—and at the same time sufficiently steady and concentrated for the observation of subtle shades of difference. I possessed a passion for research, a power of suspending judgment with patience, of meditating with pleasure, of assenting with caution, of correcting false impressions with readiness, and of arranging my thoughts with scrupulous pains. I had no hankering after novelty, no blind admiration for antiquity. Imposture in every shape I utterly detested. For all these reasons I considered that my nature and disposition had, as it were, a kind of kinship and connection with truth.

"But my birth, my rearing and education, had all pointed, not towards philosophy, but towards politics : I had been, as it were, imbued in politics from childhood. And, as is not unfrequently the case with young men, I was sometimes shaken in my mind by [other men's] opinions.[1]   I

---

[1] This translation is in accordance with Bacon's general use of the word "opinio" in the sense "false opinion." If this is correct, the meaning is that he was disturbed by false opinions suggesting doubts of the truth of his philosophic theories.

also thought that my duty towards my country had special claims upon me, such as could not be urged by other duties of life. Lastly, I conceived the hope that, if I held some honourable office in the state, I might thus secure helps and supports to aid my labours, with a view to the accomplishment of my destined task. With these motives I applied myself to politics, and with all due modesty I also recommended myself to the favour of influential friends. There was one other consideration that influenced me. The objects of philosophy just now mentioned, be they what they may, do not extend their influence beyond the condition and culture o this present mortal life. Now, as my life had fallen on times when religion was not in a very prosperous state, it occurred to me that in the discharge of the duties of political office it might be also in my power to make some provision even for the safety of souls." [1]

Here then we have an unmistakable statement of Bacon's principal object in life. *No work* seemed to him so meritorious as the discovery of an Art of Invention, and for this he considered himself best adapted. If he deviated into politics, urged by a sense of duty to his country, it was partly because he had been " shaken by opinions " in his philosophic studies, and partly because he conceived that " if he held some honourable office in the State, he might thus secure helps and supports to aid his labours with a view to the accomplishment of his destined task," *i.e.* the discovery of the Art of Invention.

To the same effect is a letter, written in January, 1592, in which Bacon once more appeals to Burghley for advancement. The appeal naturally makes us ask the reason for the great man's unwillingness to help his wife's nephew. Did he think Francis Bacon too showy to be sound ? Or too supple and versatile to be quite trustworthy ? Or was he afraid of a rival for his own son ? Bacon afterwards declared that " in the times of the Cecils able men were, of purpose, suppressed : " and the letter itself indicates a latent suspicion that he was being kept down out of a fear that his rise might interfere with the rise of his cousin Robert Cecil. If he could not rise with the help of Burghley, he might perhaps rise with the help of Essex : but in any case, before giving up all hope of Burghley, it would be well to make one last attempt to remove the Lord Treasurer's jealousies and suspicions; and accordingly toward the beginning of his thirty-second year, Bacon writes to

[1] Spedding, iii. 518.

Burghley as follows, avowing his readiness not to interfere with Robert Cecil's prospects, if the Lord Treasurer would help him : on the other hand, if his Lordship "will not carry him on," he will shift for himself, sell his inheritance, and turn plain student.

"To my Lord Treasurer Burghley

"My Lord,

"With as much confidence as mine own honest and faithful devotion unto your service, and your honourable correspondence unto me and my poor estate, can breed in a man, do I commend myself unto your Lordship. I wax now somewhat ancient ; one and thirty years is a great deal of sand in the hour-glass. My health, I thank God, is confirmed ; and I do not fear that action shall impair it, because I account my ordinary course of study and meditation to be more painful than most parts of action are.

"I ever bare a mind (in some middle place that I could discharge) to serve her Majesty ; not as a man born under Sol, that loveth honour ; nor under Jupiter, that loveth business (for the contemplative planet carrieth me away wholly) ; but as a man born under an excellent sovereign, that deserveth the dedication of all men's abilities. Besides, I do not find in myself so much self-love but that the greater part of my thoughts are to deserve well (if I were able) of my friends, and namely of your Lordship, who, being the Atlas of this commonwealth, the honour of my house, the second founder of my poor estate, I am tied by all duties, both of a good patriot, and of an unworthy kinsman, and of an obliging servant, to employ whatsoever I am to do you service.

"Again, the meanness of my estate doth somewhat move me ; for though I cannot accuse myself that I am either prodigal or slothful, yet my health is not to spend nor my course to get. Lastly, I confess that I have as vast contemplative ends as I have moderate civil ends ; for I have taken all knowledge to be my province, and if I could purge it of two sorts of rovers (whereof the one with frivolous disputations, confutations, and verbosities, the other with blind experiments and auricular traditions and impostures, hath committed so many spoils) I hope I should bring in industrious observations, grounded conclusions, and profitable inventions and discoveries —the best state of that province. This, whether it be curiosity, or vain glory, or nature, or (if one take it favourably) *philanthropia*, is so fixed in my mind as it cannot be removed.[1] And I do easily see that place of any

---

[1] We here see that Bacon considers his philosophic ambition—" if one take it favourably," and there is little doubt that he "took it favourably"—to be *philanthropia*. What he understood by the word is apparent from *Essays*, xiii. 2 : " I take Goodness in this sense—the affecting of the weal of men, which is that the Grecians call *Philanthropia ;* and the word *humanity* (as it is used) is a little too light to express it. . . . This, of all virtues and dignities of the mind, is the

reasonable countenance doth bring commandment of more wits than of a man's own—which is the thing I greatly affect.

" And for your Lordship, perhaps you shall not find more strength or less encounter in any other. And if your Lordship shall find now, or at any time, that I do seek or affect any place whereunto any that is nearer unto your Lordship shall be concurrent, say then that I am a most dishonest man.

" And if your Lordship will not carry me on, I will not do as Anaxagoras did, who reduced himself with contemplation unto voluntary poverty. But this I will do. I will sell the inheritance that I have, and purchase some lease of quick revenue, or some office of gain that shall be executed by deputy, and so give over all care of service, and become some sorry book-maker, or a true pioner[1] in that mine of truth which (he said) lay so deep.

" This which I have written unto your Lordship is rather thoughts than words, being set down without all art, disguising, or reservation. Wherein I have done honour to your Lordship's wisdom in judging that that will be best believed of your Lordship which is truest, and to your Lordship's good nature in retaining nothing from you. And even so I wish your Lordship all happiness, and to myself means and occasion to be added to my faithful desire to do you service. From my lodging at Gray's Inn."

The exact correspondence of this letter with the autobiographical passage above quoted, will not fail to strike the attention: his " civil ends " are as moderate as his " contemplative ends " are vast : he is " not born under Sol that loveth honour, nor under Jupiter that loveth business (for the contemplative planet carrieth me away wholly) ; " he desires " place " indeed, but some " middle place that he could discharge," and one reason for desiring it is because he sees " that place of any reasonable countenance doth bring commandment of more wits than of a man's own—which is the *thing I greatly affect.*" Very similar is the language in which (1597), he dedicates to his brother Anthony the first edition of the *Essays* :—

" I sometimes wish your infirmities translated upon myself, that her Majesty mought have the service of so active and able a mind, and I mought be with excuse confined to these contemplations and studies for which I am fittest."

greatest, being the character of the Deity," No one will understand Bacon's character who does not bear in mind that *throughout his life* he regarded himself as the benefactor of mankind inspired by this, " the greatest of all virtues and dignities of the mind, *the character of the Deity.*"

[1] In modern English " pioneer."

Many a politician sighs after leisure for literature who never seriously entertains the notion that the claims of literature are superior to those of politics ; but with Bacon this longing for leisure and for scientific study was something more than a mere transient desire for greater freedom or for change of occupation. In 1605 he writes to Sir Thomas Bodley :—

" I think no man may more truly say with the Psalm, *multum incola fuit anima mea* than myself.[1] For I do confess since I was of any understanding, my mind hath been absent in effect from that I have done ; and in absence are many errors which I do willingly acknowledge ; and amongst the rest this great one that led the rest—that knowing myself by inward calling to be fitter to hold a book than to play a part, I have led my life in civil causes, for which I was not very fit by nature, and more unfit by the preoccupation of my mind."

When his public career is closed in disgrace (1621) and he pours forth his sorrows and confessions to the Searcher of Souls, the great sin of all is, in his judgment, his desertion of philosophy and his having allowed himself to be diverted into politics :—

" Besides my innumerable sins, I confess before Thee that I am debtor to Thee for the gracious talents of Thy gifts and graces, which I have neither put into a napkin, nor put it as I ought to exchangers, where it might have made most profit, but misspent it in things for which I was least fit, so as I may truly say my soul hath been a stranger in the course of my pilgrimage."

So it remains even to the last ; and, in giving to the world his great work, the *De Augmentis* (1623), he can contrive to forget the long assiduous suing and scheming by which after much patient striving and many disappointments he forced his way up to office, and can actually lay the blame on " destiny " for carrying him into the vortex of a political career, being, as he says, " a man naturally fitted rather for literature than for anything else, and *born by some destiny against the inclination of his genius*, into the business of active life." [2]   It is the same story throughout—*multum incola ;* with this Bacon's public life begins, and with this it ends.

Taking all these autobiographical passages into consideration written at six different periods in his life, two of which were

---

[1] The same quotation is repeated (1609) in a letter to Isaac Casaubon (Spedding, iv. 147).   [2] Spedding, *Works*, v. 79.

intended to be secret—for in the days of his greatness he cancelled the Prelude to the *Interpretation of Nature*, perhaps as
exposing in rather too glaring a manner, the inconsistency between his theoretical preference of science and his practical
preference of politics—I do not see how we can doubt Bacon's
distinct affirmations ; 1st, that he considered himself less fit for
" business " than for " contemplation," to which he was wholly
devoted ; 2nd, that one reason for seeking office was that he
might thereby be able to help on his philosophic projects, which
with him were paramount ; 3rd, that in 1592, when he was
thirty-one years old, this had become a habit of mind with him
(the mind which he " ever bare) ; " and that, towards the end
of his life, as well as in the middle, he regretted, as an " error,"
his desertion of philosophy for business.

§ 6 Bacon Suing

The proem or preface to the *Interpretation of Nature* reveals
the proud self-confidence which never wholly disappeared from
Bacon, although in the days of his greatness it was occasionally
concealed beneath a veil of compliance.   Reading his letters
to Villiers and to James, no one would accuse Verulam or
St. Alban of pride ; but plain Mr. Francis Bacon not only felt
himself superior to the world—as the Author of the *Greatest
Birth of Time* could hardly help feeling—but also took no
trouble to disguise his sense of superiority.   He writes to Lady
Burghley in his twentieth year, justifying rather than excusing
his behaviour : " My thankful and serviceable mind shall be
always like itself, howsoever it vary from the common disguising."
In the same spirit of proud unbending rectitude he offers his
services to Lord Burghley in the year 1580, subject to the
proviso that " public and private bonds vary not, but that my

---

[1] Professor Gardiner, commenting on Bacon's letter to Bodley, says, "This
confession must not be taken too literally.   Every man deeply engaged in politics
sighs at times for a freer life, and if Bacon had a special reason for longing for it,
in order that he might develop his scientific work, it is unnecessary to suppose
that, except in moments of weariness, he regarded his political work as unworthy
of himself."—*Dict. Nat. Biog.* ii. 337.

I do not maintain that he regarded his political work as absolutely, but as
relatively, "unworthy"—as work for which he was "less fit" than for science,
and into which, consequently, he felt that he had done wrong to deviate.

service to God, her Majesty and your Lordship draw in a line."
His uncle reports to him (1586) some complaints of his pride,
intimating that there are good grounds for them; and, a year
or two earlier (1583) we find a friend of his brother Anthony
complaining of the "strangeness" which had been repeatedly
used to him by Francis. Some years later (1595) Essex, apologising for Bacon's behaviour, describes it as being "only natural
freedom and plainness which he had used with me, and, in
my knowledge, with some other of his best friends." But Bacon
himself comes nearer to the truth in his reply to Lord Burghley
(1586), when he connects his so-called pride with "bashfulness,"
while, at the same time, he promises amendment.

"For that your Lordship may otherwise have heard of me, it shall make
me more wary and circumspect in carriage of myself. Indeed, I find in
my simple observation that they which live as it were *in umbra*, and not in
public or frequent action, how moderately and modestly soever they behave
themselves, yet *laborant invidia*. I find also that such persons as are of
nature bashful (as myself is), whereby they want that plausible familiarity
which others have, are often mistaken for proud. But once, [1] I know well
and I most humbly beseech your Lordship to believe, that arrogancy and
overweening is so far from my nature as, if I think well of myself in anything, it is in this, that I am free from that vice. And I hope, upon this
your Lordship's speech, I have entered into those considerations as my
behaviour shall no more deliver me for other than I am."

A certain kind of "bashfulness" is the natural companion of
a student's self-estimation; and, while the student fit predomi-
nated, Bacon may have felt himself ill at ease as a courtier.
At all events, we find him, even in his forty-eighth year,
remarking this defect in his note-book, and devising means for
the attainment of a "plausible familiarity."

"To suppress at once my speaking with panting and labour of breath and
voice. Not to fall upon the main too sudden, but to induce and intermingle
speech of good fashion. To use at once, upon entrance given, of speech,
though abrupt, to compose and draw myself in. To free myself at once
from payment of formality and compliment, (even) though with some show
of carelessness, pride and rudeness. . . . To correspond with Salisbury
(Robert Cecil) in a habit of natural but noways perilous boldness." [2]

Whether the cause was bashfulness or pride, the mistrust of
his uncle Burghley, the jealousy of his cousin Cecil, or the

---

[1] *i.e* "Once for all."   [2] Spedding, iv. 93, 52.

Queen's doubts of his stability and capacity for business, something stood in the way of Bacon's suit for place; and after twelve years of fruitless suing he gradually separated himself from Burghley. In 1592 Anthony, soon after his return from his travels on the continent, describes his brother Francis as being "bound and in deep arrearages to" a new patron; and during the next three years (1593-5) Bacon's correspondence exhibits him pressing his suit, first for the place of Attorney-general, and afterwards for the Solicitorship, no longer through his uncle, the Lord Treasurer, but through the Earl of Essex.[1]

In his *Apology*, written twelve years afterwards (1604), Bacon tells us that his reason for dedicating his "travels and studies" to Essex was not because he thought the Earl the likeliest means of his own advancement, but because he considered him to be the fittest instrument to do good to the State. But, as we learn from the *Essay on Friendship*, friendship between the superior and inferior implies that the fortunes of the one comprehend the fortunes of the other;[2] and it was obvious to every one that the fortunes of the Queen's new favourite would comprehend those of his new counsellor. Bacon himself, in a letter to the Earl (1596), acknowledges this almost in the words of the *Essay*: "Look about, even jealously if you will, and consider whether I have not reason to think that your fortune comprehendeth mine." Possibly, as Professor Gardiner suggests, Bacon meant by these words that he looked to Essex to realise also the projects he had formed as a political reformer, and not merely his aspirations after promotion. Few, however, will be much surprised if the correspondence between the two friends, during the first two or three years of their friendship, turns entirely on Bacon's suits and Bacon's prospects, with few or no references to the interests of Essex, or even to any suggestions of political reform.

---

[1] Anthony Bacon expressed, in very plain words, his sense of Burghley's ingratitude for his own services. It had been at his uncle's suggestion that he had undertaken (1579) his long tour on the continent, in the course of which he had for more than ten years, at great expense, supplied the Government with information of great value; and on his return he received only "such words as make fools fain; and yet, even in these, no offer or hopeful assurance of real kindness, which I thought I might justly expect at the Lord Treasurer's hands, who had inned my ten years' harvest into his own barn without any halfpenny charge."—*Dictionary of National Biography*, "Anthony Bacon," ii. 325.

[2] *Essays*, xlviii. 51.

But in the very month in which his suit for the Attorney's place began (February, 1593), Bacon, who now sat for Middlesex, barred his own path by a speech in the House of Commons. Subsidies had been asked by the Government to an amount, and under circumstances, that seemed oppressive to the theorist, who could not be expected to know that during the last few years the national wealth had quadrupled itself. The burden might well seem all the more objectionable to a politician who always advocated an aggressive foreign policy, and who maintained that a people "overlaid with taxes" can never become valiant and martial.[1] It was, therefore, in entire good faith that Bacon protested against the subsidies, declaring that "The gentlemen must sell their plate, and the farmers their brass pots before this will be paid." The House was unanimous against him, and the subsidies were paid without difficulty. But the speech, though made in manifest sincerity, did not on that account conciliate the Queen; and Bacon's conscientious opposition brought on him the penalty of exclusion from the royal presence.[2]

In vain did the Earl of Essex beseech the Queen in season and out of season to restore his friend to her favour. A year passes, and Bacon (1594) is now content to offer himself for the lower post of the Solicitorship, his rival, Coke, being destined for the Attorney's place. Stung by repeated failures, he no longer preserves the dignity with which he entered on his suit; the delay, he says, has almost "overthrown his health;" no man ever received a more "exquisite disgrace." Once more he casts his thoughts on a student's life; he will retire with a couple of men to Cambridge, and there spend his life in his studies and contemplations. On the day after he avows this determination, Coke receives his Patent, and Bacon is left out in the cold.

But he cannot now give up the chase. Cambridge and literature are not to be blessed by his threatened desertion from a courtier's to a student's life. He has lost his old pride and indifference to success in civil business. He hungers now, he pines, for office. Lady Ann, his mother, hears on all sides that

---

[1] *Essays*, xxix. 91.

[2] In the same session Anthony Bacon, now member for Wallingford, opposed a Government Bill for imposing new penalties on Recusants, *Dict. Nat. Biog.* ii. 325—7.

his health is suffering from his disappointment, and writes to
Anthony (5 August, 1595), with an exhortation that Francis
should think less of preferment and more of religion, health, and
the simple duty of keeping out of debt :—

> " I am sorry your brother with inward secret grief injureth his health.
> Everybody saith he looketh thin and pale. Let him look to God and confer
> with Him in godly exercises of hearing and reading, and contemn to be
> noted to take care.[1] I had rather ye both, with God His blessed favour, had
> very good health and well out of debt, than any office. Yet, though the
> Eαρλ showed great affection, he marred all with violent courses . . . . Let
> your brother be of good cheer."

But it is all in vain. This year, like the last, is spent in
writing petitionary letters to men in power ; in hanging about
the Court stairs in expectation of a royal summons ; in currying
favour with the Vice-Chamberlain, hurrying from chambers to
Court, from Court to chambers, distracted between his legal
work and his suit ; " asserviling himself," as he himself says, " to
every man's charity ; " now beseeching and now reproaching the
great ones whom he suspects of thwarting him ; and all to fail
again (1595) with no result, nor prospect of a result, except that
the Queen is said to have expressed her satisfaction that Mr.
Francis Bacon has begun " to frame very well."

Certainly if by " frame " the Queen meant " stoop to the
usages of Courts ; " if what she desired to effect was the complete destruction of the stiff uncourtier-like pride which had
brought upon young Francis Bacon the rebuke of his uncle-in-
law, and the substitution of a temper approaching to a supple
servility, her success is apparent to anyone who contrasts Bacon's
earlier language to Lord Burghley with his present language to
Lord-Keeper Puckering. To the former he had written thus
in 1580 :—

> " To your Lordship, whose recommendation, I know right well, hath
> been material to advance her Majesty's good opinion of me, I can be but a
> bounden servant. *So much may I safely promise and purpose to be, seeing
> public and private bonds vary not, but that my service to God, her Majesty,
> and your Lordship draw in a line.*"

---

[1] That is, "despise the thought that his anxiety should be generally remarked."
In the next sentence, " the Eαρλ " is the Earl of Essex, written, according to Lady
Ann's manner, in Greek characters.

But now, after an apprenticeship of fourteen years to the manners of the Court, Bacon proffers himself as a "servant" to Puckering—if only the latter will procure him the Solicitorship —without any such lofty proviso as he thought fit to append to his promises of gratitude to Burghley:

"A timorous man is every body's, and a covetous man is his own. But if your Lordship consider my nature, my course, my friends, my opinion with her Majesty (if this eclipse of her favour were past) I hope you will think *I am no unlikely piece of wood to shape you a true servant of.*" (19 April, 1594).

And finally when he fails, while smarting from what he describes to Essex as an "exquisite disgrace," he can nevertheless write to the Queen that he "acknowledges the providence of God towards him that findeth it expedient for him to *bear the yoke in his youth.*"

It has indeed been pointed out by Mr. Spedding and Professor Gardiner that at least in one respect Bacon remained true to himself during the whole of this miserable business. As might have been supposed, the Queen had by no means forgiven that speech of his against the subsidies in 1593, for which she had excluded him from her presence; and in June 1595 she gave Burghley to understand her mind. But if she was waiting for a retractation or apology, none was forthcoming. In his reply to Burghley he refuses to believe that the Queen is really offended with him on these grounds. It is well known, he says, that he was the first of the independent members of the House who spoke for the subsidy; "and that which I after spake, in difference, was but on circumstances of time and manner; which methinks should be no great matter, since there is variety allowed in counsel, as a discord in music, to make it more perfect. But I may justly doubt, *not so much her Majesty's impression on this particular, as her conceit otherwise of my insufficiency;*" and accordingly the rest of the letter is devoted to the proof that he is "sufficient."

This letter is described as "most creditable to Bacon." But it is hard to see how, even as a place-seeker, he could have written otherwise. Was he to confess that he had been guilty of popularity-hunting, or of captious opposition, and to promise

that he would not repeat the offence? Or to declare that,
although he had honestly and conscientiously given counsel for
the best, he would never thus give counsel again? By so doing
he would for ever have disqualified himself for any position of
trust, and rendered himself for ever incapable of tendering
advice with any hope that it would be received. The best thing
that he could do was to extenuate his opposition and to show
that his suggestions were merely differences of "circumstance."
In reality he had opposed the Government on *principle* and not
merely on circumstance: "This being granted in this sort, other
Princes hereafter will look for the like; so we shall put an ill
precedent upon ourselves and to our posterity"[1]—thus he had
spoken in the House; and similarly in his letter to Burghley
immediately after his speech, "It is true that from the beginning,
whatsoever was above a double subsidy, I did wish might (*for
precedent's sake*) appear to be extraordinary, and (for discontent's
sake) might not have been levied upon the poorer sort;"[2] and
he had also maintained that the payment should be extended
over six years instead of three. Rather important differences,
these, to be described as unimportant "circumstances" of time
and manner, mere "variety" of counsel, like "discord in music"
to make it more perfect! Yet with his usual inaccuracy Bacon
persuades himself, and endeavours to persuade the Queen, that
what is not convenient is not true. He could not, with any
hope of a useful result, confess that he had been disloyal, and
promise not to be disloyal again; but he could gloss the truth
and adapt facts; and what he could do, he did.

All this while he is plunging deeper and deeper into debt,
receiving driblets of money from his brother Anthony, who
alienates an estate mainly for his sake; begging his mother to
consent to the alienation of a second estate; borrowing money
upon his reversionary clerkship; and dunned by creditors who
complain that they can get from him neither principal nor
interest. The generosity of the Earl of Essex, however, alle-
viated these latter burdens. On the final failure of his suit
(October or November, 1595), Bacon had written to his patron
a letter, in which he regrets especially his loss of "means";

[1] Bacon's speech on the Subsidy, Spedding i. 223.
[2] *Ibid.* 234.

expresses his determination henceforth to follow philosophy and not law; but adds that, though he reckons himself "a common" —born, as he says elsewhere, "for the service of mankind"— there was still at the Earl's service "as much as is lawful to be enclosed of a common."

"To my Lord of Essex,

"It may please your good Lordship,

"I pray God her Majesty's weighing be not like the weight of a balance ; *gravia deorsum, levia sursum.* But I am as far from being altered in devotion towards her as I am from distrust that she will be altered in opinion towards me, when she knoweth me better. For myself, I have lost some opinion, some time, and some means. This is my account. But then, for opinion, it is a blast that cometh and goeth ; for time, it is true it goeth and cometh not ; but yet I have learned that it may be redeemed.

"For means, I value that most, and the rather because I am purposed not to follow the practice of the law (if her Majesty command me in any particular I shall be ready to do her willing service), and my reason is, only because it drinketh too much time, which I have dedicated to better purpose. But even for the point of estate and means, I partly lean to Thales' opinion, that a philosopher may be rich if he will. Thus your Lordship seeth how I comfort myself ; to the increase whereof I would fain please myself to believe that to be true which my Lord Treasurer writeth, which is, that it is more than a philosopher morally can digest. But without any such high conceit, I esteem it like the pulling out of an aching tooth, which I remember when I was a child and had little philosophy, I was glad of it when it was done.

"For your Lordship, I do think myself more beholding to you than to any man. And I say I reckon myself as a *common* (not popular, but *common*) ; and as much as is lawful to be enclosed of a common so much your Lordship shall be sure to have.

"Your Lordship's to obey your honourable commands,

More settled than ever."

It was probably in response to this letter that Essex presented him with a piece of land worth at that time eighteen hundred pounds, or between seven and eight thousand pounds of our money.[1]

---

[1] My reason for thinking that this letter (which is undated) was written before, and not after, the gift of Essex, is that in speaking of his loss of "means" he makes no allusion whatever to the Earl's munificence. It seems scarcely possible that a man writing to a patron who had given him a gift amounting to seven or

Thus for a time Bacon's most pressing necessities were met and his suit for office, for the present, terminated.

Much as we may regret the tone and temper in which Bacon sought for office and endured failure, we ought at least to do him so much justice as to keep constantly before our minds, even if we cannot altogether accept, his own statement of his motives. He wished, so he tells us, to make money not for its own sake, but in order to have time and means for the study of philosophy. Apparently he made little by his practice at the bar, and without "place of some reasonable countenance" he could not hope for leisure, still less for the power of employing others, or, as he expresses it in his letter to Burghley, "commandment of more wits than a man's own." Conscious of this motive, conscious also of abilities superior to those of many who distanced him at the time in the competition for office, and apparently marked by birth and brain for office of some kind, he may not unnaturally have felt a more than commonly poignant irritation at a rejection which not only overthrew his highest hopes but conveyed the impression of being intended as a mark of censure or contempt.

§ 7 Bacon's "Devices;" "Mr. Bacon's Discourse in the Praise of his Sovereign;" "Promus"

During the period of Bacon's suit for office his pen had been almost idle. He had composed a couple of political pamphlets

eight thousand pounds of our money a week or two ago, should thus talk of his loss of "means," his especial regret for this loss, and his belief that a philosopher can yet become "rich if he will," without a word of special acknowledgment for the liberal gift which had gone far to cancel the loss.

But the question is certainly complicated by another consideration. The address, "It may please your good Lordship," is more stiff and formal than is usual from Bacon to Essex. In the large collection of Bacon's letters to Essex there is only *one*, *up to this date*, that has this address; and of that letter Mr. Spedding (i. 351) very justly says that "it was probably *intended for the Queen to read.*" It is by no means improbable that *this letter was intended for the same purpose:* and, if so, all mention of the Earl's gift might be purposely omitted, the object being to show the Queen that Francis Bacon was as loyal to her as ever, and that his devotion to Essex was limited by higher considerations.

In the *Apology* Bacon tells us that he accepted the gift with a verbal reservation of allegiance to the Sovereign : " I said, ' My Lord, I see I must be your homager and hold land of your gift; but do you know the manner of doing homage in law ? Always it is with a saving of his faith to the King and his other Lords.' " Spedding, iii. 144. But the *Apology* cannot be depended on, as an exact account of facts, see below, pp. 58, 61.

and two or three *Devices*. The pamphlets call for no special mention; but the *Devices* are noteworthy as exhibiting an apparent change in Bacon's attitude towards philosophy. He has described himself in an autobiographical passage above quoted, as being, at one period of his life, "shaken by opinions," and temporarily diverted from philosophy. Some such diversion may, I think, be traced if we compare the treatment of philosophy by Bacon, first in his *Conference of Pleasure* in 1592, then in the *Gesta Grayorum* in 1594, and last in the *Device on the Queen's Day* in 1595. These works of Bacon are so little known that no apology is needed for giving ample extracts from them.

The first represents Bacon, unused as yet to failure, triumphantly proclaiming the advent of a new philosophy that will carry all before it :—

"THE PRAISE OF KNOWLEDGE (1592)

" Silence were the best celebration of that which I mean to commend ; for who would not use silence there where silence is not made, and what crier can make silence in such a noise and tumult of vain and popular opinions ?

" My praise shall be dedicate to the mind itself. The mind is the man and knowledge mind ; a man is but what he knoweth. The mind itself is but an accident to knowledge, for knowledge is a double of that which is. The truth of being and the truth of knowing is all one.

" Are not the pleasures of the affections greater than the pleasures of the senses, and are not the pleasures of the intellect greater than the pleasures of the affections ? Is not that only a true and natural pleasure whereof there is no satiety ? Is not that knowledge alone that doth clear the mind of all perturbations ? How many things be there which we imagine are not ? How many things do we esteem and value more than they are ? These vain imaginations, these ill-proportioned estimations, these be the clouds of error that turn into the storms of perturbations. Is there then any such happiness as for a man's mind to be raised above the confusion of things, where he may have a respect of the order of nature and the error of men ?

" Is there but a view only of delight and not of discovery ? Of contentment and not of benefit ? Shall we not discern as well the riches of nature's warehouse as the beauty of her shop ? Is truth barren ? Shall we not thereby be able to produce worthy effects and to endow the life of man with infinite commodities ?

" But shall I make this garland to be put upon a wrong head ? Would any man believe me if I should verify this upon the knowledge that is now in use ? Are we the richer by one poor invention by reason of all the learning that hath been this many hundred years? The industry of artificers maketh some small improvements of things invented, and chance sometimes in experimenting makes us stumble upon somewhat that is new. But all the disputations of the learned never brought to light one effect of nature before unknown. When things are known and found out, then they can descant upon them; they can knit them into certain causes; they can reduce them to their principles. If any instance of experience stand against them, they can range it in order by some distinctions. But all this is but a web of the wit: it can work nothing.

"I do not doubt but that common notions which we call reason, and the knitting of them together, which we call logic or the art of reason, may have use in popular studies; but they rather cast obscurity than give light to the contemplation of nature. All the philosophy of nature which is now received is either the philosophy of the Grecians or that other of the Alchemists. That of the Grecians hath the foundation in words, in ostentation, in confutation, in sects, in auditories, in schools, in disputations. The Grecians are, as one of them saith, 'You Grecians ever children.' They knew little antiquity. They knew (except fables) not much above 500 years before themselves. They knew but a small portion of the world. That of the Alchemists hath the foundation in imposture, in auricular traditions and obscurity. It was catching hold of religion, but the best principle of it is *populus vult decipi*: so as I know no great difference between these great philosophers, but that the one is a loud crying folly, the other a whispering folly: the one is gathered out of a few vulgar observations, and the other out of a few experiments of the furnace: the one never faileth to multiply words, and the other oft faileth to multiply gold.

"Who would not smile at Aristotle, when he admireth the eternity and invariableness of the heavens, as if there were not the like in the bowels of the earth. They be the confines and borders of these two great kingdoms, where the continual alterations and incursions are. The superficies and upper part of the earth is full of variety, the superficies and lower part of the heavens, which we call the middle region of the air, is full of variety. There is much spirit in the one place which cannot be brought into mass, there is much massy body in the other place which cannot be refined into spirit: the common air is as the waste ground between the borders.

"Who would not smile at astronomers, I mean not these new car-men which drive the earth about, but the ancient astronomers that feign the moon to be the swiftest of the planets in motion, and the rest in order, the higher the slower, and so are compelled to imagine a double motion? Whereas how evident is it that that which they call a contrary motion is but an abatement of motion! The fixed stars overgo Saturn, and Saturn leaveth behind him Jupiter, and so in them and the rest all is but one motion, and the nearer the earth the slower. A motion also whereof the air and the water do participate though much interrupted.

"But why do I in a conference of pleasure enter into these great matters in sort that, pretending to know much, I should know not season ? Pardon me, it was because almost all things may be indued and adorned with speeches, but knowledge itself is more beautiful than any apparel of words that can be put upon it.

"And let me not seem arrogant, without respect to these great reputed authors. Let me so give every man his due, as I give time his due, which s to discover truth. Many of these men had greater wits, far above mine own, and so are many in the universities of Europe at this day. But alas ! they learn nothing there but to believe ; first to believe that others know that which they know not, and after [that] themselves know that which they know not. But indeed facility to believe, impatience to doubt, temerity to assever, glory to know, doubt to contradict, end to gain, sloth to search, seeking things in words, resting in a part of nature, these and the like have been the things which have forbidden the happy match between the mind of a man and the nature of things, and in place thereof have married it to vain notions and blind experiments. And what the posterity and issue of so honourable a match may be it is not hard to consider.

"Printing, a gross invention ; artillery, a thing not far out of the way ; the needle, a thing partly known before ; what a change have these three made in the world in these times, the one in the state of learning, the other in the state of war, the third in the state of treasure, commodities and navigation ! And these were, as I say, but stumbled upon and lighted on by chance.

"Therefore no doubt the sovereignty of man lieth hid in knowledge wherein many things are reserved which kings with their treasure cannot buy, nor with their force command ; their spies and intelligencers can give no news of them : their seamen and discoverers cannot sail where they grow. Now we govern nature in opinions, but are thrall to her in necessities. But if we would be led by her [in] invention, we should command her in action."[1]

The second eulogy of knowledge is couched in humbler terms. It has less of the imperious, arrogant, and almost wilfully obscure and mystical tone of the eulogist in the *Conference of Pleasure*. It is more practical, and while adhering to the inductive method, lays greater stress on the influence of wealth and power in furthering philosophic investigations :—

"THE SECOND COUNSELLOR, ADVISING THE STUDY OF PHILOSOPHY (1594)

"It may seem, most excellent Prince, that my Lord, which now hath spoken, did never read the just censures of the wisest men, who compared great conquerors to great rovers and witches, whose power is in destruction

[1] Mr. Spedding's edition of the *Conference of Pleasure*. Longmans, 1870, or *Life and Letters*, i. p. 123.

and not in preservation. Else would he never have advised your Excellency to become as some comet or blazing star, which should threaten and portend nothing but death and dearth, combustions, and troubles of the world. And whereas the governing faculties of men are two, force and reason, whereof the one is brute and the other divine, he wisheth you for your principal ornament and regality, the talons of the eagle to catch the prey, and not the piercing sight which seeth into the bottom of the sea. But I contrariwise will wish unto your Highness the exercise of the best and purest part of the mind, and the most innocent and meriting conquest, being the conquest of the works of nature ; making this proposition, that you bend the excellency of your spirits to the searching out, inventing, and discovering of all whatsoever is hid and secret in the world ; that your Excellency be not as a lamp that shineth to others and yet seeth not itself, but as the Eye of the World, that both carrieth and useth light.

" Antiquity, that presenteth unto us in dark visions the wisdom of former times informeth us that the [governments of] kingdoms have always had an affinity with the secrets and mysteries of learning. Amongst the Persians, the kings were attended on by the Magi. The Gymnosophists had all the government under the princes of Asia ; and generally those kingdoms were accounted most happy that had rulers most addicted to philosophy. The Ptolemies in Egypt may be for instance ; and Salomon was a man so seen in the universality of nature that he wrote an herbal of all that was green upon the earth. No conquest of Julius Cæsar made him so remembered as the Calendar. Alexander the Great wrote to Aristotle upon the publishing of the Physics, that he esteemed more of excellent men in knowledge than in empire.

" And to this purpose I will commend to your Highness four principal works and monuments of yourself. First, the collecting of a most perfect and general library, wherein whatsoever the wit of man hath heretofore committed to books of worth, be they ancient or modern, printed or manuscript, European or of other parts, of one or other language, may be made contributory to your wisdom. Next, a spacious, wonderful garden, wherein whatsoever plant the sun of divers climates, out of the earth of divers moulds, either wild or by the culture of man, brought forth, may be, with that care that appertaineth to the good prospering thereof, set and cherished ; this garden to be built about with rooms to stable in all rare beasts and to cage in all rare birds, with two lakes adjoining, the one of fresh water, the other of salt, for like variety of fishes. And so you may have in small compass a model of universal nature made private The third, a goodly huge cabinet, wherein whatsoever the hand of man by exquisite art or engine hath made rare in stuff, form, or motion ; whatsoever singularity, chance, and the shuffle of things hath produced ; whatsoever nature hath wrought in things that want life and may be kept, shall be sorted and included. The fourth, such a still-house, so furnished with mills, instruments, furnaces, and vessels as may be a palace fit for a philosopher's stone. Thus, when your Excellency shall have added depth of knowledge to the fineness of [your] spirits and greatness of your power, then indeed shall you be a Trismegistus, and then, when all other miracles and wonders shall cease, by reason that you shall have discovered their natural causes, yourself shall be left the only miracle and wonder of the world."[1]

The third eulogy differs greatly from the first two. It eulogises contemplation rather than knowledge, and it is put into the mouth of a hermit, who is but one of three servants of Philautia, or Selfishness, seeking to decoy the Squire's Master (Essex) from the love and service of the Queen.

"THE HERMIT'S SPEECH IN THE PRESENCE (1595)

"Though our ends be diverse, and therefore may be one more just than another, yet the complaint of this Squire is general, and therefore alike unjust against us all. Albeit he is angry that we offer ourselves to his master uncalled, and forgets we come not of ourselves, but as the messengers of Self-Love, from whom all that comes should be well taken. He saith when we come we are importunate. If he mean that we err in form, we have that of his master, who, being a lover, useth no other form of soliciting. If he will charge us to err in matter, I for my part will presently prove that I persuade him to nothing but for his own good. For I wish him to leave turning over the book of fortune, which is but a play for children, where there be so many books of truth and knowledge better worthy the revolving; and not fix his view only upon a picture in a little table, where there be so many tables of histories, yea to life, excellent to behold and admire.

"Whether he believe me or no, there is no prison to the prison of the thoughts, which are free under the greatest tyrants. Shall any man make his conceit, as an anchor, mured up with the compass of one beauty or person, that may have the liberty of all contemplation? Shall he exchange the sweet travelling through the universal variety for one wearisome and endless round or labyrinth? Let thy master, Squire, offer his service to the Muses. It is long since they received any into their court. They give alms continually at their gate, that many come to live upon; but few have they ever admitted into their palace. There shall he find secrets not dangerous to know, sides and parties not factious to hold, precepts and commandments not penal to disobey.

"The gardens of love wherein he now playeth himself are fresh to-day and fading to-morrow, as the sun comforts them or is turned from them. But the gardens of the Muses keep the privilege of the golden age: they ever flourish and are in league with time. The monuments of wit survive the monuments of power; the verses of a poet endure without a syllable

[1] Spedding, i. 335.

lost, while states and empires pass many periods.   Let him not think he
shall descend, for he is now upon a hill as a ship is mounted upon the
ridge of a wave ; but that hill of the Muses is above tempests, always
clear and calm ; a hill of the goodliest discovery that man can have, being
a prospect upon all the errors and wanderings of the present and former
times.   Yea, in some cliff [?] it leadeth the eye beyond the horizon of
time, and giveth no obscure divinations of times to come.

"So that if he will indeed lead *vitam vitalem*, a life that unites safety
and dignity, pleasure and merit ; if he will win admiration without envy ;
if he will be in the feast and not in the throng, in the light and not in the
heat ; let him embrace the life of study and contemplation.   And if he
will accept of no other reason, yet because the gift of the Muses will
enworthy him in his love, and where he now looks on his mistress's outside
with the eyes of sense, which are dazzled and amazed, he shall then behold
her high perfections and heavenly mind with the eyes of judgment, which
grow stronger by more nearly and more directly viewing such an object."[1]

Contrasted with the first passionate *Praise of Knowledge*
written in 1592, the *Praise of Contemplation*, in 1595, seems
cold indeed.   The Hermit's speech is addressed to a Squire who
is represented as being lured from the service of her Majesty
by three different ministers of Philautia or Selfishness, the
Hermit, the Soldier, and the Statesman.   The Squire rejects
them all.

"'You, Father, that pretend to *truth and knowledge*'—thus he addresses
the Hermit—'how are you assured that you adore *not vain chimeras and
imaginations ?* that in your high prospect, when you think men wander up
and down, that they stand not indeed still in their place, and it is some
smoke or cloud between you and them which moveth, or else the dazzling
of your own eyes ?   Have not many *which take themselves to be inward
counsellors with Nature proved but idle believers,* that told us tales which
were no such matter ?'"[2]

It is of course Essex, not Bacon, who is intended to speak
through the Squire, and to assure the Queen that for her sake
he renounces the works of Philautia, and will devote himself to
her Majesty's service : but I find it hard to resist the conviction
that in the contrast between the *Device* of 1592 and the *Device*
of 1595, one may read a change in the mind of Bacon also.
The vagueness of the prospects of philosophy seems at this
time to have impressed him with new force, and to have been

---

[1] Spedding, i. 378-80.   [2] Spedding, i. p. 383.

contrasted with the present and substantial realities of a life of
action.   There is no other period in Bacon's life to which we can
point with more probability as being the time when he was
" made to waver," [1] as he tells us, and tempted to set Science on
one side.   There was interest enough and variety enough in the
study of the New Philosophy; but who would guarantee that it
should not prove a chase after mere phantoms ?   " Attend," says
the Squire to the Hermit, " attend, you beadsman of the Muses,
you take your pleasure in a wilderness of variety ; but *it is but
of shadows.*"

Where a man has two motives, the love of power and the love
of knowledge, and these two conflicting, and now one, now the
other uppermost, it must necessarily be impossible without a
great mass of evidence, to determine which motive from time to
time prevails with him.   If we are to believe Francis Bacon,
power and wealth had always been in his mind subordinate to
the interests of philosophy.   He coveted office—so we found
him writing to Lord Burghley years ago—not for its own sake
but because it would give him command of wits other than his
own.   To the same effect he expresses himself in the theories
of his later years.   " No man's fortune," he writes in the
Advancement of Learning, " can be an end worthy of his being
. . . . but nevertheless fortune as an organ of virtue and merit
deserveth the consideration." [2]

Elsewhere he blames " the tenderness and want of compliance
in some of the most ancient and revered philosophers, who
retired too easily from civil business that they might avoid
indignities and perturbations, and live (as they thought) more
saint-like." [3]   And again, " it is of no little importance to the
dignity of literature that a man, naturally fitted rather for
literature than for anything else, and borne by some destiny,
against the inclination of his genius, into the business of active
life, should have risen to such high and honourable appointments."[4]   This then is Bacon's own explanation of his motives :
he professes to seek knowledge first (the highest kind of
power), and place or office, second ; and he seeks office mainly

[1] See note on p. 27, above.   [2] Spedding, *Works,* iii. 456.
[3] Spedding, *Works,* v. p. 10.   [4] *Ib.* v. 79.

as a step to the attainment and diffusion of knowledge, but also as an " organ of virtue and merit " generally.

Whether Bacon was not deceiving himself in this account of his own motives may very reasonably be questioned : but there seems little doubt that this self-deceit, if it was self-deceit, was as sincere as most of such convenient self-deceits usually are. It must always be very hard to determine where self-deceit ends and hypocrisy begins, and Bacon seems to have had more than ordinary powers of deceiving himself. Let us admit that he came by degrees to admire and to seek power and wealth for their own sakes—yet the high tone of self-respect which he retained to the very last, indicates that, in his own estimation at all events, he was pursuing fortune throughout his life, only as " an organ of virtue and merit."

Up to this point in his career he has done nothing greatly inconsistent with his professions of allegiance to truth first, and to power only as a means towards the attainment of truth. But now there are symptoms that he is beginning to waver. The independent attitude which he had assumed towards the Crown, had issued in consequences for which he had been unprepared. The *fiat* of the Queen had kept him in torture for three years. Such a power was not to be trifled with ; and it is not surprising if he conceived a new respect for it.

> " Four lagging winters and four wanton springs
> End in a word ; such is the breath of kings,"

—this is the exclamation of Bolingbroke musing on the delightful powers of monarchy. Very similar seems to have been the feeling of Bacon towards the high powers which had made him " bear the yoke in his youth." In comparison with so present and real a power, what were the dreams of science ? In case the realm of philosophy, which he had mapped out for himself in habitable and culturable provinces, should turn out, as the Squire had predicted, to be nothing but an unsubstantial " wilderness of shadows," would it not be well to secure the favour of the Queen, and a definite position in the Court, which might receive him into substantial habitations ?

The same occasion which gave rise to the *Discourse in Praise of Knowledge* produced also *Mr. Bacon's Discourse in the Praise of his Sovereign.*   That Bacon's admiration for the Queen was sincere, we know for the best of all reasons, because he praised her during the reign of her successor ; [1] and although the *Discourse* abounds with what we should now describe as adulation, it shows some discretion in the delicate handling of her defects ("a certain dryness and parsimony" in expenses " for the honour of her house" is partly denied, partly defended by " the universal manners of the times ") as well as in the just selection of her best characteristics, and especially her " magnanimity " in the face of the Spanish foe :—[2]

" No praise of magnanimity, nor of love, nor of knowledge can intercept her praise that planteth and nourisheth magnanimity by her example, love by her person, and knowledge by the peace and serenity of her times ; and if these rich pieces be so fair, unset ; what are they, set, and set to all perfection ?

" Magnanimity no doubt consisteth in contempt of peril, in contempt of profit, and in the meriting of the times wherein one liveth.

" For contempt of peril, see a lady that cometh to a crown after the experience of some adverse fortune, which for the most part extenuateth the mind, and maketh it apprehensive of fears. . . . . See a Queen, that when her realm was to have been invaded by an army the preparation whereof was like the travail of an elephant, the provisions whereof were infinite, the setting forth whereof was the terror and wonder of Europe ; it was not seen that her cheer, her fashion, her ordinary manner, was anything altered ; not a cloud of that storm did appear in that countenance wherein peace doth ever shine ; but with excellent assurance and advised security she inspired her council, animated her nobility, redoubled the courage of her people ; still having this noble apprehension, not only that she would communicate her fortune with them, but that it was she that would protect them, and not they her ; which she testified by no less demonstration than her presence in camp.   Therefore that magnanimity that feareth neither greatness of alteration, nor the vows of conspirators, nor the power of the enemy, is more than heroical."

As a specimen of the adulatory style—pedantical as well as adulatory—for which we might perhaps plead that Bacon's own taste is not so much to blame as his chameleon-like instinct of adapting his style to his atmosphere—take the following :—

" Now pass to the excellencies of her person. The view of them wholly and not severally do [*sic*] make so sweet a wonder, as I fear to divide them again.

[1] See below, p. 159.   [2] Spedding, i. 126.

E

"Nobility, extracted out of the royal and victorious line of the kings of England ; yea, both roses, white and red, do as well flourish in her nobility as in her beauty.

"Health such as was like she should have that was brought forth by two of the most goodly princes in the world, in the strength of their years, in the heat of their love ; that hath been injured neither with an over-liberal nor over-curious diet ; that hath not been softened by an umbratile life still under the roof, but strengthened by the use of the pure and open air ; that still retaineth flower and vigour of youth.

"For the beauty and many graces of her presence, what colours are fine enough for such a portraiture ? Let no light poet be used for such a description, but the chastest and the royalest.[1]

"Of her gait, *Et vera incessu patuit Dea ;*
"Of her voice, *Nec vox hominem sonat ;*
"Of her eye, *Et laetos oculis afflavit honores ;*
"Of her colour, *Indum sanguineo veluti violaverit ostro*
        Si quis ebur ;
"Of her neck, *Et rosea cervice refulsit ;*
"Of her breast, *Veste sinus collecta fluentes ;*
"Of her hair, *Ambrosiaeque comae divinum vertice odorem*
        Spiravere.

"If this be presumption, let him bear the blame that oweth [2] the verses."

Special circumstances may have given to this eulogy a peculiar and serious interest. Only a week before its delivery, a copy of a pamphlet had been sent to Anthony Bacon by one of the Lord Keeper's secretaries, entitled *Responsio ad Edictum Reginae Angliae,* supposed to have been written by Father Parsons, attacking the anti-Roman legislation which had followed the defeat of the Armada, and charging the Queen's Government with all the evils of England and all the disturbances of Christendom. It is possible that Bacon's Discourse was meant to be, as in fact it was, a reply to the pamphleteer. In any case when he was subsequently encouraged to undertake a direct reply to Parsons, he worked up a great deal of the material of the *Discourse* into another much larger treatise entitled *Certain Observations made upon a Libel Published this Present Year,* 1592. The title indicates that it must have been composed 25 March, 1593, according to our present reckoning.

The conflict in Bacon's mind during this period is curiously illustrated by a little collection of extracts, proverbs, and thoughts

---

[1] Virgil.   [2] *i.e.* owneth.

jotted down by him in the Christmas vacation of 1594 and called a *Promus* (*i.e.* Dispenser, or Steward) *of Formularies and Elegancies.*[1] Many of the extracts bear witness to his aversion to the practice of the law and to his love of philosophy, such as :—

> (1.) Vae vobis, juris periti !
> (2.) Nec me verbosas leges ediscere, nec me
>   Ingrato voces prostituisse foro.

Others express his desire to return to his old philosophic life :—

> (1.) Vitae me redde priori.
> (2.) I had rather know than be known.

Others express his contempt for the existing standard of knowledge :—

> (1.) In academiis discunt credere.
> (2.) Vos adoratis quod nescitis.
> (3.) Vos, Graeci, semper pueri.
> (4.) Scientiam canimus inter perfectos.

Others express his sense of the grandeur of his philosophic plans, and, at one time, the possibility of failure, at another time, the glorious completeness of the ultimate fulfilment :—

> (1.) Quem si non tenuit, magnis tamen excidit ausis.
> (2.) Conamur tenues grandia.
> (3.) Aspice venturo laetentur ut omnia saeclo.

Independently of other interests, many of the notes in the *Promus* are valuable as illustrations of the manner in which Bacon's method of thought influenced him even in the merest trifles. Analogy, with him, is all-pervasive. If you can say " good-morrow," why should you not also say " good-dawning " ? If you can anglicise some French words, why not others ? Why not, for example, say " good-swoear " (*i.e.* " good-soir ") for " good night," and " good-matens " for " good morning " ? Instead of " twi-light," why not try " vice-light " ? In the place of " adventurous," how much more novel and choice is " remuant " ! On the other hand, is not the usual Latin-derived " impudent " less forcible than the vernacular but novel " brased " ?

---

[1] Published for the first time in full by Mrs. Henry Pott.   Longmans, Green and Co., 1883.

Other extracts from the *Promus* have quite a different, and more than a merely linguistic, interest. They are repartees and retorts, occasionally of an uncomplimentary nature—such as in his note-book of 1608 he systematically entitled " Disparagement." In some of these Bacon deliberately writes down some good quality, and, opposite to it, a disparaging description of it. If, for example, your adversary speaks easily, you are to say, " Yes, but *not wisely ;*" if he puts *pros* and *cons* in a dramatic way by question and answer, you are to remark with a sneer, " *Notwithstanding his dialogues,* he proves nothing," and so on :—

(1.) No wise speech, though easy and voluble.

(2.) Notwithstanding his dialogues (*of one that giveth life to his speech by way of question*).

(3.) He can tell a tale well (*of those courtly gifts of speech which are better in describing than in considering*).

(4.) A good comediante (*of one that hath good grace in his speech*).

It is impossible to read these forms of " disparagement," without being reminded that Francis Bacon, in his recent suit, had probably found occasion to use them. More than once at that time he is found urging his intimate friend Essex to remember the " exceptions " against Coke and his other competitors, as when he begs him to " drive in the nail for the Huddler." [1]   But it is a terrible falling off that the man who wrote the *Greatest Birth of Time* in 1585 should think it right or seemly in 1594, not only to suffer his mind to rest on such petty tricks of the Art of the *Architecture of Fortune* (as he afterwards called it), but even to commit them to paper. " How can a man comprehend great matters," asks Bacon in the Essays, " that breaketh his mind too much to small observations ! " [2]   It is characteristic of a philosopher that he apprehended most, not the moral, but the intellectual dangers, attendant on petty pursuits. But in reality the moral danger was the more imminent of the two. No one could pursue the petty arts of Court-advancement without becoming morally callous. Bacon has already

---

[1] *i.e.* Bacon's rival, Coke, Spedding, i. 262—3. I do not know why this name was given to Coke, unless because Essex (or Bacon) wished to imply that the great lawyer rather " *huddled* " together precedents and isolated instances, than distinguished principles. Comp. Chamberlain's expression (Spedding, iii. 21), " The Parliament *huddles* in high matters."

[2] *Essays,* lii. 19.

lost the youthful indifference to wealth and power with which he had entered on Court-life when he was determined to be "like himself:" he has now begun to "frame." But will the "framing" be favourable to the moral development of the philosopher who is "born for the utility of mankind"? Is it possible to pursue office and power with so much passion, and to cultivate the arts of pushing and disparaging so assiduously without ultimately forgetting that fortune is only worthy of consideration when it is "the organ of merit and virtue"? That is a question which the further life of Bacon may perhaps help us to answer.

[1596—9]

§ 8 BACON AS THE COUNSELLOR OF ESSEX

A vacancy in the Mastership of the Rolls in the spring of 1596 gave Bacon a new prospect of office; but he no longer openly makes Essex the medium of his application. He wished to have it believed and to be able himself to assert, if necessary, that he had had no communication with Essex on the subject; and this motive suggested a petty falsehood not pleasant to record. Writing to the Earl *he makes no mention of the vacancy;* but the letter to the Earl is *inclosed in one to Anthony Bacon,* in which Francis begs his brother to secure the Earl's interest, but to say that he (Francis) *has no knowledge of the communication between Anthony and Essex.*

Although, however, Francis Bacon had probably resolved that he would for the future avoid so far committing himself to the Earl as to incur the enmity of the Cecils, it is clear that he had not yet determined to give up Essex. The Favourite's influence with the Queen was undoubtedly not so great as had been supposed; but it was yet possible that he might regain and retain at its highest the royal favour, if only he could be induced to adopt wise counsels; and in spite of all his faults, his impulsiveness, changeableness and hot temper, he had at least the merit of being ready to listen to advice and even to rebuke. " I would have given a thousand pounds to have had one hour's speech with you," writes the Earl to an old friend in a fit of passionate despair after one of his earliest quarrels with the

Queen ; and Bacon himself, noting this characteristic, writes to
an agent of Essex : "The more plainly and frankly you shall
deal with my Lord, admonishing him of any error which in this
action he may commit, such is his Lordship's nature the better
he will take it."

Appearing now therefore (October, 1596), for the first time so
far as we know, in the character of the Earl's counsellor, Bacon
addresses himself at once to the object which Essex should aim
at, and the means by which he should attain it.   The object was
the Queen's favour ; and the means, obsequiousness—or, as
Bacon calls it, "correspondence and agreeableness" to the
Queen. The Favourite had attained his position as a mere
youth and retained it hitherto by his hold on Elizabeth's
affections ; but his counsellor foresaw that "favour of affection" is more transitory and untrustworthy than "favour of
correspondence."

But by nature Essex was eminently unfitted to " correspond ; "
the task demanded a constant self-suppression, not to say
dissimulation, and Essex was the frankest and most open of
courtiers, " a great resenter," says Wotton, "and no good pupil
to my Lord of Leicester who was wont to put all passions in
his pocket ;" "one that always carried on his brow either love
or hatred and did not understand concealment" writes Cuffe,
his private secretary. To such a character, utterly devoid of
that "discreet subtlety in the composition," and that " comparity
and conformity of manners " without which, says Clarendon,
"no man in any age or court shall be eminent in the aulical
function "—Francis Bacon now undertakes to offer advice on
the Arts of a Courtier.

The Queen, he says, is in danger of receiving five unfavourable impressions of the Earl, which impressions must be avoided
by five remedies. The first impression is that he is " opiniastre
and not rulable ; " this is to be avoided by pretending to take
up projects which he is to drop at the Queen's bidding, " as if
you would pretend a journey to see your living and estate
towards Wales and the like." The second is, "of a militar
dependence ; " this Essex must "keep in substance but abolish
it in shews to the Queen," pretending to be as bookish and
contemplative as he was in the days of his youth, before the

Earl of Leicester—to quote Wotton again—drew him first into "the fatal circle from a kind of resolved privateness at his house at Lampsie in South Wales, when, after the academical life, he had taken such a taste for the rural as I have heard him say that he could well have bent his life to a retired course." The third is the fear of "a popular reputation." The only remedy is to quench it "verbis" not "rebus;" to take occasion to blame popularity in all others, "but nevertheless to go on in your honourable commonwealth courses as you do." The fourth and fifth impressions are that the Earl is careless about money matters, and that he takes advantage of his position as favourite. The former is to be remedied by increased prudence and by changing some of his servants; the latter by introducing a tool of his own into the position of minor favourite.

In this counsel there is much that is sagacious, especially in the advice to avoid military expeditions and to shun the suspicion of popularity; but from first to last it is spoiled by the trickiness which breathes through every precept; and Bacon ought to have known that it was peculiarly unfit for Essex, who was the last man in the world to be able to carry into effect such a scheme of systematic dissimulation. Essex might attempt to carry out the letter of some of these precepts—indeed, as we shall immediately see, he did make the attempt in one case, with no satisfactory results—but he could not imbue himself with their spirit. It is possible that if the Earl had been frankly warned that it was his duty, not only "in shews" but also in "substance," to subordinate some of his own inclinations to the will of the Queen, in order that he might the better serve his country, some real good might have been done; but, as it was, this and similar advice may not improbably be considered responsible (see p. 57) for at least one false step on the Earl's part; and on the whole we may say, in the language of the *Essays*, that few things did Essex more harm than that the friend in whom he placed most trust gave him advice that was rather cunning than wise.[1]

At the time when this advice was given, the Earl was in high favour; but in the spring of the next year (1597) he was once

---

[1] *Essays*, xxii. 119.

more quarrelling with the Queen, and we find him so far adopting Bacon's advice that he " pretended a journey toward Wales," from which he desisted at the command of the Queen. But the abruptness of his behaviour neutralised the concession; and his passion for adventure and distinction in war induced him wholly to disregard that most valuable part of Bacon's warning which touched on " militar dependence."

During the next two years there is little extant correspondence between the two friends, and Bacon's *Apology* declares that Essex discontinued asking his advice. But such evidence as we possess tends rather to show that Essex continued to ask for it, but Bacon discontinued giving it. In 1598 we find Bacon writing that he has *no time to attend his patron,* " nor now to write fully;" in the same year Essex sends him information about affairs in Ireland and *desires his advice thereon* ; and in the following year Essex even *complains of Bacon's silence* on matters affecting the Earl's interests. This is but one of many interests where Bacon's *Apology* seems to be at variance with his letters.

It is probably not without significance that the first edition of the *Essays* which appeared about this time (1597) was not dedicated to Essex, but to Anthony Bacon. There is no reason to suppose that Francis Bacon considered this little volume unworthy of being dedicated to the Earl. The second edition was dedicated (originally) to Prince Henry ; the third, to Buckingham. Equally small, or smaller, treatises were inscribed with the names of the Marquis of Salisbury, and Prince Charles. The probability is, therefore, that he would not dedicate the book to the Earl of Essex for fear of offending the Cecilian faction; and this probability is increased by the manner in which Anthony, as it were, re-dedicates the work to Essex and begs " leave to transfer my interest unto your Lordship."

The special need of advice in 1598 arose from the critical position of Ireland at that time, owing to the rebellion of Tyrone. In a first letter Bacon advises him to turn his attention to affairs in Ireland ; in a second (March 1598) he goes further :

"But that your Lordship is too easy in such cases to pass from dissimulation to verity, I think if your Lordship lent your reputation in this case—that is to pretend that, if peace go not on, and the Queen mean not to make a defensive war, as in times past, but a full reconquest of those parts of the country, you would accept the charge--I think it would help to settle Tyrone in his seeking accord, and win you a great deal of honour *gratis.*''

It is scarcely credible that in such a crisis the Cecilian and Essexian factions should have aimed at utilising the Irish troubles for mere party aggrandisement ; still less that both parties should seek to impose the burdensome command of the forces in Ireland upon a political enemy.   But a previous letter of Essex proves that he had some time before suspected the Cecils of a desire to ruin him by sending him away from the Court to fail in Ireland ; and on the present occasion there was no disguise.   Essex was for sending Carew, the friend of Cecil ; Cecil named Knollys, Essex's uncle—each with the view of discrediting the opposite party by failure.   In a stormy councilmeeting, the insolent conduct of Essex so infuriated the Queen that she struck him, and had him ignominiously thrust from the council chamber.   He went into a sullen retirement, whence he did not emerge till after the death of Burghley, when the disaster of Blackwater (14 August 1598), and the consequent rebellion of the whole of Ireland, had caused "the full reconquest" of that country—to repeat the words of the Earl's counsellor—to become the main problem of the time.   In an evil hour Essex now adopted that counsellor's too subtle address to "pretend" that he would accept the command.   In vain did he afterwards attempt to draw back.   "Passing from dissimulation to verity" (the very danger against which Bacon had warned him, but to which he had exposed him) he committed himself irrevocably.

His genuine unwillingness to accept the command is proved by a recently published letter (1 January, 1599) from the Earl to his intimate friend Southampton, who vehemently dissuades him from going.[1]   "I am tied in my own reputation to use no tergiversation ; the Queen hath irrevocably decreed it, the Council do passionately urge it."   He is aware of all the dangers of absence from Court, and the designs of enemies, but

---

[1] This letter was communicated to me by the late Professor Brewer and first published in *Bacon and Essex*, p. 110, where it is given in full.

there is no help for it; "into Ireland I go." Vain are his attempts to disengage himself by alleging pretexts of insufficient supplies and forces: "he could ask nothing," says Camden, "which he did not obtain by the officious, not to say crafty, assistance of his adversaries." Such was his dread of the Cecilian plots at Court in his absence, that even at the last moment he refused to depart without an express permission under the broad seal to return whenever he pleased.

A few days before the Earl's departure (27 March, 1599) Bacon, in answer to his friend's complaint, that he had been "silent in his occasions," writes a letter in which he presages success, enlarges on the honour bestowed on him by the Queen in selecting him for this duty, and adds that the success is not to be depreciated by calling the Irish "barbarians;" for the Romans highly esteemed their triumphs gained over similar races, such as "the Germans, Britons, and divers others." It is a curious instance of Bacon's unphilosophic tendency to adapt his memory to his desires, that in the *Apology*, by a slight addition to the context, he completely reverses the tenor of this letter, and, in particular, the reference to the Britons and Germans. *He did protest*, he then writes, *against the Earl's going*, warning him that he would "exulcerate the Queen's mind" and adding that *the Irish would prove no less troublesome enemies than "the ancient Gauls or Germans or Britons"* had proved to the *Romans in old times.* This is but one among many reasons for preferring the indirect evidence of Bacon's letters to the direct testimony of the *Apology* wherever we have both, and for placing very little confidence in the *Apology* where it is unsupported by external evidence.[1]

---

[1] Professor Gardiner (*Dict. Nat. Biog.*, ii. 333) while admitting the possibility that Bacon's memory played him false, adds, "It is also possible that there were really two (letters) written, the one before Essex had made up his mind, and the other after he had determined on his course, and that Bacon might urge at one time that people like the Britons and Gauls were hard to conquer, and at the other that glory might be achieved by bringing them into order. Such repetitions are very much after Bacon's style."

Here is the passage from the actual letter :—

"And if any man be of opinion that the nature of the enemy doth extenuate the honour of the service, being but a rebel and a savage—I *differ from him*. For I see the justest triumphs that the Romans in their greatness did obtain were of such an enemy as this, that is, people barbarous and not reduced to civility, magnifying a kind of lawless liberty, prodigal in life, *hardened in body, fortified in woods and bogs, and placing both justice and felicity in the sharpness of their swords. Such were the Germans and the ancient Britons and divers others.*"

Here is the account in the *Apology:*

The same administrative incapacity which in the French campaign of 1591 enabled Essex to waste away an army of four thousand Englishmen to one thousand, without having any result to show for it, now joined with bad weather and the Earl's ill-health to produce a no less miserable failure in Ireland. Indignant at his want of success, the Queen cancelled her promise of permission to return, and ordered him to advise her " particularly in writing " of the terms on which he had made a truce with Tyrone. But Essex had pledged his word to Tyrone (so he asserted) that the terms should not be committed to writing, lest his enemies should send them to Spain. Taking advantage of this dilemma, the Earl determined to act upon the Queen's cancelled promise, and to break her last orders by returning to Court to plead his cause in person. The *Declaration of the Treasons of Essex* accuses him of intending at this time to surprise the Court with the aid of " some two hundred resolute gentlemen." But he had no more than six attendants with him when, early in the morning of the 28th of September, 1599, he threw himself on his knees before the Queen.

§ 9 THE FALL OF ESSEX

For the next eleven months Essex was under restraint, and for the greater part of the time a close prisoner. The document entitled " Tyrone's Propositions," [1] on the ground of which it has

"Touching his going into Ireland it pleased him expressly and in a set manner to desire mine opinion and counsel. . . . . And because I would omit no argument, I remember I stood also upon the difficulty of the action ; setting before him out of histories that the Irish were such an enemy as *the ancient Gauls or Germans or Britons* were : and we saw how the Romans, yet when they came to do with enemies which placed their *felicity only in liberty and the sharpness of their swords,* and had the natural elemental advantages of *bogs and woods and hardness of bodies,* they ever found they had their hands full of them ; and therefore concluded that going over with such expectation as he did, and through the churlishness of the enterprise not likely to answer, it would mightily *diminish his reputation."*

Is any one prepared to believe that there were *two* discourses addressed by Bacon to Essex, *within the space of three or four months,* both arising from the express request of Essex, and *both* mentioning the " Romans," the " Germans," and " Britons," the " bogs and woods," the " sharpness of their swords," and " hardness of their bodies "—but the one inferring success, the other failure, from these identical considerations ? Surely such a " repetition " as this is not in Bacon's style, and would have been equally discreditable to his intelligence, and to the Earl's. Bacon often repeats the same or similar arguments, and uses the same language and figures of speech, to prove the same or similar conclusions ; but never, so far as I know, does he thus use *similar* words to prove *dissimilar,* or rather opposite, conclusions.

[1] Mr. Spedding's *Life,* vol. ii. p. 154.

been supposed that he was already practically committed to treason, has been shown to be devoid of all authority.[1] Disobedience in returning to Court and miserable incapacity, were the only charges that could be brought against him ; and no hint of anything treasonable was mentioned in the Declaration made in the Star Chamber (29 November, 1599,) of the grounds of the Queen's displeasure, nor in the quasi-judicial proceedings, before a special commission in the Lord Keeper's house, on 5 June, 1600.

But Essex was now fast drifting into treason. Even when released from restraint in August, 1600, he was informed that he must regard himself as still under the royal displeasure ; and this, says Cecil, made " very few resort to him but those of his own blood." He was also overwhelmed with debt ; and next month (Sept. 1600) the lease of wines whence he derived the principal part of his fortune was about to expire. If the Queen would not renew it, he was a ruined man. Oscillating between hope and despair, he at one time petitions, flatters, fawns ; at another he execrates the Queen and raves of treason. Coming from the Earl in one of these latter fits, one of his friends declares that " the man's soul seemeth tossed to and fro like the waves of a troubled sea. His speech of the Queen became no man who hath *mens sana in corpore sano*."

Meantime, although we cannot be surprised that Bacon, with his avowed notions of friendship, should no longer hold communications with one whose fortunes no longer " comprehended " his own, we may nevertheless be hardly prepared to find him pointed at by the public suspicion as the enemy of his former patron. Yet such was the general belief. Even his own brother Anthony seems not to have been entirely free from it. At all events we find Anthony at this time writing a letter to the Earl, in which he assures Essex that, dearly as he loves his brother, he would sooner that Francis died than that he should live to the Earl's prejudice. And the author of the Sydney papers, speaking of some slight offered at this time by the Queen to Essex, says,

---

[1] *Bacon and Essex*, pp. 134-147. The opinion of the late Mr. J. R. Green was that the document was not genuine ; and I presume that the silence of Professor Gardiner, who makes no mention of it, amounts to the same verdict. If it were genuine, the treason of Essex would be unquestionable.

" Mr. Bacon is thought to be the man who moves her Majesty unto it."

But from this, the gravest of all charges ever brought against Francis Bacon, we can at least partly exculpate him, and at the same time explain how the charge may have arisen.   A letter is extant in which Bacon excuses himself to the Queen for his absence from the proceedings against Essex in the Star Chamber (Nov. 1599).   As usual, the account in the letter is inconsistent with the account of the same incident given in the *Apology*.   In the latter he takes credit for absenting himself from the proceedings, and says that he excused himself on the ground of " some indisposition of body."   But the letter itself exhibits Bacon excusing himself, not on the plea of illness, but because of the violence of the Earl's followers, whom he charges, not obscurely, with a purpose to take the Queen's life :—

" My life hath been threatened and my name libelled.   But these are the practices of those whose doings are dangerous, but yet not so dangerous as their hopes ; or else the devices of some that would *put out all your Majesty's lights and fall on reckoning how many years you have reigned.*"[1]

We need not accuse Bacon of deliberately intending by these words to poison the Queen's mind against his former friend ; we may acquit him of everything but a cold-blooded indifference to his friend's interests, and a supreme desire to pose (even at a friend's cost) as a loyal and much persecuted subject of the Queen : but who can feel surprise that such language produced a result not very different from that which might have been attained by a treacherous slanderer aiming at a friend's destruction ?   Even Cecil, the Earl's chief enemy, although he expressed his disbelief in the popular report concerning Francis Bacon, nevertheless remonstrated with his cousin on the incautious conduct which had given rise to these rumours, begging him to be at least passive, and not active in insuring the fallen Favourite's utter ruin :

" Cousin, I hear it, but I believe it not, that you should do some ill service to my Lord of Essex ; for my part I am merely passive and not

---

[1] Professor Gardiner adduces this letter as a proof that Bacon was liable to " occasional ill-temper."   We could more easily believe this if the letter were in any degree injurious to his own interests.

active in this action, and I follow the Queen, and that heavily, I lead her not. . . . and the same course I would wish you to take."

In the first proceedings against Essex, (November, 1599) Bacon was allowed no part. Finding himself also likely to be excluded from the second proceedings (in York House, June, 1600), he wrote to the Queen expressing his willingness to serve her. But in spite of his request to have a substantial part assigned to him, he received instructions merely to animadvert on the Earl's indiscretion in permitting a treatise on Henry IV. to be dedicated to him in unseemly terms. Passing lightly over his prescribed task, however, he dilated on some passionate expressions in a letter from Essex to the Lord Keeper, in which the Earl had declared that the Queen's heart was obdurate, and that there was no tempest to be compared to the passionate indignation of a prince. Bacon said—and probably he persuaded himself that he thought—that he was herein actuated by a desire to keep himself in credit with the Queen, the better to serve the Earl. But this last latent motive was naturally not perceptible to the friends of Essex, one of whom singles out Bacon, above all the prosecutors, as the object of his indignation: "My Lord was charged by the Sergeant, Attorney, the Solicitor and Mr. Bacon—who was very idle, and will, I hope have the reward of that honour in the end." [1]

Bacon's display of zeal in these legal proceedings did not, however, prevent him from offering his services to Essex, a fortnight after his release from restraint (20 July).[2]

"To the Earl of Essex.

" My Lord,

"No man can better expound my doings than your Lordship, which maketh me say the less. Only I humbly pray you to believe that I aspire to the conscience and commendation of first, *bonus civis*, which with us is a good and true servant to the Queen, and next of *bonus vir*, that is an honest man. I desire your Lordship also to think that, though I confess I love some things much better than I love your Lordship, as the Queen's

---

[1] I am indebted for this letter (which is published in full in *Bacon and Essex*, p. 174) to the late Professor Brewer.

[2] In the *Apology* Bacon says that he wrote to Essex "*as soon as ever* he was at his liberty, whereby I might, without peril of the Queen's indignation, write to him."

service, her quiet and contentment, her honour, her favour, the good of
my country and the like, yet I love few persons better than yourself, both
for gratitude's sake and for your own virtues, which cannot hurt but by
accident or abuse. Of which my good affection I was ever and am ready
to yield testimony by any good offices, but with such reservations as
yourself cannot but allow. For as I was ever sorry that your Lordship
should fly with waxen wings, doubting Icarus' fortune, so for the growing
up of your own feathers—especially ostrich's or any other save of a bird
of prey—no man shall be more glad. And this is the axle-tree whereupon
I have turned and shall turn. Which to signify to you, though I think
you are of yourself persuaded as much, is the cause of my writing. And
so I commend your Lordship to God's goodness. From Gray's Inn, this
20th day of July, 1600.

Your Lordship's most humbly,
Fr. Bacon."

Bacon's letter found the Earl in one of his melancholy
despairing fits, when he was crying *Vanitas vanitatum*, after
his manner, and vowing to lead henceforth a life of contemplation. But he frankly accepted Bacon's proffered services for
the future. As for Bacon's past actions during his imprisonment, not having heard from his friend for the last nine months,
he owns himself unable to expound them, " being ignorant of
all of them save *one* "—he knows that Bacon attacked him in
the proceedings of York House. The illustration of Icarus he
treats as new and inapplicable to himself, and defends himself
against the implied charge of ambition.

" Mr. Bacon,

" I can neither expound nor censure your late actions, being ignorant of
them all save one, and having directed my sight inward only to examine
myself. You do pray me to believe that you only aspire to the conscience
and commendation of *bonus civis* and *bonus vir ;* and I do faithfully assure
you that while that is your ambition (though your course be active and
mine contemplative), yet we shall both *convenire in eodem tertio,* and *convenire inter nos ipsos.* Your profession of affection and your offer of good
offices are welcome to me. For answer to them I will say but this : that
you have believed I have been kind to you, and you may believe that I
cannot be other, either upon humour or mine own election. I am a
stranger to all poetical conceits, or else I should say somewhat of your
poetical example. But this I must say, that I never flew with other wings
than desire to merit, and confidence in, my sovereign's favour, and when
one of these wings failed me, I would light nowhere but at my sovereign's
feet, though she suffered me to be bruised with my fall. And till her

Majesty—that knows I was never bird of prey—finds it to agree with her will and her service that my wings should be imped [1] again, I have committed myself to the mue. No power but my God's and my sovereign's can alter this resolution of

Your retired friend,
ESSEX."

One point in this letter requires notice. It must be apparent, I think, that the comparison between himself and Icarus strikes Essex as not only unjust, but as novel. " I am a stranger to all poetical conceits, or else I could say somewhat of your poetical example "—these are not the words of one who had had the warning of Icarus dinned into his ears by a familiar friend who now for the hundredth time was repeating that warning. Yet in the *Apology*, Bacon would have us believe that " Icarus " was as a household word between him and Essex.

"Another point was, that I always vehemently dissuaded him from seeking greatness by a military dependence, or by a popular dependence, as that which would breed in the Queen jealousy, in himself presumption, and in the State perturbation ; and I *did usually compare them to Icarus' two wings, which were* joined on with wax, and would make him venture to soar too high and then fail him at the height."

Now there is not only no mention of Icarus, but also no warning against *seeking* " popularity " in any extant letter from Bacon to Essex. That he had warned the Earl against the *suspicion* of popularity is true : but in what terms ?

"The third impression is of a popular reputation ; which because it is a thing good in itself, being obtained as your Lordship obtaineth it, that is *bonis artibus*—and besides well governed, it is one of the best flowers of your greatness both present and to come—it would be handled tenderly. The only way is to quench it *verbis* and not *rebus*. And therefore to take all occasions to the Queen to speak against popularity and popular causes vehemently, and to tax it in all others ; but *nevertheless to go on in your honourable commonwealth courses as you do.*"[3]

On the whole, this is probably one of the many instances in which Bacon allowed his memory of facts to be biassed by what happened after these facts. He *had* warned Essex against

---

[1] *i.e.* "refitted with fresh feathers " " the mue," a word of falconry, is metaphorically used for " retirement."

[2] Spedding, iii. 145.   [3] *Ib.* ii. 42.

" seeking greatness by a military dependence," but not against
seeking it by " a popular dependence."   Also, when the Earl
was in disgrace and suspected by the Queen, Bacon had warned
him in a single letter against following the example of Icarus.
So much is true : but in after years, sitting down to write his
Apology, Bacon throws the Icarian warning back into a remoter
past, and taking as it were a bird's-eye view of the whole career
of Essex, persuades himself into the belief that he had all
along deprecated not only his friend's love of war, but also his
craving for " popularity," and had repeatedly warned him against
trusting to the waxen wings of ambition.

But however the *Apology* may misrepresent the extent of
Bacon's foresight, there is no reason to suppose that it exagge-
rates the assiduity with which at this time he endeavoured to
conciliate the Queen to Essex.   Among other services, he composed a correspondence—ostensibly between Essex and his brother
Anthony—which, when copied in the handwriting of the supposed
writers, was to be shown to the Queen, in order to exhibit Essex
loyally and passionately deploring that the malignity of his
enemies seemed destined for ever to exclude him from the royal
favour and affection.

These letters are well worth studying as specimens of Bacon's
literary and, we may almost say, dramatic power.   No one can
fail to be struck by the skill with which he distinguishes the
somewhat quaint, humorous, cumbersome style of Anthony, from
the abrupt, incisive, antithetical, and passionately rhetorical style
of Essex; and the manner in which Anthony, the sickly invalid,
divided between his devotion to his brother and his patron,
pours forth his somewhat lengthy conjectures about the Queen's
motives, affords a truly dramatic contrast with the peremptory
despair of Essex.   Noteworthy also are the references to Francis
Bacon in the two letters.   If the Queen read them, she could
hardly fail to think the better of Francis in consequence of
them.   He is described as being " reserved " even to a fault,
yet as giving the most favourable account of the Queen's gracious
intentions.   Essex must expect an eclipse at least for a time :
but Anthony desires and hopes to see his brother Francis
"established *by her Majesty's favour*, as he thinks him well
worthy, *for that he hath done and suffered.*"   If the Queen was

F

jealous lest Francis Bacon should be still too well loved by Essex, and too much devoted to Essex, nothing was more likely to disarm her jealousy than the Earl's almost sullen admission to Anthony, " For your brother, I hold him an honest gentleman, and wish him all good, *much the rather for your sake.*"

Again, the whole tenour of the letter appeals to the Queen's sense of administrative policy as well as to her sense of power. The enemies of Essex are represented as triumphant. The Queen has desired to be merciful; but the "enemies" have thwarted and will thwart her. The Queen is still prepared to forgive; but the "enemies" will not allow her to have a chance of forgiving, and for that purpose will keep Essex from Court and force him to despair. To a Queen who had an opinion that "government, with respect to factions was a principal part of policy," it might well seem that it was not wise thus to allow one faction of her Court to be completely crushed. Considered artistically, and as means to an end, these letters must be admitted by all to be truly admirable compositions.

The commencement of Anthony's letter implies that the Earl —who was intensely religious with a somewhat narrow Protestantism—was just now in one of his religious moods. Francis makes Anthony hint that people will say that Essex is like Leicester, and will call his religion mere hypocrisy; and by that very hint he both suggests to the Queen—who was fully aware of the difference between Essex and Leicester—that it is not hypocrisy, and also paves the way for the Earl to quit his religious melancholy and to enter on a new course of application to the Queen.

"Two letters framed by Sir Francis Bacon, the one as in the name of Mr. Anthony Bacon, his brother, to the Earl of Essex; the other as the Earl's answer thereunto.

" *Both which, by the advice of Mr. Anthony Bacon, and with the privity of the said Earl, were to be shewed Queen Elizabeth upon some occasion, as a mean to work her Majesty to receive the Earl again to favour and attendance at Court. They were devised while my Lord remained prisoner in his own house.*

" MY SINGULAR GOOD LORD,

" This standing at a stay in your Lordship's fortune doth make me in my love towards your Lordship jealous lest you do somewhat, or omit somewhat, that amounteth to a new error ; for I suppose of all former errors there is a full expiation. Wherein for anything that your Lordship doth, I, for my part (who am remote), cannot cast nor devise wherein any error should be, except in one point, which I dare not censure nor dissuade ; which is, that (as the prophet saith) in this affliction you look up *ad manum percutientem*, and so make your peace with God. And yet I have heard it noted that my Lord of Leicester (who could never get to be taken for a saint) nevertheless in the Queen's disfavour waxed seemingly religious ; which may be thought by some and used by others as a case resembling yours, if men do not see, and will not see, the difference between your two dispositions.

" But to be plain with your Lordship, my fear rather is, beause I hear how some of your good and wise friends, not unpractised in the Court and supposing themselves not to be unseen in that deep and inscrutable centre of the Court, which is her Majesty's mind, do not only toll the bell, but even ring out peals, as if your fortune were dead and buried, and as if there were no possibility of recovering her Majesty's favour, and as if the best of your condition were to live a private and retired life, out of want out of peril, and out of manifest disgrace ; and so in this persuasion of theirs include a persuasion to your Lordship to frame and accommodate your actions and mind to that end—I fear, I say, that this untimely despair may in time bring forth a just despair, by causing your Lordship to slack and break off your wise, loyal, and seasonable endeavours and industries for redintegration to her Majesty's favour ; in comparison whereof all other circumstances are but as *atomi*, or rather as *vacuum* without any substance at all.

" Against this opinion it may please your Lordship to consider of these reasons which I have collected, and to make judgment of them, neither out of the melancholy of your present fortune, nor out of the infusion of that which cometh to you by others' relation (which is subject to much tincture), but *ex rebus ipsis*, out of the nature of the persons and actions themselves, as the trustiest and least deceiving rounds of opinion. For though I am so unfortunate as to be a stranger to her Majesty's eye and to her nature, yet by that which is apparent, I do manifestly discern that she hath that character of the Divine nature and goodness, ' Quos amavit amavit usque ad finem ; ' and where she hath a creature, she doth not deface nor defeat it. Insomuch as, if I observe rightly, in those persons whom heretofore she hath honoured with her special favour, she hath covered and remitted not only defects and ingratitudes in affection, but errors in state and service.

" Secondly, if I can spell and scholar-like put together the parts of her Majesty's proceeding now towards your Lordship, I can but make this construction—that her Majesty in her royal intention never purposed to call your Lordship's doings into public question, but only to have used a cloud without a shower, in censuring them by some temporary restraint only of liberty, and debarring you from her presence. For first, the handling the cause in the Star Chamber, you not called, was enforced by the violence of libelling and rumours, wherein the Queen thought to have satisfied the world, and yet spared your Lordship's appearance. And then after, when that means which was intended for the quenching of malicious bruits, turned to kindle them (because it was said your Lordship was condemned unheard, and your Lordship's sister wrote that piquant letter), then her Majesty saw plainly that these winds of rumours could not be commanded down without a handling of the cause by making you party, and admitting your defence. And to this purpose I do assure your Lordship that my brother, Francis Bacon, who is too wise (I think) to be abused, and too honest to abuse, *though he be more reserved in all particulars than is needful, yet in generality he hath ever constantly and with asseveration affirmed to me that both those days, that of the Star Chamber and that at my Lord Keeper's, were won from the Queen merely upon necessity and point of honour, against her own inclination.*

"Thirdly, in the last proceeding I note three points, which are directly significant, that her Majesty did expressly forbear any point which was irreparable, or might make your Lordship in any degree incapable of the return of her favour, or might fix any character indelible of disgrace upon you. For she spared the public place of the Star Chamber ; she limited the charge precisely not to touch disloyalty ; and no record remaineth to memory of the charge or sentence.

"Fourthly, the very distinction which was made in the sentence, of sequestration from the places of service in State, and leaving your Lordship the place of Master of the Horse, doth to my understanding, *indicative*, point at this—that her Majesty meant to use your Lordship's attendance in Court, while the exercises of the other places stood suspended.

"Fifthly, I have heard, and your Lordship knoweth better, that now, since you were in your own custody, her Majesty in *verbo regio* and by his mouth to whom she committeth her royal grants and decrees, hath assured your Lordship she will forbid and not suffer your ruin.

"Sixthly, as I have heard her Majesty to be a prince of that magnanimity that she will spare the service of the ablest subject or peer when she shall be thought to stand in need of it ; so she is of that policy as she will not lose the service of a meaner than your Lordship, where it shall depend merely upon her choice and will.

"Seventhly, I hold it for a principle, that generally those diseases are hardest to cure whereof the cause is obscure ; and those easiest whereof the cause is manifest. Whereupon I conclude that, since it hath been your errors in your courses towards her Majesty which have prejudiced you, that your reforming and conformity will restore you, so as you may be *faber fortunæ propriæ*.

"Lastly, considering your Lordship is removed from dealing in causes of State, and left only to a place of attendance, methinks the ambition of any man who can endure no partners in State matters may be so quenched, as they shall not laboriously oppose themselves to your being in Court.

"So as, upon the whole matter, I can find neither in her Majesty's person, nor in your own person, neither in former precedents, nor in your own case, any cause of dry and peremptory despair. Neither do I speak this, but that, if her Majesty out of her resolution do design you to a private life, you should be as willing upon her appointment to go into the wilderness as into the land of promise. Only I wish your Lordship will not preoccupate despair, but put trust, next to God, in her Majesty's grace, and not be wanting to yourself.

"I know your Lordship may justly interpret that this which I persuade may have reference to my particular, because I may truly say, 'te stante,' not 'virebo' (for I am withered in myself), but 'manebo' or 'tenebo'; I shall in some sort be able to hold out. But though your Lordship's years and health may expect[1] a return of grace and fortune, yet your eclipse for a time is an 'ultimum vale' to my fortune ; and were it not that I desire and hope to see my brother established by her Majesty's favour (as I think him well worthy for that he hath done and suffered) it were time to take that course from which I dissuade your Lordship. But now in the meantime, I cannot choose but perform these honest duties to you, to whom I have been so deeply bounden."

"The Letter framed as from the Earl in answer of the former Letter.

"Mr. Bacon,

"I thank you for your kind and careful letter. It persuadeth me that which I wish strongly and hope for weakly ; that is, a possibility of restitution to her Majesty's favour. Your arguments, that would cherish hope, turn to despair. You say the Queen never meant to call me to public censure ; but you see I passed it, which sheweth others' power. I believe most steadfastly her Majesty never intended to bring my cause to a sentence ; and I believe as verily that, since the sentence, she meant to restore me to attend upon her person. But they that could use occasions (which it was not in me to let[2]) and amplify occasions, and practise occasions, to represent to her Majesty a necessity to bring me to the one, can and will do the like to stop me from the other.

"You say my errors were my prejudice and therefore I can mend myself. It is true. But they that know that I can mend myself, and that, if I ever recover the Queen, I will never lose her again, will never suffer me to obtain interest in her favour. You say the Queen never forsook utterly

---

[1] *i.e.* await.   [2] *i.e.* prevent.

where she inwardly favoured. But I know not whether the hour-glass of time hath altered her : but sure I am the false glass of others must alter her, when I want access to plead my own cause.

"I know I ought doubly infinitely to be her Majesty's, both 'jure creationis,' for I am her creature, and 'jure redemptionis,' for I know she hath saved me from overthrow. But for her first love, and for her last protection, and all her great benefits, I can but pray for her Majesty. And my endeavours are now to make my prayers for her and myself better heard. For, thanks be to God, they that can make her Majesty believe I counterfeit with her, cannot make God believe that I counterfeit with Him. And they which can let me from coming near unto her, cannot let me from drawing near unto Him, as I hope I do daily.

"For your brother, I hold him an honest gentleman, and wish him all good, *much the rather for your sake.* Yourself, I know, hath suffered more for me than any friend I have. But I can but lament freely, as you see I do, and advise you not to do that which I do, which is, to despair.

"You know letters, what hurt they have done me,[1] and therefore make sure of this. And yet I could not (as having no other pledge of my love) but communicate freely with you for the ease of my heart and yours."

It is of course impossible to determine with certainty from these letters whether Bacon was encouraging the Earl in a hypocritical affectation of religious melancholy, or simply expressing the Earl's actual feelings in the manner in which he thought they would be most acceptable to the Queen. Bacon, as we know from his *Essays* and from his practice, did not condemn dissimulation nor even simulation where "there is no remedy : " still we can hardly conceive that he would have written in Essex's name, "Thanks be to God, they that can make her Majesty believe I can counterfeit with her, cannot make God believe that I counterfeit with Him," and "They which can let me from coming near unto her, cannot let me from drawing near unto Him, as I hope I do daily"—unless he believed that the Earl was really now, as he often had been before, in one of his religious moods. The mood might be transient, but it would appear that Bacon wrote under the impression that it was genuine. Yet compare this with the corresponding passage in

---

[1] Perhaps the reference is to the letter written by Essex to Egerton for which he was attacked by Francis Bacon at York House. "Make sure of this" of course means "destroy this." It is a very artistic insertion in a letter written, not to be burned or "made sure of," but to be preserved by Anthony and to be given by him to Francis, and to be shown by Francis to the Queen.

the *Declaration of the Treasons of Essex*, penned by Bacon for the Court:—

"Neither was the effect of the sentence that there passed against him any more than a suspension of the exercise of some of his places : at which time also Essex, that could vary himself into all shapes for a time, infinitely desirous (as by the sequel now appeareth) to be at liberty to practise and revive his former purposes, and hoping to set into them with better strength than ever, because he conceived the people's hearts were kindled to him by his troubles, and that they had made great demonstra-tion of as much—he did transform himself into such a strange and dejected humility, as if he had been no man of this world, with passionate protestations that he called God to witness, 'That he had made an utter divorce with the world ; and he desired her Majesty's favour not for any worldly respect, but for a preparative for a *Nunc dimittis;* and that the tears of his heart had quenched in him all humours of ambition.'"[1]

It is just possible that Essex may have been dissembling. We know that Bacon persistently urged him to dissemble long ago, and to "pretend to be bookish and contemplative : " but if Essex was really dissembling at Bacon's advice, and expressing his dissimulation in Bacon's own words, then it is intolerable that Bacon himself should afterwards turn round upon the Earl and charge him (by way of proving treason) with the dissimulation which he had himself put into the Earl's mouth. But this al-ternative is not probable. It is almost incompatible with Essex's character that he should have dissembled in religious matters. In such things he was timid even to superstition.[2] Far more probably he was not dissembling at all, and Bacon, at the time, knew that he was expressing the Earl's true feelings. "But," it may be urged, "the 'sequel' showed Bacon afterwards that the Earl had really been dissembling." It is just this "sequel" that pervades the whole of Bacon's *Apology* and *Declaration*, making them both historically worthless. Bacon cannot look at the past with a simple eye, but always views it through the "sequel," doing violence to facts, converting impulsiveness into treason,

[1] Spedding, ii. 260.
[2] See Dr. Barlow's account of the Earl's confession, how that "sometimes in the field encountering the enemy, being in any danger, the weight of his sins lying heavy upon his conscience, being not reconciled to God, quelled his spirits and made him the most timorous and fearful man that might be."—*Dr. Barlow's Sermon*, Ed. 1601.

and seeing in transient religious melancholy a deep-laid
hypocritical plot.[1]

To return however to Essex in disgrace. The Queen's
coronation day (17 November, 1600) passed, and still there was
no relenting. Essex had lost his fortune, and was now hopeless of regaining it. He believed that the enemies who had
deprived him of his fortunes were plotting to deprive him of
his life; he believed (sincerely, as was afterwards proved)
that Cecil was plotting for the succession of the Spanish Infanta;
and he now began to persuade himself into the belief that
the safety of his country, as well as his own, demanded the
removal of the Queen's present advisers. Once before, in
Ireland, he had made mention of such a course; and now he
seriously recurred to it. It is a curious illustration of the
factious feeling rife at this time, that the manifestly treasonable
project of surprising the Court and forcibly removing the Queen's
counsellors was regarded—even by so honourable a man as Sir
Henry Neville, but lately the Queen's ambassador in France—
as essentially different from rebellion. Under a fresh alarm that
he should be committed to the Tower, Essex determined
(February 1601) not to wait for Parliament and quiet remedies,
but to execute his project at once. One only of the Earl's
adherents suggested that the City should be roused to arms
before surprising the Court; but this suggestion found no
favour, and on 4 February the meeting broke up, having
resolved on nothing.

On Saturday, 7 February, when nothing had been as yet

---

[1] A version of Bacon's own speech in Essex's trial, printed below (see p. 76),
and taken from the Lambeth MSS. 931]61, charges Essex with "carrying a shew
of religion."

When Coke brings this accusation of "hypocrisy in religion," Mr. Spedding
ustly says "the imputation was not only irrelevant, but unjust."

It may be urged that Bacon—who describes himself as nothing but "the pen"
wherewith the Court drew up the *Declaration*—was not responsible for its truth.
But few will admit that a man is justified in so far subordinating his own per-
sonality as to make himself a mere "pen," especially for the purpose of penning
about a benefactor and former friend what the "pen" knows to be false.

[2] The sincerity of his belief was proved by the fact that he afterwards brought
against Cecil a definite charge of supporting the claims of the Spanish Infanta.
This charge indeed collapsed; but he would hardly have been so foolish as to
injure himself by bringing forward an accusation which he knew to be baseless.
It is certain that Cecil, if not now, was at all events subsequently, in receipt of a
pension from Spain. This Essex may have suspected to be the case; and it may
have aroused suspicions, though it could not supply proof, of intended treason.

determined, the Government, suspecting the concourse at Essex House, summoned the Earl before Her Majesty's Council. Essex excused himself on the plea of health, and called his friends together. By Saturday night three hundred had gathered round him, but still no plans had been settled. On Sunday morning the Lord Keeper, with three others, coming to demand from Essex the cause of this gathering, found him in a state of great distraction, vociferating that his life was sought, that his hand had been counterfeited, and that he and his friends were there to defend their lives. The crowd forced their way into the library. " Kill them," cried some ; " keep them prisoners," cried others. In his confession, a few days before his death, Essex speaks of the " confusion his followers drew him to even in his own house, that day he went into the City ; " and indeed, the " confusion " was such, that when, a few moments afterwards, he issued from the gates, leaving the Lord Keeper and the rest, detained as hostages, no plan had been even now settled. " To the Court ! To the Court ! " was the general cry. But Essex had just received word that the Court was prepared, and that the guards had been doubled. He, therefore, turned toward the City. For this change of plan horses were needful ; but not a single horse had been provided. Without horses, without a plan, and without a leader—for who could give the name of leader to a man now distracted to madness, and described by an eye-witness as " extremely appalled and almost molten with sweat by the perplexity and horror of his mind "— the revolt had miscarried when it began. By 10 o'clock that night Essex and his friends had surrendered to the Lord Admiral, and the Earl was committed to the Tower.

§ 10 The Death of Essex

The details of this clumsy and abortive outbreak are necessary for the appreciation of Bacon's subsequent conduct in the prosecution which brought the Earl to the block. That Essex was guilty of treason there could be no doubt, and that his execution was justifiable, if not necessary, there can be equally little doubt. But the Government desired to strengthen their position by proving that the plot had from the first contemplated not a mere change of the Queen's advisers, but a subversion of the State. For this purpose it was necessary to suppress all passages in the evidence which showed either that there had been an intention to avoid violence, or that the attempt on the City was an afterthought and not the original plan. It was also desirable to show that the Earl's fears of "enemies" at Court were mere pretexts assumed as a cloak for his ambitious treason.

Accordingly, in their *Declaration of the Treasons of Essex* (which professed to contain "the very confessions *taken word for word from their originals*") the Government suppressed or mutilated *seven passages which showed that no violence was intended, and six others which proved that the outbreak in the City had not been premeditated.* The internal evidence is sufficient to show the reason for these omissions; but there is other testimony that they were deliberate. Opposite to these passages in the originals stands the mark *om.*, sometimes in Coke's handwriting, sometimes in that of Bacon.[1]

But although the Government could with impunity mutilate the evidence of Essex's treason after his death, they could not do it as yet while he was alive and able (19 February, 1601) to defend himself. True, the evidence relied on by Essex to prove that Cecil was selling the State to the Spaniards altogether collapsed; yet, on the other hand, Essex indignantly disclaimed the intention of taking the Queen's life, imputed to him by Coke, and all original purpose of rousing the City; and the Government could prove neither of these two points. If the Earl could be believed, if he was not a hypocrite, he was guilty of a treasonable act, it is true, but still of no deliberate disloyalty aiming at the Crown. It was, therefore, necessary for the Government to show that he could not be believed, and that he was not only a traitor, but also a hypocritical traitor.

To aid them at this juncture, by convicting his former friend of deep-laid treachery and hypocrisy, Bacon now rose. He ought not to have been in the court at all. The decencies of friendship demanded that, if the Government assigned him a part in the prosecution, he should decline it. Peace and order having been now assured, it could not be maintained that the

---

[1] See *Bacon and Essex*, pp. 207—210.

interests of the country would have suffered if Bacon had been absent. He was neither Attorney-General nor Solicitor, nor had he any regular position as a law officer of the Crown ; he was merely one of the " Learned Counsel." There was no reason why one in so subordinate a position should have been called to so responsible a duty—no reason except that his intimacy with Essex made him an invaluable instrument in the hands of the prosecutors for pressing home a personal charge of hypocrisy. Combining the characters of barrister and witness, he could at once impute motives to the accused and also testify to them. Two or three years afterwards, Bacon was not employed in the trial of Raleigh nor in the subsequent trials arising out of the Gunpowder Plot. He was summoned now, not as one of the " Learned Counsel," but in the special capacity of " friend to the accused." There is no evidence at all that Bacon had ever deprecated the task ; and he now performed it with a ferocious efficacy. Skilfully confusing together the *proposed* plan of surprising the Court and the actually *executed* plan of raising the City, he insists that Essex's action, instead of being a sudden afterthought, was the result of three months' deliberation, and he concentrates all his efforts on proving that Essex was not only a traitor but a hypocritical traitor.

" In speaking of this late and horrible rebellion which hath been in the eyes and ears of all men, I shall save myself much labour in opening and enforcing the points thereof, insomuch as I speak not before a country jury of ignorant men, but before a most honourable assembly of the greatest peers of the land, whose wisdoms conceive far more than my tongue can utter.[1] Yet with your gracious and honourable favours I will

---

[1] I append another version of this speech from the Lambeth MSS. 931]61, manifestly an unrevised copy of notes taken by some one present at the trial. It is principally noticeable for charging Essex with the "shew of religion."
"Then Mr. Francis Bacon spake to this effect. I expected not (quoth he) that the matter of defence should have been alleged for excuse, and therefore I must alter my speech from that I intended. To rebel in defence is a matter not heard of. In case of murder, to defend is lawful ; but in this case to do all that was done that day and then to go about to blanch it—I cannot allow. I speak not to simple men, I speak to those that can draw proof out of the nature of things themselves. It is known by books, by experience, and by common talk, that no unlawful intendments are bent directly against the Piince, but there is a [!] waltering of government, *as the phrase is in Scotland*. These go [!] by no ways, but by particular someways. My Lord, I cannot resemble your proceedings more rightly than to that of Pisistratus in Athens, who lanced himself to the intent that by the sight of bleeding wounds the people might believe he was set upon. Your Lordship gave out that your life was sought by the Lord Cobham and

presume, if not for information of your Honours, yet for the discharge of my duty, to say thus much. No man can be ignorant that knows matter of former ages—and all history makes it plain—that there was never any traitor heard of that durst directly attempt the seat of his liege prince but he always coloured his practice with some plausible pretence. For God hath imprinted such a majesty in the face of a prince that no private man dare approach the person of his sovereign with a traitorous intent. And therefore they run another side course, *obliquè et a latere;* some to reform corruptions of the State and religion ; some to reduce the ancient liberties and customs pretended to be lost and worn out ; some to remove those persons that being in high places make themselves subject to envy. But all of them aim at the overthrow of the State and the destruction of the present rulers. And this likewise is the use of those that work mischief of another quality : as Cain, that first murderer, took up an excuse for his fact, shaming to outface it with impudency. Thus the Earl made his colour, the severing some great men and councillors from her Majesty's favour, and the fear he stood in of his pretended enemies lest they should murder him in his house. Therefore he saith he was compelled to fly into the city for succour or assistance ; not much unlike Pisistratus, of whom it was so anciently written how he gashed and wounded himself, and in that sort ran crying into Athens that his life was sought and like to have been taken away : thinking to have moved the people to have pitied him and taken his part by such counterfeited harm and danger ; whereas his aim and drift was to take the government of the City into his hands and alter the form thereof. With like pretences of dangers and assaults the Earl of Essex entered the City of London and passed through the bowels thereof, blanching rumours that he should have been murdered and that the State was sold—whereas he had no such enemies, no such dangers—persuading themselves that if they could prevail, all would have done well. But now, *magna scelera terminantur in haeresin:* for you, my Lord, should know that, though princes give their subjects cause for discontent, though they take away the honours they have heaped upon them, though they bring them to a lower estate than they raised them from, yet ought they not to be so forgetful of their allegiance that they should enter into any undutiful act, much less upon rebellion, as you, my Lord,

Sir Walter Raleigh, *and carried always such a show of religion in you that men's eyes were not able through such a mist to behold the deceit.* But you imprisoned the Council. What reference had that fact to my Lord Cobham or the rest ? You alleged that matter to have been resolved upon the sudden. No : *you were three months in deliberation.* My Lord, descend into yourself, and strip you of excuse. The persons you shoot (? shot) at, if you could have rightly understood them, were your best friends."

The ingenious allusion to " the phrase in Scotland " adds point to this bitter charge. Essex was known to be in favour of the Scottish accession, and thought to be keeping up communications with the King of Scotland. To these communications Bacon afterwards confessed that he was himself privy ; but that confession was not made till the accession of James I., when the confession became profitable. (See below, pp. 94, 96).

have done. All whatsoever you have, or can say in answer hereof, are but shadows. And therefore methinks it were best for you to confess, not to justify.''

Essex felt, and the Peers must have felt, the tremendous force of this unexpected attack. If the brother of the Earl's most trusted secretary, Anthony Bacon, if one of the Earl's chief friends and councillors, who had but a few months ago professed himself more beholden to the Earl than to any human being, could now thus confidently asseverate his belief in the Earl's hypocrisy, and accuse him of feigning " enemies " and dangers out of his own imagination, to suit and cover his own treasonable purposes, then indeed the Peers might well be disposed to take the same view. Logically and formally the speech of Bacon should have had little weight; but informally it may well have had immense weight, and Essex at once endeavoured to meet it. He instinctively felt that all the force of Bacon's speech was derived, not from its logic, but from his personal relations with himself: and he therefore endeavoured to bring forward what had passed in those personal relations, as a disproof of Bacon's charge. Bacon had asserted that " there were no such enemies, no such dangers." Here then the Earl retorted that :—

" The speeches of Mr. Bacon gave him occasion to place himself against himself. For, saith he, Mr. Bacon being a daily courtier and having access to her Majesty, undertook to go to the Queen on my behalf. He drew a letter very artificially which was subscribed with my name. Also another letter was drawn by him to occasion that [?] herewith others should come from his brother, Mr. Anthony Bacon, both which he should shew the Queen. Gosnold brought me both the letters, and in my letter he did plead for me as feelingly against those enemies, and pointed them out as plainly as was possible." [1]

[1] I quote from the version in the Lambeth MSS. quoted above. The version printed by Mr. Spedding runs thus :—" To answer Mr. Bacon's speech at once, I say this much and call Mr. Bacon against Mr. Bacon. You are then to know that Mr. Francis Bacon hath written two letters, the one of which hath been artificially framed in my name, after he had framed the other in Mr. Anthony Bacon's name to provoke me. In the latter of these two he lays down the grounds of my discontentment and the reasons I pretend against mine enemies, pleading as orderly for me as I could myself. . . . If those reasons were then just and true, not counterfeit, how can it be that now my pretensions are false and injurious ? For then Mr. Bacon joined with me in mine opinion, and pointed out those to be mine enemies, and to hold me in disgrace with her Majesty, whom he seems now to clear of such mind towards me. And therefore I leave the truth of what I say and he opposeth unto your Lordships' indifferent considerations." ii. 227.

The retort was a home-thrust; and, in his first irritation, Bacon could only reply that "these digressions were not fit, neither should be suffered ; but that the honour and patience of that assembly was great." Had the letters been in the hands of the Peers, it is possible that the prejudice produced by Bacon's speech might have been dispelled : and they might have been enabled to realise—from seeing how Bacon encouraged the Earl's dread of "enemies"—the extent to which Essex, rightly or wrongly, did actually dread them. But, as they were not produced, Bacon was quite safe in adding, when he recovered his equanimity, that " he had spent more hours to make him a meet servant for her Majesty than ever he [?] desired. For anything contained in these letters, it would not blush in the clearest light." [1]

The confessions of three of the Earl's followers were now read ; and if they were read as they were printed in the Government Declaration—that is, with *the omission of all of the passages* tending to show, first, the intention to abstain from violence ; secondly, the intention not to raise the City, but only to surprise the Court ; and, thirdly, the suddenness and unpremeditatedness of the attempt upon the City—it is not surprising that the Peers were convinced that Essex was guilty of premeditated treason, amounting to an attempt to subvert the State. Still pressing his charges of hypocrisy and deliberateness, Coke desired to add, as a proof, Essex's intended tolerance of Roman Catholics.[2] But the earnestness with which Essex refuted the charge of trifling with religion told on the Peers, and they refused to allow Coke to proceed with this charge.

The opinion of the judges had been ascertained that the mere

---

[1] Lambeth MSS. 931]61, quoted above ; see also Spedding, ii. 227.

[2] Coke probably quoted Blount's evidence, Sp., ii. 304 : " Being asked upon his conscience, whether the Earl of Essex did not give him comfort that, if he came to authority, there should be a toleration for religion ? He confesseth he should have been to blame to have denied it [*for in the Earl's usual talk he was wont to say that he liked not that any man should be troubled for his religion.*"] The words in italics are marked in the original *to be omitted* (in Coke's handwriting). The reason is obvious. The only basis for Blount's statement is the Earl's " usual talk ; " such a basis was felt to invalidate the evidence, and therefore the Government *omit the basis of hearsay in order to strengthen the evidence.*

For a similar omission, where evidence is based on mere vague talk compare ii. 301. " Being asked what they would have done after ? He saith, they would have sent to have satisfied the City, and have called a parliament [*as he hath heard them talk.*"]

" rising to go to Court with such a company only to present my Lord of Essex his complaints" constituted treason, even though unaccompanied by any purpose of violence. Clearly, therefore, Essex and Southampton were traitors. But this was not enough for Coke and Bacon. They must be proved to be traitors as well in *intention* as in act, and of this the Peers did not appear as yet to be convinced to Coke's satisfaction. " Our law," said the Attorney, "judgeth the intent by the overt act." " Well," saith the Earl, "plead your law, and we will plead conscience." [1]

Once more, therefore, Bacon rose to press the charge of deliberate and hypocritical treason. Ignoring the Earl's unreasonable fears, his impulsive nature, and his complete want of self-control and forethought, he again treated Essex as though the whole of his defence was a mere afterthought to excuse a treasonable plot deliberately planned and deliberately carried out. As if Essex had not committed himself past recall by summoning round him the noisy crowd in Essex House, Bacon lays stress upon the warning of the Lord Keeper, and then on the proclamation of the herald. The disregard of these, he says, if nothing else, constitutes Essex a deliberate traitor.

"I have never yet seen in any case such favour shewn to any prisoner ; so many digressions, such delivering of evidence by fractions, and so silly a defence of such great and notorious treasons. May it please your Grace, you have seen how weakly he hath shadowed his purpose and how slenderly he hath answered the objections against him. But my Lord, I doubt the variety of matters and the many digressions may minister occasion of forgetfulness, and may have severed the judgments of the Lords ; and therefore I hold it necessary briefly to recite the Judges' opinions."

This being done, he proceeded to this effect :—

"Now put the case that the Earl of Essex's intent were, as he would have it believed, to go only as a suppliant to her Majesty. Shall their petitions be presented by armed petitioners ? This must needs bring loss of liberty to the prince. Neither is it any point of law, as my Lord of Southampton would have it believed, that condemns them of treason, but it is apparent in common sense. To take secret counsel, to execute it, to run together in numbers armed with weapons—what can be the excuse ? Warned by the Lord Keeper, by a herald, and yet persist. Will any simple man take this to be less than treason ?"

[1] Spedding, ii. 229.

The Earl of Essex answered that, if he had purposed anything against others than those his private enemies, he would not have stirred with so slender a company. But Bacon crushed him with an illustration from modern history far more damaging to Essex, and likely to make him far more suspected by Elizabeth, than the previous reference to Pisistratus.

" It was not the company you carried with you, but the assistance which you hoped for in the City, which you trusted unto. The Duke of Guise thrust himself into the streets of Paris on the day of the Barricadoes, in his doublet and hose, attended only with eight gentlemen, and found that help in the City which (thanks be to God) you failed of here. And what followed ? The King was forced to put himself into a pilgrim's weeds, and in that disguise to steal away to scape their fury. Even such was my Lord's confidence too ; and his pretence the same—an all-hail and a kiss to the City. But the end was treason, as hath been sufficiently proved. But when he had once delivered and engaged himself so far into that which the shallowness of his conceit could not accomplish as he expected, the Queen for her defence taking arms against him, he was glad to yield himself, and, thinking to colour his practices, turned his pretexts, and alleged the occasion thereof to proceed from a private quarrel."

" To this," adds the reporter, " the Earl answered little :" and indeed to an assertion of this kind, not based upon any fresh evidence, but deriving all its weight from the fact that the asserter had been one of the Earl's most intimate friends and might be supposed to be best acquainted with his nature, it is hard to see what the Earl could have found to answer. Both the prisoners were found guilty, and sentence was passed in the usual form.

[1] Professor Gardiner would excuse Bacon in part on the plea that his error was not so much moral as intellectual, a mistake arising from "the weak side of his intellect."

"In the second place it has been alleged (ABBOTT, *Bacon and Essex*, 194-242) that Bacon sinned in charging Essex with a consistent purpose of treason which was foreign to his nature. It is no doubt true that Essex never did anything deliberately, and that an analysis of character would spare his heart at the expense of his head. It does not, however, follow that Bacon went deliberately wrong. On the day of the trial he had only very recently become acquainted with the Earl's very questionable proceedings in Ireland, and it was only *in consonance with the weak side of his intellect to adopt a compact theory* rather than one which left room for vagueness and uncertainty." *Dict. Nat. Biog.* ii. 335.

I presume that the word "proceedings" refers to one or two *conversations* not acted upon (see *Bacon and Essex*, 125-133), although the Government, by garbling the evidence, endeavoured to give the impression that they were acted on.

The answer appears to be, first, that Bacon had access to the complete *ungarbled* evidence, and *indeed was a party to the garbling of it*, so that he might have known (as we know) that no treasonable project was ever seriously enter-

A few days before his execution (25 February, 1601) the composure which Essex had hitherto preserved gave way before the fear of death, or of that which follows death ; and he poured forth a torrent of exaggerated accusations (some of which were afterwards proved to be groundless) against his secretary, his friends, his sister, and himself. "Would your Lordship have thought this weakness and this unnaturalness in this man !" writes the Earl of Nottingham to Montjoy. But this outburst proceeded neither from " unnaturalness " nor from vindictiveness; but from one whose mind was now thrown off its balance by superstition, yielding in death, as he had always yielded in life, to the impulse of the moment. The vague general self-reproaches wrung from a man on the verge of the grave by superstitious fears ought not to be allowed to exaggerate his crime ; and the verdict of history must be that Essex, though guilty of treason, was not a deliberate traitor.

On Bacon's conduct different judgments will be pronounced according as each one judges more or less severely sins proceeding not from an occasional succumbing to temptation, but from an original and natural deficiency in moral taste and in the instinct of honour. Probably in consenting to contribute to the destruction of his friend, Bacon was acting under, what must have seemed to him, considerable pressure. If he had refused the task assigned to him by the Crown, he must have given up all chance of the Queen's favour and with it all hope of promotion. Very inferior men have made as great, or greater, sacrifices ; but Bacon was not the man to make such a sacrifice. He had known once what it was to be in the cloud and under the displeasure of his royal mistress, and he was unwilling to renew that experience. Debts were pressing him, and poverty staring him in the face. Recent circumstances may have quickened his appreciation of the Queen's wisdom and judgment as well as his desire for her favour, and his feeling that Essex was a reckless, wilful, incorrigible outcast from the Court, capable now, neither of helping nor of being helped, doomed to

tained ; second, that a man who, against evidence, leaps to a "compact theory" that a friend is a deliberate and consistent hypocrite, rather than adopt a " vague " theory that his friend may be a combination of ambition, weakness, recklessness, and a number of other qualities good and bad—has " a weak side " in his affections or emotions, as well as in his intellect.

G

ultimate destruction. Bacon had a keen sense of the value of fortune, of the possibilities of a learned leisure, of the importance of his own colossal plans for the benefit of the human race; on the other hand he had a very dull sense of the claims of honour and friendship. Forced to choose between prosperity and friendship, he preferred to be prosperous even at the cost of facilitating the ruin of a friend for whom ruin, in any case, was ultimately inevitable.

As it was, he gained less than he expected. But two years more remained for Elizabeth to reign, and Bacon was not destined to receive any office from her hands. Some reward, indeed, he received in shape of money; but he naturally considered £1,200 as very insufficient price for services which no one but himself could have rendered. Excusing himself to a friendly creditor, whom he cannot at once pay, owing to the delay of the promised reward, he says, " The Queen hath done somewhat for me, though not in the perfection I hoped." [1]

§ 11 The End of the Old Reign

The detailed discussion of the first edition of the *Essays* (published in January, 1597), will find a fitter place in the pages devoted to Bacon's works; but it is interesting here, to note how this, the most popular of his books, sprang out of, and illustrates, his own recent experiences.[2] The writer assumes that the world is full of evil, and that men cannot get on in the world without a knowledge of evil arts, an assumption thus definitely expressed in the *Advancement of Learning*: " We are much beholden to Machiavel and others, that wrote what men do, and not what they ought to do. For it is not possible to join serpentine wisdom with the columbine simplicity, *except men know all the conditions of the serpent*." [3]   The axiom that a man

[1] Of the relations between Francis and Anthony Bacon during the trial of Essex we have no knowledge ; but a long anonymous letter addressed (30 May, 1601) to Anthony—he died a few days before he could have received it—shows that " Anthony was interesting himself to the last—to prove his patron innocent of the worst accusations against him."—*Dictionary of National Biography*, " Anthony Bacon."

[2] The first edition included only the *Essays* on Study, Discourse, Ceremonies and Respects, Followers and Friends, Suitors, Expense, Regiment of Health, Honour and Reputation, Faction, Negociating.

[3] *Adv. of Learn.* II. xxi. 9.

who wishes to succeed must "know all the conditions of the serpent" underlies the whole of the *Essays*.

But Bacon's theory is not quite consistent with his practice. His theory is that we are to know the Evil Arts, merely that we may be on our guard against them; but in practice he often puts forward some of the minor Evil Arts as though for general use. For any man who will regard life as a game of chess and human beings as the pieces, the *Essays* will afford useful hints for winning the game; hints that go straight to the mark and are always practicable and always suggestive of more than they actually say. There is no waste of words or sentiment. Everything is to the point and tends to practice. How terse, for example, and how practical is the *Essay on Negociating*, which tells you that "If you would work any man, you must either know his nature and his fashions and so lead him; or his ends, and so win him; or his weaknesses and disadvantages, and so awe him; or those that have interest in him and so govern him!"[1] And what wisdom there is in the reason given for the advice to employ lucky people; "For that breeds confidence; and they will strive to maintain their prescription!"[2]

Perhaps the passage in the *Essays* that contains the most feeling recognition of right and wrong is—characteristically enough, as coming from one who was smarting under the rejection of a protracted suit—to be found in the *Essay on Suitors* where the writer protests that in every suit there ought to be some higher consideration than mere favour: "Surely there is, in some sort, a right in every suit: either a right of equity if it be a suit of controversy, or a right of desert, if it be a suit of petition."[3] But even here he assumes that his readers will occasionally favour the wrong side and only asks them not to carry their injustice to the length of oppression or slander.

In the little volume of 1597 there is not much of the philosophic enthusiasm which breathes in some of the later *Essays*. The subjects are for the most part on a common-place level, and the language is correspondingly homely. We must wait till 1620 for the splendid eulogy on *Truth* as "the sovereign good of human nature." In the *Studies* of 1597 we have only

---

[1] *Essays*, xlvii. 43.   [2] *Ib.* 26.
[3] *Ib.* xlix. 17.

the common sense view that "simple men admire them, wise men use them." This word "use" is indeed the key-note to the ethics of the earlier *Essays*. Everything is to be "used" for some purpose—studies, discourse, money, men, friends, and factions. The purpose ought to be a good one—so the Essayist occasionally protests—but he shows you how to make these things subserve *any* purpose, good or bad. On the frank world-liness of Bacon's views of friendship, comment has been already made; but the *Essay on Faction* is no less frank in its recognition of self-interest as a natural and prevailing motive, and almost cynical in its suppression of resentment against ratters and traitors. "Mean men," *i.e.* men of low station, are told that if they wish to rise, they must "adhere," *i.e.* take a side; yet even for beginners, he adds, it generally answers to be the most popular man of your faction with the opposite faction[1] (just as Francis Bacon of the Essexian faction was at this time (1596-7) keeping on terms with the Cecilians); and again, "the traitor, in factions, lightly goeth away with it; for when matters have stuck long in balancing, the winning of some one man casteth them and he getteth all the thanks."[2]

Bacon's part in drawing up the work described by Lord Clarendon as a "pestilent libel," but published by the Govern-ment as a *Declaration of the Treasons of Essex*[3] may be passed over the more briefly because he tells us (and we have no evidence to the contrary), that his task was little more than that of an amanuensis to the Council and the Queen.

"About that time her Majesty, taking a liking for my pen . . . . commanded me to pen that book, which was published for the better satisfaction of the world ; which I did, but so as never secretary had more particular and express directions and instructions in every point how to guide my hand in it. And not only so ; but after that I had made a first draught thereof, and propounded it to certain principal Councillors, by her Majesty's appointment, it was perused, weighed, censured, altered and made almost a new writing, according to their Lordships' better consideration ; wherein their Lordships and myself both were as religious and curious of truth, as desirous of satisfaction ; and myself indeed gave only words and form of style in pursuing their direction."[4]

[1] *Essays*, ii. 10-15.
[3] Spedding, ii. 247—363.
[2] *Ib*. 38.
[4] *Ib*. iii. 159.

But we cannot so lightly pass over the *Apology*,[1] which, (though printed in 1604) was probably written in 1603, and naturally demands consideration at this period when we are bidding farewell to Essex. It was dedicated to Montjoy (by that time Earl of Devonshire) and its object was to vindicate the Author, not in the estimation of the vulgar sort (whom, he says, he does not so much regard), but in the judgment of certain other persons, from the charge of having been false to the Earl of Essex. Speaking of " the noble but unfortunate Earl " throughout in terms of respect and tenderness, it states that the Author, during a long and entirely disinterested friendship, neglected the Queen's service, his own fortune, and, in a sort, his vocation, first to retain, and then to redintegrate, Essex in the royal favour; in which course he protests that he continued faithfully and industriously " till his last impatience, for so I will call it "— but he had once called it the hypocrisy of a Pisistratus and the treachery of a Judas when his benefactor's life was hanging in the balance—" after which day there was not time to work for him."

That Bacon's *Apology* is full of inaccuracies will be admitted by all who, without prejudice and with sufficient attention, will compare it with Bacon's letters; but it would be a hasty inference to conclude that he deliberately and consciously misrepresented a single incident. We have abundant proof that he was eminently inattentive to details. His scientific works are full of small inaccuracies; King James found in this defect of his Chancellor the matter for a witticism, " de minimis non curat lex ; " his most friendly biographer, Mr. Spedding, admits that his memory was "not very accurate in counting time," and Rawley, his private chaplain and devoted admirer, tells us that he habitually altered and improved upon the utterances of any author whom he happened to quote.

A slippery memory, and inattention to facts, especially to inconvenient facts, in a man of determined self-complacency, may easily lead to a complete distortion of history without definite and conscious falsehood. Just as Bacon habitually " improved on " the authors from whom he quoted, giving us, not what they said, but

[1] Spedding, iii. 141—160.

what he thought they ought to have said, so in the *Apology* he has improved upon himself, by slight touches and minute divergences from the truth, conveying to us the picture, not of his actual conduct, but of what he felt his conduct ought to have been. But however interesting the *Apology* may be, from a literary and rhetorical point of view, for the ease and smoothness of its style, and for the dexterity with which it colours facts without greatly falsifying them, it can never be regarded as a contribution to history—unless it be a psychological history of the manifold and labyrinthine self-deceptions to which great men have been subjected.

A few words on Bacon's money matters are needful at this point. Enriched with twelve hundred pounds as his reward for contributing to the conviction of Essex, he was now somewhat relieved from pecuniary distractions ; and we may here take our last notice of this aspect of his life, which is not without importance in attempting to estimate the motives which led him to sue for lucrative office. Having failed (in spite of the vehement advocacy of Essex) in an attempt (1597) to make a wealthy marriage with the widow of Sir William Hatton, he was arrested in the autumn of next year (1598) for a debt of £300. It appears that he had been previously sued for this debt, and that the payment had been excused till the beginning of Michaelmas term. But the impatient creditor anticipated the term by a few days ; and on the 24th of September, Bacon writes to Egerton and Cecil from a " handsome house in Coleman Street," where he is under restraint, complaining of the insult to which he has been subjected in being arrested on his way from the Tower, where he had been discharging the Queen's business, as one of the learned counsel. His straitened circumstances may be inferred from the fact that, although the " beginning of Michaelmas Term" was certainly not far off, he cannot pay his debt without great inconvenience ; " I have an hundred pounds lying by me, which he may have, and the rest upon some reasonable time and security ; or, if need be, the whole ; but with my more trouble."

In the previous year (1597) he had attempted to secure the Mastership of the Rolls by favour of the Lord Keeper Egerton. In return for this, he privately promised to Egerton's son the reversion of his Clerkship to the Council—the present Clerk, Mill, being under trial for irregularities, for which he might possibly be dismissed. As the Lord Keeper was already either appointed, or likely to be appointed, one of Mill's judges, this secret application, conveyed in obscure and circuitous terms, was scarcely creditable to Bacon. But the scheme failed and Mill retained his post.[1]

However, from a petition of Francis Bacon to the Queen in 1600, we gather that he had hopes of getting into his own hands an estate which his brother Anthony was proposing to alienate; and an improvement in his circumstances may also be inferred from the fact that we find him, about this time, undertaking to clear off his debts. In this process his unbusinesslike, over-hopeful, and self-favouring disposition becomes once more curiously prominent. His principal creditor was an old friend of the name of Trott, of whose kindness and consideration Anthony speaks in the highest terms; but Trott and Francis Bacon cannot agree upon the amount due. Into the details of this petty dispute space forbids us to enter; but the result is not without interest. Bacon offered £1,259 12s.; his friend (besides expenses amounting to about £140) claimed £1,897 12s. The Lord-Keeper Egerton (one of the most honourable men of the day and a special friend of Bacon's, to whom they referred the dispute), awarded £1,800—a decision that seems to show that Bacon's vehement complaints of his old friend's extortionate demands were, to say the least, not quite justifiable.

The reign of Elizabeth was now drawing to a close, and the time was at hand when Bacon, at least for a time, must bid farewell to politics and resort to that alternative which he had mentioned to his uncle Burghley—become a "sorry book-maker and pioneer in the mine of Truth."

---

[1] For a full discussion of the matter see *Bacon and Essex*, pp. 83-88. Professor Gardiner says on this point "The mere proposal would properly shock us at the present day; and if, as seems probable, Bacon's second letter of 12 November, in which his offer was repeated, was written after he knew that Egerton had been chosen a member of the Commission which had been appointed to examine the charges which had been brought against the actual holder of the Clerkship, the transaction assumes an aspect which ought to have opened Bacon's eyes to its questionable character—though, judging from his subsequent proceedings as Chancellor, his eyes were very hard to open." (*Dict. of Nat. Biography*, "Bacon.")

Among his enemies under the new reign he must henceforth reckon Coke, the Attorney-General. The two had been
competitors before, when Coke had been promoted from the
Solicitor's place to be Attorney-General (1594) in spite of
Bacon's suit for the same place ; they had also been rivals
(1597) in suing for the hand of Lady Hatton, and here also
Coke had been successful. Not improbably Coke had been
irritated by Bacon's attempt to come between him and the
Attorneyship. Sir Francis Bacon, Solicitor-General himself in
1611, describes the Attorney's place at that time to the King as
" the natural and immediate step and rise, *which the place I now
hold hath ever, in a sort, made claim to, and almost never failed
of.*" Why then, Coke might well have asked, should an attempt
have been made to debar him—the acknowledged head of
the legal profession in knowledge, ability, and practice—from
his " natural and immediate step and rise " by a young barrister
of thirty-three, his junior by nine years, whose legal attainments
were comparatively untried. Nothing in Coke's nature tended
to soften any pre-conceived irritation of this kind, if such irritation existed. He was rough, uncouth, and overbearing ; loving
money next to Law and utterly destitute of refinement, taste, or
appreciation for his rival's wider studies.[1] The Common Law he
regarded as the perfection of wisdom and morality ; and he was
contemptuously disregardful of any question that could not be
settled on technical grounds and by appeal to legal precedents.
Yet either the spirit and fairness of the Common Law, or perhaps
the habits of a Judge, had so far imbued him that even the in-
stincts of his narrow nature guided him occasionally to more just
conclusions than the broader and freer theorising of the philosopher who would have regarded the King as the fountain of
justice and the Judges as mere conduits. He was dogged and

---

[1] In his copy of the *Novum Organum*, received *ex dono auctoris*, Coke wrote
these words :—

"*Auctori consilium.*
Instaurare paras veterum documenta sophorum :
Instaura leges justitiamque prius."

He added, with allusion to the ship in the frontispiece of the *Novum
Organum*,

" It deserveth not to be read in schools,
But to be freighted in the ship of Fools."

Church, *Bacon*, p. 149.

stubborn; but it was not mere stubbornness and love of opposition that led him afterwards to confront and contradict the King and to be crushed rather than submit.[1]   He prized the growing independence and purity of the Bench, and manfully resisted all attempts to revive the once customary but almost disused interferences with the course of justice by the Crown, which Bacon desired to restore and systematize as part of the foundation for his ideal Monarchy.   Thus pitted against one another by circumstances, and having natures at all points antithetical, the lawyer and the philosopher could hardly fail to feel, from the first, a certain degree of mutual antipathy : but the ill-will between the two exploded in a quarrel of which Bacon himself gives the following account to his cousin Cecil.   Coke appears to have taken fire at some implied charge, or what Coke regarded as a charge, on the part of Bacon, that, in his capacity of Attorney he had been too lenient, or too neglectful of the in terests of the Crown, in dealing with a Recusant.

"To Mr. Secretary Cecil.

"It may please your Honour,

"Because we live in an age where every man's imperfections is but another's fable, and that there fell out an accident in the Exchequer which I know not how, nor how soon may be traduced—though I dare trust rumour in it, except it be malicious or extreme partial—I am bold now to possess your Honour, as one that ever I found careful of my advancement and yet more jealous of my wrongs, with the truth of that which passed, deferring my farther request until I may attend your Honour ; and so I continue

Your Honour's very humble,
And particularly bounden,
Fr. Bacon.

"Gray's Inn, this 29th of April, 1601."

---

[1] In February, 1609, the King became so furious with Coke's arguments against the jurisdiction of the Ecclesiastical Courts, that he "clenched his fists as if about to strike the Chief Justice.   Coke fell grovelling on the ground and begged for mercy." Gardiner, *History*, ii. 42.   This may seem inconsistent with the statement in the text ; but a good deal depends upon what is meant by "grovelling." It was customary for Bishops and Lord Chancellors to fall on their knees before the King, whenever they intended to contradict him or take a liberty. (Gardiner, *History*, i. 153, ii. 330) ; and kneeling and "grovelling" might be confused by an unfriendly reporter, or through the mere love of exaggeration.   At all events, if Coke "grovelled," he did not yield ; for the debate was postponed.

"A true remembrance of the abuse I received of Mr. Attorney-General publicly in the Exchequer the first day of term; for the truth whereof I refer myself to all that were present.

"I moved to have a reseizure of the lands of Geo. Moore, a relapsed recusant, a fugitive and a practising [1] traitor ; and showed better matter for the Queen against the discharge by plea, which is ever with a *salvo jure*. And this I did in as gentle and reasonable terms as might be.

"Mr. Attorney kindled at it, and said, 'Mr. Bacon, if you have any tooth against me pluck it out; for it will do you more hurt than all the teeth in your head will do you good.' I answered coldly in these very words : 'Mr. Attorney, I respect you ; I fear you not ; and the less you speak of your own greatness, the more I will think of it.'

"He replied, 'I think scorn to stand upon terms of greatness towards you, who are less than little ; less than the least ;' and other such strange light terms he gave me, with that insulting which cannot be expressed.

"Herewith stirred, yet I said no more but this : 'Mr. Attorney, do not depress me so far ; for I have been your better, and may be again, when it please the Queen.'

"With this he spake, neither I nor himself could tell what, as if he had been born Attorney-General ; and in the end bade me not meddle with the Queen's business, but with mine own ; and that I was unsworn, etc. I told him, sworn or unsworn was all one to an honest man ; and that I ever set my service first, and myself second ; and wished to God that he would do the like.

"Then he said, it were good to clap a *cap. utlegatum* upon my back ! To which I only said he could not ; and that he was at fault, for he hunted upon an old scent. He gave me a number of disgraceful words besides, which I answered with silence and shewing that I was not moved with them."

Although Coke appears, and probably was, mainly to blame for this discreditable squabble, it is not unlikely that he received some provocation from the manner in which Bacon "showed *better matter* for the Queen." It was a point of policy with the latter to endeavour to gain credit at the expense of rivals. We shall find him, later on, committing to paper a determination to "win *credit comparate* to the Attorney [Hobart] by being more short, round, and resolute." [2]   But

---

[1] *i.e.* "plotting."

[2] See p. 153, and compare *Essays*, lv. 20 : "Honour that is *gained and broken upon another* hath the quickest reflection, like diamonds cut with facets ; and, therefore, let a man contend to excel any competitors of his honour in outshooting them, if he can, in their own bow."

the present Attorney was a very different man from Hobart, and not a man to allow " credit comparate " lightly to be won at his cost. The threat of the *capias utlegatum*—no doubt referring to Bacon's arrest for debt in September, 1598—must have been extremely galling to a man who was still not free from money difficulties, and who, throughout almost all his life, was never out of debt ; and he sent the Attorney the following letter of expostulation :

" Mr. Attorney,

" I thought best, once for all, to let you know in plainness what I find of you, and what you shall find of me.

" You take to yourself a liberty to disgrace and disable my law, my experience, my discretion.   What it pleaseth you, I pray, think of me : I am one that knows both mine own wants and other men's : and it may be perchance that mine mend, and others stand at a stay.   And surely I may not endure in public place to be wronged without repelling the same to my best advantage to right myself.

" You are great and therefore have the more enemies which would be glad to have you paid at another's cost.   Since the time I missed the Solicitor's place (the rather I think by your means) I cannot expect that you and I shall ever serve as Attorney and Solicitor together ; but either to serve with another upon your remove, or to step into some other course ; so as I am more free than ever I was from any occasion of unworthy conforming myself to you, more than general good manners or your particular good usage shall provoke.   And if you had not been shortsighted in your own fortune (as I think) you might have had more use of me.   But that tide is passed.   I write not this to show my friends what a brave letter I have writ to Mr. Attorney ; I have none of these humours.   But that I have written is to a good end, that is to the more decent carriage of my Mistress' service, and to our particular better understanding one of another.   This letter, if it shall be answered by you in deed and not in word, I suppose it will not be worse for us both.   Else it is but a few lines lost, which for a much smaller matter I would have adventured.   So this being but to yourself, I for myself rest."

The enmity thus published to the world did not end here ; and through the web of Bacon's destiny and various vicissitudes, the antagonism of Coke runs like a dark thread interwoven with his most signal triumphs and his ultimate humiliation and fall.

About this time Bacon lost his brother Anthony.[1]   His health,

---

[1] Chamberlain, writing on 27 May, 1601, says "Anthony Bacon died not long since."

always infirm, had perhaps received a shock from the outbreak and death of Essex, to whom he remained faithful to the last: at all events his correspondence breaks off at that point, and from that time forward we have no record of the relations between the two brothers.   More impulsive, more free-spoken, more lavish and reckless of expenditure, and (we must add) more single-hearted than Francis, he had spent his fortune first in travelling, and afterwards in procuring foreign information for Essex, and in maintaining himself and (in part) his younger brother while the latter was prosecuting his suit for the Attorneyship and Solicitorship.   But by this time the tide had turned, and whereas he had sold estate after estate for Francis, it is now Francis who hopes (1600) to get into his own possession the land that Anthony is forced to sell ; and Anthony died, says Chamberlain, "so far in debt that I think his brother will be little the better by him." [1]

In the last Parliament of the Queen, which met 17 Oct., 1601, Bacon, who had been returned both for Ipswich and St. Albans, took an active part.   He opposed a Bill against Monopolies, declaring that the House must not interfere with the Prerogative, but proceed by petition.   He also spoke against the Repeal of the Statute of Tillage, maintaining " that it stands not with the policy of the State that the wealth of the kingdom should be engrossed in a few pasturers' hands." [2]   During the same year, in a letter to Cecil on Irish policy he ventured to advocate conciliation and toleration of the Roman Catholics, at least for a time, and the establishment of courts for the administration of justice, released from the technicalities of English law :   "English and Irish were to be treated as one nation.   In Ireland, however, the difficulty of maintaining order—in consequence of the inability of the English exchequer to maintain there a large military force—always stared the reformer in the face ; and Bacon, like the rest of his contem-

[1] This quotation from Chamberlain is important, because it seems to show that there was, at all events, no known and open rupture between the brothers consequent on the fall of Essex.   The suspicion of such a rupture might have been suggested by Bacon's language to the Queen : "I have just fears my brother will endeavour to put away Gorhambury, which—if your Majesty enable me by this gift—I know I shall be able to get into mine own hands."   But it is quite characteristic of Bacon to use such language in order to convey to the Queen the impression that he and his Essexian brother were not on the best of terms.

[2] *Essays*, xxix. 125.

poraries, had no better remedy to propose than the introduction
of English settlers as a standing garrison, a plan which, when
actually adopted, spoiled the whole scheme of reform." [1]

§ 12 THE NEW REIGN

The death of Elizabeth (24 March, 1603) made a complete
change in all Bacon's prospects.   Several letters show the
assiduity with which he endeavoured to recommend himself
to the new King through those who might have influence with
him.   Three or four days before the Queen's death (19 March,
1603) he writes to Mr. Michael Hickes, Cecil's confidential man
of business :

> "The apprehension of this threatened judgment of God, *percutiam pas-
> torem et dispergentur oves gregis*, if it work in other as it worketh in me,
> knitteth every man's heart more unto his true and approved friend. . . .
> And as I ever used your means to cherish the truth of my inclination
> towards Mr. Secretary, so now again I pray, as you find time, let him know
> that he is the personage in this State which I love most.   And this, as you
> may easily judge, proceedeth not out of any straits of my occasions, as
> mought be thought in times past, but merely out of the largeness and
> fullness of my affections."

To the Earl of Northumberland, the patron of Harriot the
mathematician, he bases an appeal on the ground of his friendship for his brother Anthony and the studies which they pursue
in common ; [2] and, as in the former letter, he disavows the
pressure of any necessity, begging the Earl " not to do so much
disadvantage to my good mind, nor partly to your own worth,
as to conceive that this commendation of my humble service
proceedeth out of any straits of my occasions, but merely out of
an election, and indeed the fullness of my heart."   His brother
Anthony is mentioned in a third letter to a Mr. David Foules,
in Scotland, in which he refers (25 March) to the correspondence which Essex had kept up, through Anthony, with the
Scottish Court.

---

[1] *Dictionary of National Biography,* " Bacon," ii. 335.
[2] Compare the *Commentarius Solutus* (1608), in which Bacon proposes "the
setting on wo(rk) my l(ord) of North(umberland), and Ralegh, and therefor
Haryott, themselves being already inclined to experiments."

"The occasion awaketh in me the remembrance of the constant and mutual good offices which passed between my good brother and yourself; whereunto (as you know) I was not altogether a stranger; though the time and design (as between brethren) [1] made me more reserved. But well do I bear in mind the great opinion which my brother (whose judgment I must reverence) would often express to me, of the extraordinary sufficiency, dexterity, and temper, which he had found in you, in the business and service of the King our sovereign lord."

The truth appears to be that, although Bacon was not at this time suffering from any pecuniary " straits of his occasions," he was not quite easy as to the reception he would meet with from the King. Essex had been the King's friend, and one of James's first acts was to liberate Southampton from the imprisonment which he was undergoing in the Tower for his part in the Earl's outbreak. Cecil might retain his place as indispensable coun- sellor; but it was possible that the man to whom the popular indignation had, rightly or wrongly, pointed as the chief instru- ment in procuring the Earl's death, might be very coldly received by one who remembered Essex with gratitude.

The desire to conciliate, and the apprehension of rebuff, may both be traced in the following letter to Southampton shortly before his release (10 April), from the Tower:—

" It may please your Lordship,

" I would have been very glad to have presented my humble service to your Lordship by my attendance, if I could have foreseen that it should not have been unpleasing unto you. And therefore, because I would commit no error, I choose to write ; assuring your Lordship (how credible soever it may seem to you at first) yet it is as true as a thing that God knoweth, that this great change hath wrought in me no other change towards your Lordship than this, that I may safely be now that which I was truly before. And so craving no other pardon than for troubling you with this letter, I do not now begin but continue to be,

Your Lordship s humble and much devoted."

It is, perhaps, for this reason that in almost all the letters of this period, Bacon dwells upon the memory and services of his brother, and claims to have known more about Anthony's secret negotiations with Scotland than in former times he had found it

---

[1] He means that the " reserve " was the result of an understanding between him and his brother ; compare the expression in the letter to the King (p. 96), " though by design (as between brethren) dissembled."

safe to acknowledge. Such a reference occurred in the letter to
Mr. Foules, quoted above ; and a second reference occurs in the
following letter (25 March) to the Abbot of Kinloss, amusingly
similar to the last :—

"The present occasion awaketh in me a remembrance of the constant
amity and mutual good offices which passed between my good brother
deceased and your Lordship, whereunto I was less strange than in respect
of the time I had reason to pretend ; and withal I call to mind the great
opinion which my brother (who seldom failed in judgment of persons)
would often express to me of your Lordship's great wisdom and soundness
both in head and heart toward the service and affairs of the King our
sovereign lord."

Sir Thomas Challoner, a confirmed Essexian, introduced to
the service of the Earl by Anthony Bacon, was now in Scotland ;
and to him also Bacon writes (28 March), in a somewhat constrained style, dispelling any dissatisfaction that Challoner may
have conceived on account of some debt unpaid, and intrusting
to him a letter to be delivered to the King.

" For our money matters, I am assured you conceived no insatisfaction ;
for you know my mind, and you know my means ; which now the
openness of the time, caused by this blessed consent and peace, will
increase ; and so our agreement, according to our time, will be observed.

" For the present, according to the Roman adage (that one cluster of grapes
ripeneth best besides another) I know you hold me not unworthy whose
mutual friendship you should cherish ; and I for my part conceive and
hope that you are likely to become an acceptable servant to the King our
Master, not so much for any way made heretofore (which in my judgment
will make no great difference [1]) as for the stuff and sufficiency which I know
to be in you, and whereof I know his Majesty may reap great service. And
therefore my general request is, that according to that industrious vivacity
which you use towards your friends, you will further his Majesty's good
conceit and inclination towards me."

Bacon's expression that what had happened " heretofore "
(meaning services performed to Essex) would " make no great
difference," probably represented his hope rather than his conviction. At all events he requests the services of another
correspondent to defend him from slanders. This letter—
addressed (28 March) to his friend, John Davies the poet,

---

[1] Mr. Spedding very justly explains these words as probably meaning " that
his having been engaged in Essex's service would not give him any special
advantage over others."

author of *Nosce Teipsum,* and afterwards Attorney-General for Ireland—is further interesting because in it Bacon apparently ranks himself among " concealed poets ; " implying, I suppose, that he had written anonymous poetry :—

"Briefly, I commend myself to your love and to the well using of my name, as well in repressing and answering for me, if there be any biting or nibbling at it in that place, as in impressing a good conceit and opinion of me, chiefly in the King (of whose favour I make myself comfortable assurance) as otherwise in that Court. . . . So desiring you to be good to *concealed poets,* I continue. . . ."

The letter to the King is in the King's own style, slightly pompous, and lengthy, and classical, beginning with a quotation from the Vulgate and ending with a line from Ovid. He appeals to his father's memory and his brother's services by way of introduction, and rejoices to see the foundation of "the mightiest monarchy in Europe." It is noteworthy that he makes no mention of his cousin Cecil, whose position perhaps at that time seemed to Bacon not perfectly assured.

" . . . . And yet further and more nearly I was not a little encouraged, not only upon a supposal that unto your Majesty's sacred ears (open to the air of all virtues) there might perhaps have come some small breath of the good memory of my father, so long a principal counsellor in this your kingdom ; but also by the particular knowledge of the infinite devotion and incessant endeavours (beyond the strength of his body and the nature of the times) which appeared in my good brother towards your Majesty's service ; and were, on your Majesty's part, through your singular benignity by many most gracious and lively significations and favours accepted and acknowledged, beyond the merit of anything he could effect. All which endeavours and duties for the most part were common to myself with him, though by design (as between brethren) dissembled.

"And therefore most high and mighty King, my most dear and dread sovereign lord, since now the corner-stone is laid of the mightiest monarchy in Europe ; and that God above (who is noted to have a mighty hand in bridling the floods and fluctuations of the seas and of people's hearts) hath by the miraculous and universal consent (the more strange because it proceedeth from such diversity of causes) in your coming in, given a sign and token what he intendeth in the continuance ; I think there is no subject of your Majesty's who loveth this island, and is not hollow and unworthy, whose heart is not set on fire, not only to bring you peace-offerings to make you propitious, but to sacrifice himself a burnt-offering to your Majesty's service ; amongst which number no man's fire shall be more pure and fervent than mine."

At this time it seemed possible, to those who were not behind the scenes, that the Earl of Northumberland, and not Cecil, might be the foremost of the new King's advisers. A few days before the Queen's death, the Council had invited the Earl to assist at their deliberations probably because he was supposed to be in favour with James. Cecil, it is true, as well as Northumberland, had been engaged for some time in secret correspondence with the Scottish Court ; but Bacon may not have been aware of this ; and the charge of favouring the Spanish succession brought by Essex against Cecil might possibly tell against the latter. Although therefore Bacon tells Hickes that Cecil " is the personage in the State " whom he " loves most," he does not hesitate to place his whole services at the disposal of Northumberland, " if I may be of any use to your Lordship, by my head, tongue, pen, means or friends, I humbly pray you to hold me your own." Accordingly it is to Northumberland, and not to Cecil, that he sends a copy of a royal Proclamation such as he thinks suitable "for the cherishing, entertaining, and preparing of men's affections : for which purpose I have conceived a draught, it being a thing familiar in my Mistress' time to have my pen used in public writings of satisfaction." By this means he seems to have desired to recommend himself to the King so that, if he could not obtain promotion at once, he might at least gain access to him, and be occasionally, though irregularly, employed by James, as he had been by Elizabeth. But the Proclamation was not used ; and though he was promised " private access " when he carried a despatch to the King from Northumberland, he was kept waiting so long that he chose rather to deliver it by the hands of others than " to cool it in my hands in expectation of access." Indeed, for a few days, by an accident, he lost even his official status as one of the learned counsel : for having no written warrant and having never been sworn in, he was not mentioned in the list of those " in office at the Queen's death," who were to be continued in office. This mistake was early remedied (21 April), but he completely failed to recommend himself to the King. " How happy I think myself," wrote the King to Cecil (27 March) " by the conquest of so faithful and so wise a councillor I reserve it to be expressed out of my own

H

mouth unto you." [1] The confidence thus early reposed was never withdrawn, and scarcely lessened till a few months before Cecil's death. Cecil remained therefore still at the head of affairs, while the Earl of Northumberland fell into the background, and with him fell Bacon's hopes of speedy legal or political advancement.

Before the King had been two months in London Bacon had been forced to recognise his position. He was to be left out in the cold more than ever; still, indeed, of the Learned Counsel as before; but not, as before, to be employed by the Sovereign on extraordinary occasions nor to have his pen "used in public writings of satisfaction." A few days ago he had expressed sanguine expectations to his friend Toby Matthew (April) : "In my particular I have many comforts and assurances : but in mine own opinion the chief is, that the canvassing world is gone and the deserving world is come. And withal I find myself as one awaked out of sleep; which I have not been this long time." But now (3 July) he writes to Cecil in tones of settled resignation. He seems to have been a second time arrested for debt, and a second time to have appealed to Cecil for money to help him out of his difficulty; and he cannot repay the money within the stipulated time. But he hopes to be able, by selling land, to leave himself, "being clearly out of debt and having some money in my pocket, 300*l.* land *per annum*, with a fair house and the ground well timbered." He had found "money so hard to come by" that he had half intended "to have become a humble suitor to your Honour to have sustained me with your credit for the present from urgent debts, with taking up 300*l.* till I can put away some land. But I am so forward with some sales as this request I hope I may forbear." It is a sorrow to him that he finds himself idle and of no use to such an honourable and kind friend. He has now bidden farewell to politics; but he would like his recent humiliation to be salved with the distinction of knighthood.

"For my purpose or course, I desire to meddle as little as I can in the King's causes—his Majesty now abounding in counsel—and to follow my thrift and practice, and to marry with some convenient advancement. For as for any ambition, I do assure your Honour mine is quenched. In the

[1] Gardiner, *History*, i. 91.

Queen's, my excellent Mistress's time, the *quorum* was small; her service was a kind of freehold and it was a more solemn time. All those points agreed with my nature and judgment. My ambition now I shall only put upon my pen, whereby I shall be able to maintain memory and merit of the times succeeding.

" Lastly, for this divulged and almost prostituted title of knighthood,[1] I could without charge, by your Honour's means, be content to have it, both because of this late disgrace, and because I have three new knights in my mess in Gray's Inn commons, and because I have found out an alderman's daughter, an handsome maiden, to my liking. So as, if your Honour will find the time, I will come to the Court from Gorhambury upon any warning.

" How my sales go forward, your Lordship shall in a few days hear. Meanwhile, if you will not be pleased to take further day with this lewd fellow " [Bacon's creditor] " I hope your Lordship will not suffer him to take any part of the penalty, but principal, interest, and costs."

At the same time he appears to have sent Cecil a memorandum of his debts, 3,700*l.* in his own name (including 500*l.* " that I was beholden to your Honour for procuring "), and 1,300*l.* in the name of his brother Anthony. Cecil's answer seems to have demurred to delay in repayment, and to have hinted that there was some fault of excess, *aliquid nimis*—whether pecuniary extravagance or what else is not quite clear[2]—which required correction on Bacon's part. The answer is good-tempered and grateful, containing a promise of amendment.

" It may please your good Lordship,

" In answer of your last letter, your money shall be ready before your day : principal, interest, and costs of suit. So the sheriff promised, when I released errors ; and a Jew takes no more. The rest cannot be forgotten, for I cannot forget your Lordship's[3] *dum memor ipse mei :* and if there have been *aliquid nimis*, it shall be amended. And, to be plain with your Lordship, that will quicken me now which slackened me before. Then I thought you might have had more use of me than now I suppose you are like to have. Not but I think the impediment will be rather in

---

[1] Before James had been three months in England he had made about 700 knights.

[2] It might possibly have been an excess of zeal in obtruding political advice, which appeared to Cecil to savour of ambition. In the *Proem to the Interpretation of Nature* Bacon complains that at this period of his life his "zeal was set down as ambition."

[3] Some word has dropped out perhaps, " your Lordship's (*kindness*) : " unless Cecil had himself used the following Latin quotation to protest his constant affection for his cousin, in which case the text may be correct.

my mind than in the matter or times. But to do you service I will come out of my religion [1] at any time.

" For my knighthood, I wish the manner might be such as might grace me, since the matter will not ; I mean, that I might not be merely gregarious in a troop. The coronation is at hand. It may please your Lordship to let me hear from you speedily. So I continue your Lordship's ever much bounden,

FR. BACON.

" From Gorhambury, this 16th of July 1603."

The marriage with the alderman's daughter, the " handsome maiden," did not take place till three years afterwards ; but he had not so long to wait for the " divulged honour," which he desired partly to please the young lady and partly to salve his recent disgrace. He did not, however, obtain even his poor petition that he might escape being " gregarious." On 22 July the Court removed from Windsor to Westminster, and on the following day the King, in his garden, dubbed as knights all the judges, all the serjeants-at-law, all the doctors of civil law, all the gentlemen ushers, and many others of divers qualities ; and on this occasion, as one of three hundred, the author of the *Greatest Birth of Time* was " gregariously " knighted.

It is interesting and instructive to compare with the actual circumstances of Bacon's rebuff and his disappointment at this period, the account given of it in the autobiographical fragment contained in the *Proem to the Interpretation of Nature.*[2] The actual fact was that Bacon had tried, by every possible means, by friends, by strangers, by enemies (as in the case of Southampton), by letters, by personal access, by the preparation of political papers, to push himself into the King's favourable notice ; and he had retired from the struggle for a time because he had completely failed, and for no other reason. How different is the impression to be derived from the autobiography ! There we find that the main cause of his retirement was the compunction of conscience. He admits indeed that one cause for this retirement was the misappreciation of his political zeal ; but the main cause was his sense that he was called to proclaim

---

[1] *i.e.*, I suppose, " I will come out of the philosophic pursuits to which I have now religiously bound myself, having forsworn politics." He was now probably writing the *Advancement of Learning.*

[2] See above p. 28.

the kingdom of Philosophy and not to play a part in civil life. "I found my zeal set down as ambition, my life past the prime, my weak health chiding me for delay, and my conscience warning me that I was in no way doing my duty in omitting such services as I could myself unaided perform for men, while I was applying myself to tasks that depended upon the will of others; and, therefore, I at once tore myself away from all those thoughts and in accordance with my former resolution I devoted my whole energy to this work," *i.e.*, to the *Interpretation of Nature*.

§ 13 The " Discourse on the Union "

In speaking of "putting his ambition on his pen" Bacon probably had in his mind the *Advancement of Learning*, the first book of which is supposed to have been written this year (1603). At this time he also wrote the brief *Proem on the Interpretation of Nature* in which he propounds his new philosophical mission, apologising for having temporarily deserted it on the plea that public duties had appeared to demand that sacrifice.

The apologetic part of the proem has been quoted above (see p. 28); but the latter part, in which he reviews the obstacles in the way of his philosophic projects, and his plans for surmounting them, is no less worthy of study; and it comes fitly here because it shows how his philosophic plans pervaded his whole life, and influenced both his political views and his applications to individual friends and patrons whom he regarded as likely to forward the great cause of Science.

"Nor am I discouraged from it because I see in the present time some kind of impending decline and fall of the knowledge and erudition now in use.

"Not that I apprehend any more barbarian invasions unless possibly the Spanish empire should recover its strength, and after crushing other nations by arms should itself sink beneath its own weight; but from the civil wars which may be expected I think (judging from certain fashions which have come in of late) to spread through many countries, from the malignity of religious sects, and from those compendious artifices and devices which have crept into the place of solid erudition I augured a storm not less fatal for literature and science. Against these evils the Printing-press is no security. And doubtless these hostile influences are destined to overwhelm that fair-weather learning, which needs the nursing of luxurious leisure and the sunshine of reward and praise, and which can neither withstand the shock of adverse opinion nor escape the imposture of quoakery.

"Far otherwise is it with Science, whose dignity is fortified by works of use and power. Therefore to the injuries that might be wrought by Time I give no heed. As for the injuries that might proceed from men, they trouble me not. For if any one charge me with seeking to be wise over-much, I answer simply that whereas in practical life there is a place for modesty, in philosophy there is no place for aught save truth. But if any one call on me for works and that at once, I say, and without any imposture, that a man in my position, not yet past middle life, retarded by ill health, who with his hands full of business, and without light or guidance, has entered upon an argument of the utmost obscurity, has done enough if he constructs the machine, though he may never set it in motion." [1]

After protesting that works, though they will ultimately be attained, must not be sought at once, and that he must not be called on to make definite promises as forecasts of results, nor to deviate from his prescribed course, he continues thus :

"My plan of publication is as follows. Those writings which aim at securing a response from the minds of others, and at purging, so to speak, the threshing-floor of the understanding, are to be published to the world at large ; the rest are to be passed from hand to hand with selection and judgment.

"I am not ignorant indeed that it is a stale trick for impostors to reserve some secrets, which are no whit better than those which they offer to the public. But in my case this resolve is not the result of imposture, but of a sober forethought. For I see that both the Formula of the Interpretation of Nature and the discoveries thereby made, will be quickened and preserved in the guardianship of a few selected minds.

"This however is not my affair, for I take no thought for anything that depends on things external. I am not chasing after fame, I am not attracted by the ambition of founding a sect after the manner of heresiarchs ; and the mere notion of aiming at private gain from so vast an undertaking seems to me as absurd as it is disgraceful. Enough for me the consciousness of well-deserving, and those practical results which Fortune herself is powerless to prevent."

Notwithstanding his resolution to " meddle as little as possible with the King's cause and to follow his private thrift and

[1] Spedding, iii. 519.

practice," Francis (now Sir Francis) Bacon does not seem to have felt precluded from tendering the King political advice.

There were some points in the new Sovereign's character— and those the most obvious on a short acquaintance—which might naturally lead Bacon to take a favourable view of the King's political future. James was learned, open to new ideas, and averse to intolerance. These characteristics might be revealed in a few hours. It needed months or years to reveal the King's fatal deficiency in earnestness, his inconstancy of purpose, his inability to sympathise with an English House of Commons, and his want of political foresight. Even a cool observer might therefore have augured well at first concerning the new reign ; and Bacon, in spite of all his professions of philosophic coolness, was one of the most blindly sanguine of observers. It is this excess of hopefulness—this determination not only to make the best, but to see the best, of everything—which explains, more adequately than any hypothesis of deliberate flattery, the language of adulation in which he addressed the King in the earlier years of his reign. Perhaps Bacon never, to the last, thoroughly realised the inherent weakness of James's character ; perhaps he found it impracticable to discontinue the habit once formed, and perceived that flattery was necessary in approaching a Sovereign who mistook deference for devotion ; be the cause what it may, he never tendered counsel to the King without disguising it in obsequiousness ; and James, in his lips, is always a sovereign incomparable, not to be mentioned in the same breath with any other except Solomon, the *Prinum Mobile*, and God.[1]

With one at all events of James's political aspirations Bacon

---

[1] James himself did not shrink from mentioning himself in a most irreverent juxtaposition with Christ (see below, p. 280) : and compare his verses composed on the comet that appeared at the Queen's death :

> "Thee to invite the great God sent his star,
> Whose friend and nearest kin good princes are."
>
> (Gardiner, *History*, iii. 295.)

Possibly Bacon's language in this respect, would not be found, not much, if at all, worse than that of many of the King's flatterers ; but it is sometimes extremely repulsive. See p. 183, where he says to James : "I will make two prayers unto your Majesty as I use to do to God Almighty, when I commend to Him His glory and cause." And elsewhere he illustrates three requests which he makes to the King by reference " to the three petitions of the Litany—*Libera nos, Domine ; parce nobis, Domine, exaudi nos, Domine.*"

could heartily sympathise.   The union of England and Scotland
was at this time a main object of the new Sovereign; and Bacon,
whose theory was that no empire should be "nice in point of
naturalisation"[1] seconded the King's efforts in a *Brief Discourse
touching the Happy Union of the Kingdoms of England and
Scotland.*[2]   This treatise, said to have been printed in 1603, em-
bodies one of Bacon's favourite doctrines, viz.: that certain
Axioms of what he calls Prima Philosophia, are as applicable to
politics as to natural philosophy.

There is a great affinity, he says, between the rules of Nature
and the true rules of policy.   The Persian magic, in old days,
was nothing but an application of the contemplation of Nature
to politics; for indeed the celestial bodies and the heavens in
their relations with the earth and sea, exhibit the relations
between king and subjects.   Everything in Nature has a private
and a public affection; as, for example, iron has a private amity
with the loadstone, but a public and general affection for the
earth.   In small matters, the private; in large, the public
affection must be obeyed.   As in Nature, so in kingdoms, there
may be "compositio," *i.e.* union without a new form, or "mistio,"
i.e. union under a new form.   The former is the easier,
but the latter, the Roman system of "commistio," is the wiser
and happier.[3]   The hand of man can in a short time bind the
graft to the stock ("compositio"); but it must be left to Time
and Nature to convert contiguity into continuity.   Another
necessary condition is that the lesser must be merged in the
greater; else there will be defection, as in the days when the
ten tribes of Israel revolted from the King of Judah.   The hint
as to the need of time may be illustrated by Bacon's letter to
the Earl of Northumberland in the April of this year (1603),
"He (the King) hasteneth to a mixture of both kingdoms and
nations faster perhaps than policy will conveniently bear."

[1] *Essays*, xxix. 151.   [2] Spedding, iii. 90.
[3] *Essays*, xxix. 156.

§ 14 BACON'S ADVICE ON CHURCH POLICY

The approaching Hampton Court Conference (deferred to January, 1604,) between the Bishops and Puritans drew from Bacon a treatise on the *Pacification and Edification of the Church.* It was written after he had received from the King a gracious recognition of his treatise on the *Union of the Kingdoms;* but the exact date of composition is uncertain. It was, however, " presented to the King at his first coming in ; " [1] and an early date is almost necessitated by internal evidence. Bacon is here exhibited speaking his own mind freely, and no longer under the pressure of the anti-Puritan influence of Elizabeth. In the *Advertisement touching Church Controversies* (1589) he had gone as far as he dared in the direction of the Puritans ; but now, in ignorance of the attitude that James might take, amid a general anticipation of change, and with a not unnatural expectation that a Scotch King would be free from the prejudices of Anglican Ecclesiasticism, he goes very much further indeed.

He advocates reform in the Church, as a remedy no less necessary in ecclesiastical than in civil matters, and especially seasonable in " the spring of a new reign " ; for in Church government, as in civil government, there may be variety according to time, place, and circumstance. A set form of prayer appears to him desirable, but it would be well to discontinue the use of the term " Priest " and the General Absolution.

" Taking the Absolution, it is not unworthy consideration whether it may not be thought unproper and unnecessary ; for there are but two sorts of Absolution, both supposing an obligation precedent ; the one upon an Excommunication, which is religious and primitive ; the other upon Confession and Penance, which is superstitious, or at least positive ; and both particular, neither general. Therefore since the one is taken away, and the other hath his proper case, what doth a general Absolution, wherein there is neither Penance nor Excommunication precedent ? And surely I may think this at the first was allowed in a kind of spiritual discretion, because the Church thought the people could not be suddenly weaned from their conceit of assoiling, to which they had been so long accustomed."

[1] Spedding, *Works*, iii. 102.

The rite of Confirmation also appears to Bacon to be a mistake, at all events in its present shape :

"For Confirmation, to my understanding, the state of the question is whether it be not a matter mistaken and altered by time ; and whether that be not now a subsequent to Baptism, which was indeed an inducement to Communion. For whereas in the primitive Church children were examined in their faith before they were admitted to the Communion, time may seem to have turned it to refer as if it had been to receive a confirmation of their Baptism."

To private Baptism he utterly objects as superstitious and unnecessary ; and the use of the ring in the Marriage Service appears to him repellent even to common sense and still more to the feelings of the learned and pious :

"For private baptism by women or lay persons, the best divines do utterly condemn it, and I hear it not generally defended. And I have often marvelled that—when the book, in the Preface to Public Baptism, doth acknowledge that Baptism, in the practice of the primitive Church, was anniversary, and but at set and certain times, which sheweth that the primitive Church did not attribute so much to the ceremony as they would break an outward and general order for it—the book should afterwards allow of private Baptism, as if the ceremony were of that necessity, as the very Institution which committed Baptism only to the Ministers should be broken in regard of the supposed necessity. And therefore this point, of all others, I think was but a *concessum propter duritiem cordis*.

"For the form of celebrating matrimony, the ring seemeth to many, even of vulgar sense and understanding, a ceremony not grave—specially to be made (as the words make it) the essential part of the action. Besides some other of the words are noted in common speech to be not so decent and fit."

He would retain the use of music in churches, while condemning "the curiosity of division and reports and other figures of music" which have "no affinity with the reasonable service of God, but were added in the more pompous times." The cap and surplice he would give up.

"For the cap and surplice—since they be things in their nature indifferent and yet held by some superstitious, so that the question is between science and conscience—it seems to fall within the compass of the Apostle's rule, which is that the stronger do descend and yield to the weaker. Only the difference is, that it will be materially said, that that rule holds between private man and private man, but not between the conscience of a private man and the order of a Church. But, since the question, at this time, is of a toleration, not by connivance which may encourage disobedience, but of a law which may give a liberty, it is good again to be advised whether it fall not within the equity of the former rule ; the rather because the silencing of Ministers by this occasion is (in this scarcity of good preachers) a punishment that lights upon the people, as well as upon the party."

The discontinued exercise of "prophesying," *i.e.*, expounding the Scriptures, at meetings of the clergy, should be revived. Ministers should be more deliberately and regularly ordained ; excommunications should be issued only for weighty offences and then not from the deputies, but from the Bishops themselves assisted by assessors. As the number of benefices exceeds the number of suitable Ministers, pluralities must be allowed, or else preachers must be allowed to serve, by turn, parishes that are without Ministers. Impropriations ought to be, but cannot be, restored to the Church ; and therefore, as the State took away the tithes from the Church it is bound to do somewhat for the support of Ministers.[1]

This treatise completely disposes of the notion that Bacon was a sound Anglican and an approver of Whitgift's attitude toward the Puritans. All the reforms he advocates, the abolition of private baptism by laymen, the discontinuance of the rite of confirmation, of the ring in the marriage service, of the cap and surplice, and of ornate church music, were demanded in the petition presented to James, on his progress to London in 1603 by Puritan Ministers, and commonly called the Millenary Petition. As far as regards religious ceremonial, Bacon was himself at this time (1604) a Puritan in his personal inclinations, though not a Puritan in the sensible, statesmanlike breadth of mind with which he regarded the bitter controversies of the extreme parties concerning matters in themselves petty. Of all the papers composed by Bacon on ecclesiastical subjects, this is by far the most important, because here, and here alone, he is speaking his own mind, freed from external pressure.[2]

---

[1] In July 1603 James informed the Universities that he intended to devote to the maintenance of preaching Ministers such impropriate tithes as he was able to set aside for that purpose. But Whitgift immediately remonstrated, and the matter was dropped.—Gardiner, *History*, i. 151.

[2] Yet Dean Church—who merely alludes to this treatise in three or four words as "a moderating paper on the *Pacification of the Church*" (*Bacon*, p. 69)—gives

In the *Advice to Queen Elizabeth* (1584) he dares not express his opinion that the expulsion of the Puritan preachers by the Bishops is " a very evil and unadvised course," without " first protesting to God Almighty " that he is not " given over, nor so much as addicted, to their preciseness; " in the treatise *On the Controversies of the Church* (1589), although he condemns principally the injuries that come from " them that have the upper hand," he does not venture to suggest any changes in the Prayer Book, and arbitrates so impartially between the two parties that he himself does not expect " to be grateful to either part." In a letter about the same date (1589-90)—apparently modified at the suggestion of Whitgift,[1] and then re-written by Bacon—in which he defends the Queen's treatment of the Puritans, he still further does violence to his own feelings and has nothing but condemnation for the Nonconformist party

three or four pages to the discussion of the paper on *Controversies in the Church*, and adds, " Certainly, in the remarkable paper on *Controversies in the Church* (1589) Bacon *had ceased to feel or to speak as a Puritan*" (*ib.* 12). Possibly Bacon was too broad-minded, too much centered in philosophy, and too much detached from formal theology, ever to "feel or speak as a Puritan." But it is certain that he advocated changes in the direction of Puritanism far more strongly in 1603 than in 1589.

[1] Spedding, i. 96, 97. It is perhaps in reference to this letter that Dean Church says (*Bacon*, p. 12), " He was *proud* to sign himself the pupil of Whitgift *and to write for him.*"

Bacon was always " proud " to write for those in authority and far too willing to make himself the " pen " for expressing opinions which he afterwards disavowed. But, apart from this general disposition of his, I do not know any evidence that he was specially " proud " to perform this rather insincere service. The letter was not written in his own name, but in the name of Walsingham, addressed to an official in France : and, though Bacon did not decline to do the work nor to " frame the alterations " dictated by the Master of his old college, there is no indication at all that he was " proud " of his work, or satisfied with the alterations. Here is his note to Whitgift to speak for itself :—

"TO MY LORD OF CANTERBURY.

"IT MAY PLEASE YOUR GRACE,
"I HAVE considered the objections, perused the statutes, and framed the alterations, which I send ; still keeping myself within the brevity of a letter and form of narration, not entering into a form of argument or disputation. For, in my poor conceit, it is somewhat against the majesty of princes' actions to make too curious and striving apologies ; but rather to set them forth plainly, and so as there may appear an harmony and constancy in them, so that one part upholdeth another. And so I wish your Grace all prosperity.
" From my poor lodging this, etc.,
Your Grace's most dutiful
PUPIL AND SERVANT."

Mr. Spedding remarks on the paper in question : " It is to be remembered indeed that it was not written in his own name, and that his was not the last judgment which was to be satisfied. Whitgift, as well as Walsingham, had a strong personal interest in the matter, nor did he want either authority or opportunity to correct his old pupil's exercise. If the original manuscript should ever be discovered I think traces will be found . . . where the style and logic halt a little, of the Primate's hand."

without a word of reproof for the Bishops. Again, later on (1616), when he found that the King was determined to make no concessions to the Puritans, he adapts himself once more to the royal views, and faces about so completely that he actually adopts the tone of one who is more conservative than the King himself and most earnestly hopeful that his Majesty will give way to no innovations. Times, no doubt, had changed. An interval of twelve years (1604-16) had introduced a temporary reaction in some quarters against extreme Puritanism, and had allowed many pleasing and hallowed associations to gather round some of those very rites and forms of the Anglican Church which had previously excited most dislike and suspicion. But we shall be doing no injustice to Bacon by supposing that the Courtier, rather than the Statesman, speaks in the following passage in which Bacon (1616) strenuously warns Villiers, the royal Favourite, against making the slightest concession to these same Nonconformists whose cause the writer had pleaded with equal strenuousness in 1604 :—

"It is dangerous to give the least ear to such innovators, but it is des-perate to be misled by them. . . . Besides the Roman Catholics, there are a generation of sectaries. . . . They have been several times very busy in this kingdom, under the colourable pretensions of zeal for the reformation of religion. The King your Master knows their dispositions very well ; a small thing will put him in mind of them. His Majesty had experience of them in Scotland ; I hope he will beware of them in England. A little countenance or connivance sets them on fire." [1]

It is for these reasons that the paper on the *Pacification and Edification of the Church*, deserves our special attention as being the truest exponent of Bacon's real ecclesiastical policy. Speaking his own mind, for once, freely, he advocates Church Reform. He pleads, not for a mere "countenance" or "connivance," but for a "law which may give a liberty." He is ready to give up such details as the surplice, the ring in marriage, the name of Priest, the use of Confirmation in its present shape, and the allow-ance of private Baptism ; but he is ready to do much more than this. It is not that he will merely concede a considerable im-mediate reform ; he goes further, and maintains the need of future and periodic reforms in the Church.

[1] Spedding, vi. 18-32.

" It is excellently said by the Prophet, *State super vias antiquas, et videte quænam sit via recta et vera, et ambulate in ea ;* so as he doth not say, *State super vias antiquas et ambulate in eis.* . . . But, not to handle this matter common-place-like, I would only ask why the civil State should be purged and restored by good and wholesome laws made every third or fourth year in Parliaments assembled, devising remedies as fast as time breedeth mischiefs, and contrariwise the ecclesiastical State should still continue upon the dregs of time, and receive no alteration now for these five-and-forty years and more ? If any man shall object that, if the like inter-mission had been used in civil causes also, the error had not been great, surely the wisdom of the kingdom hath been otherwise in experience for three hundred years at least. But if it be said to me that there is a difference between civil causes and ecclesiastical, they may as well tell me that churches and chapels need no reparations, though houses and castles do ; whereas commonly, to speak truth, dilapidations of the inward and spiritual edification of the Church of God are in all times as great as the outward and material."

Had these sensible and statesmanlike views been adopted, the Church of England might have been made to include, and might perhaps now include, all but a small minority of the nation; and the adoption of this ecclesiastical policy might have gone far to conciliate the House of Commons and to prevent the civil war which was to fall upon the next generation. But the King peremptorily rejected such advice. " I will have none of that," said he to the Puritan Doctors who pleaded for elasticity of ceremonial, " I will have one doctrine, one discipline, one religion, in sub-stance *and ceremony.* Never speak more on that point— how far you are bound to obey." The Church historian Fuller, after relating the King's determination, remarks that " thence-forward many cripples in conformity were cured of their former halting therein ; and such who knew not their own, till they knew the King's, mind in this matter, for the future quietly digested the Ceremonies of the Church." It is hard to decide to which of these two classes Bacon should be assigned. A sound Anglican would certainly call him " a cripple in Con-formity ; " on the other hand, his extraordinary power of uncon-scious self-adaptiveness may perhaps justify the assertion that " he knew not his own mind till he knew the King's." Be that as it may, he obeyed to the letter the royal command " never to speak more on that point." The printed copies of the treatise appear to have been "called in" immediately after the King's decision was known;[1] and, as we have seen above, when he undertakes afterwards to advise Villiers on the subject, the King himself could not be more conservative, and more averse to the countenancing or conciliating of "sectaries," than the converted author of *Certain Considerations touching the better Pacification and Edification of the Church of England.*

Here then once more we have to lament the extraordinary suppleness, the portentous power of adapting his mind to the mind of others—much as if he had "never known his own mind"—which made Bacon one of the most pernicious of counsellors for any man in authority who had not insight enough to perceive at once the wisdom of his advice. He had not the same courage in maintaining his moral, as in maintaining his intellectual convictions; he could "strive for the truth unto death"[2] in Science, but not in Politics. None knew better than he that "it is one thing to understand persons, and another thing to understand matters,"[3] and he prided himself upon understanding both, and did understand both : but he deliberately sacrificed "the real part of business" in order to retain his hold on the "humours" of great persons—always in the hope of hereafter influencing the great for some good end, and always with the result of making himself their tool. And hence he met the fate ordained for those who know but will not "strive for the truth" : he made himself "an underling to foolish men, and accepted the person of the mighty."

§ 15 Bacon is made Solicitor-General

In the Parliament which met 19 March, 1604, Sir Francis Bacon was again returned for Ipswich and St. Albans, and at once assumed a position prominent in the House and conciliating to the new Sovereign. He spoke in favour of a proposal to compound with the King for the extinction of Purveyance, at the same time maintaining the royal rights of Preemption and Prisage, and extolling the Prerogative as being no less ancient

---

[1] Spedding, iii. 102.   [2] *Ecclesiasticus*, iv. 27, 28.
[3] *Essays*, xxii. 8.

than the Law : "*caput inter nubila conditur.*" Charged with a petition to the King touching the abuses of Purveyors, he recommended (27 April) the suppression of their malpractices by appeal to two examples ; the one, of King Edward the Third, who in his time made ten laws against this abuse ; "the second is the example of God himself who hath said and pronounced that He will not hold them guiltless that take His name in vain ; for all these great misdemeanours are committed in, and under, your Majesty's name."

Besides warmly siding with the King in the proceedings for the Union (to consider the details of which he was the first of the Commissioners appointed by the House), he also advocated in characteristic language a subsidy to the Crown : "Let not this Parliament end, like a Dutch feast, in salt meats ; but like an English feast, in sweet meats ;" but the doubtful reception given to the project induced the King to express his wish that it should be dropped. In the discussions of the Commissioners on the Union, Bacon played a leading part ; and to him, in conjunction with the Lord Advocate of Scotland, was intrusted the task of reducing the articles to a coherent whole. The instruments were signed and sealed on 6 December, 1604 ; but before this time Bacon had received his first token of the favour of the new Sovereign ; it did, not, however, amount to much, being no more than the gift by Patent of his office of Learned Counsel, which hitherto he had held merely on verbal warrant. At the same time he received (18 August, 1604) a pension of £60 a year for life ; but this was not in the way of a salary, but expressly granted " in consideration of the good services " of *his brother Anthony*, the intimate and faithful friend of Essex,[1] who had co-operated with the Earl in keeping up a correspondence with the Court of James, for the purpose of facilitating the Scotch succession.[2] So far as concerns promotion, Bacon was

[1] Rymer's *Fœdera*, xvi. 597.

[2] Dean Church (p. 75), without mentioning the "pension" given in Anthony's name, says : "Bacon, who had hitherto been an unsworn and unpaid member of the Learned Counsel, now received his office by patent, *with a small salary ;*" but I can find no record of any "salary." Even Professor Gardiner says (*History*, i. 165) : "Bacon retained, indeed, the title of King's Counsel, *and he drew the salary such as it was ;*" and again (*ib.* 195) : "On August 18, Bacon was established by Patent in the position of a King's Counsel, *with which he received a pension of* £60 " no mention being made of the grounds on which the "pension" was given.

still neglected, and he himself appears to have expected nothing better; for two or three months afterwards, when the Solicitor's place was filled (October 1604) he did not even apply for it. In the summer of 1605, when the place of Chief Justice of Common Pleas was vacant, Bacon was again passed over; and in the trials and investigations that followed the discovery of the Gunpowder Plot in November 1605, his services were not required by the Government.

The length of the interval between December 1604, and the reassembling of Parliament in November 1605, gave Bacon leisure for working at his *Advancement of Learning* (for a summary of which see Appendix II), and apparently induced him to alter his purpose of publishing the first book by itself. In any case the two books appeared in October 1605. Sending a copy to Sir Thomas Bodley he repeats the protestation which he had made to Cecil two years before, that he has renounced " civil causes," and devoted himself to philosophy : " I think no man may more truly say with the Psalm, ' *Multum incola fuit anima mea* ' (My soul hath long dwelt with them that are enemies unto peace) than myself. For I do confess since I was of any understanding my mind hath in effect been absent from that I have done ; and in absence are many errors which I do willingly acknowledge, and amongst the rest this great one that led the rest ; that knowing myself by inward calling to be fitter to hold a book than to play a part, I have led my life in civil causes, for which I was not very fit by nature, and more unfit by the preoccupation of my mind."

When Bacon wrote thus, he had good cause for thinking that his chance of legal promotion was small. Yet, however he might write as a philosopher to a philosopher, disavowing aptitude for civil causes, there can be no doubt that afterwards he bitterly felt his non-advancement. Writing to the Lord Chancellor (July 1606) he says that his non-promotion makes him "a common gaze and a speech," and that the little reputation which by his industry he gathers is scattered and taken away by continual disgraces, every new man coming above him. Simultaneous letters to the King and Cecil prove that he had been for some time assiduously seeking and expecting office. Among other reasons for pressing his suit he alleges his desire

I

to satisfy his wife's friends; for Sir Francis Bacon was now a married man. On 10 May, 1606, being now in his forty-seventh year, he married Alice Barnham, no doubt the alderman's "handsome daughter," whom he had mentioned three years before in his letter to Cecil.[1] In answer to a cousin's congratulations on his marriage, he replies that his fortune is improved by it, and that he has no cause to be dissatisfied : " I thank God I have not taken a thorn out of my foot to put into my side; for as my state " (*i.e.* fortune) " is somewhat amended, so I have no other circumstance of complaint." Bacon's letters make scarcely any mention of her.[2] The remarks in the *Essays* on " nuptial love " as compared with " friendly love "—" Nuptial love maketh mankind, friendly love perfecteth it," [3]—would not lead us to infer that Bacon's experience caused him to form a very high estimate of married life. But, passing over a good-natured anecdote of Bacon's biographer, Rawley—which implies that Lady Bacon had a somewhat unruly tongue—we only know that after her husband's death she married his gentleman usher, and that Bacon (1625) revoked " for just and great causes " the provision he had previously made for her in his will, and left her " to her right only." [4]

Bacon soon found an opportunity of again serving the King in Parliament. During the debate on Naturalization in February 1607, violent invectives were made against Scotland and Scotchmen in England, which Bacon answered (17 February) in a speech that usefully illustrates the *Essay on Greatness of Kingdoms*. Ridiculing the danger of overcrowding England with Scotchmen, he pointed out that England is thinly populated, Ireland fertile and desolate, and as a last resource, there is always open for a valorous and warlike nation some honourable war for the enlargement of their borders.[5] After a rapid history of Naturalization, the wise liberality

[1] Lady Bacon's father was Benedict Barnham, a draper of London, elected alderman of Bread Street Ward in 1591, and sheriff in the same year ; her eldest sister, Elizabeth, married Mervin, Lord Audley and Earl of Castlehaven, who was executed on Tower Hill in 1631.

[2] The brief commendation in a letter to Hickes (27 August, 1610, see p. 163, below), is the only exception I can remember.

[3] *Essays*, x. 64.

" Of his domestic life," writes Professor Fowler (*Francis Bacon*, p. 12) " we hear nothing, and may therefore infer that it was peaceful, if not happy."

[5] *Essays*, xxix. 227-37.

of Rome in extending her franchise to foreign subjects is contrasted with the fatal jealousy of Sparta.[1] He predicts that union under one Government, unless accompanied by Naturalization, will be followed by jealousies, quarrels, and ultimately by war between the two nations. England, when firmly united to Scotland, " with Ireland reduced, the sea provinces of the Low Countries contracted (?) and shipping maintained," would be one of the greatest monarchies that hath been on the earth.

A very prominent place is given in this speech to a warlike policy. After endeavouring to remove the alarm of an influx of poor Scotch immigrants by arguing, first, that the Scotch will not come without means to support themselves, secondly, that England and Ireland are not yet fully peopled, so that there is room for all, he goes on to suggest that, in the last resort, more room may easily be obtained by a foreign war.

" The third answer (Mr. Speaker) which I give, is this : I demand what is the worst effect that can follow of surcharge of people ? Look into all stories, and you shall find it never other than some honourable war for the enlargement of their borders which find themselves pent upon foreign parts ; which inconvenience in a valorous and warlike nation, I know not whether I should term an inconvenience or no ; for the saying is most true, though in another sense, *Omne solum forti patria.* . . And certainly (Mr. Speaker) and I hope I may speak it without offence, that if we did hold ourselves worthy, whensoever just cause should be given, either to recover our ancient rights, or to revenge our late wrongs, or to attain the honour of our ancestors, or to enlarge the patrimony of our posterity, we would never in this manner forget the considerations of amplitude and greatness, and fall at variance about profits and reckonings, fitter a great deal for private persons than for Parliaments and Kingdoms."

The greatness of a nation, he continues, is based on its military power ; and it is not gold, but the sinews of men, that make the sinews of war ; witness Persia, Macedon, Rome, the Turks, and in modern times the Swiss.

" All which examples (Mr. Speaker) do well prove Solon's opinion of the authority and mastery that iron hath over gold.   And therefore, if I shall speak unto you mine own heart, methinks we should a little disdain that the nation of Spain—which, howsoever of late it hath grown to rule, yet of ancient time served many ages, first under Carthage, then under Rome, after under

---

[1] *Essays,* **xxix.** 151.

Saracens, Goths, and others—should of late years take unto themselves that spirit as to dream of a Monarchy in the West,' according to that device, *Video solem orientem in occidente*, only because they have ravished from some wild and unarmed people mines and store of gold ; and, on the other side, that this Island of Brittany, seated and manned as it is, and that hath (I make no question) the best iron in the world, that is, the best soldiers of the world, should think of nothing but reckonings and audits, and *meum* and *tuum*, and I cannot tell what." [1]

Deprecating the imputation of courtier-like flattery, " it were much alike," he says, " to rest a ' tacebo ' as to sing a ' placebo ' [2] in this business. But I have spoken out of the foundation of my heart. ' *Credidi propter quod locutus sum* ' (I believed, therefore I spake). So as my duty is performed. The judgment is yours. God direct it for the best."

There is no doubt that in this speech, and especially in his advocacy of a warlike policy, Bacon was expressing his genuine convictions. We have not only the *Essay on Greatness of Kingdoms* but also the trustworthy and unmistakable evidence of his private entries in the *Commentarius Solutus*,[3] to show that he deliberately desired an aggressive foreign policy in order to divert the attention of the English people from questions affecting the royal Prerogative. But it was natural that such constant and valuable support should be none the less appreciated in high quarters because it was sincere; and two or three days afterwards Bacon received the promise of the Solicitor's place when next vacated. The promise was soon fulfilled, and on 25 June, 1607, in his forty-seventh year, Sir Francis Bacon became Solicitor-General, with an income of £1,000 a year (about £4,000 of our money) and the prospect of further promotion.

At this point in Bacon's career we may introduce a friend of his, the principal confidant of his literary projects. Toby Matthew, son of the Bishop of Durham, seems to have been fond

---

[1] Considering the space and emphasis which Bacon gives to war as at least a possible outlet for superfluous population I think it deserved at least a word of mention in the rather long summary of this speech given by Professor Gardiner (*History*, i. 332, 333), who thus states that part of the argument which deals with the fear of over-population : " He denied that England was fully peopled. The country could with ease support a larger population than it had ever yet known. Fens, commons, and wastes, were crying out for the hand of the cultivator. If they were too little, the sea was open. Commerce would give support to thousands. Ireland was waiting for colonists to till it, and the solitude of Virginia was crying aloud for inhabitants."

[2] *Essays*, xx. 165.   [3] See p. 148, below.

of literature and travel, and Bacon had a great respect for his literary judgment and a strong personal affection for him. Their friendship lasted unbroken till Bacon's death; and in the last year of his life he wrote the enlarged *Essay on Friendship*, as a kind of memorial of the bond that had united them. While travelling on the Continent from 1605 to 1607 he was converted to the Roman Catholic faith, and consequently, upon returning to England was committed to safe custody (probably in Lambeth) while his case was under consideration. The following letter, written (at the end of 1607) to put off a proposed visit from Matthew, shows how Francis Bacon valued his friend's criticisms.

" SIR,

" Because you shall not lose your labour this afternoon, which now I must needs spend with my Lord Chancellor, I send my desire to you in this letter, that you will take care not to leave the writing which I left with you last, with any man, so long as that he may be able to take a copy of it; because first it must be censured by you and then considered again by me.

" The thing which I expect most from you is, that you would read it carefully over by yourself; and to make some little notes in writing where you think (to speak like a critic) that I do perhaps *indormiscere;* or where I do *indulgere genio;* or where, in fine, I give any manner of disadvantage to myself. This, *super totam materiem,* you must not fail to note, besides all such words and phrases as you cannot like; for you know in how high account I have your judgment."

As Matthew refused to take the oath which, at the King's command, was tendered to him, he was committed to the Fleet. Meanwhile Bacon, although he interceded for him, wrote him the following letter, which is interesting as an illustration of the *Essay on Superstition,* and of Bacon's attitude towards Roman Catholicism.

" MR. MATTHEW,

" Do not think me forgetful or altered towards you. But if I should say I could do you any good I should make my power more than it is. I do hear that which I am right sorry for, that you grow more impatient and busy than at first; which maketh me exceedingly fear the issue of that which seemeth not to stand at a stay. I myself am out of doubt that you have been miserably abused when you were first seduced ;[1] but that which I take in compassion, others may take in severity. I pray God (that understandeth us all better than we understand one another) contain you (even as I hope He will) at the least within the bounds of loyalty to his Majesty, and natural piety towards your country. And I entreat you much sometimes to meditate upon the extreme effects of Superstition in this last Powder Treason ; fit to be tabled and pictured in the chambers of meditation, as another hell above the ground ; and well justifying the censure of the heathen that superstition is far worse than atheism ; by how much it is less evil to have no opinion of God at all, than such as is impious towards His divine majesty and goodness."[2]

"Good Mr. Matthew, receive yourself back from these courses of perdition. Willing to have written a great deal more, I continue. . . ."

Not long afterwards (February, 1608) Matthew was released from prison on condition of going into exile : but his literary correspondence with Bacon was not broken off, as will be here-after seen.

§ 16   Signs of the Coming Revolution

Four years under the new Sovereign ought to have sufficed to prepare the most short-sighted of political prophets for some great struggle between the Crown and the House of Commons.

As early as 1604, when Parliament was prorogued (7 July), the breach between the King and the Commons was "practically final."[3] James appeared to have no knowledge of the privileges of Parliament, and no sense of the spirit which had originated them and which should have regulated his relations with his subjects. "The privileges of our House, and therein the liberties and stability of the whole kingdom, hath been more universally and dangerously impugned than ever, as we suppose, since the beginning of Parliaments :" such was the ominous remonstrance provoked by the King's arbitrary conduct in the very first year in which he met a House of Commons. Every-thing tended to widen the gulf between James and his people. James, as he fondly hoped, had settled ecclesiastical questions at the Hampton Court Conference, but the Commons immediately

---

[1] Matthew was converted after " seeing some of the miracles of the Church."— Spedding, iv. 9.

[2] *Essays,* xvii. 1.

[3] *Dictionary of National Biography,* "Bacon," ii. 336.

afterwards urged reforms in the interest of the Nonconformists; the King had taken steps for the revocation of injurious Monopolies, but the Commons, with a view to the liberation of trade, were preparing a large measure aimed at the Monopolies of the great Companies; the discussion of the proposed composition for Wardships and tenures had led to inconvenient inquiries into the condition and sources of the Crown revenues; and now the renewal of complaints of long standing arising from the disputed jurisdiction of the Council of Wales, threatened to trench on the royal Prerogative.[1] And beneath all these particular grievances there was the less definite and far more fatal evil, which no statesman could hope to remove, the want of sympathy and confidence between the House of Commons and the King, arising from an unalterable difference of natures, interests, and opinions.

Even if James had been the Solomon Bacon believed, or tried to believe, him to be, Solomon himself would have found all his powers tasked in the endeavour to solve the political problems of the time. Everywhere the nation was outgrowing the machinery of national Government: and the problem of adjustment was almost insoluble. The ordinary income of the Crown was no longer equal to the ordinary demands on it, and, whatever may have been the reason, the subsidies brought in less than formerly. Three subsidies in the beginning of James's reign brought in less than two in the beginning of Elizabeth's; yet the people thought they were paying more.[2] Even with the strictest economy James would have had to spend a tenth more than his receipts; and James was so far from an economist that, by 1608, his ordinary expenditure exceeded his ordinary income by £83,000 and his debt had risen to a million.[3] The great problem, therefore, was how to obtain the double result of replenishing the King's coffers without discontenting the people— a problem that was always before the minds both of Cecil and his supporter, Bacon. The 'latter familiarly alludes to it in his private notebook, as "*poll. è gem.*," *i.e.* "*politica è gemino*," or

---

[1] Spedding, iii. 210.   [2] Spedding, iv. 149.
[3] To understand the meaning of these figures the reader must remember that the average of the twelve Supplies voted in the reign of Elizabeth amounted to no more than £160,000; in other words, during the *whole of her reign* she received from the House of Commons not more than *two millions*.

" the *double* policy :" " To correspond to Salisbury (Cecil) in the
invention of suits and levies of money, and to respect *poll. è gem.*
for emptying coffers and alienation of the people," and again, " To
think of matters against next Parliament for satisfaction of King
and people in my particular" (*i.e.* so as to make himself acceptable to both), " otherwise with respect *ad Poll. è gem.*"

Closely connected with the *Poll. è gem.* was another difficulty,
the use and abuse of the royal Prerogative. The old feudal
system assigned to the Crown many rights which, being in
former times intelligible as well as valuable, had, therefore, been
once borne without complaint. There was for example *Escuage,*
or Knight's service, due from one who held land in Knight's
tenure, whereby the tenant was bound to follow his Lord into
the Scottish or Welsh wars at his own charge. Since these wars
were no longer possible, was this to be still exacted ? Again, a
Minor, being unable to serve in the field, might naturally be
assigned in feudal times as a Ward to the Crown, and the
profits of the estate might naturally be made chargeable with
the service which the Ward could not perform ; and this right,
continued into the seventeenth century, was a source of considerable revenue to the Crown ; but was this also to continue,
when the reason for it had disappeared ?[1] Another source of
revenue was the granting of Monopolies. Elizabeth had allayed
the popular discontent by suppressing many of these ; but she
had not disclaimed the right thus to exercise her royal Prerogative : and the question, therefore, remained undecided.
Most important of all, there was the question of Impositions,
that is, of the King's right to impose duties at will upon exports
and imports. This involved the fundamental question of
supremacy in the State. For if the King could levy Impositions
at will, he could govern without the aid of Parliament ; if not,
Parliament could always control the Government by refusing
supplies. On the one side it was alleged against Impositions
that the Edwards had bound themselves not to levy them, and
that none had been levied from the time of Richard II. to Queen
Mary ; on the other side, that they had been levied for a hundred
years during the times of the Edwards, and also during the last

---

[1] " The whole system " (of Wardship) " was one huge abuse ; but, whatever it
was, it was strictly legal."—Gardiner, *History,* i. 174.

sixty years ; and a recent decision in the Exchequer [1] supported the right of the Crown. Here, therefore, was a subject for dispute, sufficient, of itself, to make a breach between even a wise King and a loyal people.

How did Cecil, and how did Bacon, propose to deal with this and other kindred questions ? Three courses appear to have been open to them.

They might have admitted that the feudal and exceptional powers attached to the Crown were unfit for the times, and might have advised the King to commute them for fixed payments, more profitable to him and less galling to his subjects. This plan would have at once allayed much popular irritation ; it would have removed much occasion for future misunderstanding ; and it might have induced a wise Sovereign to study economy, by enabling him to ascertain the exact amount of his income, and by stimulating him to suit his expenditure to his receipts. The disadvantage would have been that, unless it left the King largely dependent upon supplementary subsidies, it would have made him independent of Parliament and not unlikely to become practically despotic. But it was, at all events, for the King's interests ; and the plan might have been prudently and even patriotically suggested by a courtier, who did not wish to exchange the personal government of the Sovereign for government by a fluctuating and irresponsible House of Commons.

A second course would have been to suppress all Monopolies and Impositions in practice, while tacitly retaining the power of granting Monopolies and levying Impositions as part of the royal Prerogative, thus not raising the question of right or legality, and trusting to the gratitude of the House of Commons for liberal and compensative Subsidies. The attention of the people might further have been diverted from burning constitutional questions by introducing, at every meeting of Parliament, popular measures for reforming the laws, encouraging commerce, and the like, so that the whole nation, as well as the House of Commons, might lay aside its antagonism to the royal Prerogative. This was the course adopted by Elizabeth towards the end of her reign, when pacifying the

[1] Bates's case, decided in 1606 ; see Gardiner, *History*, ii. pp. 5-7.

popular discontent at Monopolies; and it succeeded for the time. But an obvious objection to it was, that the royal self-sacrifice might not bear fruit for some years; and meantime the royal necessities were rapidly growing. Elizabeth succeeded; but she succeeded because she had the good fortune to die soon afterwards, bequeathing her debts to her successor; James had no such prospect before him. And it might also be asked, Was it worth while to retain, in a dormant state, rights which every year of inaction would make it more difficult for the Crown to recall to life ? In any case, this course, if practicable at all, was not compatible with delays, hesitations, bickerings, half-concessions; if the King was to adopt this course, he must adopt it quickly and heartily.

A third course would have been to divert the attention of the nation from Constitutional questions by a spirited and popular foreign policy, championing the cause of the Protestants in Europe, and making Great Britain the centre of a powerful Protestant League. It is hardly necessary to mention as a fourth course, the plan of giving up, as obsolete, without contract or bargain, all exercise of the royal Prerogative that had become obsolete and unduly burdensome to the subject, and all that excited suspicion by reason of abuses in the past and anticipations of abuses for the future. To a very much nobler and wiser king than James, such advice might well have seemed quixotic; and even if James had been the king to accept it, Cecil and Bacon were not the counsellors to offer it. It might have been the best course : but, in the circumstances we are considering, it was impracticable, and may, as such, be dismissed.

There remain then the three policies described above, the first, the Prudent or Mercantile Policy; the second, the Distractive and Paternal Policy; the third, the Distractive and Spirited Foreign Policy. Of these Cecil chose the first, and Bacon systematically and (as far as we can see) sincerely supported it during his life, although he bitterly inveighed against it as soon as its author was in the grave. It was frustrated by the inconstancy or insincerity of the King; and, after it had failed, Bacon, instead of trying to recur to it, resorted to the Distractive and Paternal Policy, with occasional vain attempts to induce the King to adopt the third course, which in his own heart he thought the best, the Distractive and Spirited Foreign Policy. But all his efforts were inevitably barren. The Prerogative question had gone too far, even in the reign of Elizabeth, to be now ignored under her successor. Settled it must be in some way; and that it must be settled was probably patent to almost every member of the House of Commons except Bacon and the tribe of courtiers who had neither ability nor desire to see, or foresee, anything that was disagreeable to the King.

It was characteristic of this most sanguine of counsellors that he should have supposed that the great constitutional question of the day could be buried by simply ignoring it. But we are startled to find him at the same time using language calculated to magnify the difficulty. At the least, it might have been supposed that, during the discussion of these questions, he would have studiously avoided every word that might have led the King to magnify, and the Commons to dread and suspect, the Prerogative of the Crown. But no: he loses no occasion for bringing the Prerogative forward; he justifies it, extols it, amplifies it. Perhaps he thought by enhancing the value of it, to enhance the price at which the Commons must expect to redeem the burdens which it entailed; more probably he perceived that this was the surest way to obtain entrance to the King's confidence; but in any case few did so much as Bacon to confirm the King in his most dangerous pretensions, and to convince the House of Commons that the Royal Prerogative might be turned against the liberties of the people.

A brief sketch of the course of Cecil's policy may throw light on much that Bacon said and did as a member of the House of Commons, and in the capacity of confidential adviser to the King, both here and afterwards.

§ 17 CECIL'S REMEDY AGAINST THE COMING REVOLUTION; "THE GREAT CONTRACT"

In April 1608, Cecil, now Earl of Salisbury, was made Lord Treasurer, and found an annual deficiency of £83,000, and a debt of a million. He immediately (June 1608) availed himself of the Prerogative to lay on new Impositions to the amount of £60,000 a year, and increased the tax on ale-houses by £10,000 a year. It is possible that he did this in order to predispose the House of Commons to purchase exemption from these and other irregular exercises of the Prerogative; in any case, when Parliament met (9 Feb. 1610) Salisbury frankly and fully set before them the King's necessities almost in the form of a balance-sheet, and at the same time mentioned a " retribution " from the Crown, as contingent on the " contribution " from the subject. Subsequently (21 Feb.) he informed them that the King required £600,000 down, to discharge his debts, and an annual contribution of £200,000. After some negotiation, the Commons, having received permission to treat of the discharge of Tenures, stated (26 March) that if Knight's service generally were turned into free and common socage,[1] they were ready to give the King £100,000 yearly. On the 26th of April they repeated their offer, explaining that the King was to retain the honour, and that they merely sought relief from the burdens of the Tenures.

But on the day before this offer (25 April 1610), the King succeeded in borrowing £100,000 from the City of London. Now independent, he at once changes his front; and Salisbury has to inform the Commons that " he feared lest some want in himself in conveying those things to them which the King propounded, had made them more obscure." And he proceeds to explain that, whereas they supposed the King was ready to *part with* certain points of his Prerogative for £200,000 a year, they were entirely mistaken; *the fact was that, on condition of their voting him £200,000 a year, and £600,000 down, the King would graciously permit them to make a bargain with him for the*

---

[1] " Socage " is " a tenure of land for which the service is fixed and determinate in quality."

Wardships and the like, paying him their worth, in addition to these sums.

It is impossible to suppose that Salisbury could have thus misinterpreted the King. He could not have wished his own project to fail; and his vexation was great when the Commons refused to allow the matter to be further discussed. On the one hand he endeavoured to soothe them by declaring that the sums propounded to them had been "tendered rather by way of estimation than of demand"; on the other, to intimidate them by a warning that for the House to dispute the legality of Impositions "were but to bark against the moon." But they could neither be coaxed into a renewal of their offer, nor frightened from a discussion of Impositions. When the Government perceived their temper, the Speaker received orders to deliver a message "as from the King, warning them that the question as to his right to impose duties upon merchandise exported and imported had been settled judicially, and was not to be disputed in the House;" to which the House, on ascertaining that the Speaker had received this message from the Privy Council, responded "that the same message, coming not immediately from his Majesty, should not be received as a message; and that in all messages from his Majesty, the Speaker, before he delivered them, should first ask leave of the House, according as had anciently been accustomed."

Matters were made still worse when the King (21 May 1610) endeavoured to convince the House of the reasonableness of his prohibition by a long speech, not only justifying his right to levy Impositions on exports and imports, but also *implying his right to tax all other property.* Concerning this speech, Chamberlain writes as follows:—

"The 21st of this present, he made another speech to both the Houses, but so little to their satisfaction that I hear it bred generally much discomfort to see our monarchical power and royal prerogative strained so high, and made so transcendent every way that, if the practice should follow the positions, we are not like to leave our successors that freedom which we received from our forefathers."[1]

The answer of the House next morning was to appoint a Committee "to devise upon some course to be taken to inform

[1] Spedding, iv. 182, whence the whole of this narrative is taken.

his Majesty how much the liberties of the subject and the privilege of the Parliament were impeached by this inhibition to debate his Prerogative." In order to divert the House from their purpose, Bacon made a clever speech, admitting indeed that "if the matter debated concerned the right or interest of any subject or the Commonwealth," he would not advise the House to desist; but alleging that, if the matter concerned the Prerogative, the House always desisted upon inhibition; as, for example, when Elizabeth had inhibited them from discussing her marriage, the succession, the appointment of a fast, and other matters: "and therefore he persuaded the House to present these matters of Impositions as grievances to the Commonwealth (which the King had given us leave to do) but not to question his power and prerogative to impose." But the House was not to be persuaded that the King's power of levying Impositions did not "concern the right or interest of any subject or the Commonwealth," or that it was on the same footing as a royal marriage or the appointment of a fast. They resolved to remonstrate, and accordingly sent messengers to the King with a Petition of Right.

The King replied by disavowing the plain meaning of the message conveyed through the Privy Council. He had not meant—so he now declared—to prohibit absolutely a discussion of the question, but only to suspend it in order that he might understand their intentions. The petition of the Commons was granted as they themselves had set it down.

In the discussion which followed (27 June 1610) on the King's right to levy Impositions, Bacon defended the Prerogative in a speech dealing almost solely with the point of law. The extract or manuscript of the speech is left unfinished; and Mr. Spedding's opinion is, that upon further consideration of the point of law or closer scrutiny of the records, Bacon saw reason to alter his conclusions, and consequently left the fair copy of the speech incomplete. However the House decided not to put the question of right, whereby they would have condemned the judgment of the Court of the Exchequer, "but to frame a petition by way of grievance, implying the right, though not in express terms."

In answer to the Petition two or three of the Impositions

were removed, and the King (10 July 1610) expressed his
willingness to assent to an Act by which his power should be
suspended from " imposing " any more upon merchandise, without
consent of Parliament. But the new Impositions, amounting to
£80,000 a year, remained unaltered ; and both the King and
Cecil defended the right of Imposition in such a manner as to
excite suspicions that, even if suspended, it might be revived.
The Commons were not likely to forget the rather unlucky
saying of Bacon in his recent speech, that " Kings shall not be
bound by general words. Samson [is] not to be bound by
cobwebs but by cords ; " and accordingly, a few days afterwards,
we find a member relating how the House was considering
" with what cords *we shall bind Samson's hands*, that is to say,
his Majesty's Prerogative." Meantime " they went away ill
satisfied : which they testified in their next day's meeting,
whenas subsidies were proposed and no more could be obtained
but one subsidy and a single fifteen : which a knavish burgess
said (but in the hearing of few) would do the King much good,
and serve as a *subpœna ad melius respondendum*." [1]

On 13 July 1610, the Commons—though many of them
suspected that the Government was not in earnest—offered
£180,000 for the proposed concessions. But Salisbury, after
reading a letter from the King offering to take £200,000,
informed them that, in the event of refusing, Parliament would
be dissolved, and the offer never repeated. In consequence of
this pressure they consented, in return for eight specified
concessions, to give the King a perpetual revenue of £200,000 a
year. On 21 July, the memorials of the Contract were
exchanged ; on the 23rd, after the King's answer to their other
grievances had been read, Parliament was prorogued till
16 October 1610.

The Crown would have been decidedly the gainer if the
contract had been carried out. The average proceeds from
subsidies, from 1605 to 1609, had been about £81,000. Add
to this the money value of the burdens from which the Commons had purchased exemption (estimated at £80,000 a year),
and we obtain a total of £161,000 a year. Instead of this
sum, the Crown was now to receive from the Commons *a*

---

[1] Carleton, 13 July ; Spedding, iv. 206.

perpetual yearly tax of £200,000, to be secured to the Crown
" by Act of Parliament in as strong sort as could be devised."
What had the Commons received for this extra gift of £40,000
a year, and for the unconditional permanence which they were
attaching to their contribution ?   Possibly they had gained
something in exemption from annoyances and occasional ex-
tortions of money which passed out of the pockets of the
subject, but not into the Treasury.   But, if we set that aside
the answer must be that they had gained nothing except a
"gracious answer" to very important statements of grievances,
including those of deprived and silenced ministers, pluralities
and non-residents, abuse of excommunication, abuse of the
ecclesiastical commission, Prohibitions, Proclamations, and
jurisdiction of provincial councils.   To those who were dissatisfied with the "gracious answer," the Contract of the
Commons may naturally have seemed too favourable to the
King ; and they might well feel that the permanent endowment
of the Crown might render it difficult for them to obtain a
more "gracious answer" hereafter.   No longer able to make
Supply conditional on the redress of grievances, they were
surrendering one of the most important of the privileges of the
House of Commons.

Meantime the Government was preparing to meet the
Commons in October ; and among other matters they had to
consider the abuse of Proclamations ; in which, by forbidding
certain acts under penalties (which could be enforced by the
Star Chamber), the Crown virtually assumed a power of
legislation.   On 20 September the Council considered the
subject, and in particular the Proclamation forbidding building
in and near London.   The Lord Chancellor was of opinion that
if the King had not this power, he ought to have it ; and that,
if it could not be justified by precedent, a precedent should now
be made by the Judges.

Such an enlargement of the Prerogative by Judge-made law
was obviously most unwise in the face of the opposition of the
Commons ; and Sir Edward Coke, the Lord Chief Justice,
naturally desired time for conference with the other judges
before giving his opinion.   But Bacon, partly perhaps because
of his habitual enmity to Coke, partly because his policy was

invariably to amplify the Prerogative both in season and out of season, reminded the Chief Justice that he had already virtually sanctioned Proclamations by his decisions on the bench, and that "he [Coke] had himself given sentence in divers cases" for the Proclamation against building. In this *argumentum ad hominem* Bacon had a manifest advantage over his adversary; but he took a course likely to be most injurious to the real interests of the Crown, however much it might for the moment commend him to James, as being a "peremptory royalist." Coke showed more wisdom in replying that "it was better to go back than to go on in the wrong way.' After conference, the judges decided that "the King by his Proclamation cannot create any offence which was not an offence before;" and to this decision the King conformed.

But although (in spite of Bacon's courtier-like and mischievous opposition) this obstacle to an understanding between the Crown and the Commons was removed, other obstacles soon arose. Courtiers and officials who were interested in collecting the dues of the Crown, could not acquiesce in a commutation which impoverished them; and it was natural that they should attempt to make the King suspect that he had been cheated in his bargain, reminding him that, until his debt was cleared off, he would still be at the mercy of Parliament. On the other hand the Commons feared that the King, by means of his permanent income, would be independent of them and neglectful of their grievances; and hence they hesitated to commit themselves. On 31 October, 1610 (fifteen days after Parliament had met), the King, incensed at their delay, required from the Commons a "resolute and speedy answer whether they would proceed with the Contract, yea, or no." Their discussion revealed their suspicious humour: provision was to be made "that this £200,000 be not doubled or trebled by enhancing of the coin by the King;" that Parliaments should be regularly held; and that the £200,000 be not alienated from the King; but no attempt was made to recede from their bargain. Meantime the King had come to the conclusion finally to break off the Contract; and he did this effectually by announcing (5 November, 1610) that *in addition to the annual £200,000 and in addition to the subsidy and fifteenth last given,* he expected

K

a Supply of £500,000 for the payment of his debts : without this, he said, it had never been his intention, much less his agreement, to proceed with the Contract. It can hardly be doubted that here again the King broke loose from his chief adviser, and that he, and he alone, was responsible for the quashing of the Contract on which Salisbury had set his heart. The Commons of course replied that they could not proceed in the matter. An attempt was made by the King (after conference with some thirty members of the Lower House) to reopen the question ; but it completely failed. On 25 November, 1610, James wrote a furious letter to Salisbury protesting that he had "had patience with this assembly these seven years, and from them received more disgraces, censures, and ignominies than ever Prince did endure." He complains that at the last meeting of the Council they "parted irresolute." He had followed their Lordships' advice "in having patience, hoping better issue. He cannot have asinine patience." He therefore gave orders for the immediate adjournment of Parliament ; which was dissolved in the following February. And so ends the story of Cecil's Great Contract.

§ 18   Bacon's Private Thoughts on Politics

Meantime, while Cecil was thus active, what was Bacon thinking of his activity, and of politics in general, of the coming Revolution, and of the best means for averting it? The answer to these questions will be found in a private note-book of his, called the *Commentarius Solutus*—i.e. "Loose, or Miscellaneous, Commentary"—in which he set down his thoughts, small and great, about all subjects, political, private, literary, philosophical, as they suggested themselves to him in July, 1608, about a month after Cecil had laid on the new Impositions.[1] These jottings are, obviously, far more trustworthy, as an index of Bacon's inmost convictions, than letters to the King, or speeches for the King, advocating the Prerogative. In

---

[1] Spedding, iv. 39—95. The pages bear the running title of *Transportata*, i.e. *transferred* (from a former note-book). Some of the notes may therefore be of older date than July, 1608 ; some, from internal evidence, are seen to have been written in July. See Spedding, iv. 22.

the latter, Bacon may have naturally been influenced by a desire of promotion; but in the former he "relates himself to paper" as to a most secret friend. The disjointed form of these entries; the frankness with which he makes the most discreditable avowals about himself; the cool directness with which he sets down plans for humouring, or utilising, the leading men of the day—including his cousin the Lord Treasurer, and the King himself—make it absolutely certain that the book could never have been written with a view to publication, or in the hope of exhibiting himself in a favourable light to posterity. Here then we are safe with Bacon: here we have his true self described by one who has the amplest information and not the slightest temptation to excuse or gloss or misrepresent : for what is the use of making misrepresentations to a sheet of paper ? Every word, therefore, that Bacon sets down here we may accept as representing what he believed to be his motives and objects. He may have been mistaken—as men are sometimes mistaken about their own motives and objects—but, unless we find him making himself out to be much better than we have reason for thinking him to be, we must be very sceptical to disbelieve the evidence afforded by the *Commentarius Solutus* as to Francis Bacon's public and private objects.

The sum of these secret records, so far as politics are concerned, is that Bacon exhibits himself in them as a resolute and determined courtier; without the slightest apprehension for the liberties of his country ; systematically aiming at the extension of the royal Prerogative ; jealous of lawyers and of the attacks of lawyers on what he deemed the rights of the Crown ; apparently approving of Salisbury's project for composition, but at the same time inclining to a policy of distracting the attention of the people from the enlargement of the Prerogative by an aggressive Foreign Policy. But all these general objects never induced him to forget the particular object of self-aggrandisement which pervades the Diary. And this is the weak point in our advocacy when we would fain urge that Bacon was, at all events, sincere in his Monarchical theories. To be a Monarchist and exalt the Prerogative was so manifestly for his own interest, and he was so manifestly addicted to the constant contemplation of his own interest, that we can never feel quite certain whether his conviction is prompted by public or private considerations. But the total impression which the *Commentarius Solutus* conveys to us is that, so far as Bacon could be sincere where his own interests were concerned, he was sincere in taking the side of the Crown against the side of the people. We, in these days, see with perfect clearness that " the Prerogative of the Crown would need to be curtailed when it was applied to less important objects than the maintainence of national unity." [1] But Bacon saw nothing of this. He liked Parliaments; but Parliament was to represent the wishes of the people, not to govern. The King, assisted by the Council, was to rule in reality as well as in name; and for that purpose the Crown needed a revenue independent of the contributions of the people (except in time of war or other emergency), and the royal Prerogative required to be strengthened, not weakened. A good and wise king could govern better than a popular assembly. Whether James was equal to such a responsibility, and whether the favourites and flatterers whom he gradually collected round him, could supplement his inadequacies, Bacon never seems to have entertained a doubt. His intellect as well as his interests disposed him to prefer to see government in the hands of the few, and made him averse to "popularity" and popular men.

The private schemes of the *Commentarius* may be deferred for further consideration; we are now dealing only with the political notes; and first among these in importance comes an entry as to the method of dealing with the great obstacle in the way of the enlargement of the Prerogative—the resistance of the lawyers. Without the lawyers, the country-gentlemen in the House of Commons could have given no expression to the constitutional claims of the people, and therefore in order to silence the House James needed only to suppress the lawyers. Here Bacon was assured of the support both of the King and of the Archbishop of Canterbury (Bancroft). During the last two or three years (1605—8) there had been complaints on the part of the Ecclesiastical Courts that the Common Law Judges had interfered with their proceedings by Prohibitions, requiring

[1] Gardiner, *History*, vol. i. p 42.

the former to proceed no further till they proved their right of jurisdiction. Bancroft, taking the part of the Ecclesiastical Courts, appealed to the King (1607) declaring that the Judges were mere delegates of the Sovereign, who therefore "had power to take what causes he pleased out of their hands and to determine them himself." Coke indignantly denied this. "Then," said the King, "I shall be under the Law, which is treason to affirm." The Chief Justice replied by quoting the saying of Bracton that "the King ought not to be under any man but under God and the Law." [1] No doubt Bacon has this dispute, and Coke especially in his mind, when he speaks of "mere lawyers," and suggests that it will be well to intimidate those who had seats in the House of Commons by the fear of losing promotion.

"Judges to consult with King as well as the King with Judges. . . . . Query, of making use of my Lord of Canterbury his opposition to the la(wyers), in point of reforming the laws and disprizing mere lawyers.

"To prepare either collect(ions), or at least advice, touching the equalling of laws.

"Rem(inder) ; to advise the K(ing) not to call sergeants before parliament, but to keep the lawyers in awe."

By the side of these entries, there is a marginal note as follows :—

"Summary justice belongeth to the King's prerogative. The fountain must run, where the conduits are stopped."

Another entry mentions a different kind of "Prohibitions" affecting non-Ecclesiastical Courts.

"Being prepared in the matter of Prohibitions. Putting in a claim for the K(ing). The 4 necessities, (1) time, as of war ; (2) place, as frontiers remote ; (3) person, as (for example) poor (persons) that have no means to sue those that come in by safe-conduct ; (4) matter, mixed with State."

This refers to a dispute concerning jurisdiction between the Court of King's Bench, and the Council in the Marches of

---

[1] Gardiner, *History*, ii. 39. Later (1608) Bancroft said it was "more likely that the poor would obtain justice from the King than from the country gentlemen who composed the House of Commons, or from the Judges who were in league with them. Juries were generally dependents of the gentry, and the cause of justice could not but suffer from their employment."—(*Ib.* 41).

Wales; of which we shall hear more hereafter. The Judges had unanimously resolved (Michaelmas, 1604) that four specified English counties were not within the jurisdiction of the Council, and that a "Prohibition" might be issued against the Council of the Marches, if the limits of their jurisdiction were exceeded.[1] But the dispute was not settled here. We shall soon have to refer to a paper drawn up by Bacon on the subject not later than June, 1606. Another entry in the *Commentarius*, dated Feb. 15, 1607 (*i.e.* 1608) shows that the quarrel about "Prohibitions" continued at that time to rage, and that the King not only took the side of the Council against the Judges, but even appeared to desire the establishment of more such irregular Councils for the purpose of "the distribution of justice" throughout the realm :—

"Feb. 15, 1607.[2] The K. assembled his Judges—not all, but certain of them—before their Circuits, and found fault with multitudes of Prohibitions. The particular which gave the occasion, was the complaints of the two Presidents of Wales and North. The K. was vehement, and said that more had been granted in four year of his Reign than in forty of former time ; and that no kingdom had more honourable Courts of Justice ; but, again, none was more cursed with confusion and contention of Prohibitions. Seemed to apprehend the distribution of justice after the French manner was better for the people and fitter for his greatness, saying that this course, to draw all things to Westminster, was to make him K. as it were of the Isle of France and not other provinces, so of a precinct about London and Westminster. Noted matter of profit was the cause why the Judges embraced so much. Warned a surceance of granting Prohibitions for the vacation following, with a dislike they should be granted but in Court, and shewed a purpose at some time to hear himself the matter and to define of it, though he spent many days about it. He said they put the subjects to Tantalus pain, that, when he thought to take the fruit of his suit, it fled from him."

Commenting upon this incident, Bacon says that "the Judges were in effect silent," but that they might have rejoined, without offence, that the question was whether the increase of Prohibitions might not have arisen from the encroachments of the lower and irregular Courts; which he appears to think at least a possible alternative.[3]

[1] Spedding, *Bacon's Works*, vii. 574 ; Mr. Heath's Preface.
[2] In modern reckoning February 15, 1608.
[3] "So late as July 1608, Bacon seems to have been *in private* inclined to the opinion that, in the general struggle then going on, the encroachments had been more on the part of the local courts."—Mr. Heath, Spedding, *Works*, vii. 575.

But whatever may have been Bacon's private and theoretical opinion as to the rights of the dispute, we see, recurring to the former entry, that he intended publicly and practically to regard it only so far as it might be turned to the enlargement of the Prerogative of the Crown. He proposed to justify the Crown's interference with the ordinary course of justice on the grounds of four contingencies, 1st, troubled times ; 2nd, possible disorder on the frontiers or Marches where the Council had jurisdiction; 3rd, expense and risk of long journeys for poor suitors, seeking redress against rich men, and unable to travel so far as Westminster ; 4th, possibility that political questions—"matter mixed with State "—might be involved in private suits.

The question of the jurisdiction of the Council of the Marches is important, in itself, as a thread in the tangled web of complications between King and Commonwealth which Bacon was bound, as a Statesman, to attempt to reduce to order; but it derives a special importance from the light which it throws on a treatise composed by him on *The Differences in Question betwixt the King's Bench and the Council in the Marches.* Although it was written (1606) two years before the *Commentarius,* yet the consideration of it falls fitly here, where we are taking a general view of Bacon's public and private attitude towards the political difficulties of his time ; and in order to understand this treatise, some preliminary account is necessary of the origin, purposes, uses, and abuses of the disputed jurisdiction.

§ 19   Bacon's Defence of the Council of the Marches

The reason for the original establishment of a Council on the Welsh Marches is easily understood. Some kind of special jurisdiction to settle disputes between Englishmen and semiforeigners might have obvious advantages. Accordingly, the Court of " the President and Council in the Dominion and Principality of Wales and the Marches of the same " originated in early times and was confirmed by Parliament, 34, 35 Hen. VIII., when it was armed with discretionary power over such matters as should be assigned to it by the King, "as theretofore had been accustomed and used." The more noted Council of York or Council of the North—instituted (1537) after the great Catholic rising in the North called the Pilgrimage of Grace—had neither statute nor custom to support it. Equally destitute of legal authority was a third Provincial Council, established for the Western Parts; which last, however, was soon dropped, owing to strong local opposition.[1]

One object of these Councils was the cheap, speedy, and impartial administration of justice between rich and poor; and they had facilities for curbing local combination, oppression and corruption. Yet it is not difficult to see how they may have been abused. The Councils had, as their Presidents, noblemen chosen by Court favour, and not generally trained in legal habits; they acted at a distance from central opinion and control; exercising a censorial as well as a criminal jurisdiction; unfettered by definite rules of proceeding; in cases of felony and treason, examining the supposed offenders, and applying torture at the discretion of the Court; in civil questions, staying, setting aside, and inverting, within ill-defined limits, the proceedings and principles of the ordinary Courts. The Court itself was partly dependent for its support on fines imposed for contempt and other offences, and on fees ascertained by a custom of which the lower officials were the ordinary interpreters. From such a system as this one might naturally expect abuses. And that mal-administration did actually exist, is proved by Orders issued by Lord Burghley for reformation of the Court of the Marches issued in 1579, and by instructions to the President in 1586, recognising, and endeavouring to remedy, delays, excessive costs, encroachments on the Common Law, extortion by means of fining, and so extensive an exercise of the inquisitional powers of the Court as even in those days was thought vexatious.[2]

In part the dislike of the English Counties to be coupled with the Welsh may have stimulated their protests against the Council: but it is only reasonable to suppose that their antipathy arose from the abuses which Lord Burghley en-

[1] Spedding, *Works*, vii. 569.
[2] See Mr. Heath's Preface to Bacon's paper on the *Jurisdiction of the Marches.* Spedding, *Works*, vii. 571.

deavoured in vain to remedy. At all events no Englishmen seem to have liked them. Chester appears to have been exempted from the jurisdiction of the Council of the Marches ; Bristol obtained exemption as a favour ; Worcester and the other Shires attempted, but failed, to gain the same exemption by petition. The answer was that the Court must be reformed, not restricted. After the reformation of the Court we hear of no quarrels till 1602, when the new President, Lord Zouch, is said to have slighted the Chief Justice of Chester ; and an opinion was expressed by the Chief Justice of Common Pleas that the Four Counties were not within the Council's jurisdiction. In 1604 a conflict of jurisdiction arose between the Council and the Court of King's Bench, and was submitted by Lord Zouch to the Privy Council. Judges being consulted, decided in Michaelmas, 1604, against the Council. Some angry letters from Lord Zouch to Cecil in 1605 indicate that the Privy Council also at first sided against the President ; and for two or three years the authority of the Council of the Marches seems to have been in abeyance ; but Coke asserts that it was not reformed in all points as it ought to have been.

Meantime Lord Zouch and his friends pressed on the King considerations tending to show that on the maintenance of the Council of the Marches depended the royal dignity and Prerogative. To give up the English Shires, because they were alleged not to be within the Act of Parliament, was, so they urged, to admit that the jurisdiction of the Court rested on Statute Law and that the royal Prerogative (on which it had rested from the time of Edward IV.), backed by the usage of four successive reigns after the Statute of Henry VIII., was to go for nothing. If this were so, all the decisions of the Council within the Shires would be invalid ; the Council of the North which was founded by mere Prerogative, would necessarily fall, and other Courts might follow. Other arguments based on the interests of the subject were not wanting : the advantages of local and summary tribunals, the inconvenience of severing the resort of the inhabitants of the two sides of the Borders to the same Civil Courts, the turbulent and Popish inclination of the gentry in those parts. The agitation against the Council was imputed to evil motives ; to a preference for trial by jury because juries could be influenced and intimidated; to a clannish following of the gentry by the common people; to the increasing number of attorneys hungry for costs and therefore averse from the cheap and speedy proceedings of the Council of the Marches. But principally the Council dwelt on the violation of the sanctity of the royal Prerogative; on the personal disgrace to the King if he gave up what the Tudors had upheld; and on the danger of allowing the Common Law Courts of England to aim at the exorbitant greatness of the Parliament of Paris. These memorials had some weight with Salisbury; and an annotation in his handwriting on the margin of one of them exhibits his fear lest the fall of the Council of the Marches might shake the throne: *antiquae substructiones nec facile destruuntur nec solae ruunt.*

While these disputes were before the Privy Council, a Bill passed the House of Commons (March, 1606) declaring the English Shires to be exempt. But it failed to pass the Lords; and in May (1606), when a similar Bill was again passing through the Commons, it was dropped in consequence of a gracious speech from the King; and a resolution was passed "to rest upon his Majesty's grace for the execution of the law," it being understood by the Commons that, after the recent decision of the Judges, the law would exempt the Shires from the jurisdiction of the Welsh Council. However, in the instructions next issued to the Council its jurisdiction in the Shires was not taken away, but limited to matters of debt and trespass where the damage was laid under £10. But the instructions were kept private, as usual; and not long afterwards they were exceeded. A strenuous resistance was now organised, headed by the Bishop of Hereford and twenty-six of the principal gentry; and in Worcestershire, the Sheriff, Sir John Packington, a veteran courtier of Elizabeth's time, supported his under-sheriff in refusing to obey the precepts of the Court (December, 1607). At a meeting of the Privy Council (6 November, 1608,) the King propounded the question whether the Article concerning the £10 jurisdiction of the Council within the Four Shires were according to law. There followed a somewhat indecorous altercation between the King and Coke, when the latter demanded time and the opportunity of hearing Counsel before replying: but it was finally resolved that the Judges were to "return their report what they had heard on both sides, and leave the judgment to the King." There are good grounds for thinking that the opinion of the Judges, delivered in writing by Coke (3 February, 1609) was unfavourable to the Crown; but it was never published, though pressed for in Parliament. The agitation was continued in the Parliaments of 1610 and 1614; and in the course of it a Grand Jury presented the Council as a nuisance, and 5,000 signatures were subscribed to some declaration to the same effect. But after 1614 it died out; and in 1617, when Bacon was Chancellor, the new instructions made no distinction between Wales and the English Shires, giving the Court a full, equitable, and Star-Chamber jurisdiction, which was not taken away till the next reign. Thus the final result, in Bacon's time, was to leave unreformed an obsolete and dangerous institution to be bequeathed as a grievance to the popular party in the next reign, and then to be swept away—along with a great deal besides.

These preliminary remarks will probably render unnecessary any further explanation of the following extracts from Bacon's *View of the Differences in Question betwixt the King's Bench and the Council in the Marches* (1606). It will be seen that he maintains the power of the King to establish a Court of Equity as a power derived from God Himself, and therefore, it would seem, inalienable by any promises of a particular Monarch, or by any Acts of Parliament. This argument is of importance because it appears to render worthless a promise said to have been made by James that he would never erect another such court but by Act of Parliament.[1]

Meeting the objections that the "Prerogatives of our Kings are only given them by law, and that by the law they have no power to establish a Court of Equity," Bacon says:[2]

"But.... the King holdeth not his Prerogatives of this kind mediately from the Law, but immediately from God, as he holdeth his Crown; and though other Prerogatives by which he claimeth any matter of revenue or other right pleadable in his ordinary courts of justice, may be there disputed, yet his Sovereign Power, which no Judge can censure, is not of that nature; and therefore whatever pertaineth or dependeth thereon, being

[1] Spedding, *Works*, vii. 582.   [2] Spedding, *Life*, iii. 370.

matter of government, and not of Law, must be left to his managing by his Council of State. And that this is necessary to the end of all government, which is preservation of the public, may in this particular appear. For no doubt but these grave and worthy ministers of justice have in all this proceeding no respect but their oaths and the duties of their places, as they have often and deeply protested ; and in truth it belongeth not to them to look any higher, because they have charge but of particular rights. But the State, whose proper duty and eye is to the general good, and in that regard to the balancing of all degrees [1]. . . will happily consider this point above Law, that Monarchies, in name, do often degenerate into Aristocracies, or rather Oligarchies, in nature, by two insensible degrees.

"The first is, when Prerogatives are made envious,[2] or subject to the constructions of Laws. The second is, when Law, as an oracle, is affixed to place. For, by the one, the King is made accomptable and brought under the Law ; [3] and, by the other, the Law is overruled and inspired by the Judge ; and, by both, all tenures of favour, privy counsel, nobility, and personal dependencies (the mysteries that keep up States in the person of the Prince) are quite abolished, and magistracy enabled to stand by itself. The states of Venice and Poland might be examples hereof. And the *Maires du Palais* in France, by making the Law great and themselves masters thereof, supplanted the whole line of their ancientest Kings. And what greater strength had the League there of late than the exorbitant greatness of the Parliament of Paris ? [4]

"And from hence also in the time of Henry III. our Parliament challenged power to elect and depose the Lord Chancellor, Treasurer, and Chief Justice of England, as officers of the State and not of the King. Whether then these popular titles of limiting Prerogatives, for subjects' birthrights and Laws, may not unawares, without any design or thought of the authors, open a gap unto new Barons' Wars, or other alteration and inconvenience in Government, the State is best able to discern. And therefore all I conclude is this, that the ordering of these matters doth belong thereunto.

"Yet God forbid (as one said) that we should be governed by men's discretions and not by the Law ; 'for certainly a King that governs not thereby can neither be comptable to God for his administration, nor have a happy and established reign.' [5] But God forbid also, upon pretence of liberties or Laws, Government should have any head but the King. For then, as the Popes of Rome, by making their seat the only oracle of God's

---

[1] Two or three words are here worn away in the MS.

[2] That is, "invidious."

[3] Compare the subsequent dispute between Coke and the King in Nov. 1607, when the former asserted, and the latter denied, that the Sovereign is under the Law ; see above, p. 133.

[4] The King, perhaps with this suggestion in his mind, said afterwards (February 1607, *i.e.* 1608) that " this course to draw all things to Westminster was to make him King, as it were, of the Isle of France and not other provinces."—Spedding, iv. 90.

[5] Quoted from King James's *True Law of Free Monarchies* (1598).

religion, advanced themselves first above religion and then above God ; so we may fear what may in time become of our Laws, when these reverend fathers,[1] in whose breasts they are safe, shall leave them to others perchance of more ambition and less faith. But because I assure myself that no soul living will charge his Majesty with any manner of encroachment upon the subjects' rights, I confess I marvel, and some perchance may doubt, why we should be so curious to wrest that right from his hand which all his progenitors have enjoyed hitherto."

Then, in order to prove the King's right to establish Courts of Equity, after quoting Scripture, and alleging the examples of King Alfred, William the Conqueror, Henry III., Edward III., Edward IV. (who set up the Councils of Star Chamber and the Marches), and Henry VIII. (the last of whom established the Courts of Requests, of Wards and Liveries, and the Council of the North) he proceeds as follows :

"Besides we say that in the King's Prerogative there is a double power : one, which is delegate to his ordinary judges in Chancery or Common Law ; another, which is inherent in his own person, whereby he is the supreme judge both in Parliament and all other Courts ; and hath power to stay suits at the Common Law ; yea, *pro bono publico*, to temper, change, and control the same ; as Edward III. did, when, for increase of traffic, he granted juries to strangers *de medietate linguae*, against the Common Law. Nay, our Acts of Parliament by his sole authority may be mitigated or suspended upon causes to him known. And this inherent power of his, and what participateth thereof, is therefore exempt from controlment by any Court of Law. For saith Britton, lib. 1, ' We will that our jurisdiction be above all jurisdictions in our realm ; so as we have power to give, or cause judgments to be given, as shall seem to us good without other form of process, when we may know the true right as judge.' "

It is difficult to imagine any language more likely to be acceptable to the King and pernicious to his posterity. Let it be admitted that Bacon was sincere ; that he did in reality believe, as he asserts, that " the power of the gentry is the chief fear and danger of the good subject " in the Four Shires ; that he considered it expedient for the Welsh and English poor, as well as for the Crown, that the Council of the Marches should divert some of the suitors who streamed to Westminster ; and that he genuinely feared the " reverend fathers of the Law " and their assaults upon the Prerogative more than any encroachments of the Sovereign on the rights of the people :—still, it seems

[1] *i.c.* the Judges—called, above, " the grave and worthy ministers of justice."

impossible to credit him with common sagacity, much less with prophetic intuition in entertaining these fears and anticipations.

But, even if his anticipation was well founded, that the Royal Prerogative might be hereafter injuriously curtailed by the fears and suspicions of the people, was he not going the very way to realise his own anticipation by deepening old fears and awaking new suspicions? Even supposing that it was theoretically justifiable, was it wise, thus to magnify the Prerogative? Here was a King utterly destitute of tact, of sympathy with the House of Commons, of practical sagacity; replete with bookish theories, and pedantical paper notions about the Constitution, all making for consistent despotism; garrulous, pompous, sultan-like in speech; good-natured, inconstant, and yielding in action; a King who thought himself a second Solomon, and believed himself entitled to the arbitrary powers of a tyrant such as Samuel had foreshadowed in his predictions of the coming line of despots over Israel; a King who had actually attempted to assign to the Court of Chancery the right of determining the validity of elections, and had told the House of Commons to their faces, that he had power to tax the property of his subjects without consent of Parliament.[1] On the other side, a Parliament jealous for its privileges, fervent for its rights, recalcitrant against many legal or semi-legal abuses which sheltered themselves under the Prerogative, uneasily conscious that it had lost ground under the Tudors and had let slip some of the safeguards of national liberty, sensitive to the disparagements of bishops and courtiers, excitable and suspicious of the least attempt at royal encroachment, and not unmindful that at their first meeting under their Scotch King (1604) they had been compelled to remonstrate against an unprecedented violation of the most elementary constitutional principles. And around these two antagonists there were gathering clouds ominous of conflict; increase of national expenditure requiring

---

[1] Mr. Green (*Short History*, p. 466) quotes from one of James's speeches in the Star Chamber : "As it is atheism and blasphemy to dispute what God can do, so it is presumption and a high contempt in a subject to dispute what a King can do, or to say that a King cannot do this or that ;" and in his *True Law of Monarchies*, published before his accession to the English throne, James wrote thus : "Although a good King will frame all his actions to be according to the Law, yet he is not bound thereto, but of his own will and for example-giving to his subjects."

increased taxation; a freer spirit of criticism, which, beginning with things ecclesiastical, passed on to criticise political administration; a general uprising from old feudal bonds, and an inclination (in some minds) towards republican rather than personal Government. Was this a time to rake up every remnant of antique and irregular exercise of the Prerogative in order to flaunt before King and people a power which, unless it could be allowed quietly to die, was obviously destined to be the cause of a contention that must last until one of the two contending parties owned himself vanquished?

How much better—even from the royalist or courtier point of view—to choose a time when deeds and not words might have been employed; to wait for a war or some other emergency when national distractions or national interests might allow the King to exercise the extreme rights of his Prerogative (the establishment of new Courts of Justice, or the suspension of Acts of Parliament, or what not) either without the notice, or with the willing assent of his unsuspecting subjects! The wedge thus silently introduced in time of war might have been left to work its way in time of peace, and a precedent might have been quietly and firmly established for the development of despotism. But Bacon's magniloquent talk could do no good at all. It alarmed the people without strengthening the King.

If Bacon's contention was justified, if the King had power to establish any Court he pleased in any part of his kingdom, with equitable or Star-Chamber jurisdiction;[1] power to stay suits at will; to temper, change, and control the Common Law; to suspend Acts of Parliament by his sole authority; and if this power was inherent in the King's person by "the ordinance of God," then no promises that James might make[2] to abstain from establishing such Councils hereafter could possibly bind his successor; and the people had no security that, under cover of opportunities afforded by war or civil disturbance, their

---

[1] *In Private*, Bacon seems to have entertained the question whether the exceptional Courts might not have their jurisdiction limited by Parliament. See his note in the *Commentarius Solutus*, "To advise some course for the Council of the Marches and the North, for the Admiralty, Court of Requests, and the Ecclesiastical Jurisdiction: *query, of limitation by Parliament.*"—Spedding, *Life*, iv. 55.

[2] Mr. Heath, asserting, on the authority of Carte, *Hist. Eng.* iii. 794 (Spedding, *Works*, vii. 582) that he did make such a promise, adds: "But I think I have seen a denial by the King that his speech was so explicit."

liberties might not be summarily suppressed. Their only
bulwark, the power of the purse, was in danger of being well-
nigh levelled by the royal claim to impose taxes upon merchandise
—a claim which both now and afterwards Bacon maintained to
be strictly legal. Common patriotism might have protested at
leaving the liberties of the English nation thus unprotected and
at the mercy of the Sovereign ; common honesty might have
revolted at this violation of the Spirit of Magna Charta, under
pretext of isolated and exceptional precedents mostly derived
from troubled times, or from the period of national lassitude
consequent on the Wars of the Roses ; common sense, without
any claim to prophetic foresight, might have anticipated that the
straining of the Royal Prerogative, in times of freer thought
and growing demand for liberty, must necessarily end in bringing
King and people into a fatal collision. But with Francis Bacon
none of these three considerations had sufficient weight to
prevent him from advocating a course which could not but
ultimately lead to conflict and revolution, but which had the
immediate effect of strongly recommending him to the King
and facilitating his own advancement.

§ 20   Bacon's Remedy against the Coming Revolution

Bacon's remedies against the coming Revolution, so far as we
can judge from the *Commentarius Solutus*, appear to have been
three : 1st, the suppression of the lawyers and the exaltation of
the King's "summary justice," by which means the Sovereign
was to conciliate his subjects, and especially the poor, ad-
ministering justice more cheaply, speedily, and impartially than
at present ; 2nd, the acquisition of a permanent royal revenue
by means similar to those proposed by Salisbury in the Great
Contract ; 3rd, the distraction of the popular attention from
political and debatable questions by the excitements of foreign
war.

All Bacon's remarks on laws, lawyers, and judges in the
Commentarius Solutus tend to the same object, the subordination
of the lawyers as a political power; and they show the peculiar
and responsible position then occupied by the legal profession.

In the existing relations between the King and his subjects there was then a debatable ground wherein the Prerogative of the former conflicted with the liberties of the latter; and in this field it was scarcely possible for a Judge to decide a special case without modifying and defining for posterity those previously indefinite relations, and to some extent trenching on the functions of a Statesman. Thus in 1606 the well-known decision of "Bates's case" had sanctioned the royal claim to levy Impositions on exports and imports, and the claim sustained by this single decision was maintained for thirty-five years. In our days Parliament can at once rectify, by a new Act, an injury arising from a judicial interpretation of statutes or from the over-riding of statutes by Common Law : but no such power existed then. This unsettled condition of things commended itself to Coke, as being providentially calculated to erect the Judges into a great constitutional Tribunal, whose duty it was to mediate impartially between the King and the people Bacon, on the other side, believing that true statesmanship consisted in the magnifying of the Prerogative, felt that no amount of knowledge of the Common Law of England would ever constitute such a Statesman as he deemed worthy of the name. Against the lawyers therefore, it is part of his policy to be always on his guard, and especially against lawyers of the type of Coke, whom he stigmatizes as "mere lawyers." [1] "Mere lawyers" are to be "disprized;" they are to be kept "in awe," that is, in dread that they may miss promotion, by "not calling Sergeants till Parliament has met:" Bacon proposes to make use of the Archbishop of Canterbury's opposition to the lawyers, in order to bring on a project of reforming the Laws. Elsewhere he mentions his intention of submitting to the King his project for revising the Laws, and apparently (though the language is not quite clear) with some special reference to the royal Prerogative: "for equalling laws, to proceed with my Method, and to shew the King title of Prerogative, as it is done." [2] No doubt, in any reform, Bacon could have removed much that was irregular and inequitable ; but there is as little doubt that his reformation would have commended itself rather to the Archbishop and the King than

---

[1] See Gardiner, *History*, iii. 23-4.   [2] Spedding, *Life*, iv. p. 94.

to the lawyers themselves, or to the party which, through the lawyers, was aiming at the defining and strengthening of the liberties of the people.

As for the financial part of Bacon's policy, the *Commentarius* contains no indication that its author did not sincerely believe (in July 1608, at all events) that Salisbury's financial projects were the best that could be devised:

"Note amongst the pores of gain thought of by my L(ord) of Salisb(ury.) He wanteth *Divites et Orbi tanquam indagine capi*," apparently referring to some project of fishing out orphans and rich people to make a profit of wardships and exceptionally large incomes—"*and matter of marchanding, which, mixed with power of estate, I conceive may do wonders. . . . To correspond*"—*i.e.* conform—"*to Sa(lisbury) in the invent(ion) of suits and levies of money* and to resp(ect) *poll. è gem.* for emp(ty) coffers and alien-(ation) of the peop(le.)*"[1]

We seek in vain throughout the *Commentarius* for some definite scheme of internal policy beyond the suppression of the lawyers, and the increase of the King's permanent revenue. And yet, if Bacon had such a scheme, he must certainly have made mention of it. For in the section which he entitles "Poll." and reserves for political notes, he states, briefly but methodically, first, all the great dangers of the day, then other minor perils, and then the means of remedying them; and in this sketch he could hardly have omitted any original scheme of his own, if he had been prepared with one. The

---

[1] "*For* empty coffers," *i.e.* "*to cure* empty coffers." I can find in the *Comm. Solutus* no trace whatever of any dissent from Salisbury's financial schemes, and no indication that they even needed improvement, unless the following rather obscure passage implies that Bacon objected to some of the impositions laid on by Salisbury : "My L. of Salisbury is to be remembered of the great expectation wherewith he *enters ;* as, that he will make the King's payments certain . . . ; that he will *moderate new Impositions,*" (Spedding, iv. 46). This is written in July 1608. Salisbury "entered" on the office of Treasurer in April 1608, and, while lessening a few existing impositions, had laid on new ones to the amount of £60,000 a year in June 1608. Bacon's meaning is there-fore (as Mr. Spedding has pointed out) not quite clear. But I have placed the passage before the reader, as the only one of the kind. It may possibly mean that people believed (in July) that Salisbury had laid on the "new Impositions" in June with the view of "moderating," or removing them in exchange for some contribution from the Commons. But could an expectation *in July* be described as "an expectation wherewith S. *enters ?*" Possibly this entry may have been written in April and "transferred" (see note on p. 130, above) to the *Comm. Sol.* in July, and it may have referred to some recent Impositions that might be called "new" in April ; but why transfer an entry, unchanged, that has become inapplicable ? I hope some critic may find a solution of the difficulty pointed out by Mr. Spedding.

danger that comes first in his list is "The bringing the King
low by pov(erty) and empt(y) cof(fers)." After this, he
passes before his mind other possible perils: danger from
Scotland ; danger from some too powerful subject, *e.g.* Salisbury;
from the Privy Council; from the Lower House in Parliament ;
the office of Lieutenant Constable is then mentioned in connection
with the possible absence of the Prince (Henry) in wars, if he
should come to the Crown. Then follow remedies. There is to be
"confederacy and more straight amity with the Low Countries."
Jurisdictions are to be limited and made more regular ; and he
asks himself what, if any, use could be made of the Presbytery
or nobility of Scotland. It would appear, but it is by no means
certain, that he has in mind the possibility of persuading the
King to abate something of the pretensions of the Prerogative ;
for the next entry mentions "books in commendation of
Mon(archy) mixed or Aristoc(racy) ; " and the next is, "persuade
the King in glory, *Aurea condet saecula.*" But this last
sentence may refer merely to the following entry : " new laws to
be compounded and collected ; lawgiver *perpetuus princeps ;*" and
Bacon's meaning may be that he will persuade the King to
support his favourite project of reforming the Laws by reminding him of the glory that attends a Lawgiver.[1]

After a suggestion as to the Church—"restore the Church to
the true limits of authority since Henry VIII.'s confusion—" he
notes "choice of persons *act(ive)* and in their nat(ure) *stir(ring)*
and assure them," apparently meaning that the King is to select,
for the struggle with his people, ambitious men whose loyalty
must be insured.[2] Possibly he himself might become chief
Minister and wield the whole power of the State, diverting the
King from domestic politics by "glory;" and hence the
following entry :—" succ(eed) Salisb(ury) and amuse the K(ing)
and P(rince) with pasti(me) and glory." In order to diffuse
his views on politics he contemplates " finishing my treat(ise) of

---

[1] In *Essay* lv. 33 "the true marshalling of the degrees of sovereign honour"
assigns the second place (above liberators and increasers of empire) to "lawgivers,
which are also called second founders, or *perpetui principes,* because they govern
by their ordinances after they are gone."

[2] "Ambition maketh men *active . . .* and *stirring.*"—*Essays,* xxxvi. 2.
"Good commanders in the wars must be taken, be they never so ambitious . . .
there is also great use of ambitious men in being screens to princes in matters of
danger and envy."—*Ib.* 21-25.

the great(ness) of Br(itain) with aspect ad pol(iticam)." Then
he mentions the names of several members of the House of
Commons, probably as being popular, who might be useful if
conciliated : "Chem. (?) pop(ular) Neville, Sandys, Herbert,
Crofts, Berkly."

Thus having touched on possible dangers and possible remedies,
without hitherto giving an opinion as to the most suitable
remedy—jotting thoughts down on paper in order to see,
as it were, how they looked—he now concludes by mentioning
the one remedy that seems to him most efficacious ; and this is
simply *an energetic foreign policy calculated to distract the people
from internal politics.* All questions that may arise concerning
domestic policy are to be turned aside by reference to the
" ampliation of a Monarchy in the Royalty."

" *The fairest, without dis(order) or per(il)*, is the gener(al) persuad(ing) to
K(ing) and peop(le) and cours(e) of infusing everywhere the foundat(ion)
in this Isle of a Monarchy in the West, as an apt seat, state, people, for it ;
so civilising Ireland ; further colonising the wild of Scotl(and), annexing
the Low Countries.

" If anything be questio(ned) touch(ing) Pol(icy), to be turned upon the
Ampliation of a Mon(archy) in the Royalty."

" Annexing the Low Countries," meant war with Spain ; and
this was the policy that Bacon had distinctly advocated in his
speech on Naturalization.[1] This advice is somewhat similar to
that which Shakespeare puts into the mouth of Henry IV.,
exhorting his son to distract the attention of the people from
his unsound title by foreign wars :

> " Therefore, my Harry,
> Be it thy course to busy giddy minds
> With foreign quarrels ; that action, hence borne out,
> May waste the memory of the former days."

An able and warlike King, following Bacon's advice, might
perhaps have united his people in an aggressive foreign policy
of " glory " and so have deferred for many years the struggle
between Crown and Commonwealth. The story of the Spanish
Armada and the exuberance of the national loyalty consequent
on the Gunpowder Plot showed how much of internal discord

[1] See above, pp. 115, 116.

could be forgotten when the nation was awakened to the presence of an external foe. But the problem would have been deferred, not solved, and this Bacon must have known. In truth he has recourse to delay, because he can devise no solution : he seems to have turned in his mind all remedies, and to have found all either useless or impracticable. Even if he succeeded Salisbury, he could not hope to carry out a policy of his own unless he could " *amuse* the King with pastime and glory : " and even then he would have found the popular party not to be " amused : " the only course therefore was to " busy giddy minds with foreign quarrels" and with extension of empire. Some praise is due to the insight with which Bacon detected the impracticability of James's temper, the insuperable obstacle it presented to any real union between King and people, and the necessity of "amusing" him; something to the clearness of vision that foresaw troubles ultimately to come ; but assuredly no claim can be laid by the writer of these notes to the practical foresight of a Statesman. He sees a danger but can discern no permanent remedy; and his only temporary remedy is a foreign war.

Too great stress can hardly be laid upon this private expression of Bacon's opinion as to " the fairest " policy; for with the exception of this, and the previous passage in the *Commentarius Solutus*, in which he " conceives " that Salisbury's financial projects may " work wonders," there are very few statements that we can accept as exhibiting what Bacon himself *thought best for the country*. Indeed he frankly avows his determination, " At Council table chiefly to make good my Lord of Salisbury's motions and speeches ; and, for the rest, sometimes one, sometimes another ; *chiefly his that is most earnest and in affection*." Possibly Bacon considered that, as in party government some sacrifice of individual opinion is deemed necessary if not meritorious, so he was justified in giving an unvarying support to Salisbury whom he believed to be generally in the right, even where he occasionally dissented from his patron. Possibly, to one who deemed all internal policies alike nugatory in the face of the coming conflict, it seemed almost a matter of indifference whom or what he supported in minor matters, so that, on the whole, he deemed himself justified in advocating any plan that might increase his own influence: "Mean men, in their rising, must adhere."

How the advice that he might give, or the political action that he might take, would affect his own prospects, is a consideration never absent from Bacon's mind. When he sets himself to "think of matters against next Parliament," he deliberately plans first of all how he can make himself personally acceptable to both sides—"for satisfaction of King and People *in my particular*"—and the great point of policy is added as a second consideration, "*otherwise* with respect *ad Poll. è gem.*" The *Commentarius* teems with passages which show how in all matters small or great, and in all places and circumstances, Bacon was perpetually scheming to gain a hold over this or that great person by studying and humouring his weaknesses or eccentricities; to rule everybody by conforming to everybody; and to increase his influence with one half of the world by appearing to have influence with the other:

"To set on foot and maintain access with his Majesty. . . . To attend some time his repasts and to fall into a course of familiar discourses.[1] To find means to win a conc(eit), not open but private, of being affectionate and assured to the Sco(tch) and fit to succeed Sa(lisbury) in his manage in that kind. . . . To have ever in readiness matter to minister talk with every of the great counsellors *respectivè*, both to induce familiarity and for countenance in public place. . . . Insinuate myself to become privy to my L(ord) of Salisb(ury's) estate. . . . To correspond" (*i.e.* conform) "with Salisbury in a habit of natural but no way's perilous boldness, and in vivacity, invention, care to cast and enterprise, but with due caution, for this manner I judge both in his nature freeth the stonds, and in his ends pleaseth him best and furnisheth most use of me. . . . M(emorandum), the point of the Four Shires[2] and to think to settle a course in it; but to listen how the King is affected in respect of the Prince, and to make use of my industry in it towards the Pr(ince). . . . Making the collections and shewing them *obiter*, spec(ially) fit for an Attorney, and to make them" (*i.e.* the Lord Chancellor and Lord Treasurer) "think they shall find an alteration to their contentment over that (Attorney) which now is[3] . . To furnish my Lord of Suffolk with ornaments for public speeches; to make him think

---

[1] This contrasts amusingly with the conduct of Coke, driving away from Windsor, after the sermon, instead of staying to dine with the King "who was fond," he said, "of asking him questions which were of such a nature that he preferred being as far off as possible."—Gardiner, *History*, iii. 14.

[2] See above, p. 141.

[3] Bacon was Solicitor, but he hoped to supplant the Attorney (Hobart or Hubbard) by showing his own superior fitness for the post.

how he should be reverenced by a L(ord) Chancellor, if I were :—princelike. .... To take notes, in tables, when I attend the Council ; and sometimes to move out of a memorial, shewed and seen.   To have particular occasions, fit and grateful and continual, to maintain private speech with every the great persons, and sometimes drawing more than one of them together, *ex imitatione* Att(orney).   This especially in public places and without care or affectation."

A man so supple and conciliatory, endeavouring to introduce into business and politics the ductility that he had found, or thought he had found, invincible in natural science, was destined to inevitable failure as a Statesman.   It was a part of Bacon's theory of life, as well as a result of his disposition and training, that a man must not be persistent in aiming at one object, if he wishes to prosper in the world.   He must " avoid repulse ; " and " in every particular action, if he cannot obtain his wishes in the best degree, he must be satisfied if he can succeed in a second or even a third ; and, if he cannot obtain his wishes at all in that particular, then *he must turn the labour spent in it to some other end.*   He must imitate Nature, which doeth nothing in vain. . . . For nothing is more impolitic than to be entirely bent on one action." [1]   Even if Bacon had had the insight of a Prophet, he could have done nothing with so pliant and self-seeking a nature.   He wanted, not only strength of convictions, but pertinacity in maintaining and imparting them.   Like St. Paul he could be all things to all men ; but he had not the Pauline art of being instant " in season and out of season" for any policy except that which would commend him to the King : and such political intentions as he had, vanished in a thousand petty attempts to lift himself into a position where he might carry his intentions into effect.   But his failure was intellectual and political as well as moral.   Faced by a difficult but inevitable problem he could do nothing but endeavour to evade it as insoluble ; and his only remedies against the Coming Revolution were the spendthrift policy of procrastination by recourse to the distractions of foreign warfare and the philosopher's dream of an ideal King.

---

[1] *De Augmentis*, viii. 2 ; Spedding, *Works*, v. 74.

21 Bacon's Private Plans

We know from Bacon's own testimony, that on the attainment (June, 1607) of the office for which he had sued so long, he was seized with a temporary melancholy.[1]

"I have found now twice, upon amendment of my fortune, disposition to melancholy and distaste, especially the same happening against the long vacation when company failed and business both. For, *upon my Solicitor's place*, I grew indisposed and inclined to superstition."

Most restless men and hard workers, if they have no children and no taste for field-sports, are liable to periods of depression in the intervals of hard work; but Francis Bacon might have other reasons for dejection. He was then in his forty-seventh year, he who, while still in youth, had written the *Greatest Birth of Time*, and taken all knowledge to be his province:— and what results had he to show?

The ardour of the chase for the Solicitorship having disappeared, he had leisure in the vacation to review his position and to contrast his philosophic results with his philosophic purposes; and it was perhaps under this stimulus that he, about this time (1607), settled the plan of his *Instauratio Magna*, or *Great Renewal of Learning*. The *Advancement of Learning* was but a popular work, treating in general terms of the excellency of knowledge, and noting in detail the successes and deficiencies in the present state of knowledge; and it was intended to prepare the minds of its readers to give a favourable reception to that new philosophy which was to interpret nature, and to govern nature by interpreting it. Bacon now desired to give some specimens of the true philosophic method applied to some particular work—an investigation, for example, into the nature of heat.[2] But, as an introduction to the account of this investigation, some preface and statement of general principles would be requisite; and such a preface Bacon about this time composed in Latin, under the title of *Cogitata et Visa*, i.e. *Thoughts and Judgments*. A year passed away and brought

---

[1] Spedding, *Life*, iv. 79.

[2] So-called from the fact that the treatise, and each section of the treatise, is introduced with the preamble, "Francis Bacon *thought thus*" (see below, § 50).

fresh prosperity with it. On the 16th July, 1608, died Mill the Clerk of the Star Chamber, and Bacon on the same day took the oath for the office for which he had waited nineteen years. As the clerkship was worth £2,000 a year, he was now a rich man, with an annual income of nearly £5,000, that is, about £20,000 of our money. He had now wealth enough (even without his Solicitorship which he valued at only £1,000 a year) to dispense with practice, and he might have easily devoted himself to those "contemplative ends" which, as he had told his uncle Burghley nineteen years ago, were as vast as his "civil ends" were moderate. The choice therefore between a student's life and a civil life at this time lay before him. Once more, as had befallen him on his promotion to the Solicitorship, a melancholy settles on this restless, sanguine spirit.

In theory Bacon depreciated all "earthly hope," as vain, frothy, and seductive; but in practice he was never happy except when hoping and working for what would have seemed to ordinary minds beyond all hope. In this mood he sits down on the 25th of July, 1608, to review his position and his plans. Beginning with a determination "to make a stock of £2,000 always in readiness for bargains and great occasions" and to set himself "in credit for borrowing," he passes to the question of the best means to attain influence with the King and Council.[1]

Then follow notes which show that Bacon wished to displace Hobart, the Attorney-general, that he might step into his office : " To have in mind and use the Attorney's weakness"—followed by some prepared expressions of depreciation : "The coldest examiner ; weak in Gunter's cause ; weak with the judges ; too full of cases and distinctions ; nibbling solemnly ; he distinguisheth, but apprehendeth not ; " and again, "To win credit comparate to the Attorney by being more short, round and resolute." After some notes on the best means for retaining his hold on Salisbury (Cecil), on the effect of certain medicines on his constitution, and on the double policy of contenting the people and at the same time filling the royal exchequer, he concludes with jottings relating to the arrangement of his books and papers.

[1] This, and other extracts from the *Commentarius Solutus* relating to Bacon's political schemes, have been quoted fully above (see pp. 131-135, 144-150).

The 25th of July having been devoted to the improvement of his fortunes, he devotes the following day to the New Philosophy. Since nothing can be done without experiments, it is desirable to secure scientific experimenters, and patrons of science, and he jots down a list; Russell the mineralogist; through him perhaps Sir David Murray his friend; and by him finally the Prince (Henry); the mathematician Harriot, and his patron, the Earl of Northumberland; Sir Walter Raleigh; also the Archbishop of Canterbury being single and "glorious," *i.e.* fond of fame; then Bishop Andrews (one of his most intimate friends) being "single, rich, sickly;" perhaps also learned men beyond the seas. He must finish his three tables of classified phenomena of heat, cold, and sound, as also his Aphorisms; his *Advancement of Learning* must be translated into Latin; his *Cogitata et Visa* circulated privately and discreetly, with choice "*ut videbitur.*"

Next comes a sketch of a popular discourse on his favourite text *plus ultra* (*i.e.* there is a *New World beyond* the intellectual pillars of Hercules which were once supposed to show the *ne plus ultra*). The reception given to the *Advancement of Learning* had probably taught Bacon that the minds of men were still too servilely subject to the authority of the "ostentatious" Greek Philosophy.[1] He therefore sketches a project of a work "discoursing scornfully of the philosophy of the Grecians, with some better respect to the Egyptians, Persians, Chaldees, and the utmost antiquity and the mysteries of the poets." This might be written in the character of an Elder discoursing to his sons; hence a note, "Query, of an oration '*ad filios,*' delightful, sublime, and mixed with elegancy, affection, novelty of conceit, and yet sensible."[2]

Then, after projecting a History of Marvels, and a History Mechanic (*i.e.* of experiments and observations of all mechanical arts,) he makes a note concerning "laying for a place to command wits and pens, Westminster, Eton, Winchester specially Trinity College in Cambridge, St. John's in Cambridge, Magdalene College in Oxford, and bespeaking this betimes with the King, my Lord Archbishop, my Lord Treasurer." Following up the project of "discoursing scornfully," he makes

---

[1] *Essays*, liv. 34.
[2] This project found fulfilment in the *Redargutio Philosophiarum* (see § 51).

this entry: "taking a greater confidence and authority in discourses of this nature, *tanquam sui certus et de alto despiciens*," ("like a man certain of his position and looking down from a height on others.")

Now, after a query on "younger scholars in the Universities,' he passes to a sketch of the ideal College for Inventors (such a sketch as he amplified some years afterwards in the *New Atlantis*), with its endowments, allowances for travelling-students and for experiments; its library and "inginery;" its rewards and penalties; its vaults, furnaces, and terraces for insulation; wherein, with characteristic sanguineness and love of stately effect, he does not omit "two galleries for inventors past, and spaces or bases for inventors to come." This section concludes with a note of an "endeavour to abate the price of professing sciences" (comp. *Advancement of Learning*, ii. 1, 8.) "and to bring in estimation Philosophy or Universality," *i.e.* the knowledge of the Axioms common to all sciences. He concludes his day's work by setting down fifteen heads for a scheme of legitimate or complete investigation (*inquisitio legitima*). All the entries on the next day (27 July) are devoted to a sketch of the complete investigation of Motion, in the course of which he enumerates more than twenty different kinds of motion, and assigns a number of phenomena to their several causal motions.

But the following day (28 July) brings him back again from "contemplation" to the subjects with which he started, viz., "civil business" and the architecture of his own fortunes. He again notes the emptiness of the royal exchequer, resolves to finish his treatise "of the greatness of Britain with aspect to pol(icy)," and then proceeds to define that policy, the "foundation in this isle of a monarchy in the west, as an apt seat, state, people, for it; so civilising Ireland; further colonising the wild of Scotland, annexing the Low Countries." Next come some "forms" of wit, and repartees, and notes on Recusants. Then, once more recurring to the Attorney-general (Hobart) whom he wishes to supplant, he proposes to draw up certain legal compilations, and by showing them casually ("*obiter*") to the Lord Chancellor and Lord Treasurer, to convince them that he is specially fit for the Attorney's place, "and to make think they shall find an alteration to their contentment *over that which now is.*"

Gradually he passes from politics to speak of his own affairs, his estate, his health, his pecuniary prospects.

In an earlier entry he had reminded himself to " send message of compliment to my Lady Dorset the widow," and he now more definitely notes the desirableness of inducing the rich widow to remember him in her will : " applying myself to be inward with my Lady Dorset *per Champners ad utilit(atem) test(amentariam).*"

Another note reminds him to think about the will of his half-sister, formerly Lady Neville ; and how to humour the eccentricities of some old-fashioned squire by calling him a *franklin :* " encouragement of Crosseby with great words (*such a Franklin*)." Then follow minute details of medicines that agree and disagree with him ; particulars of his lands and goods ; and so at last he comes back to politics again.

After another note about the Recusants he returns for the third time to the Attorney, this time with a separate heading, " Hubbard's [1] disadvantage : "

" Better at shift than at drift. *Subtilitas sine acrimonia.* No power with the judge. He will alter a thing but not mend. . . . Sociable save in profit. Solemn goose, stately leastwise nodd (?) not crafty. They have made him believe he is wondrous wi(se). He never beats down unfit suits with law. In persons as in people, some shew more wise than they are."

The next heading is " Customs adapted to the individual," and the contents show the writer ascending in thought even above the place of the Attorney and deliberating how he can adapt his customs to the humours of great men, so as to win his way by their favour to the highest legal position in the State. The first "individual" selected is the Earl of Suffolk, Lord Chamberlain to the Household, a pompous man, fond of adulation, who might naturally be supposed to have influence with the King ; concerning him he makes the following note, " To furnish my Lord of Suffolk with ornaments for public speeches. To make him think how he should be reverenced by a Lord Chancellor, if I were : Princelike." At the Council table he

---

[1] Bacon generally spells the name " Hubbard " or Hubberd."

resolves "chiefly to make good my Lord of Salisbury's (Cecil's motions and speeches," he will efface every vestige of his natural and student-like shyness and nervousness : " to suppress at once my speaking with panting and labour of breath and voice. Not to fall upon the main too sudden ; but to induce and intermingle speech of good fashion. To free myself at once from payment of formality and compliment, though with some shew of carelessness, pride, and rudeness." The note-book ends as it began, with money matters.

These extracts supply a sufficient answer to the question, Which will Bacon choose, Philosophy or Politics ? Obviously, he will serve neither of these two masters ; he will attempt to serve both. It is equally clear that, although he may still consider that his civil ends are subordinated to his contemplative ends, the former are no longer " moderate," and that his projects for his own advancement occupy almost as much of his attention as Philosophy and Politics.

In commenting on his deliberate and calculated flattery of great men, and disparagement of rivals, we must repeat that Bacon at all events avowed and justified such conduct. In his *Advancement of Learning*,[1] he censures the " tenderness and want of compliance in some of the most ancient and revered philosophers, who retired too early from civil business that they might avoid indignities and perturbations, and live (as they thought) more pure and saint-like ; " he cannot " tax or condemn the morigeration or application of learned men to men in fortunes." The resolution registered in his private note-book to win " credit comparate to the Attorney in being more short, round and resolute,"[2] is at least consistent with the public avowal that " Honour that is gained and broken upon another, hath the quickest reflection."[3] Those who are startled by Bacon's secret plans for showing off his abilities to the best advantage, should refer to the precepts published in the *De Augmentis*,[4] for attaining success in life. One of these is that a man should set forth to advantage before others, with grace and skill, his own virtues, fortunes and merits, and " cover

---

[1] I. iii. 10.

[2] He even adds "forms" for correcting the poor Attorney. "(All this is nothing except) (There is more) (*Oportet istaec fieri, finis autem nondum*)."— Spedding, iv. 46.   [3] *Essays*, lv. 18.   [4] viii. 2.

artificially his weaknesses, defects, misfortunes and disgraces."
For this end he inculcates dissimulation and adaptability of
mind; "if a man is dull, he must affect gravity; if a coward,
mildness;" and he "must strive with all possible endeavour to
render the mind obedient to occasions and opportunities;" "for
nothing is more politic than to make the wheels of the mind
concentric and voluble with the wheels of fortune." It is true
that Bacon begins this little treatise (called "The Architect of
Fortune ") in the *De Augmentis* with the warning that no man's
fortune can be a worthy end in itself, and that fortune only
deserves this "speculation and doctrine," so far as it is "an
instrument of virtue and merit;" but he concludes it with the
practical precept that the Architect should accustom his mind
to judge of the proportion and value of all things as they
conduce more or less to his own fortune and his own ends.

No mistake can be greater than to suppose that Bacon
reminded himself in this extraordinary fashion of the duty of
advancing himself in life, because he was by nature disposed to
be extraordinarily forgetful of that duty. The *duty* was *always*
present to his mind: it was only the ways and means of which
he desired to make systematic note. He saw all men desiring
self-advancement, but few aiming at it systematically and
scientifically. Feeling a contempt for so half-hearted a pursuit
of fortune, he desired to reduce the chase to a science, and to
make all his acts in every department of life conduce towards
it—his friendships, compliments, conversations, legal business,
House of Commons business, access to the King—everything was
to be made subservient to two objects, and one of these was
" his own particular."

The differences therefore between Bacon and an ordinary
pushing man of the world appear to be two. Firstly, he succeeded
in persuading himself that his own advancement was essential
to the advancement of Philosophy, and therefore to the benefit
of the human race for whose service he believed himself to have
been born; secondly (in consequence, partly of this self-per-
suasion, partly of a natural cold-bloodedness of disposition), he
did unscrupulously, and with his eyes open, what even men of
the world cannot do without some reluctance or blinking. Many
will study and flatter the humours of great men, but few will

do it deliberately and avowedly; some few may stoop to disparage a rival in order to obtain his place; but far fewer will do it in a business-like, thorough, and methodical manner, setting down on paper, under the formal heading of their rival's "Disparagement," elaborate entries of points and epigrams, so that, beneath the guise of casual utterances, they may undermine his influence; and still fewer—perhaps only one in the human race—could be found to jot down these petty details of a rival's depreciation among sketches of schemes for the establishment of a great Protestant Monarchy in the West, and for the foundation of a Philosophy which was to make mankind lords over the material world.

§ 22 LITERARY WORK

This year and the next (1608, 1609) still found Bacon's political path obstructed by Salisbury, and consequently gave him leisure for literature. Besides a treatise on Queen Elizabeth (*In felicem memoriam Elizabethae*)—interesting because it shows the respect which he entertained for a sovereign from whom he could no longer hope anything, his admiration for her administrative ability, and his approval of her policy towards Recusants —he also wrote (1609) *Considerations touching the Plantation in Ireland*, in which he deprecates excess of paper-government ("that there be not too much of the line and compass"), and advocates freedom from taxes and customs, and the addition of an Irish title to the Prince of Wales. But the paper does not touch the really important part of the question, the treatment of the native population.

The *Great Instauration* was not neglected. "My *Instauration* sleeps not"—so he writes (1609) to Toby Matthew; and again in the same year:—

" As for the *Instauration*, your so full approbation thereof I read with much comfort; by how much more my heart is upon it, and by how much less I expected consent and concurrence in a matter so obscure. Of this I can assure you, that though many things of great hope decay with youth (and multitude of civil businesses is wont to diminish the price, though not the delight, of contemplations) yet the proceeding in that work doth gain with me upon my affection and desire, both by years and business."

During this year (1609) he carried out two projects sketched (1608) in the *Commentarius Solutus*. " To discourse scornfully of the Grecians with some better respect to the Ægyptians, Persians, and Chaldees, and the utmost antiquities and the mysteries of the poets "—so he had written in the note-book of 1608; and accordingly he produced in 1609 a short contemptuous treatise on Greek philosophy entitled *Refutation of the Philosophies (Redargutio Philosophiarum)*, which he sent to Toby Matthew with the following letter :—

"For your caution for churchmen and church matters, as for any impediment it might be to the applause and celebrity of my work, it moveth me not ; but as it may hinder the fruit and good which may come of a quiet and calm passage to the good port to which it is bound, I hold it a just respect : so as, to fetch a fair wind, I go not too much about. But the truth is, I shall have no occasion to meet them in my way, except it be as they will needs confederate themselves with Aristotle, who, as you know, is intemperately magnified with the Schoolmen ; and is also allied (as I take it) to the Jesuits by Faber, who was a companion of Loyola and a great Aristotelian.

" I send you at this time the only part which hath any harshness ;[1] and yet I framed to myself an opinion, that whosoever allowed well of that preface which you so much commend, will not dislike, or at least ought not to dislike, this other speech of preparation ; for it is written out of the same spirit, and out of the same necessity. Nay, it doth more fully lay open that the question between me and the ancients is not of the virtue of the race, but of the rightness of the way. And to speak truth, it is to the other but as *palma* to *pugnus;* part of the same thing more large. . . . Myself am like the miller of Huntingdon, that was wont to pray for peace amongst the willows ; for while the winds blew, the wind-mills wrought, and the water-mill was less customed. So I see that controversies of religion must hinder the advancement of sciences. Let me conclude with my perpetual wish towards yourself, that the approbation of yourself, by your own discreet and temperate carriage, may restore you to your country, and your friends to your society. And so I commend you to God's goodness.

" Gray's Inn, this 10th of October, 1609."

Matthew's caution about " churchmen and church matters " refers to the great pen-and-ink war in which Cardinal Bellarmin, having answered King James's book in defence of the oath of allegiance against the Pope, was himself answered by Bishop

---

[1] The *Redargutio Philosophiarum*, for the details of which see § 51.

Andrews, who had been selected by the King as his champion.[1] This will also explain the following letter which accompanied a copy of the *Cogitata et Visa* sent by Bacon to the Bishop about October, 1609 :—

"MY VERY GOOD LORD—Now your Lordship hath been so long in the church and the palace disputing between kings and popes, methinks you should take pleasure to look into the field, and refresh your mind with some matter of philosophy ; though that science be now through age waxed a child again, and left to boys and young men ; and because you were wont to make me believe you took liking to my writings, I send you some of this vacation's fruits [2] and thus much more of my mind and purpose.

"I hasten not to publish ; perishing I would prevent. And I am forced to respect as well my times as the matter. For with me it is thus, and I think with all men in my case, if I bind myself to an argument, it loadeth my mind ; but if I rid my mind of the present cogitation, it is rather a recreation. This hath put me into these miscellanies ; which I purpose to suppress, if God give me leave to write a just and perfect volume of philosophy, which I go on with, though slowly. I send not your Lordship too much, lest it may glut you.

"Now let me tell you what my desire is. If your Lordship be so good now, as when you were the good Dean of Westminster, my request to you is that not by pricks, but by notes, you would mark unto me whatsoever shall seem unto you either not current in the style, or harsh to credit and opinion, or inconvenient for the person of the writer ; for no man can be judge and party : and when our minds judge by reflection of ourselves they are more subject to error. And though for the matter itself my judgment be in some things fixed, and not accessible by any man's judgment that goeth not my way, yet even in those things the admonition of a friend may make me express myself diversely. I would have come to your Lordship, but that I am hastening to my house in the country. And so I commend your Lordship to God's goodness."

---

[1] A choice creditable to the King's judgment, as Mr. Spedding remarks, if only he could have refrained from interfering with his champion. See Carleton's letter (11 November, 1608), "I doubt he [Andrews] be not at leisure for any bye matters, the King doth so hasten and spur him on in this business of Bellarmin's ; which he were likely to perform very well (as I hear by them that can judge) if he might take his own time, and not be troubled nor entangled with arguments obtruded to him continually by the King."
There is an interesting note about him in the *Commentarius Solutus* (1608) showing how Bacon valued his aid : "Not desisting to drawe in the Bp. Aund(rews) being single, rych, sickly, a professor to some experiments."
[2] This must not be taken literally ; for at the beginning of the vacation in July, 1608, Bacon speaks of "imparting my *Cogitata et Visa*, with choice, *ut videbitur.*" Probably he had revised or re-written the work in the vacation of 1609.

M

The second project mentioned in the *Commentarius Solutus* was a treatise on what Bacon calls " the utmost antiquities and mysteries of the poets." It was his genuine belief that the old Greek and Latin myths contained secrets of religion and policy, " sacred relics or abstracted arts of better times, which, by tradition from more ancient nations, fell into the trumpets and tunes of the Grecians." His attempt to interpret these myths and unfold their secrets he embodied in a little Latin treatise called the *Sapientia Veterum* or *Wisdom of the Ancients*.[1] This he sent to Matthew with the following letter :—

" MR. MATTHEW,

" I do heartily thank you for your letter of the 24th of August from Salamanca ; and in recompense thereof I send you a little work of mine that hath late begun to pass the world. They tell me my Latin is turned silver and become current. Had you been here you should have been my inquisitor before it came forth : but I think the greatest inquisitor in Spain will allow it. But one thing you must pardon me, if I make no haste to believe that the world should be grown to such an ecstasy as to reject truth in philosophy because the author dissenteth in religion.

" My great work goeth forward ; and after my manner I alter ever when I add : so that nothing is finished till all be finished.

" This I have written in the midst of a term and parliament, thinking no time so precious but that I should talk of these matters with so good and dear a friend. And so with my wonted wishes I leave you to God's goodness.

" From Gray's Inn, the 17th of February, 1610."

This was a busy time with Bacon. Parliament had met (9 February, 1610), and all through the session he had his hands full, supporting the Great Contract, defending the King's rights or claims, and endeavouring to keep the House of Commons in good humour. Whether on account of the pressure of political work, or for whatever reason, no literary production of this year has been handed down to us beyond a fragment which he sent to James entitled *A Beginning of a History of His Majesty's Time*. It is fortunate that the King gave him no encouragement that induced him to continue his work. No courtier should write contemporary history, least of all such a courtier as Francis Bacon, who volunteers a readiness to alter anything in his book upon the King's " least beck."

[1] For a description of this, see § 52.

" It may please your Majesty,

"Hearing that you are at leisure to peruse story, a desire took me to make an experiment what I could do in your Majesty's times. Which being but a leaf or two, I pray your pardon if I send it for your recreation, considering that love must creep where it cannot go. But to this I add these petitions, first, that if your Majesty do dislike anything, you would conceive that I can amend it upon your least beck. Next, if I have not spoken of your Majesty encomiastically, your Majesty will be pleased only to ascribe it to the law of an history, which doth not clatter together praises upon the first mention of a name, but rather disperseth and weaveth them throughout the whole narration ; and as for the proper place of commemoration (which is in the period of life) I pray God I may never live to write it. . . ."

In this year (1610) his mother died, over eighty years of age. The last mention of her is in 1600, when her health is said to be " worn." In 1608, making an entry of his property, Bacon includes Gorhambury, his mother's estate, and makes no deduction from the income of the estate on her account ; a circumstance that confirms the statement of Bishop Goodman, who writes that Bacon's mother was " little better than frantic (mad) in her age." In the following letter Bacon invites his kindly friend Sir Michael Hickes to be present at the funeral :—

" SIR MICHAEL HICKES,

" It is but a wish, and not any ways to desire it to your trouble. But I heartily wish I had your company here at my mother's funeral, which I purpose on Thursday next in the forenoon. I dare promise you a good sermon to be made by Mr. Fenton, the preacher of Gray's Inn ; for he never maketh other. Feast I make none. But if I might have your company for two or three days at my house I should pass over this mournful occasion with more comfort. If your son had continued at St. Julian's it mought have been an adamant to have drawn you : but now, if you come, I must say it is only for my sake. I commend myself to your Lady, and commend my wife to you both, and rest

Yours ever assured

FR. BACON.

" This Monday the 27th of August, 1610."

§ 23 The Decline of Cecil

As long as Cecil lived there was no chance of Bacon's having free access to the King and influence over his policy. This Bacon avowed afterwards to the King, when he declared that during his cousin's life he was like a hawk tied to another's wrist, which may flutter and "bate," but cannot fly; and he obscurely hints it in the last quoted note to the King, in which he says that his love "must creep since it cannot go" (*i.e.*, walk upright). But there were now signs that the great man's influence was on the wane. The King had been warned by one of his nobles on his death-bed that, under cover of the Great Contract, he was being stripped of his royal dignities, and that "the subject was bound to relieve him and to supply his occasions without any such contractings;"[1] and we are told that "ever after, the Earl of Salisbury, who had been a great stirrer in that business, began to decline."[2] On 25 November, 1610, the King wrote a letter to Salisbury soundly rating him for expecting from him an "asinine patience," and commanding the adjournment of Parliament, and on 29 February, 1611, Parliament was dissolved.

At the same time a favourite was coming to the front. A young Scotchman named Robert Carr, who had been one of the King's pages in Scotland but had been dismissed on James's accession to the English throne, coming to Court soon afterwards, had the good fortune to break his leg at a tilting match (1606) in the royal presence. This accident, combined with his great physical vigour and activity and strong animal spirits, sufficed to place the lad at once high in the King's favour. He was knighted without delay, and by the good offices of Cecil—who seems to have courted the rising Favourite—advantage was soon taken of a flaw in a legal conveyance to dispossess Sir Walter Raleigh's wife and children of the Manor of Sherborne, and to bestow it (1609) upon Carr. In March, 1611, still rising in royal favour, Sir Robert Carr was created Viscount Rochester.

---

[1] Goodman, see Spedding, iv. 223.

[2] The Spanish ambassador (Sarmiento) declared that Salisbury also began to fall into disgrace from the time when he advocated a war with Spain.—(Gardiner, *History*, ii. 220, note).

Meanwhile honours and preferments were flying about. The Speaker of the last House of Commons, who had assisted the Great Contract and had made himself generally useful to the King on critical occasions, had been rewarded with the Mastership of the Rolls; and another of the King's supporters had been promised the reversion of the office. Finding himself unable to trust the good-will or ability of Salisbury to help him to the Attorney's place at the next vacancy, Bacon determined (early in 1611) to make a direct appeal to the King. The following letter, in which he expressly disclaims appealing to the intercession of those "friends" who are "near and assured" (obviously meaning Salisbury), and in which he gracefully touches on the possibility of his retiring from the "laborious place" of the Solicitorship, without actually threatening resignation, could hardly fail to make James feel how great a loss he would sustain if his Solicitor were to throw up his "course of painful service" and devote himself to literature :—

"It may please your Majesty,

"Your great and princely favours towards me in advancing me to place, and, that which is to me of no less comfort, your Majesty's benign and gracious acceptation from time to time of my poor services, much above the merit and value of them, hath almost brought me to an opinion, that I may sooner perchance be wanting to myself in not asking, than find your Majesty's goodness wanting to me in any my reasonable and modest desires. And therefore, perceiving how at this time preferments of the law fly about mine ears, to some above me and to some below me,[1] I did conceive your Majesty may think it rather a kind of dullness, or want of faith, than modesty, if I should not come with my pitcher to Jacob's well, as others do. Wherein I shall propound to your Majesty that which tendeth not so much to the raising of my fortune as to the settling of my mind : being sometimes assailed with this cogitation that, by reason of my slowness to see and apprehend occasions upon the sudden, keeping one course of painful service, I may *in fine dierum* be in danger to be neglected and forgotten.

"And, if that were so, then were it much better for me, now while I stand in your Majesty's good opinion (though unworthy) and have some little reputation in the world, to give over the course I am in, and to make proof to do you some honour by my pen—either by writing some faithful narrative of your happy but not untraduced times, or by recompiling your

[1] The Speaker of the last House of Commons had been rewarded with the Mastership of the Rolls ; and Sir Julius Cæsar had received a grant of the reversion of the office.

laws (which I perceive your Majesty laboureth with and hath in your head as Jupiter had Pallas), or by some other the like work—(for without some endeavour to do you honour I would not live)—than to spend my wits and time in this laborious place wherein I now serve, if it shall be deprived of those outward ornaments and inward comforts which it was wont to have in respect of an assured succession to some place [1] of more dignity and rest ; which seemeth to be an hope now altogether casual, if not wholly intercepted.

"Wherefore, not to hold your Majesty long, my humble suit to you is that which I think I should not without suit be put by, which is, that I may obtain your assurance to succeed (if I live) into the Attorney's place, whensoever it shall be void ; it being but the natural and immediate step and rise which the place I now hold hath ever in a sort made claim to, and almost never failed of.

"In this suit *I make no friends to your Majesty*,[2] *though your Majesty knoweth that I want not those which are near and assured*, but rely upon no other motive than your grace ; resting your Majesty's most humble subject and servant."

That he received the assurance he desired may be inferred from another letter written soon afterwards, during the Attorney's illness, in the summer or autumn of 1611 :—

"It may please your most excellent Majesty,

"I do understand by some of my good friends, to my great comfort, that your Majesty hath in mind your Majesty's royal promise (which to me is *anchora spei*) touching the Attorney's place. I hope Mr. Attorney shall do well. I thank God I wish no man's death ; nor much mine own life more than to do your Majesty service. For I account my life the accident and my duty the substance.

"But this I will be bold to say if it please God that I ever serve your Majesty in the Attorney's place, I have known an Attorney Cooke (Coke) and an Attorney Hubberd (Hobart), both worthy men and far above myself : but if I should not find a middle way between their two dispositions and carriage, I should not satisfy myself. But these things are far or near as it shall please God. Meanwhile I most humbly pray your Majesty accept my sacrifice of thanksgiving for your gracious favour. God preserve your Majesty. I ever remain. . . ."

The Attorney, however, recovered ; and although Bacon may have felt in secret that Salisbury gave him no effectual help, he nevertheless did not think it prudent to neglect his cousin and patron, to whom he protests unshaken devotion in the

---

[1] *i.e.* the Attorney's place.
[2] Meaning, that he would not employ the intercession of his cousin Cecil.

following New Year's letter (January, 1612). In his usual sympathetic style, writing to a man who was broken down with cares and infirmities, and fast nearing the grave, Bacon discovers that *he himself* also finds "age and decays" growing upon him :—

" It may please your good Lordship,
    " I would entreat the new year to answer for the old, in my humble thanks to your Lordship, both for many your favours, and chiefly that upon the occasion of Mr. Attorney's infirmity I found your Lordship even as I could wish. This doth increase a desire in me to express my thankful mind to your Lordship ; hoping that—*though I find age and decay grow upon me*—yet I may have a flash or two of spirit left to do you service. And I do protest before God, without compliment or any light vein of mind, that if I knew in what course of life to do you best service, I could take it, and make my thoughts, which now fly to many pieces, be reduced to that centre. But all this is no more than I am, which is not much, but yet the entire of him that is. . . ."

A pleasing instance of Bacon's familiar humorous style is afforded by the following letter to Sir Michael Hickes, Cecil's business man, a patient and friendly creditor of Bacon's, and seemingly a man of kindly, genial disposition. He was an old servant of Lord Burghley's, and Bacon appears to have had a genuine liking for him. It is a New Year's letter written on making restitution for a pair of scarlet stockings borrowed on some occasion of need either from Lady Hickes or her daughter :—

" To my very good friend Sir Michael Hickes, Knight,
    "SIR MICHAEL,
        " I do use as you know to pay my debts with time. But indeed if you will have a good and parfite colour in a carnation stocking, it must be long in the dyeing. I have some scruple of conscience whether it was my Lady's stockings or her daughter's, and I would have the restitution to be to the right person, else I shall not have absolution. Therefore I have sent to them both, desiring them to wear them for my sake, as I did wear theirs for mine own sake. So wishing you all a good new year, I rest,
                                        Yours assured
                                            FR. BACON."

§ 24 THE "COURT OF THE VERGE;" DEATH OF CECIL

About this time we have a glimpse of Bacon for the first time in a judicial position. Some complaints had been made that the Court of the Marshalsea, which had a special jurisdiction over the King's servants and over offences committed within the "verge" or precincts of the King's court, was in the habit of exceeding its limits ; and the disputes involved some doubtful questions. The King therefore decided, probably at Bacon's suggestion, to establish (8 June, 1611) a new Court by Patent, to be called the " Court of the Verge," in which Sir Francis Bacon was appointed a Judge. Accordingly it devolved upon him to open the new Court. On this occasion he delivered a magniloquent charge to the Grand Jury, which is almost redeemed from the accusation of being too courtier-like and obsequious by a kind of grandiose unction which gives us the impression that he really did mean a great deal of what he said. It is possible that the creation of this new Court was stimulated by the assassination of the French King (Henry IV.) in the previous year, and by the consequently increased anxiety of James to secure his own personal safety.

" You are to know and consider well the duty and service to which you are called, and whereupon you are, by your oath, charged. . . . This happy estate of the subject will turn to hurt and inconvenience, if those that hold that part which you are now to perform, shall be negligent and remiss in doing their duty. For (as of two evils) it were better men's doings were looked into overstrictly and severely, than that there should be a notorious impunity of malefactors ; as was well and wisely said of ancient times, a man were better live where nothing is lawful than where all things are lawful. . . . David saith (who was a king) *The wicked man shall not abide in my house;* as taking knowledge that it was impossible for kings to extend their care to banish wickedness over all their land or empire, but yet at least they ought to undertake to God for their house. We see further that the Law doth so esteem the dignity of the King's settled mansion-house, as it hath laid unto it a plot of twelve miles round (which we call the Verge) to be subject to a special and exempted jurisdiction depending upon his person and great officers. This is as a half-pace, or carpet, spread about the King's Chair of Estate, which therefore ought to be cleared and voided more than other places of the kingdom ; for if offences shall be shrouded under the King's wings, what hope is there of discipline and good justice in more remote parts ? We see the sun, when it is at the brightest ; there may be perhaps a bank of clouds in the North, or the West or remote regions, but near his body few or none : so where the King cometh, there should come peace and order and an awe and reverence in men's hearts."

Offences are divided into four classes, those that concern (1) God and his Church ; (2) the King and his Estate ; (3) the King's people (being capital) ; (4) the King's people (not being capital) :

" . . For contempts of our Church and service, they are comprehended in that known name,[1] Recusancy ; which offence hath many branches and dependencies. The wife-recusant, she tempts ; the church-papist, he feeds and relieves ;[2] the corrupt school-master, he soweth tares ; the dissembler, he conformeth and doth not communicate. Therefore, if any person, man or woman, wife or sole, above the age of sixteen years, not having some lawful excuse, have not repaired to church according to the several statutes, the one for the weekly, the other for the monthly repair, you are to present both the offence and the time how long. . . . And of these offences of Recusancy take you special regard. Twelve miles from Court is no region for such subjects. In the name of God, why should not twelve miles about the King's Chair be as free from Papist Recusants, as twelve miles from the city of Rome (the Pope's Chair) is from Protestants.

" . . For matter of division and breach of unity, it is not without a mystery that Christ's coat had no seam ; nor no more should the Church, if it were possible. Therefore if any minister refuse to use the book of Common Prayer, or wilfully swerveth in divine service from that book ; or if any person whatsoever do scandalise that book and speak openly and maliciously in derogation of it—such men do but make a rent in the garment and such are by you to be enquired of."

After touching on perjury and witchcraft, the Charge refers matters of Supremacy, Jesuits, and seminaries, to the second head, viz. offences against "the King and his Estate ;" under which he treats amply of them, and also includes prophecies.

" Lastly, because the vulgar people are sometimes led with vain and fond prophecies,[3] if any such shall be published to the end to move stirs or tumults, this is not felony, but punished by a year's imprisonment and loss of goods ; and of this also shall you enquire. You shall likewise understand that the escape of any prisoner committed for treason, is treason ; whereof you are likewise to enquire."

---

[1] The MS. is here corrupt.
[2] Meaning, I suppose, feeds and relieves the cause of Recusancy.
[3] *Essays*, xxxv. 67.

Under the third head, he is as severe as James himself could have desired against duelling.

" . . I must say unto you, in general, that life is grown too cheap in these times. It is set at the price of words, and every petty scorn or disgrace can have no other reparation. Nay, so many men's lives are taken away with impunity that the very life of the Law is almost taken away, which is the execution.[1] And therefore, though we cannot restore the life of those men that are slain, yet I pray let us restore the Law to her life by proceeding with due severity against the offenders. And most especially this plot of ground (which as I said is the King's carpet) ought not to be stained with blood, crying in the ears of God and the King."

Under the fourth head are included matters of force and outrage, fraud and deceit (as the use of false weights and measures), public nuisances and grievances, breach and inobservance of certain wholesome and politic laws ; and herein the Jury is to inquire concerning (1) the King's pleasure, (2) the people's food, wares, and manufactures.

" You shall therefore enquire of the unlawful taking partridges, and pheasants or fowl, the destruction of the eggs of the wild-fowl, the killing of hares or deer, and the selling of venison or hares ; for that which is for exercise and sport and courtesy, should not be turned to gluttony and sale victual.

" You shall also enquire whether bakers and brewers keep their assize,[2] and whether as well they as butchers, inn-holders and victuallers, do sell that which is wholesome, and at reasonable prices, and whether they do link and combine to raise prices.

" Lastly you shall enquire whether the good statute be observed whereby a man may have that he thinketh he hath, and not be abused or mis-served in that he buys : I mean that statute that requireth that none use any manual occupation but such as have been seven years apprentice to it. . . . There be many more things enquirable by you. . . . but those which I have gone through are the principal points of your charge, which to present you have taken the name of God to witness ; and in the name of God perform it."

The reader will perceive that the jurisdiction of the new court was to be very wide. That of the old court of the Marshalsea was limited in the twenty-eighth year of Edward I.,

---

[1] *Essays*, iv. 4.

[2] That is, keep "due measure," the word "assize" meaning "a fixed quantity or dimension" (Skeat, *Etymological Dictionary*.)

so that henceforth the Stewards and Marshals should hold plea " only of trespass done within the House and of other trespasses done within the Verge and of Contracts and Cove- nants *that one of the King's House shall have made with another of the same House, and in the same House and none otherwise.*" These words left room for doubt whether the authority of the court in matters of trespass was intended to include *all* trespasses within the Verge or only those of persons in the King's House; and the exclusive view was strengthened by the clause that thenceforth the Steward should "not take cognizance of debts *nor of other things but of people of the same House.*"

Upon this point an action was at this time pending; and, if it had come before Sir Edward Coke as one of the Common Law Judges, Bacon might well have reason to fear that the issue would have been unfavourable to the Marshalsea. Availing himself, therefore, of the right of the Prerogative (as then inter- preted) to erect a new Court of Record,[1] Bacon appears to have advised the King to get round, or override, the difficulty, by establishing this new Court with unmistakable jurisdiction over *all* trespasses, *whether committed by the King's servants or the King's subjects;* and by extending the word "trespass" to mean any offence tending to injure the King or the King's subjects generally. Thus quietly and unobtrusively did Bacon procure the establishment, in the King's interest, of a Court having a jurisdiction over almost all offences except breach of private contract, throughout a circle of twelve miles radius round the King's residence, for the time being.

A brief summary must suffice of another important paper written by Bacon at this time, entitled *Advice to the King touching Sutton's Estate.* Thomas Sutton, who died on the 12 December, 1611, had by his will endowed the Charterhouse with £8,000 a year for the sustenance of a hospital and school. The will had been disputed; and the possible heir-at-law had been bound over by the Council, "if he do evict the will, to stand to the King's award and arbitrement." Hereupon Bacon writes to the King protesting that to turn the Charterhouse, a

---

[1] See above, p. 139. As to Bacon's views on the King's "power to establish Courts of Equity," see Spedding, iii. 373.

palace fit for a prince,[1] into a hospital, is all one as if one should give in alms a rich embroidered cloak to a beggar. The master of the hospital, some great person, will take the sweet; the poor, the crumbs. If, therefore, the heir has a right, and if that right is submitted to the King, the three following changes are desirable :—First, instead of a hospital—a corporation of declared beggars, a cell of loiterers, cast serving-men and drunkards—let there be a beneficence that shall *prevent* beggary and ease hardworking honesty, viz., houses of relief and correction where disabled labourers can be relieved and sturdy beggars buckled to work. Secondly, instead of teachers for children (of whom there are already too many) raise up teachers for men by adding to the niggardly endowments of existing Chairs at the Universities. Thirdly, instead of a Preacher, establish a College of Controversies, a " Receipt (I like not the word Seminary ") for converts to the Reformed Religion, or for preachers in remote and superstitious corners of the realm." Thus, " that mass of wealth that was in the owner little better than a stack or heap of muck may be spread over your kingdom to many fruitful purposes." [2]

Cecil's health had been for some time failing, and his death (4 May, 1612) deprived Bacon of a patron to whom he had faithfully, or perhaps we should say closely, adhered for fourteen years, and to whom his letters express an entire devotion. It was impossible that the two cousins could ever have cordially co-operated. Cecil, a man of systematic, orderly, and accurate mind, without a spark of genius or originality, could not but regard Bacon as a mere visionary, versatile student, whose law was to be distrusted, and whose statesmanship was unworthy of serious consideration. To Bacon Cecil appeared a mere man of detail, a broker and accountant in finance ; a man in whom cunning served as a substitute for wisdom ; one who, having no merit himself, deliberately suppressed the merit of others. It speaks much for the self-control of the younger cousin that for so long a period he so assiduously cultivated his senior and

---

[1] From a letter of Chamberlain's (18 December, 1611) we find that there had been a rumour that Sutton intended to leave it to the Prince : " He hath left £8,000 lands a year to his College or Hospital at the Charterhouse (which is not bestowed on the Prince as was given out)."

[2] Compare *Essays*, xv. 153, "Money is like *muck*, not good except it be spread."

more powerful relative. Even in the years in which he has
" no leisure " to write to Essex, and not long before the Earl
complained of his " silence in his vocations," Bacon finds time
to write to Sir Robert Cecil a letter " empty of matter, but
out of the fullness of my love," to signify " my continual and
incessant love for you, thirsting for your return," followed
by another in which he addresses his cousin as another self :
" I write to myself, in regard of my love to you, you being
as near to me in heart's blood as in blood of descent." When
he is insulted by Coke (1601) it is to Cecil that he complains,
as to " one that I have ever found careful of my advancement
and yet more jealous of my wrongs ; " and just before the
Queen's death (1603) he fears that his superabundant affection
for his great kinsman may make him almost intrusive : " If it
seem any error for me thus to intromit myself, I pray your lordship to remember I ever loved her Majesty and the State, and
now love yourself ; and there is never any vehement love without some absurdity ; " while at the same time he begs that
Cecil's private secretary will " let him [Cecil] know that he is the
personage in the State which I love most." Cecil is his refuge
when he is twice arrested for debt, first in 1598 and again in
1603 ; Cecil is his intercessor when he desires the honour of
knighthood ; and in the *Commentarius Solutus* (1608) Cecil appears as a generous lender of money *sine die* and without interest. His continuous kindness extorts from Bacon (forgetful
for once of the wise " precept of Bias," never to love a friend to
such a degree as not to remember that he may become your
enemy) the rash expression " I cannot forget your Lordship, *dum
memor ipse mei.*"

The sincerity of Bacon's belief that he was forwarding his own
interests in supporting Cecil appears from private entries in the
Commentarius.

" To insinuate myself to become privy to my Lord of Salisbury's estate.
To correspond [1] with Salisbury in a habit of natural but no way's perilous
boldness, and in vivacity, invention, care, to cast and enterprise ; but with
due caution ; for this manner I judge both in his nature freeth the
stonds,[2] and in his ends pleaseth him best and promiseth him most use of me."

---

[1] That is " to conform to."
[2] *i.e.*, " impediments." Compare *Essays*, 1. 39. " There is no *stond* or
impediment in the wit, but may be wrought out by fit studies."

He assures his patron (1608) that he esteems whatsoever he has or may have in this world but as trash—

"In comparison of having the honour and happiness to be a near and well-accepted kinsman to so rare and worthy a counsellor, governor, or patriot. For having been a studious, if not curious observer, as well of antiquities of virtue as of late pieces, I forbear to say to your Lordship what I find or conceive."

And in the year 1611, not long before his cousin's death, he writes this last protest of allegiance :—

"I do protest before God, without compliment, that if I knew in what course of life to do you best service, I would take it, and make my thoughts, which now fly to many pieces, be reduced to that centre."

These words he writes thanking Cecil for his promises of help, "upon the occasion of Mr. Attorney's infirmity ; " and they seem to imply that, if Cecil would hereafter secure his promotion to the Attorney's place, Bacon would give up philosophy and every other distraction that might prevent him from devoting his whole life to his patron's service.

But on 24 May, 1612 Salisbury died; and in less than a week afterwards, on 31 May, Bacon, offering his services in his cousin's place, writes of him thus to the King.

"He was a fit man to keep things from growing worse,[1] but no very fit man to reduce things to be much better ; for he loved to keep the eyes of all Israel a little too much upon himself, . . . and, though he had fine passages of action, yet the real conclusions came slowly on." [2]

Elsewhere he writes that " my Lord of Salisbury had a good method, if his means had been upright; " and, in less than four months after his death (18 Sept.), he can congratulate the King upon his deliverance from the incapable counsellor who had planned and mismanaged the Great Contract :

"To have your wants and necessities in particular, as it were hanged up in two tablets before the eyes of your Lords and Commons, to be talked of for four months together ; to stir a number of projects and then blast them and leave your Majesty nothing but the scandal of them ; to pretend even carriage between your Majesty's rights and the ease of the people, and to satisfy neither—these courses and others the like, I hope, are gone with the deviser of them."

---

[1] Comp. *Essays*, xix. 45.　　　　　　　　　[2] *Ib.* xxii. 124.

Then follow these words, which are cancelled in the MS., and which therefore (it is to be presumed) he did not send to the King; but that he should have even thought of sending them is sufficiently remarkable :—

"I protest to God, though I be not superstitious, when I saw your Majesty's book against Vorstius and Arminius, and noted your zeal to deliver the Majesty of God from the vain and indign comprehension of heresy and degenerate philosophy. . . . *perculsit ilico animum* that God would set shortly upon you some visible favour ; and let me not live if I thought not of the taking away of that man."

Two or three months later appeared the second edition of the *Essays*, commenting on which—only seven months after the decease of "so rare and worthy a counsellor, governor and patriot"—Chamberlain writes as follows : "Sir Francis Bacon has set out new Essays; where (in a chapter of Deformity)," *Essay* xliv. "the world takes notice that he paints out his little cousin to the life."

§ 25 BACON SUING FOR PROMOTION

From 1608 to 1620 Bacon seems to have spent such leisure as he could snatch from business in revising the *Novum Organum*. But the disadvantages under which he pursued his great wish are well illustrated by a brief treatise on the Intellectual Sphere (*Descriptio Globi Intellectualis*) written in 1612. Beginning with a division of the provinces of the world of knowledge, it speedily passes into a detailed account of astronomy ; a subject to which his attention may not improbably have been directed by Galileo's invention of the telescope and the discovery of Jupiter's satellites (May 1609—January 1610). But the work of a Solicitor-General desiring and scheming to be Attorney-General was not favourable for scientific study. In the *Thema Coeli* (which is the second part of the *Descriptio*) he constructs a theory of the Universe in which he denies the density and solidity of the moon, as well as the revolution of the earth. True, he admits that his own theory resembles all existing theories in being hypothetical; but in reality he had not given the subject even that decent degree of attention which would have justified him in forming a hypothesis on it.

The researches of Kepler, published in 1609 and known in

England at least as early as 1610, are left unnoticed by Bacon in 1612; and he speaks briefly and unappreciatively of those famous discoveries of Galileo concerning which, two years before, the able mathematician Harriot had written, "Methinks my diligent Galileus hath done more in his threefold discovery than Magellane in opening the straits to the South Sea." Harriot indeed might have said of the Solicitor's speculations in this direction what Harvey said of the Lord Chancellor's physiology, that he wrote astronomy like a Solicitor-General—or, still worse, like a Solicitor-General aspiring to be Attorney-General. Yet such as it is, this little quasi-astronomical attempt, with its Appendix, is almost the only literary work (besides the revision of the *Novum Organum*) for which Bacon will find leisure during the next eight years.[1]

Bacon's determination to obtain promotion in his profession may naturally have turned his attention to the duties of a judge and may have induced him to include that subject among the *Essays* published in 1612. The Essay on *Judicature* breathes a spirit of loyalty and almost of subservience, which might well commend the aspiring lawyer to the King. Besides many admirable remarks on the mischief that may be wrought by a judge who is unjust, dilatory, impatient, or avaricious, he speaks emphatically on the necessity of consultation between the judges and the Sovereign. In accordance with old custom judges were sometimes consulted by the King before, or during, a trial in which the interests of the Government were affected. But already in the time of Sir Thomas More the custom, or the abuse of it, seems to have been considered irregular; for the author of *Utopia*[2] protests against those who give the King counsel "to endaunger unto his grace the judges of the Realme, that he maye haue them euer on his side, and that they may in euerye matter despute and reason for the kynges right. Yea, and further, to call them into his palace and to require them there to argue and discusse his matters in his owne presence." But Bacon sees none of the dangers seen by Sir Thomas More. He desires to extend, not to curtail, the royal control over the judges. No one contended that, where individual interests were

---

[1] The *New Atlantis* (see § 58) was written before 1614.
[2] Arber's reprint, p. 60.

concerned, the Crown had any right to interfere with the ordinary course of justice; but the Solicitor-General, in his essay on *Judicature*, acutely suggests that cases affecting individuals (" *meum* and *tuum* ") may indirectly affect the State, and therefore be liable to State interference.

" It is a happy thing in a State when Kings and States [1] do often consult with judges, and again when judges do often consult with the King and State. . . . For many times, the thing deduced to judgment may be *meum et tuum* when the reason and consequence thereof may trench to point of Estate." [2]

After Bacon's promotion, we shall in due course see a practical application of this theory concerning the fitness of consultation between King and judges.   Meantime, he is merely an expectant ; but with prospects greatly improved by the death of Salisbury.   But it naturally occurred to him that the path of influence and power might now be more open and rapid through the King's Privy Council than through the routine of legal promotion.   Salisbury's death had vacated the place of Secretary as well as that of Treasurer.   Elizabethan traditions had passed away with Cecil, and there was room for a new man and new notions at the Council board. And new notions were sadly needed. The total result of Salisbury's financial policy (as shaped or thwarted by the King) had been to halve the debt at the cost of almost doubling the annual deficiency.   The debt was now £500,000 ; the annual deficiency £160,000. The Great Contract had failed ; the constitutional problems put forward in the last session all remained unsolved ; the House of Commons had entered new paths of jealousy and suspicion. For all reasons the King needed a new Councillor, one who should be in fact his Prime Minister ; and that *he* was the man, selected at once by circumstances and by natural fitness for this position, Bacon never for a moment questioned. His only doubt was as to the wording and expression of the delicate offer which he desired to make to the King.   Here is his first rough draft ; partly written (for privacy's sake) *in Greek characters*, after his mother's fashion.

[1] That is, I suppose " governments." The Latin translation has " status."
[2] *Essays*, lvi. 122-130.

"The Beginning of a Letter to the King, immediately after my
Lord Treasurer's Decease.[1]

May 29, 1612.

"It may please your Majesty,

"If I shall seem in these few lines to write *majora quam pro fortuna*,
it may please your Majesty to take it to be an effect not of presumption
but of affection. For of the one I was never noted ; and for the other I
could never shew it hitherto to the full ; having been as a hawk tied to
another's fist,[2] that mought sometimes bate [3] and proffer, but could never
fly. And therefore if—as it was said to one that spoke great words,
Amice, verba tua desiderant civitatem—so your Majesty say to me, 'Bacon,
your words require a place to speak them,' I must answer that place, or
not place, is in your Majesty to add or refrain : and, though I never go
higher but to Heaven, yet your Majesty. . . ."

Here the letter breaks off, and two days afterwards (31 May)
he tried again, in a second draft, much less egotistical, more
biblically adapted to the King's style, and more calculated to be
persuasive by putting the King's needs in the fore-front :

"31 May : Letter to the King, immediately after the Lord
Treasurer's Death.

"It may please your excellent Majesty,

"I cannot but endeavour to merit, considering your preventing graces,
which is the occasion of these few lines.

"Your Majesty hath lost a great subject and a great servant. But if I
should praise him in propriety, I should say that he was a fit man to keep
things from growing worse, but no very fit man to reduce things to be
much better. For he loved to have the eyes of all Israel a little too much
upon himself, and to have all business still under the hammer, and like
clay in the hands of the potter, to mould it as he thought good ; so that he
was more *in operatione* than *in opere*. And though he had fine passages of
action, yet the real conclusions came slowly on. So that although your
Majesty hath grave counsellors and worthy persons left, yet you do as it
were turn a leaf, wherein if your Majesty shall give a frame and constitution
to matters, before you place the persons, in my simple opinion it were not
amiss. But the great matter and most instant for the present, is the consideration of a Parl:ament, for two effects : the one for the supply of your
estate, the other for the better knitting of the hearts of your subjects unto

---

[1] Cecil died on 24 May, so that this letter was written five days afterwards.
[2] Cecil's.
[3] *i.e.* beat (*battre*) or flutter its wings.
[4] Compare the expression in the Prayer-book, "that thy *grace* may always
prevent and follow us." Bacon is fond of applying the language of religious
prayer to the King ; see p.103.

your Majesty, according to your infinite merit ; for both which, Parliaments have been and are the antient and honourable remedy.

" Now because I take myself to have a little skill in that region, as one that ever affected that your Majesty mought in all your causes not only prevail, but prevail with satisfaction of the inner man ; and though no man can say but I was a perfect and peremptory royalist, yet every man makes me believe that I was never one hour out of credit with the lower house ; my desire is to know, whether your Majesty will give me leave to meditate and propound unto you some preparative remembrances touching the future Parliament.

" Your Majesty may truly perceive that, though I cannot challenge to myself either invention, or judgment, or elocution, or method, or any of those powers,[1] yet my offering is care and observance : and as my good old Mistress was wont to call me her watch-candle, because it pleased her to say I did continually burn (and yet she suffered me to waste almost to nothing) so I must much more owe the like duty to your Majesty, by whom my fortunes have been settled and raised.   And so, craving pardon, I rest

Your Majesty's most humble servant devote,

F. B."

The epigram on his cousin, contained in the first sentence of the above letter, is contained in the *Apophthegms* as being *spoken* to the King.   Possibly it was ; and nothing but some very outspoken condemnation of Cecil on the King's part can have encouraged Bacon to adopt towards the deceased Lord Treasurer the virulent tone which characterises the next letter. But he speaks as he feels.   Bitterness, suppressed for years while suppression was expedient, breaks out from the very heart of the courtier, now that the King is bitter too, and bitterness pays.

" My principal end being to do your Majesty service, I crave leave to make at this time to your Majesty this most humble oblation of myself. I may truly say with the psalm, *Multum incola fuit anima mea ;* for my life hath been conversant in things wherein I take little pleasure.   Your Majesty may have heard somewhat that my father was an honest man, and somewhat you may have seen of myself, though not to make any true judgment by, because I have hitherto had only *potestatem verborum,* nor

---

[1] Compare Cicero's famous saying, " Si quid est in me ingenii, judices, quod sentio quam sit exiguum," and *Julius Cæsar,* iii. 2, 225–6, the speech of Antony :

" For I have neither wit, nor words, nor worth,
Action, nor utterance, nor the power of speech
To stir men's blood : I only speak right on,"

that neither. I was three of my young years bred with an ambassador in France ; and since, I have been an old truant in the school-house of your council-chamber, though on the second form ; yet longer than any that now sitteth hath been upon the head form. If your Majesty find any aptness in me, or if you find any scarcity in others, whereby you may think it fit for your service to remove me to business of State ; although I have a fair way before me for profit (and by your Majesty's grace and favour for honour and advancement), and in a course less exposed to the blasts of fortune, yet now that he is gone, *quo vivente virtutibus certissimum exitium*, I will be ready as a chessman to be wherever your Majesty's royal hand shall set me. Your Majesty will bear me witness, I have not suddenly opened myself thus far. I have looked upon others, I see the exceptions,[1] I see the distractions, and I fear Tacitus will be a prophet, *magis alii homines quam alii mores.* I know mine own heart, and I know not whether God that hath touched my heart with the affection may not touch your royal heart to discern it. Howsoever, I shall at least go on honestly in mine ordinary course, and supply the rest in prayers for you, remaining . . . ."[2]

None of these applications succeeded. If Bacon had come into power, he would have advised (as he implies in his second letter) the calling of Parliament ; and this course was distasteful to the King and still more to some of the great persons about him. For the present therefore Bacon was left without promotion ; but the King appears now to have accepted counsel more freely from him, and from the time of Salisbury's death his political correspondence becomes more ample and important.

§ 26 TRIAL OF LORD SANQUHAR ; BACON BECOMES ATTORNEY-GENERAL

A short speech delivered about this time by Bacon at the conclusion of a trial for murder is too characteristic to be passed over. A certain Lord Sanquhar, having had one of his eyes struck out accidentally by a fencing master named Turner, determined, five years afterwards, to be revenged, and returned to England from his continental travels with this intention. Finding that he could not himself safely kill Turner, he intrusted

---

[1] *i.e.* " objections."

[2] He had at first written (but with true tact suppressed) "and I wish to God your M. case were not to require extraordinary affection, for of ability I cannot speak. Sending my best prayers, I rest," &c.

the business to two friends, while he retired to the Continent to
avoid suspicion. When his friends failed him, he again came
to England and induced two of his servants to do the business;
and by one of these Turner was shot, while drinking with his
murderer. Sanquhar at first maintained his innocence, but the
arrest and evidence of the murderer and his accomplice made it
hopeless to persist in denials ; and at last he confessed everything. It is not easy to conceive a murder more cold-blooded
and dastardly than this; but Sanquhar was a nobleman and a
Scotchman, with powerful friends at Court ; and therefore Bacon
begins by commending the criminal's " Christian and penitent
course," admitting that "though it be foul spilling of blood, yet
there are more foul." After dilating upon the justice and power
of the King, he concludes thus :

" Lastly, I will conclude towards you, my Lord, that though your offence
hath been great, yet your confession hath been free, and your behaviour
and speech full of discretion ; and this shews that, though you could not
resist the tempter, yet you bear a Christian and generous spirit, answerable
to the noble family of which you are descended. This I commend in you,
and take it to be an assured token of God's mercy and favour, in respect
whereof all worldly things are but trash ; and so it is fit for you, as your
state now is, to account them. And this is all I will say for the present."

Language admirably adapted, this, to gratify the " chief Lords,"
who, as Chamberlain tells us, were suitors to the King for
Sanquhar's life ! But to the credit of James be it recorded
that their intercession was unsuccessful ; and Lord Sanquhar
was hanged (29 June, 1612) in front of the great gate of
Westminster Hall.

By the death of Cecil the lucrative position of the Mastership
of the Wards was vacated. The prerogative of Wardship being,
at this time, a popular grievance, it was considered desirable to
retrench the profits of the Mastership and to entrust it to some
man who could be content with the curtailed office. Bacon drew up
a paper of suggestions for the reform of the office, and it obtained
the royal approval : but, as he said, it was a case of *sic vos non
vobis*; he laboured for another. " The King," writes Chamberlain on 11 June, 1612, " saith he will make trial if a meaner
man cannot perform it as well as a great ; . . . . it is thought it

will light on Sir Francis Bacon." It lighted elsewhere; but this remark of Chamberlain's shows that Bacon was now considered to be winning favour with the King.

The place at the Council Board left vacant by Cecil was at this time partially filled by Henry Howard, Earl of Northampton, Lord Privy Seal, a great artist with his pen, according to the fashionable taste of the day, but a man of no principle, who had secured the support of Rochester by the marriage of the latter with his niece, the notorious Countess of Essex, whose divorce from Essex Northampton had supported. He was a concealed Romanist, a pensioner of Spain, and a hater of parliaments. To him Bacon now attempted to commend himself by his efforts for the King's finances. The Council was just now busy with the collection of an "Aid," due by ancient custom on the marriage of the King's eldest daughter. The last Aid had been collected two years before, when the Prince Henry had been knighted; and the Attorney-General had done the work under the supervision of Salisbury. Now therefore, mindful of his rule to "win credit comparate to the Attorney"—Bacon contrives to persuade Northampton that he could improve on the old arrangement; and accordingly Northampton (3 August) writes as follows to the King's Favourite, Rochester:

"Mr. Solicitor this day was ready to have informed the Board touching his own industry and care in drawing the matter of the Aid for the marriage of her Grace and the circumstances that belong to it, *in some better form and method than was used at the creation of the Prince.*"

Before calling another Parliament, a commission had been appointed to ascertain whether the deficit might not be met or diminished by the income from the Crown lands, more economically managed; and the King appears to have specially commended this question to Bacon's attention. Accordingly (17 September 1612) he writes to the King declaring that, besides the joint account which he, in company with the other sub-commissioners, will be prepared to give to the Lords, he hopes to be able to give his Majesty *somewhat ex proprio,* delicately suggesting that he can give the King information "not fit to be communicated to all those with whom I am joined." He is ready to give an account of the project for converting the lands into rents, but he warns the King not to expect everything from one remedy, nor to expect much at once :

"Generally upon this subject of the repair of your Majesty's means, I beseech your Majesty to give me leave to make this judgment : that your Majesty's recovery must be by the medicines of the Galenists and Arabians, and not of the Chemists and Paracelsians. For it will not be wrought by any one fine extract or strong water, but by a skilful compound of a number of ingredients, and those by just weight and proportion ; and that, of some simples which perhaps, of themselves or in over great quantity, were little better than poisons ; but, mixed and broken, and in just quantity, are full of virtue. And secondly, that as your Majesty's growing behindhand hath been the work of time, so must likewise your Majesty's coming forth and making even. Not but I wish it were by all good and fit means accelerated, but that I foresee that, if your Majesty shall propound to yourself to do it *per saltum*, it can hardly be without accidents of prejudice to your honour, safety, or profit."

In this advice we recognise the cautious language of one who conceives that he is, or may soon become, a responsible adviser. He is anxious that the King shall not expect too much, or too soon ; or neglect many right remedies, by thinking none needful but one. And he not obscurely hints that some indirect methods, wrong if carried into excess, but right in moderation, may be at this time expedient ; perhaps preparing the way (if only he could have had his own way) for a policy that shall savour of " popularity," concession, dissimulation of the royal necessities, private negotiations with influential members of the House of Commons, and above all—the policy most unpalatable to James —wars or rumours of war with external enemies.

The next two or three paragraphs contain far more doubtful advice—addressed as it is to a Sovereign incapable of economy and unable to refuse anything to those about him. The King is not to trouble himself if he is in debt :

" Lastly, I will make two prayers unto your Majesty, as I use to do to God Almighty when I commend to him his glory and cause ; so I will pray to your Majesty for yourself.

" The one is, that these cogitations of want do not anyways trouble or vex your Majesty's mind. I remember Moses saith of the land of Promise, that it was not like the land of Egypt that was watered with a river, but was watered with showers from heaven ; whereby I gather God preferreth sometimes certain uncertainties before certainties, because they teach a more immediate dependence upon his providence. Sure I am *nil novi accidit nobis.* It is no new thing for the greatest kings to be in debt ; and if a man shall *parvis componere magna,* I have seen an Earl of Leicester, a Chancellor Hatton, an Earl of Essex, and an Earl of Salisbury all in debt ; and yet was it no manner of diminution to their power or greatness."

All this time the reader may have been waiting for some exposition of the remedies by which Bacon hopes to meet the present necessities. But he will wait in vain. There is nothing beyond a furious attack upon the policy of Cecil which Bacon had hitherto publicly supported, and (as we know from the *Commentarius Solutus* [1]) privately approved :

> " My second prayer is that your Majesty, in respect of the hasty freeing of your State, would not descend to any means, or degree of means, which carrieth not a symmetry with your majesty and greatness. He is gone from whom those courses did wholly flow. To have your wants and necessities, in particular, as it were hanged up in two tablets before the eyes of your Lords and Commons, to be talked of for four months together : To have all your courses to help yourself in revenue or profit put into printed books, which were wont to be held *arcana imperii :* To have such worms of Aldermen to lend for ten in the hundred upon good assurance, . . . as if it should save the bark of your fortune : To contract still where mought be had the readiest payment and not the best bargain : To stir a number of projects for your profit, and then to blast them and leave your Majesty nothing but the scandal of them : To pretend even carriage between your Majesty's rights and the ease of the people and to satisfy neither—these courses and the like I hope are gone with the deviser of them : which have turned your Majesty to inestimable prejudice."

The letter concludes with protests that the writer is not moved by meddlesomeness or interested motives : his " state is now free from all difficulties " and he has other interests and occupation in his " large field of contemplations." He is entirely moved by " love and affection."

In a letter from the Lord Chancellor and Northampton to the King (11 October, 1612) honourable mention is made of his " two faithful and painful servants " the Solicitor and the Serjeant for their industry in digesting masses of evidence relating to the customs, from which it was sought to draw increased profits ; and a few days later (20 October) Northampton is found, at Bacon's special request, urging the Favourite (Rochester) to

---

[1] See above, p. 116.

send a few lines indicating that the King was satisfied with the Solicitor's zeal :

> "I beseech you to move the King that in your next private letter to me you may give some touch of his Majesty's gracious acceptance of the diligence and industry of the Solicitor. . . . *I am put in trust with the care of laying open of this point;* and, therefore, for a testimony of my discharge and an argument of his Majesty's gracious acceptance of the party's endeavour, *a character under your hand which I may shew to himself only will be authentical."*

This is the first instance of Bacon's endeavouring to gain the good will of Rochester. A few days afterwards, on the death of the recently appointed Master of the Wards, he made a direct application (13 November, 1612) to the Favourite in a short straightforward letter, that he might succeed to the vacancy. This time he felt certain of success; for, says the commonplace book of Dr. Rawley, his chaplain—"Sir Francis Bacon, certainly expecting the place, had put most of his men into new cloaks. Afterward, when Sir Walter Cope carried the place, one said merrily that Sir Walter was Master of the Wards and Sir Francis Bacon of the Liveries." However, the failure did not elicit any signs of discontent or fretfulness from the Solicitor-General, whom we find next year (June 1613) vigorously engaged in the congenial task of defending the Prerogative.

In an attempt to resist the action of a commission instituted to reform some abuses in the navy, James Whitelocke, a barrister,[1] had maintained, while pleading for his client, "that the King cannot by commission, nor by his own person, meddle with the body, goods, or lands of his subjects, but only by indictment, arraignment and trial, or by legal proceedings in his ordinary Courts of Justice." This opinion was attacked on the ground that it tended to "overthrow the King's martial power and the authority of the Council Table, and the force of his Majesty's Proclamation, and other actions and directions of State and Policy applied to the necessity of times and occasions which fall not within the remedies of ordinary justice, nor cannot be tied to the formalities of a legal proceeding *propter tarda legum auxilia."* [2] The notes of Bacon's speech show that he

---

[1] Afterwards appointed Chief Justice of Chester.

[2] These words are extracted from the summary report of the proceedings which does not distinguish the speeches of the different counsel.

laid stress upon his usual distinction between "matters of *meum* and *tuum*," and "matters of State." It was part of his policy for preparing the way for an ideal Monarchy, to bring it about that the King "should be able to command respect by some means of inflicting punishment on those who resisted his authority, more certain than an appeal to the juries in the Courts of Law." [1]

"I make a great difference between the King's grants and ordinary commissions of justice, and the King's high commissions of regiment, or mixed with causes of State.

"For the former, there is no doubt but they may be freely questioned and disputed, and any defect in matter or form stood upon, though the King be many times the adverse party.

"But for the latter sort, they are rather to be dealt with (if at all) by a modest and humble intimation or remonstrance to his Majesty and Council than by bravery of dispute or peremptory opposition."

Whitelocke is said to have made "a full and unreserved submission;" but a book, now lost, in which he gave his own account of the matter is said to have contained a note "which was his own and which was Sir Francis Bacon's addition." [2] "These proceedings," says Professor Gardiner, "are of no small importance in the history of the English Revolution. They drew forth a declaration from the Privy Council, against which the Judges made no protest, to the effect that, if it could be shown that a political question were involved in a case, it was an offence even to question the legality of the exercise of judicial powers by persons appointed by the Crown to act without the intervention of a jury." [3] If this principle could be established, the Government might easily make itself independent of juries in all political trials; and to establish it Bacon in no small measure contributed.

Amid such labours, the Solicitor-General was now on the point of receiving promotion. The death of the Chief Justice of the King's Bench took place in August, 1613; and the King, by Bacon's advice, transferred his enemy, Coke, from the Court of Common Pleas to the vacancy; promoted Hobart, the Attorney, to Coke's place; and made Bacon Attorney-General. The reasons

---

[1] Gardiner, *History*, ii. 192.   [2] Spedding, iv. 357.
[3] *History*, Vol. ii., p. 191.

alleged by Bacon for these changes were, first, that " the removal
of my Lord Coke to a place of less profit (though it be with his
will) yet will be thought abroad a kind of discipline to him for
opposing himself in the King's causes ; " secondly, the present
Attorney, a man timid and scrupulous, only fit for the late
Lord Treasurer's (Cecil's) bent (which was to do little with
much formality and protestation,[1] " sorteth not with his present
place."

On 27 October, 1613, Coke, loth to lose a part of his income
and still more loth to leave the Common Pleas, parted dolefully
from the Court, " not only weeping himself but followed with
the tears of the Bench and most of the officers of the court ; "
and on the following day Bacon received his long-sought office.
" A full heart," writes the new Attorney to the King, " is like a
full pen, it can hardly make any distinguished [2] work. . . . I shall
take to me in this procuration, not Martha's part to be busied in
many things, but Mary's part "—the very same advice and by
the same Biblical contrast, which he had addressed years ago to
poor unheeding Essex [3]—" which is to intend your service." It
is not surprising that many began to dread the rise of a lawyer
who, though he professed, and truly, to have never yet been
a day out of credit with the Lower House, nevertheless pro-
claimed himself a " peremptory Royalist." His doctrine that
matters of *meum* and *tuum* might trench on matters of State,
and might therefore require reference to the Sovereign from the
ordinary Courts, was evidently capable of being made the basis
for encroachments on liberty. " There is a strong apprehension,"
writes Chamberlain, " that little good is to be expected by this
change, and that Bacon may prove a dangerous instrument."

We have seen that Bacon had recently attempted to gain the
favour of the favourite Rochester, partly through the Earl of
Northampton and partly by a direct appeal. Two years afterwards he disclaimed any obligation to Rochester (created in
November, 1613, Earl of Somerset). " When I moved your
Majesty for the Attorney's place, it was your sole act ; more than
that Somerset, when he knew your Majesty had resolved it,

[1] *Essays*, xxvi. 7.

[2] *i.e.* it blurs everything that it attempts to express.

[3] " I said to your Lordship last time, *Martha, Martha, attendis ad plurima,*
unum sufficit : win the Queen " (5 Oct. 1596), Spedding, ii. 40.

thrust himself into the business for a fee." Though the promotion may have been the King's "sole act," Bacon probably
knew pretty well that Rochester's favour was a necessary condition; and he recognised the obligation by supplying, at his
own expense, a sumptuous masque, played by the gentlemen of
Gray's Inn in honour of the marriage of the favourite with
Lady Frances Howard, the divorced wife of the Earl of Essex.
"Sir Francis Bacon," writes Chamberlain, "prepares a masque
to honour this marriage, which will stand him in above £2,000.
And though he have been offered some help by the House, and
specially by Mr. Solicitor, Sir Henry Yelverton, who would have
sent him £500—yet he would not accept it, but offers them the
whole charge with the honour.   Marry, his obligations are such
as well to his Majesty as to the great Lord [Somerset] and to
the whole house of Howards, as he can admit no partner."

One of the first duties of the new Attorney was to deliver a
charge on duelling before the Star Chamber.[1] This evil had
recently grown to a great height :—" The many private quarrels
among great men," says Chamberlain, "prognosticate troubled
humours ; " and he enumerates a number of pairs of noble com-
batants who had gone, or were going, to settle their differences
on the Continent.   Accordingly Bacon had urged the King to
put forth a "grave and severe proclamation," fining and
banishing from the royal presence any one who should send,
carry, or accept a challenge.   He supports his condemnation of
the practice by the fine saying of Consalvo, "the great and famous
commander, who was wont to say that a gentleman's honour
should be *de tela crassiore*, of a good strong warp or web that every
little thing should not catch in it.[2] . . . A man's life is not to be
trifled away ; it is to be offered up and sacrificed to honourable
services, public merits, good causes, and noble adventures."   Yet
there is something cold and unemotional, unnaturally cold even
for a dispassionate philosopher, in Bacon's commendation of the
insensibility of the great men of Greece and Rome to "words
of reproach and contumely (whereof the lie was esteemed
none) ; " so that "no man took himself fouled by them, but
took them but for breath and the stile of an enemy, and either
despised them or returned them ; but no blood spilt about them."

---

[1] Spedding, iv. 399-416.   [2] *Essays*, lviii. 40.

Before the forthcoming meeting of Parliament, Bacon was again engaged before the Star Chamber in prosecuting one Talbot, who had refused to repudiate the doctrine of Zuares concerning the duty of Catholic subjects towards heretical kings. In the execution of this task he delivered a speech in which he exhibits his usual detestation of the Church of Rome as being the head-quarters of those "Roman soldiers" who "do either thrust the spear into the sides of God's anointed or at least crown them with thorns." As for Professor Zuares himself, the Attorney can despise "a fellow that thinks with his magistrality and goose-quill to give laws and manages[1] to crowns and sceptres;" but abhorrence, not contempt, is due to a superstition through which Henry III., in the face of his army, was stabbed by a wretched Jacobin friar;[2] Henry IV. likewise was "stiletted by a rascal votary;" Queen Elizabeth oftentimes "attempted by like votaries;" and "our excellent Sovereign King James, the sweetness and clemency of whose nature were enough to quench and mortify all malignity (in the chair of majesty, his vine and olive branches about him) attended by his nobles and the third estate in Parliament, ready in the twinkling of an eye, as if it had been a particular doom's day, to have been brought to ashes dispersed to the four winds."

But from these contests in the Law Courts we must now turn to the great impending struggle between King and Commons to be fought in the approaching Parliament; and so we pass from Bacon the Attorney-General to Bacon the King's Counsellor.

§ 27 THE POLICY " È GEMINO "

We have now to see an attempt to give practical effect to Bacon's *policy è gem.*—as he was in the habit of calling it—in other words, the policy of filling the King's coffers and at the same time contenting the people. Our view of this practical application of his theory may help us to some additional insight into the theory itself, which at present is probably not very clear to the reader. The problem was definite enough, being simply this, to reconcile and harmonise a king who claims the right of

---

[1] *i.e.* "curbs."   [2] *Essays*, xxxix. 13.

imposing taxes on merchandise at his own pleasure, and a House of Commons which protests against that right. Upon the decision of this question depended the possession of ultimate supremacy in the State. If the King could "impose" at his will, then the Commons had already little practical power over the national purse, and consequently little security for the redress of grievances; and when an increasing commerce increased the amount resulting from the "Impositions," the King might very soon become altogether independent of subsidies, and the Commons might lose every vestige of power. On the other hand, if the King had not the right of "imposing," he was dependent upon the contributions of the Commons, and consequently ultimately dependent upon their good-will.

The state of the royal exchequer cried for some prompt remedy. The Sub-Committee, appointed to investigate the finances, had proposed curtailments and improvements; but the adoption of their plans resulted in little benefit. The King could not pay even his most pressing debts. Ambassadors without allowances, sailors without pay, fortifications on the coast falling into decay, liabilities to the amount of £680,000, a probable standing deficit of £200,000 a year—all this was beyond a Sub-Committee, beyond any Imposition except such as would have raised an insurrection, beyond all remedy except such as could be supplied by Parliament. Northampton and his friends, who hated the very name of the House of Commons, were forced at last to give way; but it was not till 16 February, 1614, that the Council resolved to recommend that a Parliament should be summoned.

We are fortunate in possessing two papers clearly setting forth Bacon's reasons for recommending that a Parliament should be called: the first, a paper of private notes; the second (based upon the first), a letter addressed to the King.

The private paper consists of two sections: the former, dealing with the reasons for attempting to obtain the desired result from a Parliament and from no other source; the latter, dealing with the means by which a good result might be secured. Under the first heading he states that Parliament is the ordinary remedy; that the avoidance and implied distrust of Parliaments weaken the King in the eyes of foreigners; that the opposition in the Commons is "dissolved, or gained over;" that, through the death of Salisbury and Dunbar, the King is now on better terms with the people, because "few actions of Estate that are harsh, have been in agitation or rumour of late; and the old grievances, having been long broached, wax dead and flat." He characteristically concludes with the argument that "in his own particular"[1] it will be expedient to advise the calling of a Parliament; for "if any man dissuade a Parliament, he is exposed to the imputation of creating or nourishing diffidence between the King and his people; he draweth upon himself the charge of the consequences of the King's wants; and he is subject to interpretation that he doth it for private doubts and ends."

How utterly Bacon was at fault here, how very far the "old grievances" were from being "dead and flat," or the popular party was from being "dissolved or gained over," the history of the forthcoming Parliament will speedily show; how much Bacon had himself done to give point to the old grievances and to give unity to the popular party by flaunting the Prerogative before the eyes of the people, and by justifying an irregular taxation that would dispense with Parliaments, and an irregular judicature that would dispense with juries, has in part already appeared. But we may pass the more rapidly from the first to the second section for the following reason which he himself alleges :

"Lastly I conceive the sequel of good or evil not so much to depend upon Parliament, or not Parliament, as upon the course which the King shall hold with his Parliament; and therefore I think good to leave the first question and to apply the case to the second."

To the second accordingly we now pass; and, as was fit, the first place in the section (which consists of more than twenty clauses) is assigned to "Impositions," and the second to "Grievances." These indeed were the great questions of the day. But when the paper is searched for a definite policy as to Impositions and Grievances *there is not a vestige of one.* The Impositions *are to be "buried and silenced;"* the discussion of the Grievances *is to be put off*—that is absolutely all.

[1] See the extract from the *Commentarius Solutus*, pp. 150, 158.

The other eighteen clauses, or more, are taken up with details of management, not easily distinguishable from trickery; suggestions of impossible projects to be "given out," with the view of showing that the King did not depend upon Parliament for supplies; suggestions of "actions of estate" that are to be "voiced" (in other words, lies that are to be circulated), as well as "laws that are to be *really propounded* ;" means for conciliating one party and intimidating another; means for electing compliant members and excluding uncompliant ; means for securing the judges, for preventing hostile combinations, and so on.   Here are the earlier clauses of the paper to speak for themselves :

"INCIDENTS OF A PARLIAMENT

" 1. The Impositions, and *how that matter may be buried and silenced.*

" 2. The Grievances, and *how the collection of them in general may be restrained, and the dealing in them at all put back,* till the King's business be set in due forwardness.

" 3. What project may be probably [1] given out to be in hand, whereby the King may repair his estate out of his own means, that the proceeding with his Parliament may be upon terms of majesty and not of necessity.

" 4. What other *opinions are to be sown and dispersed,* and what actions of estate are to be set on foot and *voiced,* as preparatives, whereby men may come to Parliament better affected, and be (when they are met) more forcibly induced and persuaded to supply the King with treasure.

" 5. What gracious and plausible laws or other matter are *really to be propounded* and handled in Parliament for the comfort and contentment of the people."

The rest of the paper is taken up with the "clauses of management."   And here, if we can bring ourselves dispassionately to admire the accuracy of aim with which Bacon, making himself a mere machine in the hands of despotism, directs his blows straight against the chief support of liberty in the House of Commons, we shall praise him for again giving the lawyers the first place among the foes of the King and the friends of freedom.   The silent relaxation of the old rule which forbade a member to sit for a place in which he did not reside, had enlarged the scope of the choice of the electors; and the ablest of the barristers, known to the public by their success at

---

[1] *i.e.* plausibly.

the bar, had rapidly come to the front in the House of Commons.
The country gentlemen had not yet produced the race of
Parliamentary statesmen which was soon to arise: for the
present therefore, " the burden of the conflict in the Commons
lay upon the lawyers, who at once gave to the struggle against
the Crown that strong legal character which it never afterwards
lost. . . . The services which this class of men rendered to the
cause of freedom were incalculable." [1]   So writes our modern
historian; and Bacon expresses the same fact in his brief, quaint
fashion.   The lawyers, he says, are the *vowels* of the House, the
rest of the members, without their aid, being poor helpless
consonants, incapable of sound or utterance.

" 6. What is fit to be done for the winning or bridling of the Lawyers
(which are the *literæ vocales* of the House) that they may further the
King's causes, or at least fear to oppose them.

" 7. What course may be taken for the drawing of that body of the House
which consisteth of citizens and burgesses of corporations to be well
affected to the King's business."

Clauses 8 and 9 mention similarly the " drawing" of the
country gentlemen, and the " courtiers and King's servants,"
that the latter especially may be zealous for the King and not
— as in the last Parliament—" fearful or popular."   Next comes
the consideration of the " popular party" and the Judges:

" 10. What courses may be taken with that combined body, being extracted of all the former sorts, which made the popular party last Parliament ; for the severing of them, intimidating of them, or holding them in
hopes, or the like, whereby they may be dissolved, weakened, or won.

" 11. What course may be held to engage and assure the Judges *in omnem
eventum* for any points of law or right which may be foreseen as likely to
come in question in Parliament."

Next follow—under veils of euphemistic expression, *e.g. bonis
artibus,* and with special protest against " packing"—what must
none the less be described as " packing clauses":

" 12. What persons in particular, in respect of their gravity, discretion,
temper, and ability to persuade, are fit to be brought in to be of the House,
bonis artibus, without labouring or packing.   What persons in particular,
as violent and turbulent, are fit to be kept back from the House, *bonis
artibus,* without labouring or packing.

[1] Gardiner, *History,* i. 161.

"13. What use may be made of the boroughs of the Cinq Ports and of the Duchy, and other boroughs at the devotion of diverse the King's counsellors, for the placing persons well affected and discreet.

"14. What use may be made of the unlawful custom and abuse of the sending up and returning of blanks which, if it be restrained, perchance it may stumble many a one's entrance that think themselves assured of places.

"15. What course may be taken that, though the King do use such providence as is before remembered and leave not things to chance, yet it may be so handled as it may have no shew, nor scandal, nor nature of the packing or bringing of a Parliament ; but, contrariwise, that it tendeth to have a Parliament truly free and not packed against him."

Last come clauses intimidatory—under pretext of securing " free " discussion—and confirmatory :

"16. To this purpose, what course may be taken to make men perceive that it is not safe to combine and make parties in Parliament, but that men be left to their consciences and free votes.

"17. To let men perceive that a guard and eye is had by his Majesty that there be no infusions, as were last Parliament, from great persons, but that all proceeding be truly free.

"18. To consider whether it be fit to strengthen the Lower House with any Counsellors of Estate, and whether it will do good.

"19. To consider whether it be fit to steer the King's business, as it was last time, by conferences with the Upper House, which will be hard to do now the Treasurer is gone, who had a kind of party in both Houses.

"20. To consider of the time fit to hold a Parliament, and to take such a course as it be not held over long, but rather that men take notice of such a resolution in his Majesty not to hold it above such a time.

"[21]. To consider of a fit Speaker for the Lower House."

Amidst all this expense of political cunning there is but a poor pennyworth of political wisdom ; and the paper suggests rather a clever and unscrupulous Parliamentary Whip than a great Statesman, or the trusted counsellor of a King. Even from the royal point of view the advice is shallow ; for it mentions evils without suggesting remedies. It is easy to say that the question of " Impositions " is to be " buried." But how ?

Perhaps it may be thought that Bacon reserved the answer to that question for another paper. But those who have studied his character and his ways of working, both in science and politics, will know that such an explanation is untenable. He has no answer to give to that question, no practical solution of that problem. And because he cannot do what is best, he proceeds to expatiate on what he can do, though it is only second best. Settle the principle of supremacy between Crown and Commons —this he cannot do; but influence elections, arrange a Parliament—these things he can do, or thinks he can. And therefore, after his manner, not being able to sweep away the obstacle, he will diverge *in alia omnia*—creep round it, under it, out of its sight—anything rather than stop still and confess inability.

But we pass from the private notes to the paper of advice. And if a lingering suspicion remained that Bacon might possibly have had some real policy in reserve, some practical suggestion for dealing with the fundamental question of Impositions, it would be dispelled for ever by his actual advice given to the King. There, if anywhere, he could not keep silence on this point, if he had anything to say. Something indeed he does say, in a parenthesis; and in order to say it he resorts—as he often does in delicate matters—to Latin phraseology, and to a newly-invented and rather fashionable word at that time, "accommodate," *i.e.*, "arrange"—in plainer English "get rid of." The King had consented, during last Parliament, to allow, on certain considerations, his right of "imposing" to be limited by an Act; but it would seem that Bacon dared not now openly suggest the expediency of giving up the right of "imposing," having himself magnified it as an inherent part of the Prerogative. However, he smuggles in the suggestion parenthetically under cover of a suggestion to open and increase trade :

"What shall be the causes of Estate given forth *ad populum*: whether the opening or increase of trade (*wherein I meet with the objection of Impositions, but yet I conceive it may be accommodate*),[1] or whether the plantation of Ireland, or the reducement and recompiling of laws—throwing in some bye-matters (as Sutton's estate or the like)—it may be left to further consideration. But I am settled in this, that somewhat be published beside the money matter ; and that in this form there is much advantage."

For the rest, his *Advice to the King* contains nothing of any practical value that is not found in the notes. He begins by

---

[1] I suppose this to mean that if the King were to profess that Parliament was summoned for the purpose of increasing trade, he would be met with the objection that this profession was inconsistent with the maintenance of Impositions, which diminished trade ; and Bacon hints that this objection may be "accommodate,' by getting rid of some, or all, of the Impositions.

confessing that the King may rebuke his presumption in taking
on himself the part of a councillor when he is not one—
" You forerun; your words require a greater place " [1] leaving
the King himself to supply the logical answer, " Then ought
not the author of such wise advice to receive a greater place ? "
He proceeds to mislead the King into supposing that the old
grievances are forgotten and that the hostility of the last
Parliament proceeded from temporary causes which have now
disappeared. Then follows his advice. The King is to " put off
the person of a merchant and contractor," and to conciliate the
Parliament even if he gets little from them at once, looking
rather to the future than to the present : " Until your Majesty
have tuned your instrument you will have no harmony. I for
my part think it a thing inestimable to your Majesty's safety and
service that you once [2] part with Parliament with love and
reverence." The objection that " his Majesty's occasions will not
endure these proceedings *gradatim*," he meets with no reply but
an opposing affirmative and a metaphor. " Yes, surely. Nay, I
am of opinion that what is to be done for his Majesty's good, as
well by the improvement of his own, as by the aid of his people,
it must be done *per gradus* and not *per saltum* : for it is the
soaking rain and not the tempest, that relieveth the ground."
His third proposition is :—

" That this Parliament may be a little reduced to the more ancient form
(for I account it but a form), which was to voice the Parliament to be for
some other business of estate, and not merely for money ; but that to come
in upon the bye, whatever the truth may be. And let it not be said that
this is but dancing in a net, considering the King's wants have been made
so notorious ; for I mean it not in point of dissimulation, but in point of
majesty and honour ; that the people may have somewhat else to talk of,
and not wholly of the King's Estate ; and that Parliament men may not
wholly be possessed with these thoughts ; and that, if the King should have
occasion to break up his Parliament suddenly, there may be more civil
colour to it."

Then follows the clause quoted above, as to the causes that
shall be alleged for summoning Parliament, (" What shall be the

---

[1] Bacon had now become bolder, since 29 May, 1612, when he wrote nearly
the same words, but did not venture to send them : " If your Majesty say to me,
' Bacon, your words require a place to speak them,' I must answer that ' Place, or
not place, is in your Majesty to add or refrain.' "

[2] *i.e.* " for once." James had not parted on good terms with his previous
Parliaments.

causes . . . . advantage "): after which he once more recurs to
the question of money and the King's wants in order to suggest another opinion to be "voiced," viz., that the King
knows of means by which he can clear himself of his debts
without the help of Parliament, if he pleases; so that the
people may not suppose that his "wants are remediless but
only by Parliament."

"I could wish it were given out that there are means found in his
Majesty's Estate to help himself (which I partly think is true) ; but that,
because it is not the work of a day, his Majesty must be beholding to his
subjects ; but as [1] to facilitate and speed the recovery of himself rather than
of an absolute necessity."

He concludes with a warning apparently directed against Sir
Henry Neville and his friends—the "Undertakers" as they were
then called—who had "undertaken" on behalf of the future House
of Commons that, if the King would concede the disputed points,
the Commons would grant the necessary supplies. Neville
wished to be made Secretary of State, and Bacon hints that he
and his friends rated their services too highly.

"Also that there be no brigues [2] nor canvasses, whereof I hear too much ;
for certainly, howsoever men may seek to value their services in that kind,
it will but increase animosities and oppositions, and besides will make
whatsoever shall be done to be in evil conceit amongst your people in
general afterwards."

The sum and substance of Bacon's advice then is this, that
the King is to make no mention of past grievances, but to invent
some high business of State for which Parliament is to be ostensibly summoned ; that he is to make no mention of his
pecuniary straits but rather to give out that he sees his way to
extricate himself from them by degrees, only that it will be discreditable to his subjects that relief should be so long delayed ;
and that by gracious words and behaviour he is to induce the
House to forget the past, and to give up all future contentions
against the Prerogative.   The House is expected to believe that
it is called together to consider the plantation of Ireland, the recompilation of laws, the increase of trade ; and the King's want
of money and need of supplies are to be mere incidents "to come

[1] *i.e.* "*so as*" ; see note on p. 254.   [2] That is, "factious intrigues."

in upon the bye " ! Is it not palpable that even a consummate
master of the art of dignified dissimulation, even Bacon himself,
must have failed in carrying out such a policy as this ! Much
more such a shambling dissembler as James ; uncouth, futile, inconstant ; despotic, yet not strong ; weak, yet not conciliatory ;
without the originality to dictate a policy of his own, and
without the trustfulness or the self-knowledge that might
induce him to obey a counsellor wiser than himself. Bacon
stands condemned for ignorance of the King, ignorance of
the House of Commons, ignorance of the English people, in
supposing that the coming Revolution could be thus " fobbed off
with a tale."

The policy of Sir Henry Neville was too generous—or perhaps
we should say, too far-sighted and prudent—to commend itself to
the King ; but at least it *was* a policy. Besides drawing up a
list of minor concessions which, he thought, might conciliate the
Commons, he, with great tact, availed himself of the offer of the
King (21 November, 1610) to restrain himself hereafter from
imposing upon merchandise. This offer had immediately followed
a speech by Salisbury in a conference between the two Houses,
mentioning eight "things to be desired by both Houses," of
which the eighth was, " No Imposition to be hereafter set, but by
Parliament ; and those that are, to be taken as confirmed by
Parliament." These eight proposed concessions Neville adroitly
assumed to have proceeded from the King through Salisbury,
and he copied them out, without expressing an opinion on them,
as if they might be taken for granted. [1] The King was to suppress books and speeches hostile to Parliament, to peruse the
grievances last exhibited, to insure the performance of past
promises, and " if he would be pleased to be gracious " in any of
the others, to *do it of himself before he be pressed.* Having
summoned Parliament to meet at Michaelmas, he was to begin
by announcing such favours and graces as he was ready to bestow,
inviting a deputation of the Commons, appointed by themselves,

---

[1] See Gardiner's *History*, ii. 203. There seems some difficulty in reconciling
this with a paper, said to be in Neville's handwriting, addressed to Rochester,
and entitled "Reasons to prove that the course propounded doth no way prejudice
his Majesty's right or claim of imposing, nor abridge his profit."—Spedding, iv.
364. Perhaps Neville meant that this source of revenue would still remain, only
subject to the sanction of Parliament, which could be given in case of need.

to confer with him about their further demands. Let him but do this, and Sir Henry Neville was ready to answer it that " in a month or five weeks this point of supplying the King and of his retribution will be easily determined, if it be proposed betimes and followed close afterwards."

By this course the King undoubtedly risked something. It was possible that some of the popular party might succeed in embittering the House against the Crown, even after the royal concessions; so that when a dissolution came, the King might find that he had granted much and the Commons given nothing in return. But it was a time when to risk something would have been wise. The mutual distrust between Crown and Commons needed to be dispelled; it was the King's unconstitutional interference that had elicited from the House of Commons (1604) the protest that the privileges of the House, and therein the liberties and stability of the whole Kingdom had been " more universally and dangerously impugned than ever, as we suppose, since the beginning of Parliaments;" and since the King had created the distrust, there now justly devolved on him the task of dispelling it. Moreover, the spirit certainly, and probably the letter also, of laws and precedents, was generally felt to be against the royal claim to levy Impositions. Soon after the last Parliament, records concerning Impositions had been disinterred which had converted Hackwill, a learned lawyer and strenuous defender of the royal right. Bacon himself had seen these; and his altered tone in the next session more than justifies Mr. Spedding's cautious conjecture that he too was converted by them. If this was so, we might have expected that Bacon would retrace his steps; but there is no hint of any kind of retractation. We have seen the alarm, expressed by a dispassionate observer like Chamberlain, lest the King's Prerogative might be magnified to the detriment of the liberties of the people. Yet Bacon knew nothing, or cared nothing, for such fears. In every possible way he was still endeavouring to increase the King's power, and we shall soon find him boasting (25 July, 1617) that, when he was Lord Keeper, his Majesty's prerogative and authority had "risen some just degrees above the horizon." Bacon's action conciliated the King, and was for the advantage of "his own particular;" but it was not for the advantage of the people, nor for the ultimate advantage of the Crown. We may excuse his error in various ways, so as to save his morality and sincerity at the expense of his statesmanship; we may point out that he contemplated in a too sanguine and unpractical spirit the immediate fulfilment of colossal schemes of law reform, colonisation, enlargement of empire, all of which would be deferred if the cumbrous machinery of a supreme popular assembly were substituted for a King; we may plead that he desired the King to be powerful merely in order that the royal power might be more effectively used for the good of the people; we may show that he was led by his student, theorizing, habit of mind to leave out of account the inevitable tendency to misgovernment which besets irresponsible power, and that his weak admiration for the splendour of the throne blinded him to the special abuses which were sure to arise from the despotism of such a king as James, and such favourites as those whom James was collecting around him: but, after all has been said that can be said in the way of excuse, we must admit that Bacon's policy was radically unsound. Far wiser, far more generous, and, under the circumstances, far more for the interest both of King and Commonwealth, was the policy suggested by Sir Henry Neville.

At all events Neville's policy was entirely free from the reproach cast by Bacon on Cecil's Great Contract; it did not exhibit the King in the attitude of a bargainer. Whatever the King gave, he was to give freely and unconditionally, making no mention of his own wants, but trusting to the good sense and good feeling of Parliament to do what was needful. The question of supply was to be raised in due course,—"betimes," but not immediately; four or five weeks were to be allowed to elapse first; but when once raised, it was to be followed close and driven home. This plan promised well, and another suggestion also, if adopted, might have been very fruitful. The King was to confer occasionally with a deputation, not selected by him, but appointed by the Commons. Immense political results might have followed from the adoption of this advice; tending to the removal of misunderstanding, the contentment of the Commons, the abasement of royal favourites, the guidance of a weak king, and the strengthening of a wise one.

Again, Neville entirely avoided the dissembling taint of Bacon's policy. The King was not to profess to have called the Parliament together to settle Ireland nor to recompile the laws; nor was he to allege, nor to cause it to be "voiced," that he could extricate himself from his debts without the aid of Parliament. He was to appear as the superior disputant in a quarrel, who, on the strength of being superior, did not shrink from making the first advances for a reconciliation. No doubt James was capable of spoiling any Parliamentary plans, however well devised; but if he could have succeeded with any, this policy of Neville's afforded the best prospect of success.

It was hardly possible that a rising politician who wished to be Secretary of State should criticize dispassionately the policy of another man who aspired to the same office: and Bacon had already experienced the mortification of being pushed into the background on an important occasion when Neville, instead of himself, was chosen by the King to represent the wishes of the Commons. About 15 November, 1610, "his Majesty," we are told, "called thirty of the Parliament House before him at Whitehall, among whom was Sir H. Neville. Where his Majesty said the cause of sending for them was to ask of them some questions, whereunto he desired they would make a direct answer. The first was, whether they thought he was in want, according as his Treasurer and Chancellor of the Exchequer had informed them. Whereunto, when Sir Francis Bacon had begun to answer in a more extravagant style than his Majesty did delight to hear, he picked out Sir Henry Neville, commanding him to answer according to his conscience." [1] It was not in human nature that the man thus put on one side should be pre-disposed to look favourably on the counsel tendered by the rival who stepped into his place. And besides, it was not in Bacon's nature, delighting as he did in subtle and circuitous operations, to approve of a frank, straightforward and slightly rash policy, such as Neville recommended. He was therefore probably sincere in dissenting from it. But none the less, looking back upon the past, and contrasting the two courses suggested, the one by the plain, blunt country

[1] Winwood, *Mem.* iii. p. 235; Spedding, iv. 231.

gentleman, and the other by the Author of the *Advancement of Learning*, we must admit that the former advised like a statesman, and an English statesman; and the latter like a student, and a student of Machiavelli.

§ 28 BACON'S DRAFT OF THE KING'S SPEECH

For some time before the summoning of Parliament, conferences went on between the King and Sir Henry Neville. In order to neutralize Neville's efforts, in a letter written shortly after the birth (9 January, 1614) of the King's grandchild, Bacon does his best to prevent James from making any substantial concessions, and to assure him of the hearty loyalty of his subjects. The pealing of church bells, he says, and " the lightning of bonfires " are sufficient proof that England is not disaffected. He advises the King to ask those gentlemen who profess to do him service in Parliament what they can propound for the good of the people; and if they reply that—

". . . . . the Parliament is so now in taste with matters of substance and profit as it is vain to think to draw them on but by some offer of that nature, then for my part I shall little esteem their service if they confess themselves to be but brokers of bargains. . . . If your Majesty had heard and seen the thunder of the bells and the lightning of the bonfires for your grandchild, you would say there is little cause to doubt the affections of the people of England *in puris naturalibus*."

On 16 February, 1614, it was resolved in Council that a Parliament should be called, and all through March, says Chamberlain, there was " much justling for places in Parliament, and letters fly from great persons extraordinarily : wherein methinks they do the King no great service, seeing the world is apt to censure it as a kind of packing." [1] In fact the very measures which Bacon had recommended to be taken quietly and skilfully, in order to bring

---

[1] Spedding, v. 20. Bacon in several passages gives the impression that this " packing " was attempted by the " Undertakers." But Chamberlain's view, that it was rather the work of " great persons "—and not of Neville and his friends in the House of Commons—is confirmed by the speech of Coke in September 1615, referring to this Parliament: " He wished also that *none of their lordships, or other of the Council, or any other great men of the land* should meddle with the election of knights or burgesses, but leave the people to their own choice ; for he had observed in the last Parliament that such interposing of great men and recommendations in these elections had been very offensive."

fit men in and keep unfit out, seem to have been taken so un-skilfully and obtrusively, that they damaged the King's cause. Bacon had some legal work to do in the Duchy, receiving an annual fee for his services;[1] but he cannot (unless other evidence be forthcoming) be held responsible for the folly of the Chancellor of the Duchy, Sir Thomas Parry, one of Bacon's fellow-commissioners in the recent financial investigations, who was at this time expelled from the House for unlawful interference with elections.[2] But the Court candidates were almost every-where rejected. Nearly two-thirds[3] of the four hundred and fifty members returned were elected for the first time to represent the rising discontent of the nation; Pym amongst the number. To add to his disadvantages, the King rejected Neville and chose Sir Ralph Winwood as Secretary of State to represent the Government in the House of Commons, a man of character, ability, and valuable experience in foreign affairs, but so new to the House that the wits declared that "the first person he heard speak in that place was himself."

The session began on 5 April with a speech from the King for which Bacon had suggested notes, entitled *A Memorial of some Points which may be touched in his Majesty's speech to both Houses*, a paper so inconsistent with Bacon's own previous advice, so destitute of dignity, so deficient in tact, so full of tedious repetitions, of timorous protests, and ill-timed depre-cations, that it is difficult to believe that Bacon was entirely responsible for it. Probably it was drawn up after conference with the King, who dictated parts of it; or else we must sup-pose that, with his usual versatility, Bacon coloured his counsel to suit the recent changes of his master's mind.[4] It begins with a protest excellently calculated to awake general mistrust:

---

[1] Spedding, iv. 53, 83.

[2] Bacon had, however, considered "What use may be made of the boroughs of the Cinq Ports, *and of the Duchy*, and other boroughs at the devotion of diverse the K.'s counsellors, for the placing persons well affected and discreet."

[3] So Gardiner, ii. 230, "three hundred members, making *nearly two-thirds* of the whole assembly;" Bacon (Spedding, v. 181) says that "*three parts*" (I presume *three-quarters*) "of the House were such as had never been of any former Parliament."

[4] For example, to attribute to Bacon the parenthesis (Spedding, v. 25)—"if his officers had made as good surveys of his lands as himself hath done of his estate, he should have lost less in his sales than he hath done;"—seems to be doing an injustice no less to his style and rhythm than to his sense of what was expected from a king and due to a parliament.

" That his Majesty conceiveth they come up with minds to perform the contents of the writ whereby they are summoned ; which calleth, not to bargain, nor to declaim, or to make long and eloquent orations, but to give counsel and consent in the hard and important causes of the Kingdom."

Proceeding to the reasons for calling Parliament, after lengthily mentioning an Act for Naturalising the issue of his daughter Elizabeth, and touching on the succession (without a word about "Ireland," or the recompilation of the laws[1]), the King is to declare that for the last two years (*i.e.* since Cecil's death) he has been his own Minister, and to dilate, with something of passion, on the perilous, undignified, and wasteful position of a monarch without money :

" Besides the peril of the Estate in case of wars and troubles, they may think what a prejudice it is to the Crown and Kingdom, for his Majesty to be known to have his coffers empty and to be indebted ; for that there can be no negotiation, nor treaty, be it of marriage, commerce, failure[2] of justice in foreigners, or whatsoever, but it maketh the foreigner to stand upon proud terms, and to presume to work his own conditions. Nay it emboldeneth the foreigner not only to treat *a cavallo*, but actually to encroach and affront the State, thinking it impuissant to resent of injuries. And lastly his Majesty shall have a true trial of the loving affections of his subjects, if they shall deal kindly and worthily with him in freeing and settling both his mind and his Estate at once ;[3] whereby he may the better exercise not only the political part of his office in that which concerneth the public, but even the very *economic*, by setting himself out of interest, making provisions beforehand, taking things at just prices, and the like, which yet hitherto he hath never been able to do. That therefore this matter of supply of treasure was the second cause of calling this Parliament and upon the ground before remembered. For to speak to his Parliament in the language of an accountant by setting forth the particulars of his debts, charge, and revenue ; or in the language of a merchant by crying of his royalties to sale ; or in the language of a tyrant by telling them that he must set upon the tenters his laws and prerogatives if they do not supply him—they were courses that were never his own, his Majesty being rather willing to rest upon their affections than to conclude them by necessities."

[1] Probably he found the King averse to these suggestions, and therefore did not repeat them. But a marginal note (printed by Mr. Spedding in italics, and not as the other marginal notes) adds, " *His M. may be pleased to consider in this place whether he will not express some particulars, as the state of Ireland, &c.*"

[2] Text, " failer."

[3] This is contrary to Bacon's previous advice (p. 183). He had warned the King not to expect to free himself *per saltum*, but *per gradus*.

Passing from what the Crown requires to what the subjects desire, the King is to declare that—

"His Majesty, for his part is resolved not to entertain his people with curious tales and vain hopes, but to prevent [1] words with deeds, and petitions with grants : wherein his Majesty for their comfort doth let them know that he intendeth to send down upon them (as the Scripture sayeth) both the first and the later rain ; for he will send them down in the end of Parliament a bountiful pardon, and at the first entrance hath given order to possess them with such Bills of grace and relief as cannot be matched in example in the time of any of his progenitors, and will descend as a new birth-right and advancement to all their posterity."

Then, after a humorous comparison of himself to Bishop Gardiner,[2] the King is to make another protest that he does not bestow these benefits by way of bargain, and that he will give them a great deal more if they will only treat him liberally :

"And if any man thinketh that his Majesty doth this chiefly to draw on a large gift from his subjects at this time when he needeth them, his Majesty will say this one word and desireth it may be remembered : that when his Majesty shall find his state recovered—which with the good help of his subjects he hath vowed seriously and instantly to go through with [3] —they shall find his Majesty *more ready then than now to confer upon them other things which now it were not seasonable to think of ;* so that they may conclude that the state that his Majesty standeth in now doth put back his bounty and not draw it on."

The meaning of this is obvious. While protesting that he does not bargain, the King is to bargain with the most bare-faced frankness. He is to say distinctly that there are certain things good for the nation which he will bestow upon them if they are liberal to him, but not otherwise. Were there the least obscurity, it would be dispelled by a marginal note—printed by Mr. Spedding in italics like the hint on Ireland above mentioned—which tells us that "*this may have a tacit reference to give hope of somewhat to be done concerning the Impositions.*"

[1] *i.e.* anticipate.

[2] Here, again, the King's style seems plainly discernible : "*For as Bishop Gardiner was wont to say that he meant to be Bishop an hundreth* [sic] *years after his death, meaning it by the long leases which he had made,* so his Ma. in a contrary sense, would be glad it should be said that King James were King many years after his decease in the benefits and grants and good laws which he made for the good of his subjects."

[3] Here for the second time Bacon advises the King to clear himself from his debts *per saltum,* and not (as he had previously advised) *per gradus.*

The price that the King is to pay for the "large gift from his subjects" is certainly left indefinite; it is only a "hope," about "somewhat;" and the reference to the Impositions is "tacit;" none the less it must have been clear to every one who heard these words, if the King uttered them, that the King thereby promised a requital to the Commons if they would enable him to pay his debts.

From the objects to be pursued by Parliament, the King is to pass to the consideration of the course of proceedings; as to which he is, first of all, to repeat a third protest against bargaining:

> "That in the last Parliament his Majesty took upon him the person of a merchant, and they took upon them the persons of purchasers or contractors. But that in this Parliament his Majesty will hold himself to the person of a gracious King, and leave them to the persons of loving and kind subjects. That in bargains the manner is for either part to hold hard for themselves; but in kindness the true proceeding is for either part chiefly to take care of the other. *Charitas non quærit quæ sua sunt.* The King to take care of his subjects, and the subjects to take care of their King."

A pretty sentiment: only not very consistent with the avowal just uttered that he would not bestow certain benefits on his subjects till they had first completely freed him from his debts. We have seen above that Bacon's Memorial twice suggests that the King should state his intention of paying off his debts *at once*, that is to say, £680,000 in addition to the annual deficit of £200,000.[1] These sums therefore he expected the House of Commons to vote in supply. But, if they voted them, and thereby placed him in a position where, for some time at all events, he could have no need of them, what security had they that the King would grant them any adequate requital? Nothing except a "hope" that the King might do "somewhat" as to the Impositions; and this conveyed in words that implied no more than a "tacit reference"!

After expressing a desire that the Commons would set forth their grievances or petitions in distinct Bills, instead of accumulating many in one Bill, and that they would settle the money question without unnecessary conference with the Lords, the

---

[1] Gardiner, *History*, ii. 228.

King is to conclude his speech by announcing four princely resolutions: the first that, as he will not give up, so he will not magnify, any part of his Prerogative. The second, repeating and emphasising what has been twice said before, declares:

"That his Majesty hath fully resolved and vowed to *free his estate at once* and not to endure any longer the afflictions or temptations of a king in want. That there be but two means to do it, the one out of his own means, and the other by the help of his subjects. That, for the former, his Majesty seeth through it and knoweth his way, and hath set it down to himself.[1] But then it must be with some diminution of the patrimony of his posterity, and perhaps with the withholding of some favours and eases which pass daily from the Crown to his people. But his Majesty is confident upon their loves and affections that he shall not be driven to that course. And that this he will assure them, that, whatsoever they shall give by way of help, there was never gift that should be more rightly bestowed according to the mind of the giver than this shall be. For that his Majesty hath set down to himself so to distinguish his receipts as there shall never thereafter be any more arrears, but always competent store for that which concerneth public services."

His Majesty is also to express his determination not to rely on the service of a few men (the Undertakers), but on the whole body of his Commons; and he is to conclude his speech with a protest that he has been misrepresented and traduced by those who assert that he does not love Parliaments. On the contrary—

" His Majesty in his own disposition hath ever loved a Parliament. For it is for kings to dislike a Parliament, that, through stupidness or pride, are like images and *statuaes*,[2] and have no fit composition to treat with their people : which is so far from his Majesty, as, for his part—were it not for the charge of his subjects, or further doubt that it should be to draw more money from them—his Majesty could wish the ancient statutes were put in ure," *i.e.* use, "of holding a Parliament every year."

To a certain extent James followed Bacon's suggestions. He inserted indeed a characteristic reference to Popery, spreading in spite of the attacks of his pen and tongue; but all the

---

[1] In Bacon's previous letter (Spedding, iv. 372, quoted above, p. 197) he admitted he could only " partly think " this true—"I could wish it were given out that there are means found in his Majesty's estate to *help himself (which I partly think is true)* "—but he now goes far beyond this moderation of statement. It is difficult to see the object of an exaggeration which could deceive no one.

[2] So here and in some other places, where we should expect *statuas (statua's)* or *statuae*. Compare Spedding, iii. 249, " *Statuaes* and Pictures are dumb histories."

wheedling, coaxing element in Bacon's Memorial appears to
have been retained in the King's speech ; all the vague offers
of graces and favours that were intended as bargains; as well
as the protests that he did not intend to bargain. With what
result upon the minds of his hearers may be gathered from the
following letter of Chamberlain :

"On Saturday, in the afternoon, the King made a speech to the whole
assembly in the Great Banqueting Chamber, wherein he laid out his wants,
and descended as it were to entreating to be relieved, and that they would
show their good affection towards him in such sort that this Parliament
might be called 'the Parliament of Love.' In which kind, to begin and
train them by the way, he offered them certain graces and favours, not in
the way of merchandising (which course he will not allow nor cannot
abide to hear of) but of mere good will and *motu proprio*."

The distrust of the King nearly caused Bacon's exclusion
from the House. He had been returned by three constituencies
—St. Albans, Ipswich, and Cambridge University—but his
eligibility was disputed on the ground of his legal office. The
last Attorney-General, after some opposition, had been allowed to
retain his seat by connivance ; but he had been elected *before*
being appointed Attorney, whereas Bacon was Attorney when
elected. There were ample precedents for the election of King's
Serjeants or King's Solicitors, but none (as it happened) for the
election of the King's Attorney ; and therefore, as to this office, a
precedent was now to be made, and some would have excluded
him from the House. It was finally decided that no Attorney-
General should hereafter sit in the House. But it was urged
on the other side that, for the convenience of passing the Bills
of Grace drawn by the King's Counsel, Bacon's presence was
specially expedient. So, after being sequestered from the
House for three days, he was allowed to take his seat (12
April) for the present Parliament only. It is not likely that
this resolution of the Commons caused the steadily-rising
Attorney-General much alarm at the prospect of future exclusion from the House : he probably anticipated that the next
Parliament would find him in the House of Lords.

§ 29 THE " ADDLED PARLIAMENT "

In the Parliament, thus inauspiciously opened by the King in accordance with Bacon's advice, everything, from the beginning to the end, went as wrong as might have been expected. On 8 April the King had a second time addressed both Houses, still on the lines of Bacon's Memorial, with tedious protestations, blandishments, and repeated disavowals of bargaining, intriguing, and the like ; all of which could have no other result than to deepen the distrust of the Commons. On 11 April, as though to stultify all the King's protests, the new and inexperienced Secretary rose to move the grant of supplies, and to read over the list of concessions which the King was prepared to make.[1] But all this time no mention had been made of Impositions. On the following day the temper of the members was made apparent by the following motions thus recorded in the Journals of the House :

" *Mr. Middleton :* That the heads of the matters of Grace tend to the Gentility, not to cities, boroughs, burgesses, or merchants : *offereth a bill concerning Impositions.*

" *Sir Maurice Berkley :* against Ecclesiastical Courts."

Here then was the question of Impositions at once coming to the fore-front, the House being by no means, like Bacon, contented with a " hope " of " somewhat to be done " in this matter. And, next to that, came a question that does not appear to have suggested itself as a difficulty, either to Bacon or to the Undertakers, viz., the Ecclesiastical grievances. In vain did the Secretary depict the miseries of the State at home and abroad for want of money, and compare the King's graces to another Magna Charta; in vain did Bacon dilate upon the state of Europe " never so dark," and on the " warm and shining graces " of the King, which needed not the Attorney-General's " little burning-glass " to enhance them. The House

---

[1] Of these concessions Professor Gardiner says that they " prove how completely he " (the King) " might have every gentleman in England at his mercy. Many of them were directly tenants of the Crown ; and those who were not might easily be entangled in the meshes of a law which gave every facility to the Sovereign in prosecuting his extremest rights." They were therefore rather acts of justice than concessions of favour.

P

was wild with suspicions, probably mixing together their jealousy
of the Undertakers, with their indignation at recent interferences with elections; and the question of supply was deferred
till the House should meet ten days hence after Easter.

On 18 April the Bill on Impositions was read a second
time. By general consent the House refused to allow a vital
constitutional question to be decided by a single judgment
in the Court of Exchequer, which they set aside as "erroneous;"
and neither Bacon, nor any of those who had previously supported the King's Prerogative, made any attempt to stem the
current. No progress was made with business; and on 2 May
they were still harping on the Undertakers. One of Bacon's
wittiest and most genial speeches failed to divert them from
pursuing this investigation, which did not drop till the full
and open explanation of Sir Henry Neville showed that there
remained nothing to investigate.

On 3 May the House discussed Impositions, and on the
4th[1] returned, not improved in temper, from the presence of
the King, who had summoned them to hear his opinions on the
matter; and they determined to ask the Lords for a conference
on the subject. At this point an attempt was made by the
King's friends to push on the question of Supply; but after a
vehement discussion it was resolved, not indeed to refuse Supply
—for there was a general disposition to be liberal when the
time should come—but "to do nothing in matters of that
nature till they had ordered somewhat for the good of the
public."

The Committee charged with preparing for the conference
with the Lords brought up its report on 12 May. When the
question was first debated, in the last Parliament, the records
had been imperfectly examined. Having now collected all the
records and examined the subject, they were confident that
Impositions were illegal and that the King had been mis-
informed. They therefore proposed first to induce the Upper

---

[1] "Mr. Delliverge, accordant, in respect of the little hope *yesterday* of relief
of Impositions."—C. J., 5th May, 1614. "Yesterday," says Mr. Spedding,
"was the day on which the King had spoken to them" (v. 55). It would seem,
therefore, that the interview with the King took place on the 4th, and that
"4th" should be written for "5th" in Spedding, v. 49, "On the 5th the King
sent for them," &c.

House to join them in a petition for the removal of the burden, and then to present the joint petition to the King, together with a remonstrance of their right, "that so, this eased, they might with better judgment and with alacrity proceed to the King's Supply, the first end of this Parliament."

At this point we are confronted with a very startling fact. "Sir Francis Bacon, Attorney-General, at the conference, was to have made the Introduction to the business, and to set the state of the question;" and here are the heads of the Introduction :

"An Introduction, briefly declaring the matter in fact and state of the question. Direction to him in three things, wherein we conceive the King to have, by misinformation, done other than any of his ancestors.

"1. *The time :* for now by letters patent, and in print, these Impositions set for him and his heirs for ever : which never done before ; which strange ; because no proclamation bindeth longer than the King's life ; so could not impose but during his own life.

"2. *Multitude of Impositions :* Queen Mary—Gascoigne wines and clothes. Queen Eliz. added only one, of sweet wines. From Ed. III. to Queen M. none. In Ed. III., Ed. II., Ed. I., but five in all.—That upon a petition last Parliament divers hundredths [1] of these taken away ; so now not remaining above 300 or 400 ; yet that those remaining far more worth than those abolished.

"3. *The Claim :* for none of his ancestors ever did so, but pretended [2] wars, needs, &c. : prayed continuance, but for a time."

This was the part "committed to Mr. Attorney :" but how could the Attorney have undertaken it with any show of consistency—having but recently been an unflinching defender of the right of Imposition—or with any prospect of retaining the King's favour ? Mr. Spedding's conjecture, that Bacon (as well as the distinguished lawyer, Hackwill [3]) had been converted to the popular view by a sight of records and precedents delivered to Bacon shortly after last Parliament, is rendered almost certain by the fact that he was selected by the House for the important task of introducing the whole question in the conference with

---

[1] That is, "hundreds."   [2] *i.e.* alleged.
[3] "*Mr. Hackwill* :—Wisheth his tongue might cleave to the roof of his mouth if not speak to this Bill : it is of that importance.—That he pitied them that last Parliament began the question, confident upon the arguments and judgment in the Exchequer.—That, after he had heard the matter argued and seen the precedents, he converted ; so now remaineth, and will do his best to convert his brethren."

the Lords. For who, in their senses, would select as an advocate one who professed himself a disbeliever in the cause, and who could not therefore be reasonably expected to be zealous or cogent? But if Bacon was a convert, then the House might naturally feel that his conversion and position as the King's servant would add weight to his authority. Still there remains the question—what motive induced Bacon thus to take a course apparently destined to destroy his prospects of promotion and influence, by depriving him of the favour of the King? Was it patriotism? or penitence? or was it a concerted arrangement with the King?

It can hardly have been mere penitence or patriotism. For surely a patriotic Attorney would have been afterwards called to account by the King, when, at the conclusion of the Parliament, he animadverted on the opposition he had received, and on some of the opposing members who had given him most trouble. And there is nothing in Bacon's conduct or correspondence during the last year or two, and nothing in Bacon's character, to make it credible that he, the private and trusted adviser of the King, should thus have thwarted his Majesty on a principal point of policy, merely upon a sudden access of legal remorse, brought about by evidence which had been in his possession for three years.

Probably both the King and his Attorney were already well aware that the desired conference with the Lords would either not take place, or else that it would result in a reinforcement of the Prerogative by the combined decision of the Lords and the Judges with Coke at their head. The Bishops could be relied on to act in a mass as King's men in any political question; so could the Privy Councillors; and between them they could easily overpower even a considerable majority of the independent peers. If that was to be so, what harm could the King's Attorney do, by both acting on his convictions, and at the same time retaining his influence with the House of Commons—an influence which he might hereafter use for the King's benefit? In the House he would pose as one who, though in high favour with the King and the Privy Council, was, if not actually converted, at least convinced that their side of the question was more fairly arguable than he had before supposed;

in the royal presence he would appear as still the unfaltering champion of the King's Prerogative, who, if he accepted the painful duty of appearing to assail it, endured that pain only because the appearance of assault would be its best defence.

If Bacon still believed in the right to "impose," he had at least no excuse for being silent in its defence. For on 16 May, —so anxious was the House to hear all sides of the question before the conference with the Lords—it was moved and resolved that "If any man can speak anything for the King's right of imposing without Parliament, they will do so," and Bacon addressed the House, expressing his willingness to accept the part assigned to him, but in no way raising again the question of the King's right.

On 21 May, the message of invitation was sent to the Lords; and on 24 May, Bacon was relieved by their reply from all anxiety —if he ever entertained any—lest the proposed meeting should take place. Finding that they could not depend upon the Judges to support the right of Imposition, the Lords replied that—

" Their Lordships, having entered into a grave and serious consideration as well of the matter itself as of divers incident and-necessary circumstances, did not think it convenient to enter into any conference of that cause concerning the point of Impositions at that time."

As might have been anticipated, it was the King's men in the Upper House, that thwarted the conference. Of the sixty-nine peers who voted, thirty were for conferring; but the phalanx of fifteen bishops, nine Privy Councillors, and two Scotch peers over-bore the independent opposition; and by a majority of nine the conference was declined. So unusual and affronting a refusal was still further embittered by some insolent expressions of a bishop, Neile by name— a principal instrument in hurrying on the shameless divorce of Lady Essex—who declared that no man who had taken the oaths of allegiance and supremacy could ever discuss Impositions, and that, if the Commons were admitted to argue their case, they would effect a breach between the two Houses, as well as between the King and his subjects, by their seditious and undutiful speeches.

Infuriated by the report of this language, aggravating the

refusal that accompanied it, many of the House of Commons (men for the most part new to the House), lost all self-control; and they resolved that all business should be put aside till satisfaction had been given to the House. At this point the King intervened. He began now to perceive that, unless he would give way on the question of Impositions, he must expect nothing from the Commons: and on this point he would not yield. He now wrote rebuking them for abstaining from business, and telling them that it did not belong to them to dissolve Parliament. A deputation of forty members, headed by the Speaker, replied that they were unfit to treat of matters of moment until they had cleared themselves from recent imputations.

Nothing could now recall the Commons to business. Possibly oil was poured on the fire by some emissaries of the Parliament-hating Northampton and his friends; but distrust, the irritation of offended dignity, and the presence of two hundred new members in a House of three hundred, seem sufficient to explain everything. Bacon, hopeless of a good result, appears henceforth to have remained silent. Not even the explanation tendered by the wretched Bishop who had caused all this stir, accompanied with "solemn protestations upon his salvation," and "expressing with many tears his sorrow that his words were so misconstrued," could pacify their fury. In vain did the Lords assure the Lower House that if they had conceived that the Bishop had intended to cast any aspersion upon the latter, they would have punished him with severity; in vain did they hint at "the better expediting of his Majesty's business:" nothing passed now among the Commons but wild and incoherent speeches.

Naturally the King lost patience. On Friday, 3 June, he sent them a message that unless they proceeded forthwith to treat of Supply, he would dissolve on the following Thursday. So wrapt up had the House been in the consideration of their own dignity, that the King's resolution took them completely by surprise. The Bishop was forgotten; some would have again taken up the question of Impositions; others—and among these Wentworth—would have at once done something to satisfy the King. Others ranted against the King, courtiers, and Scotchmen. They could settle on nothing at once except a Committee of the whole House to prepare an answer to his Majesty. It was too late. The anti-Parliamentary party had triumphed. On Saturday the Speaker was (perhaps conveniently) ill, and the House did not sit: on Monday they were informed that, if they did not proceed to Supply at once, they would be dissolved on the following day (instead of Thursday); and accordingly on Tuesday, 7 June, 1614, Parliament was dissolved by commission.

It was believed by contemporaries—and on grounds deemed solid by modern authorities [1]—that some of the violent speeches in the House, those that had most irritated the King and had tended to the dissolution of Parliament, had been instigated by great persons, and especially by the "popishly-affected" Earl of Northampton, and Sir Charles Cornwallis, the late ambassador in Spain. It is probable that a friendly interview between James and the Spanish ambassador—together with the prospect of a rich portion from the Infanta whereby his debts might be paid, in the event of a marriage between Prince Charles and the Infanta—induced the King to precipitate the dissolution. But whatever part the Spanish wire-pullers may have had in animating the Parliament and the King with mutual resentments, there were other causes at work to produce this abortive result. First and foremost, there was the King's natural antipathy to popular assemblies of any kind, and especially to the English House of Commons; then the distrust inspired by the King's inconstant disposition, by his extravagant pretensions, and by the recent tendency of the King's servants (and more especially Bacon), to seize every occasion for straining and magnifying to the utmost the royal Prerogative. And this distrust must have been immensely increased by the royal speeches to the House, made, as it would seem, in accordance with Bacon's suggestions, and certainly in accordance with his extant Memorial, in which—without one word of mention of the fundamental question of Impositions which stood like a gulf between Crown and Commons—he endeavoured, at the cost of a few trifling concessions, to bribe them to bestow upon him such Supplies as would henceforth render him independent of them. Such tactics as these were too transparent. "If thou wilt be a servant unto this people

[1] Spedding, v. 72 ; Gardiner, ii. 246.

this day, and wilt serve them, and speak good words to them,
then they will be thy servants for ever,"—this was in effect the
advice given by Bacon to James : but Pym and Wentworth
and Sandys, and the other leaders of the popular party, knew
their Bibles as well as Bacon, and were not to be taken in by
the modern Solomon endeavouring to put in practice the counsel
given by the astute elders to Solomon's foolish son.

Nor can Bacon probably be acquitted of having in other ways
contributed indirectly to the ill-will between King and Commons.
To "win and bridle the lawyers" in the House ; to "sever,
intimidate, hold in hope" the popular party; to "engage and
assure the Judges *in omnem eventum ;*" to "make men perceive
that it is not safe to combine and make parties in Parliament,"
—these were some of the courses that he suggested, and it was
the suspicion of these and similar courses that went far to make
agreement between King and Commons impossible. Bacon was
not, like Northampton, guilty of a deliberate attempt to estrange
the King from the Parliament ; he honestly and earnestly
desired to see them reconciled : but he would not, or could not,
see the only means to a reconciliation ; he shrank from the unpleasant task of telling the King that he must recede from the
position he had taken up on the question of Impositions ; it
was not enough to promise that he would levy no more, and to
confirm an Act of Parliament embodying that promise ; they had
been unjustifiable from the first and never ought to have been
levied ; and the right course was to acknowledge that they could
not be justified, and to sweep away all that now existed : but
this, though Bacon seems to have felt, he had not moral strength
enough to say. And so it came to pass that his advice precipi-
tated rather than delayed the collision. Do what he might, he
could not have completely succeeded; for he could not have
persuaded James to change his nature. But, doing what he did,
he accelerated failure, and must be regarded as one of the main
agents in bringing about the abortive results of the Addled
Parliament, and in preparing the way for a Civil War.[1]

[1] "The Civil War came about," says Professor Gardiner (*History*, ii. 209) "not
because Coke's principles prevailed, but because half of Bacon's principles
prevailed without the other " ; and the next sentence explains wherein the other
unfulfilled half of Bacon's principles consisted. "*If James and his son had stood
towards Parliament as Bacon wished them to stand*, there would have been no

§ 30 TRIALS OF ST. JOHN AND PEACHAM

The death of Northampton (15 June) prevented him from obtaining the office of Lord Treasurer, which was bestowed upon the Earl of Suffolk. During the last year, the financial condition had been somewhat improved: but the new Treasurer succeeded (10 June), to an annual deficit of £101,000, which, even when diminished by the yearly instalment of the Dutch debt, was not less than £61,000; there were also other extraordinary expenses, and a debt of about £700,000.[1]

To relieve the King's necessities it was proposed that voluntary contributions should be made by the well-affected. Such contributions, rarely voluntary in fact (whatever they might be in name), and always tending to compulsion, might naturally be suspected by the popular party as superseding the action of Parliament; and Benevolences were expressly forbidden by an Act of Richard III. enacting "that the subjects and commons of this realm from henceforth should in no wise be charged *by any charge or imposition called a Benevolence, or any such like charge, and that such exactions called a Benevolence* shall be damned or annulled for ever." Accordingly Bacon warned the Council, first, that the term "Benevolence" ought not to be used, as being forbidden by Act of Parliament; and secondly, that no official recommendations of it must be issued. Moral pressure and no other was to be used. It was to be "given out abroad" that the King and the Prince daily inspected the names of the givers and the amounts of the gifts. Moreover, copies were to be "spread abroad, especially of such as give most bountifully, that others

danger to be feared from Coke." In other words, if James and his son could have become ideal monarchs, using for the good of the people that practically irresponsible power which Bacon desired to establish for them, then Bacon's statesmanship would have averted the Civil War. But surely statesmanship that depends on such an "if" must be pronounced no statesmanship at all, but a mere philosopher's dream. For some months before Bacon was preparing to manage and bridle this refractory Parliament, the King was severing himself from his Council and taking as his chief adviser his favourite Carr, a mere animal (though a high-spirited animal), as destitute of policy as of morality and refinement: "The Viscount Rochester (Carr) sheweth much temper and modesty without seeming to press or sway anything; but afterwards the King *resolveth all business with him alone.*" Sarmiento's despatch, sent home by Digby, 22 Sept. 1613 (Gardiner, *History*, ii. 218).

[1] Gardiner, *History*, ii. 260.

of their rank may perceive they cannot, without discredit and note, fall too low." But although no one was to be compelled to give, Bacon did not hesitate to recommend that no one should be permitted with impunity to dissuade others from giving: "That, howsoever no manner of compulsory means is to be used, nor no show thereof, yet if any malicious person shall deride or scorn or slander the frank disposition of the King's subjects, or purposely dissuade it, or seek to defeat it or divert it, that (he) be questioned and severely punished."

Both Bacon's warnings were disregarded. The Council sent out circulars to sheriffs, justices of the peace, and mayors, recommending the Benevolence, and repeated them when the money came slowly in. A gentleman of Marlborough, named Oliver St. John, on receiving from the mayor an application to attend a meeting for the purpose of contributing, sent to the mayor a reply, to be laid before the meeting of the justices if he thought fit, in which he described the Benevolence not only as illegal but also as a perjury on the part of the King. The task of prosecuting this recalcitrant devolved upon Bacon. Instead of glossing over the use of the illegal word "Benevolence" (which he had himself dissuaded) the Attorney, justifies it *by distinguishing between "a charge called a Benevolence" and "a Benevolence:"* [1]

"There is a great difference between a *Benevolence* and *an exaction called a Benevolence.* . . . . This was *a true and pure Benevolence,* not *an imposition called a Benevolence* which the statute speaks of. There is a great difference, I tell you (though Pilate would not see it), between *Rex Judæorum* and *se dicens Regem Judæorum.* . . . . This was a Benevolence wherein every man had a prince's Prerogative, a negative voice; and this word, *excuse moy,* was peremptory."

As Bacon himself had recommended the King to take steps to ensure that the contributors should perceive that they could not be niggardly "without discredit and note," it is obvious that this "prince's Prerogative" was rather shadowy; however, the offender had the letter of the law against him, and Coke himself had already declared to an assembly of justices that this Council "had done nothing contrary to the laws of the realm."

[1] Coke also recognised this distinction, as will be seen below.

St. John was therefore (April, 1615) condemned; but he escaped the severe penalties imposed by the Star Chamber by a submission not less intemperate in its servility than his original intemperate protest.

The Benevolence did not bring in what had been hoped. The labour of nine months produced little more than £23,000; the City of London gave £10,000 rather than lend £100,000; and the bishops and courtiers gave £13,500: but the total amount in two years amounted to little more than £66,000, and this though the Council had used every exertion and taken the utmost advantage of the condition of affairs abroad and the dangers that threatened the King's allies. Some counties protested, and appealed to the Act of Richard III.; others gave little or nothing; others gave less than they promised: in every county the sheriffs were told that the King would have no difficulty in obtaining a Supply if he would call a Parliament.

The ill-feeling aroused by the sudden dissolution of the last Parliament appears in the course of another trial at this time (1615) in which Bacon prosecuted for the Crown. During the search of the house of a clergyman named Peacham, consequent on some ecclesiastical charge, a sermon was found predicting, or suggesting, that the people might rise against oppressions; that the King might die like Ananias or Nabal; and that the Prince might be slain by those who dreaded the calling back of the crown-lands. The sermon had neither been published nor preached; but it was deemed by the King's advisers to imply a conspiracy, and Peacham was put to the torture (Jan. 1615). " In *the highest cases of treasons*," wrote Bacon in 1603, " torture is used for discovery and not for evidence;" that is to say, for the disclosure of information about other conspirators, but not for evidence against the accused; for he adds that " by the laws ot England no man is bound to accuse himself."

But a majority of the judges decided—so says the report of the trial—that Peacham's offence, even though proved, did not amount to treason, much less to the highest treason; and the interrogatories upon which Peacham was examined were of such a nature that, if he had answered them in the affirmative, he would have " accused himself." It is therefore doubtful whether Bacon could consistently have justified the use of torture in this case and for such a purpose. He was not indeed responsible for the issue of the warrant for torture; but he was Attorney-General and one of the examiners to whom the warrant was addressed, and a protest from him might have had weight. Such evidence as we have, goes to prove that Bacon saw no reason for protesting. Recommending (in 1620) the application of torture to one Peacock, probably mad, who was accused of having "practised, or pretended, to have infatuated the King's judgment by sorcery," he writes to the King, "he deserveth it *as well as Peacham did.*" In any case the wretched Peacham, after being examined in Bacon's presence "before torture, in torture, between torture, and after torture," upon interrogatories which assumed his guilt, revealed absolutely nothing; and two days afterwards Bacon's comment to the King is that the man's "raging devil seemeth to be turned into a dumb devil."

At the time when Bacon wrote these words he had doubts whether the Judges would hold Peacham's guilt to amount to treason; he hopes "the end will be good. But then every man must put to his helping hand." In other words he trusts that Peacham will be convicted of treason; but the Judges must lend their help and must be unanimous. The King was about this time in a paroxysm of panic, not even venturing to sleep without a barricade of beds around him; and his alarm induced him to command, and Bacon unhesitatingly to adopt, unprecedented measures to secure a verdict. In order to prevent Coke from influencing the Judges against the Court, it was decided, in taking their opinion as to the treasonableness of Peacham's conduct (if proved), *to consult them separately, and not, as usual, jointly.* The result of this will be, so Bacon hopes, that "my Lord Coke himself, when I have in some dark manner put him in doubt that he will be left alone, will not continue singular." Great pressure was put upon all the Judges to induce them to deliver the opinion desired by the Court. The King himself drew up a paper of vehement argument, asseverating that "the only thing the Judges can doubt of is of the delinquent's intention," and if the Judges can doubt of that, in the face of the evidence, "happy then are all desperate and seditious knaves, but the fortune of the Crown is more than miserable. *Quod Deus avertat.*"

The gratitude of every Englishman is due to Coke for the protest that he made against "the particular and auricular" taking of the opinions of the Judges, as "not being according to the custom of the realm." That the Judges should allow themselves to be consulted by the Crown *collectively* about a pending case appearing to affect the Crown's interests may seem to us unfair in the extreme ; yet it was at least sanctioned by custom, and only beginning to be deemed irregular.[1] But that the Judges should be consulted secretly and separately was a novel abuse which James himself appears to have been the first to suggest, and could have but one object, to bias or intimidate them more effectually by depriving them of the power of collective consultation and action. Both at the Council Table and in his interview with Bacon, Coke protested against this innovation, declaring "that Judges were not to give opinion by fractions, but entirely ; according to the vote whereupon they should settle in conference" (January, 1615). In this case he was overborne ; but his resistance seems to have not been without effect. The King was so much in love with his new stratagem for brow-beating the Judges in detail, that he gave instructions that the same course should be taken in another criminal case which came on next month ; but both the Lords of the Council, and the Learned Counsel ("holding it, on a case so clear, not needful") did not attempt to coerce Coke a second time to "auricular confession."

From no point of view can Bacon's conduct in this trial be pronounced creditable. Setting aside the separate consultation of the Judges—which he must have known to be an innovation most dangerous to the liberties of the subject—he was also guilty of advising the King to use deceit in every direction. He first proposes to deceive Coke by putting him in doubt "in

---

[1] We have seen above (p. 176) how Sir Thomas More protested against the custom of summoning the Judges to the King's palace "to argue and discuss his matters in his own presence ; " and a recent instance had shown how hard it was for them to resist such pressure. In a dispute between the High Commission Court and the Court of Common Pleas (1611) the Judges were first summoned before the Council ; then this having proved fruitless, the Judges of the Court of Common Pleas were sent for separately, but remained unshaken ; then all the other Judges were sent for, but still in vain ; lastly the Judges of the King's Bench and the Barons of the Exchequer were summoned before the King himself, Coke and his colleagues of the Common Pleas being excluded ; "before this ordeal some of those who were consulted gave way."—Gardiner, *History*, ii. 123.

some dark manner, that he will be left alone;" then the
wretched prisoner (28 February, 1615) is to be deceived with
"a false fire;" and lastly the public is to be deceived as to the
opinion of the Judges, and to be told that the Judges agree that
the Sermon contains treasonable matter, and hesitate as to their
decision merely on the technical ground that it was not published.

"I think also it were not amiss to make a false fire, as if all things
were ready for his going down to his trial, and that he were upon
the very point of being carried down, to see what that will work
with him.

"Lastly, I do think it most necessary, and a point principally to be
regarded, that (because we live in an age wherein no counsel is kept, and
that it is true there is some bruit abroad that the Judges of the King's
Bench do doubt of the case that it should not be treason) it be given
out constantly—and yet as it were in secret, and so a fame to slide—that
the doubt was only upon the publication, in that it was never published."

In Peacham's case, moreover, there were special circumstances of novel injustice. The Judges were required to hear
all the arguments alleged, and the precedents, "*selected*," *as
well as arranged*, by the Counsel for the prosecution, without
hearing anything that might be alleged on the other side.
They were also pressed—Coke, certainly, and the rest apparently—for an immediate answer. When Coke, after hearing
all that Bacon had to say, desired him to leave the precedents
with him that he might advise upon them, Bacon replied that
the delay thus caused would be imputed to the Judge's back-
wardness rather than to the Attorney's negligence. Whatever
may be the legal merits of the case, it is at least creditable to
Coke's moral constancy that he delivered an opinion that
Peacham's conduct did not amount to treason. This was also
(according to the report of the trial), the opinion of many of the
Judges; and Peacham, though condemned, was allowed to die
in prison, which he did seven months afterwards.

From the Attorney-General's management of Peacham's trial
it is refreshing to turn to a little piece of Bacon's English, a
specimen of his grand yet familiar style. It is from a speech
—or rather notes of a speech—which he delivered about
Michaelmas, 1614, in the Star Chamber on a case of deer-
stealing: and it exhibits him posing, in the character of

Attorney, as the humble but loving defender of the King's comfort and pleasure, who has himself "noted" (no doubt as Clerk of the Council) the wholesome effect of the chase on his Majesty's deliberations and resolves.

"My Lords, these offences of deer-hunting and stealing, and malefactors in parks, forests, and chases, I hold them in their nature great, though these instances are not the greatest.

"1. Forests, Parks, and Chases, they are a noble portion of the King's Prerogative : they are the verdure of the King ; they are the first marks of honour and nobility, and the ornament of a flourishing kingdom.   You never hear Switzerland or Netherland troubled with forests.   It is a sport proper to the nobility and men of better rank ; and it is to keep a difference between the gentry and the common sort : and so I hold this fault not vulgar.

"2. And are an excellent remedy against surcharge of people and too many of inhabitants, that the land through it grow not to sluttery.   And these green spots of the King are an excellent ornament to the beauty of the realm.

"3. They are excellent for the preservation of woods, and if the Druids and Ancients of England should now live, they would scarce get a cell or sacrarie under shady trees.   It is parcel of the King's prerogative and such as formerly they would not communicate. . . .   So if it be not a royal flower of the Crown, it is a green leaf at the least.

"4. Lastly *Affectus Regis :* the King's pleasure is known and should work in the King's subjects their due obedience in a thing not vulgar.   It is excellent for the health, and one of the cheerfullest exercises for his Majesty when he doth withdraw himself from greater affairs.   It is *subdiale exercitium,* and yet a kind of artificial solitude.   And, as I have noted, many excellent resolutions and counsels some time came to this table out of the wood. . . .   Other sorts of robberies proceed upon necessity, and rape and battery upon passion : But this is a bravery, petulancy, wantonness, lustfulness, and riotousness of the people, to do as they think good ; and in that respect the more severely to be punished."

§ 31   BACON'S PREPARATIONS FOR A NEW PARLIAMENT

During the intervals of rest from his legal practice, Bacon appears to have given a good deal of thought to the consideration of the King's finances, and his relations with his subjects.   In May, 1614, Chamberlain expresses the hope that the Commons "would not stand too stiff, but take some moderate course to supply him (the King) by ordinary means, *lest he be driven to* ways of worse consequence, wherein he shall not want colour both from law and pulpit." And accordingly soon after the Dissolution, Bacon writes to the King that there is an opinion "sometime muttered, that his Majesty will call no more Parliaments," and speaks of " rumours dispersed that now his Majesty, for the help of his wants, will work upon the penal laws." These sinister reports he proposes to disperse by persuading the King to appoint a commission " for the review of penal laws," with a view to " the repeal of such as are obsolete and snaring," and the substitution of better laws. He also proposes to him to reduce the Common Law of England, from a mere " succession of Judicial Acts," to a course or digest of books of competent volumes to be studied, and of a nature and content rectified in all points." Such a digest, " rectified in all points " by the Attorney-General wielding the authority of the King and absolutely uncontrolled by Parliament, might have been a most useful engine for preparing the way for a systematic despotism. Bacon commends the work to the King, as being—

" . . . a work which needeth no Parliament, and is one of the rarest works of sovereign merit which can fall under the acts of a King. For Kings that do reform the body of their Laws are not only *Reges* but *Legis-latores*, and (as they have been well called) *perpetui Principes*, because they reign in their Laws for ever." [1]

After the next vacation (26 April, 1615) he sent to the King a series of papers, most unfortunately lost, which would probably have exhibited in a most striking form his excessive sanguineness, and his incapacity for finance : for it was nothing less than a scheme by which the King might release himself from debt with perfect ease, and apparently without appeal to Parliament. It contained a paper mentioning possible "increasements "—or as he calls them, " sperate," and a " discarding card," intended to warn the King against the fanciful suggestions of "projectors." A single sentence cleverly and happily suggests that if this fascinating project fails, it will fail because others will supervise the execution of it, and because *he* (Bacon) is not in a position of authority where he can carry his own measures into effect.

[1] Compare *Essays*, lv. 33.

" I do now only send your Majesty these papers enclosed, because I do greatly desire so far forth to preserve my credit with you, as thus, that— whereas lately (perhaps out of too much desire which induceth too much belief) I was bold to say that I thought it as easy for your Majesty to come out of want as to go forth out of your gallery), your Majesty would not take me for a dreamer or a projector. I send your Majesty therefore some grounds of my hopes. And for that paper which I have gathered of increasements sperate, I beseech you to give me leave to think that, if any of the particulars do fail, it will be rather for want of workmanship in those that shall deal in them, than want of materials in the things themselves."

The King's finances again engaged the attention of the Council in September, 1615, and four or five of the Privy Councillors, without venturing to suggest that the Impositions must be given up, maintained that the question must be settled in some way : James, however, favoured the recommenda- tions of the Lord Chancellor (Ellesmere), who assured the Board that " he would not speak of his Majesty's right of imposing, nor even give consent it should be spoken of in Parliament or elsewhere," and proposed an investigation into proposals for improving the King's financial position, or increasing his popularity.[1]   But all alike seem to have been in favour of the calling of Parliament. About the same time Bacon tendered his advice in a long letter, much of which is spent in pointing out the errors of last Parliaments, and in inferring that, by avoiding these, the King may now anticipate a better result. Describing the Parliament of 1606 and its loyal contributions, he conveniently forgets that the Commons were then acting under a strong impulse of loyalty, consequent on the discovery of the Gunpowder Plot. He hopes that the same liberality will be manifested if the King will but call together Parliament for the business of the nation, and wait till Subsidies are spontaneously offered.   After laying all the blame of the last two Parlia- ments on Salisbury and Neville, he then proceeds from the negative to give " affirmative counsel for the future," at the same time expressing a hope that the troubled condition of affairs abroad " will give fire to our nation, and make them aspire to be again umpires of those wars ; or at least to retrench and amuse the greatness of Spain for their own preservation."

<hr/>

[1] Gardiner, ii. 366.

The "affirmative counsel" contains only one suggestion that has not already been worn threadbare by repetition : and this proceeds not from Bacon, but from Sir Lionel Cranfield, a London prentice with a head for figures, who had married his master's daughter and had made his way by sheer ability. He had recently suggested a new plan for dealing with Impositions, which had commended itself to all the Council; and Bacon—with just that touch of condescension with which his broad mind was apt to patronise specialists such as Coke in law and Gilbert in magnetism—now approves and adopts it : "I do allow well the proposition of Sir Lionel Cranfield, being more indeed than I could have looked for from a man of his breeding."[1] For the seventeenth century, Cranfield's project was very ingenious. All, or nearly all, of the new Impositions on *exports* were to be given up : but the same sum was to be collected by new rates levied on *imports*. To our notions this seems like taking with the right hand what is given with the left; but Cranfield and Bacon, and the political economists of those days, argued differently : this money would be levied—so argues the Attorney-General in his letter to the King—"for the advantage of the kingdom, and the disadvantage of the stranger;" it would "*de vero* mend the case of the realm in point of trade;" it would "silence all the voices of the out-ports which made the rattle, and which, in these, are little, or not at all, interested;" it would also leave intact the power of levying Impositions hereafter. In these terms Bacon supports Cranfield's project. Had the plan been adopted, a very short experience would have proved its commercial and political futility; it would have burdened trade without contenting the House of Commons. There is little in it to procure for its projector, and still less for its adopter, the reputation of a Statesman.

The rest is old matter in new form. In order to convince the

---

[1] Mr. Gardiner says (*History*, ii. 366-367) "The Councillors were all aware of the importance of the question of the Impositions. Not one of them, however, really suggested a way out of the difficulty. . . . In many respects his [Bacon's] view coincided with that of the Councillors ; *but he had a definite plan for dealing with the Impositions.*" But in fact Bacon's "definite plan" had *not only been originated by Cranfield but also approved, at the Council Board, by Sir Thomas Lake*, who recommends for consideration a project touching Impositions : "a project delivered unto his Majesty by Sir Lionel Cranfield, *and once moved unto your Lordships at this Board.*"—Spedding, v. 197.

people that he sees his way to releasing himself from his debts, the King may do two things :

"The one, to put it upon the profit patrimonial expected from this enfranchisement of copyholds and improvement of wastes, adding (for though the King should never do it, if such be his mind, *yet he may make use of the opinion*) the disforesting of forests in the remote parts ; and likewise upon a revenue upon wards of Recusants. The other, to turn it also upon the opinion of some great offer for a marriage of the Prince with Spain ; not that I shall easily advise that that should be really effected ; but I say *the opinion of it may have singular use*, both because it will easily be believed that the offer may be so great from that hand as may at once free the King's Estate ; and chiefly because it will be a notable attractive to the Parliament that hates the Spaniard, so to do for the King as his state may not force him to fall upon that condition."

In order to raise an immediate sum of money for pressing needs, he advises the King to make eight Barons, who are to pay £500 apiece for their titles. He is to secure the favour of the Commons, not by " offer of any flowers or sprigs of the Crown or Prerogative," but by " the embracing of worthy causes, and the advancing of worthy persons, and the protecting of his people in true religion, peace, and justice; and to gain their confidence by assigning to definite expenses definite parts of the revenue."

In all this there is no political interest : it argues a complete misapprehension of the issues between the Crown and the nation, and of the tone of the House of Commons. The real interest in this paper is in the courtier-like suppleness with which Bacon contrives to tell the King two or three home-truths, in accordance with his courtly recipe, *laudando praecipere.* The Scotch favourite, Rochester—or rather Somerset, for he had recently been made an Earl—was now declining in favour ; and the English Villiers was on the ascent. Taking advantage of this fact, Bacon cleverly praises the King for his impartial dealing between Scotch and English and suggests that he is to continue in this course; he is also to be less prodigal when he is not in or near London; he is to put down the Popish Howards and their ally, Somerset (whose fall must have been already pretty certain in Bacon's opinion, to induce him to speak so freely), so as to secure unity in his counsels; and, above all, he is not to make speeches to the House of Commons:

" As for the *medietate linguae* of Sir Charles Cornwallis, I will not be so saucy as to speak of it, the rather because somewhat hath been happily and in good time done by his Majesty in that kind already.[1] . . . The other is that which I must induce with a preface. I am of opinion that the King should not for profit diminish one iota of majesty, and I think it more needful for him so to do, being in want, than if his coffers were full ; and, if it be observed, the whole spirit of this discourse worketh in that faculty. So that, if his Majesty's abode were chiefly at London or standing-houses near London, I had not what to say. But since it is far the greatest part of the year otherwise, I know no reason in the world but he may keep greater state and majesty when he comes to London, or to other standing-houses near about, than ever he did, or ever his predecessors did, and yet nevertheless save and abate a marvellous deal of charges, which now is obscured away.

" Twelfthly and lastly, I wish the first day of the opening of the Parliament his Majesty would be pleased to speak in person, and to deliver, according to his excellent and incomparable ability, the causes of the assembling thereof. . . . *and after that (as I have heard his Majesty himself protest he would not)* so I *think he is in the right if he speak no more,* except it be upon some occasion of thanks or other weighty particular ; keeping Horace his rule, *Nec Deus intersit, nisi dignus vindice nodus inciderit.*"

What part Bacon expected to have played if the proposed Parliament had been called, we have no evidence to indicate. As Attorney, he was excluded by the recent decision of the Commons from sitting in the Lower House; but perhaps he expected that his recognised utility would have caused him to be transferred to the Upper House. However, Parliament was not yet to be called. Vacillating between the Spanish and anti-Spanish parties, the King at last decided (7 December) to go on with the negotiations for the Spanish marriage—which Bacon had recommended him to do in appearance but not in reality, with the view of frightening the Commons into liberality —and a few weeks later (20 January) he laid aside all thought of summoning Parliament. Partly he may have been afraid that the warlike spirit now rising in England, might have forced him into hostilities with Spain ; partly he was attracted

---

[1] " Alluding probably to the rise of Villiers, who was not a Scot. Sir C. Cornwallis had advised the King to distribute his favours more equally between the two nations."—Spedding, v. 186. Villiers had been made a Gentleman of the Bedchamber on 23 April, 1615, in spite of the remonstrances of the declining Favourite, Somerset.

by the prospect of the Infanta's rich portion. Meantime he so far took Bacon's advice that he procured a supply of money for his immediate needs; not, however, from the creation of Barons—which would have gone but a little way—but by surrendering to the Dutch the cautionary towns which had been pledged by them to Elizabeth as security for their debt to her. The immediate receipt (23 April, 1616) of £215,000 enabled him to defer for some time longer the unwelcome meeting of a Parliament.

§ 32 BACON'S PREPARATION FOR THE WORK OF A LORD CHANCELLOR

A new Favourite was soon to rise and the old Favourite was on the point of being tried for his life. Sir Thomas Overbury, formerly an intimate friend of the present Favourite, the Earl of Somerset, and vehemently opposed to his marriage with the divorced Countess of Essex, had been recently poisoned in the Tower by his revengeful wife, under circumstances which appeared to implicate Somerset also. His guilt, or innocence, has never been satisfactorily proved. We only know that the King—who, after much patience and remonstrance had now completely discarded his overbearing and ungrateful Favourite —earnestly desired that he should be condemned; and that Bacon's part in the prosecution was rendered difficult, partly by the insufficiency of the evidence, partly by the apparent fear that Somerset might make some disclosures prejudicial to the King. On 22 Jan. 1616, Bacon congratulates Villiers on the intended gift of a valuable Patent which had been bought by Somerset, but which the King intended to bestow on the new Favourite, as soon as it could legally be taken from the old. On the same day he also writes thus to the King concerning the pending trial : " The evidence is of a good strong thread, considering impoisoning is the darkest of offences ; but the thread must be well spun and woven together." If a conviction is to be secured, he warns the King that he must select " a Steward of Judgment that may be able *to moderate the evidence and cut off digressions ;* for I may interrupt but I cannot silence." Elsewhere he describes the evidence as being " so balanced as it may have sufficient matter for the consciences of the Peers to convict him and yet leave sufficient matter in the conscience of the King to pardon his life."

Lest the evidence should introduce inconvenient irrelevancies he proposes to take measures not only for the knitting of it but also, "to use your Majesty's own word, for the confusing [1] of it." He consults the King what step is to be taken in case of an acquittal, and receives the reply that " this case requireth that, because there may be many high and heinous offences (though not capital) for which he may be questioned in the Star Chamber or otherwise . . . . that therefore he be remanded to the Tower as close prisoner."

As the crisis approached, Bacon seems to have become still more doubtful of the result; for he recommends the King to make some promises to Somerset beyond the mere saving of his life, in order to induce him to confess; and he adds one or two precedents for the restoration of lands after attainder. Finding James resolute in his refusal, Bacon does not blush to suggest that Somerset should at all events be deceived into false expectations of royal favour; the King need not commit the deception ; a messenger can do it for him :

"I am far from opinion that the re-integration or resuscitation of Somerset's fortune can ever stand with his Majesty's honour or safety ; . . . but yet the glimmering of that which the King hath done to others, by way of talk to him, cannot hurt, as I conceive. . . . I would not have that part of the message as from the King, but added by the messenger as from himself."

Still Somerset was refractory; and Bacon recommends, in the last resort, that—

"After he [Somerset] is comen into the hall, the Lieutenant shall tell him roundly that, if in his speeches he shall tax the King, that the justice of England is that he shall be taken away and the evidence shall go on without him ; and all the people will cry 'Away with him ;' and then it shall not be in the King's will to save his life, the people will be so set on fire."

The Countess of Somerset pleaded guilty; and the Earl (who to the last maintained his innocence) was on the following day

---

[1] We may certainly give the King credit for using the word "confuse," not in our present sense, but in the sense "to fuse," "blend into one."

(25 May, 1616) unanimously condemned.   But the lives of both were spared.   One of the Countess's tools, Weston, before his trial, had expressed a hope that the Government would not make a net to catch the little fishes and let the great ones break through ; but his hope was not fulfilled.   Weston himself was hanged, with others ; but both the Earl and Countess of Somerset were ultimately pardoned, and on Bacon fell the duty, not only of drawing up a pardon for the Countess, the prime mover in the crime, but of "reforming" the pardon (1 July, 1616) [1] " in that main and material point of inserting a clause that she was not a principal, but an accessory before the fact, by the investigation of base persons."

To us, with our modern methods of conducting a criminal trial, it must of course seem intolerable that the Attorney-General should communicate with the King, pending a trial, concerning the "knitting" or "confusing" of the evidence ; the appointment of a Steward to "moderate digressions; " and the immediate re-arrest of the prisoner, in the event of an acquittal. But, if we are not to be unjust to Bacon, we must try to place ourselves in the position of an Attorney-General in the seventeenth century conducting a trial, criminal, it is true, but also in some sense political.   By the legal officials of the Government the trial was regarded as practically concluded when the preliminary investigation and examinations had satisfied them of the prisoner's guilt; the public trial was rather to satisfy the public than to elicit the truth, which (so the King's Counsel considered) was already known.   For the Government to fail in securing a condemnation would be a discredit and a source of weakness.   Yet even when these and all possible allowances are made for Bacon's conduct, it is hard to avoid the feeling that he knows himself to be working, not only for the Government, but also for the King personally, and for his own credit with the King. The old Favourite, if he is not condemned and at least disgraced, will be in the way of the new ; it is for the King's convenience that the accused should be put out of the way ; hence, the Attorney's sole object is to put him out of the way.   The possibility of the prisoner's innocence is not so much as considered ; and this though Bacon himself admits that the

---

[1] Professor Gardiner, by a misprint, dates the letter "11 July" (*Hist.* ii. 361).

evidence was so inadequate as to make it doubtful whether a conviction could be procured even from a jury of hostile Peers. As for the deception which Bacon deliberately suggests to the King, in order to extort a confession from Somerset by some false "glimmering," it cannot be in any way defended or extenuated, even by an appeal to the low moral standard according to which State trials in those days were conducted.

Somerset was kept in the Tower for six years with the judgment of death hanging over his head, probably for the purpose of inducing him to procure a pardon by the intercession of Villiers, whom he was to recompense by the gift of his estate at Sherborne.[1] But this he steadily refused to do ; and it was not till January, 1622, that he was allowed to leave his prison, still maintaining his innocence. A few months before the King's death, he received a formal pardon for his real or supposed crime.

The Favourite having been cast down, Bacon might possibly hope to realise his dreams of stepping into Salisbury's place as the chief and recognised adviser of the Sovereign. He was not then aware how impotent he or any man of real genius would be to sway the King in comparison with a handsome, active and fluent youth like Villiers. But in any case there still remained one other powerful enemy to overcome before Bacon could rule supreme over English Law as Lord Chancellor. That enemy was the Chief Justice, Sir Edward Coke. The need of the services of Coke during the investigations into the murder of Sir Thomas Overbury, had suspended, but only for a time, Bacon's persistent efforts to overthrow his rival in order to secure the subservience of the Judges, under the King as master, and himself as overseer. An occasion had been afforded by an incident that had occurred some three or four years before. About that time, Mr. John Murray, of his Majesty's bedchamber, had procured a new patent office for making writs in the Common Pleas, and had thereby interfered with the profits of the Prothonotary ; by whom an action had consequently been brought in the King's Bench, raising the question of the legality of the Patent.[2] Conceiving that this was a question in which the King's interests

---

[1] Gardiner, ii. 363.
[2] An attempt had been made by Elizabeth to create the very same office ; but it had been resisted by the Judges, and the Queen had withdrawn her claim.

were affected, Bacon desired to transfer it from the King's Bench to the jurisdiction of the Lord Chancellor, who would be always likely to favour the rights of the Crown. For this purpose he had attempted to stop the proceedings in the King's Bench by a writ *De non procedendo, Rege inconsulto* ("about not proceeding without consulting the King"); for which a second hearing had been appointed for 20 November, 1615. But when that day drew on, Overbury's death was engaging general attention, and Coke's in particular. By Bacon's advice the King therefore instructed Coke to defer the hearing of the case. It came on again on 27 January, 1616; and on the same day Bacon describes to the King how his faithful Attorney did battle for the Prerogative against the Bar and the Bench:

"There argued on the other part Mr. George Crook, the Judge's brother, an able book-man and one that was manned forth with all the furniture that the Bar could give him (I will not say the Bench) and with the study of a long vacation. I was to answer, which hath a mixture of the sudden; and of myself I will not nor cannot say anything but that my voice served me well for two hours and a half; and those that understood nothing [1] could tell me that I lost not one auditor that was present in the beginning but staid till the later end. If I should say more, there were too many witnesses (for I never saw the Court more full) that mought disprove me."

At the conclusion of the speech, " my Lord Coke was pleased to say that it was a famous argument;" and the Attorney, expressing a belief that he has almost turned the tide in favour of the Prerogative, dilates on the importance of a successful issue:

"Sire, I do partly perceive that I have not only stopped but almost turned the stream; and I see how things cool by this, that the Judges—that were wont to call so hotly upon the business—when they had heard me, of themselves took a fortnights-day to advise what they will do; by which time the term will be near at an end; and I know they little expected to have the matter so beaten down with book-law (upon which my argument wholly went) so that every mean student was satisfied."

But Bacon will not depend upon his own eloquence. He begs the King, " because the times are as they are," to command Coke

---

[1] Perhaps, Lady Bacon.

not to proceed further till he (Coke) has spoken with his Majesty :

"It concerneth your Majesty threefold : first, in this particular of Murray ; next, in the consequence of fourteen several patents, part in Queen Elizabeth's time, some in your Majesty's time, which depend upon the like question ; but chiefly because this writ is a mean provided by the ancient law of England, to bring *any case that may concern your Majesty in profit or power from the ordinary Benches, to be tried and judged before the Chancellor of England* by the ordinary and legal part of this power. And your Majesty knoweth *your Chancellor is ever a principal counsellor and instrument of monarchy, of immediate dependence on the King ; and therefore like to be a safe and tender guardian of the regal rights.*" [1]

No one can mistake this policy. At a time of transition, when on the one side the Commons were striving to shake off the old but legal burdens handed down from feudal times, and when the Stuart dynasty on the other side was attempting to re-animate with increased life and vigour the half-dead powers of Impositions, Monopolies, Patents, Councils of the Provinces, and the like—Bacon sided against the Commons and with the Crown. The former aimed at Constitutional Monarchy, an anomalous kind of government, displeasing to logical minds ; the latter, more logically, aimed at Despotism ; and Bacon, like a philosopher as he was, drifting further and further out of the current of patriotic sympathies into the vortex of Court influence —deliberately espoused the cause of Despotism against that of Constitutional Monarchy—Despotism that was to be tempered indeed by the deepest affection for the subjects, by profound regard for fundamental traditions, by preservation of all the rights and distinctions of burgesses, gentry and nobility ; Despotism that was to be wielded by an ideal King doing all things for the people ; but, none the less, Despotism alike in the Church and in the State ; and in order that the King might achieve despotism in the State, it was necessary that the Judges in this time of flux—when the nation was striving to accommodate ancient traditions to modern life—should not be allowed to take a dispassionate or impartial view of inevitable conflicts. They were not to regard themselves as umpires arbitrating between

---

[1] Bacon did not succeed in this case in establishing the principle for which he was contending ; the matter was terminated by a compromise.

the King and the Commons, in all matters of disputed law.
Wherever the King's rights were concerned, they were to regard
themselves not as Judges but as advocates, as the King's
servants; "lions" towards the offending subject, but in relation
to the supreme Master, "lions under Solomon's throne." A
narrow and short-sighted theory, which every Englishman must
regard with aversion; but the persistency and skill with which
the Attorney-General endeavoured to carry this theory into
effect—in spite of the overwhelming disadvantages of attempting
to establish an ideal Monarchy under a Monarch who was so far
from being ideal—cannot but extort our admiration for Bacon's
pre-eminence in the smaller arts of political management.

We have seen from Bacon's private note-book that he invariably regarded politics from three points of view; there was the
double view of strengthening the King without discontenting
the people; but there was also "his own particular." In thus
exalting the Chancellor's Court above all the ordinary Courts of
Justice, and in putting forward the Chancellor as "a principal
instrument of Monarchy" and "a safe and tender guardian of
regal rights," he could not possibly ignore Ellesmere's sinking
health or his own peculiar fitness to succeed to the seat on the
woolsack. Accordingly on February 9 (1616) he began a letter
to the King in which he ventured to introduce the subject of a
successor to Ellesmere:

"My Lord Chancellor's sickness falleth out *duro tempore*. I have always
known him a wise man and of a just elevation for a monarchy. But your
Majesty's service must not be mortal. And if you leese[1] him, as your
Majesty hath now of late purchased many hearts by depressing the wicked,[2]
so God doth minister unto you a counterpart to do the like by raising the
honest."

But before sending this letter he heard that the King had
himself written to the sick Chancellor. In the true spirit of
a courtier, Bacon (probably on 11 February) re-wrote his letter:

"My Lord Chancellor's sickness falleth out *duro tempore*. I have always
known him a wise man and of a just elevation for monarchy. I understood this afternoon by Mr. Murray that your Majesty hath written to
him, and I can best witness how much that sovereign cordial wrought

---

[1] That is, "lose."   [2] No doubt, "Somerset."

with him in his sickness this time twelvemonths. . . . I purpose to see my Lord to-morrow, and then I will be bold to write to your Majesty what hope I have either of his continuance or of his return to business, that your Majesty's service may be as little passive as can be by this accident."

But on the following day (12 February) he had seen the Chancellor; and now, without any hesitation, he offers his services to the King, making " oblation " of his heart, his service, his place of Attorney (worth £6,000 a year), and his Clerkship in the Council, which was worth £1,600 more, and reminding him that his father filled the place under Elizabeth and filled it well :

"Your worthy Chancellor, I fear, goes his last day. God hath hitherto used to weed out such servants[1] as grew not fit for your Majesty. But now he hath gathered to himself a true sage, or *salvia*, out of your garden. But your Majesty's service must not be mortal. . . .

" Now I beseech your Majesty let me put you the present case truly. If you take my Lord Coke, this will follow : first, your Majesty shall put an over-ruling nature into an over-ruling place, which may breed an extreme. Next, you shall blunt his industries in matter of your finances, which seemeth to aim at another place. And lastly, popular men are no sure mounters for your Majesty's saddle. If you take my Lord Hubbard, you shall have a Judge at the upper end of your Council-board and another at the lower end, whereby your Majesty will find your Prerogative pent. For, though there should be emulation between them, yet as legists they will agree in magnifying that wherein they are best. He is no statesman, but an economist, wholly for himself ; so as your Majesty—more than an outward form—will find little help in him for your business."

If Bacon himself should become Chancellor, his Majesty " shall only be troubled with the true care of a King, which is to think what he would have done in chief, and not of the passages." Having always been " gracious in the Lower House," and having " some interest in the gentlemen of England," Bacon trusts that he will be able to " rectify that body of Parliament-men which is *cardo rerum*." By "that body of Parliament-men " he appears to mean, not the country-gentlemen, but the Lawyers in the House. These elsewhere he devises how to " win or bridle," as being " the *litterae vocales* of the House," that is the " vowel sounds," which are necessary for vocal utterance, and without

---

[1] *i.e.* Cecil and Northampton ; the fall of Somerset was then impending.
[2] Spedding, iv. 367 ; and see above, p. 193.

which the consonants (*i.e.* the country-gentlemen) cannot find expression of their grievances; and by "rectifying" them, he means keeping them in the straight path of loyalty by the hope of promotions and other rewards. That at least is the natural inference from the words immediately following:

> "For let me tell your Majesty that that part of the Chancellor's place which is to judge in equity between party and party, concerneth your Majesty least. But it is the other parts, of a moderator amongst your Council, of *an overseer over your Judges, of a planter of fit Justices and governors in the country, that importeth your affairs and these times most.*"

Professor Gardiner says:[1] "Perhaps if any date can be fixed as that on which Bacon's chance of serving the nation politically was at an end, it is that of the dissolution which took place on 7 June, 1614; James then deliberately took one way, and the nation another." But here, two years afterwards, we seem to see Bacon, not following, but guiding the King on the path that led him from the nation, and brought his successor to destruction. He positively invites the King to make a tool of him for the purposes of despotism. It is indeed to be a kindly despotism, and he himself is to be selected as an instrument, partly because he is in favour with the people:

> "To conclude : if I were the man I would be, I should hope that, as your Majesty hath of late won hearts by depressing,[2] you should in this case leese no hearts by advancing : for I see your people can better skill of *concretum* than *abstractum*, and that the waves of their affections flow rather after persons than things : so that acts of this nature (if this were one) do more good than twenty bills of grace."

The sum of which is, that if the King will but avail himself of the services of an ideal Chancellor provided him by Providence, the Commons of England will gradually allow themselves, by kind words, gracious manners, and wise and philanthropic measures for the Commonwealth, to be lured into forgetfulness of all past and present grievances, and will suffer the constitution of England to glide into that firm and fixed mould of paternal Monarchy which seemed to Bacon the logical consequence of past precedents and present needs.

[1] *Dictionary of National Biography*, "Bacon."
[2] Depressing Somerset.

Bacon received a promise of the Chancellorship; but it was conveyed in a manner that showed him he had made one slight mistake. In his letter to the King he had laid stress upon the fact that his former promotion to the Attorneyship was the King's "own sole act," not that of the Favourite Somerset; "more than that Somerset, when he knew your Majesty had resolved it, thrust himself into the business for a fee." And therefore he had appealed directly to the supreme Master: "I have no reason to pray to saints." There he was wrong. The old saint was cast down from the niche; but a new saint already filled its place. The promise of the Chancellorship was conveyed to him, not directly from the King, but through Villiers. Bacon's consummate tact immediately appreciated and accepted the lesson that he must henceforth approach the King through the new Favourite; and in the following letter he promises Villiers (15 February, 1616) that he will for the future wholly rely upon him and employ no other intercession with the King:

"SIR,

"The message which I received from you by Mr. Shute hath bred in me such belief and confidence, as I will now wholly rely upon your excellent and happy self. When persons of greatness and quality begin speech with me of the matter and offer me their good offices, I can but answer them civilly. But these things are but toys. I am yours, surer to you than to my own life. For, as they speak of the Turquois stone in a ring, I will break into twenty pieces before you have the least fall. God keep you ever.

Your truest servant,
FR. BACON.

"My Lord Chancellor is prettily amended. I was with him yesterday almost half an hour. He used me with wonderful tokens of kindness. We both wept, which I do not often."

§ 33 THE FALL OF COKE

Ellesmere was moved to fresh life and vigour by an unwarrantable attack of Coke upon the Chancery jurisdiction. Two fraudulent creditors having obtained judgments in their favour in the King's Bench, their victims had sought and obtained relief from Chancery. Indignant at this and at the recent attempt to take causes from his Court to the jurisdiction of the

Chancellor, Coke instigated the creditors to prefer (12 February, 1616) indictments of Præmunire in the King's Bench against all the persons who had been concerned in the proceedings in Chancery—the plaintiffs, the counsellors, the solicitors, and the Master of the Chancery; but this attack was baffled by the resolute refusal of the Grand Jury to find a true bill; a refusal in which they persisted in spite of Coke's remonstrances and threats, seconded by the other Judges of the King's Bench. Coke had now made a false step, of which Bacon was not slow to discern the advantage that might hereafter be taken. But as Somerset's case was still pending, nothing could have been at present more untoward for the King's purposes than this quarrel. "There is no thinking of arraignments," writes Bacon (21 February, 1616), "until these things be somewhat accommodate, and some outward and superficial reconciliation at least made between my Lord Chancellor and my Lord Chief Justice; for this accident is a banquet to all Somerset's friends." But he advises the King to take the first convenient opportunity of utilising Coke's presumption, in order to make the Judges know their places :

"My Lord Coke at this time is not to be disgraced, both because he is so well habituate for that which remaineth of these capital causes, and also for that which I find is in his breast touching your finances and matters of repair of your estate. On the other side . . . use is to be made thereof for the settling of your authority and strengthening of your Prerogative according to the true rules of Monarchy. And to be plain with your Majesty, I do not think there is anything a greater *polychreston, ad multa utile* to your affairs, than upon a just and fit occasion to *make some example against the presumption of a Judge in causes that concern your Majesty, whereby the whole body of those magistrates may be contained in better awe ;* and it may be this will light upon no unfit subject of a person that is rude and that no man cares for."

Even if none of the Puisne Judges have so behaved as to forfeit their place, "yet the very presumption of going so far in so high a cause" deserves, he thinks, that they should answer it upon their knees before his Majesty and the Council, and receive a sharp admonition. Summing up, he lays stress upon two points : one is, that each Court is to keep within its own prescribed limits and precedents :

" The other, that in these high causes that touch upon State and Monarchy, your Majesty give them strait charge that upon any occasions intervenient hereafter they do not make the vulgar party to their contestations by public handling them before they have consulted your Majesty, to whom the reglement of those things only appertaineth."

Before this letter was written, Bacon had already suggested to Villiers the propriety of his being made a Privy Councillor. But now, if the Judge were to be called before the Council, and there to be censured, it was more than ever necessary; and as the Chancellor seemed now likely to recover, there was little prospect of Bacon's speedily coming into the Council *ex officio.* He, therefore, renewed (21 February) his former suit to Villiers, and repeated it within a week (27 February) on the ground that he was liable to the charge of " interloping " in giving his Majesty counsel without the official right to do so, and that " there were never times which did more require a King's Attorney to be well armed." In the course of April next he received from the King and Villiers assurances of support; but no special mention is found of the Councillorship.

Meantime, a second collision with Coke was at hand. A living had been granted by the King to the Bishop of Lincoln [1] in *commendam,*[2] and the claimants of the right of presentation had brought an action against the Bishop. It had come before the twelve Judges in the Exchequer Chamber on April 20, and was to be reheard on Saturday, April 27. As the case might affect the Prerogative—*e.g.* the right to grant *Commendams* under any circumstances—the King had instructed the Bishop of Winchester [3] to watch the case and report to him; and upon the Bishop's report he directed Bacon to signify his pleasure to Coke that the case should be adjourned till the King had spoken to them. Bacon appears to have been in no hurry to convey this command ; for, though he received it on Wednesday

---

[1] Dr. Neile, who had facilitated the divorce of Lady Essex from her husband, and had been charged with expressions derogatory to the House of Commons (see pp. 213, 214).

[2] A *commendam* is a benefice which, being void, is *commended* to the charge of some sufficient clerk, to be supplied until it may be conveniently supplied with a pastor. An Act of William IV. (1836) prohibited future bishops from holding in *commendam* the livings they held when consecrated.—Haydn's *Dictionary of Dates.*

[3] Dr. Bilson.

afternoon, he did not send word to Coke till Thursday evening,
nor to the other Judges till Friday, 26 April. It is possible
that some sense of personally injured dignity, as well as of
public expedience, instigated the Judges to disobey the royal
mandate thus conveyed. They proceeded with the case on the
day appointed (27 April), and drew up a joint letter expressing
the reasons for their disobedience.

April had passed, and May almost passed; yet Bacon was still
not Privy Councillor. Coke's Præmunire had failed, because the
Grand Jury had returned an *ignoramus*; but a renewal of it was
threatened. The *Commendam* case was to come on again on
8 June. Something like impatience now breathes in Bacon's
repeated request (30 May, 1616) to Villiers. He reminds him
of "what is past" (his services in the conviction of Somerset)
and "what is to come" (his expected services in the impending
conflict with Coke):

SIR,
"The time is, as I should think, now or never for his Majesty to
finish his good meaning towards me, if it please him to consider what is
past and what is to come.

"If I would tender my profit and oblige men unto me by my place and
practice, I could have more profit than I desire, and could oblige all the
world and offend none : which is a brave condition for a man's private.
But my heart is not on these things. Yet on the other side I would be
sorry that worthless people should make a note that I get nothing but
pains, and enemies, and a little popular reputation which followeth me
whether I will or no. If anything is to be done for yourself, I should
take infinite contentment that my honour mought wait upon yours. But
I would be loth it should wait upon any man's else. If you would put
your strength to this business, I know it is done. And, that done, many
things more will begin. God keep you ever. I rest,
                         Your true and devoted servant,
                                             FR. BACON.
"30 May, 1616."

In consequence of this appeal we may suppose that Villiers
did "put his strength to the business." Yet the answer might
well have disappointed a man who felt that an "understanding"
with a King was equal to a promise. The previous correspondence shows that Bacon had responded effusively to both the

King and Villiers in answer to certain intimations with respect to the Chancellorship; but now we find him writing (3 June) "A letter to Sir G. Villiers upon the choice his M. gave him, whether he would be sworn Councillor, or have assurance to succeed the Chancellor." With perfect good temper, and without one word of reproach or remonstrance, Bacon prefers the present to the prospective. In his own heart he was probably confident that, whenever the woolsack was vacant, the King's necessities would point to him, and to no other, as the fit successor of Ellesmere:

"Sir,

"The King giveth me a noble choice, and you are the man my heart ever told me you were. Ambition would draw me to the later part of the choice. But in respect of my hearty wishes that my Lord Chancellor may live long, and the small hopes I have that I shall live long myself; and above all, because I see his Majesty's service daily and instantly bleedeth—towards which I persuade myself (vainly perhaps, but yet in mine own thoughts firmly and constantly) that I shall give them, when I am of the Table, some effectual furtherance (as a poor thread of the labyrinth which hath no other virtue but an united continuance without interruption or distraction)—I do accept of the former, to be Councillor for the present and to give over pleading at the Bar. Let the other matter rest upon my proof, and his Majesty's pleasure, and the accidents of time."

Between the 1st and 6th of June Bacon drew up a Memorial for a Declaration which the King was to make in Council concerning the indictments instigated by Coke in the preceding February. His Majesty, not instigated thereto either by the Chancellor or by the Attorney, was to express his regret that an attempt, apparently encouraged by the Judges of the King's Bench, has been made to disgrace the Chancery for proceedings which, as he has ascertained from his Learned Counsel, are entirely within the jurisdiction of that court; nor has any precedent been brought for indictment (on which action has been taken) in the King's Bench against the Chancery; he therefore purposes that an inquiry shall be held into the conduct of the Judges of the King's Bench by the Council, who shall be attended by the Learned Counsel. Secondly, as to the *Commendams*, the King conceives the action of the Judges to be indiscreet, presumptuous, and contemptuous; in disobeying his commands to adjourn the case; in alleging that the Attorney's letter (that is to say, his Majesty's commandment) was against the Law; and in breaking their oath, which binds them to give the King counsel.[1]

As the re-hearing of the *Commendam* case had been fixed for Saturday, 8 June, the meeting of the Council was arranged to come on before; and on 6 June, the twelve Judges being in attendance, the King came in person to the Council. The proceedings seem to show that the technical advantage and right of precedent were on the side of the King, while Coke had nothing but an instinctive aversion to forms which, however technically correct, were obviously liable to be so strained as to become oppressive. Unfortunately this was not a plea that could be very well expressed in words; and Coke—who invariably took his stand on narrow technical grounds wherever he could do so—was not the man to give it fitting expression. Consequently he made a very poor defence, resorting to such arguments as "that the stay required by his Majesty was a delay of justice, and therefore contrary to law and the Judges' oath;" that the Judges knew that the case would not concern his Majesty's power to grant *Commendams;* and that they could not adjourn it, "because Mr. Attorney's letter mentioned no day certain, and an adjournment must always be to a day certain." Certainly the King had the best of it here, in calling this last argument "mere sophistry," as the Judges might have fixed a day at their discretion.

The Learned Counsel were now called upon to deliver their opinions. But Coke simply answered that the King's Counsel ought not to plead or dispute with the Judges, for they were to plead before the Judges, and not to dispute with them: whereupon the King's Attorney replied:

"That he found that exception strange: for that the King's Learned Counsel were by oath and office (and much more where they had the King's

---

[1] It may be worth while to note one slight discrepancy between Bacon's *Memorial* and the facts. The *Memorial* says that "his Majesty's Attorney signified so much" (*i.e.* the King's command to adjourn) "*by his letters (the next day after he had received his commandment) to all the Judges.*" But the fact is that Bacon received the King's command on *Wednesday* afternoon, but did not write to Coke till *Thursday* afternoon, and to the other Judges till *Friday;* and it is not improbable that the shortness of the notice increased the resentment of the Judges at what they deemed the insulting interference of the Attorney-General.

express commandment) without fear of any man's face to proceed or declare against any the greatest peer or subject of the kingdom ; and not only any subject in particular, but any body of subjects or persons—were they Judges, or were they an Upper or Lower House of Parliament—in case that they exceed the limits of their authority, or take anything from his Majesty's royal power or Prerogative : and so concluded, that this challenge (and that in his Majesty's presence) was a wrong to their places, for which he and his fellows did appeal to his Majesty for reparation."

On this the King intervened. It was the duty of the Counsel, he said, to do what they had done, and he would maintain them in it. Coke replied that he would not dispute with his Majesty; and the King, not without humour, remarked that the Judges would not dispute with *him*, and would not allow the Learned Counsel to dispute with *them*, so that, " whether they did well or ill it must not be disputed." After this, the Lord Chancellor, concluding the statements of the Learned Counsel, delivered his opinion that the delay required by his Majesty would not have involved any breach of a Judge's oath. And now the Judges were separately called on to answer this question : " Whether, if at any time in a case depending before the Judges, which his Majesty conceived to concern him either in power or profit, and therefore required to consult with them and that they should stay proceedings in the meantime, they ought not to stay accordingly ? " It is probable that, as was the custom in taking the opinions of the Council, the junior or lowest in standing of the Judges was asked his opinion first. All assented, except Coke, who replied that " When that case should be, he would do that should be fit for a Judge to do." Taking courage from this, " the Chief Justice of the Common Pleas (who had previously assented with the rest) now added that he would ever trust the justness of his Majesty's commandment."

Nothing could have been nobler, wiser, and more temperate than Coke's answer. It was noble because the speaker, to his own apparent ruin, and unsupported by his own brethren on the Bench, upheld justice to the best of his power against the straining of an ancient practice which was likely to become oppressive : it was wise and temperate because he did not at once cast off and renounce old customs however obsolete and

possibly injurious. There might come a case before him where
the King's policy and Government were definitely and seriously
interested and where no private injustice could be contemplated ; such a case might be honourably deferred at the King's
command. Another case might come before him, where some
manifest injustice or some tedious and ruinous delay of justice
was intended by a King or a King's favourite ; such a case he
would not delay : " he would do that should be fit for a Judge
to do."

How vague and fluctuating an interpretation might be set
upon the King's right to consult the Judges in cases concerning
his "power or profit" is shown by the passage in Bacon's
Essay on Judicature : in which, after insisting that Kings and
States must consult Judges in cases that " trench to *point of
Estate*," he proceeds to define these last words as follows :

"I call *matter of Estate*, not only the parts of Sovereignty, *but
whatsoever introduceth any great alteration, or dangerous precedent, or
concerneth manifestly any great portion of people.*" [1]

A King's Attorney must be very dull who could not show
that almost any pending case "manifestly," though indirectly,
"concerned a great portion of people ; " and thus the King
could claim an almost general right of interference. In any
such case the Counsel were to be forbidden (if Bacon had his
will) to argue against the King's Prerogative ; the Judges were
to be compelled to take private counsel with the King or the
King's Lawyers ; they might be even separately summoned
to simultaneous interviews where they would have to hear
all that could be said on the King's side, without hearing anything that could be said on the other side : and finally they
might be asked or coerced by silent pressure to say what opinion
they intended to give, before they had heard more than one
side of the case. In the present instance, for example, " Mr.
Justice Doddridge said that *he would conclude for the King
that the Church was void and in his Majesty's gift.*" Thus the
scene closes in just such a triumph for the King as Bacon had
anticipated :

[1] *Essay* lvi. 122-133.

"The Judges having thus far submitted and declared themselves, his Majesty admonished them to keep the bounds and limits of their several courts, and not to suffer his Prerogative to be wounded by rash and unadvised pleading before them, or by new inventions of law : for as he well knew that the true and ancient common law is the most favourable, for kings, of any law in the world,[1] so he advised them to apply themselves to the study and practice of that ancient and best law . . . and therefore gave them leave to proceed in their argument."

On 26 June Coke was called before the Council to answer certain charges preferred against him by the Solicitor-General, and, in particular, to explain his conduct in the matter of the Præmunire. Here he stated that, when the Judges received his Majesty's command that no Bill of that nature be hereafter received, he and his brethren *" caused the same to be entered as an order in the same Court ; which shall be observed ; "* so that whatever his opinion may have been as to the justice or injustice of the settlement, he at least acquiesced in the King's authority to settle the question. But the King determined not only to humiliate him but also to use him as an instrument, if possible, for purifying the law from popular innovations : and the greatest Lawyer in England was to be compelled to adapt his Law Reports to the superior judgment of James. His Majesty therefore directed the Council (30 June, 1616) to call Coke again before them and to inform him that it was the King's pleasure he should forbear for the present to sit at Council or on the Bench, and that he must employ this enforced leisure in correcting in his Reports "many exorbitant and extravagant opinions set down and published for positive and good law ; . . . and having corrected what in his discretion he found meet in these Reports, his Majesty's pleasure was that he should bring the same privately to himself that he might consider thereof, as in his princely judgment should be found expedient."

[1] This was by no means an unmixed exaggeration. Sir Henry Neville, in the King's presence (Spedding, iv. 231) complained that "in matter of justice they (the King's subjects) could not have an indifferent proceeding ; " and see note on p. 209), where Professor Gardiner is quoted as saying that the King "might have every gentleman in England at his mercy" by entangling him " in the meshes of the law."

§ 34 Bacon becomes Lord Keeper

Villiers had been for some time rapidly rising in favour. "This is now the man," writes a friend to Carleton (27 August, 1616), "by whom all things do and must pass; and he far exceeds the former (Somerset) in favour and affection." His affable and winning nature contrasted agreeably at this time with the moroseness of the former Favourite; and he appears to have looked up to Bacon as a respected counsellor. Bacon, on the other side, was not alone in thinking much better of Villiers than he deserved, and in forming about him anticipations that were not destined to be realized. If he erred here, he erred with Archbishop Abbot and the Privy Council, who had introduced Villiers to the notice of the King in the hope of supplanting Somerset. Although therefore Bacon had a customary blindness to the defects of those in power who could be useful to him, it was probably not all flattery when he praised the rising Favourite (12 August, 1616) to the King as "a safe nature, a capable mind, an honest will, generous and noble affections, and a courage well lodged; and one that I know loveth your Majesty unfeignedly, and admireth you as much as it is in a man to admire his Sovereign upon earth." The King of course showed this letter to Villiers, and declared that the latter was "beholding" to Bacon for such kind expressions. Bacon will not allow that there can be any obligation for merely speaking the truth (20 August): "It was graciously and kindly done also of his Majesty towards me to tell you that you were beholding to me; but it must be then for thinking of you as I do; for otherwise, for speaking as I think, it is the part of an honest man." The reader will not fail to note the fatherly tone—a tone not long to be preserved—in which he addresses and advises the young Favourite. It is in a letter forwarding (12 August) to the freshly created Viscount Villiers his patent of creation:

"And now, because I am in the country, I will send you some of my country fruits; which with me are good meditations; which, when I am in the city, are choked with business.

"After that the King shall have watered your new dignities with his bounty of the lands which he intends you, and that some other things concerning your means which are now in intention shall be settled upon you, I do not see but you may think your private fortunes established ; and therefore it is now time that you should refer your actions chiefly to the good of your Sovereign and your country. It is the life of an ox or beast always to eat, and never to exercise; but men are born (and specially Christian men) not to cram in their fortunes but to exercise their virtues ; and yet the other hath been the unworthy and (thanks be to God) sometimes the unlucky humour of great persons in our times. Neither will your further fortune be the further off : for assure yourself that fortune is of a woman's nature, that will sooner follow you by slighting than by too much wooing."

He then encouraged him to a deed "which was never done since I was born, and which, not done, hath bred almost a wilderness and solitude in the King's service," *i.e.* to promote merit : "for in the time of the Cecils able men were by design and of purpose suppressed ; " and though the condition of things is bettered, yet still promotion depends too much on "money and turn-serving and cunning canvasses and importunity."

"Above all, depend wholly (next to God) upon the King, and be ruled, as hitherto you have been, by his instructions ; for that is best for yourself. For the King's care and thoughts concerning you are according to the thoughts of a great king ; whereas your thoughts concerning yourself are, and ought to be, according to the thoughts of a modest man. But let me not weary you. The sum is, that you think goodness the best part of greatness, and that you remember whence your rising comes, and make return accordingly. God ever keep you."

Thus Bacon expresses to Villiers all the good thoughts he had about the King, and to the King all the good thoughts he had about Villiers ; probably not forgetting that, being together, each would thus hear Bacon's good opinion of him from the other—a much more delicate compliment than flattering a person to his face. Villiers at all events took Bacon's counsel in such good part that he asked for more : and Bacon responded to this request in a long *Letter of Advice* of which two different versions are extant.

In this paper, after some excellent advice on the division and arrangement of business, coming to Church-matters, Bacon gives up every trace of his old feeling in favour of Reform, and avows himself in all respects an ecclesiastical Conservative. If any question be moved as to the doctrine of the Thirty-nine Articles, "give not," he says, "the least ear to the movers thereof." The tenets of the "Romish Catholics (so styling themselves)," and of the sectaries, are inconsistent, the former with the truth of Religion, the latter with monarchy: "for the regulating of either, there needs no other coercion than the due execution of the laws already established by Parliament." As regards Church-discipline also, he has now forsworn the old protest that "the contentious retention of custom is a turbulent thing," that "a good husbandman is ever proyning and stirring in his vineyard," and that "the constitutions and orders of the Bishops have reformed little." [1] Times had changed; and the Nonconformist feeling, though still deep and strong, was not so manifest now as in the days of Elizabeth. Besides, the royal will had pronounced against all Reform beyond the settlement of the Hampton Court Conference; and a star does not move more obediently from east to west, than Bacon obeys, and appropriates as his own, the motion of his *primum mobile,* the King.

" If any attempt be made to alter the discipline of our Church, although it be not an essential part of our religion, yet it is so necessary not to be rashly altered as the very substance of religion will be interested in it. Therefore I desire you, before any attempt be made of an innovation by your means, or by any intercession to your Master, that you will first read over—and his Majesty call to mind—that wise and weighty Proclamation which himself penned and caused to be published in the first year of his reign, and is prefixed in print before the Book of Common Prayer (of that impression); in which you will find so prudent, so weighty reasons not to hearken to innovations, as will fully satisfy you that it is dangerous to give the least ear to such innovators, but it is desperate to be misled by them. But, to settle your judgment, mark but the admonition of the wisest of men, King Solomon, *Prov.* 27, *v.* 21, *My son, fear God and the King, and meddle not with those who are given to change.*"

Concerning the Laws, that is, " the Common Laws of England," Bacon speaks with an enthusiasm which shows that, however far he was prepared to go in the direction of utilising them for the strengthening of the King's Prerogative, he would not be a party to recasting them with the view of bringing about an

[1] See above, p. 24.

avowed despotism : " if they be rightly administered, they are the best, the equallest in the world between the Prince and the People ; by which the King hath the justest Prerogative, and the People the best liberty." But then he sketches a plan by which the Judges are to be employed by the King as a kind of provincial police under the Chancellor as Head Inspector : a plan tolerable, perhaps, under the sway of a perfect Ruler, but likely to be perverted to the most oppressive purposes under a needy and prodigal Sovereign, driven to doubtful or illegal expedients for the sake of procuring money without recourse to Parliament. In Bacon's theory, however, the King was not to use the Judges as his instruments, but rather as his counsellors :

"Let the King take a care (and, as much as in you lies, do you take care for him) that the Judges of the Law may always be chosen of the learnedst of the profession (for an ignorant man cannot be a good judge) and of the prudentest and discreetest, because so great a part of the Civil Government lies upon their charge. And indeed little should be done in legal consultation without them, and very much may be done by their prudent advices, especially in their Circuits, if right use were made of them . . . if the King, by himself (which were the best) or by his Chancellor, did give them the charge according to occurrences at their going forth, and receive a particular accompt from them at their return home. They would then be the best intelligencers of the true state of the kingdom and the surest means to prevent or remove all growing mischiefs within the body of the realm."

The Laws themselves, though they are to be administered in the interests of the King, are not to be subverted :

" In the laws we have a native interest. It is our birthright and our inheritance, and I think the whole kingdom will always continue that mind which once the two Houses of Parliament publicly professed *Nolumus legem Angliae mutare*. Under a Law we must live ; and under a known Law and not an arbitrary Law, it is our happiness that we do live. And the Justices of Peace, if a good choice be made of them, are excellent instruments to this state."

Foreign policy is briefly despatched ; it is fixed by the King, who is resolved on peace ; " God send we surfeit not with it."

As to trade and political economy Bacon is found here, as elsewhere, by no means in advance of his times. He would lay the foundation of a profitable trade, by providing that exports shall exceed imports, so as to insure for the nation a balance of bullion, and by admitting as imports nothing but solid merchandise, not luxuries. Vanity in apparel is to be restrained as well as excess in diet. Native commodities and artisans are to be preferred to foreign. How far Bacon was prepared to carry the practical realization of his theories of Political Economy is shown by a curious piece of advice given by him to the King in the course of this very year. A struggle was at this time going on between English and Dutch commerce. James and his Council desired to retain in English hands not only the process of spinning, but also those of dyeing and dressing wool, and for that purpose had taken their charter from the old Company of cloth-workers, and given a charter to a new Company ; which was bound not to export wool till it had been dyed and dressed. As the Dutch would not buy wool in this state, preferring their own methods, the English trade slackened, and complaints arose from men out of work. Bacon proposes (13 September, 1616,) a drastic remedy "which certainly would do the deed," viz., that the King should, by Proclamation, *"forbid (after fourteen days, giving that time for suiting men's selves) the wearing of any stuff made wholly of silk without mixture of wool for the space of six months."* It is to be regretted that this piece of paper legislation was not carried into effect ; for it would have been interesting to note whether the results would have opened Bacon's eyes to the unpractical nature of some of his theories. But the previous interferences had at least one definite effect ; they diminished the good understanding which every wise statesman would have desired to maintain between England and the States ; and for this end Bacon, with others, must bear the blame.

Now that Villiers was established in the position of Favourite, Bacon perhaps thought that, by the aid of his influence, he might induce the King to consider a *Proposition touching the Compiling and Amendment of the Laws of England.* This was a task that had, for a long time back, engaged his attention. In the first of his reported Parliamentary speeches (1592) he digresses to mention it ; and many passages might be quoted to show how his philosophic and order-loving mind revolted from the chaotic condition of English Law, and how ardently he longed to see the commencement of a revision which he

commended as an "heroical" undertaking. In his present paper
he rejects, as a perilous innovation, the proposal to "reduce the
common laws of England to a text-book as the statutes are."
He recommends, as regards the common laws: 1st, a book *De
Antiquitatibus Juris,* "to be used for reverend precedents but
not for binding authorities;" 2nd, a series of Year Books from
Edward I. downwards, containing typical cases and "noting and
resolving" (by assembly of all the Judges in the Exchequer
Chamber or by Parliament) all contradictory cases. As auxiliaries
for the study of the Common Law there will be needed: 1st,
Institutions; 2nd, a Dictionary of legal terms; 3rd, a Treatise
on the Rules of Law. For the reform of Statute Law, it will be
needful, 1st, to discharge obsolete statutes; 2nd, to repeal statutes
sleeping, but still "snaring," and in force; 3rd, to mitigate
penalties; 4th, to reduce concurrent statutes heaped one upon
another to one clear, uniform law.

While recommending to the King this vast and "heroical"
project, the expectant Chancellor has a word of characteristic
self-confidence to say about his own part in it: "I do assure
your Majesty I am in good hope that, when Sir Edward Coke's
Reports and my Rules and Decisions shall come to posterity,
there will be (whatever is now thought) question who is the
greatest lawyer." Coke was at this time suffering from a double
disgrace. He, the greatest lawyer of his day, had not only been
suspended from his judicial duties, but also ordered by the King
to employ his leisure in correcting some "exorbitant and
extravagant opinions" which, so the King had been informed,
were "set down and published in his reports for good and
positive law." The corrections were to be submitted to the
King's "princely judgment," and after four months Coke appeared (17 October, 1616) before the Chancellor and the
Attorney to give an account of his corrections. At this interview a selection was made of five, out of a much larger number
of opinions, on which the King required explanation; and on
these five points Coke (21 October) returned his "humble and
direct answer." In every case but one, he maintained that his
words neither implied, nor were meant to imply, any interference
with the power of the Crown. But his fall had been determined. It is creditable to Bacon that he treated the Chief

Justice at this time with something of the respect due to his learning and character. " The Attorney," says Chamberlain (26 October), " is thought to be come about; as well that he ever used him with more respect than the rest, as for divers speeches he gives out in his favour, as that " A man of his learning and parts is not every day found, nor so soon made as marred." Herein, perhaps, the King himself had led the way.   Angered by the report that some of the Chancellor's servants—perhaps after the interview on 17 October—had insulted the great lawyer in his disgrace, his Majesty had sent word " that he would have him well used." But on 10 November, James announced to the Council his intention to remove Coke from the Bench. A paper in Bacon's hand contains suggestions to the King for the censuring of his rival. His Majesty is to declare that he might have proceeded on the grounds of deceit, contempt, and slander of his government, not only to have put him from his place of Chief Justice, but also to have brought him in question in the Star Chamber; but that (for the present) he refrains from all but the first.   After censuring his actions, his Majesty is to add that—

" Besides the actions themselves, his Majesty in his princely wisdom hath made special observation of him . . . that he, having in his nature not one part of those things which are popular in men, being neither liberal, nor affable, nor magnificent, he hath made himself popular by design only, in pulling down government."

It is probable that the King did not approve of, or use, this paper; for Chamberlain tells us that, in the presence of the Council, while signifying his intention to remove Coke, he " yet gave him this character, that he thought him no way corrupt, but a good justicer; with so many words as if he meant to hang him with a silken halter." Possibly the influence of Villiers was used to break his fall; for Coke was by this time making overtures for the marriage of his daughter to the Favourite's brother; and we already find Bacon (13 Nov.) keeping from Villiers his communications with the King concerning Coke : " I send not these things which concern my Lord Coke by my Lord Villiers, for such reason as your Majesty may conceive." In any case we know that, a few months afterwards, Bacon had to excuse himself to the King if he was " sometimes sharp (it may

be too sharp) " in matters affecting Coke which came before the
Council ; and it may well be that even James, irritated as he
was against the most self-willed and inconvenient of Judges,
nevertheless revolted from the tone of the censure which
Bacon would have put into his mouth, censure of a fallen man
proceeding from an acknowledged rival or enemy.   However,
Bacon's long series of assiduous, obsequious, and valuable
services, was too obvious to be ignored.   Scarcely a week passed
without a letter giving the King some new proof of the activity
and usefulness of his Attorney, and some suggestion how much
more useful he would be as a Chancellor, plastic as clay, and
making all the Judges equally plastic beneath the pressure of
the King's hand.   For example, a few days after Coke's fall (21
Nov. 1616,) he writes thus :

" But while your Majesty peruseth the accounts of Judges in circuits your
Majesty will give me leave to think of the Judges here in their upper
region.   And because Tacitus saith well *opportuni magnis conatibus transitus
rerum*, now, upon this change (when he that letteth [1] is gone) I shall endeavour, to the best of my power and skill, that there may be a consent and
united mind in your Judges to serve you and strengthen your business.'

In particular, Bacon used his utmost efforts to carry out the
King's wishes by the suppression of duelling : and here he gives
a specimen of the way in which the Judges, by their co-operation
with the King, might do something to rid the kingdom from a
growing evil.   Sending to Villiers an account of a speech of his
before the Council on this subject, he says :

"Yesterday was a day of great good for his Majesty's service and the
peace of this kingdom concerning duels by occasion of D'Arcy's case.   I
spake big, and, publishing his Majesty's strait charge to me, said it had
struck me blind as,[2] in point of duels and cartels, I should not know a
coronet from a hat-band. . . .   In this also I forgot not to prepare the judges,
and wish them to profess, and as it were to denounce, that in all cases of
duel capital before them, they will use equal severity towards the insolent
murder by the duel and the insidious murder, and that they will extirpate
that difference out of the opinions of men . . . which they did excellent
well."

As a specimen of Bacon's "big" style, the notes of his speech
before the Council (27 Nov.) to which he refers in the letter just
quoted, are not without interest :

[1] *i.e.* Coke.   [2] *i.e.* "*so* as," or "*so* that ;" see note on p. 197.

"The duel to which your[1] chartel hath introduction shall never have better terms at my hands than to be the inceptive act to murder. . . . It always carries this with it, that it is a direct affront of Law, and tends to the dissolution of Magistracy. They, being men, despising laws divine and human, they become like Anabaptists that do as the Spirit moves them, and according to the boundings and corvets of their own wills, and for this they have made acts, and have rules, distinctions, and cases. This is right as[2] the Scripture saith—to imagine mischief as a law.

". . . . These swelling tumours that arise in men's proud affections must be beaten flat with justice ; or else all will end in ruin. It is to set a vile price upon the blood of the subject. . . . Will you have the sacrifices of men, not of bulls or oxen ?

"You say the Law is such. But, my Lords, the Law of England is not taken out of Amadis de Gaul, nor the book of Palmerin, but out of the Scripture, out of the laws of the Romans and Grecians, where never a duel was ; and they had such excellent reproachful speeches as we read in their writings, and yet never no sword drawn.

"But the King hath taken away all excuse, having given a fair passage ; and nothing can be offered as a wrong, but he hath left sufficient remedy. My Lords, when his Majesty spake lately unto me of this business—and no man expresseth himself like him—he said, ' I come forth and see myself nobly attended, but I know not whether any of them shall live four-and-twenty hours ; for it is but the mistaking of a word in heat, and that brings the lie, and that a challenge, and then comes the loss of their lives.' "

An Attorney who could thus give expression to every wish of the King, and diffuse it through the kingdom by the instrumentality of the Judges, might well be regarded by James as likely to be a Chancellor after his own heart. The present Chancellor Egerton, Lord Ellesmere, who had recently been created Viscount Brackley, had indeed served him faithfully—so faithfully that the lawyers of Westminster Hall nicknamed him Viscount "Break-law" ; but though he constantly maintained the King's Prerogative, he had not the energy or ability which Bacon possessed, to enlarge and extend it. Besides, he had been long ailing and desirous of resigning. On 5 March, worn out with disease, he at last succeeded in persuading the King to accept his resignation ; and on 7 March, 1617, with the best wishes of his predecessor, Sir Francis Bacon received the Great Seal with the title of Lord Keeper.[3]

---

[1] "Your" is used contemptuously, or familiarly, as often in Shakespeare : "the chartel (*i.e.* challenge,) with which you are so well acquainted."

[2] That is, "just as."

[3] Dean Church (p. 108) observes, "There was a curious hesitation in treating

§ 35 THE LORD KEEPER'S ACTIVITY

"The rising unto place is laborious, and by pains men come to greater pains ; and it is sometimes base, and by indignities men come to dignities :" so wrote the Solicitor-General in 1612.[1] But the Lord Keeper was now to learn the truth of the converse proposition—that "by dignities men come to indignities ;" for never, during all the patient drudgery of his Solicitorship, nor even in earlier days during his long, fruitless suit for place under Elizabeth, had he experienced such humiliations as were now to fall upon him. The Essay speaks, indeed, of "downfall," and hints at the difficulty of maintaining one's position in office : "The standing is slippery and the egress is either a downfall or at least an eclipse, which is a melancholy thing ;" but it says nothing of the misery of only being allowed to stand at the cost of having first stooped to the most ignominious self-prostration. It describes the responsibilities of place as having "license to do good and evil ;" but it is silent on the degradation of using a high place for nothing but an ampler exercise of obsequious arts, and for a more effectual servility to the will of an unworthy patron.

One of Bacon's first tasks in his capacity of Lord Keeper (23 March, 1617) was to find good reasons for the project of the Spanish match, from which he had formerly been averse, but to which he now assented in company with the rest of the Council. In a paper submitted to the King he suggests the good of Christendom arising from this union between Spain and England, whereby religious differences may be laid aside and forgotten ; the extinction of piracy by the united fleets; the opportunity of a Holy War against the Turk so as to "suffocate and starve Constantinople ;" the erection of a tribunal or praetorian power to decide controversies between Christian countries ; and lastly, the opportunity for checking the growth

him as other men were treated in like cases. He was *only Lord Keeper*. It was not till the following January that he received the office of Lord Chancellor. It was not till half a year afterwards that he was made a Peer." But this appears to be a mistake ; for "during the whole of Elizabeth's reign *no one had borne the title of Lord Chancellor, and no Lord Keeper had been made a Peer.*"—*Dictionary of National Biography,* "Bacon," ii. 345.

[1] *Essays,* xi. 7.

of a disposition in some places to make "popular estates and leagues to the disadvantage of monarchies."

But in company with the rest of the Council he incurred a rebuke for using their discretion in keeping back a royal Proclamation commanding the nobility to leave London. It had been ordered at a time when most of the nobility had left, and was thought likely to be needlessly distasteful; but no such excuse availed with James; who signified to them (April, 1617) that "obedience is better than sacrifice, and that he knoweth he is King of England." Already therefore the new Lord Keeper had received some warning of the limits within which he must confine himself when (7 May, 1617), he took his seat in the Court of Chancery, exceeding all his predecessors, says a correspondent of Carleton, in "the bravery and multitude of his servants."

Writing to Villiers (now Earl of Buckingham), an account how he yesterday took his seat in Chancery, the Lord Keeper deplores the pomp of the proceedings:

"Yesterday I took my place in Chancery, which I hold only from the King's grace and favour, and your friendship. There was much ado and a great deal of world. But this matter of pomp, which is heaven to some men, is hell to me, or purgatory at least."

We cannot here forget what the writer tells us elsewhere: "You shall observe that the more deep and sober sort of politic persons in their greatness, are ever bemoaning themselves what a life they lead, chanting a *quanta patimur!* Not that they feel it so, but to abate the edge of envy." [1]

His speech on taking his seat, abounds in promises of amended procedure. Beginning with the charge of the King, "the absolutest [2] prince in judicature that hath been in the Christian World," he promises to keep within due bounds the jurisdiction of the Court; he will grant no injunction merely on priority of suit, nor "make it a horse-race who shall be first at Westminster Hall." So far from neglecting the assistance of the reverend

---

[1] *Essays*, ix. 98. Professor Gardiner no doubt expresses the truth in saying (*History*, ii. 198): "*He* [Bacon] *liked the pomp and circumstance of power,* its outward show and grandeur, the pleasant company and the troops of followers which were its necessary accompaniments."

[2] That is, "most perfect."

S

Judges his coadjutors, he protests that, should there be any main diversity of opinion in his assistants from his own, he should probably have recourse to the King's own judgment before he should pronounce. Condemning the excess of deliberation in his predecessor on the Bench —" of whom I learn much to imitate and (with due reverence to his memory let me speak it) somewhat to avoid " [1]—he declares that " fresh justice is the sweetest," and that " the subject's pulse beats swift, though the Chancery pace be slow." On the other hand he condemns no less that affectation of despatch [2] which turns utterly to delay and length, like Penelope's web, doing and undoing. As for the plaintiffs who make delays, after having obtained an injunction to stay a suit in Common Law—" by the grace of God I will make injunctions an hard pillow to sleep on." In an interesting little personal digression the Lord Chancellor hints that he may possibly cut short his life by hard work, and he takes his hearers so far into his confidence as to tell them what he intends to do with his long vacations :

"Again, because justice is a sacred thing, and the end for which I am called to this place, and therefore is my way to heaven (and if it be shorter, it is never a whit the worse) I shall, by the grace of God (as far as God shall give me strength) add the afternoon to the forenoon, and some fortnight of the vacation to the term, for the expediting and clearing of the causes of the Court. *Only the depth of the leisure of the three long vacations I would reserve in some measure free for business of Estate, and for studies, arts, and sciences, to which, in my nature, I am most inclined.*"

In conclusion, the chief comfort to him under the burden of his new duty is that he serves so wise and good a Master, that he needs "to be but a conduit for the conveyance only of his goodness to the people."

A very interesting letter (8 May), to Buckingham, shows with what a mixture of graciousness and authority he intended to play his part of overseer of the Judges, whose assistance would be of inestimable advantage for the purpose of systematically magnifying the royal Prerogative :

"Yesterday, which was my weary day, I bid all the Judges to dinner (which was not used to be) and entertained them in a private withdrawing

---

[1] The text varies, one version having "*much* to avoid."
[2] *Essays*, xxv. 1.

chamber with the Learned Counsel. When the feast was passed I came amongst them, and set me down at the end of the table, and prayed them to think I was one of them, and but a foreman. I told them I was weary, and therefore must be short, and that I would now speak with them but upon two points.

" Whereof the one was that I would tell them plainly that I was firmly persuaded that the former discords and differences between the Chancery and other Courts was but flesh and blood ; and now the men were gone the matter was gone ; and that for my part, as I would not suffer any the least diminution or derogation from the ancient and due power of the Chancery, so, if anything should be brought to them at any time touching the proceedings of the Chancery which did seem to them exorbitant or inordinate, that they should freely and friendly acquaint me with it, and we should soon agree ; or if not, we had a Master that could easily both discern and rule. At which speech of mine, besides a great deal of thanks and acknowledgment, I did see cheer and comfort in their faces as if it were a new world.

" The second point was that I let them know how his Majesty, at his going, gave me charge to call and receive from them the accounts of their circuits, according to his Majesty's former prescript, to be set down in writing, and that I was to transmit the writings themselves to his Majesty ; and accordingly, as soon I have received them, I will send them to his Majesty."

Another means of increasing the King's power would be to extend the jurisdiction of the Court of High Commission. This Court had been established at the beginning of Elizabeth's reign, to deal with the extraordinary crisis caused by the national transition in religion. " Its powers were enormous, and united both those forms of oppression which were repulsive to moderate Englishmen. It managed to combine the arbitrary tendencies by which the lay courts were at that time infected, with the inquisitional character of an ecclesiastical tribunal." [1] Yet it is to this Court that Bacon now desires to give extended powers if he can persuade the Judges to consent. The letter concludes with a most courtly and dexterous insinuation that James can govern England as well in his absence, through the Lord Keeper, as by his own presence.

" Some two days before, I had a conference with some Judges (not all, but such as I did choose), touching the High Commission and the extending of the same in some points ; which I see I shall be able to despatch by consent, without his Majesty's further trouble.

[1] Gardiner, *History*, i. 34.

"I did call upon the Judges' Committees also for the proceeding in the purging of Sir Edward Coke's *Reports*, which I see they go on with seriously.

"Thanks be to God, we have not much to do for matters of counsel, and I see now that his Majesty is as well able by his letters to govern England from Scotland, as he was to govern Scotland from England."

A few days afterwards (having recovered from a short illness which made some think that the new Lord Keeper had "so tender a constitution of body and mind that he would hardly be able to undergo the burden of so much business as his place required,") he took the opportunity of the promotion of certain Judges, to deliver two or three weighty speeches, in all of which he magnifies to the utmost the King's Prerogative. A Judge, he says to Mr. Serjeant Hutton, is "not to be headstrong but heartstrong;" and then follows a sentence of which the Lord Keeper thought so well, that he afterwards (1625) inserted it in the enlarged edition of the *Essays*: "The twelve Judges of the realm are as the twelve lions under Solomon's throne; they must be lions, but yet lions under the throne." Sir John Denham receives similar advice: "Above all, you ought to maintain the King's Prerogative, and to set down with yourself that the King's Prerogative and the Law are not two things; but the King's Prerogative is Law and the principal part of Law." To the same effect is his charge to all the Judges in the Star Chamber on 10 July: the Judges are "the planets" of the Kingdom; the King is their "first mover," that is, the *primum mobile* of the old astronomy.[1] "Do therefore," he charges them, "as the planets do: move always and be carried with the motion of your First Mover, which is your Sovereign; a popular Judge is a deformed thing." On 8 June he writes to Buckingham that he has cleared off the business in Chancery: "Not one cause unheard. Not one petition unanswered. And this, I think, could not be said in our age before."

---

[1] Compare *Essays* xv. 5: xvii. 24; li. 59.

§ 36 The Lord Keeper out of Favour

But meanwhile, a storm was preparing for the Lord Keeper. There had been, as far back as November, 1616, a project for the marriage of Sir John Villiers, a brother of Buckingham, to Coke's daughter; and although it had been at one time broken off by Coke's refusal to pay the needful dowry, the negotiations had been reopened, and Coke was now (June, 1617) on good terms with the Favourite. The mother, Lady Hatton, averse to the match, had carried the girl away; but Coke, after vainly attempting to obtain a warrant from Bacon through the mother of Sir John Villiers, had obtained one from Winwood. Then, accompanied by several servants, he had "repaired to the house where she was remaining, and with a piece of timber cr form, broken open the door and dragged her along to his coach."

Bacon of course regarded this affair, like all others, from a double point of view—the political, and "his own particular." In both aspects, the proposed marriage seemed to him most objectionable. If, by an alliance with the Favourite, Coke were again restored to the sunshine of the royal favour, and perhaps to his place in the Council, it might have the effect of discouraging the friends and encouraging the enemies of the Prerogative; and his own position would assuredly be shaken by an enemy always at the King's hand to blacken his motives and to laugh at his law.[1] But Bacon made the very great mistake of thinking that, because this step would unquestionably be injurious to him privately, and possibly to his political schemes for the King's interests, therefore the King himself could not possibly be in favour of it. He altogether overrated his own influence and underrated the Favourite's; and in expostulating with the latter, he forgot that a young man who

---

[1] "It is true," he says, in his first letter (July 12) to Buckingham, "my judgment is not so weak to think it can do me any hurt;" and he protests to the King that it is absurd to suppose that he should fear Coke or "take umbrage at him in respect of mine own particular;" but in a subsequent letter he confesses that, from the very first, he was alarmed *on his own account,* lest he should lose the friendship of the Favourite (August 23): "*I did ever fear that this alliance would go near to leese me your lordship,* that I hold so dear; and that was the *only respect particular to myself* that moved me to be as I was till I heard from you."

will endure a moral or spiritual exhortation couched in general terms, will be far less patient when his adviser not only warns him against a particular course on which he is resolved, but also gives point to the warning by telling him that his disobedience will end in his ruin.

The Lord Keeper's head must have been a little turned by all that "pomp and world" through which he had lately passed; or else he could hardly have shown such a curious want of tact as characterises the letter to the Earl of Buckingham in which (12 July) he protests against the proposed marriage. The Earl's brother, he says, purposes to marry into a disgraced house, and the Earl himself will go near to lose all his friends, himself (Bacon) only excepted. Since by his great experience in the world he must needs see further than his Lordship can, he trusts Buckingham will accept this, his faithful service. On the same day he gives Lady Hatton a warrant for the recovery of her daughter. Three days afterwards Coke was called before the Council, and orders were given that an information should be preferred against him in the Court of the Star Chamber. But a short interval sufficed to change all this. Taxed at the Council Board with abetting Coke, Winwood produced a "letter of approbation of all his courses" from the King, which struck the Council dumb. They immediately undid everything they had done, and informed the King (about 19 July) of their retractation.

A fortnight had now elapsed since Bacon had written to Buckingham, and still neither the King nor the Favourite had vouchsafed any reply. He therefore writes to the King (25 July) declaring that "if there be any merit in drawing on that match," it is due to the Council, who "have so humbled Sir Edward Coke, as he seeks now that with submission which (as your Majesty knows) before he rejected with scorn." Yet he ventures to protest that, if Coke is to be restored, his Majesty must expect divisions in the Council, not from anything that could arise from Bacon himself—"for I can be *omnia omnibus* for your Majesty's service "—but because of Coke's unsociable and intolerable nature. In the same strain he writes also to Buckingham. On 23 August, a short and angry note from the Favourite, and a sharp rebuke from the King, awakened the Lord Keeper to

a sense of his true position.   Another letter from him couched
in a strain of pathetic humility—humbly confessing that he had
been " a little parent-like " in his advice to the Favourite " (this
being no other term than his Lordship hath heretofore vouchsafed to my counsels), but in truth (and it please your Majesty),
without any grain of disesteem for his Lordship's discretion"
—elicited from the King only a second rebuke, and from
Buckingham the laconic reply that " time would try all."

Meantime, Bacon's faithful friend and admirer, Yelverton, the
Attorney-General, had gone to meet the King who was now
returning from Scotland ; and he sent a report of the state of
things at Court, which showed Bacon that his position was
endangered.   Coke had arrived before him and had been well
received.   Buckingham was burning with a fierce and undis-
guised resentment ; he plainly told Yelverton that " he would
not secretly bite," but would openly oppose those who had set
themselves against the match ; " and they should discern what
favour he had by the power he would use."   Yelverton, who
would truckle neither to the Favourite nor to the King, protested that Sir Edward Coke himself by his violence, and not
the Lord Keeper, had thrown obstacles in the way of the marriage.   Then follows a graphic account of the storms which the
Lord Keeper must be prepared to face.

" Now, my Lord, give me leave out of all my affections that shall ever
serve you, to intimate touching yourself :

" 1st. That every courtier is acquainted that the Earl professeth openly
against you as forgetful of his kindness, and unfaithful to him in your love
and in your actions.

" 2nd. That he returneth the shame upon himself, in not listening to
counsel that dissuaded his affection from you, and not to mount you so high ;
not forbearing in open speech (as divers have told me and this bearer, your
gentleman, hath heard also) to tax you, as if it were an inveterate custom
with you to be unfaithful to him as you were to the Earls of Essex and
Somerset.

" 3rd. That it is too common in every man's mouth in court, that your
greatness shall be abated, and as your tongue hath been a razor to some, so
shall theirs be to you.

" 4th. That there is laid up for you, to make your burden the more
grievous, many petitions to his Majesty against you. . .

" My noble Lord, if I were worthy, being the meanest of all to interpose
my weakness, I would humbly desire :—

" 1. That your Lordship fail not to be with his Majesty at Woodstock. The sight of you will fright some.

" 2. That you single not yourself from the other Lords, but justify all the proceedings as your joint acts ; and I little fear but you pass conqueror.

" 3. That you retort the clamour and noise in this business upon Sir Edward Coke, by the violence of his carriage.

" 4. That you seem not dismayed, but open yourself bravely and confidently, wherein you can excel all subjects ; by which means I know you shall amaze some and daunt others."

But Yelverton did not know the real cause of Buckingham's and the King's displeasure. It was not the definite action of Bacon and the Council in opposing Coke's illegal violence ; it was rather the position assumed by the Lord Keeper of authoritative adviser to the King's Favourite, that had irritated both of them. They were angry, and from their point of view naturally angry, that Bacon did not know his place. He had been guilty of the folly of holding it out almost as a threat, that the Favourite of the King would " go near to lose " many of his friends, if he persisted in allying himself with Coke : as though the friendship of any one were in the least doubtful, or were of the least importance, for one who enjoyed his Majesty's chief affection ! In Coke or Yelverton, such a mistake would have been pardonable : they were both blunt, straightforward men, who had never professed such absolute devotion as the Lord Keeper had to the royal will. But Bacon had repeatedly asserted that if he were raised to that high place he would make it his business and pride to be a mere instrument in the hands of the King ; he could promise his master nothing but the homage of a perfect obedience, *gloria in obsequio.* The King and the Favourite had accepted these professions as sincere ; they meant to use Bacon as a mere instrument for carrying out their desires ; and in proportion to their previous credence in his professions they were now disappointed and irritated that they had placed at the head of the Council a man who apparently meant to have a will of his own. First in the suppression of the Royal Proclamation,[1] and now again in this intolerable attempt to intimidate Buckingham, he had manifested an independence which his previous suppleness justified them in

[1] See above, p. 254.

regarding as a treacherous ingratitude. Why had he not at least consulted the King before siding against Sir John Villiers? Why had he not taken for granted that the Favourite's brother was supported by the Favourite, and that his will must not be disputed, at all events till the King's pleasure were known? Perhaps Bacon was fondly hoping to carry out the resolution he had committed to paper in the *Commentarius Solutus* in 1608 [1] —to "amuse the King with pastime," so that while James was enjoying himself in Progresses or diverting himself with Scotch distractions, it might be left to the Lord Chancellor to be the real ruler of England. But if so, he was vastly mistaken. James could be led anywhere by a handsome, fluent, empty-headed Favourite, but not by Bacon. Flatter as he might, Bacon must always be inherently disqualified from playing the part of a Cecil, and still more of a Carr or a Villiers; for he could never succeed in altogether divesting himself of an element of greatness, and James "never attached himself to any man who was truly great." [2]

Under these circumstances, no excuses, nor justifications, nor evasions were of the least use to the wretched Lord Keeper. Submission, and nothing else, was his way out of the difficulty. He was to be punished—and he richly deserved punishment— for supposing that after rising to office by subservience, he could maintain himself in office by independence; for supposing that under such a King as James, working through such a Favourite as Villiers, it would be possible for a versatile, philosophic mind, deficient in moral rigidity, to do anything except what he had promised to do—*gloria in obsequio*—submit and obey. He submitted accordingly; nay, he even offered the Favourite *to put his submission into writing,* if that would pacify him. Two years of the King's concentrated affection had so degraded that affable young man that he actually felt no pain in receiving this offer from a man old enough to be his father, and so richly endowed with intellectual gifts, that even a Favourite should have felt some touch of admiration for him; to whom Buckingham, in a relenting and compassionate mood, sends a pencil note after this fashion:—

---

[1] See above, p. 147.   [2] Gardiner, *History,* i. 49.

" I do freely confess that *your offer of submission unto me, and in writing* (*if so I would have it*), battered so the unkindness that I had conceived in my heart for your behaviour towards me in my absence, as out of the sparks of my old affection toward you I went to sound his Majesty's intention how he means to behave himself towards you, specially in any public meeting ; where I found on the one part his Majesty so little satisfied with your late answer unto him, which he counted (for I protest I use his own terms) *confused and childish,* and his vigorous resolution on the other part so fixed, that he would put some public exemplary mark upon you, as I protest the sight of his deep-conceived indignation quenched my passion, making me upon the instant change from the person of a party into a peace-maker ; so as I was forced upon my knees to beg of his Majesty that he would put no public act of disgrace upon you, and, as I dare say, no other person would have been patiently heard in this suit by his Majesty but myself, so did I (though not without difficulty) obtain thus much :—that he would not so far disable you from the merit of your future service, as to put any particular mark of disgrace upon your person. . . .

" Thus your Lordship seeth the fruits of my natural inclination ; and I protest all this time past it was no small grief unto me to hear the mouth of so many upon this occasion open to load you with innumerable malicious and detracting speeches, as if no music were more pleasing to my ears than to rail of you : which made me rather regret the ill-nature of mankind, that like dogs love to set upon him that they see once snatched at. And to conclude, my Lord, you have hereby a fair occasion so to make good hereafter your reputation by your sincere service to his Majesty, as also by your firm and constant kindness to your friends, as I may (your Lordship's old friend) participate of the comfort and honour that will thereby come to you.   Thus I rest at last

Your Lordship's faithful friend and servant,

G. B."

In return, Bacon pours on Buckingham a gratitude even more profuse than that which he had once offered to Cecil :—

" My ever best Lord, now better than yourself, your Lordship's pen, or rather pencil, hath portrayed towards me such magnanimity and nobleness and true kindness, as methinketh I see the image of some ancient virtue and not anything of these times. It is the line of my life and not the lines of my letter that must express my thankfulness ; wherein, if I fail, then God fail me, and make me as miserable as I think myself at this time happy by this reviver through his Majesty's clemency and your incomparable love and favour."

Whatever other resolutions Bacon may have broken, none can accuse him of breaking this. The " lines of his life " will henceforth exhibit him in undeviating conformity with the

Favourite's will. On 28 September, Coke was restored to the Council Table, and having paid down £30,000 as her dowry, saw his daughter united to Sir John Villiers: but the Lord Keeper was restored to favour, and never again forfeited it.

§ 37 BACON AS LORD CHANCELLOR

Shortly after the Lord Keeper's submission and restoration to favour, Buckingham began to test Bacon's promise to " express his thankfulness by the lines of his life," by making constant applications to him in favour of Chancery suitors. In so doing, he was acting against an excellent precept which Bacon inserted in the *Advice* (see p. 248): " By no means be you persuaded to interpose yourself by word or letter, in any cause depending, or like to be depending, in any Court of Justice . . . . If it should prevail, it prevents justice; but if the Judge be so just as not to be inclined thereby, yet it always leaves a taint of suspicion." [1] In November, 1617, we find Buckingham "renewing " a motion which he appears to have made before in behalf of parties in a cause depending. It would seem that Bacon expostulated with him; for three days afterwards Buckingham writes that he " had resolved to give the Lord Keeper no more trouble in matters of controversy depending before him; " yet he desires Bacon's favour in the plaintiff's behalf, with the qualification " so far only as the justice of their cause shall require."

In January, 1618, the Favourite again pleads for one Sir George Tipping, who " is willing to perform a decree made in Chancery . . . . *but that he is persuaded*," &c., in other words, declines to obey the decree except upon conditions. For this man, Buckingham desired the Lord Keeper's further favour, and hopes that he will " find out some course how he may be exempted from the fear of the sale of his land." Once more (February, 1618) Bacon's expostulations may have touched Buckingham,

---

[1] This paragraph "only appears in the second form of the *Advice*, written after 1619, when Bacon had had personal experience of the proceedings of Villiers " (Gardiner, *History*, iii. 29). But, from the next two sentences in the text above, it appears that Bacon had previously remonstrated on the subject in 1617 ; and Bacon's worst enemies can hardly believe that he did not repeat the remonstrance between 1617 and 1619.

who writes that he had resolved not to write to his Lordship on any matter between party and party, yet—

". . . at the earnest request of my noble friend, the Lord Norris, to whom I account myself much beholden, I could not but recommend unto your Lordship's favour a special friend of his, Sir Thomas Monk, who hath a suit before your Lordship in the Chancery with Sir Robert Basset ; which, upon the report made unto me thereof, seemeth so reasonable, that I doubt not that the cause itself will move your Lordship to favour him, if upon the hearing thereof it shall appear the same unto your Lordship as at the first sight it doth unto me. I therefore desire your Lordship to show in this particular what favour you lawfully may for my sake, who will account it as done unto myself."

But after this date there appears to be no further evidence, direct or indirect, that Bacon protested against the "taint of suspicion" which the Favourite continued to cast upon his judgments. Among a number of other letters (1618) one recommends some officers of his Majesty's household against the Lady Vernon, in which Buckingham doubts not "but, as his Majesty has been satisfied of the equity of the cause in his Officers' behalf who have undergone the business by his Majesty's command, your Lordship will also find their cause worthy of your favour." He desires a "speedy end" that his Majesty "may be freed from further importunity ; and the Officers from the charge and trouble of following the suit."

Under the circumstances—after he had once resolved to tolerate these attempted interferences with the course of Law—some may perhaps think it creditable to Bacon that, so far as is yet known, the pressure of the Favourite did not coerce him to any deliberate perversion of justice, except in one (the following) case, which lasted from the summer of 1617 to the winter of 1618. To the plaintiff (eight years old at his father's death) had been left a legacy of £800. His uncle, Dr. Steward by name, trustee and executor, mixed the trust money with his own ; and, when the plaintiff came of age, he disputed his nephew's claim to interest. When the case, on being heard in the Court of Chancery, went for the plaintiff, the defendant, after repeated acts of contumacy, appealed to Buckingham. Buckingham immediately wrote two letters to Bacon, saying in the first, that he owed Dr. Steward "a good turn ; " and in the second, that Dr. Steward was "a stout man," and "I should be sorry he should make any complaint against you." Upon this, Bacon saw the parties privately, and annulling all the deliberate decisions of the Court, compelled the youth to assent to the ceasing of all proceedings, and to accept the bare £800 without interest. To cover this disgraceful transaction, Bacon awarded a commission appointed by both parties for the further investigation of the disputed points. Of this commission it is said by Mr. Heath (to whom Mr. Spedding intrusted the investigation of the case) "I do not suppose that anything was ever meant by it except to ease the Lord Chancellor of his burden." [1]

For all his services and submissions, the Lord Keeper was now about to receive his reward. On 1 January, 1618, the Earl of Buckingham, freshly elevated to be Marquis of Buckingham, gave a great feast at which the Lord Keeper was made Lord Chancellor with a salary fixed for his life, and with an increase of £600 a year above his salary as Lord Keeper. "His Lordship," writes Chamberlain, "hath of late much insinuated into the King's and Marquis's favour." Among other services performed in return for these favours Bacon probably drew up the *Declaration* justifying the execution of Sir Walter Raleigh. It received additions from the King; and we have no evidence but that of style for supposing that it proceeded from Bacon's pen. That evidence, however, is strong.[2] But whether he composed it or not, it is probable that he regarded Raleigh as little better than a pirate ; and we learn from a letter in the archives of Simancas that on the 22nd of October the Lord

---

[1] For a fuller account of this case see the Introduction, above. Professor Gardiner (*National Dictionary of Biography*, "Bacon," ii. 345) says that Bacon "was exposed to a constant flow of letters from Buckingham, asking him to show favour to this person or that, *of course under the reservation that he would do so only so far as was consonant with justice.*" But Mr. Spedding has admitted that this reservation is not infrequently omitted (vi. 259-260).

[2] On the *Declaration*, see Gardiner, *History*, iii. 152, 153. "It was founded on the evidence which had been taken, and there is not the smallest reason to suspect that any false statement was intentionally inserted by James or his ministers. . . . . But in starting from the theory that the mine was a mere figment of Raleigh's imagination, it left out of sight the fact that he had reason to believe the mine existed, though he certainly had no conclusive evidence on the point." In other words, the Government, using Bacon as its pen, endeavoured to prove Raleigh to be a hypocrite, just as they had endeavoured to prove Essex to be a hypocrite (see above, pp. 75-80). The gold-mine in the case of Raleigh corresponded to the "enemies" in the case of Essex.

Chancellor censured him greatly when he informed him that he must die.

Among other proofs of the devotion of the Lord Chancellor to Villiers, we must reckon the part played by the former in expediting the disgrace of one of the Favourite's most prominent enemies, the Earl of Suffolk, who was then Lord Treasurer. The attack on Suffolk—though justified by the corruption of his wife, if not his own—was but part of a general assault against the Howards, the only obstacle that still remained to Buckingham's ambition. Besides Suffolk himself, who was a Howard, there was his son-in-law, Viscount Wallingford, the Master of the Wards; there was another Howard, the Earl of Nottingham who was Lord High Admiral; and Sir Thomas Lake, Secretary of State, with Sir Henry Yelverton, Attorney-General, were both dependents of this powerful family. The mere fact that they were powerful and did not owe their power to him, would have been sufficient cause for the hostility of the Favourite; but they had also attempted (about the beginning of 1618) to supplant him in the King's affections, by introducing another favourite. Their failure had made Buckingham stronger than ever; the King had bestowed new rewards on him, and publicly professed his desire to advance the house of Villiers above all others: "Of myself," he said, "I have no doubt, for I live to that end; and I hope that my posterity will so far regard their father's commandments and instructions as to advance that house above all others whatever." But the King's increased affection by no means quenched the Favourite's desire for vengeance; and substantial grounds were not long wanting to enable Buckingham to commence a course of retaliation on the Howards. Almost every Crown official in those times derived part of his income from bribes, or presents, or perquisites, universally recognised in practice, but not to be justified in a Court of Law. Suffolk, yielding to the influence of his wife, had transgressed even the recognised limits of irregularity, and had rendered himself peculiarly open to charges of corruption. Accordingly on the day after the first accusation was brought against him, he was deprived (19 July) of the Treasurership, and the Treasury was put into commission.

In vain had the Secretary, Lake, anticipating that he would

share the downfall of his patron Suffolk, thrown himself at Buckingham's feet, and offered him a bribe of £15,000 to be restored to favour. The money probably found its way into the pockets of the Favourite's mother, but the restoration to favour was only temporary. It was said (and with, at least, some grounds) that he had allowed himself to be drawn by a scheming daughter into misuse of his authority for the purpose of supporting her false accusations; and in February, 1619, he was condemned to fine and imprisonment, and compelled to resign his office. Against Wallingford, the Master of the Wards, a man of spotless character, it was impossible to proceed in the same way; but Lady Wallingford had lampooned the faction of Buckingham, and therefore James informed him that he did not wish to be served by the husband of such a wife. Wallingford courted inquiry, but was at last induced to resign his office on promise of compensation. The Earl of Nottingham was more justly removed from office. The report of the Navy Commission showed extensive abuses; the expenses of the navy were increasing, and its efficiency decreasing, with unexampled rapidity. Already in January, 1618, it had been proposed that Buckingham should take the place of the old and incapable High Admiral, and in the following year Nottingham resigned the post, pensioned by the King, and compensated by Buckingham; and thus at last the Favourite, besides remaining Master of the Horse, became Lord High Admiral of England.

Along with the fall of the Howards there had been proceeding a searching inquiry into administration of the finances. In the Household, the Treasury, the Wardrobe, and the Admiralty, retrenchment and beneficial reforms had been carried out, with the valuable and original aid of Sir Lionel Cranfield, but with the encouragement and co-operation of Buckingham. Their financial efforts were aided by the growing commercial prosperity of the country; and thus, without adding a penny of taxation, the King's revenues from the great customs and the wine duties was raised from £90,000 to £156,000 a year. Although he was still beset by pressing difficulties, it is not surprising that the King was led by these financial improvements to place increased confidence in the Favourite, who had introduced them in despite of his enemies the Howards.

The trial of Suffolk did not come on for hearing till October, 1619. In answer to those who interceded for him, the King replied that a trial was necessary in order to prove that he had been justly deprived of his office. About the guilt of the Countess, who was simultaneously accused, there is no doubt whatever; but it is possible that Suffolk himself may have been merely lax in the permission and extension of recognised official irregularities. In any case he had to do with a Judge who was perhaps even more formidable on the Bench than if he had been prosecuting as Attorney-General. By a strange irony of circumstances Bacon now found himself called to try that same nobleman about whom—in the old days of his plans for advancement—he had jotted down this private note in the *Commentarius Solutus*: "to make him think how he should be reverenced by a Lord Chancellor, if I were." But he readily adapted himself to the changed position. All his sympathies were naturally with Buckingham, and against the accused. The cause of the Howards was identified with inefficiency, with promotion on the ground of family connections, with corruption, and with financial difficulties. Bacon therefore took up the case for the Crown with the zeal of an advocate. He regularly reports the progress of the trial to the Favourite; he takes credit for refusing to delay the case to allow Suffolk time to obtain witnesses from Ireland; he refuses to stop the proceedings upon Suffolk's offer of submission, or even to forward Suffolk's letter to the King; he describes his care " of this case, in a number of circumstances and discretions, which, though they may seem but small matters, yet they do the business and guide it right." " The evidence," he writes on one occasion, " went well; I will not say I holp it; " and again, " This day the evidence went well; and, a little to warm the business when the misemployment of treasure which had relation to Ireland was handled, I spake a word, that he that did draw treasure from Ireland did not *emulgere* (milk) money but blood." At last (13 November, 1619) the Lord Chancellor is able to report that the goal of his labours is reached, and the Earl of Suffolk sentenced, with his wife, to a fine of £30,000, and imprisonment in the Tower.

Bacon's political and legal labours at this time furnish a

curious contrast to the philosophical work which he was on the point of publishing.[1] Among other services for the Crown we find him supervising the prosecution of certain Dutch merchants who had been accused of exporting bullion, from whom Bacon secures fines for the King's coffers to the amount of £180,000; suggesting the application of torture to a crack-brained fellow named Peacock, who was said to have attempted to "infatuate the King's judgment by witchcraft"; encouraging the King to pull goose-quills, *i.e.* to punish pamphleteers; and generally trying every device to relieve the King's poverty, "which," he writes, "if I should now die and were opened, would be found at my heart, as Queen Mary said of Calais."

Yelverton, the Attorney-General, the plain blunt man who had refused to purchase his office by bribes or by flattery—the single friend who had remained staunch and constant to the Lord Keeper Bacon in the hour of his temporary disgrace when the King and Buckingham had set their faces against him and all the courtiers were yelping at his heels—was now the only one of the little group of the Howards and their friends who had not been overthrown ; and his turn was soon to come. There were not wanting premonitory symptoms. We find the Lord Chancellor suggesting that "Mr. Attorney" was remiss, first in Suffolk's trial (6 May), and then in the matter of the Dutch merchants (9 Oct.), in which it would seem that the Government had a very weak case, and was behaving in a very arbitrary, not to say oppressive manner. Bacon seems to have had "much ado" in persuading the two Chief Justices to be "firm to the cause and satisfied;" and in spite of the efforts of the three he expresses a fear that "the major part of the votes" may go the other way; "but that which gives me most to think, is the carriage of Mr. Attorney, which sorteth neither with the business nor with himself; for as I hear from divers and partly perceive, he is fallen from earnest to be cool and faint." There is no pretence of impartial justice. When the Dutchmen were fined after the proceeding in the Star Chamber, Buckingham writes back word that "*this victory* hath so well pleased his Majesty that he giveth thanks to all;" in particular he *returns thanks to the Lord Chancellor and would have him*

---

[1] The *Novum Organum*, published in 1620.

deliver the same to Coke and the Judges. The omission of
Yelverton's name is ominous ; and soon afterwards (October 14)
Mr. Attorney is again complained of as mismanaging Suffolk's
case.

In other ways, Yelverton now came into collision with the
Favourite ; and this time it was in connection with a Monopoly,
or Monopoly Patent, for making gold and silver thread, enjoyed
by a Company in which Sir Edward Villiers, the half-brother of
the Favourite, had invested £4,000 and therefore had a considerable interest. In theory (see below, p. 286) a Monopoly was
supposed to be for the good of the people (very much like our
modern Patents) by encouraging inventions; and in days when
bullion was believed to constitute the only real wealth of a nation,
the Government might fairly claim to supervise so important
a manufacture and to encourage a Company which engaged
to manufacture thread from *imported* gold. But in practice
this Monopoly resulted in nothing but resistance on the part
of merchants and oppression on the part of the Government.
Proceedings against the recalcitrant goldsmiths in the Court
of Exchequer were instituted in 1617, but abandoned, as they
were certain to fail. Hereupon the King wrote from Scotland
to Yelverton ordering him summarily to imprison the offenders ;
but this letter Yelverton "kept by him, thinking the King not
well informed." In March, 1618, both the manufacture and the
profits were taken into the King's hands. This transference
was made at Bacon's suggestion, and his motive—or at least one
motive—is obvious. Sir Edward Villiers was to receive £500
a year out of the profits in return for his investment; and
Christopher Villiers, another brother of the Favourite's, was to
receive £800 a year out of the profits for no reason at all.
However much therefore Bacon may have been influenced by
considerations of political economy and high policy, few will
doubt that one object of this suggested transference was
to bring money into the pockets of the brothers of the
Favourite, by taking the Monopoly under the direct protection
of the Government and making it a paying concern.

The Lord Chancellor accordingly now took up the cause of the
Government Monopoly with a most oppressive energy. Against
the goldsmiths—who urged that they had made gold thread many

years before the existence of the Company with whom the Monopoly had originated—he raked up an old Act of Henry VII. expressly forbidding goldsmiths to melt gold and silver except for special objects, amongst which the manufacture of gold and silver thread had not been mentioned. This obsolete statute placed the goldsmiths at Bacon's mercy ; and he showed them none. But as repeated seizures of instruments and imprisonments of artificers still failed to suppress competition, a fresh commission was issued (October, 1618) to hunt offenders down; and to this body the notorious Mompesson was added, a friend and kinsman of Buckingham's, whose energy in suppressing offences against his own Patent for inns promised equal success in suppressing offenders against the gold-thread Monopoly. The Commissioners were authorised to institute prosecutions before the Star Chamber; and a prosecution was accordingly instituted, but dropped. Thus for the second time legal proceedings had been abandoned; first, in the Court of Exchequer, and now in the Star Chamber; yet the seizures and imprisonments were as frequent as ever.

At this time (1619) a new coercive measure was suggested to James by Bacon and Montague (the Chief Justice of the King's Bench). The goldsmiths and silk mercers *were to be forced to enter into bonds not to sell their wares to unlicensed persons.* Mompesson told the silk mercers that, if they refused to seal these bonds, "all the prisons in London should be filled, and thousands should rot in jail." This persistent oppression had now gone to such unprecedented lengths that Yelverton, who had hitherto gone with Bacon and Montague, began to hang back. Sir Edward Villiers, naturally alarmed for his pension, which depended upon the profits of the manufacture, made a personal appeal to the Attorney—all would be lost, he said, if Yelverton did not help him. Yelverton was afraid to disoblige the Favourite's brother; but he also had a conscience which—not being the conscience of a philosopher or a political economist or a great person—entertained some fears of carrying oppression beyond customary limits. He therefore determined to throw the whole responsibility upon Bacon, as the official who was the main mover in the whole business. To oblige Villiers, he committed the mercers to prison; to satisfy his conscience, he declared that, unless the Lord Chancellor confirmed the commitment, he would instantly release them. Having gone thus far—and being probably convinced that he was acting from the purest motives and simply for the good of the nation—Bacon was not the man now to shrink back; after hearing what the mercers had to say, he recommitted them to prison. The whole of the City was at once in an uproar; bail was offered in £100,000; and a deputation proceeded to the King, who at once released the prisoners. Even those who are most familiar with Bacon's extraordinary blindness to inconvenient truths must marvel that this series of abuses and oppressions could not open his eyes to the fact that there must be something wrong in his theory and conduct. Instead of now abolishing the Monopoly and the tyrannical Commission, a Proclamation was issued justifying the system on grounds of high national policy[1]: and the abuses and oppressions went on as before; unlicensed goods were still seized; bonds were still forced upon the silk mercers; the bullion which was to have been imported was not imported; the coin of the realm was melted down; the City was exasperated; and all—if we set aside high national policy as being an inadequate explanation of this persistent oppression—for the purpose of obtaining £500 a year for one Villiers and £800 a year for another. There is only one refreshing circumstance in the whole of this miserable business— these leeches of the Commonwealth gained next to nothing. What Edward may have received we do not know, but the Government manufacture proved so complete a failure that the sum total of Christopher's receipts did not exceed £150 during the whole existence of the Monopoly. If however the Favourite's brothers were disappointed, that was not Bacon's fault: no one could accuse Bacon that he had allowed public opinion, or the Laws of England, or self-respect, or considerations of the King's interest in maintaining a good feeling between him and his subjects, to stand in the way of obliging the brothers of Buckingham. Yelverton, not Bacon, was to blame: and Yelverton must now be sacrificed on the Favourite's

---

[1] The words of the Proclamation, says Professor Gardiner, from whom this sketch is taken (*History*, iv. 9—19) "may fairly be taken as Bacon's defence of himself."

altar. Very ominous was it for the poor Attorney that the Lord Chancellor wrote (February, 1620)—perhaps in reference to some protests of Yelverton against his own unconstitutional courses and against the impolicy of further exasperating the City—" Mr. Attorney groweth pert with me of late, and I see well who they are that maintain him."

It was not long before Yelverton gave his adversaries a handle against him. In drawing up a charter for the City of London he had inadvertently inserted clauses for which he was unable to produce a warrant. The worst that could be charged against him was that he had misunderstood the King's verbal directions. But his enemies determined to proceed to the severest measures, and the Council advised that his offer of submission by letter be refused, and that an information be laid against him in the Star Chamber on 27 October. On the 24th of October Bacon made notes of his intended remarks upon the case, in which he meets the Attorney's plea (that he has merely committed an error of judgment) by declaring that the highest contempt and excess of authority is termed by the law of England " misprision " or " mistaking," whereof he takes the reason to be that "mistaking" is ever joined with contempt ; " for he that reveres will not easily *mistake ;* but he that slights and thinks more of the greatness of his place than of the duty of his place, will soon commit *misprisions.*"

One feels that there is something of hypocrisy in the whole conduct of this trial, as though every one did not know that Yelverton's real offence was that he had always refused to cringe to Buckingham. But Bacon's behaviour is peculiarly cold-blooded and ungrateful. Yelverton had faithfully stood by him, almost alone, when the King and the Favourite were ready to crush him, and when all the Court had turned against him ; and whatever might have been his faults of carelessness in the present instance, no one accused the Attorney of corruption. Yet when the case came on, and when " the bill was opened by the King's Sergeant briefly, with tears in his eyes . . . and Mr. Attorney, standing at the Bar amid the ordinary Counsellors, with dejected looks, weeping tears, and a brief, eloquent, and humble oration, made a submission, acknowledging his error, but denying the corruption "—the Lord Chancellor endeavoured to resist the merciful proposal of the majority of the Councillors, viz., to defer proceedings till his Majesty was informed of the Attorney's submission :

"This," he writes to Buckingham, "was against my opinion, then declared plain enough ; but put to votes and ruled by the major part, though some concurred with me. I do not like of this course, in respect that it puts the King in a strait ; for either the note of severity must rest upon his Majesty if he go on ; or the thanks of clemency is in some part taken away, if his Majesty go not on. I have *cor unum et via una*, and therefore did my part as a judge and the King's Chancellor. What is further to be done I will advise the King faithfully when I see his Majesty and your Lordship. But before I give advice I must ask a question first."

On 8th November the Chancellor announced that the King would not interfere with the course of justice, so that the hearing of the case must continue; and on the 11th he thus announces the termination to Yelverton's great enemy :

"My very Good Lord,
   "Yesternight we made an end of Sir Henry Yelverton's cause. I have almost killed myself with sitting almost eight hours. But I was resolved to sit it through. He is sentenced to imprisonment in the Tower during the King's pleasure, the fine of £4,000, and discharge of his place, by way of opinion of the Court, referring it to the King's pleasure. How I stirred the Court I leave it to others to speak : but things passed to his Majesty's great honour. *I would not for anything but he had made his defence ; for many chief points of the charge were deeper printed by the defence.*"

§ 38 The Publication of the "Novum Organum"

Foreign politics occupy, just now, little of the Lord Chancellor's time. But in a *Short view of Great Britain and Spain* (1619) he had drawn up reasons *against* an alliance with Spain, which compare amusingly with the paper drawn up in 1617, *in favour* of it. Two years before, he had advocated the alliance on the ground of the peace of Christendom, the extinction of religious animosity, and the destruction of piracy. Now he inveighs against Spain as an empire whose policy has been bloody, corrupting, treacherous, and unnatural ; cruel to Christendom, while negligent of infidels and pirates. Between England and

Spain there never can be a secure peace—·such is the nature of
the religion of the latter; England was never so well as now
prepared for its fitting task, to take the Indies from Spain.
To this task the King of England is summoned; first, as
wielding the greatest naval power in Christendom; secondly, as
being the Defender of the Faith, and a monarch of such understanding, learning, and godliness, that the sacred work of
planting the true Church in foreign parts devolves upon him,
as it were, by office.   A sonorous piece of English—to which
however the King appears to have given little heed, while very
ready to use his Lord Chancellor's services for the purpose of
overthrowing his Favourite's enemies, enlarging his Prerogative,
enforcing his monopolies, and procuring a harvest of fines.

But the sudden invasion of the Palatinate (Sept. 1620) by
the Spaniards—determining the King to support his son-in-law
and to summon a Parliament for the purpose of obtaining
supplies for a war—made the Chancellor hope that his services
might now be used for nobler purposes.   Never had Bacon—in
spite of his unflinching championship of the Prerogative—shown
the slightest personal or public distrust of the House of
Commons: and it is one among innumerable instances of his
sanguine complacency and his blindness to the course of public
opinion that no one was more zealous than himself for the
assembling of the very Parliament that was destined to bring
about his own downfall.   When he received his Majesty's
instructions to consult with a few others how to prepare a
Parliament " without packing or degenerate arts," he replies
(2 Oct.), " All your Majesty's business is *super cor meum*, for
I lay it to heart.   But this is a business *secundum cor meum.*"

At the very time, however, when the preparations for a
Parliament were going on, the Lord Chancellor used such " new
doctrine " about the Prerogative as led some observers to
suppose that there would be no Parliament at all.

"The first day of term,[1] Sir Thomas Chamberlain, Chief Justice of
Wales and Chester, was sworn a judge of the King's Bench; at whose
admission the Lord Chancellor took occasion to enlarge himself much upon
the Prerogative, and how near it was akin and of blood (as he termed it) to

---

[1] October 9 : Chamberlain writes thus on October 14 to Carleton.

the Common Law ; saying further (whatsoever some unlearned lawyers might prattle to the contrary) that it was the accomplishment and perfection of the Common Law. Which new doctrine, but now broached, is perhaps to prepare the way to a purpose in hand, that all men shall be rated and pay, by way of subsidy, as if it were done by Parliament ; and those that refuse, their names to be certified, that other order may be taken with them."

What the Lord Chancellor meant by saying that the Prerogative was "the accomplishment and perfection" of the Common Law, was probably quite clear to those who had often heard him in the Law Courts. It meant that, wherever the Common Law was imperfect or incomplete, the Prerogative was to step in and to supply what was wanting for the State, or, in other words, for the King; and how this doctrine might be utilised in a sudden war, nominally to meet a particular emergency, but really to the general endangering of the liberties of the subject, could be readily conjectured by many others less keen-sighted than Chamberlain. It might have been supposed that, by this time, Bacon's eyes would have been opened to the nature of the Sovereign whose powers he was so strenuously attempting to extend; taught by experience, he might have at last discerned that, in working for James, he was really working for Villiers, or for some future Favourite. But this he could not, or would not, see. The King's language about his Favourite had been long ago (1617) sufficiently explicit to undeceive him : " I James am neither a god nor an angel, but a man like any other. . . . I wish to speak in my own behalf and not to have it thought to be a defect; for Jesus Christ did the same, and therefore I cannot be blamed. Christ *had his John and I have my George*." But Bacon would not be undeceived. To have seen the truth, would have forced him to acknowledge the error of all his fine monarchial theories, by which he had done such great things for himself in raising himself to office, and by which he was to do such great things for the people. Such a disappointment would have been too bitter for endurance; and he avoided it by shutting his eyes to patent facts.

Meantime Bacon had prepared and sent to the King a Proclamation of which his Majesty by no means approved. It set forth the condition of affairs abroad and especially in the Palatinate, stating that the King was resolved to employ the uttermost of his force and means to recover and re-settle the said Palatinate to his son and his descendants, and had therefore determined to resort to the good affections and aids of his loving subjects. It added monitions as to the kind of men who should, and should not, be chosen as members. In his reply, the King (19 Oct.) expressed his dislike of the introduction of "matters of state and the reasons of calling a Parliament, whereof neither the people are capable, nor is it fit for his Majesty to open now unto them; but to reserve to the time of their assembling, according to the course of his predecessors, which his Majesty intendeth to follow." It seems probable that Bacon's Proclamation, in the excited and warlike condition of the people, might have gone much further than any other devices of management to secure a Parliament devoted to the King's interests; however, the King rejected all but the latter " monitions," and expressed his intention of drawing up a Proclamation of his own.

Amidst all these preparations for Parliament and the efforts to procure a conspicuous downfall for Yelverton, Bacon appears once more in a character which he might seem almost to have laid aside—as a Philosopher, as the herald of the Kingdom of Man over Nature. Fifteen years had elapsed since the publication of the *Advancement of Learning*, in English. Now he gave to the world a volume in Latin, containing a prospectus of the *Instauratio Magna* followed by a series of Aphorisms " Concerning the Interpretation of Nature and the Kingdom of Man," together with a set of directions for the formation of a Natural and Experimental History. This is all that was ever completed of the *Novum Organum*, the New Instrument by which human reason was to obtain supremacy over Nature.[1]

It is melancholy to note that there is little in the work now published which may not be discovered, in a less developed shape, in some one of his many previous tentative and unpublished treatises, most of which were written before he climbed into office. Even when it should be completed, the *Novum Organum* professed to be but a very small part of the

---

[1] For an account of the *Novum Organum* see § 53 and § 54.

Great Instauration. But it was sent into the world uncompleted, because, says the Author, he had begun to number his days, and " would have it saved." Well might he despair of perfecting even a single part of the *Instauration*, when he looked back at the philosophic results of the last seven years. Yet he fondly hoped that the King, whom he had so assiduously courted, studied, and served, would do something to aid the compiling of " the Natural and Experimental History" which was to be the basis of his philosophy, and which he had always described as a " royal work " exceeding the powers of a subject. It is mainly with this view that he thus addresses himself (12 Oct.) to the King :—

" The work, in what colours soever it may be set forth, is no more but a new Logic, teaching to invent and judge by Induction (as finding Syllogism incompetent for sciences of Nature) and thereby to make philosophy and sciences both more true and more active. . . . There be two of your Council and one other Bishop of this land, that know I have been about some such work near thirty years ; so as I made no haste. And the reason why I have published it now, specially being imperfect, is, to speak plainly, because I number my days, and would have it saved.

"There is another reason of my so doing ; which is to try whether I can get help in one intended part of this work, namely the compiling of a Natural and Experimental History, which must be the main foundation of a true and active philosophy. This work is but a new body of clay, whereinto your Majesty, by your countenance and protection, may breathe life. And to tell your Majesty truly what I think, I account your favour may be to this work as much as an hundred years' time : for I am persuaded the work will gain upon men's minds in ages, but your gracing it may make it take hold more swiftly ; which I would be glad of, it being a work meant not for praise or glory, but for practice and the good of men.

" One thing, I confess, I am ambitious of, with hope ; which is, that after these beginnings and the wheel once set on going, men shall suck more truth out of Christian pens than hitherto they have done out of heathen. I say, with hope ; because I hear my former book of the *Advancement of Learning* is well tasted in the Universities here and the English Colleges abroad ; and this is the same argument sunk deeper."

It is refreshing to see Bacon for once addressing the King in the language of conscious greatness. He is certain that his work will succeed ; and although his courtly pen allows him at first to declare that the royal protection will " breathe life " into his " new body of clay," he cannot long continue insincere, when speaking of himself as a philosopher; and he proceeds to avow his belief that the King can do no more than accelerate a success which, with or without the royal favour, is ultimately certain. Perhaps the King was a little irritated at what he not improbably considered an exaggerated self-estimation. At all events in his reply (15 Oct.) he quietly assumes his capacity to judge and criticise the *Novum Organum,* and pretty clearly hints that he should have to blame some obscurities, and that a principal reason for commending the work is that it agrees in some measure with his own notions.

" MY LORD,

"I have received your letter and your book, than the which you could not have sent a more acceptable present unto me. How thankful I am for it cannot better be expressed by me than by a firm resolution I have taken : first, to read it through with care and attention, though I should steal some hours from my sleep (having otherwise as little spare time to read it as you to write it); and then, to use the liberty of a true friend in not sparing to ask you the question in any point whereof I shall stand in doubt *(nam ejus est explicare cujus est condere),* as on the other part I will willingly give a due commendation to such places as in my opinion shall deserve it.

" In the meantime I can with comfort assure you that you could not have made choice of a subject more befitting your place and your universal and methodick knowledge ; and in the general I have already observed that you jump with me in keeping the mid way between the two extremes, as also in some particulars I have found that you agree fully with my opinion. And so praying God to give your work as good success as your heart can wish and your labours deserve, I bid you heartily farewell."

In his very interesting answer Bacon (19 Oct.) urges the King to state all his objections ; and, while putting in a kind of protest against the judgment of any critic who is not initiated into the experimental philosophy, he is ready to bow to the King's judgment as a unique exception to this rule : and repeating his former petition in plainer terms, he again presses on his Majesty the expediency of " breathing life " into the " body of clay " by setting on foot collections for a Natural History.

" I cannot express how much comfort I received by your last letter of your own royal hand. . . . Your Majesty shall not only do to myself a singular favour, but to the business a material help, if you will be graciously pleased to open yourself to me in those things wherein you may be unsatisfied.   For though this work—as by position and principle—doth disclaim to be tried by anything but by experience and the resultats [1] of experience in a true way ; yet the sharpness and profoundness of your Majesty's judgment ought to be an exception to this general rule,[2] and your questions, observations, and admonishments, may do infinite good.

"This comfortable beginning makes me hope further that your Majesty will be aiding to me in setting men on work for the collecting of a Natural and Experimental History, which is *basis totius negotii;* a thing which, I assure myself, will be from time to time an excellent recreation unto you—- I say to that admirable spirit of yours that delighteth in light : and I hope well that even in your times many noble inventions may be discovered for man's use.   For who can tell—now this Mine of Truth is once opened — how the veins go, and what lieth higher and what lieth lower ? "

In these philosophic hopes of royal assistance Bacon was doomed to be disappointed.   The high place which he declared he had coveted from the first principally because of the command which it would give " of other men's wits," procured neither from others nor from the King the support he had anticipated.   Nor did James ever go beyond the very moderate praises he had bestowed in his letter ; indeed, at other times and to other ears he is said to have expressed his opinion much more epigrammatically, and less favourably, about this new and unintelligible book : " It was like the peace of God," he said, " which passeth all understanding."

§ 39   The Lord Chancellor in Peril

The climax of Bacon's favour and greatness had now been reached, and there was no warning of decline.   In the same month in which he published the *Novum Organum* he welcomed with unfeigned delight the King's expressed intention to summon a Parliament.   He did not in the least perceive what a storm of opposition he had been rousing up by his persistent straining of

[1] *i.e. results :* the word is elsewhere used by Bacon (Spedding, viii. 172), "the *resultate* of their counsels."

[2] When we consider how thoroughly Bacon was in earnest in all matters relating to philosophy, we shall be disposed to think this, perhaps, the most flattering compliment he ever paid to James.   It reminds one a little of the preacher, in the royal presence, who, after incautiously committing himself to the general statement, " *Nous mourrons, nous mourrons tous,*" qualified it as he bowed to the royal pew—" *presque tous.*"

the King's Prerogative; for he had been sincere, or thought he
had been sincere, in pursuing that policy, and "he was never
able to understand what a gulf there was between his own
principles and those of the representatives of the people."[1]
From some Monopoly Patents he anticipates a little trouble
with the new Parliament; but it never occurs to him that he
personally has anything to fear. Of all the suitors that had
appeared before him, only one or two had as yet publicly
complained; and their complaints, when referred to the Council, had been pronounced baseless. Everything at this time
seemed to point towards an uninterrupted career of public and
private splendour. Near the fish-ponds of Gorhambury he had
built himself a delightful and ingeniously constructed house for
recreation and study, to which perhaps he now hoped to be able
to devote an ampler leisure.

On 22 Jan. 1621, he kept his sixtieth birthday in the house
of his birth, amid a goodly assemblage of guests, of whom Ben
Jonson was one. The poet has recorded in glowing lines the
"smile" that lit up York House, "the fire, the wine, the men;"
and as if he had been in the secrets of Destiny, he sings of—

> "England's High Chancellor, the destin'd heir,
> In his soft cradle, to his father's chair;
> Whose even thread the Fates spin round and full
> Out of their choicest and their whitest wool."

Five days afterwards (27 Jan. 1621) he was created Viscount
St. Alban "with all the ceremonies of robes and coronet,"
says Chamberlain. This was his eighth promotion, "a diapason
in music," as he himself calls it in a letter to the King; and
then he adds an unconscious prophecy almost too dramatically
ironical, "a good number and accord for the close."

Yet, amidst all these deceitful flatteries and caresses of fortune, one obscure voice, whose sound has come down to our
times, seems to have raised a note of warning which, by the
passionate sincerity of its remonstrance, might well have caused
the Lord Chancellor to feel some apprehensions. Thomas Peyton,
author of the *Glass of Time* (1620), appears (like the unfortunate

---

[1] Gardiner, *History*, ii. 193.

nephew of Dr. Steward, see p. 269) to have obtained a decree
from the Lord Chancellor which was afterwards annulled or not
acted on, owing to the superior interest of his powerful
adversaries ; and he vents his indignation in a poem, almost as
remarkable for the emphasis with which he acquits the Chancellor of avarice or self-prompted injustice, as for the boldness
with which he hints, or more than hints, at his subservience to
higher evil influences.

> " Most honourable [1] Lord, within whose reverend face
> Truth, mercy, justice, love and all combine,
> Heaven's dearest daughters of Jehovah's race
> Seem all at full within thy brows to shine,
> The King himself (t' immortalize thy fame)
> Hath in thy name [2] fore-typèd out the same.

> " Great Verulam, my soul hath much admired
> Thy courtly carriage in each comely part,
> Worth, merit, grace, when what the land desired
> Is poured upon thee as thy just desert,
> Grave, liberal mind contending with the rest
> To seat them all in thy judicious breast.

> " Thrice noble Lord, how dost thou prize of gold,
> Wealth, treasures, money and such earthly cash ?
> For none of them thou hast thy justice sold,
> But held them all as base infected trash
> To snare, allure—out from a dunghill wrought—
> The searèd conscience of each muddy thought.

> " Ah, dearest Lord, *hold but the scales upright,*
> *Let Court nor favour over-sway my cause,*
> To press me more than is beyond my might
> Is but their reach *to cross thy former laws.*
> Let me have peace, or that which is mine own,
> And thy just worth shall o'er the world be blown."

A Lord Chancellor less sanguine and less self-complacent than
Bacon might also have apprehended with some personal mis-
givings the action of the Parliament touching Monopolies, with
which he had had a great deal to do of late. A Patent, or
Monopoly Patent, was, in theory, a licence or a restriction given

[1] I think "honourable" must have been abbreviated in pronunciation.
[2] A play on "Verulam" and "verum."

by the Crown for the encouragement of invention, or to remedy a glut, or to improve or stimulate manufacture; and it must be pronounced good in law by the Judges as well as certified to be " convenient " by the King's advisers.[1] For example, one Patent gave a monopoly of the manufacture of glass, because the patentees offered to use coal instead of wood, so as to spare the timber of the country; another Patent gave a monopoly of gold and silver lace, because the patentees promised to use imported bullion, thereby (according to the political economy of those days) adding to the wealth of the nation. In theory, therefore, a Monopoly Patent ought to be " good and beneficial to the commonwealth."

But Bacon, against his better judgment, to oblige Buckingham, had certified as " convenient," and enforced most oppressively, Patents in which the Favourite's brothers had a pecuniary interest, and which he himself can hardly have regarded as generally beneficial; except so far as he was able to persuade himself that almost anything was beneficial, if, for the time, it was his interest to do or sanction the thing in question. How bitter a discontent had been aroused by these Patents and by the general action of the Council over which Bacon presided, may be inferred from a letter written by Chamberlain in the preceding summer (8 July, 1620):

" Indeed the world is now much terrified with the Star Chamber, there being not so little an offence against any Proclamation but is liable and subject to the censure of that Court; and, for Proclamations and Patents, they are become so ordinary that there is no end, every day bringing forth some new project or other. In truth the world doth even groan under the burthen of these perpetual Patents; which are become so frequent that whereas, at the King's coming in, there were complaints of some eight or nine Monopolies then in being, they are now said to be multiplied by so many scores."[2]

---

[1] In 1601 Francis Bacon spoke as follows in the House of Commons defending the Queen's right to grant Monopolies: " If any man out of his own wit, industry, or endeavour, find out any thing beneficial to the Commonwealth, or bring any new invention which every subject of this kingdom may use; yet, in regard of his pains and travel therein, her Majesty perhaps is pleased to grant him a privilege to use the same only, by himself or his deputies, for a certain time. This is one kind of Monopoly. Sometimes there is a glut of things, when they be in excessive quantity, as perhaps of corn; and perhaps her Majesty gives licence of transportation to one man. This is another kind of Monopoly. Sometimes there is a scarcity or a small quantity; and the like is granted also."—Spedding, iii. 27.

[2] Gardiner, *History*, iv. 1.

That Bacon had been guilty of a certain degree of corruption in this matter—sacrificing the interests of the people to the interests of his patron or his patron's brother—appears pretty clearly from the tone in which he himself and his fellow-councillors speak of the Monopolies, and from the language used by the House of Commons and even by the King.

We have seen above (p. 267) that in the enlarged edition of Bacon's *Advice* to Buckingham, written (1619 or 1620) after some years of experience of the Favourite's habits, the Lord Chancellor had inserted a warning against interference with cases pending in Courts of Law. It is no less noteworthy that in the same edition he also inserted a special clause against Monopolies, not condemning such as are injurious, but including all in a sweeping condemnation :—

" But especially care must be taken, that Monopolies, (which are the canker of all trades), be by [no] means admitted under the pretence or the specious colour of the public good." [1]

The small committee over which the Lord Chancellor presided, to which was intrusted (7 Oct. 1620) the duty of " perusing of the former grievances and of things of like nature which have comen in since," reports (29 Nov.) that, as regards Patents of Monopolies, they have chosen out only those " that are most in speech, and do most tend either to the vexation of the common people, or the discontenting of the gentlemen and Justices. . . . There be many more, of like nature but not of like weight, nor so much rumoured ; which to take away now in a blaze, will give more scandal that such things were granted, than cause thanks that they be now revoked." Writing to Buckingham on the same day, the Lord Chancellor uses language that can hardly be mistaken.

" Your Lordship may find that in the number of Patents which we have represented to his Majesty as like to be stirred in by the Lower House of Parliament, we have set down three which may concern some of your Lordship's special friends, *which I account as mine own friends ; and so showed myself when they were in suit.*"

What can this mean except that the Lord Chancellor, when the Favourite's friends sued for Patents of an injurious, or, at least,

[1] Spedding, vi. 49.

doubtful tendency, "showed himself *their friend*" by straining
a point in their favour ?

After mentioning the three objectionable Patents and their
owners, he continues :

> "These in duty could not be omitted, for that, specially the first two of
> them, are *more rumoured both by the vulgar and by the gentlemen, yea, and
> by the Judges themselves, than any other Patents at this day.* Therefore I
> thought it appertained to the singular love and affection which I bear you,
> upon so many obligations, to wish and advise that your Lordship (whom
> God hath made in all things so fit to be beloved) would put off the envy of
> these things (which I think in themselves bear no great fruit) and rather
> take the thanks for ceasing them than the note for maintaining them."

And then, after his manner, as if for the express purpose of undoing all the effect of his excellent advice, he adds a qualification—that fatal qualification which, whether expressed or
unexpressed, is to be read between the lines of all his advice
to the King and the King's Favourite, and by which, like
Penelope, he was always unweaving the web of his wisest
counsel—

> "But howsover let me know your mind, and your Lordship shall find I
> will go your way."

It would seem that the King and Buckingham left it an open
question, and threw the decision on the Council. Naturally
Coke and others of the Council (who had no share, as the Lord
Chancellor had, in the responsibility of certifying these obnoxious
patents as " beneficial to the commonwealth "), were not so anxious
as the Lord Chancellor to cancel them before the meeting of
Parliament. It was therefore decided that they should be left
in force. The Chancellor himself was probably distracted
between his regard for what was politically just and expedient
(as well as for his own interests) and his dread of injuring the
Favourite's friends and a second time incurring the Favourite's
displeasure. He thus characteristically describes to Buckingham
(16 Dec. 1620) his attitude on the Monopoly question :

> "The King, by my Lord Treasurer's signification, did wisely put it upon
> a consult, whether the Patents which we mentioned in our joint letter were
> at this time to be removed by Act of Council before Parliament ; I opined

(but yet somewhat like Ovid's mistress—that strove, but yet as one that would be overcomen—) that yes."

No doubt Bacon felt confident in the support of the King and Buckingham, in the event of any attack being made on him in Parliament. Some such feeling at least appears to be indicated by a cancelled expression in a letter to Buckingham (16 Dec.), " it is true the speech of these things in the Lower House *may be contemned.*" It is only in the notes of the Lord Chancellor's speech " intended to be spoken after the King's speech to the two Houses," that we, for the first time, find a trace of anxiety on his own account. Here he warns Parliament against meddling with *Arcana Imperii* and reserved points of sovereignty, " as the marriage of the King's children ; as making of war and peace ; *choice and trust of counsellors or officers.*" These last words (as well as the clause about " the marriage of the King's children ") are cancelled in the MS., but they appear to point to a feeling that the House of Commons was likely to attack some of the King's " counsellors or officers ; " and the Lord Chancellor must have known that no one presented so prominent a mark as himself. The cancelling of both the passages just quoted points in the same direction : Bacon was beginning to feel a little alarmed at what might be said about him in the House of Commons ; but it was not a pleasant subject, and he desired to say nothing about it, and to think about it as little as possible.

The House met on 30 January, and at once (5 Feb.) appointed a Committee of Grievances. They soon fell upon the Monopolies, and especially on those mentioned above as being most objectionable. The question arose whether Mompesson's Patent for Inns was, 1st, against law ; 2nd, good in law but ill in execution ; 3rd, neither good in law nor execution. We must do Bacon the justice to say that both Coke and other members of the Lower House *at first* (19 Feb.) placed the Patent in the second class, *i.e.* as being good in law but ill in execution. But after going into the case, the Committee reported through Coke (21 Feb.) that they found this Patent an exorbitant grievance *both in itself* and in the execution. Sir Giles Mompesson, in a petition to the House, confessed that " so general a Patent cannot but be a great grievance to the subject;" and the King (March, 1621) came to the House and made a long speech "to satisfy the Upper House that he was not guilty of those grievances which are now discovered, but that he grounded his judgment upon others who have misled him." As Bacon had certified to the *conveniency as well as to the legality* of the Patent (13 Nov. 1616), he could not plead that he was not, in part, responsible for the mischiefs that had resulted from it. On the whole, bearing in mind that Bacon himself had confessed that he had "*shown himself the friend*" of the suitors for these oppressive Patents, and that he would be naturally disposed to go great lengths to oblige Buckingham's friends, we are led to the conclusion that here, as in the case of Dr. Steward, Bacon's action was contrary to the interests of justice, and that he shut his eyes to obvious evils sure to result from the proposed Patents, rather than disoblige the Favourite. If he had been made responsible for this misconduct and displaced in consequence of it, the loss of office would not have been too severe a penalty, and by no means so severe as the sentence which Bacon had himself advocated and pronounced on Yelverton.

But there was another vulnerable point in the Lord Chancellor's armour, through which the fatal wound was actually dealt, though ideal justice would have struck down its victim in almost any other way. For however great and numerous Bacon's faults may have been, he was not in the ordinary sense a taker of bribes. Such gifts as he received, irregular and doubtful though they may seem to us, were, in all but a very few cases, justified by the etiquette of an age when every great person about the Court was in some sense a bribe-taker. The King himself encouraged both of his Favourites to take bribes; Rochester spent £90,000 in twelve months and never took a bribe without the King's sanction; Buckingham with a princely income of £15,000 a year, yet insisted on receiving some tribute for every promotion or distribution of Court favour; the Lord Treasurer's place was said to be worth "some thousand pounds to him who after his death would go to heaven; twice as much to him who would go to purgatory; and no one knows how much to him who would adventure to a worse place:" "If," said James to a Venetian ambassador, "I were to begin to punish those who take bribes, I should soon not have a single subject left." [1] Bacon unquestionably took presents, and sometimes from persons who had cases pending before him ; yet at least it cannot be shown that he was ever led by them to pervert justice. He was not avaricious ; on the contrary, he was free-handed to an excess. But his very liberality, his extravagance, his love of pomp and splendour, together with his negligence of all details, and his especial carelessness about pecuniary details, combined to lay him open to the same accusations which might have been more justly levelled against an ordinary corrupt and avaricious Judge.

If we may trust an account of the Chancellor's receipts for one quarter, he had an income of more than £16,000,[2] or between £60,000 and £70,000 of our money. Yet he never had money enough for his extravagances. He loved to be attended by a large retinue of "gentlemen waiters," and when he was made Lord Chancellor, his increase of salary apparently so far fell beneath his expectation that he "at one clap cashiered sixteen of his gallants." A few months afterwards we find him applying to the King (Oct. 1618), to farm the profits of the Alienations as a reward that will "a little warm the honour" of the barony of Verulam, newly bestowed on him. Again he suggests (but "in a jest merrily,") that the King might give him £2,000 out of a fine due from one Vanlore, a creditor of his ; and as this hint appears not to have been taken, he (again unsuccessfully) requests Buckingham to obtain for him from the King the valuable privilege of "making a Baron." Among his various shifts to obtain money, the Lord Chancellor even stooped to borrow money from those who actually had, or were likely to have, causes before him, so that, at least on one occasion, he had

---

[1] Gardiner, *History*, iii. 74-6 ; ii. 212.

[2] Mr. Spedding says somewhere that the legitimate receipts were £2,790 ; but he infers (from a report that £20,000 were offered for the office at the time of Ellesmere's resignation) that the actual receipts may have been £3,000 a year. But the Lord Chancellor's accounts show (Spedding, vi. 327) that the total of the moneys received from the 24th of June, 1618, till the 29th of September following amounts to £4,160 12s. 10d. As this would be the least lucrative quarter, it would seem that his annual receipts were not much less than £20,000 a year, *i.e.* more than £80,000 a year of our money. Elsewhere (vii. 266) Mr. Spedding quotes from an old MS. referring to the year 1614, showing that in that year the fees and allowances assigned to the Lord Chancellor were no more than £1,047 15s.

to issue a decree against a creditor from whom he had recently borrowed £500.

Where the money all went may easily be conjectured from the evidence of the Chancellor's account book. From this it appears that, after cashiering "sixteen of his gallants" six months before, he still had twenty-six "gentlemen-waiters" and other servants in proportion; and that his annual expenditure for mere "rewards"—mostly gratuities given to servants and messengers for bringing him presents of grapes, pheasants, stags, &c.—was at the rate of £1,000 a year, or between £4,000 and £5,000 of our money.[1] Interspersed among the items of this profuse expenditure on footmen, are disbursements indicating that the Lord Chancellor was paying ten per cent. for petty loans, and that the bills of his tradesmen were discharged "in part."[2]

A large part of the receipts of the Lord Chancellor (in those days), as of other judicial officers, arose from presents and "gratifications" paid by parties whose suit had been decided. But this practice was already regarded as unsatisfactory by the better sense of the time; and bad as it was, it was far less scandalous than the acceptance of a gift from any suitor whose cause was still pending, or was likely to return to the Court. Yet Bacon himself afterwards confessed that he had taken presents under these latter circumstances. "Keep your hands clean," said the Lord Chancellor (29 June, 1620), quoting Solomon against bribery in an impressive charge to Mr. Whitelock in the Court of Chancery, on the promotion of the latter to be Chief Justice of Chester; but *on the same day* he made a final order in the case of a party from whom, two or three days before, he had received

---

[1] Spedding, vi. 327-333.

[2] Here is an extract from the account for the year 1618 (Spedding, vi. 333):—

July.	£	s.	d.
8. Paid the La. Hicks for the interest of 200*lb.* for 6 months	10	0	0
8. Paid Mr. Neave the upholster, in part of his bill of 647*lb.* 7*s.* 6*d.* 200*lb.*, so there now *remains due unto him* 447*lb.* 7*s.* 6*d.*	200	0	0
8. Paid Mr. Bate, haberdasher of small wares, *in part of his bill*	10	0	0
9. Paid Mr. Durant his bill for necessaries for your Lps. use	0	13	0
9. Paid Mr. Parkinson the Linen Draper by your Lp. order *in part of his bill* of 158*lb.*	50	0	0
9. Paid Mr. Wade the Grocer by your Lp. order *in part of his bill* of 26*lb.*	20	0	0
9. Paid Mr. Harwood the Perfumer in full of all due to him till this present 9th of July	7	17	0

a purse of £100, having at different times received from her, *pendente lite*, £310.[1]

On another occasion a French Wine Company had promised him £1,000 if he could break down a combination of vintners who refused to buy their wines ; and he attempted to gratify them by persuading the vintners. But afterwards, the business being referred to him by the King, as a matter that concerned royal customs, Bacon took up the matter more peremptorily, and imprisoned some of the most obstinate of the vintners; after which he received his thousand pounds. There is no proof of corruption in this, nor in any case that came before Bacon (except that of Dr. Steward's nephew quoted above); but there is abundant proof of a culpable inattention to ordinary rules of self-respect, and a strong suspicion that his extreme readiness to believe that what was convenient was also right, disposed him not to look too carefully into the sources of his receipts.

§ 40 The Lord Chancellor's Fall

When the King declared that he " had grounded his judgment upon others who had misled him," all knew that the Lord Chancellor was now implicated. But he had not yet had an opportunity of defending himself against any specific charge when (14 March) a suitor presented a petition to the House of Commons, stating that, two years and a half before, the Lord Chancellor had received money from him for the better despatch of a pending suit. Conscious, but as yet only half conscious, that his conduct would not bear investigating, Bacon wrote on the same day to Buckingham :

" My very good Lord,

" Your Lordship spake of Purgatory. I am now in it, but my mind is in a calm ; for my fortune is not my felicity. I know I have clean hands and a clean heart ; and I hope a clean house for friends or servants. But Job himself, or whosoever was the justest judge, by such hunting for matters against him as hath been used against me, may for a time seem foul, specially in a time when greatness is the mark, and accusation is the game. And if this be to be a Chancellor, I think if the great seal lay upon

---

[1] Spedding, vii. 253.

Hounslow Heath, nobody would take it up. But the King and your Lordship will, I hope, put an end to these miseries one way or other. And in troth that which I fear most is lest continual attendance and business together with these cares, and want of time to do my weak body right this spring by diet and physic, will cast me down ; and then it will be thought feigning or fainting. But I hope in God I shall hold out. God prosper you."

A second accusation, of receiving money *pendente lite*, having been brought against the Lord Chancellor immediately after the first, the Commons (19 March), desired a conference with the Lords, " having found abuses in certain eminent persons." Under this sudden shock Bacon's health gave way, and the examination of witnesses proceeded in his absence. Although he had desired that his defence might be reserved to him, a letter which he wrote to the King on the 25th shows that he was gradually giving up all hope of defence. He still protests against being supposed to have perverted justice, and to have taken bribes as a " depraved habit ;" but he admits that he may have partaken of the abuse of the times ; finally, he makes himself an oblation to the King to "do with me as may best conduce to the honour of your justice, the honour of your mercy, and the use of your service, resting as clay in your Majesty's gracious hands."

The strange feature in this letter is that the writer appears to be sincerely and honestly under the impression that he is a single-hearted patriot, and quite amazed at the hostile feeling that he found rising up against him in both Houses.

" When I enter into myself, I find not the materials of such a tempest as is comen upon me. I have been (as your Majesty knoweth best) never author of any immoderate counsel, but always desired to have things carried *suavibus modis*. I have been no avaricious oppressor of the people. I have been no haughty, or intolerable, or hateful man, in my conversation or carriage. I have inherited no hatred from my father, but am a good patriot born. Whence should this be ? "

But the reader will find in the conclusion of this very letter an answer to the question, " Whence should this be ? " For, with perfect truth, he adds this appeal to the King : "I have been *ever your man*, and counted myself but an usufructuary of myself, the property being yours." This was one reason why many in the House of Commons were not ill-pleased to see the great

Chancellor's fall ; he had, indeed, chosen to be " the King's man," and not " the nation's man." Dispassionate and sensible political observers like Chamberlain had feared him as a " dangerous instrument," and had remarked on his " new doctrine" as to the King's Prerogative ; and, in a manner all the more dangerous to the liberties of the people because it was *suavibus modis*, he was gradually subjecting the Judges to the Crown, and steadily amplifying in the interests of the King those very powers which true lovers of English freedom desired to see gradually extinguished. Moreover, men of common sense and ordinary morality were outraged by the contrast between the Lord Chancellor's professions and actions. Never had any man lectured the judges upon a judge's duties with more dignity and authority than he; and yet on the very day when he was teaching them to " keep their hands clean," he was making an order in a case in which he had taken gifts from suitors *pendente lite*. Again, in the matter of the Monopolies, he had shut his eyes to facts ; he " had shown himself a friend" to the Favourite's friends, and had allowed himself (though in company with others) to certify both to the legality and to the expediency of Patents, which—in the opinion of the House of Commons at all events—he ought to have known to be, if not illegal, at least inexpedient, and to which the King himself declared that he would never have assented if he had not been " misled" by his counsellors. Lastly—though this the House of Commons did not know, nor perhaps did even Coke suspect—he had deliberately perverted justice in at least one case in the Court of Chancery, brow-beaten by the importunity of Buckingham. But what was known and patent to all was quite enough to make all lovers of justice and national liberty earnestly desire that an example should be made of the highly-gifted man who had sinned against these two great causes. It was not Coke's enmity, nor Cranfield's resentment for past slights, it was Bacon's own conduct and policy that stirred up this storm in the Lower House against one whom almost all admired as much as they condemned. And no doubt many felt that in striking down the Lord Chancellor they were indirectly establishing a precedent for something like ministerial responsibility. Bacon, in 1607 (see above, p. 140), defending in his high style the Prerogative

which the King derived from God Himself, and maintaining
that the King was not "accomptable to Law," had stigmatized
as a democratic innovation, an attempt of the Parliament in old
days to "depose the Lord Chancellor" *as if he were an officer*
"*of the State and not of the King.*" The Commons were not
sorry now to show the Lord Chancellor that he would have done
well to consider himself an officer *of the State, as well as an
officer of the King.* But this he had never done. In particular
instances he had sacrificed the nation to the King's Favourite,
and he had in all instances tried to go as far as possible in the
direction of magnifying the King's power to the detriment
of the nation ; for these things they could not definitely attack
him ; but indirectly they could punish him for these, by punish-
ing relentlessly the definite acts that brought him under the
charge of corruption.

What answer the King returned to the Lord Chancellor's letter
we do not know ; but on the following day (26 March), going to
the House of Lords, James left judgment wholly to them, declaring his readiness to carry their sentence into execution, and
to "strike dead" the three Monopolies principally complained
of. Meanwhile, as Bacon's illness increased upon him, he made
his will (10 April), bequeathing his soul to God above, his
body to be buried obscurely, his name to the next ages and to
foreign nations. A slight token is left to Prince Charles, who is
also to have the offer of the reversion of Gorhambury and
Verulam ; but no mention is made of the King or of Buckingham. It is possible that at this critical moment Bacon felt that
his trust and devotion had not been rewarded with the protection which they deserved. At the same time he composed
a prayer, in which, while making a general confession of
"innumerable sins," he also protests that he has been free
from certain specified faults, and concludes with this particular
confession :

"Besides my innumerable sins, I confess before thee that I am debtor to
thee for the gracious talent of thy gifts and graces, which I have neither
put into a napkin, nor put it (as I ought) to exchangers, where it might
have made best profit, but misspent it in things for which I was least fit ;
so as I may truly say, my soul hath been a stranger in the course of my
pilgrimage."

Recovering from his illness, he made notes for an interview with the King which was to take place on 16 April; and there is a passage in these notes which, though cancelled by the writer, clearly shows that he felt his judicial conduct would not bear inspection. He begins by distinguishing three kinds of bribery, 1st, bargain, or contract for reward, to pervert justice *pendente lite ;* 2nd, where the judge conceives the case to be at an end, but does not take sufficient care to ascertain this ; 3rd, when the cause is really ended. As to the third class, he conceived it to be no fault, though now, he adds, he is willing to be better informed ; as to the second, he fears in some particulars he may be faulty. But as to the first class—where at least we might have expected unqualified denial—he seems to have felt that whatever his motives might have been, his actions exposed him to the charge of corruption. This at least is a natural inference from some cancelled words in the MS. :

" But, for the first of them, I take myself to be as innocent as any born upon St. Innocent's day in my heart. [*And yet perhaps, in some two or three of them, the proofs may stand pregnant to the contrary*].[1] For the second, I doubt in some particulars I may be faulty ; and, for the last, I conceived it to be no fault ; but therein I desire to be better informed that I may be twice penitent, once for the fact and again for the error."

In a subsequent letter to the King (21 April), begging that " the cup may pass from him," he beseeches the King, if not by direct use of the Prerogative, at least by indirect influence, to quash the proceedings against him. The surrender of the Seal, accompanied by a general submission, will surely, he thinks, be a sufficiently severe punishment. The conclusion of his letter indicates that the writer (possibly in anticipation of the King's intervention) has almost recovered his self-complacency.

---

[1] I quote from the *first* draft of the notes, Spedding, vii. 236. Prof. Gardiner (*History*, iv. 88), quoting from the same draft, but (here alone, as far as I remember) not from Spedding, but from Montagu's edition of Bacon's works (xvi. note, G. G. G.), omits the cancelled words, and makes no reference to them.
    The words "in my heart" obviously demand some antithesis ; "*in my heart* I was guiltless, though *in appearance* guilty." In the *second* draft or "improved version," as Mr. Spedding calls it, which probably represents more nearly what Bacon ultimately said, the words run thus :—
    "The first is, Of bargain, contract, or promise of reward, *pendente lite*. And this is properly called *venalis sententia,* or *baratria* or *corruptelae munerum.* And of this *my heart tells me* I am innocent ; that I had no bribe or reward in my eye or thought, when I pronounced any sentence or order."

> " But because he that hath taken bribes is apt to give bribes, I will go
> further and present your Majesty with a bribe. For if your Majesty give
> me peace and leisure, and God give me life, I will present your Majesty
> with a good history of England and a better digest of your laws."

But the King had taken the Chancellor at his word and had
no intention of preventing the course of justice from making
the clay into a " vessel of dishonour."

Closely following his last letter to the King a general submission was sent to the Upper House (22 April) entitled " The
humble submission and supplication of the Lord Chancellor."
He begins by expressing his satisfaction at the utility of the
precedent, calamitous though it is for himself, because hereafter
" the greatness of a Judge or Magistrate shall be no sanctuary
or protection of guiltiness," and because Judges will " fly from
anything that is in the likeness of corruption (though it were
at a great distance) as from a serpent." He understands that
some justification is expected of him. He will offer none but
that of Job :

> " For after the clear submission and confession which I shall now make
> unto your Lordships, I hope I may say and justify with Job in these words ;
> *I have not hid my sin as did Adam, nor concealed my faults in my bosom.*
> This is the only justification which I will use.
>
> " It resteth therefore, that, without fig-leaves, I do ingenuously confess
> and acknowledge that, having understood the particulars of the charge, not
> formally from the House, but enough to inform my conscience and memory,
> I find matter sufficient and full, both to move me to desert the defence,
> and to move your Lordships to condemn and censure me.
>
> " Neither will I trouble your Lordships by singling those particulars
> which I think may fall off.
> *Quid te exempta juvat spinis de pluribus una ?* "

He then shows at some length, by a story from Livy (" But
herein I beseech your Lordships to give me leave to tell you a
story,") that moderate punishment may deter as effectually as
mercilessness, and begs them to behold their " chief pattern, the
King our Sovereign, a King of incomparable clemency, and
whose heart is inscrutable for wisdom and goodness : "

> " Yourselves are either nobles (and compassion ever beateth in the veins
> of noble blood) or reverend Prelates, who are the servants of Him that
> would not break the bruised reed nor quench the smoking flax. You all

sit upon one high stage, and therefore cannot but be more sensible of the changes of the world and of the fall of any of high place.

" Neither will your Lordships forget that there are *vitia temporis* as well as *vitia hominis*, and that the beginning of reformations hath the contrary power of the pool of Bethesda ; for that had strength to cure only him that was first cast in, and this hath commonly strength to hurt him only that is first cast in. And for my part I wish it may stay there and go no further. . . .

"And therefore my humble suit to your Lordships is, that my penitent submission may be my sentence and the loss of the Seal my punishment ; and that your Lordships will spare any further sentence, but recommend me to his Majesty's grace and pardon for all that is past. God's Holy Spirit be amongst you."

It cannot but occur to those who have closely followed the narrative of the Lord Chancellor's doings for the last few months, that he was strangely inconsistent in measuring out for Yelverton so ample a cup of bitterness for much less culpable acts, and in desiring that a Lord Chancellor, making a general submission in answer to charges of corruption, should demand that the cup should pass almost, if not altogether, from him. Yelverton's sole fault (setting aside the unpardonable sin of being out of favour with Buckingham) was that he had made mistakes of judgment. Of corruption he was expressly acquitted. Yet his submission (mainly owing to Bacon's opposition) was not allowed to stay the proceedings against him ; he was deprived of his office, fined £4,000, and sentenced to imprisonment in the Tower during the King's pleasure ; and this sentence Bacon reports to Buckingham with the utmost satisfaction.

It was not likely that the Lords would be moved by a few impassioned words, or by a "story" from Livy, to content themselves with the slight and inadequate sentence which the Lord Chancellor desired—a sentence which would have made them condoners of corruption in high places, and would have brought upon them the just indignation of the Lower House. When (24 April) Bacon's letter of submission was read to the Lords, "No Lord spoke to it, after it was read, for a long time." At last the Lord Chamberlain spoke : "The question is whether this submission be sufficient to ground your Lordship's judgment for a censure, without further examination." The House having resolved itself into Committee to consider this, the twenty-three charges of corruption were read, and then the Lord Chancellor's submission was read a second time. The Prince and Buckingham wished to accept the submission and to spare further sentence; but they found no support. Some would have ignored the submission altogether, as being too late to stop proceedings, and too general to ground a censure. By declining to "single out particulars," and to rebut any possibly false or weak charges, Bacon might have seemed at first sight to have gained this great advantage, that he avoided the definite admission of those charges which were true and strong. But it proved otherwise. "It is not sufficient," said the Lord Chamberlain: "for the confession is grounded upon a rumour . . . . He neither speaks of the particular charge, nor confesseth anything particular." The same view was taken by Southampton, who pointed out that amidst many lengthy and general submissions and confessions there was no confession of corruption: "He is charged by the Commons," said Southampton, "with corruption: and no word of confession of any corruption in his submission. It stands, with the justice and honour of this House not to proceed, without the parties' particular confession; or to have the parties to hear the charge, and we to hear the parties' answer." This was the only fair and reasonable course to adopt; and after some discussion it was decided that, instead of summoning him to hear the charges, the particulars should be sent to him (but without the "proofs"), and that he should be requested to send his answer with all convenient expedition. A letter from the Lord Chancellor to the Chief Justice excited some anticipation that he would defend himself: but, in answer to their inquiry on this point, there came back his written answer:

"The Lord Chancellor will make no manner of defence to the charge, but meaneth to acknowledge corruption, and to make a particular confession to every point; but humbly craves liberty that, where the charge is more full than he finds the truth of the fact, he may make declaration of the truth in such particulars; the charge being brief and containing not all circumstances."

For this purpose time was given him, and on 30 April there was read in the House of Lords a full and detailed confession, admitting the truth of twenty-eight charges, of which about six imported the acceptance of money from suitors *pendente lite.* The twenty-eighth charge is that "The Lord Chancellor hath given way to great exactions by his servants, both in respect of private seals, and otherwise for sealing of Injunctions;" to which he replies, "I confess it was a great fault of neglect in me that I looked no better to my servants." And there is attached to the particular confessions the following general statement :

> "I do again confess that, in the points charged upon me, although they should be taken as myself have declared them, there is a great deal of corruption and neglect, for which I am heartily and penitently sorry, and submit myself to the judgment, grace, and mercy of the Court."

A committee of twelve of the Lords was at once sent to Bacon, to inform him that they conceived it to be an ingenuous and full confession, and to ask him whether the subscription was in his hand, and whether he adhered to it : "My Lords," he replied, "it is my act, my hand, my heart. I beseech your Lordships be merciful to a broken reed." The King was at once moved to sequester the Seal. The Lords who came to receive it (1 May) on finding him very ill, "wished it had been better with him." His reply was, "The worse the better. By the King's great favour I received the great Seal; by my own great fault I have lost it."

On 2 May the Upper House agreed to proceed in the business of the Lord Chancellor. The Usher and Sergeant were ordered to summon him to appear in person on the following day; the Judges to be there in their robes (save one in each court), the Lower House to be sent for. The Sergeant to carry his mace and show it him, but not to carry it before him as he did when he had the Seal." But from this humiliation Bacon was to be spared. The Gentleman Usher and Mr. Sergeant reply that they find the Lord Chancellor sick in bed : "He answered that he is so sick that he is not able to repair hither; that this is no excuse; for, if he had been well, he would willingly have come." The Lords therefore proceeded (3 May) in his absence; and, instead of discriminating the charges (some of which referred to complimentary gifts

received *after* the end of a suit) they came to a general conclusion that "the Lord Chancellor is guilty of the matters
wherewith he is charged." It was probably felt, even by
Bacon's best friends, that no good purpose would be served by
going again into the particulars of the several accusations
against him : such a course might have destroyed the effect of
his submission, and have embittered the feeling against him;
accordingly the resolution was passed *nemine dissentiente*.
About the penalty there was much difference of opinion. There
was an almost unanimous feeling that he ought to be disqualified for any public office : but the majority were successful
in resisting the proposal to degrade him; yet even the Earl of
Arundel, who was one of his strongest supporters, declared " his
offences foul, his confession pitiful." In the end it was resolved
that he should be fined £40,000, imprisoned in the Tower during
the King's pleasure, declared incapable of any office, place, or
employment in the State or Commonwealth, and that he should
never sit in Parliament, nor come within the verge of the Court.
It is at least creditable to Buckingham's constancy that to the
last he stood by the fallen man who had served him only too
well. When the question was put "whether these punishments
above shall be inflicted upon the Lord Viscount St. Alban, or
no," it was "agreed, *dissentiente* Lord Admiral."

Those who have followed Bacon's career with attention up to
this point will not be surprised to find that, in spite of his
public confession, he did not, in his own heart, believe that he
had been guilty of corruption. And indeed we have already
recognised that he ought certainly to be called guiltless, if " corruption " meant merely the deliberate perversion of justice for
money: but if the word is fitly used (as it must be) to denote
the misconduct of a judge who, for any motives whatever—not
money merely but " Court or favour " as poor Peyton expresses
it [1]—wrests justice to the wrong side, then the investigation of
Dr. Steward's case shows that Bacon cannot be pronounced
incorrupt. However, that the fallen Chancellor himself in
private took a brighter view of his own conduct, is proved by
this sentence written by himself in cipher: " I was the justest
judge that was in England these fifty years, but it was the justest

---

[1] See above, p. 286.

sentence in Parliament that was these two hundred years."
Until it can be shown that Coke or Egerton reversed a legal
decision to oblige a Favourite, or through some other corrupt
motive, this self-acquittal cannot be accepted: but we may
readily acknowledge that the prosecution of the charges of
judicial misconduct was sharpened by political dissatisfaction
with the Government of which Bacon had made himself the
instrument.

§ 41 BACON'S DEATH

The remaining five years of Bacon's life—"a long cleansing
week of five years' expiation and more," as he himself calls it—
were divided between suing for means, and prosecuting his
philosophical work. His imprisonment in the Tower, delayed
at first owing to the state of his health, was pressed by the
Lords (12 May) "that the world may not think," as Southampton
said, "our sentence is in vain." But it lasted for no more than
two days. Even two days were almost more than he could
bear: and he implores the Favourite (31 May) for immediate
release:

"GOOD MY LORD,
      "Procure the warrant for my discharge this day. Death, I thank God,
is so far from being unwelcome to me, as I have called for it (as Christian
resolution would permit) any time these two months. But to die before
the time of his Majesty's grace, and in this disgraceful place, is even the
worst that could be ; and when I am dead, he is gone that was always in
one tenor, a true and perfect servant to his master ; and one that was never
author of any immoderate, no, nor unsafe, no (I will say it) nor unfortunate
counsel ; and one that no temptation could ever make other than a trusty,
and honest, and thrice loving friend to your Lordship ; and (howsoever I
acknowledge the sentence just, and for reformation sake fit) the justest
Chancellor that hath been in the five changes since Sir Nicholas Bacon's
time. God bless and prosper your Lordship, whatsoever become of me,
      Your Lordship's true friend, living and dying,
                                                          FR. ST. ALBAN.
"Tower, 31st May, 1621."

Released from the Tower he is at once himself again, and
(with his usual irresistible restlessness and sanguineness) imploring (4 June) to be employed by the King. To the last he never

seemed to understand that in declaring him incapable of public office, and excluding him from the Court and from his place in Parliament, the Lords had deliberately intended to disqualify him for the post of confidential adviser to the King, and that the King could not replace him in his old position without setting himself in opposition to their decision.

" I heartily thank your Lordship for getting me out of prison ; and, now my body is out, my mind nevertheless will be still in prison, till I may be on my feet to do his Majesty and your Lordship faithful service. Wherein your Lordship, by the grace of God, shall find that my adversity hath neither spent nor pent my spirits. God prosper you."

In the same cheerful spirit he writes (4 June) to the King :

" I humbly thank your Majesty for my liberty, without which timely grant any further grace would have come too late. But your Majesty, that did shed tears in the beginning of my trouble, will I hope shed the dew of your grace and goodness upon me in the end. Let me live to serve you ; else life is but the shadow of death to,

Your Majesty's most devoted servant,

FR. ST. ALBAN."

His fine, being assigned by the King to some of his friends, was an actual benefit to him, in that it protected his property even from the just claims of his creditors by the shelter of the prior royal claim. But he had now to live on the scraps of his former fortunes. The Provostship of Eton was denied to him, and he had to part with York House and Gorhambury and retire once more to chambers in Gray's Inn.

Letters of this period exhibit him struggling against the influx of adversity. " I do not think," he says, "any except a Turk or a Tartar would wish to have another chop out of me." An additional sting was added to his calamities by the attitude of Buckingham, who—manifestly regarding his friend's political career as now concluded—intimated that he could no longer need York House, and offered to buy it of him. Bacon's refusal so alienated the Favourite, that he no longer stood his friend with the King, and even declined to see him. The following letter is the first draft (for two other copies were written before Bacon could cool down enough to write with such moderation as not altogether to break with his former patron) of the passionate protest in which he declares that to give up his father's house, the house where he himself was born, would be a second sentence :

" MY LORD,

 " I say to myself that your Lordship hath forsaken me, and I think I am one of the last that findeth it, and in nothing more than that twice at London your Lordship would not vouchsafe to see me, though the latter time I begged it of you.

 " If your Lordship take any insatisfaction about York House, good my Lord, think of it better ; for I assure your Lordship that motion was to me as a second sentence, for I conceived it sentenced me to the loss of that which I thought was saved from the former sentence, which is your love and favour. But sure it could not be that pelting matter, but the being out of sight, out of use, and the ill offices done me perhaps by such as have your ear. Thus I think and thus I speak ; for I am far enough from any baseness or detracting, but I shall ever love and honour you, howsoever I be,

    " Your forsaken friend and freed servant,

        " FR. ST. ALBAN."

Soon afterwards we find him writing a petition to the Lords in which he describes his wretchedness in language that might have been borrowed straight from Lear, " I am old, weak, ruined, a very subject of pity ; " appealing again and again to Buckingham for help ; declaring that he is " cast for means ; " and lastly —as if a piece of paper with the King's name on it could cure the disease from which his good name had suffered—imploring a royal pardon " to the end that blot of ignominy may be removed from me and from my memory with posterity, that I die not a condemned man, but may be to your Majesty, as you to God, *nova creatura.*" But these few extant letters in which he appears complaining, petitioning, and piteously supplicating, do not represent the deeper current of his life. He was now steadily devoting himself to labours for which he was better fitted than for politics or state-trials. At the time when his guilt had first been brought home to him, he had particularly deplored as his greatest offence his fault in mispending the talent of his gifts and graces in things for which he was least fit. Now he was resolved to make amends ; and these five years of humiliation brought forth a rich crop of literary work, which testifies that the days of his fall were not spent in repinings and supplications. Whatever language of irritation or importunity he may have occasionally used to the great persons from whom he hoped to obtain favours, all his most intimate friends—those who knew him in the privacy of his domestic life—concur in praising the patience and good temper with which he met adversity, and the unruffled perseverance with which he pursued his philosophic studies.

The *De Augmentis,* the completed edition of the *Essays,* the *History of Henry VII.,* and the *Dialogue on a Holy War,* beside the *Sylva Sylvarum,* and a number of tracts (intended as contributions to the *Natural History* without which his *Novum Organum* could not be applied to action) all proceeded from his pen during these five years of enforced retirement. When a comparison is made between these literary fruits of his downfall and the barrenness of the years of his official greatness, one is tempted to wish either that he had never become great, or that his greatness and his downfall had come earlier. If he had carried out his intention long ago expressed (perhaps in a transient fit of sullenness) to his uncle Burghley, to retire to Cambridge and there to become " a sorry bookmaker," how much we might have gained from the books he would have written, how easily could we have dispensed with the few papers of political advice that he would have left unwritten, and how gladly should we miss his name in the state trials that he would not have conducted ! One consolation was still left to him amid all his troubles and humiliations—the delusion of bright anticipations. Fond though he was of declaiming against hope—all hope at least except that which looked forward to a life beyond the grave—he was himself one of the most conspicuous examples of the sustaining power of the virtue which he despised. He was hopeful and hopefully employed to the very last.

In the summer of 1625, when the plague was raging in London, he seems to have been seriously ill ; yet he writes to a foreign correspondent, one Father Fulgentio, in a spirit of complacent satisfaction with his past philosophic work, mingled with ardent expectations of future success. He cannot indeed complete the *Natural History,* which he intends to form the Third Part of his *Instauratio*. That is plainly a work for a King, or a Pope, or some college or order, and cannot be done, —not at least as it should be done—by a private man's industry. But he trusts to complete all the rest, except the *Second Philosophy*, which is to form the Sixth Part of the *Instauratio ;* and he is supported by hope, partly because the nobility of the work seems fit to obtain God's sanction, partly "because of the ardour and constancy of my own mind, which, in this pursuit, has not grown old nor cooled in so great a space of time ; it being now forty years, as I remember, since I composed a juvenile work on this subject, which with great confidence and a magnificent title I named the *Greatest Birth of Time.*"

One of the strongest helps that a man can have in the time of trouble seems to have been denied to Bacon. No record in any letter or document hitherto has attested that his wife sympathised with his pursuits, or shared any of his aspirations. Her name is scarcely mentioned in his voluminous correspondence, except in a letter indicating that her convenience, as well as his own, required that York House should be retained. But the conclusion of the will which he made (December, 1625) not long before his death, revoked "for just and great causes" the provision made for her in her former part, and leaves her "to her right" only.

The same document affords one more curious and final instance of his sanguine temperament, and of his ignorance of money matters. After making provision for several legacies, amounting to three or four thousand pounds, he conceives there will be a "good round surplusage," out of which he proceeds to endow two lectureships in either of the two Universities. One of these lectures is to be on Natural Philosophy, and he trusts that the salary of neither will be below £200 a year. But it was not destined that any Professorship should perpetuate the name of Verulam or St. Alban at Cambridge or Oxford. The proceeds of his estate amounted to little more than £7,000, while his debts amounted to £20,000, and neither the "good round surplusage" nor the lectureships ever had any other than an imaginary existence.

Not many days of life now remained for him, and his last letter explains the cause of his death. Riding from London to Highgate, toward the end of March, 1626, on a sunny day when he was turning in his mind certain experiments concerning the conservation and induration of bodies, he was seized with a desire to try the effect of snow in preserving flesh from putrefaction. He alighted from his coach at a cottage where, as the story goes, he bought a fowl, and with his own hands stuffed it with snow. A chill and sudden sickness supervening, forced him to resort at once to the neighbouring house of Lord Arundel; and there, in ignorance of his approaching end, he dictates a letter to the host whose hospitality he had been compelled to claim.

"MY VERY GOOD LORD,

"I was likely to have had the fortune of Caius Plinius the elder, who lost his life by trying an experiment about the burning of the mountain Vesuvius. For I was also desirous to try an experiment or two, touching the conservation and induration of bodies. As for the experiment itself, it succeeded exceedingly well ; but in the journey (between London and Highgate) I was taken with such a fit of casting, as I knew not whether it were the stone, or some surfeit, or cold, or indeed a touch of them all three. But when I came to your Lordship's house I was not able to go back, and therefore was forced to take up my lodging here, where your housekeeper is very careful and diligent about me ; which I assure myself your Lordship will not only pardon towards him, but think the better of him for it. For indeed your Lordship's house was happy to me ; and I kiss your noble hands for the welcome which I am sure you give me to it.

"I know how unfit it is for me to write to your Lordship with any other hand than mine own ; but in troth my fingers are so disjointed with this fit of sickness, that I cannot steadily hold a pen."

Those fingers were never to hold a pen again. He died on the morning of Easter Sunday, 9 April, 1626.

§ 42 BACON AT HOME

Before proceeding to discuss Bacon's character, it seems fair to hear the best that can be said about him by a witness who knew him very well, or at all events had very good opportunities for knowing him; and such testimony we find in the brief memoir about him composed by his chaplain, Dr. Rawley. Making allowance for a little courtliness, a little disposition to omit or gloss over anything unpleasing or ungraceful,[1] a little excess of admiration, and here and there, perhaps, a tinge of obsequiousness such as may fairly be pardoned in a Lord Chancellor's chaplain, we can hardly deny that the writer felt a real and hearty affection for his great patron. The memoir scarcely touches on Bacon's public career, at all events during the reign of James; but the latter portion of it gives some quaint and interesting details about his domestic life and habits, and illustrates the feelings with which he was regarded by his dependents and familiar friends. We have seen Bacon in the Law Courts, in the Star Chamber, in Parliament, and in what may be described as the King's Cabinet; we are now to see him as he appeared to his chaplain at home.

"There is a commemoration due as well to his abilities and virtues as to the course of his life. Those abilities which commonly go single in other men, though of prime and observable parts, were all conjoined and met in him. Those are, *sharpness of wit, memory, judgment,* and *elocution.* For the former three his books do abundantly speak them; which with what sufficiency he wrote, let the world judge; but with what celerity he wrote them, I can best testify. But for the fourth, his *elocution,* I will only set down what I heard Sir Walter Raleigh once speak of him by way of comparison (whose judgment may well be trusted), *That the Earl of Salisbury was an excellent speaker, but no good penman; that the Earl of Northampton (the Lord Henry Howard) was an excellent penman, but no good speaker; but that Sir Francis Bacon was eminent in both.*

"I have been induced to think, that if there were a beam of knowledge derived from God upon any man in these modern times, it was upon him. For though he was a great reader of books, yet he had not his knowledge from books,[2] but from some grounds and notions from within himself; which, notwithstanding, he vented with great caution and circumspection. His book of *Instauratio Magna* [3] (which in his own account was the chiefest

---

[1] Rawley avoids, for example, any mention of the pecuniary difficulties to which Bacon was reduced in his later years; and he not only omits all reference to the domestic difference which finally induced Bacon to revoke in his last will the dispositions previously made in his wife's favour, but even "speaks of their married life in terms which almost exclude the supposition of any (difference)."— Spedding, vii. 524, 538.

[2] *i.e.* not from books *only : Ex libris tamen solis scientiam suam deprompsisse handquaquam concedere licet.* This and the following notes (except where bracketed) are from Mr. Spedding, *Works,* i. 10—18.

[3] For *Instauratio Magna* in this place, and also for *Instauration* a few lines further on, the Latin version substitutes *Novum Organum.* Rawley, when he spoke of the *Instauration,* was thinking no doubt of the volume in which the *Novum Organum* first appeared, and which contains all the pieces that stand in this edition before the *De Augmentis.*

of his works) was no slight imagination or fancy of his brain, but a settled and concocted notion, the production of many years' labour and travel. I myself have seen at the least twelve copies of the *Instauration*, revised year by year one after another, and every year altered and amended in the frame thereof, till at last it came to that model in which it was committed to the press ; as many living creatures do lick their young ones, till they bring them to their strength of limbs.

" In the composing of his books he did rather drive at a masculine and clear expression than at any fineness or affectation of phrases, and would often ask if the meaning were expressed plainly enough, as being one that accounted words to be but subservient or ministerial to matter, and not the principal. And if his style were polite,[1] it was because he would do no otherwise. Neither was he given to any light conceits, or descanting upon words, but did ever purposely and industriously avoid them ; for he held such things to be but digressions or diversions from the scope intended, and to derogate from the weight and dignity of the style.

" He was no plodder upon books ; though he read much, and that with great judgment, and rejection of impertinences incident to many authors ; for he would ever interlace a moderate relaxation of his mind with his studies, as walking, or taking the air abroad in his coach,[2] or some other befitting recreation ; and yet he would lose no time, inasmuch as upon his first and immediate return he would fall to reading again, and so suffer no moment of time to slip from him without some present improvement.

" His meals were refections of the ear as well as of the stomach, like the *Noctes Atticae*, or *Convivia Deipno-sophistarum*, wherein a man might be refreshed in his mind and understanding no less than in his body. And I have known some, of no mean parts, that have professed to make use of their note-books when they have risen from his table. In which conversations, and otherwise, he was no dashing [3] man, as some men are, but ever a countenancer and fosterer of another man's parts. Neither was he one that would appropriate the speech wholly to himself, or delight to outvie others, but leave a liberty to the co-assessors to take their turns. Wherein he would draw a man on, and allure him to speak upon such a subject, as wherein he was particularly skilful, and would delight to speak. And for himself, he contemned no man's observations, but would light his torch at every man's candle.

"His opinions and assertions were for the most part binding, and not

---

[1] The Latin version adds : *Siquidem apud nostrates eloquii Anglicani artifex habitus est.*

[2] In the Latin version Rawley adds gentle exercise on horseback and playing at bowls : *Equitationem, non citam sed lentam, globorum lusum, et id genus exercitia.*

[3] The word "dash" is used here in the sense in which Costard uses it in *Love's Labour's Lost*. "There, an't shall please you ; a foolish mild man ; an honest man, look you, and soon *dashed.*" Rawley means that Bacon was not a man who used his wit as some do, to *put his neighbours out of countenance : Convivantium neminem aut alios colloquentium* pudore suffundere *gloriae sibi duxit, sicut nonnulli gestiunt.*

contradicted by any ; rather like oracles than discourses ; which may be imputed either to the well weighing of his sentence by the scales of truth and reason, or else to the reverence and estimation wherein he was commonly had, that no man would contest with him ; so that there was no argumentation, or *pro* and *con* (as they term it), at his table : or if there chanced to be any, it was carried with much submission and moderation.

" I have often observed, and so have other men of great account, that if he had occasion to repeat another man's words after him, he had an use and faculty to dress them in better vestments and apparel than they had before ; so that the author should find his own speech much amended, and yet the substance of it still retained ; as if it had been natural to him to use good forms, as Ovid spake of his faculty of versifying,

Et quod tentabam scribere, versus erat.

" When his office called him, as he was of the king's counsel learned, to charge any offenders, either in criminals or capitals, he was never of an insulting and domineering nature over them, but always tender-hearted, and carrying himself decently towards the parties (though it was his duty to charge them home), but yet as one that looked upon the *example* with the eye of severity, but upon the *person* with the eye of pity and compassion. And in civil business, as he was counsellor of estate, he had the best way of advising, not engaging his master in any precipitate or grievous courses, but in moderate and fair proceedings : the king whom he served giving him this testimony, *That he ever dealt in business* suavibus modis ; *which was the way that was most according to his own heart.*

" Neither was he in his time less gracious with the subject than with his sovereign. He was ever acceptable to the House of Commons [1] when he was a member thereof. Being the king's attorney, and chosen to a place in Parliament, he was allowed and dispensed with to sit in the House ; which was not permitted to other attorneys.

" And as he was a good servant to his master, being never in nineteen years' service (as himself averred) rebuked by the king for anything relating to His Majesty, so he was a good master to his servants, and rewarded their long attendance with good places freely [2] when they fell into his power ; which was the cause that so many young gentlemen of blood and quality sought to list themselves in his retinue. And if he were abused by any of them in their places, it was only the error of the goodness of his nature, but the badges of their indiscretions and intemperances.

" This lord was religious, for though the world be apt to suspect and prejudge great wits and politics to have somewhat of the atheist, yet he was conversant with God, as appeareth by several passages throughout the

---

[1] The Latin version adds, *in quo saepe peroravit, non sine magno applausu.*

[2] *Gratis*, in the Latin version ; *i.e.* without taking any money for them, an unusual thing in Bacon's time, when the sale of offices was a principal source of all great men's incomes.

whole current of his writings. Otherwise he should have crossed his own principles, which were, *That a little philosophy maketh men apt to forget God, as attributing too much to second causes ; but the depth of philosophy bringeth a man back to God again.* Now I am sure there is no man that will deny him, or account otherwise of him, but to have him been a deep philosopher. And not only so ; but he was able *to render a reason of the hope which was in him,* which that writing of his of the *Confession of the Faith* doth abundantly testify. He repaired frequently, when his health would permit him, to the service of the church, to hear sermons, to the administration of the Sacrament of the blessed body and blood of Christ; and died in the true faith, established in the church of England.

" This is most true—he was free from malice, which (as he said himself) *he never bred nor fed.*[1] He was no revenger of injuries ; which if he had minded, he had both opportunity and place high enough to have done it. He was no heaver of men out of their places, as delighting in their ruin and undoing. He was no defamer of any man to his prince. One day, when a great statesman was newly dead, that had not been his friend, the king asked him, *What he thought of that lord which was gone ?* he answered, *That he would never have made His Majesty's estate better, but he was sure he would have kept it from being worse ;* which was the worst he would say of him : which I reckon not among his moral, but his Christian virtues.[2]

" His fame is greater and sounds louder in foreign parts abroad, than at home in his own nation ; thereby verifying that divine sentence, *A prophet is not without honour, save in his own country, and in his own house.* Concerning which I will give you a taste only, out of a letter written from Italy (the storehouse of refined wits) to the late Earl of Devonshire, then the Lord Candish ; *I will expect the new essays of my Lord Chancellor Bacon, as also his History, with a great deal of desire, and whatsoever else he shall compose : but in particular of his History I promise myself a thing perfect and singular, especially in Henry the Seventh, where he may exercise the talent of his divine understanding. This lord is more and more known, and his books here more and more delighted in ; and those men that have more than ordinary knowledge in human affairs esteem him one of the most capable spirits of this age : and he is truly such.* Now his fame doth not decrease with days since, but rather increase. Divers of his works have been anciently and yet lately translated into other tongues, both learned and modern, by foreign pens. Several persons of quality, during his lordship's life, crossed the seas on purpose to gain an opportunity of seeing him and discoursing with him ; whereof one carried his lordship's

---

[1] " He said he had breeding swans and feeding swans ; but for malice, he neither bred it nor fed it."—From a commonplace book of Dr. Rawley's in the Lambeth Library.

[2] [But see above, pp. 174, 175. Dr. Rawley appears not to have known, or to have forgotten " the worst that Bacon could say of Cecil."]

picture from head to foot [1] over with him into France, as a thing which he foresaw would be much desired there, that so they might enjoy the image of his person as well as the images of his brain, his books. Amongst the rest, Marquis Fiat, a French nobleman, who came ambassador into England, in the beginning of Queen Mary, wife to King Charles, was taken with an extraordinary desire of seeing him ; for which he made way by a friend ; and when he came to him, being then through weakness confined to his bed, the marquis saluted him with this high expression, *That his lordship had been ever to him like the angels, of whom he had often heard, and read much of them in books, but he never saw them.* After which they contracted an intimate acquaintance, and the marquis did so much revere him, that besides his frequent visits, they wrote letters one to the other, under the titles and appellations of father and son. As for his many salutations by letters from foreign worthies devoted to learning, I forbear to mention them, because that is a thing common to other men of learning or note, together with him.

" But yet, in this matter of his fame, I speak in the comparative only, and not in the exclusive. For his reputation is great in his own nation also, especially amongst those that are of a more acute and sharper judgement ; which I will exemplify but with two testimonies and no more. The former, when his *History of King Henry the Seventh* was to come forth, it was delivered to the old Lord Brook, to be perused by him ; who, when he had dispatched it, returned it to the author with this eulogy, *Commend me to my lord, and bid him take care to get good paper and ink, for the work is incomparable.* The other shall be that of Doctor Samuel Collins, late provost of King's College in Cambridge, a man of no vulgar wit, who affirmed unto me,[2] *That when he had read the book of the Advancement of Learning, he found himself in a case to begin his studies anew, and that he had lost all the time of his studying before.*

" It hath been desired that something should be signified touching his diet, and the regimen of his health, of which, in regard of his universal insight into nature, he may perhaps be to some an example. For his diet, it was rather a plentiful and liberal diet, as his stomach would bear it, than a restrained ; which he also commended in his book of *The History of Life and Death.* In his younger years he was much given to the finer and lighter sorts of meats, as of fowls, and such like ; but afterward, when he grew more judicious,[3] he preferred the stronger meats, such as the shambles afforded, as those meats which bred the more firm and substantial juices of the body, and less *dissipable*, upon which he would often make his meal, though he had other meats upon the table. You may be sure he would not

---

[1] This picture was presented to him by Bacon himself, according to the Latin version.

[2] In the Latin version Rawley has thought it worth while to add that this may have been said playfully : *Sive festive sive serio.*

[3] More judicious (that is) by experience and observation : *experientiâ edoctus* is the expression in the Latin version.

neglect that himself, which he so much extolled in his writings, and that was the use of nitre ; whereof he took in the quantity of about three grains in thin warm broth every morning, for thirty years together next before his death.   And for physic, he did indeed live physically, but not miserably ; for he took only a maceration of rhubarb,[1] infused into a draught of white wine and beer mingled together for the space of half an hour, once in six or seven days, immediately before his meal (whether dinner or supper), that it might dry the body less ; which (as he said) did carry away frequently the grosser humours of the body, and not diminish or carry away any of the spirits, as sweating doth.   And this was no grievous thing to take.   As for other physic, in an ordinary way (whatsoever hath been vulgarly spoken [2]) he took not.   His receipt for the gout, which did constantly ease him of his pain within two hours, is already set down in the end of the *Natural History*.

" It may seem the moon had some principal place in the figure of his nativity : for the moon was never in her passion or eclipsed, but he was surprised with a sudden fit of fainting ; and that, though he observed not

---

[1] In the Latin version Rawley gives the quantity : *Rhabarbari sesquidrachmam.*

[2] [Rawley's words indicate that Bacon was popularly supposed to be a constant valetudinarian, and certainly the Memoriæ Valetudinis (Spedding, iv. 78—9) in his *Commentarius Solutus* would lead us to infer that he was in the habit of watching his own constitution and symptoms very attentively.

" I doe find nothing to induce stopping more and to fill the head and to induce languishing and distast and fevrous disposicion more I say then any maner of offer to sleep at afternoon, eyther ymmediately after dynner or at 4 of clock. And I could never yet fynd resolucion and strength enough in my self to inhibite it.

" I have fownd a dyett to feed of boyld meat, coole salletts, abstinence of wyne, to doe me much good, but it may not be contynued for palling and weakenyng my stomach.

" I have fownd good of 3 spoonefulls of Syrope of vinegar simple or (*sic*) syrope of lemans taken ymediately before supper, for it quickneth appetite and raiseth yᵉ expulsive vertue for any remayn of collection in yᵉ stomach.

" I have ever had opinion that some comforting drink at 4 a clock howre wᶜʰ is the howre of my languishing were proper for me."

Still more suggestive is the manner in which a valetudinarian note is suddenly interpolated in the midst of other notes about " forms," *i.e.* retorts, witticisms, &c. (Spedding, iv. 57).

"To send message of complemᵗ to my La. Dorsett the wydowe.

"*fo.* Princes when in justs triumphes or games of victorye men deserve crownes for their perfourmance, doe not crown them beloe whear they perfourmed but calleth them up.   So God by death " [evidently a note applying to Lord Dorset and intended for the consolation of Lady Dorset].

"*fo.* It is not for me to seek this without your favour but rather to desire your favour without it.

" *When I was last at Gorhambury I was taken much wᵗʰ my symptome of melancholy and dout of yʳsent perill, I found it first by occasion of soppe wᵗʰ sacke taken midde meal and it contynued wᵗʰ me that night and yᵉ next mornyng, but note it cleared and went from me without purge and I turned right and disposed of myself.*

"*fo.* My L. Chanc. will not ayd legacies of mariage where the woman is gott away without yᵉ consent of her frendes, and his By woord is, Yf you provyde flesh for your self provyde bread likewise."]

nor took any previous knowledge of the eclipse thereof ; and as soon as the
eclipse ceased, he was restored to his former strength again.

" He died on the ninth day of April in the year 1626, in the early morning of the day then celebrated for our Saviour's resurrection, in the sixty-
sixth year of his age, at the Earl of Arundel's house in Highgate, near
London, to which place he casually repaired a week before ; God so ordaining
that he should die there of a gentle fever, accidentally accompanied with a
great cold, whereby the defluxion of rheum fell so plentifully upon his
breast, that he died by suffocation ; and was buried in St. Michael's Church
at St. Albans ; being the place designed for his burial by his last will and
testament, both because the body of his mother was interred there, and
because it was the only church then remaining within the precincts of old
Verulam : where he hath a monument erected for him in white marble
(by the care and gratitude of Sir Thomas Meautys, knight, formerly his
lordship's secretary, afterwards clerk of the King's Honourable Privy
Council under two kings) ; representing his full portraiture in the posture
of studying, with an inscription composed by that accomplished gentleman
and rare wit, Sir Henry Wotton.

" But howsoever his body was mortal, yet no doubt his memory and
works will live, and will in all probability last as long as the world lasteth.
In order to which I have endeavoured (after my poor ability) to do this
honour to his lordship, by way of conducing to the same."

It is possible that Rawley's reticence on the straits to which
his patron was reduced led him to omit a " memorable relation,"
which he reported to Tenison as an illustration of Bacon's
patience during his last five years of adversity.   One day Bacon
was dictating to Dr. Rawley some experiments in his *Sylva*.   In
the midst of his work a friend called in to bring him a final
answer concerning some grant from the King, from which Bacon
had hoped to repair his fortunes : " His friend told him plainly
that he must thenceforth despair of that grant, how much soever
his fortunes needed it.   *Be it so,* said his Lordship ; and then he
dismissed his friend very cheerfully, with thankful acknowledg-
ments of his service. His friend being gone, he came straightway
to Dr. Rawley and said thus unto him, *Well, sir, yon business
won't go on: let us go on with this, for this is in our power.*
And then he dictated to him afresh for some hours, without
the least hesitancy of speech or discernible interruption of
thought."

Similar testimony is borne by his apothecary and secretary,
Peter Boëner, who was in his service till the beginning of 1623 :

"Though his fortune may have changed, yet I never saw any change in his mien, his words, or his deeds, towards any man. *Ira enim hominis non implet justitiam Dei:* but he was always the same both in sorrow and joy, as a philosopher ought to be."

§ 43 BACON'S CHARACTER : THE PROBLEM

In well-known words, Bacon has bequeathed his "name and memory to men's charitable speeches, and to foreign nations, and the next ages." It is a pity he could not have bequeathed it to the great dramatist who died ten years before him; for none but Shakespeare could do justice to the singular and complex combinations of good and evil in this strange character. Some of the evil of it may be gathered from almost every chapter (except the last) of the preceding narrative; much more from a detailed study of his own letters; and most of all from his private notes; for never was man franker in committing to paper his own defects and infirmities. On the other hand, many of his better characteristics cannot receive great prominence in a biography dealing mainly with definite and important facts and utterances. I have not knowingly omitted a single good or kind action of any importance that is recorded in Mr. Spedding's copious biography to have been performed by him : but naturally the correspondence of a Lord Chancellor and a philosopher turns on political or philosophical subjects, and not on the quiet amenities or philanthropies of the inner life. Bacon's better traits have to be inferred, not from anything that he himself said or did on particular occasions, but from the brief testimony of one or two of his most intimate friends, whose disinterested eulogies after his disgrace and death prove that to them at least he seemed not only genial, kindly, and affectionate, but also a bright example of lofty virtue.

There seems something of the nature of a psychological problem in the contradiction between Bacon as he appeared to his friends, and Bacon as he appears to us. We have noted already the spirit of genuine affection which breathes through the short memoir of him written by his chaplain Rawley. His domestic apothecary and secretary, Peter Boëner, expresses a wish that a statue of him may be erected, not for his learning and researches, but " as a memorable example to all, of virtue, kindness, peacefulness, and patience." Ben Jonson speaks in the same strain of his " virtue;" he could never bring himself, he says, to condole with the great man after his fall, because he knew that no accident could do harm to his virtue, but rather serve to make it manifest. To the same effect writes Sir Toby Matthew, one of his most intimate friends, who was in the secret of his philosophic projects, and to whom he dedicated his *Essay on Friendship:* "It is not his greatness that I admire, but his virtue. It is not the favours I have received of him that have enthralled and enchained my heart, but his whole life and character; which are such that, if he were of an inferior condition, I could not honour him the less, and if he were my enemy, I should not the less love and endeavour to serve him."

In all this, it may be said, there is nothing strange, nothing that deserves to be called a problem : it is no new thing to find in the same man private virtues sharply contrasting with public defects. True; but if we enumerate the faults of which in the preceding narrative Bacon seems to stand convicted, they will appear to be precisely of the kind which would repel inferiors and familiar friends in private life. His behaviour, for example, to his long-suffering and friendly creditor Trott, a small matter in itself, is important as an indication of a selfish unreasonableness. His treatment of Essex can hardly be termed, even by those who attempt to extenuate it, other than cold-blooded, ungenerous, and ungrateful; and a deficiency in generosity and in honourable instinct more easily alienates familiar dependents than a coarseness in open vice. As for his gross and persistent flattery to Cecil up to the day of his patron's death, followed by censorious criticism, almost before the same patron could be laid in his grave, and then by fervent congratulations to the King upon the goodness of God in delivering him from a pestilent counsellor—it argues a disposition so lost to all sense of consistency and shame that we can hardly understand how a man guilty of such time-serving can have attracted a single sincere friend. His rancour towards his enemy Coke, the want of moral discrimination indicated by his language at the trial of Lord Sanquhar, and his cruel ingratitude to his friend Yelverton,[1] all point in the same direction, revealing an absence of healthy moral instinct, a deficiency which—one might have expected—Bacon's immediate dependents and friends would not have been slow to detect. Again, his servile submission to the Favourite in a matter in which he professed to believe himself in the right and the Favourite in the wrong; his deliberate and persistent attempts to lower the reputation of Hobart, the Attorney-General; his advice to the King to delude Somerset, when on his trial, by promises never intended to be kept—are all faults of the same kind, appearing to indicate a cold, passionless, we may almost say crooked, nature; such as could not excite any enthusiasm in those who knew it well. On his confession that he had received gifts from suitors in cases pending before him, not much stress need be laid, regard being had to the customs of the times. Even the much more serious case of judicial dereliction in which Bacon reversed a decision in compliance with Buckingham's dictates, may possibly (though very improbably) have been an isolated act of injustice. Nevertheless these irregularities contribute to our difficulty in understanding how the man who was responsible for them can have presented to such intimate associates as Rawley, Boëner, and Toby Matthew, a character of ideal "virtue."

But the problem does not stop here. We have not merely to explain how a man could occasionally creep like a snake in public, and pose as an angel in private; we have further to explain how he could do a great number of doubtful and dishonourable actions, and yet always retain so high an opinion of himself, that self-respect is too weak a name for it. Many a man does all sorts of bad things, and persuades others that he is good, but it is seldom that a man (unless under the domination of some religious superstition) can do bad things and yet believe in his own peculiar goodness. Again, many men do base things unpremeditatedly, on the spur of self-interest, and with more or less of unwillingness, and forget them, or try to forget them afterwards. They do them, but are ashamed of doing them.

---

[1] See p. 278.

But Bacon did them deliberately, and gave the best proof that he looked them in the face before doing them, by setting them down on paper.

Take, for example, his paragraphs in his *Commentarius Solutus*, mentioned above (p. 153), and headed "Hubbard's Disadvantage." It is just possible that in our own days a lawyer or other professional man may now and then not be deterred by feelings of delicacy from expressing unfavourable opinions of some rival in his profession, occupying a superior position which he himself desires to obtain; nay, that he may even do this habitually whenever an occasion presents itself; but it is hardly conceivable that any one should deliberately set down on paper terms of "disparagement" intended to be dropped, as if *ex tempore*, in course of conversation. Or take the paragraph in the same note-book referring to Bacon's relations with Cecil at the Council-board. That Bacon, against his better judgment, should support his cousin's and patron's propositions, is wrong, but intelligible; but it is almost unintelligible that he should set down on paper a determination to abuse his position at the Council-board: "At the Council-table chiefly to make good my Lord of Salisbury's motions and speeches, and for the rest, sometimes one, sometimes another: chiefly his that is most earnest and in affection." Or again, take his note with reference to Suffolk: "To furnish my Lord of Suffolk with ornaments for public speeches. To make him think how he should be reverenced by a Lord Chancellor, if I were." How is it possible that a man should thus write himself down a flatterer, and yet speak and think of himself as "born for the service of mankind," and in his moments of deepest contrition, when confessing his sins to God—deplore, not his servility nor his self-seeking, but chiefly his misuse of God's "gracious talent of gifts and graces," which he had misspent in things for which he was least fit?

A most inadequate explanation has been offered for Bacon's faults in the suggestion that they arose from want of money: "Carelessness about money was probably the root *from which all Bacon's errors and misfortunes sprang.* And the want of money led him to seek preferment more openly and more keenly than we in these days, when we are more given to mask our ambitions, should regard as consistent with dignity." [1] It is indeed true that, in Bacon's earlier life, want of money caused need of office, and need of office drove him to strenuous and scarcely dignified office-seeking. But this cause will not explain the systematic flattery and place-seeking sketched out in the *Commentarius Solutus.* Those notes were written in July, 1608, when Bacon was Solicitor-General, with an income of nearly £3,000 a year (his Solicitorship being reckoned at only £1,000) and *nine days before he began to write,* the death of the Clerk of the Chamber, and Bacon's succession to the Clerkship, had added £2,000 a year to his income, making a total of nearly £5,000 a year, or about £20,000 of our money. Yet it was after this recent accession to his income that Bacon sat down to write out schemes for disparaging the Attorney-General, and for ultimately becoming Lord Chancellor. These simple facts dispose of the excuse that at this period of his life Bacon was driven to seek preferment by want of money.

Pope's epigram on " the wisest, brightest, meanest of mankind," and the usual commentaries on the epigram, are equally beside the mark as explanations of the point at issue. For we are not questioning the compatibility of scientific excellence, or political insight, or even patriotic spirit, with grave moral deficiency. Our problem is to explain how the so-called " meanest of mankind "—who certainly stooped at times to conduct that would in ordinary persons be called despicably " mean "—not only persuaded others who were on intimate terms with him and had opportunities for knowing him well, that he was a pattern of " virtue," but also to the last retained a high self-respect.

§ 44 BACON'S CHARACTER: THE SOLUTION

Bacon's own letters and works suggest a very different and much more complicated explanation of his career than the simple solution of "want of money." All men lead double lives, a private and a public; but, if we may believe his own account about himself—and it agrees with many casual and

---

[1] *Francis Bacon,* by Professor Fowler, p. 28.

unpremeditated indications in his writings—he was a man in whom the two lives were to an extraordinary degree separable ; not however that in his case we should divide the public from the private, but rather the public from the scientific.

Bacon considered himself, so he has told us in the Proem to the *Interpretation of Nature*,[1] born for the service of mankind, and especially to serve men by extending their dominion over Nature. Birth and education, and the importance of the political crisis, diverted him for a time to politics ; but even then he was stimulated by the hope that *if he rose to eminence in the State he should have a larger command of industry and ability to help him in his philosophic work.* Some may dispute the sincerity or the deliberateness of the very similar avowal made to Burghley (1592) ; but I do not see how those who give any credit at all to Bacon's professions, can withhold their belief from the statement in the Proem, written when he was over forty years of age (at a time when he thought he had forsworn all pursuits but Philosophy, so that he could dispassionately review the political distraction of his earlier manhood), and supported as it is by many similar autobiographical statements, made at different periods of his life.[2] The importance of this evidence is increased, not diminished, by the fact that Bacon cancelled the passage later in life, when he had suffered himself a second time to be allured into the political vortex. And it is confirmed by the private notes in the *Commentarius Solutus*, which exhibit Bacon still planning how to use his influence and position for the purpose of drawing in great and learned men among his contemporaries, as recruits in the army of Science.

But as the Philosopher plunged deeper and deeper into the excitements of civil life, he began to love place and pomp and power more and more for their own sakes. The formidable and unexpected difficulties which he found barring the way to immediate scientific success, co-operated with the importance of the political crisis and the charms of office to throw Science more and more into the background. The claims of politics pressed themselves on his attention with increasing strength. Here was a King ignorant of Parliaments, but wise in statecraft, willing to

---

[1] See above, p. 27.   [2] See above, pp. 30-32.

be advised ; on the other side, a democratic feeling "creeping on
the ground;" a disposition on the part of an irresponsible assembly of country gentlemen and lawyers, variable, unorganised,
and untrained in politics, to interfere with government; and
between the two stood, in his own imagination, the Philosopher
as a mediator, the faithful servant of the King, but the trusted
friend of the Commons, able to advise the former and to manage
the latter, and hopeful that *suavibus modis* he might reconcile
the two in such a way as to strengthen and amplify the monarchy
without exciting the active discontent of the people. Did not
patriotism itself dictate that, in these exceptional circumstances,
he should break the letter of his ascetic resolution, and tear
himself away from Philosophy in order to do his duty to his
country? And might not Science herself reap some benefit
from this temporary desertion, if her gospel were soon afterwards preached from the steps of the throne by the confidential
adviser of the King?

"Good thoughts, though God accept them, yet towards men are little
better than good dreams, except they be put in act, and that cannot be
without power and place."[1]

The temptation must be admitted to be great; and one
moral to be deduced from Bacon's life appears to be this, that
a man who desires to preserve his self-respect, and who is
conscious of a too supple, self-deceiving, self-indulgent nature,
in deciding between the two Voices which would lead him in
opposite directions, should make a rule—wherever he finds the
considerations on either side almost exactly balanced—of choosing that course by which he will not make most money. So
deciding, he may still go astray on the paths of ambition,
fanaticism, Phariseeism, and in countless other ways : but on
the whole, for a weak, moral nature, with good intentions, but
a tendency to worldliness, it seems safe advice.

When the choice of a political life had once been made, the
rest inevitably followed. If, for the sake of Philosophy and
the interests of his country, success in civil life was to be attained, Bacon believed that he must not despise the ordinary
means of attaining it. It is absurdly inconsistent, he says, or—

[1] *Essays*, xi. 34-40.

to use his own words—" it is the *solecism* of power to think to
command the end, and yet not to endure the means." [1]   These
means Bacon felt to be morally imperfect ; but, for the sake of
the object, the Philosopher must not shrink from them : " sometimes by indignities men rise to dignities." [2]   Human nature.
like other nature, must be governed by being studied and
humoured, not by being forced.   No Philosopher, unless he
intends to be a useless recluse, ought to be above "morigeration," that is, above applying himself to the humours of great
persons.   Men must be managed, persuaded, cajoled ; led somehow, and, only in the last resort, driven.   The Philosopher is
really managing Nature when he is flattering, and therefore
ought to feel no more shame at flattery than at performing an
experiment in chemistry.

Human nature being imperfect must be influenced by imperfections : " there is in human nature generally more of the
fool than of the wise." [3]   " Most people understand not many
excellent virtues : the lowest virtues draw praise from them ;
the middle virtues work in them astonishment or admiration ;
but of the highest virtues they have no sense or perceiving at
all : " [4] if men are selfish, or even malignantly mischievous,
they are merely acting in accordance with their nature, and it is
unreasonable to expect they will act otherwise : [5] " If you would
work any man, you must either know his nature and his fashions
and so lead him ; or his ends, and so win him ; or his weakness
and disadvantages and so awe him, or those that have interest
in him, and so govern him." [6]   In politics and in civil life, as in
science, we must take nature as it is, not as we suppose it ought
to be.   If we are not trained to know the wiles of wicked men,
our virtue will be an undefended prey to wickedness ; so that
" we are much beholden to Machiavelli and other writers of that
class, who openly and unfeignedly declare and describe what men
do, and not what they ought to do, for without this, virtue is
open and unfenced." [7]   However much, therefore, Bacon may
laud Truth and Goodness, he lauds them only as ideals, to which

[1] *Essays*, xix. 56.   [2] *Essays*, xi. 9.
[3] *Ibid.*, xii. 12.   [4] *Ibid.*, liii. 6.
[5] *Ibid.*, iv. 17.   [6] *Ibid.*, xlvii. 42-46.
[7] *De Augmentis*, vii. 2.

none must approach too close who wish for success. "It is one thing," he says, "to be perfect in things and another to be perfect in the drifts and humours of men:" but the statesman must endeavour to be perfect in both, and in accommodating oneself to human nature, some personal self-adaptation or subservience is needful. Bacon does not disguise from himself or from his readers the necessity imposed upon every man who would succeed, to temper his virtue with some alloy of imperfection. Throughout the *Essays* there is assumed a contrast between ideal virtue and a standard of practical conduct; and the morality of Bacon's most popular work, as well as of Bacon's life itself, is not unfairly represented in the following words of Machiavelli : " The present manner of living is so different from the way that ought to be taken, that he who neglects what is done to follow what ought to be done, will sooner learn how to ruin than how to preserve himself. For a tender man, and one that desires to be honest in everything, must needs run a great hazard amongst so many of a contrary principle." [1]

There appear to have been moments in Bacon's life when he judged himself by a higher standard of morality; when he described the choice of a courtier's career as an " error," and the "great error " of his life ; when he confessed that his conscience reproved him for deserting the tasks of philosophy and applying himself to " tasks that depended upon the will of others ; " and when he accused himself of thereby mis-spending God's talent " in things for which he was least fit." Such statements, frequently repeated in various circumstances, and combined with the deliberate statement in the Proem to the *Interpretation of Nature*, seem to indicate a deeply-rooted though often stifled consciousness in the writer of these confessions that he was morally as well as intellectually unfit for a life in the Court.

Generally, however, Bacon succeeded in suppressing this self-accusing conviction, and maintained the theory (more than once described in the preceding pages) that a philosopher is to be blamed for retiring from the world. He even censures the tenderness and want of compliance in some of the most ancient and revered philosophers, who retired too easily from civil business that they might avoid indignities and perturbations

---

[1] See Appendix I., Note on Professor Fowler's defence of Bacon's morality.

and live (as they thought) more pure and saintlike." "Pragmatical men," said he, must be taught that "learning is not like a lark which can mount and sing and please itself and nothing else; but it partakes of the nature of a hawk which can soar aloft and can also descend and strike upon its prey at leisure." What, therefore, men of the world do for the purposes of self-advancement unsystematically, unwillingly, and with more or less of shame, that Bacon did systematically, and, for the most part, without a particle of shame or regret, feeling that he was therein not serving himself alone, but also Philosophy: "It is of no little importance to the dignity of learning that a man, naturally fitted rather for learning than for anything else, and borne by some destiny against the inclination of his genius into the business of active life, should have risen to such high and honourable appointments under so wise a king."[1]

In part, therefore, Bacon's enthusiasm for Science may explain some of his moral derelictions. As religious enthusiasts are tempted, so scientific, æsthetic, and political enthusiasts may be tempted, to do a little wrong in order to secure a great good, and to suppress the instinctive promptings of common-sense morality, when morality appears to stand in the way of a great Cause. But there were also in this many-sided genius certain inherent deficiencies and qualities which predisposed him to accept the doctrine of the Architecture of Fortune, and to work it out (within certain limits) with a novel and unconventional thoroughness. An ordinary man of general goodness and benevolence might have been saved by mere moral instinct from some of Bacon's errors, from his morigeration, simulations, and ostentations; but instinct and emotion in him were unduly subordinated to reason. He stood apart from, and unswayed by, the current of popular and contemporary emotions, whether good or bad; never fervent in Puritanism even when he supported the Puritans; never a warm Anglican even when he turned against all Nonconformity; he had no sympathy with the general resentment against unjust and obsolete oppressions (except so far as they presented anomalies in law); no conception of the growing force of the craving for more liberty; no percep-

[1] *De Augmentis*, viii. 2; Spedding, *Works*, v. 73.

tion at all of the great gulf that divided him from that
very House of Commons which he prided himself on understanding so well. He was above the prejudices of his race as
well as those of his age and nation. He praises, for example,
the ancients for despising "words of reproach and contumely
(whereof *the lie* was esteemed none);" and even blows "are not
in themselves considerable, save that they have got upon them
the stamp of a disgrace, which maketh these light things pass
for great matters." Caution in forming friendships may be
prescribed ; but no one of ordinary moral instinct would accept
Bacon's often-repeated precept of Bias, "Love as if you were
sometime to hate, and hate as if you were sometime to love."
He was probably not happy in marriage ; but even a disappointed
husband might have found something better to say of the divine
purpose of domestic life than that wife and children, though
they are "a kind of discipline of humanity," are "impediments
to great enterprises." But what else was to be expected from
the man who asks, as though there could be but one answer
to the question, "Are not the pleasures of the intellect
greater than the pleasures of the affections?"

Again, the marvellous versatility of Bacon's mind was not
without some moral danger. Applied to philosophy, this faculty
was helpful in enabling him to adapt his thoughts to the Pro-
tean windings of Nature, and it has been justly called by
Hallam an "incomparable ductility." But it pervaded his
whole character and his most minute actions. Even in his
varied handwriting we may trace it and still more in his composition, which adapts itself with singular flexibility to every
subject, to every shade of thought, and sometimes, in his letters,
to the characters of his several correspondents. This "ductility,"
carried into the practical life of a Councillor and Judge,
was not an advantage. He prided himself upon his capacity
for becoming *all things to all men;* but when he applied this
maxim to his intercourse with the great, it always resulted in
his becoming nothing but a flatterer or an obsequious adviser.
As he bowed to Nature in the certainty of overcoming her by
obedience, so he bowed to kings and favourites ; but with the opposite result, that he became not their master but their servant.
"I am bold to think it, till I think that you think otherwise"—

thus pliantly we have found him expressing himself in one of
his earliest papers of advice to Queen Elizabeth; and one of
his latest letters to Buckingham—after pointing out the inex-
pediency and oppressiveness of certain Monopolies for which,
as certifier, the Lord Chancellor would be considered responsible
—concludes as follows, "Howsoever, let me know your will, and
I go your way." This is the tenour of all Bacon's political
action. He always intended and endeavoured to go his own
way : but if he could not, then, sooner than not be employed,
he was always ready to go the way of his employers; and his
endeavour to be independent was so slight, and his endeavour
to be employed was so strong, that the result was always the
same. His employers never had any difficulty with him : they
let him know their will, and he went their way.

His high estimate of his own character was sustained not
only by the dangerous support of the consciousness of vast plans
of universal philanthropy, but also by an habitual inaccuracy of
mind, combined with an unusually sanguine disposition, disposing him always to take the most favourable views of everything
that concerned himself. His inaccuracy in matter of detail, as
for example in quotations, is admitted by his earliest biographer,
and attracted the King's good-humoured comment, "De minimis
non curat lex." Mr. Spedding admits that this inaccuracy
extended to dates; Mr. Ellis shows that it pervaded all his
science. I have also noted this disposition in Bacon's estimate
of his own debts as compared with the estimate of Egerton,
one of the most upright and respected of his friends; and the
crowning instance of all was afforded by the mention in his last
will of that imaginary "good round surplusage" which was to
be devoted to the foundation of lectureships at the Universities.
But this same inaccurate and over-hopeful disposition, influencing his reviews of his own conduct, invariably disposes him to
form a too favourable opinion of himself and his surroundings,
extending even to his friends and patrons for the time being;
so that even his gross flattery of Cecil, Villiers, and the King was
probably not all flattery. Like many others who have taken low
views of human nature in general, he seems to have made some
compensation by taking sanguine views of particular persons, and
especially of those whom, at the time, he desired to prosper,

because his own prosperity was involved in theirs. His inordinate restlessness and greediness for work co-operated with, and stimulated, this over-hopeful disposition. Well and wisely had his mistress Elizabeth called him in old days " her watch-candle " because " he did continually burn." Some fuel, either of active thought, or else of action itself, was constantly needed to keep alive the consuming flame of that ever-burning intellect which, whenever it could find no other food, preyed upon itself in inward melancholy.[1] Something therefore he must always be doing; and, if the best was impracticable, then, sooner than do nothing, he could make himself believe that what was practicable was also best. All men have a self-illusive power; but Bacon had it enormously developed. Abundant illustrations of this complacent tendency may be found in extracts from Bacon's letters, quoted in the preceding biography; but most of all in the famous *Apology*, which, however historically worthless, will always retain a value not only for the biographers of Bacon but for all students of human nature who wish to know the lengths of mis-statement, without absolute untruthfulness, to which a man of strong imagination and of slippery memory may be led, who aims at doing too many things, and is too ready to think well of himself.

The sum is, that we accept in great part Bacon's description of his own career, and especially of " that great error that led the rest." He was not by nature the " fittest timber to make a politique of"; but he undertook to become a " politique," and, having undertaken it, he took Machiavelli's advice—so far as concerns the lesser arts of self-advancement—and " hardened himself in order to subsist." But, although he did this systematically and unblushingly, he never altogether forgot that his real calling was to further the Kingdom of Man over Nature, and that to this object all the fruits of his civil successes must be devoted. Supported by this never-failing consciousness, in the midst of all his schemes for self-advancement, he could never feel like a commonplace self-seeker. When he seeks wealth and stoops to take doubtful gifts, he never becomes sordid or avaricious; even when he perverts the truth or recommends falsehood to the King we gaze on him as a portent, with sorrow

[1] See above, p. 152.

rather than with pity or unmixed contempt. Something of the support that Religion gives to its votaries was afforded to Bacon by Philosophy: and just as a Jesuit's simulation may be more mischievous, but must be always less vulgar than that of a selfish man of the world, so it was with the petty immoralities of the Founder of the New Philosophy. Even while creeping in the service of the great Cause, he did not feel himself to be "mean" at all, much less "the meanest of mankind"; nor did his contemporaries feel him to be so; nor can we; and yet, on sufficient occasion, he could creep like a very serpent.

With all his faults, he is one who, the more he is studied, bewitches us into a reluctance to part from him as from an enemy. He has "related to paper" many of his worst defects; but neither his formal works nor his most private letters convey more than a fraction of the singular charm with which his suavity of manner and gracious dignity fascinated his contemporaries, and riveted the affections of some whom it must have been hardest to deceive. It would seem that whenever he found men naturally and willingly depending on him and co-operating with him—so that there was no need to scheme about them, and humour them, and flatter them—his natural and general benevolence found full play; and where he esteemed them so far as to make them partners in his philosophic aspirations and labours, something perhaps of his passionate enthusiasm for Truth in Nature ennobled his intercourse with them, and placed him on a footing of such cordial fellowship with his brother-workers that he really loved them. At least it is certain that he made them love him.

In part, perhaps, the adversities and humiliations of that "long cleansing week of five years' expiation" may have chastened his moral character and generated in him an increased affection for those few friends who remained faithful to the last, even when their interests were no longer "included in his." During those five years he devoted himself (at one time under a vow, literally observed) to the prosecution of his scientific labours; and in these he persevered, in spite of all distractions and discouragements, until the end came. The men who were intimate with him during this student-period, may well have seen cause (like Boëner) to admire his patience, and to find in him an illustration of the saying in one of his own writings, "Virtue is like precious odours, most fragrant when incensed or crushed." And from this point of view, his best friends may see no reason to deplore the circumstances of his end. Fallen from his high place, with shattered fortunes, cast out from his father's house, he died under the roof of a stranger, cutting short his life in a petty experiment which any scullion could have performed for him. But if he had prolonged his Chancellorship for thirty years of wealth and official splendour, it would have been but to "misspend" still further his time and talents in "things for which he was least fit": and surely to die thus homeless in the independent and honest performance of even the humblest research in the cause of Truth, was better than to lie in state in York House, struck down in the climax of his greatness and complacency, while "applying himself to tasks" that depended upon the will of such a king as James, and "constraining the lines of his life" to express his thankfulness to such a patron as Villiers.

PART II

BACON'S WORKS

§ 45 THE REVOLT AGAINST ARISTOTLE

ALTHOUGH Bacon always speaks of his own philosophy as quite new and different from all philosophic systems that had gone before, yet he was at least partially aware that, on its negative side, and in its protest against excessive deference to the authority of Aristotle, his work had been anticipated. He had entered into the fruits of the labours of many predecessors, some of whom are mentioned in his pages; and without a brief review of their work, it would be difficult to realise the nature of the task he undertook.

As early as the thirteenth century his namesake, Roger Bacon (born about 1214), had protested against the Aristotelian despotism, in behalf of a new learning which should be based on experience and should produce fruit. In language which reminds us of Francis Bacon's *Idols*, he imputes human ignorance to four causes: authority, custom, popular opinion, and the pride of supposed knowledge. Nor could the author of the *Novum Organum* have uttered a more confident prediction of the results to be expected from the practical application of the New Learning than is found in the passage where Roger Bacon declares that, as Aristotle by ways of wisdom gave Alexander the kingdom of the world, so Science can enable the Church to triumph over Antichrist by disclosing the secrets of nature and art.

But the Schoolmen were too strong for Roger Bacon. Beginning with John Scotus Erigena in the ninth century, and ending with William of Ockham in the fourteenth, these philosophers made it their endeavour to arrange and support the orthodox doctrine of the Church in accordance with the rules and methods of the Aristotelian dialectics ; and at the very time when Roger Bacon was rebelling against the yoke, Thomas Aquinas was riveting it more firmly than ever by fashioning the tenets of Aristotle into that fixed form in which they became the great impediments to the progress of knowledge. The adoption of the Aristotelian philosophy by the Dominican and Franciscan Orders in the form in which Aquinas had system-atised it, helped to defer for three centuries the reform which Roger Bacon was already urging as a crying necessity. Pastur-ing, and content to pasture, on Aristotle instead of Nature, the Schoolmen despised experiment and observation. It was such students as these whom Francis Bacon likened, not to the bees, who mould what they gather, nor even to the ants, who at least collect, but to the spiders, evolving unsubstantial theory from self-extracted argument.

Yet during the fifteenth and sixteenth centuries theoretical innovation and practical reform were in secret mutiny, preparing the way for the open revolt against Aristotle and his viceroy of Aquinum. During these two centuries the fundamental doctrines of mechanics, hydrostatics, optics, magnetism, and chemistry were established and promulgated ; and their startling and irrefutable results forced on men's minds the power given to mankind over nature by the New Philosophy. Over these fresh provinces of learning, since Aristotle had not discovered them, Aristotle could claim no dominion. In this revolution the prin-cipal part was played by a class described by Whewell as the " Practical Reformers " ; but to Francis Bacon they were compa-ratively unknown and unappreciated, and we will therefore give precedence to that other class which receives more frequent and prominent mention in his works, and which may be called the class of "Theoretical Innovators."

Telesius (Bernardinus), born in 1508, in his treatise on the *Nature of Things* (1565), says : " The construction of the world, and the magnitude and nature of the bodies in it are not to be investigated by reasoning, as was done by the ancients; but they are to be apprehended by the sense and collected from the things themselves." He complains that his predecessors in philosophy during their laborious examinations of the world, "appear never to have looked at it, but to have made an arbitrary world of their own. We then, not relying on ourselves, and of a duller intellect than they, propose to turn our regard to the world itself and its facts." But the execution of his work was not equal to his conception of it; and we find him deserting the path of experiment and falling into the old track of assumptions. Ramus (born in 1515) maintained as his thesis, when proceeding to his degree of Master of Arts in Paris (1535), that " all that Aristotle has said is not true." In 1543 he published his *System of Logic*, with animadversions upon Aristotle. After being deprived of his Professorship and restored, he was put to death in 1572, during the massacre of St. Bartholomew's day. Campanella (who was born in 1568, and died in 1639) warns men against mere books and definitions, proclaiming his own resolution to " compare books with that first and original writing, the world," and declaring that men must begin to reason from sensible things: " definition is the end and epilogue of Science."

Among the " Practical Reformers," Leonardo da Vinci (1452—1519) is the first who took the true view of the laws of equilibrium of the lever in the most general case. He anticipates Francis Bacon in his remarks on experiment: " The interpreter of the artifices of Nature is Experience, who is never deceived. We must begin from experiment and try to discover the reason." Copernicus (1543), in his *Revolution of the Heavenly Bodies*, introduced the heliocentric theory, though (and this must be borne in mind when we discuss Bacon's rejection of the Copernican system) he nowhere asserts that it is a certain truth, but merely describes it as " a better explanation of the revolution of the celestial orbs."

Tycho Brahé (1560—1601), the prince of observers, without a telescope and with a globe no bigger than his fist, detected the errors of existing astronomical tables, and by his mechanical skill in the construction of instruments discovered the means of remedying these errors; and to his observations we owe the deduction of the real laws of a planet's motion by Kepler (1609 —1618), and of the fundamental law of attraction by Newton (1687). Though he rejected the Copernican theory (a very

different theory then from the theory as modified by Newton)
he discovered that the old Ptolemaic spheres of the planets and
of the Primum Mobile [1] could not possibly be solid; and thus
he struck the first decisive blow against the Ptolemaic system.

Napier (1550—1615) by the publication (1614) of his *Logarith-
mic Tables*—on which he was busied before 1594, but of which
Francis Bacon never appears to have had any knowledge—
bestowed on astronomy a benefit which has been described by
Laplace as "doubling the life of astronomers by reducing to a
few days the labour of many months."

Galileo (1564—1642) by his experiment from the leaning tower
of Pisa (before 1592), disproved the Aristotelian doctrine that
bodies fall quickly or slowly in proportion to their weight. Rebuking the "paper philosophers" who thought that philosophy
could be studied like the *Æneid* or the *Odyssey*, he employs the
same language as Campanella concerning the Book of the Universe : "Philosophy is written in that great book, I mean the
Universe, which is constantly open before our eyes; but it cannot
be understood except we first know the language and learn the
characters in which it is written." But more effective than his
sublimest denunciations of paper philosophy was his invention
of the thermometer (before 1597), and the construction of his
wonder-working telescope in 1609.

Gilbert, physician to Queen Elizabeth and author of a treatise
On the Magnet (1600), deserves special attention as being not
only the contemporary but also the countryman, of Francis
Bacon (1540—1603). Like Bacon, he strongly maintains the
superiority of experimental knowledge; like Bacon he desires
to see more fruit from philosophy; and like him he also inveighs
against Aristotle and Galen as the two Lords of Philosophy,
worshipped as false gods; but he differs from Bacon in consistently adhering to the Copernican system of astronomy, rejecting
the Ptolemaic as absurd. Galileo writes of him, "I extremely
admire and envy this author," and Whewell (from whom this
sketch is taken) declares that his work "contains all the fundamental facts of Magnetism so fully stated that we have at this
day little to add to them:" but to Francis Bacon, impatiently
aspiring after vast and general conclusions, Gilbert's researches

---

[1] *Essays*, xv. 22 ; xvii. 21 ; xli. 59 ; and compare *Paradise Lost*, iv. 592.

seemed petty and narrow; and for some faint praise of this original worker he takes ample compensation by declaring that Gilbert has so lost himself in his subject, that " he has himself become a magnet."

From this brief summary of the thoughts and works of the Theoretical Innovators and the Practical Reformers, it will be seen that Francis Bacon (1561—1626) being in his early manhood the contemporary of Galileo, Tycho Brahé, and Kepler, and of his countrymen, Gilbert and Napier, was living in the midst of an intellectual revolution which had already almost shaken off the yoke of the tyrant Aristotle, and was preparing to set up Experience on the vacated throne.

But the new *de facto* Government was not yet recognised by the outside world, and was suspected by many who spoke authoritatively as the appointed champions of Religion. At this particular time therefore there was need of some herald of Philosophy to proclaim the new kingdom and to summon the world to a solemn coronation of the new sovereign. " I am but a trumpeter not a combatant," writes the author of the *De Augmentis;* and whatever more he did or failed to do, certainly he succeeded in sounding forth through the civilised world a note of triumph, preparing the way for the welcome of the New Philosophy by men of letters, by men of the world, by prelates, nobles, and kings.

Neither the tone, nor the merits, nor the results, of Bacon's philosophical works will be appreciated by any who have not learned to sympathise with the social timidity of the discoverers in the sixteenth, and even in the seventeenth centuries. Fundamental innovations in Natural Philosophy were at that time regarded with something of the fear and hatred inspired by theological heresies. Galileo (1597) writes to Kepler that he had personally adopted the Copernican system some years before, but that *he continued to teach in public the Ptolemaic system.* Even as late as 1628, not in Italy but in England, and not dealing with Astronomy (which might have seemed a Biblical province) but with the circulation of the blood, Harvey writes : " So new and unheard of are my discoveries that I not only anticipate some evil from the envy of particular persons, but even dread incurring the enmity of all."

Z

Hence, in part, may we explain Bacon's anxiety to obtain a peaceable entrance for his philosophy, and his desire to gain the help of kings, nobles, and bishops ; hence his various literary experiments, anonymous or otherwise, some attacking the old philosophy, some recommending the new ; some abstruse, some popular ; some directly and avowedly philosophical, some (as for example the *Wisdom of the Ancients*) indirectly suggesting his philosophic tenets or (as in the *New Atlantis* or the *Redargutio Philosophiarum*) blending his view with a mixture of attractive fiction. To express his conciliatory purpose, he frequently uses an illustration derived from the peaceable occupation of Italy by the French under Charles VIII. As those invaders had no need to fight, but only to " chalk up quarters " for their troops, so he hopes to find " chalked up quarters " for the New Philosophy in the hearts of men.

The absence of encouragement for scientific work, and the isolation of scientific workers, were other disadvantages against which Bacon had to contend : and hence in the *Advancement of Learning* [1] we shall find him advocating the endowment of readers in sciences and the provision of expenses for experiments, and by his last will attempting to supply this deficiency. He dislikes the religious controversies of the day, among other reasons because they divert the minds of men from science, and, in his earnest desire for a theological peace, he compares himself to the miller of Huntingdon, who " prayed for peace among the willows that his water might have the more work." [2] Gilbert, Napier, Harriot, and in later times Harvey, found it necessary to prosecute their studies abroad. Of English scientific isolation Bacon himself presents a striking and blamable instance; for he appears to have known nothing of the results of Kepler's calculations, nor of Napier's logarithms,[3] nor of Galileo's experiments on falling bodies. Harriot is a still more striking instance of this isolation, not indeed that, like Bacon, he is ignorant, but rather that he is ignored. Not till 1788 was it ascertained from the inspection of his papers

---

[1] II. viii. 9, 10.   [2] See above, p. 160.
[3] Yet Napier was in correspondence with Anthony Bacon (before 1603) and sent him mathematical papers.—(See *Dictionary of National Biography*, " Anthony Bacon," ii. 326).

that he had been the first to discover the solar spots, and that he had observed the satellites of Jupiter simultaneously with Galileo. For the leisure necessary for these researches he was indebted to the Earl of Northumberland, who, besides maintaining many other learned men, had settled on him a pension of £300 a year. Concerning this great mathematician Bacon makes a note in his *Commentarius Solutus;* but it is merely to the effect that he is "inclined to experiments." We cannot be surprised if hereafter we find Bacon—in his keen realization of the evils arising from the isolation of the labourers in the field of science—laying great, and perhaps too great, stress on the advantages to be expected from systematic division of labour and co-operation.

§ 46 The Scheme of the "Magna Instauratio"

We have briefly considered the obstacles that Bacon saw before him in his path to scientific discovery — prejudice, suspicion, contempt, isolation, want of facts, want of means. But, of all the enemies of the New Philosophy, Aristotle and the Aristotelian spirit appear to have been regarded by him as the most dangerous; and perhaps a few words on the antagonism between the ancient and the modern philosopher may be no unfit preparation for understanding the objects of the latter. We cannot well understand what Bacon tried to effect, and how he tried, unless we first know what Aristotle failed to effect, and why he failed: and we may be led by Bacon's virulent invective against his great predecessor to judge the inveigher somewhat harshly unless we have a clear notion of the immense mischief which Aristotelianism had done, and was doing, to all science and all progressive thought. The mere completeness and literary symmetry of some of Aristotle's physical theories commended them to bookish, non-observant students, interested in natural science rather because of its bearing on theology than for its own sake; and their adoption barred the way for progress. One or two instances may suffice. Aristotle's theory of astronomy was based on the belief that the heavens and all the heavenly bodies must be incorruptible, free from change and from irregularity: consequently the motions of all the orbs *must be in the perfect figure,* the circle, and all the orbits *must be concentric.* Moreover the incorruptibility of the stars demanded that they should be made, not of the perishable four elements, but of an imperishable *fifth essence* or " quintessence."

These propositions he proved by appeal, not to observation nor to experiment, but to what is *good* and *bad,* to what is *natural* and *unnatural.* Thus, concerning the motion of the heavenly bodies, he argued that their motion " must go on constantly, and therefore must be either continuous, or successive. Now what is continuous is more properly said to take place constantly than what is successive. Also the continuous *is better ; but we always suppose that which is better to take place in nature,* if possible." Again as to the fifth element, or *quintessence,* he argued after this fashion : " We have proved that the heavenly bodies move in circles and for ever ; but *it is the nature* of earth and water to move down, and of air and fire to move up : therefore the heavenly bodies either do not belong to the four elements, or else move in a motion contrary to their nature. But *unnatural motions decay speedily.* Therefore to the heavenly bodies (having been proved to move *for ever*) the circular motion must be *natural.* Therefore they do not belong to the four elements. Therefore they are composed of a fifth element or quintessence." For similar reasons Aristotle gives his verdict against the possibility of a vacuum in nature : " In a void there could be no difference of up and down ; for as in nothing there are no differences, so there are none in a privation or negation : but a void is merely a privation or negation of matter : therefore in a void bodies could not move up and down, *which it is their nature to do.* Therefore a void is against nature and impossible." [1]

Such theories and such arguments commend themselves at once to children : and it is not surprising that for many ages during the infancy of European civilisation, this symmetrical Aristotelianism took captive the imaginations of many minds, even after Ptolemy and Copernicus had published their astronomical hypotheses. It was against such a yoke as this that Bacon protested when he declared that " Aristotle's temerity and false reasoning had begotten for men a fantastic heaven,

[1] Whewell, *History of Inductive Sciences,* i. pp. 43, 45, 54.

composed of a fifth essence, free from change ; " [1] and Aristotle is always in Bacon's mind when he declaims against the easy assent of the multitude to authority, and against the willingness of most men to receive, without discussion, symmetrical and agreeable, but fictitious, theories—no better than mere *stage-plays*—which we shall presently find our philosopher branding with the name of the *Idols of the Theatre*.

It is a popular belief that Aristotle was led into the errors of his physical philosophy because he did not know Induction, which, it is thought, was first invented by Francis Bacon. This, however, is an error. Induction is nothing more than the *intro-duction* or *induction* of a number of particular instances to prove a general statement ; and, consciously or unconsciously, every child is constantly in some sense practising Induction. All that we can say as to Aristotle's Induction is, that it was so different from Bacon's proposed Induction in certainty and completeness as almost to be different in kind. An important part of Bacon's Induction was the system of "exclusions ; " that is to say, a method of gradually excluding such supposed causes of any phenomenon as do not invariably co-exist with the phenomenon. This, and other methods of increasing the efficiency of Induc-tion were neglected by Aristotle. His Induction was for the most part what Bacon describes as "puerile" and "enumera-tive," without due selection or variation of circumstances (as though a child were to infer that all men are white because all the men whom he has met are white) ; and although Aristotle did occasionally experimentalize in physiological researches, his Induction was not systematically accompanied by experiment. Moreover, the disadvantages and limitations under which he worked, necessarily made his observations inadequate and in-sufficient ; and in setting before himself scientific problems he sometimes hastily adopted (as if they were scientific terms) popular words implying popular notions, which were really vague, unscientific, and misleading. To say, for example, that a feather floats in the air because it is *light,* and that a stone falls in the air because it is *heavy,* and to infer that light things have a *nature* or *appetite* for rising, and heavy things have a *nature* or *appetite* for falling—this is not only untrue but an

---

[1] Spedding, *Works*, v. 525.

untruth that is all the more dangerous because it is, as it were, democratic and suited to the minds of the multitude. It enthrones popular expressions, giving them supremacy over facts. In this particular error — which, strengthened by Aristotle's authority, blocked up for centuries the path towards the scientific explanation—Bacon himself appears to have shared; but the multitude of similar mistakes arising from the quasi-philosophic adoption of such terms as "hot," "cold," "moist," "dry," "nature," "appetite," and the like, appears to have induced the modern philosopher to single out for reprobation this mischievous reaction on the mind resulting from popular words and notions, as being one of the special obstacles in the way of attaining the Truth; and—as this error sprang from the intercourse and common *traffic* of thoughts, represented by popular and inadequate words—he called it the *Idol of the Market-place*.

The reader of Bacon's works must not accept as exactly and literally true all his attacks on Aristotle. Against the exaggerated depreciation of Francis Bacon, Roger Bacon's words should be placed in the other scale : "Aristotle arranged all the departments of philosophy according to the possibilities of his time."[1] When we compare his results with his means the work of the great Stagirite may be regarded as almost superhuman. True, he sometimes fell into the error of too hastily adopting some neat and consistent physical theory that conformed itself to his favourite metaphysical distinctions; but occasionally Bacon makes the teacher bear the blame that should fall on the scholars. It was not Aristotle, as Bacon declared,[2] but Aristotle's followers, who asserted that one measure of earth is transmutable into ten of water; and one of water into ten of air. But the very fact that the Aristotelians could base such a dogma upon a mere misinterpretation of part of a single sentence of their master, attests most eloquently the servitude in which this "Ottoman," as Bacon calls him, enchained posterity for ages. Under this Sultan the Schoolmen served as Mamelukes. By arguing, as Aristotle had done, from assumptions of what is *best*, or most *wonderful*, or most *natural*, and by a judicious use of the mystical meanings of numbers, it was possible to deduce,

---

[1] Professor Fowler's *Novum Organum*, p. 73.
[2] Spedding, *Works*, ii. 235.

by mere reasoning, most ample and satisfying accounts and explanations of all things in earth and heaven—especially in the latter. It was in the strength of Aristotle and the Aristotelian logic that Duns Scotus (1307), disputing before the University of Paris, demolished "two hundred objections" to the doctrine of the Immaculate Conception and resolved the knottiest syllogisms of his adversaries as Samson did the bonds of Delilah ; and the same philosophy could be trusted to settle for mankind, by simple logic, the precise number of angels that could stand on the point of a pin. The syllogistic and meta-physical method admirably suited those who wished to systema-tize a vast system of ecclesiastical and theological doctrine, apart from all experience of human nature. Thus a universal science, obtained by reasoning alone, and intimately connected with the scholastic theology, was established with the authority of a religious creed ; and theology came to be considered the only philosophy. It is said, though possibly it may be in hyperbole, that in some part of Germany the *Ethics* of Aristotle were read in the churches on Sunday, in the place of the Gospel : but there is no hyperbole in the saying of Francis Bacon that " the Schoolmen, having made Divinity into an art, have almost incorporated the contentious philosophy of Aristotle into the body of Christian religion." [1]

These considerations may enable us, while doing full justice to the great Greek philosopher, to understand, and in large measure to sympathise with, the burning indignation with which Bacon assails him. For " Aristotle," let us substitute " the Aristotelians," and every word of Bacon's invective will be true : their philosophy was barren ; their induction was an im-posture ; and if they ever summoned Experience, it was, in the words of Bacon's bitter accusation, not to consult her as an adviser but to drag her at their chariot-wheels as a captive.[2] Yet, for Bacon's own sake, we must regret the excess of his contempt and scorn for Aristotelianism. It placed a real and serious obstacle in the way of his own scientific work. Seeing so clearly where Aristotle had gone wrong, he was too apt to think that, by simply avoiding the mistakes of his predecessor,

---

[1] *Filum Labyrinthi, Works,* iii. 499.
[2] See the *Redargutio Philosophiarum,* p. 369, below.

he himself would inevitably go right. Aristotle's failures, so far from discouraging him, seem rather to have inspired him with an excess of presumption, as if, when these obstacles were removed, no others would remain to bar the secrets of Nature. Revolting from the unscientific doctrine of the Aristotelian "natures," "appetites," and "qualities," he conceived a sanguine prejudice not only that Nature was orderly, but that her secrets must be readily discovered in an orderly and almost mechanical manner. The recent discoveries of Tycho Brahé, Kepler, Galileo, Harvey, and Gilbert, might have taught him useful lessons of patience, of reverence for the vastness of Nature, and, at the same time, of respect for the indirect results which might spring from the researches of a specialist working in one small corner of her vast domain: but he did not learn these lessons because he did not know or did not appreciate their achievements. They were not grand enough for him; and he merged them all in an indiscriminate condemnation of the barrenness of scientific study from Aristotle's days to his own. The discoveries of science up to his time, he said, had been mainly accidental; no wonder that the Egyptians worshipped beasts as gods; for the instinct of beasts had discovered more healing herbs than the art of men. But why should there not be an art of discovery?

At present, he reflected, some were content to rest in empiricism and isolated facts; others ascended too hastily to first principles; all alike often wasted time and labour in experiments that led to no results, and in observing phenomena that would teach nothing. These evils must be remedied. After the minds of men had been cleared from their inherent imperfections and taught to regard Nature evenly and impartially, philosophers must then be taught to pursue a fixed path of inductive experiment which would guide the feeblest intellect aright, as infallibly as the compasses would guide even the most inaccurate draughtsman to trace a perfect circle. Instead of seeking after experiments which would produce immediate fruit, the philosopher must seek those which would give him light and would direct him towards higher and yet higher experiments, so that he might proceed ever further in the analysis of Nature, and at last reach the real Laws or Forms of all existence, the knowledge of which would bring with it the power of reproducing all existing things.

"How few are the letters of the alphabet, and yet how innumerable are the words and thoughts which they can be made to represent! Might it not be so in the Book of Nature likewise; and as we can take words to pieces and find the single letters, can we not also take the phenomena of Nature to pieces and find their simple constituent elements, the 'simple natures,' so to speak, which in various combinations make up all existences? Heat for example: what can be easier than to *introduce*, one after another, the bodies that contain heat, and to show what common fact there is in each which, amid countless diversities of circumstance, *is never absent whenever heat is present?* Thus, by examining a sufficient number of instances of heat, we shall be able to reject some superficial appearances of cause, which after a time we shall find *not* to be invariably present where heat is present, and we shall be left with a residuum of invariably present fact, through which we shall be able to produce heat at will; and thus we shall at last attain the knowledge of heat by attaining the knowledge of its causes. This *introduction* or *induction* of instances with a view to arrive at causes, requires skill, no doubt; it must not be conducted at haphazard; it is an Art in itself, the Art of Induction; but with patience and docility applying ourselves to things and not to words, to Nature and not to Aristotle, we shall surely attain this Art of Induction: and this, once attained, will be a Key to unlock all the secrets of Nature and to enable us to perform all her processes." Thus Bacon appears to have reasoned: and, as he was by nature over-hopeful; disposed to exaggerate similarities and (with all deference to his own judgment of himself[1]) to underrate the dissimilarities of phenomena; as also he had sufficient general knowledge of recent discoveries to appreciate (more than most men of his time) the orderliness and uniformity of Nature, and had not sufficient special knowledge of recent discoveries to make him aware (as Gilbert and Harvey and Harriot would have been aware) of the indefinable

---

[1] See p. 27 above, where he says he found in himself a capability for discerning dissimilarities.

combination of scientific imagination with scientific toil and
observation, necessary to constitute an original Discoverer—he
early persuaded himself into the belief that it would be a matter
of no great difficulty for him to elaborate such an Art of Induction as would make the discovery of Nature's secrets little more
than a mechanical routine.

All that was needed in addition to the Art of Induction, or
New Instrument for the Interpretation of Nature—was a
sufficient supply of natural phenomena to work on. For that
purpose it would be necessary to compile a new Natural History,
not on the old plan (which aimed at collecting a number of
unarranged, exceptional, and marvellous phenomena for the
purpose of exciting mere amusement or amazement) but a
History classified in accordance with scientific conceptions. To
compile such a Natural History would be a work exceeding the
compass of one man's ability, and suitable rather for a crowned
head. Bacon therefore determined in his earlier years to apply
himself to the former object, the elaboration of the New
Induction, or as he calls it the New Instrument or Organ
(Organum) by which Nature is to be interpreted. But, later in
life—perhaps because the New Instrument had not been found
so efficacious as had been at first anticipated—we shall find him
laying greater stress on the Natural History, and declaring that,
with such a classified History, much advance might be made,
even without the New Instrument.

We must also bear in mind that he presupposes that the
work of interpreting Nature will not be a solitary but a "collegiate" pursuit, wherein a multitude of labourers, having had
their several provinces of observation and experiment mapped
out for them by a superior director, will obtain results of different grades of importance, the lower preparing the way for the
higher, and the whole ascending as it were like the layers of a
pyramid. The apex of this pyramid was to be the highest
knowledge of all, which consists in knowing the axioms common
to all sciences.

The object of all his efforts, Bacon was wont to describe,
not as a rebellion against philosophic despotism, nor yet as a
revolution, nor even as a new institution of philosophy, but
rather as a *renewal* of the wholesome ancient philosophy of the

Egyptians and earlier Greeks, which had been perverted and suppressed by the innovations of Aristotelian ostentation.[1] This description, which he adopted in his youth, he never afterwards discarded; and to this day his philosophic work is known to us as the *Magna Instauratio* or Great Renewal of Learning.

Bacon's own account of the scheme of the *Magna Instauratio* is found in a section of the *Novum Organum* called the *Distributio Operis*, which will be described in due course;[2] but meanwhile the remarks of Mr. Ellis will throw light both on the scheme as a whole, and on all those Baconian treatises which chronologically precede the *Novum Organum*.

"The *Instauratio*," says Mr. Ellis, "is to be divided into six portions of which the *first* is to contain a general survey of the present state of knowledge.

"In the *second*, men are to be taught how to use their understanding aright in the investigation of Nature.

"In the *third*, all the phenomena of the universe are to be stored up, as in a treasure-house, as the materials on which the new method is to be employed.

"In the *fourth*, examples are to be given of its operation and of the results to which it leads.

"The *fifth* is to contain what Bacon had accomplished in Natural Philosophy *without* the aid of his own method ; *ex eodem intellectus usu quem alii in inquirendo et inveniendo adhibere consueverunt*. It is therefore less important than the rest, and Bacon declares that he will not bind himself to the conclusions which it contains. Moreover, its value will altogether cease when—

"The *sixth* part can be completed ; wherein will be set forth the New Philosophy—the results of the application of the new method to all the Phenomena of the Universe. But to complete this Bacon does not hope ; he speaks of it as a thing *et supra vires et ultra spes nostras collocata.*

"The greater part of the plan traced in the *Distributio* remained unfulfilled."[3]

It is a curious and instructive fact that, in spite of all that Bacon wrote to publish, elucidate, and exemplify his philosophic system, there is no general consent among his readers and commentators as to what the system really was. Mr. Ellis however —whose criticisms, although unfortunately incomplete, appear to me to be far superior in depth and clearness to those of any

---

[1] See p. 403, "Deus *Instaurator*."   [2] See p. 377.
[3] Spedding, *Works*, i: 71-2.

other commentator—believes that no account of it can be adequate which does not recognise in it an improvement and perfection of logical machinery. Mr. Spedding on the other hand thinks that the classified Natural History was the most important part of the system, more important than the Key of Interpretation itself. Quotations may undoubtedly be produced from Bacon's works to support the latter view. But I think they will be found to be in every case drawn from Bacon's later works; when, having tried the Key of Interpretation and found it fail, he had been driven to some other refuge for his disappointment. The importance attached to the Natural History appears to have arisen from a change of front. The History would be of little use unless it was classified in accordance with the rules suggested by the Key of Interpretation; and the Key itself—some perfected Logic by which an ordinary mind could discover secrets of Nature not to be detected by the highest unassisted genius—was the central point of the Baconian philosophy.

We proceed to consider one of the many early tentative forms in which some of the principles of the *Instauratio* are set forth.

§ 47 " PARTUS MASCULUS TEMPORIS ;"[1] " VALERIUS TERMINUS."[2]

In the autumn of 1625, Bacon confessed to a correspondent that, some forty years before, he had written a work, which with juvenile audacity and a presumptuous title " he had called *The Greatest Birth of Time, or the Great Renewal of the Empire of Man over the Universe* (*Partus Maximus Temporis sive Instauratio Magna Imperii Humani in Universum*)." No such work is extant; but we have a short fragment proved to be very early by internal evidence, the title of which is *Partus Masculus Temporis*, or *the Male Birth of Time*. There are grounds for thinking that, under a title slightly changed and toned down, we have here the *Partus Maximus*, the first germ of the *Magna Instauratio*.

After a prayer to God that the kindling of the new light of Nature may not dazzle the eye of the soul so as to

---

[1] Spedding, *Works*, iii. 521-539.   [2] *Ibid.* 215-252.

darken it against the reception of the light of spiritual truth, the author proceeds to complain that the minds of all men are blocked or branded with false fancies (*idols*) which preclude the acceptance of truths. This "universal insanity" requires skill in preparing the way for the truth. In a second chapter (which may have been composed or revised later) the author asserts that the object of the New Philosophy is to bring about a lawful wedlock between the mind and *things* (as distinct from fancies) whence shall spring a brood of heroic inventions which (like Hercules of old) shall clear the earth from pests and miseries. There follows a bitter onslaught on all the philosophers from Aristotle downwards. He concludes with the warning that we must begin putting away the *idols*, as well those of the home (*hospitii*) as those that beset us abroad (*viae*).

So ends the *Male Birth of Time*, of which the title is perhaps the most noteworthy part. By "male" he means "generative," or "fruitful," as opposed to the barren philosophy of Aristotle. The exact date of this fragment is not known; but it is characteristic of Bacon's sanguine spirit that this early (perhaps earliest) effort at the *Magna Instauratio* contains little more than a grand title and a prayer against the dangers of an immoderate success.

We can not be surprised that an author who stigmatized the present state of learning as "universal insanity," should contemplate the anonymous publication of works likely to make himself widely disliked, suspected, or ridiculed. Accordingly Bacon's earliest connected work on Philosophy was intended to be published with the title *Valerius Terminus, Of the Interpretation of Nature, with the annotations of Hermes Stella*—a work intended for a select few, and requiring the aid of an *interpreter* (Hermes) to cast a helpful *star-light* (Stella) on the wanderings of the reader towards the philosophic *goal* (Terminus).

Bacon begins by defending the search after the knowledge of Nature from the charge of impiety, supporting his defence by an appeal to the examples of Moses and Solomon, and describing his object as a discovery of all operations and possibilities of operations, from immortality (if it were possible), to the merest mechanical practice.

The external impediments of knowledge, he says, have been

want of steadfastness, want of co-operation, want of tradition from the past, incompleteness, and premature subdivisions. One of the first needs is to make a Kalendar or Inventory of the present intellectual wealth of mankind, not for the purpose of parading any "universality of sense or knowledge," but in order to give some awakening note both of the wants in man's present condition, and the nature of the supplies to be wished. But, as the object is not only to stir up hopes but to direct men's labours, he proceeds to the main business, viz., the discovery of operations.

In order to produce a result we must not only have "certainty" but also "liberty;" that is to say, we must not only ascertain some causes that are *certain* to produce the result, but also such causes as we are at *liberty* to command; and the wider our choice of causes can be, the less we shall be "restrained" to some definite means, and the greater will be our "liberty."

Thus, to produce whiteness; the first "direction" given may be, to intermingle air and water, as in foam, snow, &c. This "direction" is certain, but "tied" to air and water; you "free" it by a second "direction," adding, instead of water, any transparent body provided that it is uncoloured and more grossly transparent than air itself, *e.g.* glass or crystal beaten to powder. The third "direction" removes the "restraint" of "uncoloured," by adding amber beaten to powder, or beer frothing. A fourth "direction" removes the "restraint" of "more grossly transparent" by adding flame, which (but for the presence of smoke) would be a perfect white. A fifth "direction" removes the restraint of air, but still retains "transparent bodies;" bringing us therefore, so far, only to this conclusion, that the nature of "whiteness" may be illustrated by the study of "transparent bodies." Here the author stops: "To ascend further by scale I do forbear, partly because it would draw on the example to an over-great length, but chiefly because it would open that which in this work *I am determined to reserve.*" In a somewhat similar way we shall find Bacon *reserving*, or leaving his investigations incomplete, at the end of the *Novum Organum.* No doubt he believed that he had something in reserve; but it is probable that his extraordinary sanguineness and self-confidence always disposed him, when he found himself at the end of his tether, to deceive himself into the belief that he stopped because he wished to stop, and not because he was compelled to stop.

Proceeding to comment on the novelty of his method, he admits however this " freeing of a direction" to be discernible in the received philosophies as far as a " swimming " (i.e. vague and shifting) " anticipation could take hold, in that which they term the *form* or *final cause*, or that which they call the *true difference*; both which it seemeth they propound rather as impossibilities and wishes than as things within the compass of human comprehension." Thence he proceeds to the internal impediments of knowledge, those inherent in the human mind itself. For the mind, instead of being a perfect mirror to reflect the truth, distorts everything that it reflects by its unevenness— " I do find therefore in this enchanted glass four Idols, or false appearances of several and distinct sorts, every sort comprehend- ing many subdivisions: the first sort I call Idols of the Nation or Tribe; the second, Idols of the Palace; [1] the third, Idols of the Cave; and the fourth, Idols of the Theatre."

Without explaining the meaning of these terms, the author passes on to make, amid much negative matter, the following statements: that the only test of the truth of knowledge is the discovery of new works and active " directions" not known before ; that we are not to seek the causes of things concrete, which are infinite, but of abstract natures, which are few (these natures being " as the alphabet or simple letters whereof the variety of things consisteth, or as the colours mingled in the painter's shell wherewith he is able to make infinite variety of faces or shapes"); that we are not to seek for the materials or dead beginnings of things, but rather for the nature of motions, inclinations and applications; that we are not to seek knowledge by anticipations; that every particular that works any effect is a thing compounded of diverse single natures, and that these particulars must be broken and reduced by exclusions and inclusions to a definite point before we can determine what it is precisely that produces the effect; that the New Philosophy " doth in sort equal men's

---

[1] Elsewhere these are called "Idols of the Market-place." "Place" is used (*Adv. of L.*, II. xxiii. 5) for " Market-place" (Lat. "in foro"). Is it possible therefore that " Palace" is here a mistake for " Place"? For the "Idols" see below, pp. 380-1.

wits," enabling all men to discover with mechanical accuracy, just as a pair of compasses enables every hand to draw a perfect circle.

The work is fragmentary ; and of the annotations of Hermes Stella, the author himself writes that " none are set down." It is supposed to have been written about 1603.

§ 48 The " Advancement of Learning " [1]

The *Advancement of Learning* (published in 1605) supplies the Inventory of the results of knowledge, and the deficiencies, suggested (as Mr. Ellis believes,[2] and as appears from the above sketch) in *Valerius Terminus*. It is written in a more popular style, avoiding many technicalities used in Bacon's other works ; describing, for example, the fallacies denoted by the Idols, but avoiding the use of the term " Idol ; " and it adopts a much more conciliatory attitude to the ancient philosophers than is expressed in Bacon's unpublished treatises.

For the general reader no work of Bacon's is better adapted (as indeed Bacon intended it to be adapted) to be a preparation for the general scheme of the Great Instauration. For although the Key of knowledge is not clearly revealed in it, the deficiencies of knowledge are so indicated, and the supplements so suggested, as constantly to keep before the reader's mind not only the weaknesses of the Old Philosophy, but also the strength of the New, and thus to lead him to conceive its character. Scarcely a page of the Second Book of the *Advancement* fails, directly or indirectly, to guide us towards the *Novum Organum*. And if any one labours under the common prejudice that Bacon's philosophy had for its sole object the increase of the material comforts of men, he cannot better dissipate that error than by gaining a clear conception of the tendency of the book which, more than any other Baconian treatise (for the *De Augmentis* is no more than a larger Latin edition of it), shows that he had taken, not material nature alone, but " all Nature to be his province." Referring the reader to the Appendix for a summary of the great body of the work (which deals with

---

[1] Spedding, *Works*, iii. 253-491 ; for the amplified Latin translation called the *De Augmentis*, see Spedding, *Works*, i. 413-837.

[2] It should be added that Mr. Spedding differs here from Mr. Ellis.

natural and human Philosophy), we shall here give merely a very brief account of the whole argument, and a summary of the earlier sections which deal with history and poetry.

The First Book is a mere introduction, showing how learning has been discredited by faults in critics or students, and bringing testimony to its excellence from divine and human sources.

The Second Book treats of "What has been done for the Advancement of Learning, human and divine, with the Defects of the same." After pointing out the defects in the places of learning, the neglect of science by states and universities, and the want of intercourse between the learned men of different countries, the Author proceeds to classify first human, and then divine learning, taking as his basis the three faculties, of memory, imagination, and reason, which he calls the "three parts of man's understanding."

Human learning is divided into three parts, History, corresponding to memory, Poetry, corresponding to imagination, and Philosophy, corresponding to reason.[1] (*Advancement of Learning*, II. i. 1 ; *De Augmentis*, II. i. 1.)

History is subdivided into natural, civil, ecclesiastical, and literary.[2] Continuing the triple division which is noticeable all through the greater part of this book, he subdivides Natural History into the history of nature in course, *i.e.* nature in its ordinary course ; nature wrought, *i.e.*, arts ; and nature erring or varying, *i.e.* marvels.

The two latter are deficient. The present histories of nature erring are fabulous or frivolous ; and the histories of nature wrought have failed through contempt of small matters and of experiments familiar and vulgar. Yet the nature of everything is best seen in its smallest portions ; and Thales, by keeping his eyes down, might have avoided the well and yet seen the stars in it. Civil history may be divided (as pictures or sculptures are unfinished sketches, or finished and still perfect, or finished but defaced by age) into memorials, perfect histories, and antiquities ; and a perfect history

---

[1] The Peripatetics, so far following Aristotle, divided knowledge into (1) speculative, (2) practical, (3) artistic or constructive (ποιητική) ; the Stoics into (1) Logic (which was to include Grammar and Rhetoric), (2) Ethics, (3) Physics (which included Theology).—See Professor Fowler's *Francis Bacon*, p. 75.

[2] In the *De Augmentis*—the amplified Latin edition of the *Advancement* published in 1623—History is either Natural or Civil ; and the latter includes Literary and Ecclesiastical, as well as Political History.

may represent a time (as a chronicle) or a person (as a biography) or an action (as a narration). Ecclesiastical history contains the history of the Church, the history of Prophecy, and the history of Providence; of these the second is deficient, and the first and third are unsatisfactory. Literary history is non-existent; and yet, without it, the history of the world is as "the statua of Polyphemus with his eye out; that part being wanting which doth most show the spirit and life of the person." Of all the appendices to history the letters of wise men are the most important, being more natural than orations and public speeches, and more deliberate and advised than conferences or present speeches.—(*Adv. of L.* II. i. 2, iii. 5; *De Augm.* II. iv—xiii.)

A single chapter suffices for Poetry.

Poetry is triply divided into narrative, representative or dramatic, and allusive or parabolical. Though for the most part restrained in words, it is in all other points extremely licensed, and it arises from the imagination. For inasmuch as the material world is in proportion inferior to the soul, the imaginative faculty devises a more ample greatness, a more exact goodness, and a more absolute variety than can be found in the nature of things; whence it appears that poetry tends to magnanimity, morality, and to delectation.—(*Adv.* II. iv. 1, iv. 5; *De Augm.* II. xiii., iii. 1.)

At a time when literary history was non-existent, that Bacon should have called attention to this deficiency, pronouncing that, without it, the history of the world is as " the statua of Polyphemus with his eye out," is one among instances of his intuition, originality, and superiority to existing preconceptions, which make the *Advancement* to this day a stimulating and interesting book. It will be noted that in parabolical poetry Bacon would include the works of the " sage and serious " Spenser, as well as the fables of Æsop and the myths of Greece and Rome; but no place seems left for lyrical poetry and hardly any for satires and epigrams. From Poetry we pass to Philosophy.

Philosophy is (1) divine, (2) natural, (3) human, coming to the mind by rays (1) refracted, (2) direct, (3) reflected.[1] But again, philosophy is like a tree; and therefore, before describing the branches (of which the above are three) we ought to describe the trunk which is common to all, and to erect one universal science by the name of Philosophia Prima, primitive or

---

[1] This is the expression used in the *De Augmentis*. In the *Advancement* it runs thus: " In philosophy the contemplations of man do either *penetrate* unto God, or are *circumferred* to nature, or are *reflected* or reverted upon himself."

summary philosophy, as the main or common way, before we come where
the ways part and divide themselves. This is practically deficient ; for
although men have reasoned *syllogistically* about quantity, similitude,
diversity, and the like, yet there is a complete silence about these common
adjuncts of things, *as they are found in nature*. Wherefore we lay down
that this Prima Philosophia is to be a receptacle for all such profitable
observations and axioms as fall not within the compass of any of the
special parts of philosophy or sciences, but are more common and of a
higher stage.—(*Adv.* II. v. 1, v 3 ; *Augm.* III. i.—ii.)

   In Divine Philosophy, *i.e.* Natural Theology, there is an excess rather
than a deficience ; for some, trying to extort from nature not merely
evidence of the existence, power, skill, and beneficence of God, but also
confirmation of points of faith, have by their commixture made an heretical
religion and an imaginary and fabulous philosophy. Leaving therefore
divine philosophy or natural theology (to be carefully distinguished from
divinity or inspired philosophy which we reserve till the last, as the haven
of our contemplations) we proceed to the second branch of Philosophy, *i.e.*
Natural Philosophy.[1]—(*Adv.* II. vi. 1, vi. 2 ; *Augm.* III. ii.—iii.)

   As an exposition of Bacon's philosophic system, the *Advancement of Learning* is of less value than many of his shorter
treatises ; but it will always be important for its literary value,
as well as for its suggestiveness and stimulating effect upon
every seeker after truth.   "It is," says a recent biographer[2] of
Bacon, "the first great book in English prose of secular interest ;
the first book which can claim a place beside the *Laws of
Ecclesiastical Polity*. As regards its subject-matter, it has been
partly thrown into the shade by the greatly enlarged and
elaborate form in which it ultimately appeared, in a Latin
dress, as the first portion of the scheme of the *Instauratio*, the
De Augmentis Scientiarum. Bacon looked on it as a first effort,
a kind of call-bell to awaken and attract the interest of others
in the thoughts and hopes which so interested himself. But it
contains some of his finest writing. In the *Essays* he writes as
a looker-on at the game of human affairs, who, according to his
frequent illustration, sees more of it than the gamesters themselves, and is able to give wiser and faithful counsel, not without
a touch of kindly irony at the mistakes which he observes.   In
the *Advancement* he is the enthusiast for a great cause and a

---

[1] See below, § 64-8, for a summary of the rest of the *Advancement of Learning*,
which treats of Natural Philosophy.
   Dean Church, *Bacon*, pp. 217-220.

great hope, and all that he has of passion and power is enlisted in the effort to advance it. The *Advancement* is far from being a perfect book. As a survey of the actual state of knowledge in his day, of its deficiencies and what was wanted to supply them, it is not even up to the materials of the time. Even the improved *De Augmentis* is inadequate; and there is reason to think the *Advancement* was a hurried book, at least in the later part, and it is defective in arrangement and proportion of parts. Two of the great divisions of knowledge—history and poetry—are despatched in comparatively short chapters; while in the division on 'Civil Knowledge,' human knowledge as it respects society, he inserts a long essay, obviously complete in itself and clumsily thrust in here, on the ways of getting on in the world, the means by which a man may be ' *Faber fortunae suae* '—the architect of his own success; too lively a picture to be pleasant of the arts with which he had become acquainted in the process of rising. The book, too, has the blemishes of its own time; its want of simplicity, its inevitable though very often amusing and curious pedantries. But the *Advancement* was the first of a long line of books which have attempted to teach English readers how to think of knowledge; to make it really and intelligently the interest, not of the school or the study or the laboratory only, but of society at large. It was a book with a purpose, new then, but of which we have seen the fulfilment. He wanted to impress on his generation, as a very practical matter, all that knowledge might do in wise hands, all that knowledge had lost by the faults and errors of men and the misfortunes of time, all that knowledge might be pushed to in all directions by faithful and patient industry and well-planned mtehods for the elevation and benefit of man in his highest capacities as well as in his humblest. And he further sought to teach them *how* to know; to make them understand that difficult achievement of self-knowledge, to know *what it is* to know; to give the first attempted chart to guide them among the shallows and rocks and whirlpools which beset the course and action of thought and inquiry; to reveal to them the ' idols' which unconsciously haunt the minds of the strongest as well as the weakest, and interpose their delusions when we are least aware,—' the fallacies and false appearances inseparable from our nature and our condition of life '—to induce men to believe not only that there was much to know that was not yet dreamed of, but that the way of knowing needed real and thorough improvement, that the knowing mind bore along with it all kinds of snares and disqualifications of which it is unconscious, and that it needed training quite as much as materials to work on, was the object of the *Advancement*. It was but a sketch; but it was a sketch so truly and forcibly drawn, that it made an impression which has never been weakened.[1] . . . It is a book which we can never open without coming on some noble interpretation of the realities of nature or the mind; some unexpected discovery of that quick and keen eye which arrests us by its truth; some felicitous and unthought-of illustration, yet so natural as almost to be doomed to become a commonplace; some bright touch of his incorrigible imaginativeness, ever ready to force itself in amid the driest details of his argument."

§ 49 PLAN OF THE SECOND PART OF THE "INSTAURATIO MAGNA"

It will be remembered that the object of the Second Part of the *Magna Instauratio* was to teach men " how to use their understanding aright in the investigation of Nature.[2] Soon after the publication of the *Advancement of Learning*, Bacon took this work in hand and composed (1606-7) the *Outline and Argument of the Second Part of the Instauratio* (Partis Instaurationis Secundae Delineatio et Argumentum). Of this work—important for its wide range, brevity, and clearness—the following is a summary.[3]

For the special purpose of the Interpretation of Nature (*Interpretationi Naturae ipsi*) there shall be three books, the third, the fourth, and the sixth (for the fifth, which will consist of Anticipations based on the ordinary use of Reason, is merely temporary; and, as soon as we can use the verification

---

[1] I omit here some words with which I am unable to agree : " To us its use and almost its interest has passed away."

[2] See Mr. Ellis's summary of the scheme of the *Instauratio* as a whole, quoted on p. 347. This should constantly be referred to, if the reader wishes to understand the exact object of each of the many treatises which were written as contributions to the *Instauratio*.

[3] Spedding, *Works*, iii. 547—557.

afforded by the legitimate use of Reason, this fifth book will pass into the sixth).[1]

As for this present book, the second, it has for its special subject the Understanding (*Intellectus ipse*) and the care and government thereof, and the equipment of reason. This may be called Logic ; but, if so, it must be understood to be a new Logic, subjecting to tests that which the old Logic takes upon trust, viz., principles, first notions, and even the information given by the senses. Moreover, it inverts the order of the old Logic ; for instead of flying at once up to principles and generalities, and deducing therefrom middle propositions, the new Logic begins with histories of facts and particulars, thence mounts to middle propositions, and thence to general principles.

We are seeking light. Now every object that is to receive light must first be polished, secondly, turned to the light, thirdly, receive the influx of the light. In precisely the same way must we deal with the human mind :

I. The mental "area," so to speak, must be levelled and cleared.

II. The mind must be "converted" or turned towards the new truths.

III. The new truths must be imparted.

I. The process of "levelling" is threefold, corresponding to the three-fold nature of the Idols that beset the mind ; for they are either external or inherent. The external Idols may have arisen from the dogmas of philosophers, or from perverse laws of demonstration. Wherefore the task of "levelling" must include first the destruction of the dogmas of philosophers, secondly, the release of the mind from the fetters of false notions about demonstration, thirdly, the eradication (or at least the branding) of the inherent Idols or perversenesses of the mind.

II. For the purpose of "conversion" the student must be delivered from prejudice and from despair, believing that the divine Will encourages the search after truth, and that the new truth (which is as different from the old as the "idols" of the human mind are from the "ideas" of the divine mind) is not a vague, wandering, or recurring eddy, but a *goal* ("errorum et vastit atis *terminum*," and compare *Valerius Terminus*).[2] It will also be well to show the causes that have produced past errors, in order that the mind may be roused to hope for the avoidance of future error. And let none suppose that this preliminary labour is superfluous or that the "idols" of the mind can easily be put away by force of will. For without help none can do this ; inasmuch as the "spirits" of the philosophers (unlike those of the prophets) are not "subject to" the philosophers ; and the author (who is leading them on a path that he has himself explored) knows by experience that it is more difficult to obtain access to the minds of men than to the secrets of Nature.

---

[1] For the six divisions of the *Instauratio*, see above, p. 347.
[2] For the "idols," see below, p. 381.

III. For the imparting of truth, or Information of the mind, we must minister to the Sense, the Memory, and the Reason.

The Sense—as it cannot well perceive causes, but only motions, alterations, and results—is apt to form wrong notions, classifying together phenomena outwardly similar but essentially dissimilar. For the witness of the senses is always proportional to man's prejudices (*ex analogia hominis*). It must (i.) be rectified by being brought into proportion with the Universe (*ad analogiam Mundi reducatur et rectificetur*). We must not speak of " fire," for example, as an element, or use " humidity " as a scientific notion. The Sense must also (ii.) be strengthened so as to perceive processes at present imperceptible owing to their minuteness ; and (iii.) must be supplied with stores of facts as materials to work on.

These then are the three Ministrations to Sense, (i.) Rectification for its deviations ; (ii) Substitutes for its weaknesses ; (iii) Natural History and Experiment to supply it with materials.

The Ministration to the Memory (it being assumed that all investigations must be conducted with the aid of writing [1] and tables of particulars) requires (i.) a statement of the points to be inquired into ; (ii.) a Provisional Table showing the order in which the several points are to be investigated ; (iii.) since no first Table is likely to hit at once the track of any Universal Law (*sequatur rei venam quae ex analogia universi sit*) and yet we must make an order—for Truth emerges sooner from wrong order than no order —it is necessary to show in the third place the method of transposing the old Tentative Tables into the New Tables, and the method of renewing (*instaurandi*) the investigation.

The Ministration to Reason (since one kind of Reason, *i.e.* Theoretical, or Contemplative, discovers all the causes of anything, and another, *i.e.* Practical or Active, selects such causes as are in our power) includes the Ministration (i.) to Contemplative, (ii.) to Active Reason.

(i.) It is the part of the Contemplative Reason to erect on the ground-plan of a Simple Notion (previously obtained by the ministrations to Sense and Memory) the solid structure of an Axiom (*haec enim est veritatis portio solida, cum simplex notio instar superficiei videri possit*). Such an Axiom must be obtained, not by the old, illegitimate, precarious, and enumerative Induction, but by the new and legitimate Induction, which by means of exclusions and rejections arrives at conclusions. To this Induction we give the name of Formula of Interpretation.

Under the Ministrations to Contemplative Reason come also, first, the art of continuing the investigation by using the discovered Axiom for the purpose of eliciting still higher and more general Axioms, which higher Axioms must be verified by reference to the experiences from which we started ; secondly, we must vary our investigations to suit the varieties of the

---

[1] Compare *Essays*, xxv. 59 : "The proceeding upon somewhat conceived in writing doth for the most part facilitate dispatch. For though it should be wholly rejected, yet that negative is more pregnant of direction than an indefinite ; as ashes are more generative than dust."

nature under consideration : and after following out a varied and adapted investigation of Forms,[1] we shall then investigate material and efficient causes ; thirdly, we must contract our investigation by selecting instances, pointing out the Prerogative of Instance and the Prerogative of Investigation, *i.e.* those instances or experiments which have as it were a paramount or " Prerogative " vote, affording more light than the rest, so that a few of these excel a multitude of others.[2]

(ii.) The Ministration to the Active Reason sets forth (1) the peculiar method to be used when we are not seeking an Axiom or Cause but the accomplishment of some work (for in seeking Axioms we have to rise from particulars to generals ; but in seeking works we must descend from generals to particulars) ; (2) the method of making general Tables fitted for practice, whereby all kinds of work may be speedily accomplished ; (3) a method of proceeding from experiment to experiment (without the previous establishment of an Axiom) a path slippery and unsafe but not to be entirely ignored.

Such is the outline of our Second Book, whereby we trust we have constructed a bridal chamber for the union of the Mind of Man with the Universe. Toward the conclusion we shall add some remarks about co-operation and succession in labour. For men will not learn their full strength until they learn division of labour.

The reader should carefully notice the order of the steps to be taken in the *Delineatio,* and in particular the statement in the last paragraph but four, that an Axiom is to be erected on the ground-plan of a Simple Notion previously obtained by the ministrations to Sense and Memory. We shall presently find Bacon departing from this order in the *Novum Organum ;* and it is on the impossibility of obtaining " a Simple Notion" that his philosophy will make shipwreck.[3]

§ 50 THE " COGITATA ET VISA "[4]

In June, 1607, Sir Francis Bacon was made Solicitor-General ; and about this time (possibly in the following vacation) he bethought himself that as time was slipping away and he was now " entangled more than he could have desired in civil business " he ought not to wait for the completion of the

---

[1] For the meaning of " Form," see note on p. 384, below.
[2] On Prerogative Instances, see below, p. 396.
[3] See below, p. 392.
[4] Spedding, *Works,* iii. 589-620.

proposed work on the *Interpretation of Nature*, but to publish at once some particular Investigation ("Tables of Invention," or " Formulæ of Legitimate Investigation ") to serve as specimens of his general work, and to excite in their readers a curiosity for the Key of Interpretation. Accordingly he composed, about this time, some Tables called a *Legitimate Investigation of Motion.* As an introduction to the Tables, he wrote a treatise entitled *Thoughts and Judgments concerning the Interpretation of Nature, or concerning Operative Science* (Cogitata et Visa De Interpretatione Naturae, sive De Scientia Operativa).[1]

When (1606-7) he wrote the *Delineatio* (described in the last section) he did not purpose to set forth his method by means of an example ; on the contrary, the three ministrations to the Sense, to the Memory, and to the Reason (of which the last is the new method of Induction) were to be set forth in order and didactically. . . . . Thus it appears that after Bacon had not only decided on writing a great work on the reform of philosophy, but had also determined on dividing it into parts (of which the Second was to contain the exposition of his new method), he in some measure changed his plan, and resolved to set forth the essential and operative part of his system chiefly by means of an example. This change of plan appears to be marked by the *Cogitata et Visa*—a circumstance which makes this tract one of the most interesting of the precursors of the *Novum Organum.*[2] The Legitimate Investigation would have covered the ground which the second book of the *Novum Organum* was meant to occupy ; the *Cogitata* covers most of the ground actually covered by the first book of the *Novum Organum.*

Science, as now existing, attains neither to certainty nor to magnitude. Medicine, Alchemy, Magic, all alike fail. The art of Mechanics slowly weaves its petty web of experience, instead of seeking light from Philosophy. Chance is the only inventor. Men have never understood that the apparent complexity of the language of Nature is based upon a simple Alphabet. The multitude has never sought truth, save for amusement, and has been content to accept in its stead the dogmas of philosophers. The absorption of men's attention by Theology and Moral Philosophy, the fears and hostility of superstition, the devotion of the Universities to narrow and stationary studies, the prejudice and wilful despair of mankind, the

[1] Spedding, *Works*, i. 78, iii. 619.
[2] Mr. Ellis's Introduction, Spedding, *Works*, i. p. 79.

vagueness of words, the quackery of impostors, and a contempt for works and experiments as being beneath the dignity of human nature—all these obstacles have stood in the way of Science.

The philosophies of the later Greeks, and especially of Aristotle, have been like stage-plays, fictions fairer than truth. And even so in modern times, Telesius, Frascastorius, Carden, and Gilbert, forming conclusions from a few instances, have but as it were touched Nature with the tip of their fingers. Taking a few well-known effects, they connect them in a kind of network of theory made to fit these known effects ; but they do not demonstrate the existence of causes that will enable them to produce hitherto unheard-of effects. As for the philosophy of the earlier Greeks, the Author knew that it would not have been difficult for him to palm off his new discoveries as the rediscovered inventions of those ancient philosophers. But he relied on evidence alone and refused every kind of imposture.

The present demonstrations are inadequate ; a defect for which the understanding is responsible. The mind of mankind, like an uneven mirror, reflects the rays of truth unevenly ; and the mind of every individual (as the result of education or disposition) has within itself a kind of seductive influence or familiar spirit (daemonem familiarem) which perturbs the understanding with diverse empty spectres.[1] Yet we must not despair. As the most helpless hand with the aid of compasses can draw a perfect circle, so is it with the mind ; for which we must seek a compass, not in the syllogism of Deductive Logic—for a syllogism is compounded of words, and therefore dependent upon the truth of pre-existing notions which are often vague or foolish—but in the New Induction.

The Old Induction of Enumeration was applied only to the general principles of Science, while the Middle Propositions were deduced by Syllogistic reasonings. But the Old Induction, compared with the New, is as water compared with wine ; the one, a raw and natural product of the intellect ; the other, carefully prepared from the Vintage of phenomena, plucked, gathered, pressed, and purified. The old and ordinary methods of discovery by reading, meditation, dialectic experience or experiment, are all casual and inefficient.

Let us stimulate ourselves by thinking of the glory of the Discoverer. For if it is a glory to have discovered single inventions, he who shall discover the one invention that shall include the potency of all inventions will be called the Discoverer of Discoverers, far above all Conquerors, Lawgivers, and Founders of Empires. An invention so fruitful may be truly called the Male Birth of Time. Such a Discovery extends the empire of Man over Nature ; for man's power is co-extensive with his knowledge (tantum

[1] This is one among many passages which show that the word "Idol" in Bacon's works is used with a kind of play on the theological meaning of the word. See also above, p. 358, where the "ideas" of God are contrasted with the "idols" of man. And elsewhere he says that whosoever has not explored the sources of errors in the motions of the mind, "he will find all things beset with spectres and incantations ; unless he can break the charm he can never interpret nature."—Spedding, Works, i. 93.

potest quantum scit). No strength, indeed, can break the chain of natural causes ; but by obeying Nature, man can conquer her.

Further, let none despise the mention of works in the New Philosophy. Just as in Religion faith is the essential, and works are needful only as a proof of the presence of living faith, so in Science works are needed, not for themselves, but to prove that the Science which originates them is living. The same Philosophy which endows men with new works will also endow them with new mental power.

As fresh grounds for hope, we must remember that Antiquity should be wiser than youth ; and it is the *later and modern ages of the world that are really old and truly deserve the title of Antiquity.* After the recent enlargement of the Material Globe by the discovery of the New World it would be intolerable that the Intellectual Globe should receive no corresponding enlargement. The prevalent weariness of religious controversy leaves room for scientific study. Lastly, if by mere chance and groping so many inventions have been discovered, how much more may be expected from systematic research !

As regards the practice of the new Art, we must (1) complete a refutation of the past (*redargutio rerum praeteritarum*) ; (2) having freed our minds from old theories, opinions, and common notions (*communes notiones*) we must approach particular phenomena afresh, without bias and with the innocent eye of a child ; (3) we must accumulate a " forest " or store of particulars (" particularum *sylvam* et materiem" ; compare *Sylva Sylvarum* below, p. 406) sufficient for our purposes, partly from natural history, partly (and principally) from experiments ; (4) this store must be so tabulated and reduced to order that the Intellect may be able to act on it (for even the divine Word did not act on chaos without order) ; (5) from these tabulated Particulars we must ascend to general " comprehensions " (*communes comprehensiones*) ; (6) here we must avoid the natural but dangerous temptation to pass at once to the highest " comprehensions," the so-called " principles." To these we must gradually ascend by a logical " ladder " (" per *scalam* veram "[1]) beginning from the nearest " comprehensions ; " (7) we must discover a form of Induction leading us to a general conclusion in such a way that we may actually demonstrate the impossibility of finding a contradictory instance ; (8) no " comprehension " can be received and approved till it has given bail for itself by pointing out for us new particulars beyond and beside those from which it was itself deduced.

The best method of drawing attention to the New Philosophy—regard being had to the prejudice, envy, and sloth of mankind—will be first to set forth a specimen of the New Method, that is to say Tables of Discovery, which may stimulate men to ask for the Key of Discovery.

---

[1] See p. 378, below, for the *Ladder of the Understanding* (Scala Intellectus)

§ 51 "Filum Labyrinthi;"[1] "Redargutio Philosophiarum"[2]

From a passage in the *Commentarius Solutus* written July, 1608, we find that Bacon was at that time contemplating " the finishing the Three Tables of Motion, Heat and Cold, and Sound, (*De Motu, De Calore et Frigore, De Sono*) ; and in the same note-book there is an attempt to construct Tables on the first of these subjects. There is also a Latin fragment on the same subject (called *Filum Labyrinthi*, or the *Thread of the Labyrinth*). In both versions the Tables are spoken of as *Machina Intellectus Inferior*, and mention is made of new Tables (*Chartae Novellae*) and of a higher instrument (*Machina Superior*) for which the old Tables and the inferior instrument are to prepare the way.

Thus it is ever with Bacon's scientific researches. Instead of being deterred by present failure, he is always able to throw himself forward into the future, and is as confident as ever on the strength of expectations. Yet that he lost confidence in the wonder-working Tables as time went on, and was driven to transfer some of his trust from them to the *Natural History*, on which, in his later days, he rested his principal hopes, seems proved by the subordinate position which he assigns to these Tables in the *Novum Organum*. There the description of the different kinds of motion is introduced merely as a part of the doctrine of the Prerogatives of Instances. To the same effect is a curious piece of manuscript evidence in the Tables on Cold and Heat. On the back of the MS. is written in a clear and careful hand (probably at the time when he was well satisfied with his work) the word *New;* but afterwards (presumably at a time when he perceived that the Tables were antiquated) he has written in a hurried and careless hand the word *Vetus.* It may be here mentioned that the Tables on Heat (composed about 1608) contain no mention of the thermometer, although the principle of it was known to Galileo before 1597, and is supposed to have been known in England by 1603. The selection of Motion as the subject for the Legitimate Investigation exhibits at once Bacon's strength and weakness as a Philosopher. It was

---

[1] Spedding, *Works*, iii. 625-640.   [2] *Ibid.* iii. 557-585.

an admirable intuition to discern that all the processes of
Nature were modes of motion, so that, if we could understand
her motions, we could command her processes ; but it was not
like a philosopher—rather it was like a Solicitor-General,
" entangled more than he could have desired in civil business"
—to depart from his prescribed order of inquiry because he
was in a hurry to obtain results ; to hasten on to the "ministrations to the Reason " before he had ministered to the Sense and
Memory ; and to neglect such an obvious " ministration to the
Sense " as had already been procured for him by the labours of
Galileo in the discovery of the thermometer. The divisions
and subdivisions of these Tables are chiefly interesting for the
rich picturesqueness of their titles, although there is not wanting
a stimulating suggestiveness in many of the classifications.

The *Commentarius Solutus*, quoted above, gives an interesting
insight into Bacon's literary and philosophical purposes in 1608.
After recording his resolution to finish the Aphorisms, *Clavis
Interpretationis* (that is the Key of Interpretation which was
published twelve years afterwards (1620) under the title of
Novum Organum),[1] he will impart his *Cogitata et Visa* to a few

---

[1] Spedding, *Life*, iv. 64-66. The whole passage deserves study.

"The finishing the 3 Tables, de Motu, de Calore et frigore, de sono.

"The finishing of the Aphorismes, Clavis interpretationis, and then setting
foorth yᵉ book. Qu. to begynne first in france to print it ; yf hear then
wᵗ dedication of advantage to yᵉ woork

"Proceeding wᵗʰ yᵉ translation of my book of Advancemenᵗ of learnyng ;
harkenyng to some other yf playfere should faile.

"Imparting my Cogitata et Visa w ʰ choyse, ut videbit .

"Ordinary discours of plus ultra in Sciences, as well the intellectuall globe as
the materiall, illustrated by discouvery in oʳ Age.

"Discoursing skornfully of the philosophy of the graecians wᵗʰ some better
respect to yᵉ Aegiptians, Persians, Caldes, and the utmost antiquity and the
mysteries of the poets.

"Comparing the case to that wʰ lyvy sayeth of Alexander, Nil aliud qᵐ bene
ausus vana contemnere.

"Qu. of an oration ad filios, delightfull, sublime, and mixt wᵗʰ elegancy,
affection, *novelty of conceyt and yet sensible*, and Superstition.

"To consyder wᵗ opinions are fitt to nourish tanquam Ansae and so to grift the
new upon the old, ut religiones solent.

"Ordinary cours of Incompetency of reason for naturall philosophy and
invention of woorks, A prety devise to buy and sell wᵗʰ, Aditus nō nisi sub persona
infantis.

"To procure an History of Marvailes, Historia naturae errantis or variantis,
to be compiled wᵗʰ Judgmᵗ and without credulity and all the popular errors
detected ; Viscentius, Jubart, Pliny, Hystorie of all sorts for matters strange in
nature told in serie temporū heare and there inter cetera ; Pancarolus, de reb.
memorabilibus, divers authores.

"To procure an History mechanique to be compiled wᵗʰ care and diligence (and

select critics. He will write an "ordinary discourse" showing
that there is *plus ultra, i.e.* something more beyond, in the
Intellectual World of Science, as well as in the Material World
enlarged by the discoveries of Columbus. He also suggests
"discoursing scornfully of the Grecians; with some better
respect to the Ægyptians, Persians, Chaldees, and the utmost
antiquity and the mysteries of the poets" (an entry interesting
as pointing to the Wisdom of the Ancients which he sent to a
friend in the following year [1609]; and soon afterwards he adds,
"To consider what opinions are fit to nourish *tanquam ansæ*,"
i.e. as handles for the introduction of the new opinions), "and so
to graft the new upon the old, as in the way with religions (*ut
religiones solent*)."

In the same context occurs the following entry : "Comparing
the case to that which Livy saith of Alexander, *Nihil aliud
quam bene ausus vana contemnere*" (His only merit was a just
contempt for empty perils).[1] "Query, of an oration *ad filios*,"
—*i.e.* in the authoritative tone in which a father would address
his sons—"delightful, sublime, and mixed with elegancy, affection, novelty of conceit, and yet sensible, and Superstition." [2]

In the following year, 1609, we find Bacon sending to Toby
Matthew a "speech of preparation," which belongs to the *Pars
Destruens*, the "levelling and clearing" of the mind, (see p. 358)
intended to prepare the way for the new by destroying the old,
and in particular by destroying the Idol of the Theatre or
Authority. It is an imaginary speech addressed by a learned
French philosopher "*ad filios*," under the title of "The Refu-

to professe it that [it] is of the experim[ts] and observations of all Mechanicall Arts.
The places or thinges to be inquyred are, first the materialls, and their quantities
and proportions ; next the Instrum[ts] and Engins requesite ; then the use and
adoperation of every Instrum[t]: then the work it self and all the processe thereof
wth the tymes and seasons of doing every part thereof. Then the Errors w[ch] may
be comytted and agayn those things w[ch] conduce to make the woorke in more
perfection. Then all observacions, Axiomes, directions. Lastly, all things
collaterall incid[t] or intervenient."

[1] The comparison is this : As Alexander found the Persian armies and other
obstacles in the way of the establishment of the Macedonian empire to be a mere
nothing, so will the Founder of the Kingdom of Man over Nature find his
obstacles insignificant, if he will only dare to despise them. See this thought
worked out in the *Redargutio*, below, p. 369.

[2] The only explanation that suggests itself of the word "superstition" is that,
the scene being laid in Paris, and the speakers presumably Frenchmen and Roman
Catholics, the fiction would conciliate foreigners by its concessions to the Roman
Catholic faith, which faith Bacon generally has in view when he uses the word
"superstition."

tation of Philosophies " (*Redargutio Philosophiarum*) and deserves
a summary as being one of the finest specimens of Bacon's
rhetoric. The dramatic machinery is simple. Bacon, conversing
with a friend in Paris on his projects in Philosophy, is supposed
to receive from him an account of a recent conference of Parisian
philosophers (having philosophic objects similar to his own)
about fifty in number, of mature age and the highest character
and position, prelates, noblemen, and others of eminence ; to
whom, after an interval of earnest expectation, there enters one
of placid, and serene countenance (save that he wore the aspect
of one who was always pitying [1]) who, after taking his seat on
the same level as his audience, without platform or pulpit, began
an oration, of which the following is a summary :

God has made you, my sons, to be not beasts, but men ; that is to say,
mortal gods, capable of receiving the knowledge of Himself by faith, and
the knowledge of His material world by sense. As touching the latter
knowledge you count yourselves to be rich, but you are poor. For all your
present, all your future, revenue, consists of the labours of six men, Aristotle,
Plato, Hippocrates, Galen, Euclid, and Ptolemy. Behold your total pos-
sessions ! Now as God will not have you bestow the faith and allegiance of
your souls on petty mortals in the place of the immortal God ; so neither
did He give you the trustworthy witness of the senses that you should
therewith contemplate the works of six men instead of contemplating the
works of God Himself as they may be discerned in heaven and earth. Yet
how shall I win you to the Truth ? For all your theological, all your
political, treatises, assume the Old Philosophy ; nay, your very literature
and language are moulded on its maxims, so that even in your cradles you
drank in perforce this Cabala of Errors ; and its influence has been confirmed
in you by the training of schools, of colleges, and of social, nay, I may
almost say, of national life. How then can I ask you to give up the Old
Philosophy ?

I will not ask you to make such a sacrifice. Keep your Old Philosophy
that you may retain your authority with the common people. Have one
way of dealing with Nature, and another way of dealing with the ignorant.
Every man of supereminent knowledge has to play a kind of part when
he condescends to instruct those of inferior knowledge. He must strip off
his true character and humour his pupil by adopting, for the time, his
pupil's condition of mind. But be warned by the old proverb, and see that
if you have Lais, Lais shall not have you ; give yourselves for a time, but
do not surrender yourselves for ever, to others. Remember also that,

---

[1] A similar expression is assigned to the "Father of Salomon's House" in the
New Atlantis ; see below, pp. 421-2, where will also be found the same description
of "the seat on the same level"—emblematic of scientific equality.

although it will be easier for you, with these concessions, to receive the New Method, yet you cannot receive it till your minds are prepared for it by being cleared and delivered from what is false ; and it is for the purpose of attaining this deliverance that we are assembled here to-day.

Let us treat then of the Old Philosophy, not as learned men, but in arguments intelligible to all. First, as to the nation whence it sprang—a nation justly censured by the Egyptian Priest in Herodotus, "You Greeks are always children." Next as to the times—a generation that had not so much as a thousand years of history to look back on, people to whom naught but a small portion of the earth was known, and whose most belauded travellers had but, as it were, visited the suburbs of their own cities ! Lastly, as to the men, we blame the teaching, not the teachers. Aristotle and Plato were men of intellect capacious, keen, sublime ; but by their pretensions and authority they did infinite mischief, and are only fit to be described as a better sort of Sophists.

Aristotle—who made a world for himself out of his Categories, and thought to settle such questions as those of Density and Rarity by mere verbal distinctions of Act and Power—if Aristotle seem to any of you to be the chief of teachers because he has drawn after him all modern as well as all ancient times, the answer is that he derives his eminence from the sloth and pride of the human race, sloth in searching for truth, pride in cloaking ignorance. It is the mark of imposture to come, not in the name of Truth, but in one's own name. " I am come," saith the very Truth, " in the name of my Father, and ye receive me not ; if another come in his own name, him ye will receive." Even so came Aristotle, and even for this cause was he received ; and he is great only because he is the greatest of impostors. As for the saying that his doctrines must be true because they are accepted by common consent, such an argument (however it may avail in religion when religion descends from heaven) is the worst of all omens in matters intellectual. For nothing can please the multitude except it be vulgar, superstitious, or ostentatious ; and just as Phocion suspected himself to be in the wrong simply because he was applauded by the Athenians, so the seeker after truth should be led by the assent of the multitude to ask himself " What error have I committed ? "

In the New Philosophy no Dictator is to be allowed either from the ostentatious later schools of the Greeks, or from the older and superior Greek philosophers who studied Nature ; for all these philosophies are no better than stage-plays. And the modern systems are equally at fault. Let no one arraign us of presumption in thus condemning others. It is our path, and not our understanding, that is superior to theirs. He that is least in the New Kingdom is greater than the greatest of the Old. In this battle-field the victory is not to the swift, nor to the proud, but to the humble and teachable. Lay aside therefore all hope of learning from antiquity, or from the modern chemists, those children of Accident and Phantasy ; and return to the consideration of the signs and tokens which convict the Old Philosophy.

The first sign is *fruits ;* which, in the Old Philosophy, were disputations, and isolated contradictions of isolated errors, resulting in not one single discovery for the enrichment and elevation of mankind. The second sign is *growth ;* but under the Old Philosophy, whereas the mechanical arts have grown, the sciences have remained stationary, like images, having admiration and worship but no life nor motion. A third sign, or rather testimony, arises from the *confessions of ignorance* made by the philosophers themselves, though they would fain excuse themselves by throwing the blame on Nature. The last and most certain sign is derived from the *methods ;* for methods of making things are (potentially) the things themselves ; and the old methods are to the new what manual labour is to machine labour ; and the old labourer is to the new what a spectator on a tower straining his eyes in the contemplation of a distant hamlet is to the same spectator when he descends from the height to view each object close at hand. Be not misled by the statement that Aristotle and others in old times practised Induction and Experience. That so-called Induction was but an imposture. After they had made their theories they would select their instances to suit their theories ; or, if any one of their instances contradicted their theories, they would explain it away by some subtlety, or dismiss it as an exception. In fine it was the custom of Aristotle not to consult Experience as a free adviser but to drag her at his chariot-wheels as a captive.

Train yourselves to understand the real subtlety of *things* and you will learn to despise the fictitious and disputatious subtleties of *words ;* and freeing yourselves from such follies, you will give yourselves to the task of facilitating (under the auspices of the divine Compassion) the lawful wedlock between the Mind and Nature. Be not like the empiric ant which merely collects ; nor like the cobweb-weaving theorists who do but spin webs from their own intestines ; but imitate the bees which both collect and fashion.

Against the " Naught beyond " of the ancients raise your cry of " More beyond." When they speak of "the not imitable thunderbolt," let us reply (not like the mad Salmoneus but in sober wisdom) that the thunderbolt is "imitable." [1] Let the discovery of the new terrestrial world encourage you to expect the discovery of a new intellectual world, remembering the words of the prophet that " many shall run to and fro, and knowledge shall be multiplied." The fate of Alexander will be ours. The conquests which his contemporaries thought marvellous and likely to surpass the belief of posterity, were described by later writers as nothing more than the natural successes of one who justly dared to despise imaginary perils. Even so our triumphs (for we shall triumph) will be lightly esteemed by those who come after us ; justly, when they compare our trifling gains with theirs ; unjustly, if they attribute our victory to audacity, rather than to humility and to freedom from that fatal human pride which has lost us everything

[1] The reference is to Salmoneus who aspired to imitate the "not imitable thunderbolt" of Jupiter.—*Æneid,* vi. 585.

and has hallowed the fluttering fancies of men (*volucres meditationes*) in place of the imprint stamped upon things by the divine seal.

Here (said the narrator) the speaker ceased ; and the audience conversed together, as men dazzled with excess of light, yet full of hope. Then, turning to me, " And now," asked he, " what say you of this ? " " It is right welcome," said I. " If so," said he, " you may perchance preserve some fruit of your travels among us by finding room for this discourse in your writings." " You say well," replied I, " and I will not forget it."

So ends the *Redargutio Philosophiarum,* one of the most rhetorical, aggressive, and negative of all Bacon's philosophical treatises and, perhaps, for these very reasons, not inferior to any of them in literary interest.

§ 52 " DE SAPIENTIA VETERUM " [1] AND THE ASTRONOMICAL TREATISES [2]

The third part of the *Magna Instauratio* [3] was to include the *Phenomena of the Universe* (that is to say, experience of all sorts of phenomena) and a Natural History of such a kind as can serve for the basis of a Natural Philosophy—a History not of bodies merely but of virtues also, " those, I mean, which may be reckoned as it were cardinal, viz. density, rarity, heat, cold, consistency, fluidity, heaviness, lightness, &c." Such a treatise is extant (supposed to have been written after 1608, and certainly written several years before 1622) having for its object the investigation of Density and Rarity ; and it is interesting as exhibiting Bacon in the character of an experimenter noting quantitative results, but still more as proving his ignorance of the works of other labourers in the same province (*Densi et Rari Historia*).[4]

In the year 1609 was published the Latin treatise " Concerning the Wisdom of the Ancients " (*De Sapientia Veterum*). We have seen (*Cogitata*, above, p. 362) that Bacon had rejected after serious consideration the plan of sheltering his new philosophy under the authority of antiquity by imputing it to the earlier Greek Philosophers. But he seems to have entertained a genuine belief not only that the early Natural Philosophers

[1] Spedding, *Works*, vi. 605-764.   [2] *Ib.* iii. 727-779.   [3] See above, p. 347.
[4] Spedding, *Works*, ii. 241-305.

among the Greeks (Pythagoras, Empedocles, Heraclitus, Democritus and the rest) had penetrated far deeper into the secrets of
Nature than their successors, but also that in the myths of the
Greek religion and in the fables of the Greek poets there lie
enshrined physical discoveries and political mysteries.   His
dedication to the Earl of Salisbury, while depreciating the Author,
extols the subject—primaeval antiquity, an object of the highest
veneration; parable, " a kind of ark in which the most precious
portions of the sciences were deposited ; " philosophy, which
is, next to religion, " the second grace and ornament of life
and the human soul; " and he avows his hope that by his
treatise he may " give some help towards the difficulties of life
and the secrets of Science."

Accordingly, in the *Wisdom of the Ancients*, Proteus is matter,
captured and constrained by Science ; the Giants, rebelling
against Jupiter, represent Sedition destroyed by Sovereignty ;
Perseus is Military Power furnished with the wings of celerity,
with the mirror and shield of forethought, and with the helmet
of secresy ; Atalanta, lured from her course by the golden apples,
is a figure of Science seduced by immediate profit from her
enterprise of the conquest of Nature ; and Cupid is the atom, or
rather the appetite and instinct, of primal matter, which, out of
Chaos, begot all things.   The discourse on this last myth was
afterward amplified by Bacon into a separate treatise on the
*Beginnings and Origins of Things according to the Fables of
Cupid and Heaven,*[1] a summary of which may serve as a specimen of his application of these ancient stories to Science.

Cupid, says the Fable, was born of an egg, which had been
laid by Night.   This teaches us not only that the instinct of
matter (being due to God Himself) is hidden in unsearchable
darkness, but also that all knowledge is bred (like Cupid) out of
darkness, that is, out of negatives.   We learn the cause of anything by rejecting the non-causes.

Again the Fable tells us that Cupid was naked.   That is to
say, primitive matter must not be endowed by our imaginations
with secondary qualities, such qualities as in reality belong not
to atoms but to bodies composed of atoms.   Those who have
thus erroneously invested matter have been guilty of clothing

---

[1] Spedding, *Works*, iii. 65-118.

Cupid; some with a veil (those who explain everything by the transformations of one element, water for example); others with a tunic (those who assume a plurality of elements); others with a cloak (those who assume an infinity of first principles each possessed of specific properties).   Contrasted with these false doctrines is the true one, that there is one first, fixed, and invariable material principle.   Then follows an exposition of the doctrine of those who have " clothed Cupid," most space being devoted to the doctrine of Parmenides revived by Telesius, viz., that there are two principles of things.

Of this unfinished tract Mr. Ellis says that it shows Bacon to have obtained a deep insight into the principles of the atomic theory which in his hands becomes a theory of forces only, " much like the theory of Boscovich, who considered that all phenomena might be explained (without matter) on the hypothesis of the existence of a number of centres of force." Probably it was of some of the sayings in this treatise that Leibnitz remarked, " We do well to think highly of Verulam ; for his hard sayings have a deep meaning in them."

If Bacon was guided sometimes wisely by his intuitions in large scientific conjectures as to first principles and possible laws, it must be admitted that in the attempt to form theories on special subjects he was not equally happy; and in many cases he was led away by inexcusable error and inaccuracy.   Of this an example is furnished by his treatise on the *Flux and Reflux of the Sea* (written probably a little before 1612).[1]   In extenuation of his errors we must remember that in those days the connection between the moon and the tides, though recognised, was not clearly understood, and that no sufficient distinction was made between the undulatory motion of *stationary water* and the progressive motion of water.   Hence Telesius compared the sea to a cauldron which boiled over (thus causing the tides) when heated by the sun, moon, and stars.

Bacon's theory was based on the belief that *the earth was fixed* and the stars moved westward.   Assuming that all things, except the earth, had *some* westward motion, he supposed that the stars moved quickest ; the higher planets less quickly ; the moon less quickly than any of the planets : and the water least

[1] Spedding, *Works*, iii. 39-64.

quickly of all, thus lagging behind the moon. The motions of
ebb and flow he explains from the configuration of the earth;
and his whole theory depends upon the supposition that the
tides of the Pacific do not synchronize with those of the Atlantic.
It is one of the most remarkable instances of his extraordinary
carelessness that, to establish this fact—the key-stone of his
theory—he quotes an author (Acosta), who, on the contrary,
asserts that the tides *do* synchronize.

Still more unfortunate are Bacon's attempts at Astronomy.
In 1612 he published a Description of the World of Thought
(*Descriptio Globi Intellectualis*).[1] Dismissing (perhaps as being
only fit for a popular and preliminary treatise), the triple division
of history in the *Advancement of Learning* (into ecclesiastical,
civil, and natural), he divides history more scientifically (as he
does also subsequently in the *De Augmentis*) into natural and
civil; and then, having stated the divisions of Natural History,
he devotes the rest of the tract to one of these divisions, the
History of Celestial Things, *i.e.* Astronomy. To this treatise is
added another (*Thema Coeli*), containing Bacon's own provisional
theory of Astronomy.[2]

The work is chiefly remarkable for its neglect of recent astronomical discoveries. He indeed refers briefly to Galileo's discovery
of Jupiter's satellites (published together with other discoveries
in the *Sydereus Nuncius*, 1611), but he does not appear to have
seen its importance in confirming the theory of Copernicus; and
concerning Kepler's Laws (two of which had been published in
the *De Stella Martis* in 1609, and had become known in England
in 1610), he is entirely silent. Yet, if he had taken the trouble
to make himself acquainted with them (or rather if the occupations of a Solicitor-General aspiring to the place of Attorney-
General, had left him leisure for astronomical studies), the adoption by Kepler of the ellipse, as the celestial curve, would have
rendered Bacon's complaint at once superfluous and false, that
all astronomers alike are prejudiced in favour of the circle as
being the only perfect curve, and alone fit for celestial motions.

Nevertheless, there is more excuse than is immediately apparent for Bacon's sweeping condemnation of all existing systems
of Astronomy. No system could be called consistent or complete

[1] Spedding, *Works*, iii. 727-768.   [2] *Ibid.* iii. 769-779.

till Newton discovered the Law of Gravitation. The Ptolemaic system itself, with its eccentrics and epicycles, was inconsistent with the strict Aristotelian Philosophy, which required all celestial motions to be simple and concentric; and it was therefore, by some philosophers, accepted only as a hypothesis, " saving the phenomena," while the more zealous Aristotelians rejected it with contempt.

Copernicus himself advocated his own system merely as a hypothesis; and in his works the term " Demonstrations " meant, not that certain causes *did* cause, but only that they *could* cause, certain phenomena. The introduction (erroneously attributed to Copernicus himself), which prefaces his great work on the Revolutions of the Celestial Orbs says, " It is not necessary that hypotheses should be true or even probable ; it is sufficient that they lead to results of calculation which agree with observations. . . . . . *Neither let any one, so far as hypotheses are concerned, expect anything certain from Astronomy ; since science can afford nothing of the kind.*" The obvious question, " *Why* should celestial bodies move in recurring orbits, and terrestrial bodies otherwise ? " could not be answered by Copernicus. Nor could he answer another question of which any child could see the force : " If the earth is moving round at the rate of several hundred miles an hour *eastward*, how is it that a stone thrown straight up from the earth into the air does not fall down on the earth at a considerable distance *westward* of the spot where it left the earth ? "—to which his only reply was that " perhaps the air carried the stone onward." The failure to answer these two questions condemned his astronomy as hypothetical. Hence Ramus, the logician, had (like Bacon) treated the Copernican system as a mere hypothesis, and had offered to resign his professorship in favour of any one who could produce an " astronomy without hypotheses ; " and it is creditable to Bacon's faith in the uniformity of nature, that he predicted that future discoveries would rest " upon observation of the common passions and desires of matter "—an anticipation of Newton's law of attraction.

But there is nothing Newtonian in the theory of his own, which he proceeds to elaborate. Making earth the centre of his system, he assumes that, the further one proceeds from earth, the more does the atmosphere become, not only rarified, but also adapted to be the home of the flamy substance of which the stars are supposed to consist. In the earthly atmosphere flame cannot exist without support; as we leave the earth, the air becomes rarer and flame acquires consistency, first in the comets, next in the body of the moon, where flame, though still weak, ceases to be extinguishable; thence, as we go still further, the flame increases in strength and purity until, in the planets Jupiter and Saturn, it begins to be exhausted by the proximity to the sidereal element.[1] Finally, all planetary form is swallowed up in a region of unmixed flame. Thus there are three regions: 1st, the region of the extinction of flame; 2nd, the region of its union; 3rd, the region of its dispersion.

Next as to celestial motions. Since rest must not be taken out of nature, and since compactness of matter (such as we find in the terrene globe), induces aversion [2] to motion, it is reasonable to look for rest in the earth if anywhere. But if there is perfect rest, we must suppose there is also perfect mobility; and those bodies which are furthest from the earth will be most perfectly mobile. Accordingly, the further planets are from the earth, the more quickly they move (regard being had to the magnitude of their orbits); and whereas the orbits of the most remote approximate to circles, those of the nearest are spirals differing most from circles; "for in proportion as substances degenerate in purity and freedom of development, so do their motions degenerate." A protest follows against present astronomical systems: "As for the hypotheses of astronomers it is useless to refute them, because they are not themselves asserted as true; and they may be various and contrary one to the other, yet so as equally to save and adjust the phenomena." The treatise concludes thus: "These then are the things that I see, standing as I do on the threshold of natural history and philosophy; and it may be that, the deeper a man has gone into natural history, the more he will approve them."

The principal reason for disinterring these well-nigh forgotten

---

[1] "In Saturni autem regione rursus natura flammae videtur nonnihil languescere et hebescere; utpote et a solis auxiliis longius remota, et a coelo stellato in proximo exhausta." Spedding, *Works*, iii. 771.

[2] The reader will not fail to notice how Bacon here and elsewhere succumbs to the power of words such as "appetite," "aversion," "nature" and the like—the very Idols against which he had so passionately protested.

treatises is because they illustrate in a very remarkable way the confidence which induced their Author, amid a multitude of engrossing occupations, to write in a tone of authority on a subject of which he himself knew so very little as not even to be able to appreciate the discoveries made by his contemporaries. During the rest of his life, immersed in State trials and attempts at politics, he was not destined to find leisure to supply his astronomical deficiencies; and accordingly we find that, the older he grew, the firmer became his conviction that the new belief in the rotation of the earth was false. In the treatise on the Flux and Reflux of the Sea, he merely notices the belief as "somewhat arbitrarily devised, so far as concerns physical reasons;" in the *Thema Coeli* (1612), he says that he now inclines to the theory of fixity ("which I now think to be the truer opinion"); but in the third book of the *De Augmentis* (1623), he is certain that the theory of the earth's motion is absolutely false (*nobis constat falsissimum esse*).[1]

At this point there is a great gap in the series of Bacon's Philosophical works. In 1613 he was appointed Attorney-General, and from that time till 1620, the year before his downfall, no literary work of any kind published, or unpublished, is known to have issued from his pen. All that he did was apparently to re-write repeatedly and revise the *Novum Organum*, which now claims attention.

§ 53 THE "NOVUM ORGANUM" (BOOK I)[2]

Fifteen years after the publication of the *Advancement of Learning* (which might serve as a first part of his *Magna Instauratio*) Bacon published (1620) the *Key of the Interpretation of Nature*, or, as he now preferred to call it, the *Novum Organum* (*New Instrument*), which was to serve as the second part of his great work.

---

[1] In the *Praise of Knowledge* (1592) he *perhaps* condemns the Copernican theory : "Who would not smile at the astronomers, *I mean not* these new carmen which drive the earth about, but the ancient astronomers, which feign, &c." (Spedding, i. 124) ; and in the *Temporis Partus Masculus* he includes the Copernicans in his general condemnation of astronomical hypotheses ; "Seest thou not, my son, that *alike these feigners of eccentrics and epicycles, and these carmen of the earth*, delight in pleading the doubtful evidence of phenomena?" (*Works*, iii. 536).

Spedding, *Works*, i. 71-223.

He had been at work upon it for a long time, and his chaplain Rawley says that he had seen " at the least twelve copies revised year by year, one after another, and amended in the frame thereof." There is reason to suppose that Bacon is referring to an early draft of this work in the *Commentarius Solutus* (1608) when he speaks of "finishing the *Aphorisms, Clavis Interpretationis,* and then setting forth the book;" and, if so, Rawley's twelve copies, revised year by year, may just cover the period between 1608 and 1620, the date of publication. How very little was done in these twelve years, and how little the *Novum Organum* contains that is not also contained in Bacon's previous works will appear from the following summary.

The title-page contains the title *Magna Instauratio* (being intended as the title of the whole work, and not of the *Novum Organum*) and a picture of a ship passing safely between the two Pillars of Hercules, with the text, *Multi pertransibunt et augebitur scientia* [1]—an allusion to Bacon's favourite comparison between the recent discovery of the new material world, and the anticipated discovery of a new intellectual world. In a Pröemium he explains that the publication of the work in an unfinished condition arose from the haste, not of ambition, but of anxiety: because he desired to leave behind him some outline of his object in the event of his death. After the Dedication to the King, a General Preface describes the present obstacles in the way of learning and the need of a new method.

Then follows an important section (entitled the Arrangement of the Work, *Distributio Operis*), which sets forth the divisions not of the *Novum Organum*, but of the whole of the proposed *Magna Instauratio* (in which the *Novum Organum* is but the second part). They are as follows :—

1. *The Divisions of the Sciences* (Partitiones Scientiarum).

2. *The New Instrument* (Novum Organum), or *Testimonies concerning the Interpretation of Nature* (Indicia de Interpretatione Naturae).[2]

---

[1] *Daniel* xii. 4. "Many shall pass through and knowledge shall be increased."
[2] In his previous works Bacon declares that he is not a "judex" but an "index," and therefore prepared to give not "judicia" but "indicia." The full title of the Second Part, as given in the *Novum Organum* itself, adds the word "Vera," *True Testimonies.*

3. *The Phenomena of the Universe,* or *History, Natural and Experimental, adapted for the foundation of Philosophy* (Phaenomena Universi, *sive* Historia Naturalis et Experimentalis ad condendam philosophiam).

4. *The Ladder of the Understanding* (Scala Intellectus). [This part was to contain examples of the operation of the New Method and of the results to which it leads.[1]]

5. *Fore-runners,* or *Anticipations of the Second Philosophy.* (Prodromi, *sive* Anticipationes Philosophiae Secundae). [This was to contain such discoveries as Bacon had made by ordinary methods; and without waiting for the New Method; and it was intended to be tentative.]

6. *The Second Philosophy,* or *Active Science* (Philosophia Secunda, *sive* Scientia Activa). [This was to contain the results of the application of the New Philosophy to all Phenomena.]

After the *Distributio Operis* a second title-page announces that the First Part of the *Instauratio* concerning the Divisions of Learning is wanting, but that it may be supplied in some measure from the Second Book of the *Advancement of Learning.* It adds these words, " Here follows the Second Part of the *Instauration,* which sets forth the Art itself of interpreting Nature and of a truer operation of the Understanding; but not in the form of a regular treatise, but only summarily *(per summas)* digested into Aphorisms." A third title introduces the *Novum Organum,* or *True Testimonies concerning the Interpretation of Nature.* Then, after a Preface—in which the author declares his willingness to accept the received philosophy as a social and literary ornament, but summons the Children of Knowledge to a truer Learning—a fourth title announces the Summary of the Second Part, digested into Aphorisms; and when a fifth title has grandiloquently heralded " Aphorisms concerning the Interpretation of Nature and the Kingdom of Man," the *Novum Organum* itself is at last presented to us.

The First Book of the *Novum Organum* was written for the same purpose as the *Cogitata et Visa,* and reproduces the substance of the latter; it was designed as an introduction to a particular example of the new method of Induction (which is

---

[1] For the description of the "scala" or "ladder," see the summary of the *Cogitata et Visa* above, p. 363.

reserved for the Second Book of the *Novum Organum*) and was intended to prepare the minds of men by removing prejudices and misconceptions.

The first Aphorism (in language borrowed from Bacon's earlier works) proclaims that " Man is the servant and interpreter of Nature ; " that is, he can do nothing save by conforming himself to her laws, and by interpreting her facts so as to ascertain her motives (which are causes). Then follow (Aphorisms 5—10) reflections on the barrenness of existing sciences, and (11—14) of existing Logic ; and the unsoundness or uselessness of existing notions (15—17) ; and an assertion that everything must depend upon a New Induction. The Old Method and the New are then placed in contrast (18—37) showing that the Old passes at once from particulars to the highest generalities, whence attempt is made to deduce all intermediate propositions ; whereas the New rises by gradual Induction and successively, from particulars to Axioms of the lowest generality, then to intermediate Axioms, and so ultimately to the highest.[1]

In the following sections (38—70) Bacon develops his well-known doctrine of the four *idols*. Roger Bacon had mentioned in his *Opus Majus* the four " stumbling-blocks " in the path towards truth : (1) authority ; (2) custom ; (3) popular and unlearned notions (*sensus*); and (4) the combination of ignorance with a pretence of knowledge. But only the first of these exactly corresponds to any of Bacon's *idols*; and the *Opus Majus* not having been printed till the eighteenth century, had probably not been read by Francis Bacon ; who seems to have known his great predecessor mainly as one who neglected theory and applied himself to mechanical inventions.[2]

The name Images, or Idols (" *Idola*, sive *Imagines*," as they are called in the *De Augmentis*), is applied by Bacon to those false phantoms which are called up by the inherent perverseness of the human mind so as to exclude, from the very first, the possibility of seeing the truth. Besides errors of observation and of reasoning, he noticed certain prejudices or infirmities which prevent men from *trying to observe and to use their reason*. The *Delineatio* and the *Cogitata* have indicated the origin of this metaphor. We are seeking light. Now the human mind, if it were a regular and even mirror, would reflect

---

[1] See the *Cogitata et Visa*, p. 363, for the need of this gradual ascent.
[2] Spedding, *Works*, i. 90, 163.

all rays of light regularly and represent the truth accurately ;
but it is irregular and distorted, so as to reflect distorted *images*
or *idols* of the true objects: it is, says the *De Augmentis* (v. 4),
"rather like *an enchanted glass, full of superstition and imposture.*" These words indicate the quasi-theological play upon the
word Idols, which pervades the whole of the Baconian doctrine
concerning them : they are "images" and "phantoms" created
by the misdirected human will, which refuses to allow the mind
to receive the "ideas of God." The *Novum Organum* (following
the *Delineatio*) expressly contrasts the "*ideas* of God" with the
"*idols* of the human mind." Until it has been levelled and
purified *by God's truth*, the mind is under the influence of a
"familiar spirit" (daemonem familiarem) which peoples it with
spectres ; and until it can be released from this magic charm, it
sees all things around it infected with phantoms and incantations
(larvata et incantata).[1] Take for example (1) the inherent habit
—common to the whole *Tribe* of mankind—of being more affected
by one affirmative instance (*e.g.* an extraordinary cure effected by
some drug) than by many negative instances of failure ; there
are also (2) special prejudices (*e.g.* in favour of exaggeration)
inherent in individuals, imprisoned so to speak in the *Caves* of
their own idiosyncrasies ; there is (3) a general disposition to be
the slave of those phrases and words (such as Church, Law of
Nature, Necessity) which in the intercourse, traffic, and as it
were the *market-place* of life, are often wont to change their
meanings and insensibly to bring the wise into subjection to the
notions of the vulgar ; there is lastly (4) an inherent indolence
which predisposes the human mind to acquiesce in the *theatrical*
fictions of any teacher who is confidently, consistently, and
speciously dogmatic.

As to the classification of these errors Bacon seems to have
felt a good deal of hesitation. In the *Valerius Terminus* (1603)
he mentions four ; the *Advancement* (1605), (which does not
mention the word "idol") makes mention of only three errors
under this head ; in the *Partis Secundae Delineatio* (1606—7)
there are three *idols* ; but the *Novum Organum* (1620) (recurring
to the number in the *Valerius Terminus*, though placing them
in a different order) mentions four *idols*, two inherent in the

---

[1] See note on p. 362, above.

mind, and two external ; lastly the *De Augmentis* (1623) while retaining the triple division of the *Advancement* admits that there is a fourth idol, and recognises the treatment of the subject in the *Novum Organum* as being more full and subtle.[1] The following is the arrangement in the *Novum Organum* :

In a quadruple division, the *idols*, or false human phantasies, are opposed to the *ideas* of the divine mind. Of the four classes of *idols* two are inherent in the human mind ; two, external :

(1) *The Idols of the Tribe*, to which the mind is exposed because of the qualities common to the whole race or Tribe of humanity.

(2) *The Idols of the Cave*, which results from the special peculiarities or circumstances of individuals, dwelling each in his own cave.[2]

(3) *The Idols of the Market Place*, resulting from the use of words, which are the coins (often spurious or deceitful) by which men exchange thoughts.

(4) *The Idols of the Theatre*, whereby men in masses, like the vast audience of a theatre, allow themselves to be swayed by the impostures of symmetrical and authoritative systems of Philosophy, which are no better than theatrical fictions. This section (69, 70) concludes with some remarks on vicious demonstrations, which are the strongholds of Idols.

The mention of defective demonstrations leads to the next section, which, covering (though more amply) the ground already covered by the *Cogitata* and the *Redargutio*, treats first of the five signs (71—77) and then of the fifteen causes (78—92) of a defective Philosophy.

This section concludes with the most important cause of all, namely despair of the possibility of success. To remove this despair the grounds of hope are stated (93—115), and herein are mentioned new equipments for the

---

[1] Spedding, *Works*, i. 643 (*De Augm.* v. 4) : " There is also a fourth kind which I call the *Idols of the Theatre*, superinduced by corrupt theories or systems of philosophy and false laws of demonstration. But this kind may be rejected and got rid of, so I will leave it for the present. *The others absolutely take possession of the mind and cannot be removed.* The full and subtle handling of these, however, we assign to the *Novum Organum.*" The italicized words seem to show that Bacon considered that the Idols of the *Market Place*, which in the *Novum Organum* are classified as external, might very reasonably be classified as inherent.

[2] That these words refer to the famous allegory of the Cave in Plato's *Republic*, is proved by *De Augm.* v. 4 : " With this emblem of Plato's concerning the Cave, the saying of Heraclitus agrees well, that " men seek the sciences in worlds of their own and not in the greater world." And to the same effect is a passage in the *Phenomena Universi* : " Every one philosophises *out of the cells of his own imagination, as out of Plato's Cave.*" (*Works*, v. 131). For previous mentions of, or allusions to, the *Idols*, see above, *Valerius Terminus*, p. 351, *Advancement of Learning*, § 65, *Delineatio*, p. 358, *Cogitata*, p. 362.

search after Truth ; (1) a Natural History classified for the information of
the Understanding in due order with a view to the foundation of Philosophy—which will include "not only variety of natural species, but also
experiments of the mechanical arts," and will be quite a different thing
from a Natural History as understood by Aristotle and his followers ;
(2) additional experiments throwing light on causes, and not merely producing results of immediate profit ; (3) an "entirely different method, order,
and process, for carrying on and advancing experience ; " (4) experiments
and experience reduced to writing ; (5) experience set down in Tables apt,
well arranged, "and, as it were, living." These classified facts, with the inferences deduced from them, will lead up first to the lower, then to the
higher Axioms ; not till afterwards will the descent be made from Axioms
to works ; (6) but our chief hope lies in the New Induction which analyses
Nature by rejections and exclusions, and is entirely different. from the
puerile and precarious enumerative Induction of antiquity.[1]

The levelling of the ground having been now effected by showing the
inability of unaided reason, received demonstrations, and received philosophies (115) the Author should pass from the destructive to the constructive
part of his work. But first he has to disarm prejudices. He protests that
he is not the founder of a sect, and that the ancient philosophies may be
set aside with perfect deference to the philosophers themselves ; just as in
the drawing of a circle one may, without disparagement, prefer to the hand
of the most cunning draughtsman the use of a pair of compasses. The New
Philosophy is not sordid, nor given up to works ; which are sought, not for
themselves, but as the pledges of truth. Nor does the New Philosophy impugn the senses or the judgment. Rightly directed, the faculties of man
may guide him into all truth in Logic, in Ethics, and in Politics, as well as in
Natural Philosophy. The last Aphorism (130) of the First Book declares
that it is now time to pass to the Art itself, which, however, is not yet perfect, nor is it absolutely necessary ; for, even without it, if men had a "just
history of Nature and Experience," and could bind themselves by two rules,
first, to lay aside received opinions, and, secondly, to restrain themselves
from seeking at once to ascend to the highest generalizations, they would be
able, by the native force of the mind, to fall into the right Interpretation
of Nature.[2]

[1] For a protest that his Induction differs from Aristotle's, see the *Redargutio*,
above, p. 369.
[2] Spedding, *Works*, i. 225-368.

§ 54 THE "NOVUM ORGANUM" (BOOK II) [1]

The Second Book of the *Novum Organum* was intended to set forth the particular example of the Art of Interpretation, for which the First Book served as a mere introduction, and accordingly Bacon selects *heat* as the object of his investigations. If we ask why he propounded his method by an example, his answer is given in the last paragraphs of the *Cogitata et Visa*. He thought that an example would be the best means of exciting curiosity as to the method ; and that it would suffice for the intelligence of the capable reader, while, for the incapable, no exposition of the method, however lengthy, would be sufficiently clear. These are the reasons that he himself alleges ; but Mr. Ellis, with great probability, suggests an additional motive : "Another reason for the course which he followed may not improbably have been that he was more or less conscious that he could not demonstrate the validity, or at least the practicability, of that which he proposed. The fundamental principle, in virtue of which alone a method of exclusions can necessarily lead to a positive result, namely that *the subject-matter to which it is applied consists of a finite number of elements, each of which the mind can recognise and distinguish from the rest*, cannot, it is manifest, be for any particular case demonstrated *à priori*. Bacon's method in effect assumes that substances can always be resolved into an aggregation of a certain number of abstract qualities, and that their essence is adequately represented by the result of this analysis. Now this assumption or postulate cannot be made the subject of a direct demonstration, and probably Bacon came gradually to perceive more or less the difficulties which it involves. But *these difficulties are less obvious in special cases than when the question is considered generally ;* and on this account Bacon may have decided to give, instead of a demonstration of his method, an example of its use." [2] It is possible also that, when he first determined on this course, he may have thought that the particular example of the *Art of Interpretation* might result in some immediate practical

---

[1] Spedding, *Works*, i. 225-368. [2] Spedding, *Works*, i. 84—5.

result—some new power, for example, of producing heat—
which might be far more effective, with most minds, than a
formal demonstration of the general principle.

The reader who is unfamiliar with Bacon's style and mode of
work may expect that, since the Second Book of the *Novum
Organum* was to set forth the Key of Interpretation, it would
proceed to do so at once : but those who have studied his earlier
treatises and know his love of prefaces and introductions will
not be unprepared for ten preliminary aphorisms.

The early Aphorisms of the Second Book deal with Forms or Laws of
things, variously defined as (Aphorism 1) "the Form, or true specific
difference, or nature-engendering nature, or source of emanation." Not
however (2) that Forms give existence ; for "in Nature, nothing really
exists besides individual bodies, performing purely individual acts according
to a fixed law. Yet in philosophy this very Law, and the investigation,
discovery, and explanation of it, constitute the foundation as well of knowledge as of operation ; and it is this Law, with its clauses (*paragraphos*)
that I mean when I speak of Forms." [1]

The discovery of Forms (3) gives a power far exceeding that which
results from the discovery of particular and efficient causes ; for an efficient
cause will only in certain circumstances produce the required nature ; but
(4) the Form of a nature is such that, when the Form is present, the nature
infallibly follows, and when the Form is removed, the nature vanishes.
Lastly, the true Form will educe the given nature from some essence
which is of a more general kind [*e.g.* it will educe the nature of heat
from the more general nature of motion, of which heat is a particular
kind]. [2]

The rule or Axiom for the transformation of bodies (5) is of two kinds.

(i.) The first regards a body as a troop or collection of *Simple Natures*.
For example, in order to transform a body into gold, you may regard gold
as a collection of simple natures, yellowness, weight, ductility, &c. These
natures you may superinduce on the body, thus educing the nature of gold
from a knowledge of the Forms of the simple natures that compose it. And
this course, though the more difficult of the two, is the only one that leads
to profound and radical operations on Nature. (For example, in all inquiries about the heavenly bodies, we cannot attain the truth without first

---

[1] " I rather adopt this name," adds Bacon (2), "because it has grown into use
and become familiar." Professor Fowler (*Novum Organum*, p. 392) says : "We
can seldom be quite sure in which of its two senses, nature or essence, and law or
cause, he is using it ; and in fact sometimes he seems to be using it in both at
once." He may have thought that heat, for example, could not otherwise be
defined than as being that kind of motion which constituted and caused heat. To
the other definitions of Form, given here and on p. 388, we may add one from the
Redargutio (*Works*, iii. 580), " Formae, sive verae rerum differentiae."
[2] For Formal and Final Causes, see the *Advancement of Learning*, p. 461.

attaining the knowledge of the nature of spontaneous rotation, attraction, or magnetism, and of many other natures which are more general than the nature of the heavenly bodies themselves.)

(ii.) The second way is to study compound bodies themselves in order to ascertain their *Latent Process* (*latens processus*) by which they are generated ; and although this pursuit deals rather with what may be called particular habits of Nature than with the universal and fundamental Laws which constitute Forms, yet it is readier and more immediately hopeful than the search for the Forms of Simple Natures.[1]

In neither of these two courses shall we succeed unless we study (6) the *Latent Configuration* (*latens schematismus*) of the given body. Here let it be remembered that, as *Latent Process* is not a succession of steps, but a continuous progress, which for the most part escapes the senses ; so (7) *Latent Configuration* is something far more subtle than is commonly supposed— something to be detected, not by the mere test of fire, but by reasoning and true Induction, combined with experiments, in the course of which we must inquire into the amount and nature of the *spirit* and *tangible essence* in each body. Let no one suppose (8) that we shall thus be led to the false doctrine of the atom implying a vacuum and the unchangeableness of matter. Nor let him be alarmed at the subtlety of the investigation : for the nearer it approaches to Simple Natures, the easier and plainer will everything become.

From the two methods given above for the transformation of bodies we may (9) deduce a double division both of the theory and of the practice of Science. First as to the theory. Let the investigation of Forms constitute Metaphysic ; then the investigation of the Efficient Cause, Matter, Latent Process, and Latent Configuration, may be assigned to Physic.[2] Next as to practice. Let (scientific) Magic be assigned to Metaphysic ; and Mechanic to Physic. Thus, having marked out the field of knowledge, we pass (10) to precepts for attaining knowledge.

I. We are to educe Axioms from Experience.

II. We are to derive new experiments from Axioms.

Again, the first Precept is divided into three parts or Ministrations ;[3] for in order to educe new Axioms from experience—

1. We must minister to the *sense* by preparing a Natural and Experimental History.

2. We must minister to the *memory* by classifying the History in Tables of Instances so arranged that the understanding may be able to deal with them.

3. We must minister to the *mind or reason* (*mentem sive rationem*) by offering it the aid of "Induction, true and legitimate Induction, which is

---

[1] The language here used by Bacon about the discovery of Forms seems less hopeful than that used in previous works. See above, p. 351.

[2] For a similar division see the *Advancement*, below, § 64.

[3] For a previous mention of these "ministrations" in the *Delineation* see p. 359.

the very Key of Interpretation." For without this, even with the aid of
the History and the Tables, the understanding, if left to itself (*intellectus
sibi permissus*), is incompetent to form Axioms.

It is with the third of the sections that we must now begin, afterwards
returning to the other two.[1]

Now therefore at last the reader is brought up to the point
where he may expect to have revealed to him that Particular
Example of the Art of Interpretation which it is the sole
object of the *Novum Organum* to introduce and expound—the
core and centre of the whole Baconian philosophy, which indeed
is not a system, but a method. All that has preceded has been
by way of introduction ; theorising, censuring, exhorting, mark-
ing out and dividing into districts the region to be conquered—
matter mostly negative, and, where positive, mostly vague and
unsatisfactory—as when the author informed us that we are to
inquire (Aphorism 7) into the *spirit* of each body "whether it
be copious and turgid, or meagre and scarce"—or else altogether unpractical and even inconsistent—as when he told us
(Aphorism 8) that we need not suppose we should be led to a
doctrine implying a vacuum. The existence of a vacuum, being
a subject quite beyond the region of experience, could neither be
denied nor asserted, on Baconian principles; and in another
Aphorism of this very book it is left an open question. Bacon
told the King (and we have every reason to suppose that he
was not exaggerating) that he "had been about some such
work" as the *Novum Organum* "near thirty years ; so as I made
no haste. And the reason why I have published it now, specially
being imperfect, is, to speak plainly, because I number my
days and would have it saved."[2] But even a Lord Chancellor
can scarcely be acquitted of haste who, writing on such
a fundamental subject as the existence of a vacuum, tells us
in Aphorism 8 that "the doctrines of *a vacuum and of the
unchangeableness of matter are both false*" ("praesupponit
vacuum et materiam non fluxam, *quorum utrumque falsum est*")
and in Aphorism 48 *of the same book*, "I am *not prepared to say
for certain whether or no there be a vacuum*" ("neque enim

---

[1] See Mr. Ellis's comment on this departure from the prescribed order, above,
p. 361.

[2] See above, p. 282.

pro certo affimaverimus utrum detur vacuum "). Bearing in mind that in the *De Principiis* and in the *Descriptio Globi Intellectualis* (1612) [1] he left it an open question, and that in the *Historia Densi et Rari* (1622—6) he decided against a vacuum, we are led to infer that Aphorism 48 of this book was written before Aphorism 8 and hastily transferred into the *Novum Organum* without due revision. This symptom of haste will strike the observant reader as ominous of evil for his expectations concerning the Key which is now about to be placed in his hands : he will do well also to be alarmed at the promise in Aphorism 8, that *when he gets a little further on, a little nearer to Simple Natures, "the easier and plainer will everything become."* This sounds like an attempt to prepare the reader not to be discouraged if the author presently avows the existence of some obstacle which bars immediate progress, and which must serve as an excuse for delay : and as Bacon stopped in the *Valerius Terminus* just when we wanted him to go on, so we must not be surprised to find him stopping now. With these cautions we now proceed to the Aphorism (11) which is to disclose the Key, simply premising that, where we should speak of Laws of Nature, Bacon (using the term introduced in Aphorism 1) speaks of *Forms.*

(11). Let the nature to be investigated be Heat.[2] We must investigate the Form of Heat by first summoning all known instances which agree in possessing Heat, to put in as it were an *appearance* at the bar of the Understanding (facienda est *comparentia* ad intellectum): for example, sun-rays, horse-dung, frost-burn, quick-lime sprinkled with water, &c. (in all twenty-eight instances) ; this is the Table of Essence and Presence (*Essentiae et Praesentiae*). Secondly (12) we make a Table of Instances, corresponding to the twenty-eight above, where Heat *might be expected to be present but*

---

[1] Spedding, *Works*, v. 497, 516, 519. The precise date of the *De Principiis* is not known : but Mr. Ellis, (*Works*, iii. 73), notes that there is another inconsistency between that treatise and the *Novum Organum*. In the *De Principiis* "there is one first material principle, idque *fixum et invariabile*. . . . In the interval between writing this tract and the *Novum Organum* Bacon's opinions seem to have undergone some change, as he has there (ii. 8) condemned the atomists for asserting the existence of 'materia non fluxa'; an obscure phrase, but which appears irreconcilable with the expression which I have just quoted, fixum et invariabile."

[2] In the *Filum Labyrinthi* (see p. 364) Bacon had chosen Motion for the nature to be investigated. Probably failure had induced him to select a new nature. Also "he had now perhaps come to regard Motion as an ultimate fact."—See Professor Fowler's *Francis Bacon*, p. 114.

is not, e.g. moon-rays, the rays of the sun in the middle region of the air and in polar regions, &c. ; this is the Table of Deviation or Absence in Proximity (*Absentiae in Proximo*).   Thirdly (13) we make a Table of Instances in which Heat is found *in different degrees*, which must be done by making a comparison either of its increase or decrease in the same subject, or of its amount in different subjects, as compared with one another ; "*for the Form of a thing is the very thing itself, and the thing differs from the Form no otherwise than as the apparent differs from the real, or the external from the internal, or the thing in reference to man from the thing in reference to the Universe.*"[1]   It therefore necessarily follows that no nature can be taken as the true Form, unless it always decrease when the nature in question decreases, and in like manner always increase when the nature in question increases.   This is the Table of Degrees or of Comparison (*Tabula Graduum sive Comparativae*).

On these three Tables (called the Presentation of Instances to the Understanding) Induction must be set at (15) work ; "for the problem is, upon a review of the instances, all and each, to find such a nature as is always present, or absent, or increasing, or decreasing, when the given nature is present, or absent, or increasing, or decreasing ; such a nature as this is (as I have said [2]) a particular case of a more general nature (limitatio naturae magis communis).   *But the human mind cannot attempt this problem affirmatively from the first, as, when left to itself (sibi permissa) it is always wont to do :* to God, the Giver and Architect of Forms, it belongs to have an affirmative knowledge of Forms immediately, and from the first contemplation.   But this is assuredly above the power of man, to whom it is granted only to proceed at first by negatives, and at last to end in affirmatives, after exclusion has been exhausted."

" The first work therefore " (16) " of true induction (as far as concerns the discovery of Forms) is *the rejection or exclusion of the several natures which are not found in some instance where the given nature is present; or are found in some instance where the given nature is absent ; or are found to increase in some instance when the given nature decreases, or to decrease when the given nature increases.*   Then indeed, after the rejection and exclusion has been duly made, all false and volatile opinions will vanish into smoke (abeuntibus in fumum opinionibus volatilibus), and there will remain, as it were at the bottom, a Form affirmative, solid, and true, and well-defined."

Here, in this Method of Exclusions, we have the key-stone of the Baconian method.   Understanding this, we can understand how it was that Bacon magnified his Induction as being a

---

[1] See the note on *Forms*, p. 384, above.

[2] See Aphorism 4, above.   The "natura communis," for example, or genus, of Heat, will be motion ; and the "limitatio" will be that *difference* which distinguishes Heat from other kinds of motion, and which is therefore said to make Heat what it is.

certain and mechanical process entirely different from the
ordinary Induction. His confidence was based on his belief—the
old belief expressed in the *Valerius Terminus*—that the letters
of the alphabet of Nature, those Simple Natures which make up
all material things, are few in number. If there are only, for
example, twenty Simple Natures that can possibly cause anything whatever ; and if you can prove that nineteen of them
are *not* the causes of a given nature, say Heat ; it follows that
the twentieth *is* the Cause or Form of Heat : and under such
circumstances it is an easy matter to "proceed from negatives
to an affirmative." It has been urged that the Plurality of
Causes is fatal to the correctness of Bacon's system of Exclusions. If, for example, the Simple Natures be represented
by the letters of the alphabet, a given nature—say Heat—may
be caused by *a, or* by *b, or* by a combination of *c* and *d*. When
therefore we find a number of instances of heat where *b, c,* and
d are not present (because in these instances the heat is caused
by *a*) and when we must (according to Bacon's system) reject *b,
c,* and *d,* shall we not be in error ? This objection Bacon
appears to endeavour to meet in the following Aphorism (17).
Though he does not frankly and expressly admit that his
Exclusion, under such circumstances, must be inaccurate, he
declares that his object is practical ; and that for the purpose of
" superinducing " the given nature, it is sufficient to ascertain
one Form. For the purpose of producing Heat it will be
practically sufficient to ascertain that it is Motion of a particular kind, even though we may have committed a *theoretical*
inaccuracy in excluding other causes or Forms which could
produce Heat. Perhaps also he tacitly assumed that if a given
nature can be produced by more than one Form, *e.g.* by *a* or *b*
or *c* or *d*, it will follow that these Forms are not really Simple
Natures, but themselves capable of being resolved into Simple
Natures of which they are combinations ; just as he thought, at
one time, that Motion, which is the Form of Heat, could itself
be resolved into some nature simpler than itself : for he says in
the following Aphorism that, although hanging, stabbing, apoplexy, and atrophy are different *causes* of death, yet they must
all "agree in the Form or Law which governs death." In other
words he assumes that the *ultimate* Cause or Form of *such*

natures as he is investigating will be always single and not plural. The cautious language of the Aphorism (17) should be noted: for he distinguishes between Compound Forms (which are combinations of Simple Natures, as of the lion eagle, rose, and the like) and the Forms of Simple Natures; and he protests that his remarks apply only to the latter.

"(17) When I speak of Forms, I mean nothing more than those laws and determinations of absolute actuality, which govern and constitute any Simple Nature, as Heat, Light, Weight, *in every kind of matter and subject that is susceptible of them.*[1] Thus the Form of Heat, or the Form of Light, is the same thing as the Law of Heat, or the Law of Light. *Nor indeed do I ever allow myself to be drawn away from things themselves and the operative part.* And therefore when I say, for instance, in the investigation of the Form of Heat, 'Reject rarity,' or, 'Rarity does not belong to the Form of Heat,' it is the same as if I said, 'It is possible to superinduce Heat on a dense body,'[2] or, 'It is possible to take away or keep out Heat from a rare body.'

" But if any one conceives that my Forms are of a somewhat abstract nature because they mix and combine things heterogeneous (for the heat of heavenly bodies and the heat of fire seem to be very heterogeneous; so do the fixed red of the rose or the like, and the apparent red of the rainbow, the opal, or the diamond; so again do the different kinds of death, death by drowning, by hanging, by stabbing, by apoplexy, by atrophy; and yet they agree severally in the nature of heat, redness, and death) . . . . he may be assured that these things, however heterogeneous and alien from each other, agree in the Form or Law which governs heat, redness, and death; and that the power of man cannot possibly be emancipated and freed from the common course of nature, and expanded and exalted to new efficients and new modes of operation, except by the revelation and discovery of Forms of this kind."

Thus, at the very moment when he introduces the fundamental part of his method, Bacon parenthetically, as it were,

[1] "Nihil aliud intelligimus quam leges illas et determinationes actus puri quae naturam aliquam simplicem ordinant et constituunt (ut calorem, lumen, pondus) *in omnimoda materia et subjecto susceptibili*." These words are hardly susceptible of any other interpretation than this, that Bacon *limits himself to those Causes, Forms, or Laws which produce the given nature whenever and wherever the given nature exists.* It is a large assumption—that a Simple Nature, Heat for example, must always have but one ultimate Cause or Form—but, if we once grant it, the objection derived from Plurality of Causes against Bacon's Method of Exclusions at once ceases to be applicable.

[2] The meaning seems to be this: "I do not say that it is *not possible* that rarity should be connected with Heat. My object is not negative and theoretical, but positive and practical: and therefore I content myself with passing from the negative and theoretical exclusion to this practical affirmative: 'It *is possible* to superinduce Heat on bodies that are not rare.'"

slips in a distinction which is of vital importance. His Method of Exclusions applied *only to those Laws or Forms which govern and constitute Simple Natures whenever and wherever those Simple Natures exist.* But who is to tell beforehand about a given Nature whether it is Simple or Complex ? And even supposing that we are led by intuition to some Simple Nature, how do we know that he is correct in his apparent assumption that it cannot be produced by two or more quite different and independent Laws or Forms ? However, without any immediate apology, Bacon now proceeds (18) to set forth fourteen instances of Exclusion applied to Heat; among which are some interesting errors, with at least one instance of remarkable insight : "On account of common fire . . . . reject the nature of the heavenly bodies. . . . On account *of the rays of the moon* [1] and other heavenly bodies (with the exception of the sun) also reject light and brightness. *On account of ignited iron, which does not swell in bulk,*[2] but keeps within the same visible dimensions, reject local or expansive motion of the body as a whole. On account of the dilation of air in calendar glasses and the like, wherein the air *evidently moves locally and expansively, and yet acquires no manifest increase of heat,*[3] also reject local or expansive motion of the body as a whole." On the other hand he shows a true intuition in rejecting the notion of an inherent "caloric" or "*principial* nature" (naturalem *principialem*) because he finds Heat generated by friction.[4] He concludes the Aphorism with a negative : "All and each of the above-mentioned natures do not belong to the Form of Heat," qualified by a more justifiable affirmative : "And from all of them man is freed in his operations on Heat."

[1] It is now known that the moon's rays give out some heat.

[2] An erroneous supposition.

[3] And yet Bacon himself, in Aph. xiii. 38, details a long experiment showing that air expands with heat, and expressly speaks of it as "*dilatatus per calefactionem.*" See also Aphorism 20 in Book ii. : "This kind of motion is best seen in air, *which continuously and manifestly dilates with a slight heat*" : yet in the same Aphorism he adds : "When the air is extended in a calendar glass without impediment or repulsion—that is to say uniformly and equably—*there is no* (?) *perceptible heat (non percipiatur calor).*" He seems to be distinguishing between two kinds of expansion, (1) *as a whole (secundum totum)*, and (2) *in the parts (per particulas minores)*, of which the *latter* alone constitutes Heat according to his theory.

[4] See Mr. Ellis's note (Spedding, *Works*, i. 260) : "The proof that caloric does not exist—in other words that heat is not the manifestation of a peculiar substance diffused through nature—rests mainly on experiments of friction."

Now that the Method of Exclusions has been tried and found wanting, it becomes necessary to explain the failure; and accordingly the next Aphorism (19) admits that our ignorance of Simple Natures stops the way. But the author adds that he sees a way to remedy this defect, and promises to do it.

The process of Exclusion cannot (19) in our present state of knowledge be complete ; for we proceed by excluding Simple Natures; (*e.g.* the nature of the heavenly bodies above) ; but as our notions of Simple Natures are often vague and ill-defined, the Understanding needs aids for the foundation of better notions ; and we must regard our Exclusions as being, for the present, tentative. "I therefore, well knowing and nowise forgetting how great a work I am about (that of rendering the Human Understanding a match for things and nature) do not rest satisfied with the precepts I have laid down ; but proceed further to devise and supply more powerful aids for the use of the Understanding ; which I shall now subjoin."

If the *Novum Organum* is to do its work, it ought now to carry out the promise of the last Aphorism and indicate to the reader some means for arriving at the knowledge of Simple Natures. For until we have this knowledge we cannot use the Method of Exclusions. But how can we attain the knowledge of Simple Natures? Let the fourteenth Aphorism of the First Book answer :

" The Syllogism consists of Propositions ; Propositions consist of words ; words are symbols of notions. Therefore, if the *notions themselves*—and here we have the root of the matter—are confused and over-hastily abstracted from the facts, there can be no firmness in the superstructure. Our only hope therefore lies in *a true Induction.*"

Is not this something like reasoning in a circle ? We cannot perform the perfect and true Induction without clear *notions* of Simple Natures ; and, if we would gain those clear notions, *our only hope lies in true Induction.*

An ordinary philosopher would have here confessed that he had failed in his attempt to obtain a mechanical process for discovering the Laws of Nature. But such confessions are not in Bacon's manner. If he cannot effect the first best, his plan is always to effect a second best, and to make the best of that, and never to allow himself to be brought to a stand by disappointments. It therefore occurred to him that, if his Method failed him, he might fall back upon his Natural History—the three positive Tables called the Presentation of Instances—which might help him to some discovery, even without the negative Table and without the Exclusions from which he had once hoped so much. It is true that in the First Book (Aph. 20) he has cautioned us against "the Understanding left to itself (*Intellectus sibi permissus*)" which "wearies of experiment" and prematurely "springs up to positions of higher generality;" but at the conclusion of the same book (Aph. 130), in a passage above quoted, he declared that if men had a regular (justam) History of Nature and Experience, and could lay aside received opinions and notions, and "refrain the mind for a time from the highest generalizations and from those next to the highest," they would be able by the native force of mind to fall into the true form of Interpretation. Accordingly Bacon now casts aside his Method of Exclusions, and with the aid of the three positive Tables he allows himself to make a tentative approach towards the Law or Form of Heat. The Aphorism (20) in which he states this intention is noteworthy, because it contains a kind of avowal that a "working hypothesis"—though no part at all of the New Induction—may accelerate scientific discovery, by tending to some kind of order in the classification of phenomena, although the classification may be erroneous.

"And yet, *since truth will sooner come out from error than from confusion*, I think it expedient that the Understanding should have permission (*ut fiat permissio intellectui*) after the three Tables of First Presentation (such as I have exhibited) have been made and weighed, to make an essay of the Interpretation of Nature in the affirmative way : on the strength, both of the instances given in the Tables, and of any others it may meet with elsewhere. Which kind of tentative process I call the *Indulgence of the Understanding (permissionem Intellectus*), or the *Incomplete Interpretation (Interpretationem inchoatam*), or the *First Vintage.*"[1]

The conclusion of the Aphorism (20) presents us (1) with a tentative "Form, or True Definition," of Heat where the identification of the two words "Form" and "Definition" is to be noted as an indication of the great importance attached by

---

[1] For a previous use of this metaphor, see the *Cogitata et Visa*, above, p. 362.

Bacon to the attainment of clear and true *notions*—and (2) with a tentative "Direction," showing us how to produce Heat :

"From this, our First Vintage, it follows that the Form, or true Definition, of Heat (Heat, that is, in relation to the universe, not simply in relation to man) is in few words as follows : 'Heat is a motion, expansive, restrained, and acting in its strife upon the smaller particles of bodies.' But the expansion is thus modified : 'While it expands all ways, it has at the same time an inclination upwards.' And the struggle in the particles is modified also : 'It is not sluggish, but hurried and with violence.'

"Viewed with reference to operation it is the same thing. For the Direction is this : 'If in any natural body you can excite a dilating or expanding motion, and can so repress this motion and turn it back upon itself, that the dilation shall not proceed equably, but have its way in one part and be counteracted in another, you will undoubtedly generate heat.'"

It will be remembered that in Aphorism 19 after admitting the inadequacy of his Method of Exclusions, Bacon promised to supply " more powerful aids (*fortiora auxilia in usum intellectus*) for the use of the Understanding." The 20th Aphorism ends with a statement that he now proceeds to supply these : "Now, however, we must proceed to 'further aids' (*ulteriora auxilia*)." Accordingly the 21st Aphorism begins thus :—

"(21) The Tables of Presentation, and the Rejection (or process of Exclusion) being completed, and also the First Vintage being made thereupon, we are to proceed to the other helps of the Understanding (ad reliqua auxilia intellectus) concerning the Interpretation of Nature and true and perfect Induction."

The "help" now wanted is a help to the formation of true conceptions of Simple Natures, without which the Method of Exclusions cannot be performed. But for this help the reader will wait in vain. Mr. Ellis expresses his opinion that Bacon himself had " never, even in idea, completed the method which he proposed :" " In order to the completion of his method . . . a subsidiary method is required, of which the object is the formation of scientific conceptions. To this method Bacon gives the name of Induction ; and it is remarkable that Induction is mentioned for the first time in the *Novum Organum* in a passage which relates, not to axioms, but to conceptions. Bacon's Induction therefore is not a mere ἐπαγωγή, it is also a method of definition; [2] but of the manner in which systematic Induction is to be employed in the formation of his conceptions we learn nothing from any part of his writings. And by this circumstance our knowledge of his method is rendered imperfect and unsatisfactory. We may, perhaps, be permitted to believe that, so far as relates to the subject of which we are now speaking, *Bacon never, even in idea, completed the method which he proposed.* For, of all parts of the process of scientific discovery, the formation of conceptions is the one with respect to which it is most difficult to lay down regular rules. The process of establishing axioms Bacon had succeeded, at least apparently, in reducing to the semblance of a mechanical operation; that of the formation of conceptions does not admit of any similar reduction. Yet these two processes are, in Bacon's system, of co-ordinate importance. All commonly received general scientific conceptions Bacon condemns as utterly worthless.[3] A complete change therefore is required; yet of the way in which Induction is to be employed in order to produce this change he has said nothing." [4]

Few, however, would infer from the language of the rest of the book that Bacon is here brought to a standstill, and that he " had not completed, even in idea," the method which he is attempting to set before his readers. Probably he was not himself fully aware of the insuperable nature of the obstacle before him; but a certain semi-consciousness of failure induces him to evade the difficulty; to creep round it and under it; to separate, so to speak, the main stream of his argument into a multitude of petty rills or runlets to which he gives grand and

---

[1] *Nov. Org.* i. 14: see the passage quoted above, p. 392: "The syllogism consists of propositions. . . . Our only hope therefore lies in a true Induction": and compare i. 18: "In order to penetrate into the inner and further recesses of nature, it is necessary that both notions and axioms be derived from things by a more sure and guarded way."

[2] Comp. Aph. 20, quoted above, p. 394: "the Form, *or true definition,* of Heat;" and Aph. 16 (p. 388), "a Form affirmative, solid, and true, and *well-defined.*"

[3] Comp. *Nov. Org.* i. 15: "There is no soundness in our notions, whether logical or physical. Substance, Quality, Action, Passion, Essence itself, are not sound notions: much less are Heavy, Light, Dense, Rare, Moist, Dry, Generation, Corruption, Attraction, Repulsion, Element, Matter, Form, and the like; but all are fantastical and ill-defined."   Spedding, *Works,* i. 37.

promising names, and which he disperses so that they may cover a great amplitude of space, and flow on somehow although to little purpose, becoming shallower as they increase in width and number, and leaving behind them unremoved and unremovable the great rock of the Simple Natures. Nowhere certainly in all his writings does Bacon more conspicuously justify the praise bestowed by Yelverton on his pre-eminent power of expressing himself "bravely and confidently"[1] than in the following Aphorism with its influx of grandiloquent promises of " helps for the use of the Understanding."

"I propose to consider, in the first place, Prerogative Instances ; 2nd, the Supports of Induction ; 3rd, the Rectification of Induction ; 4th, Varying the Investigation according to the nature of the subject ; 5th, Prerogative Natures with respect to Investigation, or what should be inquired first and what last ; 6th, the limits of Investigation, or a Synopsis of all Natures in the Universe ; 7th, the Application to Practice, or things in their relation to Man ; 8th, Preparations for Investigation ; 9th, the Ascending and Descending Scale of Axioms."

The rest of the book is devoted to the first of these nine sections, viz., the Prerogative Instances, of which twenty-seven are enumerated and illustrated by examples. Prerogative Instances are those which are distinguished from ordinary instances by having, as it were, a kind of royal "Prerogative," a superior claim on our attention, because they afford more light than ordinary instances, so that a few of the former are more valuable than a multitude of the latter.[2] For example, first among the twenty-

[1] Spedding. vi. 2—8 : "That you seem not dismayed, but open yourself *bravely and confidently*, wherein you can excel all subjects." See above, p. 264.

[2] "*Prerogativa*" was the name given to the Tribe or Century that *gave the first vote* in the Roman Comitia ; their vote was usually followed by the rest, so that it was almost always *paramount*. Hence the word came to be applied to royal rights ; and hence (with one, or both, of these allusive meanings) it is used by Bacon to denote instances of *paramount importance*. See the summary of the *Delineatio* above, p. 360, for a previous mention of them.

The titles of the twenty-seven Instances may perhaps be stimulative to the memory of those who have read the *Novum Organum*, and suggestive to the imagination of those who have not. They are as follows : (1) Solitary ; (2) Migratory ; (3) Striking or Shining (ostensive) ; (4) Clandestine, or of the Twilight ; (5) Constitutive ; (6) Conformable, or, of Analogy ; (7) Singular, or Heteroclites ; (8) Deviating ; (9) Bordering, or Participles (limitaneæ) ; (10) of Power, or, of the Fasces ; (11) of Companionship and Enmity ; (12) Ultimity or Limit ; (13) of Alliance ; (14) of the Finger-post (*crucis*), hence the well-known *crucial* instance ; (15) of Divorce ; (16) of the Door ; (17) Summoning Instances ; (18) of the Road, or Travelling Instances ; (19) Supplementary or Substitutive ; (20) Dissecting or Awakening Instances ; (21) of the Rod or Rule ; (22) of the

seven come what are called *Solitary Instances.* These "exhibit the nature under investigation in subjects which have nothing in common with other subjects except that nature;" *e.g.* suppose we are investigating colour; then prisms, crystals, dews, &c.—which show colours, not only in themselves, but externally on a wall—are *Solitary Instances*; for these have *nothing in common* with the colours fixed in flowers, coloured stones, metals, &c., *except the colour :* " from which we easily gather that colour is nothing more than a modification of the image of light received upon the object, resulting in the former case from the different degrees of incidence, in the latter from the various textures and configurations of the body." In this and many others of the *Prerogative Instances* Bacon exhibits something of the intuition of a discoverer; and in the selection of the two examples just mentioned he was peculiarly happy; for it was by means of them that Newton afterwards found out the composition of light. But no amount of admiration for the ingenuity of occasional observations and for the keenness of occasional insight can blind us to the fact that they bring us little if at all nearer to the formation of a true conception of Simple Natures, without which the Method of Exclusions will not work, and consequently the Key of Interpretation will unlock nothing. Yet hopeful to the last, the author concludes this small fragment of an immense work with a promise couched in the language of undaunted faith :

" But now I must proceed to the supports and rectifications of Induction ; and then to Concretes and Latent Processes and Latent Configurations, and the rest, as set forth in order in the twenty-first Aphorism ; that at length (like an honest and faithful guardian) I may hand over to men their fortunes, now that their Understanding is emancipated, and as it were come of age ; whence there cannot but follow an improvement in man's estate and an enlargement of his power over nature. For man, by the Fall, fell at the same time from his estate of innocency and from his dominion over creation. Both of these losses however can, even in this life, be in some part repaired ; the former by religion and faith, the latter by arts and sciences."

Course or Water (*i.e.,* the water-clock) ; (23) of Quantity, or Doses of Nature ; (24) of Strife or Predominance ; (25) Intimating Instances ; (26) Polychrest, or of General Use; (27) Magical Instances.

§ 55 Contributions to the Third Part of the " Instauratio Magna "

The Third Part of the *Instauratio Magna* was to be (see the *Distributio Operis*, p. 378 above) the *Phenomena of the Universe, or History Natural and Experimental*, adapted for the foundation of Philosophy. Accordingly in the same year in which Bacon published the unfinished *Novum Organum*, he also published a short treatise entitled *Preparation for a Natural and Experimental History (Parasceue ad Historiam Naturalem et Experimentalem).*[1]

A Preface informs us that his object is to incite others to co-operate with him in the vast work of preparing the materials for the *Natural History;* this he cannot hope to perform unaided, whereas that which relates to the work of the Understanding itself he may accomplish by his own efforts. Another reason that he gives for busying himself with a task somewhat beneath him is the desire to prescribe the plan of the proposed History, lest his followers should imitate the pattern of the cumbrous useless histories of his predecessors. Without such a History nothing can be effected, no, not even though all the world should convert itself into a University for the study of Philosophy. But with it—if there be added to it such auxiliary and light-giving experiments as, in the very course of Interpretation, will either present themselves or will have to be found out—the investigation of nature and of all sciences will be the work of a few years.

Repeating the division used in the *Advancement of Learning*, he would divide Nature triply into (1) Nature free, in her generations ; (2) Nature free, in her errors ; (3) Nature in bondage, under art or experiment. The Universe is not to be contracted to suit the prejudices of the Understanding ; but the Understanding is so to expand itself as to embrace the spirit of the Universe ; that philosophers may no longer skip like fairies in their own little enchanted rings, but move in a circuit wide as the world itself.

In collecting instances from arts, we are to choose those that

[1] Spedding, *Works*, i. 369-414.

conduce not to the perfection of arts themselves, but to Axioms; and we are to be guided in our choice by the study of the Pre-rogatives of Instances. Everything relating both to bodies and virtues in Nature is to be set forth (as far as may be) numbered, weighed, or measured. As to the history of Cardinal Virtues in Nature mentioned in the *Distributio Operis*, this must be indeed collected before we come to the work of Interpretation; " but I reserve this part for myself, since, until men have come to be a little more familiar with Nature, I cannot venture to rely very much on other people's industry in that matter."

The *Parasceue* resembles the *Novum Organum* in ending with an unfulfilled promise and a long list of titles :

"And now we ought to proceed to the delineation of the Particular Histories. But I have at present" (this was 1620, the year before his fall, and he was then Lord Chancellor) "so many distracting occupations that I can only find time to subjoin a catalogue of their titles. As soon however as I have leisure, I mean to draw up a set of questions on the several sub-jects. . . . In other words (according to the practice in civil suits) even so in this great Plea and Suit granted by the divine favour and providence, whereby Mankind seeks to recover its right against Nature, I intend to subject both Nature and the Arts to an examination upon interrogatories."

Here follow one hundred and thirty titles of Histories (beginning with Nature " free in generations "); 1—21 dealing with parts of the elements; 22—25 with the four elements themselves; 26—40 with species; 41—128 with human nature and arts (including even the arts of cooking, dyeing, riding, &c.); 129 and 130 with the history of the natures and powers of numbers and figures.

Having completed in the *Parasceue*, or *Preparation*, his sketch of that part of the third portion of the *Instauratio Magna* (*Phenomena of the Universe, or History Natural and Experimental*) which his followers might be trusted to execute, Bacon proceeded, two years afterwards (1622), to execute that part which he had " reserved for himself "—the *History of the Cardinal Virtues*. This was published in parts under the title, *Natural and Experimental History for the Foundation of Philosophy, or Phenomena of the Universe, being the Third Part of the " Instauratio Magna."* At this time (the year after his fall) Bacon had bound

---

[1] Spedding, *Works*, ii. 3-228.

himself "as by a vow" to complete and set forth, every month,
one or more parts of the Natural History; and this treatise
contains titles for the labours of six months: viz. the Histories
of (1) the Winds; (2) Dense and Rare, or the Contraction and
Expansion of Matter in Space; (3) Heavy and Light; (4)
the Sympathy and Antipathy of Things; (5) Sulphur, Mercury,
and Salt; (6) Life and Death.

But, like the *Novum Organum* and the *Parasceue*, this treatise
also promises more than was performed. Of several of these
Histories nothing but the Introduction was completed. That
Bacon still retained his confidence in his scheme of a Natural
History, appears from the language in which he dedicates the
Phenomena to the Prince of Wales: "A thing like a grain of
mustard-seed, very small in itself, yet a pledge of those things
which, by the grace of God, will come hereafter. . . . . For a
small and well-ordered Natural History is *the Key of all knowledge and operation.*" There is no trace of any disappointment
at his inability to perfect the *Novum Organum*, nor any vestige
of suspicion that the *Novum Organum* might possibly prove
unworkable. He admits indeed that not a few things, "and
these amongst the most important," remain to be completed in
the *Organum;* but he *advisedly* passes them over for the
present, his design being, so he informs his readers, rather to
advance the universal work of the Instauration in many things
than to perfect it in a few; for even if the *Organum* were
completed, and men willing to use it, *they could make little
progress without the Natural History,* "whereas the Natural
History without the *Organum*, would advance it not a little."
The Introduction to the *Phenomena* concludes with a prayer
that God will protect and direct the work. But all this
devotion and pathetic confidence cannot conceal the fact that
his trust in the New Natural History appears to increase
in proportion to his distrust of the New Induction: and it is
startling indeed to find the term "Key" now transferred from
the latter to the former; which he now ventures to call "the
Key of all knowledge and operation."

To come however to the plan of the work. It will be
remembered that the conclusion of the *Novum Organum* contains
a promise to proceed "to the supports and rectifications of

Induction, and next, to *Concretes*, and Latent *Processes*, and Latent *Configurations*." The plan of the *Phenomena* (*Norma Historiae Praesentis*) exhibits Bacon apparently attempting to carry out this resolution.

Although, he says, we have previously sketched our plan of History in the *Parasceue*, we will now give a more detailed scheme of it. To the Titles included in the Catalogue of the *Parasceue*, "which pertain to *Concretes*, we superadd titles concerning Abstract Natures,[1] whereof, in the same work, we made mention, as being a History reserved for our own efforts. These are (1) Diverse *Configurations* of Matter, or Forms of the First Class ; (2) Simple Motions ; (3) Sums of Motion " (see *Summae Motuum*, or Compound Motions, *De Augmentis*, iii. 4) ; " (4) Measures of Motions ; some others. Of these I have completed a New Alphabet and placed it at the end of this volume."

Under each title, after an Introduction, particular Topics or Articles of Inquiry, will be propounded, to throw light on present, and to stimulate future, investigations. Histories and Experiments will occupy the first place, but, where they are wanting, there will be injunctions for Experiments, forming a kind of " Designed History " ; and there will be indications of the method of experimenting, and cautions against fallacies. There will also be the Author's Observations on the History and Experiments, and speculations or rudimentary Interpretations concerning causes (*Commentationes et tanquam rudimenta quaedam Interpretationis de Causis*) sparingly interspersed. There will also be Provisional Rules or Imperfect Axioms (*Canones Mobiles, sive Axiomata Inchoata*) ;[2] Reminders concerning Practice ; and a list of Works Impossible, or Undiscovered.

The Plan concludes thus :

" It is evident, from what has been said above, that the present History not only supplies the place of the Third Part of the Instauration " (*Phaenomena Universi*, see p. 378), " but is no mean preparation for (1) the Fourth Part " [*i.e. Scala Intellectus*, the *Ladder of the Understanding*, which was to contain examples of the New Method and of the Topics of Inquiry] ; " and it is also a preparation for (2) the Sixth Part *Secunda Philosophia* " [the Second Philosophy or Active Science, which was to contain the results of the application of the New Philosophy to all phenomena] " by reason of the Major Observations, the Speculations, and the Provisional Rules."[3]

First in the Histories comes the History of the Winds, in which the Designed History, or sketch of proposed Experiments or Inquiries, far exceeds in length the actual History ; the latter

---

[1] *i.e.* the Cardinal Virtues of Nature, see p. 399.
[2] An apparent recognition of the use of *Working Hypotheses*.
[3] Spedding, *Works*, ii. 17, 18.

being taken mainly from Pliny, Aristotle, and Acosta. On windmills Bacon appears to write from his own experiments; and his remarks reveal that looseness of mind which he occasionally evinces when he descends to detail. Finding that, by increasing the number of vanes, the effect of the wind is increased, he ascribed the motion of the vanes, not to the direct action of the wind, but to a lateral reaction of the air compressed between the vanes; forgetting that, while increasing the vanes, he had also increased the surface exposed to the wind, and that, according to his theory, a windmill with one sail only ought to remain stationary. On the other hand he suggests several observations which, if they could have been set on foot throughout Europe, might by this time have issued in results of great practical value.[1]

Next to the History of Winds comes the History of Life and Death, taken by Bacon out of proper place, " because in a matter of so great importance the least delay is costly." His theory is to this effect:

> In living bodies two kinds of spirits exist: 1st, a crude, mortuary spirit, such as is present also in inorganic bodies, a spirit imponderable, intangible, and discernible in its operations only; 2nd, an animal or vital spirit, which gives rise to the phenomena of life. This vital spirit tends to slip out of the body, and also, like a slow fire, to consume the body; and it acts (1) by attenuating moisture; (2) by escaping through the pores; (3) by causing the contraction of the grosser parts of the body, as is apparent immediately after the emission of the spirit in death. We ought therefore to inquire about the Nature of durable and non-durable bodies (stones and vegetables, as well as animals) and to neutralize the destructive action of the mortuary and the vital spirits by diet and medicine.

Whatever may be said about Bacon's theory, the manner in which it has been set forth and the remarks by which it is accompanied "have been much commended," says Mr. Ellis, " by one of the greatest of medical writers (Haller)."[2]

The New Alphabet has not yet been described; yet it deserves description as showing Bacon's fondness for subdivisions and lengthy titles, and his confidence, to the last, that Nature can be conquered by mere accumulation of facts classified in mechanical arrangements.

[1] Spedding, *Works*, ii. 19-78.   [2] *Ibid.* ii. 91-228.

" Greater Masses. Sixty-seventh Inquiry, or that concerning the Earth ; denoted by τ τ τ.[1] Greater Masses. Sixty-eighth Inquiry, or that concerning Water ; denoted by υ, υ, υ.[1] Greater Masses. Sixty-ninth Inquiry, or that concerning Air ; denoted by φ, φ, φ." [1]

After three more of these titles of the " Greater Masses," he comes to " Conditions of Beings " :

" We must institute an inquiry concerning Existence and Non-Existence, which comes seventy-third in order, and is marked by *a a a a*.

" Conditions of Beings ; or concerning Existence and Non-Existence ; denoted by *a a a a*.

" Possibility and Impossibility are nothing else than Potentiality or Non-Potentiality of Being. Let the seventy-fourth inquiry be on this subject, and be marked β β β β.

" Conditions of Beings. Concerning Possibility and Impossibility ; denoted by β β β β.

" Much and Little, Rare and Common, are the Potentialities of Being in Quantity. Let the seventy-fifth inquiry be concerning them, and be marked by γ γ γ γ.

" Conditions of Being (*sic*). Concerning Much and Little ; denoted by γ γ γ γ." [2]

With the same tedious prolixity follow three more titles— Concerning the Durable and the Transitory ; the Natural and the Monstrous ; the Natural and the Artificial. The treatise terminates with the same prayer as that which introduces the *Phenomena*.

" Such then is the rule and plan of the Alphabet. May God the Maker, the Preserver, the Renewer (" Instaurator ") of the Universe (of His love and compassion to man) protect and guide this work, both in its ascent to His glory, and its descent to the good of man, through His only Son, God with us."

As we peruse these unnecessary repetitions of merely mechanical signs, who can escape the impression that the Author takes a pleasure in lingering over the mere appearance of order and accomplishment in his unfinished system, and that he is, unconsciously, glad of any pretext by which he can find scope for his restless activity, and at the same time deceive himself into the belief that he is making progress, while shutting his eyes to unforeseen obstacles which have made progress impossible !

[1] The Greek letters denote respectively 67, 68, and 69.
[2] Spedding, *Works*, ii. 85-88.

In the same year (1623) was written (though not published till 1658) the *History of Density and Rarity*, principally noteworthy because Bacon appears from it to have been ignorant of the method of calculating specific gravities published by Ghetaldus twenty years before and substantially in use now. He gives, instead, a method of his own which has not commended itself to modern science.[1]

A short paper entitled *Topics of Inquiry concerning Light and Luminous Matter* would be interesting if it could be shown that it was written this year, as exhibiting an arrangement different from that of the other treatises in the *Phenomena*, and more similar to that in the *Novum Organum*, with its Tables of Presence, of Absence in Proximity, and of Degrees. But the absence of all mention of the telescope, to which Bacon refers in the year 1612, indicates that this fragment was written before that year.[2]

§ 56 "De Augmentis";[3] "Sylva Sylvarum"[4]

In 1623 was published the *De Augmentis et Dignitate Scientiae*, a greatly amplified Latin Translation of the *Advancement of Learning*. It will be remembered that the *Advancement of Learning* consisted of two books, one on the Dignity of Learning, the other on the Divisions of Learning, and that on the title-page of the *Novum Organum* in 1620, occur these words: "The First Part of the Instauration, which embraces the *Divisions of Learning*, is wanting; but these Divisions may be in some measure obtained from the Second Book of the *Advancement of Learning*." The Latin Translation accordingly amplifies the "Divisions" contained in the Second Book of the *Advancement* into eight books. The First Book of the *Advancement*, though retained in the Translation, is treated as a mere Introduction on the Dignity of Science, and is not even mentioned in the Introductory Table of the Divisions of Learning.

---

[1] Spedding, *Works*, ii. 229-306.   [2] *Ibid.* ii. 313-324.
[3] *Ibid.* i. 414-837. For a summary of the English version, the *Advancement of Learning*, see Appendix I., pp. 461-475, below.
[4] *Ibid.* ii. 325-686.

Writing to a correspondent in Italy two years after the publication of this work,[1] Bacon describes the *De Augmentis* as the
First Part of the Instauration. But although the work acquires
additional importance from the definite place thus assigned to
it in his system, it does not greatly differ, except in amplitude
of detail and illustration, from the *Advancement of Learning.*
Among the more important differences, it is to be noted that,
whereas the *Advancement* divides History into Natural, Civil,
Ecclesiastical and Literary, the *De Augmentis* adopts the dual
division into Natural and Civil; Civil History being made to
comprise Ecclesiastical and Literary. Again in the *Advancement* there are three fallacies, in the *De Augmentis* there are
four Idols. Instead of dividing the Operative part of Natural
Philosophy into three parts (Experimental, Philosophical, and
Magical) the *De Augmentis* divides it into two (Mechanic and
Magic). And generally the passages dealing with Science are
amplified, while allusions to England and English History are
omitted or subordinated. A work intended to be read in Italy
must needs avoid condemnation of Romish errors, and it is
interesting to note how many of such condemnations and other
references to religion are omitted in the Latin Translation :
Bacon himself tells the King [2] that he had this object in view :
" I have been mine own *Index Expurgatorius* that it may be
read in all places."

The *Sylva Sylvarum*, published in 1627 after Bacon's death,

---

[1] Spedding, vii. 530–2, letter to Father Fulgentio.

[2] Spedding, vii. 436.

[3] Professor Fowler (*Francis Bacon*, p. 182) appears to attribute the theological
differences between the *Advancement of Learning* and the *De Augmentis* to some
change of mind in the Author. " How far Bacon's confidence in ' the ship of the
church ' was implicit, and without exception, is, I think, somewhat doubtful.
For it is a notable fact (which I have not seen elsewhere noticed) that the passage
on the nature and attributes of God, including certain statements on the Trinity
and the division of the elect or reprobate, which occurs towards the end of the
Advancement of Learning, is altogether left out in the *De Augmentis*, published
eighteen years afterwards."

But it will be found that *the whole of the section* on theology in the *Advancement of Learning* is condensed or modified in the Latin version, so as to give less
offence to readers in France or Italy. And the same care to remove anything
offensive to foreign readers will be found to have modified the *whole of the text* of
the Latin Translation both of the *Advancement* and of the *Essays*. Take for
example the following passage (*Adv.* I. iii. 3) : "The Jesuits, of whom, although
in regard of their superstition I may say, *Quo meliores, eo deteriores*, &c."—on
which Mr. Aldis Wright remarks, " the whole clause is modified in the *De
Augmentis to avoid giving offence to Roman Catholics.*"

is supposed to have been written about 1624.[1] As a collection
of observations was called in Bacon's metaphorical language
Sylva (see p. 363, above, *Sylva vel Materies*) this treatise is
naturally called *Sylva Sylvarum*, being a Collection of Collections. It has been shown by Mr. Ellis that the order of many
of these observations, which are the results of Bacon's reading,
*follows the order of the book from which they happen to have
been extracted ;* so that, for example, it is possible in the *Sylva*
to trace the travels of Sandys from Lemnos to Constantinople
and thence to Egypt. This *Sylva* therefore is not a classified
Natural History, but rather a haphazard collection of raw
material. Although to modern readers many of the observations may seem to savour too much of the wonderful and occasionally of the absurd, yet as compared with the contemporary
standard of Natural History, they are declared by Mr. Ellis to
be philosophical and suggestive.

Written after the *Sylva Sylvarum* come two brief papers, one
called *Scala Intellectus,* or *Ladder of the Understanding,* and the
other *Prodromi sive Anticipationes Philosophiae Secundae,* that is,
Forerunners or Anticipations of the Second Philosophy.[2] In
these—Bacon's last philosophical efforts—we see him still
pressing forward on his career of imaginary conquest, leaving
behind him half-conquered or unconquered regions for others
to occupy. The *Scala* tells us that:

The beginning of the path has been marked out in the Author's second
work, the *Novum Organum.* Entering forthwith upon that path he has
treated of the Phenomena of the Universe and their History in a third
work, wherein he has penetrated and passed through the dark and tangled
Wood of Nature.[3] It now remains to ascend to a more open but a more
arduous region, emerging from the Wood to the spurs of the mountain. He
therefore proposes to give, as a Ladder of the Understanding, examples of
the Legitimate Investigation of which he had set forth the theory in the
Organum. Let but the object be indicated, and others with more leisure
and fewer obstacles will easily achieve it.[4]

Prodromi, or *Forerunners,* is the title of the Fifth Part of the
Instauration (see p. 378). In the short Preface thus entitled

---

[1] Spedding, *Works,* ii. 325-686.
[2] See above, p. 378, for the place these were to fill in the *Magna Instauratio.*
[3] Note the play on " Wood " or " Sylva " ; and see " Sylva Sylvarum " above.
[4] Spedding, *Works,* ii. 687-689.

(for it is no more than a Preface), Bacon declares that a compromise between the New and Old Philosophy is not unjustifiable, at least thus far:

> A man of average ability may investigate the secrets of Nature without the exact use of the *Organum*, if he will but cast aside the Idols and study things instead of books. Such a student may lay more successful siege to Nature than the mere reader of books, even though the former has not employed the regular engines of war (*machinas non admoverit*) nor followed the Rule of Interpretation. Much more is it lawful for him to entertain this hope about himself, since his mind has been strengthened by the practice and exercise of interpreting Nature. Yet he will not bind himself by these anticipations, but will reserve everything for the final decision of the Second and Inductive Philosophy ; and he will set them forth sparsely, not connectedly, because this method is most suitable for fresh-sprung and budding sciences.[1]

Thus, with a Preface, and an unfulfilled intention, ends the *Magna Instauratio*.

§ 57 THE MERITS AND DEMERITS OF BACON'S PHILOSOPHY

As to the demerits of Bacon's Philosophy there is a general agreement, so far as this, that it has been of no direct use in making discoveries. Modern Science recognizes as an effectual aid in research the " working hypothesis " which Bacon is generally said to ignore. Yet even in some of his earlier teatises, he accepts a *Provisional Table* which was to prepare the way for the New Table (*Chartae Novellae*) ;[2] and the same tendency may be discerned in the *Prima Vindemiatio, or Permissio Intellectus* (see p. 393) as well as in the *Provisional Rules* (*Mobiles Canones*, see p. 401) and in the *Anticipationes Secundae Philosophiae*. In his later works, at all events (as for example in the *Historia Vitae et Mortis*) he seems to recognize the utility or necessity of provisional hypotheses. We have also seen in the extract from the *Prodromi* quoted in the last paragraph that the *Instauratio Magna* closes with a recognition of the occasional utility of this

[1] Spedding, *Works*, ii. 690-692.
[2] See the summary of the *Delineatio*, twelfth para raph, p. 359, above.

irregularity. No doubt, in his Astronomical treatises, he inveighs against all astronomical hypotheses, even against that of Copernicus. But there was much excuse for such invective. The Introduction to the *Copernican Astronomy* itself declared not only that the Copernican system was hypothetical, but also that in astronomy *no absolute truth could be expected ;* [1] and it was against this habit of despair in Science that Bacon principally directed his attacks. It must be admitted, however, that generally Bacon does not sufficiently recognize the necessity of some guiding conception (of the nature of a hypothesis) in selecting phenomena from the first.

A more serious objection is, that he starts with, and never consciously divests himself of, *a prejudice in favour of the simplicity of Nature, disposing him to exaggerate the facility of its analysis.* He believes for example that the surest way to make gold is to ascertain the causes of its qualities, viz., weight, colour, closeness of parts, pliancy, freedom from rust, together with the Axioms that concern those Causes, and then it is only necessary to superinduce these qualities upon any nature in order to transform that nature to gold. His theory is that Nature speaks, as it were, a language of an infinite vocabulary, but of a limited alphabet. Master the alphabet, and you can reproduce the countless variations of the words. This is the problem stated in the *Valerius Terminus,* and, so stated, it seems easy of solution.

But it has been pointed out by Dr. Whewell that, instead of investigating *simple natures,* modern discoverers have succeeded by investigating the Laws of *special phenomena.* Thus, instead of investigating Heat, men of science have studied the Laws of Conduction, Radiation, Specific Heat, Latent Heat; then have followed hypotheses about Heat itself, which have been verified, amended, and finally adopted.

Subsequently Bacon became aware that it is not so easy to form a right conception of a single letter of Nature's Alphabet. Our very notions of "simple natures" are often wrong and require correction. Hence in the *Partis Secundae Delineatio* he had awakened to the necessity of the task of constructing a *bona notio,* or *right conception of a simple nature.* This task

[1] See above, p. 374.

was to have been performed in the *Novum Organum*, as it was then designed; and *the omission of it indicates that Bacon found it impossible*. At the time of writing the *Novum Organum* he seems to have perceived that the formation of a *bona notio* and the establishment of an Axiom were so closely intertwined that the one could not be presented independently of the other and his view now became, that at first Axioms must be established by means of the commonly received conceptions, and subsequently these conceptions must be rectified by means of the ulterior aids to the mind (the *fortiora auxilia in usum intellectus*) which he promises in the nineteenth Aphorism of the Second Book of the *Novum Organum*, but never actually gives. But, with this failure, there falls at once the chief claim of the New Philosophy, the claim of the New Instrument to be (like the compasses in the hand of an inferior draughtsman) unerring in its operation, even when employed by an operator of only average ability. These then appear the two internal causes of the failure of Bacon's Natural Philosophy; first, the undue neglect of the use of the Imagination in scientific research, secondly, a prejudice in favour of a particular kind of simplicity in Nature.

But a third charge has been in times past frequently, and is still occasionally, brought against the Baconian philosophy; it is accused of being vulgarly "utilitarian," devoted to the material utilities of men.

This charge, thus worded, is easily refuted. No reader of the *Advancement of Learning*, or even of the brief summary of it given further on,[1] can deny that Bacon "took *all Nature* for his province,"—not material nature merely, but human nature also with its faculties, the memory, the will, the imagination. It is true indeed that he gives little attention to the discussion —and probably he had not much fitness or ability for the discussion—of those fundamental conceptions which have dazzled and attracted many so-called philosophers from the time when philosophy began, such as Time, Space, Necessity, Free Will, Cause, Effect, and the like. And, as to the investigation of Final Causes, he used a language of deprecation which Pope perhaps had in his mind when he described a Philosophy of

---

[1] See Appendix II. pp. 461-475.

"Second Causes" as forerunning the Advent of the Goddess of Dulness:

> "Philosophy, that leaned on Heav'n before,
> Shrinks to her second cause, and is no more."

But at least a Baconian may reply not only that the so-called philosophical discussions of these primary notions have been barren, but also that the Baconian philosophy itself has indirectly illustrated them. Our conceptions of Time and Space, for example, have been amplified and ennobled far more by the Newtonian Philosophy of "second causes"—which has led us to the knowledge of stars so remote that centuries elapse before a ray from them can reach us—than by whole disquisitions on the mere meaning or origin of the notions Space and Time. And the same may be said, when Bacon is charged with a loose and superficial treatment of questions bearing on human nature. Certainly he has not put forth much that was new, nor has he even collected much that was old and worth collecting; but he has at least warned us off from trespassing on the pleasant paths of Cloudland speculators, the inventors of names without meanings, the hair-splitting discriminators, the cobweb-theory spinners; he has set up a finger-post pointing to the poets, the historians, and the physicians,—in other words to the records of the *facts* of human nature, when human nature is surrounded by the most various circumstances and subjected to the most various tests,—as being a more promising source whence we may hope to gain some fresh knowledge as to what we are, and how we may be made better than we are.

Physical Science, with Bacon, rises to the level of a Religion. It is God's will that His Laws should be discovered by the faculties which He Himself has given to men. The discovery of these Laws would no doubt result in the increase of the material powers and comforts of men; but the discovery *in itself* seemed to Bacon a great and holy work, as being an exercise of God-given faculties in the way in which God intended them to be exercised. Not only therefore pity for men, but also allegiance to God stimulates him on the path of investigation. The errors of the ancient philosophers, their brain-creations, and power-displays, their "invented systems of the Universe like so

many arguments of plays," their elegant philosophies, "out of
the cells, each of his own imagination, as out of Plato's cave,"[1]
are all, in Bacon's estimation, not mere errors, but almost—
now, at all events, when the mischief of their errors has been
revealed—of the nature of sins.

"We copy the sin of our first parents while we suffer for it. They wished
to be like God, but their posterity wish to be even greater. For we create
worlds, we direct and domineer over nature, we will have it that all things
are as in our folly we think they *should be*, not as seems fittest to the
Divine wisdom, or as they are found to be in fact ; and I know not whether
we more distort the facts of nature or of our own wits ; but we clearly impress the stamp of our own image on the creatures and works of God,
instead of carefully examining and recognizing in them the stamp of the
Creator himself. Wherefore our dominion over creatures is a second time
forfeited, not undeservedly ; and whereas after the fall of man some power
over the resistance of creatures was still left to him—the power of subduing
and managing them by true and solid arts—yet this too through our inso-
lence, and because we desire to be like God and to follow the dictates of our
own reason, we in great part lose.

"If, therefore, there be any humility towards the Creator, any reverence
for, or disposition to magnify, His works, any charity for man and anxiety
to relieve his sorrows and necessities, any love of truth in nature, any
hatred of darkness, any desire for the purification of the understanding, we
must entreat men again and again to discard, or at least banish for a while,
these volatile and preposterous philosophies which have preferred theses to
hypotheses, led experience captive, and triumphed over the works of God.
Drawing nigh in all humility and reverence they must unroll the volume of
Creation ; thereon must they dwell and meditate ; this must they peruse
purely and sincerely with minds washed clean from preconceived opinions.
For this is that sound and language which ' went forth into all lands,' and
did not incur the confusion of Babel ; this should men study to be perfect
in, and, becoming again as little children, condescend to take the alphabet of
it into their hands, and spare no pains to search and unravel the interpretation thereof, but pursue it strenuously and persevere even unto death."[2]

The study of Physical Science, pursued in this spirit and
with these objects, can hardly be described as vulgarly utilitarian or as ministering to the merely material wants of men.

About the merits of Bacon's philosophy there is not the same
agreement as about the demerits. Some have asserted, and not
without show of reason, that whereas Bacon's system was,
according to his own account, quite new, it is in reality, so far as

---

[1] The *Phenomena of the Universe*, *Works*, v. 131.
[2] *Ib.* 131–133, and ii. 14–15.

it is true, not new; and so far as it is new, not true. But this language, however plausible, is not a fair way of putting the case, when we are speaking of merit. Because Bacon exaggerated the novelty and utility of his philosophy, it does not follow that it was not to some extent new, and, to a still greater extent, useful. To have concentrated and vitalized a great multitude of diffused, scarce-recognized, and inert truths, is not a very different work from discovering truth; and this at least Bacon did.

Never before had scientific Induction been so clearly set before the world and so sharply distinguished from the "puerile" enumerative Induction prevalent among the Aristotelians; and although the pretensions of the new method to facility and certainty were raised too high, they cannot be dismissed as altogether false. Again, the cautions against the inherent fallacies of the mind; the inculcation of the study of nature and not books, of things and not words; the subordination of the Syllogism to Induction; the directions to use, to vary, and to select experiments, illustrated by many experiments of Bacon's own devising, some of which are by high authority deemed valuable as well as original; the erection of a scientific standard for Natural History; the recommendation, practically exemplified, to attend to the small things and unpretending processes of Nature; the great stress laid upon the advantages of the intelligent co-operation of many workers to one end; and, above all perhaps, the hopeful confidence with which the Founder of the New Philosophy urges his disciples to cast away old conceptions and devote themselves anew to the study of Nature in the perfect certainty that her secrets will be so revealed as to make man her Master—all these unquestionable characteristics of Bacon's works produce on his readers an impression which, even now in these days of scientific achievement, cannot be regarded as false, or useless, or antiquated.

It is in the application of his philosophy to special subjects that he appears at his weakest. What the discoverer of the circulation of the blood thought of his writings, so far as they touched on physiology, we have already heard;[1] his astronomical theories would now be deemed monstrosities;

[1] See above, p. 176.

and from his works on the Winds, Tides, Density, and Heat, might be collected a long list of errors and inaccuracies. Against these may be set however observations and precepts so intuitively felicitous that they have elicited the approval of Haller and Herschel, the latter of whom declares that some of Bacon's suggested experiments on light might well be supposed to have been borrowed from Newton; and the results at which he arrived, in the investigation of Heat, he sets forth in language not greatly differing from that which in modern times describes Heat as a Mode of Motion. On the whole, however, the balance (so far as concerns special subjects) is decidedly against Bacon; for many of his inaccuracies and errors are due to his own carelessness, and still more to his ignorance of the previous discoveries of his contemporaries. His first treatise on Heat, which must have been written long after the discovery of the principle of the Thermometer, makes no reference to it, and even in the *Novum Organum*, where he mentions the air thermometer, he still proceeds on the old theory that some things are hot, others (liquids for example) cold: "Experiments with a thermometer would have shown that they were not. But these Bacon did not try" (Ellis). Similarly the want of attention to the discoveries of Galileo made him commit himself to an opposition (the more pronounced as he grew older) against the Copernican theory of astronomy.

Whether the avoidance of these errors would have suggested to him any modification of his whole system, may be doubted; correct views of astronomy,[1] it is said, would probably not have helped him to perfect the *Novum Organum*. But these and other glaring errors have always been blemishes on his reputation as a philosopher, and have led many to under-rate his industry and scientific intuition. This is perhaps a just retribution. It was not want of industry, but want of leisure, and the desire to do many things, that engendered this habit of inaccuracy and this negligence of the discoveries of others: and for his want of leisure he was himself to blame, because he deliberately preferred the life of a courtier and a politician to the life of a seeker after truth.

Yet, as a popularizer of truth, he gained from his position, of

[1] Professor Fowler's *Francis Bacon*, p. 196.

a great person in the Court, some advantages which may be
thought to compensate for the disadvantages to which he
subjected himself, as a worker in the field of Science. The
study of things instead of words, and the practice of the Art of
Experimentation—which had been degraded by its association
with the Alchemists—received dignity when they were recommended by the precept and example of a Lord Chancellor.
"There can be little doubt" says Professor Fowler,[1] "that the
foundation of the Royal Society in England (and possibly the
same origin may be assigned to some similar societies on the
continent) was due to the impulse given by Bacon to the study of
experimental science and the plans which he had devised for its
prosecution." These words point to a vague, indefinite kind of
influence, by no means such as Bacon himself would have
preferred. Although in one or two famous passages he describes
himself as a mere " bell-ringer " to "call the other wits together,"
he elsewhere states his claims for himself, or rather for his work,
in a far higher tone. But, after all, we may recognize in the
result a certain fitness of things. If, according to Harvey's sneer,
he wrote about philosophy like a Lord Chancellor, at all events
it may be retorted that he also popularized philosophy like a
Lord Chancellor. If his influence is vague and indefinite, it
will probably on that very account be all the more lasting.
Few men now read the works of Copernicus or Kepler.
Their great discoveries are transferred to the works of later
authors. But no English-speaking author can ever hope to
transfer to himself the Baconian charm. By a strange irony of
Providence, the great depreciator of words and the professed
despiser of "terrestrial hope" seems destined to derive an
immortal memory from the rich variety of his style and the
vastness of his too sanguine expectations.

[1] *Francis Bacon*, p. 196.

LITERARY WORKS

§ 58 THE "NEW ATLANTIS;"[1] "HISTORY OF KING HENRY VII."[2]

As early as 1608 we find Bacon in the *Commentarius Solutus* (see p. 154) seriously considering the possibility of securing some College for combined research subject to his direction; "laying for a place to command wits and pens; Westminster, Eton, Winchester, Trinity or St. John's at Cambridge, Magdalene College, Oxford."[3]   He even enters into details of the arrangements for the proposed College :

" Giving pensions to four, for search to compile the two histories *ut supra* (*i.e.* the *History of Marvels* and the *History of Mechanical Arts*). Foundation of a college for Inventors. Two galleries with statuas for Inventors past, and spaces, or bases, for Inventors to come. And a Library and an Inginary. Query, of the order and discipline, to be mixed with some points popular to invite many to contribute and join. Query, of the rules and prescripts of their studies and inquiries. Allowance for travelling. Allowance for experiments. Intelligence and correspondence with the Universities abroad. Query, of the manner and prescripts touching secrecy, tradition, and publication. Query, of removes and expulsions in case, within a time, some invention worthy be not produced. And likewise query of the honours and rewards for inventions. Vaults, furnaces, terraces for insulation, workhouses of all sorts."

Going further back, to 1594, we find Bacon, in the *Gesta Grayorum*,[4] suggesting as a work fit for a mighty Prince, the creation of a great Palace of Invention, with "a most perfect and general library," "a spacious, wonderful garden," "a goodly huge cabinet or museum," and "such a still-house, so furnished with mills, instruments, furnaces, and vessels, as may be a palace fit for a philosopher's stone."   It seems probable that soon after the death of Cecil in 1612, when Bacon aspired to be the King's chief counsellor as well as the founder of a new philosophy,

---

[1] Spedding, *Works*, iii. 119-166.
[3] Spedding, iv. 66.
[2] *Ibid.* vi. 1-264.
[4] See above, p. 44.

and when the distractions of political and legal business prevented him from doing any serious work at philosophy, he sat down to amuse himself, and perhaps to excite the co-operation of others, by painting a bright picture of an ideal Palace of Invention in an ideal State. To this fragment he gave the name of the *New Atlantis*.[1]

It was published by Dr. Rawley, Bacon's Chaplain, in 1627, at the end of the volume containing the *Sylva Sylvarum*, with a Preface in which the editor informs us that the object of the work was not only to sketch the model of "Salomon's House" —the name given to the imaginary College instituted for the interpretation of nature—but also to describe the laws and constitution of an ideal commonwealth.

> "This fable my Lord devised to the end that he might exhibit therein a model or description of a college instituted for the interpreting of nature and the producing of great and marvellous works for the benefit of men, under the name of Salomon's House, or the college of the Six Days' Works. And even so far his Lordship hath proceeded, as to finish that part. Certainly the model is more vast and high than can possibly be imitated in all things, notwithstanding most things therein are within men's power to effect. His Lordship thought also in this present fable to have composed a frame of Laws, or of the best state or mould of a Commonwealth ; but foreseeing it would be a long work, his desire of collecting the Natural History diverted him, which he preferred many degrees before it."

The earlier part of the fragment, describing the landing of certain voyagers on the before unknown island called New Atlantis and their first impressions of the natives, dwells in a very interesting way on the qualities which Bacon appears to have rated highest in every nation and perhaps to have regretted most as being absent from his own. The main characteristic of the Atlantic citizens is *orderliness*. They are orderly and seemly alike in their pleasures and in their tasks ; their enjoyments are sober, their splendour is tasteful ; a due division of labour and of the results of labour diffuses universal contentment ; they are humane, courteous, and systematically

---

[1] "The *New Atlantis* has hitherto been ascribed to a later period in Bacon's life, but . . . is twice mentioned by him in an unpublished paper (*Harleian Charters*, iii. D. 14), the date of which lies between the dissolution of Parliament in 1614 and Bacon's appointment as Lord Keeper in 1617."—*Dictionary of National Biography*, "Bacon," by S. R. Gardiner, ii. 344.

liberal to strangers. Special stress is laid on the incorruptibility of all officials, who accompany their rejection of gifts
with the saying that they refuse to be "twice paid."

Bacon is always at his best in prayers, prefaces, thanksgivings,
and dreamy descriptions of what he is intending to do. Moreover this dream was written, not in Latin, like the *Sapientia
Veterum* and almost all the rest of Bacon's more important
works, but in English, and in a very interesting style. An
Oriental love of colour pervades the book; Hebrews and
Hebrew words and Hebrew customs play a prominent part in
it; and no language less dignified than Spanish is tolerated in
its pages. Rich, majestic pomp; sage and solemn ceremonies;
a recognition of degrees, ranks, and orders in the State as being
appointed by God and necessary for the happiness of man; a
religion that combines the charity and breadth of the New
Testament with something of the more earthly and material
thoughts and ritual of the Old; an exaltation of material
wealth, comfort, and prosperity, as being the natural results of a
devout pursuit of Science in an orderly and religious country—
such are the salient features of this most interesting fragment.
Bacon has put into it perhaps more of his own self, his tastes,
his preferences, his ideals, than into any other of his writings
and, as it is comparatively unknown, the reader may be glad
to see a few specimens of it.

The first few lines skilfully transport us far away from home
and from all known regions. After a year's sojourn at Peru,
certain mariners sail for China and Japan by the South Sea,
taking with them victuals for twelve months. A prosperous
voyage of five months is succeeded by contrary winds which
carry them for more than seven months out of their course, so
that their victuals fail. Finding themselves without food "in
the midst of the greatest wilderness of waters in the world,"
they gave themselves up for lost; yet "did they lift up their
hearts and voices to God above who showeth His wonders in the
deep;" and it came to pass that presently they discerned a land
"flat and full of boscage;" but they are prevented from landing
by "divers of the people, with bastons in their hands; yet
without any cries or fierceness, but only as warning us off by
signs that they made." Soon comes one aboard bearing "a

E E

tipstaff of a yellow cane tipped at both ends with blue," and a scroll of yellow parchment, on which was written "in ancient Hebrew, and in ancient Greek, and in good Latin of the School, and in Spanish," a prohibition to land, but a permission to remain in harbour fourteen days and to have all their wants supplied; "this scroll was signed with a stamp of cherubins' wings, not spread but hanging downwards, and by them a cross." [1] Troubled by this prohibition to, land they send a request to be exempted for the sake of their sick. To the servant who takes back their petition, they offer " some reward in pistolets, and a piece of crimson velvet to be presented to the officer; but the servant took them not, nor would scarce look upon them." About three hours afterwards there approaches in a boat a person, as it seemed, of place :

> " He had on him a gown with wide sleeves, of a kind of water chamolet, of an excellent azure colour, far more glossy than ours ; his under-apparel was green ; and so was his hat, being in the form of a turban, daintily made, and not so large as the Turkish turbans ; and the locks of his hair came down below the brims of it. A reverend man was he to behold. . . . (He) stood up, and with a loud voice, in Spanish, asked ' Are ye Christians ?' We answered 'We were' ; fearing the less, because of the cross we had seen in the subscription. At which answer the said person lifted up his right hand towards heaven and drew it softly to his mouth (which is the gesture they use when they thank God) and then said : 'If ye will swear (all of you) by the merits of the Saviour that ye are no pirates, nor have shed blood lawfully nor unlawfully within forty days past, you may have licence to come on land.' "

Soon comes a notary to tender the oath, "holding in his hand a fruit of that country, like an orange, but of colour between orange-tawney and scarlet, which cast a most excellent odour. He used it (as it seemeth) for a preventative against infection." He also refused pistolets with a smile, saying " ' He must not be twice paid for one labour ' : meaning (as I take it) that he had salary sufficient of the State for his service. For (as I afterwards learned) they call an officer that taketh rewards *twice*

---

[1] This combination of the " cherubin " and the " cross " is typical of the combination of the Jewish and the Christian element which may be traced throughout the book. Note, for example, below (as an instance of Hebrew feeling), that even the " lawful " shedding of blood, within forty days, would have precluded the mariners from landing.

paid." Speedily they are escorted into the Strangers' House,
" a fair and spacious house, built of brick, of a somewhat bluer
colour than our brick; and with handsome windows, some of
glass, some of a kind of cambric oiled," with " handsome and
cheerful chambers furnished civilly," and containing, for the
sick, " seventeen cells, very neat ones, having partitions of
cedar wood." And here their guide leaves them—he also
declining pistolets with the exclamation " Twice paid ! "—to
enjoy " right good viands, both for bread and meat, better than
any collegiate diet that I have known in Europe," with " store
of those scarlet oranges for our sick " and " a box of small grey
and whitish pills " to hasten their recovery. After a probation
of three days there enters " a new man that we had not seen
before, clothed in blue as the former was, save that his turban
was white, with a small red cross on the top. He had also a
tippet of white linen. At his coming in, he did bend to us a
little, and put his arms abroad." The new-comer, introducing
himself as the Governor of the House of Strangers, and by
vocation a Christian Priest, announced that the State has
licensed the strangers to remain six weeks ; only none must go
" above a *karan* (that is with them a mile and a-half) from the
walls of the city, without special leave."

On the morrow the Governor, answering such questions as
they like to put, informs them how " this island of Bensalem (for
so they call it in their language) " miraculously received a copy
of the New Testament twenty years after the Ascension. A
pillar of light surmounted by a cross, appearing in the East and
then vanishing, disclosed a small ark of cedar, containing " all
the Canonical books of the Old and New Testament . . .
And the Apocalypse itself, and some other books of the New
Testament *which were not at that time written, were nevertheless
in the book.*" Therewith was a letter from the Apostle St.
Bartholomew, declaring that he had sent this ark. And then
was " wrought a great miracle, conform to that of the Apostles
in the original gift of tongues. For there being at that time
in this land Hebrews, Persians, and Indians, besides the natives,
every one read upon the Book and Letter, as if they had been
written in his own language. And thus was this land saved
from infidelity."

On the next day an account is given of the early history of
the island and an explanation of its isolation, and of the causes
of its being unknown to Europe, while Europe is known to the
islanders; and then reference is made to a great King who
ruled the island nineteen hundred years ago. "His name"
says the Governor "was Solamona; and we esteem him as the
lawgiver of our nation. This King had a *large heart*, inscrutable
for good, and was wholly bent to make his kingdom and people
happy."[1] Of all the excellent acts of this monarch the most
excellent is the erection and institution of an Order or Society
called "*Salomon's House*, the noblest foundation that ever was
upon the earth, and the lantern of this Kingdom;" dedicated
to the study of the Works and Creatures of God, and so called
after Salomon, the son of David, because Solamona found
himself "to symbolize in many things with that King of the
Hebrews."[2]

At this point a digression introduces us to a "Feast of the
Family, a most natural, pious, and reverend custom," given, at
the cost of the State, "to any man"—whom they call a *Tirsan*
—"that shall live to see thirty persons descended of his body,
alive together, and all above three years old." After the *Tirsan*
has taken his seat on a daïs under a canopy of ivy "curiously
wrought with silver and silk of divers colours, broiding or
binding in the ivy"—the mother in a separate gallery where
she sitteth but is not seen, and "all the lineage" on the daïs
behind and around the *Tirsan* in order of years—there
approaches a *Taratan*, or herald, in a mantle of sea-green
satin streamed with gold, who, "with three curtesies, or rather
inclinations," presents a charter from the King containing gifts
of revenue, and many privileges, exemptions, and points of
honour granted to the *Tirsan*, who is addressed in it as *Such an
one our well-beloved friend and creditor:* "which is a title
proper only to this case. For they say the King is debtor to no
man but for propagation of his subjects." Then the herald
takes a cluster of grapes wrought of gold, the grapes being in

---

[1] Compare Spedding, vii. 244 "Our Sovereign, a King . . . whose *heart is
inscrutable* for wisdom and *goodness*."

[2] Mr. Ellis is (no doubt) right in saying that Bacon here alludes to James I.
Mr. Spedding's dissent is based upon the hypothesis of a late date for the *New
Atlantis*, which has been shown to be incorrect; see note above, p. 416.

number as many as there are descendants of the family, and presents it to the *Tirsan*, who delivers it to one of the sons, called ever after the Son of the Vine. After this, the *Tirsan* is served at dinner by his own children, such as are male, " who perform unto him all services of the table upon the knee ; " and then a hymn commemorates the praises of Adam, Noah, and Abraham, " concluding ever with a thanksgiving for the nativity of our Saviour, in whose birth the births of all are only blessed." [1] Finally the *Tirsan*, calling forth his lineage in order, gives to each his blessing in a solemn prescribed form, together with a jewel : and the day is ended with music, dances, and other recreations.

The traveller then relates how he " fell into straight acquaintance" with a Jewish merchant : " for they have some few *stirps* of Jews yet remaining among them, whom they leave to their own religion : which they may the better do, because these Jews give unto our Saviour many high attributes, and love the nation Bensalem extremely." With this Jew he has some conversation concerning the relations between the sexes in the island of Bensalem, and from him he learns that in a few days he may witness a rare sight. One of the Fathers of Salomon's House (of whom they have seen none this dozen years) is to enter the city in state.

" The day being come he made his entry. He was a man of middle stature and age, comely of person, and had an aspect as if he pitied men.[2] He was clothed in a robe of fine black cloth, with wide sleeves and a cape. His under-garment was of excellent white linen down to the foot, girt with a girdle of the same ; and a sindon or tippet of the same about his neck. He had gloves that were curious, and set with stone ; and shoes of peach-coloured velvet. His neck was bare to the shoulders. His hat was like a helmet, or Spanish montera ; and his locks curled below it decently ; they were of colour brown. His beard was cut round, and of the same colour with his hair, somewhat lighter. He was carried in a rich chariot without wheels, litter-wise ; with two horses at either end, richly trapped in blue velvet embroidered ; and two footmen at each side in the like attire. The chariot was all of cedar, gilt, and adorned with crystal ; save that the fore-end had pannels of sapphires, set in borders of gold, and the hinder-end the like of emeralds of the Peru colour. There was also a sun of gold

---

[1] *i.e.* "in whose birth *alone* the births of all are blessed."
[2] Compare the description of the Father in the *Redargutio*, above, p. 366.

radiant, upon the top, in the midst ; and on the top before, a small cherub of gold, with wings displayed. The chariot was covered with cloth of gold tissued upon blue. He had before him fifty attendants, young men all, in white satin loose coats to the mid-leg ; and stockings of white silk ; and shoes of blue velvet ; and hats of blue velvet; with fine plumes of divers colours, set round like hat-bands. Next before the chariot went two men, bare-headed, in linen garments down to the foot, girt, and shoes of blue velvet ; who carried the one a crosier, the other a pastoral staff like a sheep-hook ; neither of them of metal, but the crosier of balm-wood, the pastoral staff of cedar. Horsemen he had none, neither before nor behind his chariot ; as it seemeth, to avoid all tumult and trouble. Behind his chariot went all the officers and principals of the Companies of the City. He sat alone, upon cushions of a kind of excellent plush, blue ; and under his foot curious carpets of silk of divers colours, like the Persian, but far finer. He held up his bare hand as he went, as blessing the people, but in silence."

Soon afterwards the good Jew comes joyfully to the travellers with the tidings that the Father will have private conference with one of them ; and accordingly the narrator, being chosen by his fellows for this purpose, is admitted to an audience. The reader may remember that, in the *Redargutio Philosophiarum*,[1] the Elder who utters the oration *ad filios* is seated on the same level as his audience "without platform or pulpit." This is apparently an emblem of the deprecation of authority in Science, where all should stand on the uniform level of reason : and probably with the same emblematic meaning here we read that the Father of Salomon's House was " in a fair chamber, richly hanged and carpeted under foot, without any degrees to the state." [2]

" He was set upon a low throne richly adorned, and a rich cloth of state over his head, of blue satin embroidered. He was alone, save that he had two pages of honour, on either hand one, finely attired in white. His under-garments were the like that we saw him wear in the chariot ; but instead of his gown, he had on him a mantle with a cape, of the same fine black, fastened about him."

When the traveller has received his blessing and has "kissed the hem of his tippet," all else depart from the chamber, and the

[1] See above, p. 367.
[2] *i.e.* " without any steps leading up to the chair of state."

Father, in the Spanish tongue, declares that he will give the
stranger the greatest jewel he has ; for he will impart to him a
true account of Salomon's House, its object, its instruments,
the functions of its inmates, and their ordinances and rites ; and
he at once states the object of the House to be " the knowledge
of Causes and secret motions of things, and the enlarging of
the bounds of human empire, to the effecting of all things
possible."

Here the literary interest ceases : for the rest of the fragment
consists of little more than an enumeration of the instruments
and the divisions of labour in Salomon's House.   Now and then
we meet with an amusing instance in which Bacon's sanguine
prophecies have been fulfilled, as when the Father prophetically
describes speaking-tubes, declaring that they have " means to
convey sounds in trunks and pipes to great distances and in
curved lines " : [1] but for the most part there is not much literary
charm—though there is something stimulating and hope-
inspiring in the description of the material microcosm in which
the Fathers reproduce all the phenomena of the Universe ; the
caverns, miles deep, in which they conserve bodies, cure diseases,
and prolong the life of hermits ; the turrets—half a mile in
height, on mountains more than two miles high—which they
use for meteorological observations ; the great and spacious
houses where they imitate and demonstrate meteors ; the
chamber of health where they qualify the air for the cure of
divers diseases ; the gardens where they produce new kinds of
flowers and fruits ; the parks and inclosures for beasts and birds
where they practise experiments of breeding and vivisection ;
the perspective houses where they make demonstrations of all
lights, radiations, and colours, making artificial rainbows, haloes
and circles of light, and conducting (by means of glasses) observations in urine and blood, not otherwise to be seen : and lastly
the houses of deceits of the senses, where they " represent all
manner of feats of juggling, false apparitions, impostures, and
illusions, and their fallacies."

From the description of the instruments the Father passes on
to describe the functions of the Fellows of the House.   Some
of them travel to obtain information ; these are Merchants

[1] I adopt here the Latin text.

of Light. Others collect experiments from books; these are Depredators. Others, called Mysterymen, collect experiments from the mechanical mysteries or crafts, while the Pioneers or Miners, who delve in Nature's secrets, try new experiments of their own. Above these is the class of Compilers (better called in the Latin translation "divisores") who classify (" draw into titles and tables ") the experiments of the four classes mentioned above, so that they may give better light for deducing Axioms from them.[1] Next to these, the Dowrymen, or Benefactors,[2] endeavour to draw out of these experiments things of use and practice for man's life and knowledge, as well for works as for plain demonstration of causes. Above these again come the Lamps, who " direct experiments of a higher light," and the Inoculators, who execute the experiments so directed and report them. Highest of all stand those who " raise the former discoveries by experiments into Greater Observations, Axioms, and Aphorisms," these are called Interpreters of Nature.

A brief but striking section is devoted to the ordinances and rites of the Fathers, in which most space is given to the Galleries of Inventors and Inventions :

" We have two very long and fair galleries; in one of these we place patterns and samples of all manner of the more rare and excellent inventions : in the other we place the statua's of all principal inventors. There we have the statua of your Columbus, that discovered the West Indies ; also the inventor of ships; your monk that was the inventor of ordnance and gunpowder; the inventor of music; the inventor of letters; the inventor of printing; the inventor of observations of astronomy; the inventor of works in metal; the inventor of glass; the inventor of silk in the worm; the inventor of wine; the inventor of corn and bread; the inventor of sugars; and all these by more certain tradition than you have. Then have we divers inventors of our own, of excellent works; which since you have not seen, it were too long to make descriptions of them; and besides, in the right understanding of these descriptions you might easily err. For upon every invention of value, we erect a statua to the inventor and give him a liberal and honourable reward."

A few words more mention their prayers for aid and blessing; their hymns and services of laud and thanks which they say

---

[1] These represent the formation of the Tables *Comparentiae, Absentiae in Proximo,* and *Graduum :* see above, p. 388.
[2] These represent the *Vindemiatio Prima :* see above, p. 393, *Novum Organum,* ii. 20.

daily to God for His marvellous works ; their natural divinations of diseases, plagues, earthquakes, inundations, comets, whereby they are enabled to advise their countrymen how to anticipate or remedy these evils: and then the book ends with a parting blessing and a present of two thousand ducats bestowed on the traveller by the Father, together with permisson to publish the narrative :

" And when he had said this, he stood up ; and I, as I had been taught, kneeled down; and he laid his right hand upon my head, and said : ' God bless thee, my son, and God bless this relation which I have made. I give thee leave to publish it for the good of other nations ; for we here are in God's bosom, a land unknown.' And so he left me, having assigned a value of about ten thousand ducats for a bounty to me and my fellows. For they give great largesses where they come upon all occasions.

[THE REST WAS NOT PERFECTED.] "

No reader of the *New Atlantis* can fail to be struck by the religious light in which the venerable Father of Salomon's House is regarded. He is no mere student or specialist; he is a benefactor of the human race, a Father of his country, a Mediator between man and the Laws of God, " having an aspect as one that pities men " ; not a rhetorician or preaching prelate, but a Priest of Science blessing the people with outstretched hand " in silence " amidst the spontaneous veneration of his countrymen. Rising from the perusal of this little book we can better understand Bacon's whole life and character, and especially his unbounded self-respect and the self-confidence which was the source of some of his best literary efforts and some of his worst political errors. Even when he was certifying to oppressive Monopolies, imprisoning goldsmiths and mercers to oblige Buckingham's brothers, presiding at State trials as Lord Chancellor and "helping the evidence " so as to bring about the issue desired by the King, he always regarded himself as a philanthropist on a large scale, a true Priest of Science, after the manner of the Father of Salomon's House, having in his heart that true *philanthropia* which is " the character of God Himself."

[1] See note on p. 29, above.

Only one other work of imagination (if we except the Dialogue in the *Redargutio*) proceeded from Bacon's pen. This is a fragment of an *Advertisement touching an Holy War* written in the form of a Dialogue, in which the interlocutors represent a Moderate Divine, a Protestant Zelant, a Romish Catholic Zelant, a Militar Man, a Politique, and a Courtier. The conversation is life-like, and the characters well sustained; but the work is so imperfect as to leave the reader doubtful as to the intended conclusion. It is probable, however, that Bacon would have inclined to a war against the Turks on grounds, not of religion, but of policy. In 1622 (the year in which the *Advertisement* was written) the Spanish marriage being still on foot, it was natural that Bacon should recur to the instructions which in 1617 he had sent to Sir John Digby, suggesting that the marriage might "be a beginning and seed of a Holy War against the Turk." The fragment is preceded by a long dedication to Bishop Andrews, and Bacon thought it worthy of being translated into Latin and included in his *Opera Moralia et Civilia*.[1]

The *History of Henry VII*.[2] was probably begun in June, 1621, soon after Bacon's release from the Tower, and presented to the King in the following October. A history of England from the Wars of the Roses to the Union of the two Kingdoms, had been noted in the *Advancement of Learning* as deficient; and a fragment, of doubtful date, but previous to 1609, shows that Bacon had previously intended to supply this deficiency. The character of Henry VII. given in that earlier fragment goes far to disprove the notion that now in 1621 Bacon idealised that monarch in order to gratify the reigning King.

The conception of Henry is clearly identical in both; a king who never failed to compass what he sought, but who—partly from his training, partly from "some great defects and main errors in his nature, custom, and proceedings"—never aimed at the highest and noblest objects. The success with which he achieved small things is recorded by Bacon with that quiet satisfaction which one naturally feels at seeing a man or instrument unerringly perform its appointed task. But, though he calls him "the Solomon of England," he emphatically declares that he

---

[1] Spedding, *Works*, vii. 1-36   [2] *Ibid*. vi. 1—263.

was keen-sighted but not far-sighted, and dexterous rather than wise. His contempt for Henry's avarice reveals itself in such expressions as that which describes how obloquy was " sweetened to him by confiscation." So far from investing the king with imaginary nobility he assumes that it was only in his earlier days that the virtues of nobleness and bounty " had their turns in his nature." It is true he describes " this great king's *felicity* " towards the end of his life, as being at the top of all worldly bliss; but he is careful to add in the same sentence that he enjoyed " the great hatred of his people," and that he needed an opportune death to deliver him from the danger of being dethroned by his own son.

This peculiar use of the word " felicity " (*felicitas*) may be illustrated by a fragment on the character of Julius Caesar.[1] If Henry's " felicity " was compatible with the " hatred of his subjects," the " felicity " of Caesar is said to have been compatible with, and a result of, an unflinching selfishness. " He referred everything to himself, and was himself the true and perfect centre of all his own actions, which was the cause of his *singular and almost perpetual felicity, i.e.* material prosperity." In judging Julius, as in judging Henry, Bacon manifests the same dispassionate appreciation of intellectual ability even when separated from moral excellence :

" He undoubtedly had greatness of mind in a very high degree . . . . yet he allowed neither country, nor religion, nor services, nor kindred, nor friendships, to be any hindrance or bridle to his purposes."

But the palm is given, not to Julius but to Augustus :

" For Julius, being of a restless and unsettled disposition, though for the compassing of his ends he made his arrangements with consummate judgment, yet had not his ends themselves arranged in any good order . . . . whereas Augustus, as a man sober and mindful of his moral condition, seems to have had his ends likewise laid out from the first in admirable order and truly weighed." [2]

Among other historical fragments the one best worth mentioning is entitled, *In Felicem Memoriam Elizabethae*.[3] It is a spirited

---

[1] Spedding, *Works*, vi. 335.   [2] *Ibid.* vi. 347.
[3] *Ibid.* vi. 233-303.

vindication of Elizabeth against Papist attacks, and as it was written in 1608, when there was nothing to gain by flattery, it has ·the authority due to a disinterested eulogy proceeding from one who knew the Queen well and owed her little. Making his will in 1621 he mentions this alone among all his works as the one that he desires to have published : " In particular I wish the *Elogium* I wrote, *In Felicem Memoriam Reginae Elizabethae,* may be published."

§ 59 Minor Literary Works

Bacon's collection of *Apophthegms* was probably intended to supply the deficiency noted in the *Advancement of Learning* and in the *De Augmentis ;* [2] in the latter of which (1623) he describes *Apophthegms* as serving " not for pleasure only and ornament, but also for action and business, being, as one called them, *mucrones verborum,* speeches with a point or edge, whereby knots in business are pierced and severed." He expresses his regret at the loss of Caesar's collection ; " for, as for any others that we have in this kind, but little judgment has, in my opinion, been used in the selection." In the following autumn (1624) while he was recovering from a severe illness, the *Apophthegms* were written from his dictation.[3]

His religious works (besides some prayers and translations into verse from the Psalms) consist of two short treatises entitled, *A Confession of Faith* and *Meditationes Sacrae.* In the *Confession* (written before 1603, but how long before is not known) there is little to indicate that the author was a man of science. At the outset, it is true, there is something Baconian in the recognition of the universality of the Law of Mediation, which, he says, pervaded the Universe from the beginning, because, "neither angel, man, nor world could stand, nor can stand, one moment in His eyes, without beholding the same in the eyes of a Mediator ; and

---

[1] This clause does not occur in the last will, made in 1625 ; but a clause in almost identical words is quoted by Tenison as being from " Lord Bacon's last will "—perhaps from an earlier draft of it in his possession. (See Spedding, *Life,* vii. 540.)

[2] *Adv.* II. iii. 4 ; *De Augm.* ii. 12.

[3] Spedding, *Works,* vii. 111-186.

therefore (before Him with whom all things are present), the
Lamb of God was shown before all worlds." For the rest, there
is little individuality in Bacon's *Confession*. The origin of Evil,
instead of being admitted to be inscrutable, is more freely than
luminously spoken of to this effect: "He made all things in
their estate good, and removed from Himself the beginning of
all evil and vanity into the liberty of the creature." God created
the constant Laws of Nature, which, however, have had three
changes, viz. 1st, when "the matter of heaven and earth was
created without forms;" 2nd, after each of the six days; 3rd,
at the curse: and there will be a fourth change at the end of
the world.

The soul of man was not produced by heaven or earth, but breathed
immediately from God, so that the ways and proceedings of God with
spirits are not included in Nature, that is, in the laws of heaven and
earth. Adam's sin consisted in "presuming to imagine the commandments and prohibitions of God were not the rules of Good and Evil, but
that Good and Evil had their own principles and beginnings." Jesus
Christ was the Word, not taking flesh, but *made* flesh, "so as the Eternal
Son of God and the ever-blessed Son of Mary was one person; so one as
the Blessed Virgin may be truly and catholicly called Deipara, the Mother
of God." Christ having man's flesh, and man having Christ's spirit, there is
an open passage and mutual imputation; whereby sin and wrath are conveyed to Christ from man, and merit and life are conveyed to man from
Christ. After the souls of those that die in the Lord have passed from
their present blessed rest into the further revelation of glory at the Last
Day, the glory of the Saints shall then be full, and the Kingdom shall
be given up to God the Father, from which time all things shall continue for ever in that being and state which they shall then receive.[1]

In the *Meditationes Sacrae* (published with the first edition of
the *Essays* in 1597) there are several thoughts which may be found
embodied in Bacon's later works.[2] Among these is the statement (repeated in the *Advancement of Learning*) that in order
to improve the vicious we must know vices:

"There are neither teeth, nor stings, nor venom, nor wreaths and folds
of serpents, which ought not to be all known, and, as far as examination
doth lead, tried; neither let any man here fear infection or pollution; for
the sun entereth into sinks and is not defiled." There are three kinds of

---

[1] Spedding, *Works*, vii. 215-226.   [2] *Ibid.* vii. 227-242.

imposture in Religion ; 1st, the formal or scholastic theology of those who, as soon as they get any subject matter, straightway make an art of it ; 2nd, the accumulation of legends ; 3rd, mystical use of high-sounding phrases, allegories, and allusions. Heresies spring from two sources, either from not knowing the Scriptures, or from not knowing the power of God ; for the Scriptures reveal God's will, the Universe God's power. The former error breeds Superstition ; the latter, Atheism. What the shell is to the kernel, what the Ark was to the Tables of the Law, that is the Church to the Scriptures.

Next to the importance attached by Bacon to the Bible as the only source of Unity, his denunciation of " terrestrial hope" claims principal attention. Himself one of the most sanguine and hopeful of mankind, Bacon would banish hope from all matters relating to life on earth, and relegate it to expectations of heaven. About earthly matters men should not hope, but only entertain reasonable anticipations. Idly do the poets fable that Hope was left in Pandora's casket to be the antidote against all diseases; rather it was itself the worst disease of all, making the mind, " light, frothy, unequal, wandering. . . . By how much purer is the sense of things present, without infection or tincture of imagination, by so much wiser and better is the soul." To the same tenour run the remarks on Hope in the *Essays*: it is a habit by which rulers can deceive the seditious into peace : " the politic and artificial nourishing and entertaining of hopes, and carrying men from hopes to hopes, is one of the best antidotes against the poison of discontentments." [1] Perhaps the most characteristic and doubtful of the *dicta* in the *Meditations* is the passage in the section on Heresies, where he asserts that those heresies are worst which deny God's power: " for in civil government also it is a more atrocious thing to deny the power and majesty of the Prince than to slander his reputation ;" the inference from which seems to be that it is a greater sin to deny God's power than to deny His goodness, and that he who worships a non-omnipotent Being of goodness is morally worse than the worshipper of an omnipotent Satan.

The *Translation of certain Psalms into English Verse* was made, like the collection of Apophthegms, during a period of illness in 1624.[2] The fact that he not only dedicated these

---

[1] *Essays*, xxv. 186.   [2] Spedding, *Works*, vii. 263-286.

translations to his friend George Herbert but actually published them in the same year, appears to require explanation. Mr. Spedding thinks it possible that " he owed money to his printer and bookseller, and if such trifles as these would help to pay it, he had no objection to their being used for the purpose." There are probably few data for determining the value of an author's profits in the early part of the seventeenth century; but it seems unlikely that a little pamphlet—for it contains no more than seven Psalms, and can hardly claim to be called a book— could have gone far in the direction of paying the printer's bill for the author of such abstruse works as the *Novum Organum* and subsequent Latin works. Perhaps he may have published them as a kind of thankoffering for his recovery. In any case the publication is a proof that he thought well of his verses; and the reader may be naturally curious to see what kind of verse was written and approved by one who in old days called himself a " concealed poet," [1] and who wrote magnificent prose in almost every conceivable style.

The following is an extract from the first Psalm, and it does not give us a high notion of Bacon's poetic powers :

" Who never gave to wicked reed [2]
    A yielding and attentive ear ;
Who never sinner's paths did tread,
    Nor sat him down in scorner's chair ;
But maketh it his whole delight
    On law of God to meditate,
And therein spendeth day and night :
    That man is in a happy state.

" He shall be like the fruitful tree,
    Planted along a running spring,
Which, in due season, constantly
    A goodly yield of fruit doth bring :
Whose leaves continue always green,
    And are no prey to winter's pow'r :
So shall that man not once be seen
    Surprisèd with an evil hour."

A translation of the ninetieth Psalm is, in parts, far more forcible and rhythmical ; but the last of the four following stanzas is both bald and cacophonous :

---

[1] See above, p. 96. [2] *i.e.* counsel.

"O Lord, thou art our home, to whom we fly,
    And so hast always been from age to age ;
Before the hills did intercept the eye,
    Or that the frame was up of earthly stage,
        One God thou wert, and art, and still shall be ;
        The line of Time, it doth not measure thee.

"Both death and life obey thy holy lore,
    And visit in their turns, as they are sent ;
A thousand years with thee they are no more
    Than yesterday, which, ere it is, is spent ;
        Or as a watch by night, that course doth keep,
        And goes, and comes, unwares to them that sleep.

"Thou carriest man away as with a tide ;
    Then down swim all his thoughts that mounted high :
Much like a mocking dream, that will not bide,
    But flies before the sight of waking eye ;
        Or as the grass, that cannot term obtain
        To see the summer come about again.

            *   *   *

"Begin thy work, O Lord, in this our age,
    Shew it unto thy servants that now live ;
But to our children raise it many a stage,
    That all the world to thee may glory give.
        Our handy-work likewise, as fruitful tree,
        Let it, O Lord, blessèd, not blasted be."

The translation of the one hundred and fourth Psalm perhaps exhibits Bacon at his best as a versifier, although even here there are occasional declensions from the elevated style, as in the reference to—

        "the great Leviathan
That makes the seas *to seeth like boiling pan.*"

But of the opening Mr. Spedding says (I think with somewhat excessive praise) that " the heroic couplet could hardly do its work better in the hands of Dryden," and it is, at least, of such merit as to claim a longer extract than the other Psalms :

"Father and King of pow'rs, both high and low,
Whose sounding fame all creatures serve to blow,
My soul shall with the rest strike up thy praise,
And carol of thy works and wondrous ways.

But who can blaze thy beauties, Lord, aright ?
They turn the brittle beams of mortal sight.
Upon thy head thou wear'st a glorious crown,
All set with virtues, polish'd with renown :
Thence round about a silver veil doth fall
Of crystal light, mother of colours all.
The compass heaven, smooth without grain [1] or fold,
All set with spangs of glitt'ring stars untold,
And strip'd with golden beams of power unpent,
Is raisèd up for a removing tent.
Vaulted and archèd are his chamber beams
Upon the seas, the waters, and the streams :
The clouds as chariots swift do scour the sky ;
The stormy winds upon their wings do fly.
His angels spirits are, that wait his will,
As flames of fire his anger they fulfil.
In the beginning, with a mighty hand,
He made the earth by counterpoise to stand ;
Never to move, but to be fixèd still ;
Yet hath no pillars but his sacred will.
The earth, as with a veil, once cover'd was,
The waters over-flowèd all the mass :
But upon his rebuke away they fled,
And then the hills began to shew their head ;
The vales their hollowed bosoms open'd plain,
The streams ran trembling down the vales again :
And that the earth no more might drownèd be,
He set the sea his bounds of liberty ;
And though the waves resound, and beat the shore,
Yet it is bridled by his holy lore.
Then did the rivers seek their proper places,
And found their heads, their issues, and their races ;
The springs do feed the rivers all the way,
And so the tribute to the sea repay :
Running along through many a pleasant field,
Much fruitfulness unto the earth they yield :
That know the beasts and cattle feeding by,
Which for to slake their thirst do thither hie.
Nay desert grounds the streams do not forsake,
But through the unknown ways their journey take :
The asses wild, that hide in wilderness,
Do thither come, their thirst for to refresh.
The shady trees along their banks do spring,
In which the birds do build, and sit, and sing ;

---

[1] *i.e.* "roughness," like the "grain" of wood.

F F

Stroking the gentle air with pleasant notes,
Plaining or chirping through their warbling throats.
The higher grounds, where waters cannot rise,
By rain and dews are water'd from the skies ;
Causing the earth put forth the grass for beasts,
And garden herbs, serv'd at the greatest feasts ;
And bread, that is all viands' firmament,
And gives a firm and solid nourishment ;
And wine, man's spirits for to recreate ;
And oil, his face for to exhilarate.
The sappy cedars, tall like stately tow'rs
High-flying birds do harbour in their bow'rs ;
The holy storks, that are the travellers,
Choose for to dwell and build within the firs ;
The climbing goats hang on steep mountain's side ;
The digging conies in the rocks do bide.
The moon, so constant in inconstancy,
Doth rule the monthly seasons orderly ;
The sun, eye of the world, doth know his race,
And when to shew, and when to hide his face.
Thou makest darkness, that it may be night,
Whenas the savage beasts, that fly the light,
(As conscious of man's hatred) leave their den,
And range abroad secur'd from sight of men.
Then do the forests ring of lions roaring,
That ask their meat of God, their strength restoring ;
But when the day appears, they back do fly,
And in their dens again do lurking lie.
Then man goes forth to labour in the field,
Whereby his grounds more rich increase may yield.
O Lord, thy providence sufficeth all ;
Thy goodness, not restrained, but general
Over thy creatures : the whole earth doth flow
With thy great largeness pour'd forth here below.
Nor is it earth alone exalts thy name,
But seas and streams likewise do spread the same.
The rolling seas unto the lot doth fall
Of beasts innumerable, great and small ;
There do the stately ships plough up the floods ;
The greater navies look like walking woods ;
The fishes there far voyages do make,
To divers shores their journey they do take.
There hast thou set the great Leviathan,
That makes the seas to seeth like boiling pan.
All these do ask of thee their meat to live,
Which in due season thou to them dost give."

Some allowance must be made (no doubt) for the fact that Bacon is translating and not writing original verse. Nevertheless a true poet, even of a low order, could hardly betray so clearly the cramping influence of rhyme and metre. There is far less beauty of diction and phrase in these verse translations than in any of the prose works that are couched in an elevated style. Possibly the nature of the subject was against him. Theological verse, like theological sculpture, might seem to require something of the archaic, and a close adherence to the simplicity of the original prose. But I cannot help coming to the conclusion that, although Bacon might have written better verse on some subject of his own choosing, the chances are that even his best would not have been very good.

A brief notice is claimed by the *Colours of Good and Evil*, published in 1597 in the same volume as the first edition of the *Essays.*[1] The title signifies the Fallacies, or "Colours," by which a persuader labours "to make things appear good or evil, and that in higher or lower degree." Each "colour" is exemplified by an instance, and followed by its "reprehension" or refutation. One of the ten Colours set forth in this treatise may serve as a specimen of the rest.

"Quod rem integram servat, bonum ; quod sine receptu est, malum. Nam se recipere non posse impotentiae genus est ; potentia autem bonum." [That course which keeps the matter in a man's power is good ; that which leaves him without retreat is bad : for to have no means of retreating is to be, in a sort, powerless, and power is a good thing.]

"Hereof Æsop framed the fable of the two frogs, that consulted together in the time of drought (when many plashes that they had repaired to were dry), what was to be done ; and the one propounded to go down into a deep well, because it was like the water would not fail there : but the other answered, 'Yea ; but if it do fail, how shall we get up again ?'" And the reason is, that human actions are so uncertain and subject to perils, as that seemeth the best course which hath most passages out of it.

"Appertaining to this persuasion, the forms are, *You shall engage*[2] *yourself;* on the other side, *Tantum quantum voles sumes ex fortuna*, &c., you shall keep the matter in your own hands.

"The reprehension of it is, that *Proceeding and resolving in all actions is necessary :* for as he saith well, *Not to resolve is to resolve ;* and many times it breeds as many necessities, and engageth[2] as far in some other sort, as to resolve.

---

[1] Spedding, *Works*, vii. 65-92.   [2] *i.e.* "entangle."

"So it is but the covetous man's disease translated into power ; for the covetous man will enjoy nothing, because he will have his full store and possibility to enjoy the more ; so by this reason a man should execute nothing, because he should be still indifferent and at liberty to execute anything. Besides, necessity, and this same *jacta est alea*, hath many times an advantage, because it awaketh the powers of the mind, and strengtheneth endeavour. *Ceteris pares necessitate certe superiores estis* [Being equal otherwise, in necessity you have the better]."

§ 60 The Method of the "Essays"[1]

The Colours of the Good and Evil are more closely connected with the *Essays* than might be supposed. Both alike are amplifications (the *Essays* being more ample and varied) of a species of rhetorical equipment called by Bacon *Antitheta*, "Opposite Maxims," or "Antitheses of Things" ; the object of which is thus set forth in the *De Augmentis* (vi. 3) :

"I would have all topics, which there is frequent occasion to handle (whether they relate to proofs and refutations, or to persuasions and dissuasions, or to praise and blame), studied and prepared beforehand ; and not only so, but the case exaggerated both ways with the utmost force of the wit, and urged unfairly as it were and quite beyond the truth. And the best way of making such a collection, with a view to use as well as to brevity, would be to contract these common places into certain acute and concise sentences ; to be as skeins or bottoms of thread which may be

---

[1] As to the word "Essay," it is interesting to contrast what Bacon and Ben Jonson say of it.

The former (in the cancelled dedication to Prince Henry, see below, p. 438) distinguishes "Essays" from "just treatises," implying that his work must be expected to be a little disconnected and abrupt : "Certain brief notes, set down rather significantly than curiously, which I have called *Essays*. The word is late, but the thing is ancient. For Seneca's Epistles to Lucilius, if one mark them well, are but *Essays*, that is, *dispersed meditations*, though conveyed in the form of Epistles."

Ben Jonson will have none of the *Essayists*. They are the writers "that turn over books, and are equally searching in all papers, that write out of what they presently find or meet, without choice : by which means it happens that what they have discredited and impugned in one work, they have, before or after, extolled the same in another. Such are all the *Essayists*, even their master, Montaigne" (Ben Jonson's *Works*, ed. Gifford, p. 747).

Considering the great admiration expressed by Ben Jonson for Bacon's style (see p. 453) one is a little surprised to find no mention of Bacon's *Essays*, and to note the assumption that Montaigne is "Master of the Essayists." It may be noted that in 1625, describing the new edition of his *Essays* to Father Fulgentio, Bacon says that in Italy the book was called *Saggi Morali*, "but I gave it a weightier name, calling it 'Faithful Discourses,' or 'The Inwards of Things.'"

unwinded at large when they are wanted. . . . A few instances of the thing, having a great many by me, I think fit to propound by way of example. I call them Antitheses of Things."

Many of the acute and concise sentences, thus propounded in the *De Augmentis*, will be found interspersed in the *Essays*, of which they often constitute a kind of framework. They are the " skeins or bottoms of thread," to use Bacon's own metaphor, while the examples, illustrations, and inferences, represent the " unwinding."

In the ten Essays which complete the earliest edition (1597), the " acuteness and conciseness " of the style are most marked and are well suited to the subjects treated of : (1) Study, (2) Discourse, (3) Ceremonies and Respects, (4) Followers and Friends, (5) Suitors, (6) Expense, (7) Regiment of Health, (8) Honour and Reputation, (9) Faction, (10) Negotiating.   These subjects do not admit of a rhetorical or periodic style, but afford scope for common sense, humour, terse force, and apt homely illustration.   Bacon was not at this time conscious that he was writing a book that would last as long as the English language.   He published these " fragments of his conceits " (as he tells us in the dedication to his brother Anthony) to prevent the circulation of pirated copies, not without an apology, likening them to " the new half-pence which, though the silver were good, the pieces were small." [1]

In October, 1612, the second and enlarged edition of forty *Essays* was entered at Stationers' Hall ; and in the following December Chamberlain writes that " Sir Francis Bacon hath set out new Essays, where in a chapter on Deformity " (Essay xliv.), " the world takes notice that he points out his little cousin to the life." The " little cousin " was Bacon's former patron Robert Cecil, Earl of Salisbury, who had died in May, 1612 ; and if " the world " was right, Bacon probably wrote the new Essay in question (and perhaps others of the new Essays) after May in that year.   That he had spent some labour upon the work appears from the intended dedication to Henry Prince of Wales (cancelled owing to the Prince's death on the 9th of November, 1612), in which he says that, although he has not had leisure

---

[1] For the early editions of the *Essays*, see Spedding, *Works*, vi. 521-591.

to write "just treatises" (*i.e.* regular treatises) by reason of his continual service, he has endeavoured to make them "not vulgar, but of a nature whereof a man shall find much in experience, little in books; so as they are neither repetitions nor fancies."

The titles of the first three Essays, Religion, Death, Goodness and Goodness of Nature, at once show that the new volume rises to a higher level than the former : and on the same level are the Essays on Empire, Atheism, Superstition, Fortune, and Greatness of Kingdoms. Yet though the language is more elevated and periodical than that of the first edition, it still so far savours of the Antitheta that he describes his work to the Prince as "certain brief notes, set down rather significantly than curiously," and thinks it necessary to defend the style by an appeal to Seneca. The word *Essays*, he says, is late—it was perhaps borrowed from the *Essais* of Montaigne, which were published in 1580—"but the thing is ancient. For Seneca's *Epistles to Lucilius* if one mark them well, are but Essays, that is, dispersed meditations, though conveyed in the form of epistles."

On the death of the Prince of Wales Bacon dedicated the new volume to his brother-in-law Sir John Constable. The new dedication is couched in an altogether lower tone than the first :

"My last Essays I dedicated to my dear brother Master Anthony Bacon, who is with God. Looking amongst my papers this vacation I found others of the same nature ; which if I myself shall not suffer to be lost, it seemeth the world will not, by the often printing of the former."

It would be unsafe to take too literally this casual "finding" of the new Essays in the course of the vacation, or to infer from it that Bacon under-rated his new work. If there is any discrepancy between the tone of the later dedication to Sir John Constable and the cancelled earlier dedication to the Prince, the latter probably best represents the labour spent on the new Essays, and the author's opinion of them.

The final edition of 1625 contains fifty-eight Essays (eighteen more than the second edition) : but the author no longer excuses them as "dispersed meditations." In number, it is true, there is less difference between the Third and Second Edition than between the Second and First; but he has enlarged them—so he writes in his dedication to the Duke of Buckingham—not only in number but also "in weight, so that they are indeed a new work." In their new form they are deemed by their author worthy of being translated into Latin, and Bacon avows his belief that "the Latin volume of them (being in the universal language) may last as long as books last."

Almost all the Essays so far adhere to their original conception—"certain brief notes rather significantly than curiously set down"—that they for the most part avoid anything like a formal introduction or periodic peroration. Thus in the late Essay on "Vicissitude of Things" (lviii.) the opening is "Salomon saith, There is no new thing upon the earth;" and the end, "As for the philology of them, that is but a circle of tales, and therefore not fit for this writing." The introduction (if it may be so called) is generally some short and abrupt maxim, metaphor, or quotation: "I cannot call riches better than the baggage of virtue;" "Houses are built to live in and not look on;" "God Almighty first planted a garden;" "What is truth? said jesting Pilate, and would not stay for an answer;" "Nature is often hidden, sometimes overcome, seldom extinguished;" "An ant is a wise creature for itself, but it is a shrewd thing in an orchard or a garden;" "Shepherds of peoples had need know the calendars of tempests in State."

Then follows the "unwinding." Plutarch, Tacitus, Seneca, Pliny, Livy, Machiavelli, are brought forward to "exaggerate the case both ways with the utmost force of wit." If a conclusion is arrived at, it is seldom ostentatiously or even decidedly set forth, but generally accompanied by prominent qualifications and modifications. The Essay, like the sonnet, loves a quiet close. The earlier edition of the Essay on Parents and Children ends with, "As the blood happens;" in the Essay on Seditions the end is, "Or else the remedy is worse than the disease;" in that on Dispatch, "As ashes are more generative than dust;" in Masques and Triumphs, "But enough of these toys;" in the Essay on Deformity, "And Socrates may go likewise with them; with others." An Essay in Bacon's sense of the word—that is, a "Dispersed Meditation," showing what may be said on both sides—naturally rejects anything in the way of a peroration or emphatic termination. Only a few of the later Essays, such as those on Truth, Adversity, and Revenge, are exceptions to this rule.

§ 61 THE SUBJECT MATTER OF THE ESSAYS

We pass from considering the method of the *Essays* to the consideration of their subject matter. And first as to their morality. Bacon claims for them in his dedications that they are "not fancies," but based on experience, and that they "come home to men's business and bosoms." This claim they fully justify. They deal with men and facts as they are, not as they ought to be ; and they lay down rules for conduct accordingly. In order to enable men to be on their guard against Evil Arts, they teach men the knowledge of Evil Arts; and in extreme cases, where there is "no remedy," they occasionally allow the use of Evil Arts. There is indeed not wanting a sincere appreciation of virtue and a theoretical preference of the better course. "Goodness of all virtues and dignities of the mind is the greatest, being the character of the Deity ; and, without it a man is a busy, mischievous, wretched thing, no better than a kind of vermin" (xiii. 5). To the same effect the Essay on Truth tells us that "Clear and round dealing is the honour of man's nature ; " "Wisdom for a man's self is, in many branches thereof, a depraved thing" (xxiii. 41); and "nothing doth more hurt in a state than that cunning men pass for wise " (xxii. 18).

But on the other hand Bacon realises as keenly as Machiavelli that the state of society is unfavourable for the full exercise of virtue : "there is in human nature generally more of the fool than of the wise " (xii. 12); most people "understand not many excellent virtues ; the lowest virtues draw praise from them; the middle virtues work in them astonishment or admiration; but of the highest virtues they have no sense or perceiving at all " (liii. 6). Men are so naturally selfish or malignant that it is absurd to be angry with them for faults which they cannot avoid : " Why should I be angry with a man for loving himself better than me ? And if any one should do wrong merely out of ill-nature, why yet it is but like the thorn or briar which prick and scratch because they can do no other" (iv. 18). Time and old age bring rather moral deterioration than improvement : "Age doth profit rather in the powers of understanding than in the virtues of the will and the affections" (xlii. 54).

Such being the corrupt and pitiable state of human nature, how is the practical man to obtain power over others except by knowing the defects of human nature, and taking advantage of them ? Herein the Essay on Negotiating goes as straight to the point as Machiavelli could desire : "If you would work a man, you must either know his nature and fashions, and so work him ; or his ends and so win him ; or his weaknesses or disadvantages, and so awe him ; or those that have interest in him, and so govern him" (xlvii. 42). Bacon, however, stops short of Machiavelli in not sanctioning the indiscriminate and liberal use of Evil Arts for the advancement of one's fortune. For the most part he teaches them only that his pupils may be on their guard against them ; but he makes an exception in favour of Dissimulation and Falsehood, the occasional use of which he not only allows but commends, although he protests against the useless folly of a general habit of deception : "Certainly the ablest men that ever were, have all had an openness and frankness of dealing, and a name of certainty and veracity. But then they were like horses well managed, for they could tell passing well when to stop and turn" (vi. 29) ; and again, "The best composition and temperature is to have openness in fame and opinion, secrecy in habit, dissimulation in reasonable use, and a power to feign if there be no remedy" (vi. 110) ; for though falsehood "embaseth" like alloy, yet it "may make the metal work the better" (i. 65).

Throughout all the *Essays* Bacon, like the Father of Salomon's House in the *New Atlantis*, has "an aspect as of one pitying mankind" ; but it is that kind of pity which is akin to contempt. He does not believe much in the purifying force of family affection. Though he admits that "wife and children are a kind of discipline of humanity" (viii. 39), yet, as compared with friendship, wedded love is inferior ; "nuptial love maketh mankind, friendly love perfecteth it" (x. 64) ; and, as for friendship, there is little of it in the world, and "least of all between equals, which was wont to be magnified.   That that is, is between superior and inferior, whose fortunes may comprehend the one the other" (xlviii. 51).   Love itself is a Siren or a Fury, "the child of folly" (x. 4, 51).

Religion is seldom or never mentioned in the *Essays* as a basis for morality.   As a subject of political interest it has a whole Essay devoted to it, treating of Unity in Religion; and the Essay on Vicissitude recognizes that sects and religions are the "orbs that rule in men's minds most," and gives precepts for staying those great revolutions.   But there is very little in the *Essays* corresponding to the important place assigned in the *De Augmentis* and *Advancement of Learning* to the Christian Faith, as imprinting Goodness or Charity on men's souls, and raising them to greater perfection than all the doctrines of morality can do.   The theoretical morality of the *Essays* appears to be based upon the recognition of a public and a private Good, and upon the nobility of preferring the wider to the narrower object.   Their practical morality is based upon the recognition of the fact that for the most part men will prefer the narrower to the wider, their own to the public interests.

The famous passage (Essay xvi. 1) in which Bacon appears to avow a preference for Atheism over Superstition, "It were better to have no opinion of God at all than such an opinion as is unworthy of Him,"[1] must be balanced with the other saying (Essay xv. 1): "I would rather believe in all the fables of the Legend, and the Talmud, and the Alcoran, than that this universal frame is without a Mind."   Bacon drew a sharp line of distinction between matters of revealed Religion and matters of Science. The former, he says, are not to be criticised nor reasoned about, but to be accepted in faith.   They are (see p. 474), like the rules of a game, purely matters of arrangement, dependent upon the will of God who arranged them, and consequently they are

---

[1] Although the context and the illustration from Plutarch imply that "having no opinion about" is the same as "having an opinion that there is no such person as," yet the Latin translation "nullam *aut incertam* opinionem," and still more the insertion of the word "good" in Bacon's letter to Sir Toby Matthew (1607) "to have no *good* opinion about God," indicate that Bacon may have wavered between three meanings, (1) "believing that God does not exist;" (2) "not believing that God exists;" (3) "believing that, though God exists, we know nothing about Him."

unfit, by their very nature, to be made subjects of reason. It followed that a few marvels or "fables" more or less in revealed Religion might be accepted without difficulty if they involved no conception "unworthy" of God.

But it is to be noted here that Bacon does not avow any preference for Polytheism over Atheism. Polytheism probably seemed to him "unworthy" of God, inasmuch as, by introducing a multitude of wills, it appeared to introduce discord and limitations to the divine power; and we have seen above (see p. 430) that in a very striking passage of the *Meditationes Sacrae* Bacon applies to God the saying that "it is a more atrocious thing to deny the *power* and majesty of the Prince than to slander his *reputation*." It was, perhaps, an intellectual even more than a moral necessity with Bacon to believe that the symmetry and order of Nature proceeded from one all-powerful Mind, and the attributes of "power" and "order" struck him more than moral attributes.[1] However, the Essay on Superstition goes a step further in the recognition of the necessity of having "good opinions" about God. Horrified by the crimes that had been perpetrated in his own days under the name of religion, the author declares that Agnosticism itself is preferable to such a belief in God as would justify murder and treason. It is not to be inferred from these words that Bacon himself had the least tendency to Agnosticism. He dreaded, indeed, for the sake of Science, the commixture of theological and scientific study; but if we may judge from the combined evidence of all his works, including some most private and trustworthy expressions of feeling, he was, or desired to be, in all matters of religion, strictly orthodox, according to the tenets of the Church of England; inclining at first somewhat to the side of the Puritans, but in his later years busying himself less with religious polemics, and manifesting aversion to any changes in the discipline as well as doctrine of the Church.

In politics the *Essays* exhibit Bacon as a patriot rather than a cosmopolite, and as a "royalist"—to use the title he claimed for himself—rather than a favourer of the extension

---

[1] Compare his saying on p. 41 above, "Are not the pleasures of the understanding greater than the pleasures of the affections?"

of popular rights.   As for external policy, " there can no general rule be given (the occasions are so variable) save one which ever holdeth.   Which is that Princes do keep due sentinel that none of their neighbours do overgrow so (by increase of territory, by embracing of trade, by approaches, or the like) as they become more able to annoy them than they were" (xix. 65).   War is regarded as essential to national life.   " No body can be healthful without exercise, neither natural body nor politic ; and certainly to a kingdom or an estate a just and honourable war is the true exercise . . . . . for, in a slothful peace, both courages will effeminate and manners corrupt" (xxix. 260).   It is a fundamental principle of foreign policy to endeavour to gain wealth at the cost of neighbour States ; for " the increase of any estate must be upon the foreigner ; for whatsoever is somewhere gotten is somewhere lost" (xv. 140).

Internal policy is to be regulated in many respects with a view to external war.   The nation that is to become great is not to be over-taxed, because it is not possible "that a people overlaid with taxes should ever become valiant and martial" (xxix. 91).   States are to " take heed how their nobility and gentlemen do multiply too fast ; for, if the gentlemen be too many, the commons will be base ; and you will bring it to that, that not the hundred poll will be fit for a helmet, especially as to the infantry, which is the nerve of an army" (xxix. 113).   Yet, within certain limits, " the splendour, and magnificence, and great retinues, and hospitality of noblemen and gentlemen received into custom doth much conduce to martial greatness" (xxix. 135) ; and " kings that have able men of their nobility shall find ease in employing them and a better slide into their business ; for people naturally bend to them as born in some sort to command" (xiv. 49).   " Sedentary and within-door arts . . . . . have in their nature a contrariety to a military disposition," and, though they cannot be now carried on by slaves, as in the ancient States, yet they should be left chiefly to strangers" (xxix. 195), the natives being reserved for agriculture and manly industries.

The expression "balance of power" which we have used to describe Bacon's external policy, may also serve to characterize the internal relations which he wished to see established between the several orders of the State.   King, nobles, merchants, yeomen, all in their several places, are to form a kind of *cosmos*, after the pattern of the revolving heavens.   The King is to be the Primum Mobile (xv. 52; xvii. 21 ; xli. 59) which moves all things ; yet each planet is also to have its private motion.   A monarchy where there is no nobility is " a pure and absolute tyranny," like that of the Turks (xiv. 5).   The greater nobles are to be kept at a distance, but not depressed (xix. 130) ; rather they should be maintained as a barrier between the King and the insolency of inferiors (xiv. 24) ; the lesser nobles are to be encouraged as a counterpoise to the high nobility, and as being most influential with the common people and able to temper popular commotions (xix. 146).   The Commons are to be kept from want and necessity, and the better sort from poverty ; for the rebellions of the belly are the worst (xv. 118).   For the purpose of increasing the national wealth Bacon advocates what we should now consider an excess of paternal legislature, " the cherishing of manufactures ; the banishing of idleness ; the repressing of waste and excess by sumptuary laws ; the improvement and husbanding of the soil ; the regulating of things vendible ; the moderation of taxes and tributes " (xv. 124) : " Above all things, good policy is to be used that the treasures and moneys in a State be not gathered into few hands.   For otherwise a State may have a great stock, and yet starve ; and money is like muck, not good except it be spread.   This is done chiefly by suppressing, or at the least keeping a strict hand upon, the devouring trades of usury, engrossing, great pasturages, and the like " (xv. 155).   In the last resort, sedition among the nobles—the Giants of the antique mythology—must be remedied by calling in the commonalty, the hundred-handed Briareus (xv. 170) ; and, for the immediate suppression of slight disturbances, the prince is always to have at hand some great person of military valour (xv. 230).

It will be seen that in this internal " balance " Bacon regards his political *cosmos* mainly from the point of view of the Primum Mobile, or King.   It appears to have been his genuine conviction that danger was to be apprehended from " the inclination of the times to popularity," *i.e.* popular government.   This phrase occurs in the private note-book called the *Commentarius*

Solutus, in which he also notes a disposition to "popular estates creeping on the ground" in many countries. With the advantage of experience many will now pronounce Bacon to have been wrong in setting himself against a beneficial or irresistible tendency : but in those days, when Government by Parliament in its present shape was an untried experiment, it is easily conceivable that even an able statesman might regard with dread the prospect of an administration conducted by a mass of incoherent and untrained legislators. Bacon appears at all events to have been sincere in his desire to subordinate all classes and interests in the State to the royal Primum Mobile ; and this feeling, in days when the boundary line between the Prerogative and popular rights was not well defined, may perhaps in part explain the strong language in which he impresses the need of deference even on the part of the judicature to the will of the Crown : "Do as the planets do ; move always and be carried with the motion of your First Mover, which is your Sovereign." Thus he addressed the judges from his place as Lord Chancellor,[1] and to the same effect he writes in the *Essays:* " Let judges also remember that Salomon's throne was supported by lions on both sides ; let them be lions, but lions under the throne, being circumspect they do not check or oppose any points of sovereignty " (lvi. 136).

It is not however the theology, nor the morality, nor the politics, nor even the fascinating language of the *Essays*, which should constitute their chief claims. They contain, compressed into the smallest compass, many of the best sayings of the phi- losophic works, based on, and occasionally illustrated by, some of the most fundamental axioms of Bacon's philosophy. But their peculiar merit is that they not only imprint on the memory a number of thoughts good in themselves, and abounding in practical use, but also reveal the path by which the author arrived at them and stimulate the reader to follow still further on that path of analogy and to reach similar thoughts for him- self. For the basis of the *Essays*, as of the philosophical works, is this fundamental thought, that in social life, as in non-human nature, results can only be attained by knowing causes, and that the processes of human nature may often be not only illustrated,

---

[1] See above, p. 260.

but even ascertained and accomplished, by the application of certain Axioms common alike to animate and inanimate Nature. Thus the Essay on Ambition is based upon the unexpressed axiom that " All things move violently to their place, but easily in their place;" the Essay on Fortune has for its basis the notion that a combination of many small causes often escapes notice; "The way of Fortune is like the milken way in the sky, which is a meeting, or knot, of small stars, not seen asunder but giving light together. So are there a number of little and scarce discerned virtues, or rather faculties and customs, that make men fortunate." Herein consists the peculiar fitness of the metaphors so richly strewn throughout the Essays : they are often more than illustrations, they are the origins of the thought which the author presents to us; and of many of them Bacon would probably say, as he says elsewhere of Analogical Instances: "These are not only similitudes, as men of narrow observation may conceive them to be ; but the same footsteps of nature treading or printing upon several subjects or matters."

§ 62   BACON AS A WRITER

Remarking on the difference in style between the earlier and later editions of the *Essays*, Lord Macaulay has been led to the conclusion that in the works of Bacon, as in those of Burke, terseness in youth gives place to rich copiousness in old age—a reversal of the natural order of rhetorical development. And this opinion has been so generally adopted without question that a refutation of it may not be without use.

I do not believe that Lord Macaulay would have come to this conclusion if he had had before him that complete collection of Bacon's works for which these and later times will remain deeply indebted to Mr. Spedding. Bacon's style varied almost as much as his handwriting ; but it was influenced more by the subject-matter than by youth or old age. Few men have shown equal versatility in adapting their language to the slightest shade of circumstance and purpose. His style depended upon whether he was addressing a king, or a great nobleman, or a philosopher, or a friend; whether he was composing a State paper, pleading in a State trial, magnifying the Prerogative, extolling Truth, discussing studies, exhorting a judge, sending a New Year's present, or sounding a trumpet to prepare the way for the Kingdom of Man over Nature. It is a mistake to suppose that Bacon was never florid till he grew old. On the contrary, in the early *Devices*, written during his connection with Essex, he uses a rich exuberant style and poetic rhythm; but he prefers the rhetorical question of appeal to the complex period. On the other hand, in all his formal philosophical works, even in the *Advancement of Learning*, published as early as 1605, he uses the graver periodic structure, though often illustrated with rich metaphor. The *Essays*, both early and late, abound in pithy metaphor, as their natural illustration; but in the later and weightier edition—in which they were enlarged not only in number, but also " in *weight* so that they are indeed a new work "—there is an intentional increase of rhetorical ornament and illustration, and, in some of the later Essays on more serious subjects, there is somewhat more of the periodic structure. But this is caused by the weight of the subject, not by weight of years.

As instances, take first the following specimens of the early florid style (a comparison between the servant of Love and the servant of Self-love) from the *Device of Essex*, 1594-5 :

"But give ear now to the comparison of my master's condition, and acknowledge such a difference as betwixt the melting hailstone and the solid pearl. Indeed it seemeth to depend as the globe of the earth seemeth to hang in the air ; but yet it is firm and stable in itself. It is like a cube or die-form, which, toss it or throw it any way, it ever lighteth upon a square. . . . His falls are like the falls of Antaeus ; they renew his strength : his clouds are like the clouds of harvest, which makes the sun break forth with greater force ; his wanes and changes are like the moon, whose globe is all light towards the sun when it is all dark towards the world ; such is the excellency of her nature and of his estate."

Next, take a passage from the *Advancement of Learning* (1605). Though published twenty years before the last edition of the *Essays*, it is no less periodic in structure, and hardly less rich in style, than the passage quoted by Lord Macaulay from the latter .

"Neither is certainly that other merit of learning, in repressing the inconveniences which grow from man to man, much inferior to the former, of relieving the necessities which arise from nature ; which merit was lively set forth by the ancients in that feigned relation of Orpheus' theatre ; where all beasts and birds assembled, and forgetting their several appetites, some of prey, some of game, some of quarrel, stood all sociably together listening unto the airs and accords of the harp ; the sound thereof no sooner ceased or was drowned by some louder noise, but every beast returned to his own nature. Wherein is aptly described the condition of men ; who are full of savage and unreclaimed desires of profit, of lust, of revenge ; which, as long as they give ear to precepts, to laws, to religion sweetly touched with eloquence, and persuasion of books, of sermons, of harangues, so long is society and peace maintained ; but if these instruments be silent, or that sedition and tumult make them not audible, all things dissolve into anarchy and confusion."

On the other hand the *History of Henry VII.*, written in 1621, although it is for the most part periodic in structure, yet by its abruptness and occasional roughness, its colloquial phrases and homely metaphor, often reminds us of the earlier *Essays :*

"So that they were now like sand without lime ; ill bound together ; especially as many as were English ; who were at a gaze, looking strange upon one another, not knowing who was faithful to their side, but thinking that the king (what with his baits and what with his nets) would draw them all unto him that were anything worth. And indeed it came to pass that divers came away by the thrid, sometimes one and sometimes another."

Or take from the same source the following humorous description (all the more humorous when it is remembered that Bacon himself had been both a " lawyer and a privy councillor ") of Henry VII.'s instruments, Empson and Dudley :

"And as kings do more easily find instruments for their will and humour than for their service and honour, he had gotten for his purpose, or beyond his purpose, two instruments, Empson and Dudley ; whom the people esteemed as his horse-leeches and shearers : bold men and careless of fame, and that took toll of their master's grist. . . . These two persons, being lawyers in science and privy councillors in authority (as the corruption of the best things is the worst) turned law and justice into wormwood and rapine."

G G

In accordance with this adaptation of style to subject, we may expect to find a richer and more rhythmical style in those essays which deal with high subjects such as Truth, Death, Adversity, Love, Envy, Friendship, and a more blunt and colloquial style in those that deal with more commonplace subjects such as Studies, Faction, Discourse, Health, Expense. But the edition of 1597 included only these latter commonplace subjects. This then (independently of the intention to add *weight* to the last edition), is a sufficient reason why the language and construction in the supplementary Essays might naturally be more sententious, periodic, and elevated than in the earlier Essays—without supposing that Bacon's style underwent any great and unusual change in his maturity and old age.

It would seem that Bacon's habit of collecting choice words and phrases, to express his meaning exactly, briefly, or ornately, had from a very early date the effect of repelling some of his hearers by the interspersion of unusual expressions and metaphors. Fresh from hearing an argument of Mr. Francis Bacon in the year 1594 "in a most famous Chequer Chamber case," a young lawyer thus records his impressions:

"His argument, contracted by the time, seemed a *bataille serrée*, as hard to be discovered as conquered. The unusual words wherewith he had spangled his speech were rather gracious for their propriety than strange for their novelty, and like to serve both for occasions to report and means to remember his argument. Certain sentences of his, somewhat obscure, and as it were, presuming upon their capacities, will, I fear, make some of them admire rather than commend him."[1]

Conscious of this temptation to be singular and obscure, Bacon would often ask his friends and secretaries (so Rawley informs us) "if the meaning were expressed plainly enough, as being one that accounted words to be but subservient or ministerial to matter;" and in letters to Bishop Andrews and Toby Matthew he asks them to "mark whatsoever shall not seem current in the style," and to correct "such words and phrases as" they "cannot like." On one occasion (as early as 1610) the King is said to have manifested his dislike for Sir Francis Bacon's

[1] Spedding, i. 263.

" extravagant style " [1] by requesting some one else to represent more soberly the wishes of the House of Commons. It would therefore be more in accordance with fact to call attention to this singularity of language, largeness of vocabulary, and richness of illustrations, as distinguishing Bacon's style to some extent *in every period, and especially in his early period,* than to lay stress upon any imaginary development of the bold early style into a florid late one.

But the leading peculiarity of Bacon's literary style is its *sympathetic* nature; that is to say, its versatile adaptation to every slightest variation of subject or aspect of a subject. As Lord Chancellor, he can be florid and discursive upon the King's Prerogative, but homely and forcible on ordinary legal business. " I do not mean to make it a horse-race who shall be first at Westminster Hall," and again, " By the grace of God I will make injunctions a hard pillow to sleep on." Even in the later additions to the earlier Essays—though for the most part purposely " weighty " and periodical in structure—yet, when the subject needs it, we find the old terse metaphor characteristic of the earliest edition : " The rebellions of the belly are the worst ; " [2] " Money is like muck, not good except it be spread ; " [3] " But then it must be a prudent king, such as is able to grind with a hand-mill ; " [4] " Distilled books are like common distilled waters, flashy things." [5]

If therefore any difference could be exhibited in detail between Bacon's later and earlier styles it would probably be found to be this, that *the later works are more free from uncommon words and phrases and are " more current in the style."* He seems gradually to have succeeded, with the aid of friendly critics, in shaking off his early tendency to " spangle his speech " with fit and terse but unusual expressions. But that he felt any pride in, or even set just value on, his unique mastery of the English language there is scarcely any indication. *Of his Latin* he was proud : " They tell me," he writes (February 1610)

---

[1] See above, p. 201. The word "extravagant" may possibly refer to the thought as well as to the language ; but those who have read Bacon's utterances in the House of Commons will find that, wherever the King is mentioned, an "extravagance " of language accompanies "extravagance " of thought.

[2] *Essays,* xv. 87.   *Ibid.* 76.   [4] *Ibid.* iv. 29.

[5] *Ibid.* iv. 30, a passage added in the later edition.

complacently to his friend Toby Matthew, "that my Latin is turned into silver and become current." His friend was then in Spain, close to the terrible Inquisition; but Bacon thinks even the Inquisition would pass his Latin: "Had you been here, you should have been my Inquisitor before it came forth: but I think the greatest Inquisitor in Spain will allow it." [1] We may search all Bacon's writings through before we shall find a sentence like this to show that he took an equal pride in his English. Yet others of his day, and those good judges, were aware that he was a master of English style. Sir Walter Raleigh pronounced him eminent both as a speaker and as a writer; and here is the judgment passed by Ben Jonson on *Dominus Verulamius*, as a speaker, after his death:

" His language (when he could spare a jest [2]) was nobly censorious. No man ever spake more neatly, more pressly, more weightily ; or suffered less emptiness, less idleness, in what he uttered. No member of his speech but consisted of his own graces. [3] His hearers could not cough or look aside from him without loss. He commanded where he spoke and had his judges angry and pleased at his devotion. No man had their affections more in his power. The fear of every man that heard him was, lest he should make an end." [4]

The same critic, in a review of the great English writers from the earliest ages, awards the palm to Bacon :

" Cicero is said to have been the only wit that the people of Rome had, equalled to their empire. We have had many, and in their several ages, ... Sir Philip Sidney and Mr. Hooker (in different matter) grew great masters of wit and language, and in whom all vigour of invention and strength of judgment met. The Earl of Essex, noble and high ; and Sir

---

[1] It is possible that Bacon's pride in his Latin may have been increased not only by his comparative unfamiliarity with that language but also by a little contemporary criticism, not always quite so favourable : " I come even now," says Chamberlain, December 16th, 1608, " from reading a short discourse of Queen Elizabeth's life, written in Latin by Sir Francis Bacon. If you have not seen or heard of it, it is worth your inquiry ; and yet methinks he doth *languescere* towards the end, and falls from his first pitch ; *neither dare I warrant that his Latin will abide test or touch.*"—(Spedding, *Works*, vi. 283.)

[2] This hints at one of Bacon's defects. Compare what the faithful Yelverton reports to Bacon himself (see above, p. 263) : " It is too common in every man's mouth in Court that your greatness shall be abated ; and, *as your tongue hath been as a razor to some, so shall theirs be to you.*"

[3] That is, I suppose, " each part of his speech had a grace of its own."

[4] Ben Jonson's Works, ed. Gifford, p. 749.

Walter Raleigh, not to be contemned either for judgment or style. Sir Henry Savile, grave, and truly lettered ; Sir Edwin Sandys, excellent in both ; Lord Egerton, the Chancellor, a grave and great orator, and best when he was provoked. But his learned and able (though unfortunate) successor is he who hath filled up all numbers,[1] and performed that, in our tongue, which may be compared or preferred either to insolent Greece, or to haughty Rome. In short, within his view and about his time, were all the wits born that could honour a language or help study. Now things daily fall ; wits grow downward, and eloquence grows backward ; so that he may be named and stand as the mark and ἀκμή of our language." [2]

But of all this, his peculiar greatness, Bacon would seem to have known little or nothing ; and perhaps for this very reason he gained the palm of style the more easily because he was indifferent to it, and hardly conscious of his claim to it. In his estimation, literary style was a snare quite as often as a help. In " civil occasions, of conference, counsel, persuasion, discourse," or the like, " a sensible and plausible elocution may be of use ; but surely to the severe inquisition of truth, and the deep progress into philosophy it is some hindrance." [3]   It is—

"The first distemper of learning, when men study words and not matter ; whereof though I have represented an example of late times, yet it hath been and will be, *secundum et majus et minus*, in all time. . . . It seems to me that Pygmalion's frenzy is a good emblem or portraiture of this vanity ; for words are but the images of matter ; and, except they have life of reason and invention, to fall in love with them is all one as to fall in love with a picture." [4]

Another reason for Bacon's indifference to English style was that he wrote for posterity and disbelieved in the permanence of the language of Spenser and Shakespeare. He rested his fame upon his Latin writings. For the sake of making his philosophy generally intelligible in his own times to the learned in all countries, we could not have been surprised if he had desired to have his words translated into the language of the learned ; but it was not of his own times that he was thinking, but of future ages. As he grew older he appears to have been more and more impressed with the hopelessness of any expectations of lasting

---

[1] A Latinism, meaning "has attained perfection."
[2] Ben Jonson's Works, ed. Gifford, p. 749.
[3] *Advancement of Learning*, Book I. iv. 2.   [4] *Ibid.*

fame or usefulness based upon English books. As early as 1607 he desired to have the *Advancement of Learning* translated into Latin ; but this was for his contemporaries in foreign parts—" the privateness of the language wherein it is written, excluding so many readers "[1]—at least, there is no mention of posterity. But after his downfall—when age, and infirmities, and poverty pressed on him, and he stretched forth a more eager expectation to those "future ages" to which he bequeathed his name and reputation—he repeatedly avows his belief that English books will not last. When he sends the Latin translation of the *Advancement of Learning* to the Prince, he says (1623) : " It is a book, I think, *will live, and be a citizen of the world, as English books are not ;* "[2] in his dedication of the last edition of the *Essays* to Buckingham (1625) he conceives that " *the Latin Volume of them (being in the universal language) may last as long as books shall last ;* " and in a letter to his intimate friend, Toby Matthew (1623), he more plainly avows both his regard for the opinion of " posterity " and his belief that posterity would not preserve works written in the " modern languages : "

" My labours are now most set to have those works which I had formerly published—as that of Advancement of Learning, that of Henry VII., that of the Essays (being retractate and made more perfect) well translated into Latin by the help of some good pens which forsake me not. *For these modern languages will at one time or other play the bank-rowtes* [3] *with books ; and since I have lost much time with this age, I would be glad, as* [4] *God shall give me leave, to recover it with posterity.* '

It is very strange, and not a little sad, to think that, owing to this deeply-rooted distrust in the destiny of his native language, Bacon threw away (so far as we can see) much of the small portion of his life devoted to philosophy and literature. The very means that he took to insure fame have tended to deprive him of it. Who, except a scholar or two at the Universities, now reads, in the Latin, the *De Augmentis,* or the *Novum Organum,* or the *Sapientia Veterum,* or that book which was to " last as long as books shall last," the Latin translation

---

[1] Spedding, iii. 301.   [2] *Ibid.* vii. 436.   [3] *i.e.* " bankrupts."
[4] So Mr. Spedding's text : perhaps " as " means " so far as." Dean Church reads " if " instead of " as.'

of the *Essays?* For the vast English-speaking race of the twentieth century, amid the increasing pressure of the claims of English authors, it seems probable that the Latin works on which Lord Bacon rested his fame with future ages, will be little better than waste paper. It will be the despised *Advancement of Learning* and the English *Essays* that will sustain his reputation as a master of words as long as the English language shall last. And the same disappointment of his expectations has befallen his Science. All that Bacon thought best in it is now unanimously rejected as worthless for present uses ; and some have even denied that it was ever worth anything for use in the past. Hence it has come to pass that the man who, more than any other, protested against " Pygmalion's frenzy" of devotion to words, himself owes in great measure that existence which he coveted in the minds of posterity to his literary style. Posterity has taken the philosopher at his word and pronounced that he spoke the truth when, in mock-modesty, he declared that he himself was but " the trumpeter to call the wits together."

Yet while a general acquiescence must be given to this verdict, it must not be adopted without discrimination. If Bacon is now no more to us than a Master of words, it must be at least admitted that Bacon's words are not as other men's. It is not " the choiceness of the phrase, and the round and clean composition of the sentence, and the sweet falling of the clauses, and the varying and illustration of his works with tropes and figures," that constitute his claim to a literary immortality : it is that his words—to use his own expression— are " male," by which he meant not impotently ornamental, but generative of such thoughts as are potent to produce action. As long as infirm human nature remains what it is, few Englishmen will fail to learn something about their infirmities from the *Essays*, and to rise from their perusal with a quickened contempt for an objectless existence, and for those who, having an object, do not go straight towards it. Progress as the Sciences may, it is difficult to believe that the *Advancement of Learning* can ever become quite antiquated or superfluous ; as long at least as it is not superfluous to inspire mankind with a confident, patient, and enthusiastic faith that there is an order and correspondence in the whole Universe of Learning; that one Law rules all the provinces of animate and inanimate Nature; that it is the will of God that His children shall approach more closely to Him by searching out His ways in heaven and earth and in the human heart; that no imaginary flaming sword of divine jealousy need deter the student from drawing near to this Paradise of Knowledge; and that no Pillars of Hercules, with their antiquated *ne plus ultra*, need now be supposed to bar the voyage of the explorer who is bent on steering out from inland seas into the untraversed ocean. And in this sense the English works of Bacon may still be regarded as a *Partus Masculus Temporis*, a veritable Male Birth of Time, bearing the inscription *Plus ultra*, "There is more beyond," and justifying that prediction of the Prophet which the author of the *Instauratio Magna* proudly placed upon his title-page, *Multi pertransibunt et augebitur Scientia*.[1]

[1] Daniel, xii. 4

APPENDIX I [1]

§ 63 Professor Fowler's Defence of Bacon's Morality

There have not been wanting modern defenders of Bacon's morality who are unwilling that he should be called in any sense a pupil of Machiavelli. "Nothing," says one of these,[2] "can well be more remote either from what is ordinarily understood by Machiavellism, or from some of the actual utterances of Machiavelli himself, when taken in their literal sense, than such passages as the following, expressing, as I believe, Bacon's genuine sentiments : ' I take Goodness in this sense, the affecting of the weal of men, which is that the Grecians call Philanthropia. This of all virtues and dignities of the mind is the greatest, being the character of the Deity ; and without it man is a busy, mischievous, wretched thing ; no better than a kind of vermin, &c.' ' Wisdom for a man's self is, in many branches thereof a depraved thing. It is the wisdom of rats, that will be sure to leave a house somewhat before it falls.' " And the same advocate defends Bacon for teaching the Art of Self-advancement, on the ground that a moralist is justified in giving " rules for bettering one's own fortune, provided, at least, that *such rules are not likely to interfere with the general welfare.*"

Such a defence does not meet the case. It is not by showing that Bacon *theoretically* admires goodness that we can disprove the fact that he was influenced by Machiavelli. Machiavelli himself is as frank as his pupil in recognizing *theoretically* the badness of the Evil Arts which he systematises.

[1] Note on p. 325.
[2] Professor Fowler, *Francis Bacon*, p. 41.

" These ways," says the teacher, " are cruel and contrary, not only
to civil, but to Christian, and, indeed, human conversation ; for
which reason they are to be rejected by everybody ; for certainly
'tis better to remain a private person than to make oneself king
by the calamity and destruction of one's people. Nevertheless,
he who neglects to take the first good way, if he would preserve
himself, must make use of the bad."

It is not, therefore, by quoting theoretical condemnations of
selfishness, or praises of truthfulness, that an advocate can hope
to justify the morality of the *Essays*. The justification must be
effected, if at all, by showing that Bacon does not " give rules
for bettering one's fortunes " without " providing that *such rules
shall not interfere with the general welfare*." But this cannot be
shown. Against the enthusiastic eulogy of Goodness above
quoted, we are forced to set the caution—true enough, but
suspicious in a treatise great part of which is taken up with
precepts concerning the art of " bettering one's fortunes "—that
" extreme lovers of their country or masters were never fortunate, neither can they be." [1]   Against the statement that "clear
and round dealing is the honour of man's nature," we must
place the admissions that, " No man can be secret except he
give himself a little scope of dissimulation," [2] and that " the
best-composition and temperature is to have openness in fame
and opinion, secrecy in habit, dissimulation in seasonable use,
and a power to feign if there be no remedy." [3] As for politicians,
tortuosity and deceit are considered by Bacon almost matters of
necessity in them : " Such (envious) dispositions are the very
errors of human nature, and yet they are the fittest timber to
make great Politiques of, like to knee-timber, that is good for
ships that are ordained to be tossed, but not for building houses
that shall stand firm." [4]   It is true that he dislikes and dreads
the predominance of cunning : " Nothing," he says, " doth more
hurt in a State than that cunning men pass for wise." [5] But in
his *Essay on Truth* he is obliged to admit that " mixture of
falsehood is like alloy in coin of gold and silver, which may
make the metal work the better," though the metal is debased

[1] *Essays*, xl. 32.   [2] *Ibid.* vi. 76.   [3] *Ibid.* vi. 110-113.
[4] *Ibid.* xiii. 68, " knee-timber " is " crooked timber."
[5] *Ibid.* xxii. 118.

by it.[1] And in practice we have found that Bacon considered this alloy not unfrequently necessary.

Again, we have seen that one part of Bacon's Art of Self-advancement—or, as he called it, the Architecture of Fortune—consisted in "morigeration," that is, in accommodating oneself to the ways of great men ; another consisted in Ostentation, or showing off one's abilities to the best advantage ; and one of the precepts of this art is that " Honour that is gained and broken upon another hath the quickest reflection, like diamonds cut with facets; and therefore let a man contend to excel any competitors of his honour in out-shooting them, if he can, in their own bow." [2] Those who defend these and other similar precepts as " not likely to interfere with the general welfare " can hardly have realised what their author meant by them, and must be referred to his own interpretation of them in the *Commentarius Solutus*. There we found Bacon making notes with the view of putting these precepts in practice ; deliberately preparing to conform himself to Salisbury's humours and to support Salisbury's propositions, whether right or wrong, at the Council Board ; seeking opportunities for attending the King at meals, and for engaging great persons in conversation in public places, thereby to increase his own reputation ; trying to show one great Lord how far he (Bacon) is superior to the present Attorney-General, and another great Lord what reverence he would receive from him (Bacon) if he were Lord Chancellor ; elaborating compliments and messages of condolence and little arrangements to induce lesser persons to remember him in their wills ; and systematically noting down a rival's weakness and shortcomings, in order that he may drop out casual epigrams holding them up to ridicule, so as to prepare the way for ousting him from his office in order that he himself might step into the vacant place. All this is very small and mean and far below the level of the villainy of the Evil Arts of Machiavelli ; but it does not cease to be bad merely because it is not colossal ; it does not cease to be hollow, false, demoralizing, fatal to all purity and nobility in social life, because it is—truth compels us to say it even of so great a genius—marvellously and portentously contemptible.　Surely

[1] *Essays*, i. 65.　　　　　　　[2] *Ibid.* lv. 20

such a doctrine of the Architecture of Fortune, to be built up upon petty untruthfulness and petty ostentation, cannot be sheltered—in the face of such plain practical illustrations of its tendency, afforded us by the author himself—under the quiet assumption that "such rules are *not likely to interfere with the general welfare.*"

[1] The author of *Daniel Deronda* appears to me to have had Francis Bacon in her mind when she wrote the following defence of dissimulation and Deronda's retort. " There's a bad style of humbug, but there's also a good style, one that oils the wheels and makes progress possible . . . . It's no use having an Order of Council against popular shallowness.   There is no action possible without a little acting."

" One may be obliged to give way to an occasional necessity," said Deronda. " But it is one thing to say, 'In this particular case I am forced to put on this foolscap and grin,' and another to buy a pocket foolscap and practise myself in grinning . . . . If I were to set up for a public man, I might mistake my own success for public expediency."

A few pages further on she speaks of such systematic dissimulation as being destructive of " that openness which is the sweet fresh air of our moral life."

APPENDIX II

SUMMARY OF THAT PART OF THE "ADVANCEMENT OF LEARNING" WHICH TREATS OF PHILOSOPHY

§ 64 THE "ADVANCEMENT OF LEARNING:" NATURAL PHILOSOPHY

In pp. 353-5 above, the reader will find a brief statement of the scheme of the whole of the *Advancement of Learning*, with its triple division of human learning into History, Poesy, and Philosophy; and a summary was given of the few sections devoted to History and Poesy. We proceed now to summarize that part which treats of Philosophy.

The truths of Natural Philosophy have been said to lie hid in mines; but art, or Vulcan, is also a great discoverer of natural truths; and, owing to the importance of experiment and practice in the study of Nature, we must discuss separately the mine and the furnace, the pioneer and the smith, the inquisition of causes and the production of effects, or in other words, Natural Science and Natural Prudence. (*Adv.* II. vii. 1; *Augm.* III. iii.)

First then for Natural Science or Theory. This is usually divided into Physic, Metaphysic, and Mathematic; but we shall place Mathematic under the head of Metaphysic, using the word Metaphysic not in its ordinary sense of "supernatural,"[1] nor as identical with Prima Philosophia (which is the parent of all sciences) but as the higher portion of Natural Science. Physic will contemplate that which is inherent in matter and therefore transitory; Metaphysic, that which is abstracted and fixed. Physic will handle that which supposes in nature only a being and moving; Metaphysic, that which supposes further in nature a reason, understanding, and plan; Physic will seek material and efficient causes, Metaphysic, formal and final causes.[2]

[1] See *Macbeth*, i. 4, 30.
[2] "Final and formal causes" are (Professor Fowler, *Francis Bacon*, p. 70) "the ultimate purposes which things subserve, and that innermost constitution or essence from which the other properties of an object or quality are derived."

To take an example, Physic will be content with noting that fire is the cause of induration in clay, and of "colliquation" in wax; but Metaphysic, not content with noting causes that produce varying effects, will ascend to the fixed causes, or laws of nature, which produce induration in the one case and colliquation in the other. Physic and Metaphysic are both based upon Natural History; and the three form a kind of pyramid in which Natural History is the lowest layer, describing the variety of things; next comes Physic, describing the causes, but variable or respective causes; higher still comes Metaphysic, describing the fixed or constant causes. As for the vertical point, the summary law of nature *opus quod operatur Deus a principio usque ad finem*, we know not whether man's inquiry can attain to it. These three stages of knowledge are to the impious no better than three steps upward to rebellion—Pelion on Ossa, and on Ossa Olympus; but to the pious they are as a Trisagion, Holy, Holy, Holy, to the Glory of God.

As to Physic, it is not deficient, though possibly inaccurate.[1] As to Metaphysic, considered as the investigation of formal causes (the form being ὁ λόγος τῆς οὐσίας, that which determines a thing to be what it is), it is deficient. For though Plato descried that Forms were the true object of knowledge, he fell into the error of supposing that Forms are absolutely abstracted from matter instead of being confined and determined by matter; and so his opinion proved barren. Others have given up the search after Forms as hopeless. But they have been led into this despair by the fruitless search after the Forms of substances, such as the Form of a lion, an oak, or gold. This search is no less useless and absurd than the attempt to seek in gross the Forms of those sounds which make whole *words*, which by composition and transposition of letters are infinite in number. But how much easier to inquire the Forms of those sounds which make simple *letters*, and hence to infer the Forms of words! In the same way it is a comparatively simple task to inquire the Forms of sense, of voluntary motion, of vegetation, of colours, of gravity and levity, of density, of tenuity, of heat, of cold, and all other natures and qualities. These (like an alphabet) are not many, and from these all created things derive their essences (upheld by matter); and to investigate these Forms is the task of Metaphysic.

Not that Physic does not deal with these qualities. But how? Only as regards the efficient and variable causes. For example, Physic asserts that the cause of whiteness in snow and frost is the subtle intermixture of air and water. But this is not the Form; it is only the Efficient Cause which is ever but the vehicle of the Formal Cause. But if the inquiry be made in Metaphysic, the answer is something of this sort, that two transparent bodies intermixed, with their optical portions arranged in a simple and regular order, constitute whiteness.[3]

---

[1] For Bacon's confidence (subsequently shaken) in the simplicity of the investigations of *Forms* see pp. 385, and 351.

[2] For *Forms*, see note on p.384, above.

[3] This is an addition only found in the *De Augmentis*. As to the investigation of "whiteness," see *Valerius Terminus*, p. 350, above.

The ways of Physic are ever narrow and restrained ; for physical causes only give light to new invention in *simili materia* ; but whosoever knows a Form knows the possibility of superinducing the nature of that Form upon any variety of matter ; and his path is like that described, though in a more divine sense, by Solomon, " When thou goest, thy steps shall not be straitened ; and when thou runnest, thou shall not stumble."

The second task of Metaphysic, namely, the inquiry of Final Causes (that is, the objects for the sake of which an agent, whether consciously or not, has been performing an action) has been not so much neglected as misplaced ; for it has been transferred from Metaphysic to Physic. Here it has proved an excuse for sluggishness, so that the atomic philosophy of Democritus (who did not suppose a Mind in the frame of things, and, therefore, neglected Final Causes) has proved more fruitful in physical science than the philosophy of Plato or Aristotle, who introduced Final Causes, the former as a part of theology, the latter as a part of logic. But in its right place, that is in Metaphysic, this inquiry into Final Causes is good ; and there is no repugnance between Formal and Final Causes. For example, to say, in Physic, that the cause of the hairs in the eyelids is to protect the sight, is misplaced and prejudicial to inquiry, but there is no repugnance between that Final Cause and the cause that " pilosity is incident to orifices of moisture." For two causes can be true and compatible, one declaring an intention, the other a consequence only ; and the wisdom of God is more admirable when Nature intendeth one thing and Providence draweth forth another.

In Mathematics there is no deficience ; but the study of pure Mathematics is not sufficiently recognized as a remedy for dull, wandering, and sensuous understandings ; and, as nature is further disclosed, there cannot fail to be more kinds of mixed Mathematics.   (*Adv.* II. vii. 1, viii. 2 ; *Augm.* III. iii.—iv.)

Passing from the Mine to the Furnace, *i.e.* from Natural Science to Natural Prudence, we divide it into three parts, experimental, philosophical, and " magical," corresponding to the three divisions in Natural Philosophy, viz., History, Physic, Metaphysic.[1] Not much can be effected by the first two of these ; and the third is altogether deficient. For the present books of monstrous Magic are to the future books of genuine and Metaphysical Magic what the story of King Arthur is to Cæsar's Commentaries—the latter being both more wonderful as well as more true.

In the present Magic it is not the ends, but the means, that are absurd. By studying weight, colour, fragility, volatility, we may superinduce these qualities upon any metal, and produce the alchemist's first object—gold ; by studying arefactions, assimilation of nourishment, the increase and clearing of the spirits, the depredations made by the spirits on the humours and solid parts ; by investigating diets, bathings, anointings, and the like, we may

---

[1] In the Latin translation the merely empiric and manual practice which he here calls experimental, is relegated to Natural History and banished from Philosophy.

attain their second object—prolongation of life. To develop the true Magic we must make a Kalendar of inventions, noting also things deemed impossible or not yet invented, and also approximations to inventions ; and we must also be careful to value inventions, not in proportion to their immediate use, but for the light they throw on the further discovery of causes.

Thus far concerning Natural Philosophy, wherein, if any readers contradict, the Author will not contend. If it be truth, the voice of Nature will consent.

" And as Alexander Borgia was wont to say of the expedition of the French for Naples, that they came with chalk in their hands to mark up their lodgings and not with weapons to fight ; so I like better that entry of truth which cometh peaceably with chalk to mark up those minds which are capable to lodge and harbour it, than that which cometh with pugnacity and contention."

It will be well, however, to add a Kalendar of doubts or problems, and of popular errors in particular matters ; and also an account of differences of opinion touching the principles of nature. (*Adv.* II. viii. 3—6 ; *Augm.* III. v.—*ad fin.*)

§ 65 THE "ADVANCEMENT OF LEARNING." HUMAN PHILOSOPHY ; MAN "SEGREGATE" : THE UNDERSTANDING

The third subdivision of Philosophy, it will be remembered, was Human Philosophy. This includes, first the knowledge of the connection and mutual influence of body and mind; secondly, knowledge concerning the body; thirdly, knowledge concerning the mind.

Again, Human Philosophy may be either simple or particular, considering man *segregate*; or else conjugate and civil, considering man *congregate* and in society.

The knowledge of " human nature entire," that is, of the connection between body and mind, has been attempted, but with doubtful success. (*Adv.* II. ix. 1—3 ; *Augm.* IV. i.) As to the knowledge of the body, medical science has been more professed than laboured, and there is a deficience in the registration of cases and in the " inquiry which is made by anatomy ; " wherein, although men might not be utilized, the needful results might be obtained from the dissection of beasts alive.[1] Cosmetic and athletic are deficient, but the deficiencies are not worth supplying. (*Adv.* II. x. 1—13 ;

---

[1] Bacon's position in the antivivisection controversy is here clearly defined.

Augm. IV. ii.) The investigation into the human mind may inquire the nature of the soul or mind, or the faculties thereof.

The soul, being inspired immediately from God, and not extracted out of the mass of heaven and earth, is therefore not a subject for philosophy, but to be inquired of by religion. As for divination and fascination—the two appendices to this part of the knowledge concerning the soul—they are deficient, not in mass, but because of the undetected mixture of verity and vanity. (*Adv.* II. xi. 1—3; *Augm.* IV. iii.—*ad fin.*)

As to the faculties of the mind, since we described three above, the Memory, the Imagination, and the Reason, it might be supposed that the knowledge of the mental faculties would deal with these three. But we were then speaking of the parts of learning produced by the several parts of the mind; now we are speaking of the sciences which handle the parts of the mind, and for this purpose we shall divide the subject into two parts, the one being the Understanding and Reason, the other, the Will, Appetite, and Affection. For whereas the Reason produces "position or decree," and the Will produces action or execution, the Imagination moves in both provinces. For Sense delivers its images to the Imagination before Reason can judge of them, and Reason delivers its judgments to Imagination before the Will can execute them. It is true that the Imagination is not always servant but sometimes dominant, for example, in matters of faith and Religion: "Nevertheless, because I find not any science that doth properly or fitly pertain to the Imagination, I see no cause to alter my former division." The knowledge of the Reason is the art of arts; for as the hand is the Instrument of Instruments, so is the mind the Form of Forms; and the intellectual arts are four—(1) *invention*, (2) *judgment*, (3) *retention or memory*, and (4) *tradition*. (*Adv.* II. xii. 1—3; *Augm.* V. 1.)

(1) As for *invention* of arts and sciences, all confess that at present it has no existence. The beasts, which were gods to the Egyptians, have been as reasonable inventors as men. The ordinary Induction, concluding upon enumeration of particulars without instance contradictory, is a mere conjecture, which may be overthrown by some new instance; as if Samuel had rested upon those sons of Jesse which were brought before him, and failed of David, who was in the field. It is not possible from mere particulars to rise at once to the principles of sciences. Even if the principles could be in some cases rightly ascertained, yet it is impossible by syllogisms to deduce middle propositions[1] from them in natural philosophy. For the syllogism consists of propositions, and propositions consist of words, and words are often only the current tokens of popular unscientific notions, having nothing in reality corresponding to them; so that no amount of

---

[1] That is, general propositions about *concretes*, distinguished from an *abstract* proposition such as "things that are equal to the same thing are equal to one another." A particular proposition about concretes would be ranked as *lowest*; a general proposition about concretes as *middle*; and an abstract proposition as highest. See the second paragraph of the summary of the *Delineatio*, above, p. 358, and the fourth paragraph of the *Cogitata*, p. 362.

H H

argument can ever correct the initial error or deduce a true conclusion. Not that the senses are in fault ; but the intellectual powers are weak, and make false inferences from the reports of the senses.

This part of *invention* the Author purposes in a future treatise to expound in two parts, one termed *Experientia Literata*, the other *Interpretatio Naturae*. These terms are explained in the Latin translation, which states that there are three ways of advancing, 1st groping in the darkness, that is, with unmethodical and casual experiment, 2nd being led by a guide's hand, that is, passing from one experiment to another (*Experientia Literata*), 3rd being led by the light itself (*Interpretatio Naturae.*) (*Adv.* II. xiii. 1–5 ; *Augm.* V. ii.)

As to *invention* of speech or argument, it is not properly invention, but resumption of that which has been already invented ; and it implies two courses, preparation (*Promptuaria*) and suggestion ('*Topica*). Both Cicero and Demosthenes approve the premeditation of theses, to be particularized and utilized as occasion may allow ; and their authority may outweigh Aristotle's ridicule of the Sophists (who, as he says, exhibit shoes ready made instead of teaching how to make a shoe) and may warn us against changing a rich wardrobe for a pair of shears. Suggestion—which directs us to marks that may excite our mind to return and reproduce its collected knowledge—is useful for inquiry as well as for invention ; for a faculty of wise inquiry is half a knowledge. Topics may be particular as as well as general ; and, in every special inquiry, we shall gain by drawing forth the subject into questions or places of inquiry. (*Adv.* II. xiii. 6–10 ; *Augm.* V. iii.)

(2) From *invention* we pass to *judgment.* The judgment of proofs and demonstrations may deal with inductive or deductive proof. But in Induction the same action of the mind which invents, judges. Therefore, for judgment of Induction, the reader is referred to what has been said above concerning the Interpretation of Nature. But in deductive proof the case is different ; for the invention of the middle proposition is one thing, and judging of the consequence of the syllogism is another thing, and therefore necessitates separate consideration. This art (of judging deductive proof) has two parts, a part of Direction, and a part of Caution ; viz. Analytic (representing Direction) which frames a true form of syllogism, by deflections from which we may judge erroneous deductions ; and Elenche (representing Caution) which exhibits the more subtle forms of sophisms with their refutations. Under the latter head should come the great sophism of sophisms, the equivocation or ambiguity of words and phrase, especially such as express the common adjuncts of essences ; majority, minority, priority, posterity, identity, diversity, possibility, act, totality, part, existence, privation and the like.

But there is a much more profound and important kind of fallacies into which no inquiry has been made. These are not external but situate in the mind itself. For the mind of man, not being a clear and equal glass, but rather like an enchanted glass, is full of inherent misrepresentations.[1] For example, it is more affected by a few affirmatives than by many negatives (an error which is the root of all superstition), and it supposes in nature a greater uniformity than there really is (an error that has perverted astronomy).[2] Secondly, there are the false appearances imposed upon us by our individual nature, imprisoned as we are in the caves of our own complexions and customs ; so, Plato intermingled his philosophy with theology, Aristotle with logic, Proclus with mathematics, and, while the alchemists extracted a philosophy from the furnace, Gilbert made one out of his observations of a load-stone.[3] Thirdly, there are the false appearances imposed by words, which are framed according to the notions and capacities of the vulgar ; and although we think we govern our words, yet oftentimes, as a Tartar's bow, they shoot back upon the understanding, and mightily entangle the judgment.[4] Lastly, the application of different kinds of proof to different subjects is an important part of judgment ; and it is deficient (*Adv.* II. xiv. 1-12 ; *Augm.* V. iv.). Passing rapidly over (3) *memory*, which is noted as "weakly inquired of," we come to the fourth intellectual art, *tradition;* wherein we may discuss the organ, the method, and the illustration.

(4) The inquiry into one kind of organ, the written signs of language (hieroglyphics, &c.), is deficient ; the inquiry into words, as being "the footsteps and prints of reason" (philology), is reported not as deficient but as "very worthy to be reduced into a science by itself." Method should be of two kinds, one, ("magistral") for teaching what is old, the other for progression toward what is new. For the latter purpose, knowledge should be delivered in the same method wherein it was discovered, transplanted as it were with the roots. The method of enigmatical tradition, once in credit, has been disgraced by the impostures of many vain persons ; but a far better method is that of aphorisms ; which test solidity, point more directly to action, and stimulate inquiry. To embody doctrine in Problems and Solutions is tedious and destructive of unity. Methods should be adapted to the subject and to the audience ; and herein should be considered the manner and limitation of the propositions and the degree of detail required (for what avails Ortelius' universal map to direct the way between London and York?)—a subject whereof the inquiry is deficient. (*Adv.* II. xvi. 1— xvii. 14 ; *Augm.* V. v.—VI. ii.)

The illustration of *tradition* is Rhetoric, a science excellent and excellently well laboured, whose object is "to apply Reason to Imagination for the better moving of the Will," or again "to fill the Imagination to second Reason."[5] For whereas Reason beholds the future and the

---

[1] See pp. 379-80, above, for this metaphor in connection with the *Idols*.
[2] These are the Idols of the Tribe, although the name is not here mentioned. For the Idols, as discussed in the *Novum Organum*, see p. 381, above.
[3] These are the Idols of the Cave. For an account of the depreciated Gilbert, see above, p. 336.
[4] These are the Idols of the Forum or Market-place.
[5] The *De Augmentis* has it thus : "Munus Rhetoricae non aliud est quam ut *Rationis dictamina Phantasiae applicet et commendet,* ad excitandum appetitum et

sum of time, affection (*i.e.* passion) beholds merely the present; and therefore, as the present fills the Imagination more, Reason is commonly vanquished; but when Rhetoric makes things future and remote appear as present, then Imagination revolts to the side of Reason, and Reason prevails. As deficiencies in Rhetoric, there are marked, first, a collection of the Colours or Sophisms which disguise good and evil; secondly, a collection of Antitheta, *i.e.* theses.argued *pro et contra* ready for oratorical applications; thirdly, a collection of Formulæ to serve as prefaces, conclusions, digressions, transitions, excusations, &c. (*Adv.* II. xviii. 1-9; *Augm.* VI. iii.)

There remain two appendices, one concerning editions, commentaries, and critical apparatus; the other concerning the art of teaching. The latter appendix includes the order of subjects taught; the variation of easy subjects with difficult; the application of different kinds of learning to the different natures of pupils; and the intermission or continuance of exercises so as to perpetuate good habits and break off bad ones. (*Adv.* II. xix. 1-3; *Augm.* VI. iv—*fin.*)

§ 66 THE "ADVANCEMENT OF LEARNING:" HUMAN PHILOSOPHY; MAN "SEGREGATE;" THE WILL

Having discussed the knowledge that deals with Reason, in all its branches, Bacon now proceeds to the knowledge that treats of the Will.

Herein most have been content to set forth patterns of virtue, without giving precepts how to conform one's life to those patterns; probably because the subject consists not in novelties nor subtleties but in common matters in which men have despised to be conversant. A treatise on the Tillage or "Georgics" of the Mind should treat, first, of the nature of good; secondly, of the rules for confirming man's will thereunto.

Concerning the nature of Good men have discoursed well and divided it well, according as it refers to mind, body, or estate (*i.e.* circumstances). But it should be more clearly recognized that all things animate or inanimate have tendencies towards a double nature of Good; first towards the Good of the individual, second towards the Good of the whole or class to which the individual belongs. Of these two tendencies the latter is the nobler.

This consideration must induce us to award the palm to the active over the contemplative life; it decides for Socrates or Zeno, and virtue, against the Cyrenaics or Epicurus, and pleasure. Hence we must censure

voluntatem." And the "filling" of the Imagination is thus explained : "Finis, denique Rhetoricae Phantasiam *implere observationibus et simulacris*, quae Rationi suppetias ferant." Hence we see that "applying Reason to the Imagination" means "adapting arguments so as to appeal to the Imagination;" and Imagination is to be "filled with such images and observations as may assist Reason."

Epictetus, who presupposes that felicity must be placed in those things which are in our power lest we be liable to fortune and disturbance. Hence also we must censure the desire to fly from perturbations rather than extinguish them, and the "tenderness" of certain ancient philosophers who retired too easily from civil business in order to avoid indignities and perturbations. (*Adv.* II. xx. 1—2 ; *Aug.* VI. i.)

Private Good is either passive or active. The latter is the worthier. Passive Good consists in the preservation or perfection of one's own nature ; active Good in imprinting one's own nature upon other things.

Passing to that Good of men which concerns society, and which we will term "duty," we are to consider it not in its relation to society (which subject is reserved for the discussion of man "congregate ") but in its effect on the individual, or man "segregate " ; and first we will treat of the fruit, then of the culture necessary to obtain the fruit. The duty of a man, as a member of the State, has been well handled by others ; but the duty of a man in his profession, vocation, and place, has been only indirectly set forth by men of different professions, who have unduly magnified their several vocations ; wherein, however, must be mentioned with special praise His Majesty's treatise on the duty of a King.

For the complete discussion of the duties and virtues of professions, we should know their vices and impostures ; for it is not possible to join serpentine wisdom with columbine innocency except men know all the conditions of the serpent. We must also treat of domestic and social relations in detail, and of the comparative importance of different and possibly contending duties. (*Adv.* II. xxi. 1-11 ; *Augm.* VII. ii.)

After discussing the fruit, *i.e.* the nature of Good, we come to the culture, *i.e.* the means by which the Will should be conformed thereto. If it be said that this culture, or cure of the mind, belongs to divinity, it may be replied that divinity has moral philosophy for her handmaid ; and this subject has been left uninquired. First, then, like true husbandmen, we must ask what depends on us, and what does not. In the culture of the mind, two things are beyond our control, points of nature and points of fortune. Human nature cannot be altered, but *vincenda ferendo*, it must be conquered by *suffering ;* not, however, by a dull suffering, but by a wise and industrious suffering, better called "accommodating" or "applying."

Now as we cannot fit or supply a garment till we have taken the measure of the body, so we cannot apply culture to the mind till we have set down varieties of human nature. For example, we must consider versatility as compared with narrowness of mind ; the disposition that conceives and executes far-reaching plans (or "longanimity ") as compared with the contrary ; the disposition to take pleasure in the good of others, or benignity as compared with malignity. Add to this the impressions of nature, imposed on the mind by age, climate, health, beauty, nobility, wealth, prosperity, and their opposites ; all of which must be as carefully studied by the cultivator of the mind as varieties of soil by the agriculturist. And as in the body, we must study not only physiology but also pathology, so, in the mind, diseases as well as ordinary nature must be known; whence it follows that we must at this point study the affections. These ought to have been handled by Aristotle directly in his Ethics, instead of collaterally in his Rhetoric; nor have the Stoics examined this subject in a practical way. But the poets and historians are the best teachers of this knowledge, showing us the complex motions of the affections, and how to set affection against affection and to master one by another; as for example by employing fear and hope to bridle the rest.

Having considered the nature of the field, and the limitations of culture, we pass now to culture proper, that is, to the work that is within our command. Here we ought to discuss custom, exercise, habit, education, example, imitation, emulation, company, friends, praise, reproof, exhortation, fame, laws, books, studies. Of these, we can but touch on one or two. Aristotle was careless in saying that of those things which consist by nature nothing can be changed by custom; for it is not true of those things wherein nature admits a latitude. The following precepts are useful for the formation of good habit: (1) Do not begin with too difficult exercises (which may discourage), nor with too easy (which stop progress); (2) practise when the mind is best disposed, so as to gain rapidity; and when it is worst disposed, so as to make the mind more supple; (3) bear ever towards the contrary extreme of that whereunto we are by nature inclined; (4) since we all naturally hate constraint, the mind is brought to anything better, and with more sweetness and happiness, when that to which you tend is not ostensibly the primary, but a secondary, object. Lastly, as regards books and studies, it is obvious that moral philosophy and political philosophy are unfit studies for youth; and as to scholastic morality, there is a danger lest it make men too precise, arrogant, and incompatible. Many other precepts might be given both as to studies, and the other points, company, fame, &c., enumerated above. But the best kind of culture of the mind is based on the fact that the minds of all men are at some times in a state more perfect and at others more depraved; whence arises the precept to fix and cherish the " good hours " of the mind and to obliterate the evil; the former object being accomplished by vows, constant resolutions, and exercises, the latter by some kind of expiation of that which is past, and the re-commencement of a new course. But this part seems sacred to religion. Wherefore we will conclude with the most compendious and noble of all methods of culture, that a man propound unto himself honest and good ends, and that he be resolute, constant, and true unto them, so that he may "mould himself into all virtue at once," not artificially and by pieces, but by a natural and general growth. For no preceptor can frame a man so excellently for the duties of life as can Love; and "if a man set before himself the good of others, and be truly inflamed with charity, it doth work him suddenly into greater perfection than all the doctrine of morality can do." Thus we conclude the Culture of the Mind, which has for its object to make the mind sound, beautiful, and active for all the duties of life. (*Adv.* II. xxii. 1-17; *Augm.* VII. iii. 3.)

§ 67 THE "ADVANCEMENT OF LEARNING :" HUMAN PHILOSOPHY ;
MAN " CONGREGATE "

Having now considered man " segregate," Bacon proceeds to
that part of Human Philosophy which considers him in his
" congregate " or civil aspect.

Civil knowledge has three parts, conversation (*i.e.* social intercourse),
negotiation (*i.e.* the carrying on of business) and government—corresponding
to the three objects sought by man in society, viz. comfort, use, and protection. Wisdom of conversation deals with behaviour ; which, being the
garment of the mind, ought to have the conditions of a garment ; it should
be in fashion, not too elaborate, so shaped as to set forth the better qualities
of the mind, and hide the worse ; and above all it ought not to be too
restrictive for exercise or motion. But this subject has been elegantly
handled. (*Adv.* II. xxiii. 1-3 ; *Augm.* VIII. i.)

On the other hand the wisdom of business, or negotiation, has not been
collected into writing ; the principal treatise on it being the Proverbs of
Solomon. There are also some fables to the point. But now that the
times abound with history, living examples are better than fictitious ; and
the best form of writing on the variable necessities of public or private
business will be found in histories, or in biographies and letters, with inferences deduced from them ; for knowledge drawn freshly from particulars
before our eyes is most readily applied to particular occasions.

But there is another part of the wisdom of business quite different from
the above ; for we have been talking of the wisdom of counsel to others ;
but there is also a wisdom for oneself consisting in the Architecture of one's
own fortune ; and this is deficient and deserving of inquiry, partly because
Science should embrace every knowledge, partly because fortune, as an
organ of virtue and merit, deserves its due consideration.

The Architect of Fortune must study the particular natures of present
actions and persons ; for these are as it were the minor propositions in his
syllogisms ; and without these, no major propositions, however true, can
issue in true conclusions. But a few general precepts may be given. For
example, the Architect must trust countenances and deeds rather than
words ; yet he must consider the motives of deeds, and not despise words
uttered under the influence of passion ; he may study men from the
evidence of their enemies, servants, and friends ; but better by consideration of their natures and objects ; judging weak impulsive men by their
natures, strong and self-controlled men by their objects. For all these
purposes the shortest way is to have acquaintance with men of general
knowledge, and to be intimate with at least one friend who has perfect
intelligence in each special subject ; you should also be frank enough to

provoke others to openness of speech, without revealing what you yourself would keep secret. Also the politic wise man should resolve in every conference and action, besides the present action, to learn something new for future action.

Further, the Architect must study his own weakness and defects, giving himself more or less scope, according as the times suit his nature or otherwise ; choosing his course of life, his friends, and his models, in conformity with his own nature, so that he may excel. He must always set forth his own merits, not neglecting the Art of Ostentation, which, "if it be carried with decency and government, doth greatly add to reputation." Not less important is the art of covering one's defects, which a man may accomplish in three ways : by caution in avoiding tasks too great ; by "colour," in tinging every defect with a hue of some corresponding virtue (representing his cowardice as mildness, dulness as gravity, &c.) ; and, thirdly by confidence, the last but surest of all remedies.

Another precept is to make the mind pliant and obedient to occasion (for nothing is more politic than to make the wheels of our mind concentric and voluble with the wheels of fortune), though we must not neglect also the art of forming our own plans and making our own occasions. Further, the Architect must not always be reserved or dissembling, but must observe a happy mean between the habits of futility and dissimulation ; for the greatest politicians have in a natural and free manner professed their desires. Lastly, men must judge aright not only of the consequences of things, but also of proportions and comparisons, preferring things of substance to things of show.

In the marshalling of men's pursuits toward their fortune, the order should be, first, the amendment of their own minds ; secondly, wealth ; thirdly, reputation ; and fourthly, honour.

Other precepts fit for the Architect of Fortune are to embrace matters which do not occupy too long time ; to imitate Nature (who never does anything in vain), and if one cannot attain one's first object, to reach a second, or else a third, or at least something ; never to commit oneself irrevocably ; and, lastly, in friendship, to remember the precept of Bias, "Love as though you may hate, and hate as though you may love."

All these arts may be called Good Arts ; with Evil Arts, such as Machiavelli has enumerated, no doubt the pressing of a man's fortune may be more compendious ; but "the shortest way is commonly the foulest, and surely the fairer way is not much about." Again, even though men refrain from Evil Arts, yet the Sabbathless pursuit of Fortune leaves no room for the duty to God. Men of the world should remember that Fortune is coy when she is much wooed ; but a better caution is "Seek ye first the Kingdom of God ; " which we may apply to the mind and say, "Seek ye first the virtues of the Mind ; " and although the human foundation (of virtue) has somewhat of the sand, the divine foundation is on a rock. (*Adv.* II. xxiii. 3—46 ; *Augm.* VIII. ii.)

As for Government, to the governed it is for the most part secret, though to Governors it should be clear; even as this world, which to us seems dark, is in the sight of God as a sea of glass before His throne.   In handling such a subject, reverence is due; for next to the crime of rebellion is the crime of futility, for which Sisyphus and Tantalus were punished.   Writing to a King that is a master of this science, the Author thinks it becoming to pass over this subject in silence.   But touching the more public part of government, the laws, he notes this deficience, that men have handled them either as philosophers imaginatively and unpractically (in discourses like the stars,[1] which give little light because they are so high,) or else as lawyers treating of what is received as law, and not of what ought to be law.

A middle course should be pursued in discussing this subject.   Men should write as statesmen, laying down what ought to be, and may be, law; not omitting the means for making laws certain and easy of execution; suggesting how they are to be penned, revised, expounded, pressed, or mitigated; considering how far laws that regulate private rights may influence the commonweal; and generally discussing all the means by which laws may be administered and endowed with such elasticity and adaptability to circumstances as to receive "animation."   As for the superiority of the Laws of England to the Civil Law, to enlarge upon it would be to intermix practical details with general science.   (*Adv.* II. xxiii. 47—50; *Augm.* VIII. iii.)

Here the Author concludes the subject of Human Philosophy which, with History and Poetry, made up the totality of human Learning.   Before passing to divine learning, he looks back upon his work and compares it to the mere tuning of instruments, which is in no way pleasant to hear, but yet is the cause why the music is sweeter afterwards.   He has hopes that posterity may play better on the instruments which he has been content to tune.   Among these grounds for hope are, the revival of learning; the intellectual ability of the present age; the accumulated learning of the past; the art of printing; the extension of navigation, introducing an extension of Natural History; the leisure for study (greater than was possible in the small republics of Greece and in the vast empire of Rome, where politics or government absorbed almost all attention); the present disposition to peace; *the consumption of all that ever can be said in controversies of religion,*[2] the perfection of the King's learning, inciting others to imitation; and, lastly, the inseparable tendency of time to disclose truth.   Now he passes to sacred and inspired divinity, the Sabbath and port of all men's labours and peregrinations.   (*Adv.* II. xxiv.)

[1] See note on p. 349, above, for an illustration from the explanation of *Hermes Stella.*
[2] Perhaps the most striking among many striking instances of Bacon's power of believing what he hoped.

§ 68 The " Advancement of Learning:" Sacred Philosophy.

The *Advancement of Learning* concludes with an account of Sacred Philosophy, its achievements, deficiencies, and limits.

Sacred [1] theology (or divinity) is grounded only upon the word and oracle of God and upon the light of Nature. Yet whereas the religion of the Greeks was based on argument and the religion of Mahomet interdicted argument, the Christian faith, preserving the golden mean, allows some use of Reason in religion. Reason must not attempt to prove or examine the mysteries of faith, any more than Reason can dispute the rules of a game, as, for example, the rules of chess; but when the principles of faith are admitted, Reason may illustrate them and deduce from them inferences for conduct.

Here may be noted a deficience, a treatise (called *Sophron* in the Latin translation) on the True Limits and Use of Reason in Spiritual Things, for want of which some men search into what is not revealed, while others dispute what is positively stated, and others again, instead of saying with St. Paul, " *I, and not the Lord,*" are too fond of saying " *Not I, but the Lord,*" and not only so but bind it with the thunder and denunciation of curses and anathemas. (*Adv.* II. xxv. 1—7.)

Divinity has two principal parts, the nature of the Revelation and the matter of the Revelation. The nature of the Revelation includes, first, the limits of it; secondly, the sufficiency of it; thirdly, the acquiring of it. As to the sufficiency, we may consider herein what points of religion are fundamental and what have been the gradations of light according to the dispensation of times ; and here the Author rather gives it as advice, than notes as a deficience, that men shall piously and wisely consider " of what latitude these points are which make men merely " (*i.e* utterly) "alien and dis-incorporate from the Church of God," suggesting a treatise On the Degrees of Unity in the Kingdom of God.

The acquiring of Revelation may be in two ways. The water of Life obtained from the Scriptures, may either be forced as it were into cisterns and thence drawn when wanted (which is the method of scholastical divinity), or it may be drawn from the Scriptures direct (*Interpretation Solute*). The former sort, though it may seem to be more ready, is more liable to corruption. Scholastic divinity seeks brevity, compact strength, and a complete perfection ; but it has never attained the first two, and ought not to seek the third ; for in divinity many things must be left imperfect, unrounded, and abrupt, breaking off with the exclamation—'O the depth of the

---

[1] The following section is in part omitted and in part condensed in the *De Augmentis*, ix., in which less stress is laid on theology and religious matters than in the *Advancement*. (See note on p. 405 above.)

wisdom and the knowledge of God ! How unsearchable are His judgments and His ways past finding out.' As to the *Interpretation Solute*, we must bear in mind that the Inditer of the Scriptures knew things which no man attains to know, and therefore the Scriptures cannot be interpreted as a profane book. (*Adv.* II. xxv. 8—14.)

The two classes of interpreters, who aspire to explain from the Scriptures the secret details of heaven, or to unravel the secrets of Nature, are both to be checked with a ' Be not high-minded, but fear.' The matter contained in Revelation comprises matter of belief and truth of opinion, and matter of service or adoration ; whence issue four branches—faith, manners (*i.e.* morals), liturgy, and government ; and these may be briefly passed over, because no deficience can be reported in them, no ground vacant and unsown ; so diligent have men been, either in sowing of good seed or in sowing of tares.

Thus has the Author made, as it were, a small globe of the Intellectual World with a note and description of the parts not constantly occupate or not well converted (Lat. "non satis excultas ") by the labour of man. (*Adv.* II. xxv. 15—25.)

INDEX

INDEX

Words printed in italics are Bacon's ; the addition of † denotes translation from Bacon's Latin.

Words printed in italics are Bacon's ; the addition of † *denotes translation from Bacon's Latin.*

Words printed in italics are Bacon's ; the addition of † *denotes translation from Bacon's Latin.*

will assist in preparing a Natural History, 282-4 ; his wife, 99, 100 ; never mentioned in his letters, 114 ; appears as the counsellor of Essex, 53-6 ; Essex complains of his "silence," 56 ; commonly supposed to instigate the Queen against Essex, 61 ; desired by Cecil not to do so, 61 ; compares Essex to Cain, Pisistratus, and the Duke of Guise, 76, 80 ; his suspicious offer to Egerton, 87 ; advice to Cecil on Irish policy, 92 ; endeavours to prevent the House from discussing an inhibition to debate the Prerogative, 126 ; defends Impositions, 126 ; defends Proclamations against Coke, 129 ; his view of Parliaments, 132 ; approves Cecil's financial projects, 145 ; on the power of the King. 141 ; his remedy against the Coming Revolution, 144-51 ; flatters Cecil while living, reviles him when dead, 173-5 ; says he was *as a hawk tied to another's* (Cecil's) *fist*, 178 ; has no suggestion to make as regards Impositions, 191 ; suggests means for controlling elections and managing Parliament, 192-4 ; makes a half-suggestion that the King should give up Impositions, 195 ; his rivalry with Sir Henry Neville, 201 ; chosen by the Commons to introduce the discussion of Impositions with the Lords, 211 ; adopts Cranfield's project for settling Impositions, 226 ; "his chance of serving the nation politically at an end in 1614," 237 ; Bacon's political economy, 226, 251 ; his dislike of duelling, 254-5 ; his advice to the Judges, 260 ; accused by Villiers of being unfaithful to Essex and Somerset, 263 ; does not understand his position with the King, 264 ; offers to put into writing his submission to Buckingham, 264 ; advises Villiers not to interpose by word or letter in any suit pending in the Courts, 267 ; rehears a case in Chancery on the Favourite's demand, 296, xxiv-xxix ; his ingratitude to Yelverton, 277-8 ; broaches "new doctrine" about the Prerogative, 280 ; guilty of corruption in certifying to oppres-

sive Monopolies, 287-91 ; writes to the King, *I have been ever your man*, 295 ; his fine, a benefit to him, 305 ; is denied the Provostship of Eton, 305 ; implores a full pardon, 306 ; seriously ill during the plague, 307 ; his view of his collective works, 308, xxxix ; Rawley's biography of, 309-17 ; "a great reader, but no plodder upon books," 310-11 ; "no dashing man," 311 ; "would light his torch at every man's candle," 311 ; his meals, 311 ; his exercises, 311 ; "was religious," 312 ; "neither bred nor fed malice," 313 ; could never resist the temptation to sleep in the afternoon, 315 ; always fainted at an eclipse of the moon, 315 ; Boëner's testimony to his patience, 317 ; Matthew's and Ben Jonson's testimony to his virtue, 318 ; not led to desert philosophy by want of money, 321 ; his temptations to politics, 322-3 ; his views of human nature, 324 ; his detachment from contemporary thought, 326-7 ; his "incomparable ductility," 327 ; light shed on his character by the *New Atlantis*, 425 ; his poetry, 430-35.

(ii) Francis Bacon (the philosopher), did not appreciate the science of his day, 336, 337, 339, 373, 175-6 ; too sanguine that the order of Nature was easily discoverable, 344-5 ; his metaphor of the Alphabet of Nature, 345-351 ; his notions of a Natural History, 346 ; attaches greater value to the Natural History when he finds his *Novum Organum* fail, 346, 348, 364, 382 ; "his incorrigible imaginativeness," 357 ; his insight into the atomic theory, 336 ; his attacks on Aristotle, 339-43, 368-9, 13 ; his extraordinary carelessness, 373, 383 ; his attempts at Astronomy, 373-6 ; his growing disbelief in the motion of the earth, 376 ; his reasons for propounding his system by means of an example, 383 ; why he relinquished the investigation of motion, 387 ; scientific errors of, 391, 402, 413 ; appears to reason in a circle, 392 ; his self-confidence, 396, 397 ; his self-deception, 403 ; merits and

Words printed in italics are Bacon's ; the addition of † denotes translation from Bacon's Latin.

Words printed in italics are Bacon's ; the addition of † *denotes translation from Bacon's Latin.*

Words printed in italics are Bacon's ; the addition of † denotes translation from Bacon's Latin.

cipline of the, not to be altered, 249 ; *restore the Church to the true limits of authority since Henry VIII.'s confusion,* 147

Church Music, *figures of music, added in pompous times,* 106

Church Reform, Bacon at first favours, 105-7 ; afterwards deprecates, 249

Churches, the Reformed, *Churchmen even impugn the validity of Holy Orders conferred in,* 24

Church, Dean, quoted, xv., xix., 107, 112, 255, 355

Cicero approves premeditated theses, 466

Cinque Ports, 194, 203

Clarendon, Edward, Earl of, on Elizabeth's "countenancing factions," 6 ; on the qualifications for eminence in "the aulical function," 10 ; describes the *Declaration of the Treasons of the Earl of Essex* as "a pestilent libel," 78, 84

Clatter, an history doth not clatter together praises upon the first mention of a name, 163

Clerkship of the Council, the, reversion of, given to Bacon, 26 ; Bacon succeeds to, 153

Clothworkers, 251

Cogitata et Visa, 360-3 ; sent to Bishop Andrews, 161 ; purpose of, 361 ; covers the ground of Book I. of *Novum Organum,* 361 ; change of plan marked in, 361 ; *imparting my C., with choice " ut videbitur,"* 365

Coke, Sir Edward (written also Cook and Cooke), Speaker in the Parliament of 1593, contrast and antipathy between him and Bacon, 88 ; Bacon alludes to him as "the Huddler," 52 ; appointed Attorney-General, married Lady Hatton, 88; his opinion of Bacon, 88 ; conducts the arraignment of Essex, 72 : his quarrel with Bacon, 90 ; Bacon's expostulation, 91 ; consulted (when Chief-Justice of the Common Pleas) on the legalty of certain Royal Proclamations,128,129; his promotion to the King's Bench recommended by Bacon, and why, 186, 187 ; protests, in the name of the Judges, against "auricular confession" in Peacham's case, 220, 221 ; pronounces the Benevolence legal, 218 ; commissioned to investigate the murder of Overbury,232,233 ; encourages an indictment of Præmunire

against the officers of the Chancery, 238,239; refuses to postpone the Commendam case, 240, 241 ; his noble answer to the King in Council, 244 ; is suspended from office and finally deprived of it, and enjoined to review and correct his *Reports,* 246, 253 ; negotiates with Villiers a marriage between the Favourite's brother and his own daughter,253; carries away his daughter from Lady Hatton,261; presents a Report from the Committee of Grievances on the Patent for Inns, 290 ; his admiration for the Common Law, 88 ; his desire that the Judges should mediate between the Crown and the Commons, 145 ; contrast between him and Bacon, in courting the King, 150 ; fond of the technicalities of law, 243 ; *an over-ruling nature,* 236 ; *neither liberal nor affable, nor magnificent,* 253 ; *he that letteth,* 254

Colour, instances of, 397 ; prominent in the *New Atlantis,* 474

Colours of Good and Evil, the, 435 ; *Colours,* or Sophisms, a collection of, needed, 468 ; *Colour,* a means of hiding one's defects, 472

College of Science, the ideal, 155

Commendam, meaning of, 240 ; the C. case, 240-5

Commentarius Solutus, the, 130, 133, 134, 146-8, importance of, 149 ; private plans noted in, 152-9 ; scientific plans noted in, 159, 415 ; political plans in, 130-5, 144-8 ; indicates approval of Cecil's policy, 146

Common Law. *See* Law

Common notions may be of use in popular studies, 42

Common Pleas, Court of, Coke transferred from, 186, 187

Commons, if the gentlemen be too many, the C. will be base, 444

Commons, House of, the, at variance with Elizabeth on the question of Church Government, 16 ; their protest against breach of privileges in 1604, 118 ; warned that the question of Impositions must not be disputed in the House, 125 ; refuses to accept the message, 125 ; Bacon suggests means for dividing, intimidating, and managing, 192-4 ; preponderance of new members in, 203 ; proposes a conference with the Lords concerning Impositions, 210; attacks Monopolies,

---

Words printed in italics are Bacon's ; the addition of † denotes translation from Bacon's Latin.

Words printed in italics are Bacon's ; the addition of † denotes translation from Bacon's Latin.

Words printed in italics are Bacon's ; the addition of † denotes translation from Bacon's Latin.

[1] The figures in parentheses indicate the *line* of the Essay quoted.

Words printed in italics are Bacon's ; the addition of † *denotes translation from Bacon's Latin.*

Words printed in italics are Bacon's ; the addition of † *denotes translation from Bacon's Latin.*

Words printed in italics are Bacon's ; the addition of † *denotes translation from Bacon's Latin.*

Words printed in italics are Bacon's ; the addition of † denotes translation from Bacon's Latin.

Words printed in italics are Bacon's ; the addition of † *denotes translation from Bacon's Latin.*

Words printed in italics are Bacon's ; the addition of † denotes translation from Bacon's Latin.

Words printed in italics are Bacon's ; the addition of † *denotes translation from Bacon's Latin.*

Words printed in italics are Bacon's ; the addition of † denotes translation from Bacon's Latin.

Words printed in italics are Bacon's ; the addition of † denotes translation from Bacon's Latin.

Words printed in italics are Bacon's ; the addition of † *denotes translation from Bacon's Latin.*

Words printed in italics are Bacon's ; the addition of † *denotes translation from Bacon's Latin.*

Words printed in italics are Bacon's; the addition of † denotes translation from Bacon's Latin.

Words printed in italics are Bacon's; the addition of † *denotes translation from Bacon's Latin.*

Words printed in italics are Bacon's ; the addition of † denotes translation from Bacon's Latin.

Words printed in italics are Bacon's ; the addition of † *denotes translation from Bacon's Latin.*

Words printed in italics are Bacon's ; the addition of † *denotes translation from
Bacon's Latin.*

382 ; † *of Essence and Presence*, 387 ;
† *of Absence in Proximity*, 388;
† *of Degrees or Comparison*, 388
Tacitus, I fear T. will be a prophet,
"*magis alii homines quam alii
mores,*" 180 ; *saith well, opportuni
magnis conatibus transitus rerum,*
254
Tantalus, 473 ; the Law Courts "put
the subjects to Tantalus' pain," 134
Tartar, words, *like a Tartar's bow, shoot
back upon the understanding,* 467
Talbot, William, charge against, xxxvi.
Taunton, represented by Bacon in Parliament, xxxi.
Taxes, *a people overlaid with, not
martial,* 444 ; *the gentlemen must
sell their plate and the farmers their
brass pots before this will be paid,*
35
Teacher, every teacher must *play a
kind of part,* when he instructs, 367 ;
teachers are needed for men, not for
children, 172
Teaching, the art of, 468
Telescope, the, when invented, 336
Telesius (Bernardinus) 335, 362 ; on
the tides, 372 ; revived the doctrine
of Parmenides, 372
Temporis Partus Maximus, the, 348
Tenderness, Bacon blames the *tenderness and want of compliance* in some
philosophers, 47
Tenison, Thomas, Archbishop of
Canterbury, his anecdote on Bacon's
patience, 316
Tenures. *See* Knight's service, Wardships
Thales, *by keeping his eyes down, might
have escaped the well and seen the stars
in it,* 353 ; *I partly lean to Thales'
opinion that a philosopher may be rich
if he will,* 39
Thema Coeli, 373
Theology, has distracted men from
Philosophy, 361
Thermometer, the, when invented,
336 ; Bacon ignorant of, 364
Theses, men prefer theses to hypotheses,
411
Things, †*master things, and you will
despise words,* 369
Tides, Bacon on the, 372 ; Telesius on
the, 372
Tillage, Bacon speaks against the repeal
of the statute of, 92 ; of small arable
farms, to be encouraged, 445
Time, the tendency of, to disclose truth,

473 ; *it must be left to Time and Nature
to convert contiguity into continuity,*
104 ; *let me so give every man his due
as I give Time his due,* 43
Time, *Greatest Birth of,* the, 348
Torture, when allowed, 219 ; applied to
Peacock and Peacham, 220
Topica, 466
Trade, Bacon's views on the encouragement of, 250, 251
Tradition, the fourth intellectual art,
467
Transformation of bodies, rule for, 384
Translation of certain Psalms, the,
430-5
Trinity College, Cambridge, Francis
Bacon goes to, 13 ; Whitgift master
of, 13 ; a practical joke in, 14
Trott, Nicholas, Bacon's creditor, 6 ;
Egerton arbitrates between Bacon
and, 87
*Truth, the truth of being and the truth
of knowing is all one,* 41 ; † *emerges
sooner from wrong order than from
no order,* 359 ; †*comes sooner from
error than from confusion,* 393
Turks, the government of, *a pure and
absolute tyranny,* 445 ; Bacon suggests
a Holy War against the T., 256,
426
Tyrone, Earl of, leader of the Irish rebellion, 56; his so-called Propositions,
59, 60

U.

UNDERSTANDING, relation of, to the
Will and Imagination, 465 ; perturbed by inherent errors, 362 ; when
left to itself (sibi permissus), 393 ;
Indulgence of the, 393 ; Bacon's first
work is to *purge the threshing-floor of
the Understanding,* 102
Understanding, the Ladder of the, 363,
378
"Undertakers," the, why so called,
197 ; excitement in the House about
them, 210 ; Bacon's allusion to them,
197
Union, different kinds of, 104
Union of England and Scotland (*see
Act for the better Grounding, &c.,
Articles or Considerations touching,
&c., A brief Discourse touching, &c.,
Certificate or Return, &c.*), 104 ; Bacon
one of the Commissioners for forwarding the, 112
Unity. *See* Church

*Words printed in italics are Bacon's ; the addition of † denotes translation from
Bacon's Latin.*

Words printed in italics are Bacon's ; the addition of † denotes translation from Bacon's Latin.

Words printed in italics are Bacon's ; the addition of † *denotes translation from Bacon's Latin.*

THE END.

LONDON RICHARD CLAY AND SONS, PRINTERS,